D1021050

Books by Phillip Margolin

GONE, BUT NOT FORGOTTEN

PHILLIP MARGOLIN

WILD JUSTICE

AVON BOOKS

An Imprint of HarperCollinsPublishers

Gone, But Not Forgotten was published in paperback by HarperTorch in February 2005.

Wild Justice was originally published in hardcover by HarperCollins in September 2000 and in paperback by HarperTorch in August 2001.

HarperCollins books may be purchased for educational, business, or sales promotional use. For information please write: Special Markets Department, HarperCollins Publishers Inc., 10 East 53rd Street, New York, NY 10022.

FIRST EDITION

ISBN-13: 978-0-06-112159-3
ISBN-10: 0-06-112159-2

06 07 08 09 RRD 10 9 8 7 6 5 4 3 2 1

GONE, BUT
NOT FORGOTTEN

For Doreen,
my law partner, my best friend and my wife
for twenty-five extraordinary years of marriage.

Acknowledgments

A lot of people helped me transform the idea for *Gone, But Not Forgotten* into the book you are reading. Dr. William Brady and Dr. Edward Colbach answered my technical questions about medicine and psychiatry; Dr. Stanley Abrams not only reviewed my manuscript but let me borrow extensively from his paper, *The Serial Murderer*; my friend and fellow novelist Vince Kohler graciously took time from writing his most recent Eldon Larkin mystery to critique my manuscript; and my brother, Jerry, gave me his "elementary" assistance.

Once a manuscript is finished, it has to find a home. I cannot speak too highly of Jean Naggar, Teresa Cavanaugh and everyone else at the Jean V. Naggar Literary Agency. Everybody should be this lucky in their choice of an agent.

I am greatly indebted to David Gernert for the time he invested in editing *Gone, But Not Forgotten*. It is a much better book now than it was when he first read it because of his suggestions. I am also grateful to Deborah Futter for her editorial assistance and everybody at Doubleday for their support.

And, of course, there is my wife, Doreen, and my fantastic children, Daniel and Amy, who critiqued the book and provided a happy home in which to write it.

Part One

WAKE-UP CALL

Chapter One

I

"Have you reached a verdict?" Judge Alfred Neff asked the eight men and four women seated in the jury box.

A heavy-set, barrel-chested man in his mid-sixties struggled to his feet. Betsy Tannenbaum checked the chart she had drawn up two weeks ago during jury selection. This was Walter Korn, a retired welder. Betsy felt uncomfortable with Korn as the foreman. He was a member of the jury only because Betsy had run out of challenges.

The bailiff took the verdict form from Korn and handed it to the judge. Betsy's eyes followed the folded square of white paper. As the judge opened it and read the verdict to himself, she watched his face for a telltale sign, but there was none.

Betsy stole a glance at Andrea Hammermill, the plump, matronly woman sitting beside her. Andrea stared straight ahead, as subdued and resigned as she had been throughout her trial for the murder of her husband. The only time Andrea had shown any emotion was during direct examination when she explained why she shot Sidney Hammermill to death. As she told the jury about firing the revolver over and over until the dull click of hammer on steel told her there were no more bullets, her hands trembled, her body shook and she sobbed pitifully.

"Will the defendant please stand," Judge Neff said.

Andrea got to her feet unsteadily. Betsy stood with her, eyes forward.

"Omitting the caption, the verdict reads as follows: 'We the jury, being duly impaneled and sworn, do find the defendant, Andrea Marie Hammermill, not guilty . . .'"

Betsy could not hear the rest of the verdict over the din in the courtroom. Andrea collapsed on her chair, sobbing into her hands.

"It's okay," Betsy said, "it's okay." She felt tears on her cheeks as she wrapped a protective arm around Andrea's shoulders. Someone tapped Betsy on the arm. She looked up. Randy Highsmith, the prosecutor, was standing over her holding a glass of water.

"Can she use this?" he asked.

Betsy took the glass and handed it to her client. Highsmith waited a moment while Andrea regained her composure.

"Mrs. Hammermill," he said, "I want you to know that I prosecuted you because I believe you took the law into your own hands. But I also want you to know that I don't think your husband had the right to treat you the way he did. I don't care who he was. If you had come to me, instead of shooting him, I would have done my best to put him in jail. I hope you can put this behind you and go on with your life. You seem like a good person."

Betsy wanted to thank Highsmith for his kind words, but she was too choked up to speak. As Andrea's friends and supporters started to crowd around her Betsy pushed away from the throng to get some air. Over the crowd she could see Highsmith, alone, bent over his table, gathering law books and files. As the assistant district attorney started toward the door, he noticed Betsy standing on the fringe of the crowd. Now that the trial was over, the two lawyers were superfluous. Highsmith nodded. Betsy nodded back.

2

With his back arched, his sleek muscles straining and his head tipped back, Martin Darius looked like a wolf baying over fallen prey. The blonde lying beneath him tightened her legs around his waist. Darius shuddered and closed his eyes. The woman panted from exertion. Darius's face contorted, then he collapsed. His cheek fell against her breast. He heard the blonde's heart beat and smelled perspiration mingled with a telltale trace of perfume. The woman threw an arm across her face. Darius ran a lazy hand along her leg and glanced across her flat stomach at the cheap digital clock on the motel end table. It was two p.m. Darius sat up slowly and dropped his legs over the side of the bed. The woman heard the bed move and watched Darius cross the room.

"I wish you didn't have to go," she said, unable to hide her disappointment.

Darius grabbed his kit off the low-slung chest of drawers and padded toward the bathroom.

"I've got a meeting at three," he answered, without looking back.

Darius washed away the sheen of sweat he had worked up during sex, then toweled himself roughly in the narrow confines of the motel bathroom. Steam from the shower misted the mirror. He wiped the glass surface and saw a gaunt face with deep-set blue eyes. His neatly trimmed beard and mustache framed a devil's mouth that could be seductive or intimidating. Darius used a portable dryer, then combed his straight black hair and beard. When he opened the bathroom door, the blonde was still in bed. A few times, she had tried to lure him back into bed after he was showered and dressed. He guessed she was trying to exercise sexual control over him and refused to give in.

"I've decided we should stop seeing each other," Darius said casually as he buttoned his white silk shirt.

The blonde sat up in bed, a shocked expression on her normally confident, cheer-leader face. He had her attention now. She was not used to being dumped. Darius turned slightly so she would not see his smile.

"Why?" she managed as he stepped into his charcoal gray suit trousers. Darius turned to look at her so he could enjoy the play of emotions on her face.

"To your credit, you are beautiful and good in bed," he said, knotting his tie, "but you're boring."

The blonde gaped at him for a moment, then flushed with anger.

"You shit."

Darius laughed and picked up his suit jacket.

"You can't mean it," she went on, her anger passing quickly.

"I'm very serious. We're through. It was nice for a while, but I want to move on."

"And you think you can use me, then toss me away like a cigarette," she said, the anger back. "I'll tell your wife, you son-of-a-bitch. I'll call her right now."

Darius stopped smiling. The expression on his face forced the blonde back against the headboard. Darius strolled around the bed slowly, until he was standing over her. She cowered back and put her hands up. Darius watched her for a moment, the way a biologist would study a specimen on a slide. Then he grabbed her wrist and twisted her arm until she was bent forward on the bed, her forehead against the crumpled sheets.

Darius admired the curve of her body from her backside to her slender neck as she knelt in pain. He ran his free hand along her rump, then applied pressure to her wrist to make her body quiver. He liked watching her breasts sway rapidly as she jerked to attention.

"Let me make one thing very clear to you," Darius said in the same tone he might use with a recalcitrant child. "You will never call my wife, or me, ever. Do you understand?"

"Yes," the blonde gasped as he twisted her arm behind her, pushing it slowly up toward her shoulder.

"Tell me what you will never do," he commanded calmly, releasing the pressure for a moment and stroking the curve of her buttocks with his free hand.

"I won't call, Martin. I swear," she wept.

"Why won't you call my wife or bother me?" Darius asked, putting pressure on the wrist.

The blonde gasped, twitching with the pain. Darius fought back a giggle, then eased up so she could answer.

"I won't call," she repeated between sobs.

"But you haven't said why," Darius responded in a reasonable tone.

"Because you said I shouldn't. I'll do what you want. Please, Martin, don't hurt me anymore."

Darius released his hold and the woman collapsed, sobbing pitifully.

"That's a good answer. A better one would be that you won't do anything to annoy me, because I can do far worse to you than I just have. Far, far worse."

Darius knelt by her face and took out his lighter. It was solid gold, with an inscription from his wife. The bright orange flame wavered in front of the blonde's terrified eyes. Darius held it close enough for her to feel the heat.

"Far, far worse," Darius repeated. Then he closed the lighter and walked across the motel room. The blonde rolled over and lay with the white sheet tangled around her hips, leaving her slender legs and smooth back exposed. Each time she sobbed, her shoulders trembled. Martin Darius watched her in the motel mirror as he adjusted his wine-red tie. He wondered if he could convince her this was all a joke, then get her to submit to him again. The thought brought a smile to his thin lips. For a moment, he toyed with the image of the woman kneeling before him and taking him in her mouth, convinced that he wanted her back. It would be a challenge to get her on her knees after the way he had crushed her spirit. Darius was confident he could do it, but there was a meeting to attend.

"The room's paid for," he said. "You can stay as long as you want."

"Can't we talk? Please, Martin," the woman begged, sitting up and turning on the bed so that her small, sad breasts were exposed, but Darius was already closing the motel room door.

Outside, the sky looked ominous. Thick, black clouds were rolling in from the coast. Darius unlocked the door of his jet-black Ferrari and silenced the alarm. In a short while, he would do something that would increase the woman's pain. Something exquisite that would make it impossible for her to forget him. Darius smiled in anticipation, then drove off without the slightest suspicion that someone was photographing him from the corner of the motel parking lot.

• • •

Martin Darius sped across the Marquam Bridge toward downtown Portland. The heavy rain kept the pleasure boats off the Willamette River, but a rusty tanker was pushing through the storm toward the port at Swan Island. Across the river was an architectural mix of functional, gray, futuristic buildings linked by sky bridges, Michael Graves's whimsical, post-modern Portland Building, the rose-colored U.S. Bank skyscraper, and three-story historical landmarks dating back to the eighteen hundreds. Darius had made his fortune adding to Portland's skyline and rebuilding sections of the city.

Darius changed lanes just as a reporter began the lead story on the five o'clock news.

"This is Larry Prescott at the Multnomah County Courthouse speaking with Betsy Tannenbaum, the attorney for Andrea Hammermill, who has just been acquitted in the shooting death of her husband, City Commissioner Sidney Hammermill.

"Betsy, why do you think the jury voted 'not guilty'?"

"I believe it was an easy choice once the jurors understood how battering affects the mind of a woman who undergoes the frequent beatings and abuse Andrea suffered."

"You've been critical of this prosecution from the start. Do you think the case would have been handled differently if Mr. Hammermill was not a mayoral candidate?"

"The fact that Sidney Hammermill was wealthy and very active in Oregon politics may have influenced the decision to prosecute."

"Would it have made a difference if District Attorney Alan Page had assigned a woman deputy to the case?"

"It could have. A woman would have been able to evaluate the evidence more objectively than a man and might have declined prosecution."

"Betsy, this is your second acquittal in a murder case using the battered wife defense. Earlier this year, you won a million-dollar verdict against an anti-abortion group and *Time* magazine listed you as one of America's up-and-coming female trial lawyers. How are you handling your newfound fame?"

There was a moment of dead air. When Betsy answered she sounded uncomfortable.

"Believe me, Larry, I'm much too busy with my law practice and my daughter to worry about anything more pressing than my next case and tonight's dinner."

The car phone rang. Darius turned down the radio. The Ferrari purred as it pulled away from the traffic. Darius glided into the fast lane, then picked up on the third ring.

"Mr. Darius?"

"Who is this?"

Only a few people knew the number of his car phone and he did not recognize the voice.

"You don't need to know my name."

"I don't need to speak to you, either."

"Maybe not, but I thought you'd be interested in what I have to say."

"I don't know how you got this number, but my patience is wearing thin. Get to the point or I'll disconnect."

"Right. You're a businessman. I shouldn't waste your time. Still, if you hung up now, I can guarantee I'd be gone but not forgotten."

"What did you say?"

"Got your attention, huh?"

Darius took a deep, slow breath. Suddenly there were beads of perspiration on his brow and upper lip.

"Do you know Captain Ned's? It's a seafood place on Marine Drive. The bar's pretty dark. Drive there now and we'll talk."

The connection was broken. Darius lowered the phone onto its cradle. He had slowed without realizing it and there was a car on his bumper. Darius crossed two lanes of traffic and pulled onto the shoulder of the road. His heart was racing. There was a shooting pain in his temples. Darius closed his eyes and leaned back against the headrest. He willed his breathing back to normal and the pain in his temples eased.

The voice on the phone was rough and uncultured. The man would be after money, of course. Darius smiled grimly. He dealt with greedy men all the time. They were the easiest to manipulate. They always believed the person they were dealing with was as stupid and frightened as they were.

The pain in his temples was gone now and Darius was breathing easily again. In a way he was grateful to the caller. He had grown complacent, believing he was safe after all these years, but you were never safe. He would consider this a wake-up call.

3

Captain Ned's was weathered wood and rain-spattered glass jutting out over the Columbia River. The bar was as dark as the voice promised. Darius sat in a booth near the kitchen, ordered a beer and waited patiently. A young couple entered, arm in arm. He dismissed them. A tall, balding salesman in a disheveled suit sat on a stool at the

bar. Most of the tables were taken by couples. Darius
scanned the other booths. A heavy-set man in a trench
coat smiled and stood up after Darius fixed on him.

"I was waiting to see how long it would take you,"
the man said as he slipped into the booth. Darius did not
reply. The man shrugged and stopped smiling. It was unsettling to sit opposite Martin Darius, even if you thought
you held the winning hand.

"We can be civilized about this or you can be
bitchy," the man said. "It don't matter to me. In the end,
you'll pay."

"What are you selling and what do you want?" Darius answered, studying the fleshy face in the dim light.

"Always the businessman, so let's get down to business. I've been to Hunter's Point. The old newspapers
were full of information. There were pictures, too. I had
to look hard, but it was you. I got one here, if you'd like
to see," the man said, sliding his hand out of his coat
pocket and pushing a photocopy of a newspaper front
page across the table. Darius studied it for a moment,
then slid it back.

"Ancient history, friend."

"Oh? You think so? I have friends on the force, Martin. The public don't know yet, but I do. Someone has
been leaving little notes and black roses around Portland.
I figure it's the same person who left 'em in Hunter's
Point. What do you think?"

"I think you're a very clever man, Mr. . . . ?" Darius said, stalling for time to dope out the implications.

The man shook his head. "You don't need my name,
Martin. You just have to pay me."

"How much are we talking about?"

"I thought two hundred and fifty thousand dollars
would be fair. It'd cost you at least that much in attorney
fees."

The man had thinning, straw-colored hair. Darius could see flesh between the strands when he bent forward. The nose had been broken. There was a gut, but the shoulders were thick and the chest heavy.

"Have you told the people who hired you about Hunter's Point?" Darius asked.

There was a brief flicker of surprise, then a flash of nicotine-stained teeth.

"That was terrific. I ain't even gonna ask how you figured it out. Tell me what you think."

"I think you and I are the only ones who know, for now."

The man did not answer.

"There is one thing I'd like to know," Darius said, eyeing him curiously. "I know what you think I've done. What I'm capable of doing. Why aren't you afraid I'll kill you?"

The man laughed.

"You're a pussy, Martin, just like the other rape-os I run into in the joint. Guys who were real tough with women and not so tough with anyone else. You know what I used to do to those guys? I made 'em my girls, Martin. I turned 'em into little queens. I'd do it to you too, if I wasn't more interested in your money."

While Darius considered this information, the man watched him with a confident smirk.

"It will take me a while to come up with that much money," Darius said. "How much time can you give me?"

"Today is Wednesday. How's Friday?"

Darius pretended to be considering the problems involved with liquidating stocks and closing accounts.

"Make it Monday. A lot of my holdings are in land. It will take me until Friday to arrange for loans and sell some stock."

The man nodded. "I heard you didn't believe in

bullshit. Good. You're doing the right thing. And, let me tell you, friend, I'm not someone to fuck with. Also, I'm not greedy. This'll be a one-shot deal."

The man stood. Then he thought of something and grinned at Darius.

"Once I'm paid, I'll be gone *and* forgotten."

The man laughed at his little joke, turned his back and left the bar. Darius watched him go. He did not find the joke, or anything else about the man, amusing.

4

A hard rain hit the windshield. Big drops, falling fast. Russ Miller switched the wiper to maximum. The cascade still obliterated his view of the road and he had to squint to catch the broken center line in the headlight beams. It was almost eight, but Vicky was used to late suppers. You put in the hours at Brand, Gates and Valcroft if you expected to get anywhere. Russ grinned as he imagined Vicky's reaction to the news. He wished he could drive faster, but a few more minutes would not make much difference.

Russ had warned Vicky he might not be home on time as soon as Frank Valcroft's secretary summoned him. At the advertising firm, it was an honor to be asked into Valcroft's corner office. Russ had been there only twice before. The deep, wine-colored carpets and dark wood reminded him of where he wanted to be. When Valcroft told him he was going to be in charge of the Darius Construction account, Russ knew he was on his way.

Russ and Vicky had been introduced to Martin Darius this summer at a party Darius hosted to celebrate the opening of his new mall. All the men who worked on the account were there, but Russ had this feeling that Darius had singled him out. An invitation to join Darius on his yacht arrived a week later. Since then, he and Vicky had been guests at two house parties. Stuart Webb, another account executive at Brand, Gates, said he felt like he was standing in a chill wind when he was with Darius, but Darius was the most dynamic human being Russ had ever met and he had a knack for making Russ feel like the most important person on Earth. Russ was certain that Martin Darius was responsible for making him the team leader of the Darius Construction account. If Russ was successful as team leader, who knew what he would be doing in the future. He might even leave Brand, Gates and go to work for the man himself.

As Russ pulled into his driveway the garage door opened automatically. The rain pounding on the garage roof sounded like the end of the world and Russ was glad to get inside the warm kitchen. There was a large, metal pot on the stove, so he knew Vicky was making pasta. The surprise would be the sauce. Russ shouted Vicky's name as he peeked under the cover of another pot. It was empty. There was a cutting board covered with vegetables, but none of them was sliced. Russ frowned. There was no fire under the large pot. He lifted the lid. It was filled with water, but the pasta was lying, uncooked, next to the pasta maker he had bought Vicky for their third anniversary.

"Vick," Russ shouted again. He loosened his tie and took off his jacket. The lights were on in the living room. Later, Russ told the police he had not called sooner because everything looked so normal. The set was on. The Judith Krantz novel Vicky was reading was open and facedown on the end table. When he realized Vicky was not home, he assumed she was over at one of the neighbors.

The first time Russ went into the bedroom, he missed the rose and the note. His back was to the bed when he stripped off his clothes and hung them in the closet. After that, he slipped into a warm-up suit and checked the cable guide to see what was on TV. When fifteen more minutes passed without Vicky, Russ went back into the bedroom to phone her best friend, who lived down the block. That was when he saw the note on the pillow on the immaculately made bed. There was a black rose lying across the plain, white paper. Written in a careful hand were the words "Gone, But Not Forgotten."

Chapter Two

As Austin Forbes, the President of the United States, walked toward United States Senator Raymond Francis Colby he passed through the rays of sunlight streaming through the high French windows of the Oval Office, creating the impression that God was spotlighting a chosen son. Had he noticed, the diminutive Chief Executive would have appreciated the vote of confidence from above. The results of his earthly polls were not nearly as complimentary.

"Good to see you, Ray," Forbes said. "You know Kelly Bendelow, don't you?"

"Kelly and I have met," Colby said, remembering the in-depth interview the President's troubleshooter had conducted just two weeks before.

Senator Colby sat in the chair the President indicated and glanced out the east windows toward the rose garden. The President sat in an old armchair that had graced his Missouri law office and followed him up the ladder of power to the Oval Office. He looked pensive.

"How's Ellen?" Forbes asked.

"She's fine."

"And are you fine? You're in good health?"

"Excellent health, Mr. President. I had a thorough

physical last month," Colby answered, knowing that the FBI would have furnished Forbes with his doctor's report.

"No personal problems. Everything's going well at home? Your finances are sound?"

"Ellen and I are celebrating our thirty-second anniversary next month."

Forbes stared hard at Colby. The good old boy vanished and the hard-nosed politician who had carried forty-eight states in the last election took his place.

"I can't afford another fiasco like this Hutchings thing," Forbes said. "I'm telling you this in confidence, Ray. She lied to me. Hutchings sat where you're sitting and lied. Then that reporter for the *Post* found out and . . ."

Forbes let the thought trail off. Everyone in the room was painfully aware of the blow that had been dealt to Forbes's prestige when the Senate voted against confirming the nomination of Mabel Hutchings.

"Is there anything in your past that can cause us problems, Ray? Anything at all? When you were c.e.o. of Marlin Steel did you ever pay a corporate bribe? Did you use marijuana at Princeton or Harvard Law? Did you knock up some girl in high school?"

Colby knew the questions were not ridiculous. The aspirations of presidential hopefuls and Supreme Court nominees had run aground on just such rocky shoals.

"There will be no surprises, Mr. President."

The silence in the Oval Office grew. Then Forbes spoke.

"You know why you're here, Ray. If I nominate you to be Chief Justice of the United States, will you accept?"

"Yes, Mr. President."

Forbes grinned. The tension in the room evaporated.

"We make the announcement tomorrow. You'll make a great Chief Justice."

"I'm indebted to you," Colby said, not trusting himself to say more. He had known the President would make the offer when he was summoned to the White House, but that did not keep him from feeling as light as a free-floating cloud.

Raymond Colby sat up as quietly as possible and shuffled his feet along the carpet until he found his slippers. Ellen Colby stirred on the other side of their king-size bed. The senator watched the moonlight play on her peaceful features. He shook his head in amazement. Only his wife could sleep the sleep of angels after what had happened today.

There was a liquor cabinet in the den of Colby's Georgetown town house. Colby fixed himself some bourbon. On the upper landing the antique grandfather clock ticked away the seconds, each movement of the ancient hands perfectly audible in the stillness.

Colby rested his glass on the fireplace mantel and picked up a framed and fading black and white photograph that had been taken the day his father argued a case before the United States Supreme Court. Howard Colby, a distinguished partner in Wall Street's most prestigious law firm, died at his desk two months after the photograph was taken. Raymond Colby may have been first at Harvard Law, c.e.o. of Marlin Steel, the governor of New York and a United States senator, but he always saw himself in relationship to his father as he had been that day on the steps of the Court, a ten-year-old boy under the protection of a wise and gruff giant whom Raymond remembered as the smartest man he had ever known.

There were fifty-three broad steps leading from the street to the entrance to the Court. Raymond had counted as he climbed them, hand in hand with his father. When they passed between the columns supporting the west portico, his father had stopped to point out "Equal Justice Under Law" engraved in the bone-white marble of the Great Hall.

"That's what they do here, Raymond. Justice. This is the court of last resort. The final place for all lawsuits in this great country."

Massive oak doors guarded the Court's chambers, but the courtroom was intimate. Behind a raised mahogany bench were nine high-backed chairs of various styles. When the justices filed to their seats, his father stood. When Howard Colby addressed the Court, Raymond was surprised to hear respect in the voice of a man who commanded the respect of others. These men in black, these wise men who towered over Howard Colby and commanded his respect, left a lasting impression. On the train ride back to New York, Raymond swore silently to sit some day upon the bench of the nation's highest court. His dream would come true when the President made his announcement at tomorrow's press conference.

The waiting had begun Friday when a White House source told him that the President had narrowed his choice to the senator and Alfred Gustafson of the Fifth Circuit Court of Appeals. This afternoon, during their meeting in the Oval Office, the President told Colby it was his membership in the Senate that made the difference. After the disastrous defeat of Mabel Hutchings, his first nominee, the President wanted a sure thing. The Senate was not going to reject one of its own, especially someone with Colby's credentials. All he need do now was pass through the nominating process unscathed.

Colby put down the photograph and picked up his

drink. It was not only the excitement of the nomination that kept him from sleep. Colby was an honest man. When he told the President that there was no scandal in his past, he was telling the truth. But there *was* something in his past. Few people knew about it. Those who did could be trusted to keep silent. Still, it concerned him that he had not been entirely candid with the man who was fulfilling his greatest dream.

Colby sipped his drink and stared at the lights of the capital. The bourbon was doing its job. His tense muscles were relaxing. He felt a bit sleepy. There was no way to change history. Even if he knew what the future would bring, he was certain he would have made no other choice. Worrying now would not change the past and the chances of his secret surfacing were very small. Within the hour the senator was sound asleep.

Chapter Three

1

The pathetic thing was that after the affairs and the lies, not to mention the divorce settlement, which left Alan Page living in the same type of shabby apartment he had lived in when he was a law student, he still loved Tina. She was what he thought about when he was not thinking about work. Going to a movie did not help, reading a book did not help, even bedding the women with whom his well-meaning friends fixed him up did not help. The women were the worst, because he always found himself comparing and they never stacked up. Alan had not been with a woman in months.

The district attorney's mood was starting to affect his staff. Last week, Randy Highsmith, his chief deputy, had taken him aside and told him to shape up, but he still found it hard to cope with bachelorhood after twelve years of what he thought was a good marriage. It was the sense of betrayal that overwhelmed him. He had never cheated on Tina or lied to her and he felt that she was the one person he could trust completely. When he found out about her secret life, it was too much. Alan doubted he would ever fully trust anyone again.

Alan pulled into the City garage and parked in the spot reserved for the Multnomah County district attorney, one of the few things Tina hadn't gotten in the divorce, he mused bitterly. He opened his umbrella and raced across the street to the courthouse. The wind blew the rain under the umbrella and almost wrenched it from his hand. He was drenched by the time he ducked inside the gray stone building.

Alan ran a hand through his damp hair while he waited for the elevator. It was almost eight. Around him, in the lobby, were young lawyers trying to look important, anxious litigants hoping for the best and dreading the worst, and a bored-looking judge or two. Alan was not in the mood for aimless social chatter. When the elevator came, he pushed six and stepped to the rear of the car.

"Chief Tobias wants you to call," the receptionist told him as soon as he entered the district attorney's office. "He said it was important."

Alan thanked her and pushed open the low gate that separated the waiting area from the rest of the offices. His private office was the first on the right along a narrow hall.

"Chief Tobias called," his secretary said.

"Winona told me."

"He sounded upset."

It was hard to imagine what could upset William Tobias. The slender police chief was as unflappable as an accountant. Alan shook out his umbrella and hung up his raincoat, then sat behind his large desk and dialed across the street to police headquarters.

"What's up?" Alan asked.

"We've got another one."

It took a moment for Alan to figure out what Tobias
was talking about.

"Her name is Victoria Miller. Twenty-six. Attractive,
blond. Housewife. No kids. The husband is with Brand,
Gates and Valcroft, the ad agency."

"Is there a body?"

"No. She's just missing, but we know it's him."

"The same note?"

"On the bed on the pillow. 'Gone, But Not Forgotten.' And there's another black rose."

"Was there any sign of a struggle this time?"

"It's just like the others. She could have disappeared
in a puff of smoke."

Both men were silent for a moment.

"The papers still don't know?"

"We're lucky there. Since there aren't any bodies,
we've been handling them like missing persons cases. But
I don't know how long we can keep this quiet. The three
husbands aren't going to just sit around. Reiser, the lawyer, is on the phone every day, two or three times a day,
and Farrar, the accountant, is threatening to go public if
we don't come up with something soon."

"Do you have anything?"

"Not a thing. Forensics is stumped. We've got no
unusual fibers or hairs. No fingerprints. You can buy the
notepaper at any Payless. The rose is an ordinary rose.
Ditto the black dye."

"What do you suggest?"

"We're doing a computer search on the m.o. and I've
got Ross Barrow calling around to other police departments and the FBI."

"Are you looking into possible connections between
the victims?"

"Sure. We've got lots of obvious similarities. The
three women are around the same age, upper middle-

class, childless, housewives with executive-type husbands. But we've got nothing connecting the victims to each other."

Tobias could have been describing Tina. Alan closed his eyes and massaged the lids.

"What about health clubs, favorite stores, reading circles? Do they use the same dentist or doctor?" Alan asked.

"We've thought of all those and a dozen more."

"Yeah, I'm sure you have. How far apart is he working?"

"It looks like one a month. We're into what? Early October? Farrar was August and Reiser was September."

"Christ. We better get something going soon. The press will eat us alive once this breaks."

"Tell me about it."

Alan sighed. "Thanks for calling. Keep me up-to-date."

"You got it."

Alan hung up and swiveled his chair so he could look out the window. Man, he was tired. Tired of the rain and this asshole with the black rose and Tina and everything else he could think of. More than anything, he wanted to be by himself on some sun-soaked beach where there were no women and no phones and the only decision he would have to make was about the strength of his suntan lotion.

2

No one ever called Elizabeth Tannenbaum stunning, but most men found her attractive. Hardly anyone called her Elizabeth, either. An "Elizabeth" was regal, cool, an eye-catching beauty. A "Betsy" was pleasant to look at, a tiny bit overweight, capable, but still fun to be with. Betsy suited her just fine.

A Betsy could also be a bit frazzled at times and that was how Betsy Tannenbaum felt when her secretary buzzed her just as she was stuffing the papers on the Morales case into her briefcase so she could work on them at home this evening, after she picked up Kathy from day care and cooked dinner and straightened the house and played with Kathy and . . .

"I can't take it, Ann. I'm late for day care."

"He says it's important."

"It's always important. Who is it?"

"He won't say."

Betsy sighed and looked at the clock. It was already four-thirty. If she got Kathy by five and rushed to the store, she would not be done cooking until six. On the other hand, if she did not keep bringing in clients she would have all day to shop. Betsy stopped pushing papers into her briefcase and picked up the phone.

"Betsy Tannenbaum."

"Thank you for taking the call. My name is Martin Darius."

Betsy caught her breath. Everyone in Portland knew who Darius was, but he did not call many of them.

"When does your staff leave?" Darius asked.

"Around five, five-fifteen. Why?"

"I need to speak to you this evening and I don't want anyone to know about it, including your secretary. Would six be convenient?"

"Actually, no. I'm sorry. Is there any way we can meet tomorrow? My schedule is pretty open then."

"How much is your normal fee, Mrs. Tannenbaum?"

"One hundred dollars an hour."

"If you'll meet me at six tonight, I'll pay you twenty-five hundred dollars for the consultation. If I decide to hire you, you will be extremely pleased by the fee."

Betsy took a deep breath. She dreaded doing it, but she was going to have to call Rick. She simply could not afford to turn down that kind of money or such a high-profile client.

"Can I put you on hold, Mr. Darius? I have another obligation and I want to see if I can get someone else to take care of it."

"I can hold."

Betsy dialed Rick Tannenbaum on the other line. He was in a meeting, but his secretary put her through.

"What is it, Betsy? I'm very busy," Rick said, making no attempt to hide his annoyance.

"I'm sorry to bother you, but I have an emergency. A client needs to meet me at six. Can you get Kathy at day care?"

"What about your mother?"

"She's playing bridge and I don't have the number at her friend's house."

"Just tell the client you'll meet him tomorrow."

"He can't. It has to be tonight."

"Damn it, Betsy, when we separated, you promised you wouldn't do this to me."

"I'm really sorry," Betsy said, as angry at herself for begging as she was at Rick for making this so difficult. "I rarely ask you to pick up Kathy, but I need you, this once. Please."

Rick was silent for a moment.

"I'll do it," he answered angrily. "When do I have to be there?"

"They close at six. I really appreciate this."

Betsy hung up quickly, before Rick could change his mind.

"Six will be fine, Mr. Darius. Do you know the address of my office?"

"Yes," Darius said, and the line went dead. Betsy put the phone down slowly and sank into her chair, wondering what business a man like Martin Darius could possibly have with her.

Betsy glanced at her watch. It was six thirty-five and Darius had not arrived. She was annoyed that he had kept her waiting after she had put herself out, but not annoyed enough to jeopardize a twenty-five-hundred-dollar fee. Besides, the wait had given her time to work on the Morales case. She decided to give Darius another half hour.

Rain spattered against the window behind her. Betsy yawned and swiveled her chair so she could look out into the night. Most of the offices in the building across the way were deserted. She could see cleaning women starting to work. By now, her own building was probably deserted, except for the night people. The silence made her a little uncomfortable. When she swiveled back, Darius was standing in the doorway. Betsy started.

"Mrs. Tannenbaum?" Darius said, as he entered the room. Betsy stood. She was almost five feet eleven, but she had to look up to Darius. He extended his hand, exposing the exquisite gold cuff links that secured his French cuffs. His hand was cold and his manner distant. Betsy did not believe in auras, but there was definitely something about the man that did not come across on television or in newspaper photos.

"I'm sorry to be so mysterious, Mrs. Tannenbaum," Darius said when they were seated.

"For twenty-five hundred dollars you can wear a mask, Mr. Darius."

Darius grinned. "I like an attorney with a sense of humor. I haven't met too many of them."

"That's because you deal with business lawyers and tax attorneys. Criminal lawyers don't last long without a sense of humor."

Darius leaned back in his chair and looked around Betsy's cluttered office. It was her first and it was small and cramped. She had made just enough money this year to think about moving to larger quarters. If she ever collected the verdict in the abortion case she would definitely move, but that case was bogged down in the appellate courts and she might never see a penny.

"I was at a charity affair for the Portland Opera the other night," Darius said. "Do you go?"

"I'm afraid not."

"Too bad. It's quite good. I had an interesting discussion with Maxine Silver. She's on the staff. A very strong-minded woman. We were discussing Greig's book. Have you read it?"

"The novel by the serial killer?" Betsy asked, puzzled by the direction the conversation was taking.

Darius nodded.

"I've seen a few reviews, but I don't have time to read anything but legal periodicals. It's not my kind of book, anyway."

"Don't judge the book by its author, Mrs. Tannenbaum. It's really a very sensitive work. A coming-of-age story. He handles the subject of his protagonist's abuse with such tenderness that you almost forget what Greig did to those children. Still, Maxine felt it shouldn't have been published, solely because Greig wrote it. Do you agree with her?"

Darius's question was strange but Betsy decided to play along.

"I'm opposed to censorship. I would not ban a book because I disapproved of the person who wrote it."

"If the publisher bowed to pressure from, say, women's groups and withdrew the book from circulation, would you represent Greig?"

"Mr. Darius . . ."

"Martin."

"Is there a point to these questions or are you just making small talk?"

"Humor me."

"I could represent Greig."

"Knowing that he's a monster?"

"I would be representing a principle, Mr. Darius. Freedom of speech. *Hamlet* would still be *Hamlet*, even if Charles Manson wrote it."

Darius laughed. "Well put." Then he took a check out of his pocket.

"Tell me what you think, after reading this," he said, placing the check on the desk between them. The check was made out to Elizabeth Tannenbaum. It was for $58,346.47. Something about the figure was familiar. Betsy frowned for a moment, then flushed when she realized the sum was her exact gross income for the previous year. Something Darius would know only if he had access to her tax returns.

"I think someone has been invading my privacy," Betsy snapped, "and I don't like it."

"Twenty-five hundred dollars of this is your fee for this evening's consultation," Darius said, ignoring Betsy's anger. "The rest is a retainer. Place it in trust and keep the interest. Someday, I may ask you to return it. I may also ask you to represent me, in which case you may charge me whatever you believe the case is worth over and above the retainer."

"I'm not certain I want to work for you, Mr. Darius."

"Why? Because I had you investigated? I don't blame you for being angry, but a man in my position can't take chances. There is only one copy of the investigative report and I'll send it to you no matter how our meeting concludes. You'll be pleased to hear what your colleagues have to say about you."

"Why don't you give this money to the firm that handles your business affairs?"

"I don't wish to discuss this matter with my business lawyers."

"Are you being investigated in connection with a crime?"

"Why don't we discuss that if it becomes necessary."

"Mr. Darius, there are a number of excellent criminal defense attorneys in Portland. Why me?"

Darius looked amused. "Let's just say that I believe you are the most qualified person to handle my case, should representation become necessary."

"I'm a little leery of taking a case on this basis."

"Don't be. You're under no obligation. Take the check, use the interest. If I do come to you and you decide you can't represent me, you can always give the money back. And, I can assure you, if I'm accused I will be innocent and you will be able to pursue my defense with a clear conscience."

Betsy studied the check. It was almost four times the largest fee she'd ever earned and Martin Darius was the type of client a sane person did not turn down.

"As long as you understand I'm under no obligation," Betsy said.

"Of course. I'll send you a retainer agreement that spells out the terms of our arrangement."

They shook hands and Betsy showed Darius out. Then she locked the door and reentered her office. When Betsy was certain Darius was gone, she gave the check a

big kiss, gave a subdued whoop and whirled around. A
Betsy was allowed to indulge in immature behavior from
time to time.

3

Betsy was in a terrific mood by the time she parked her
station wagon in her carport. It was not so much the retainer, but the fact that Martin Darius had chosen her
over all the other attorneys in Portland. Betsy was building a reputation with cases like *State* v. *Hammermill,* but
the big-money clients were still going to the big-name
criminal defense attorneys. Until this evening.

Rick Tannenbaum opened the door before Betsy
fished her key out of her purse. Her husband was slender
and an inch shorter than Betsy. His thick black hair was
styled to fall across his high forehead, and his smooth skin
and clear blue eyes made him look younger than thirty-
six. Rick had always been overly formal. Even now, when
he should be relaxing, his tie was still knotted and his suit
coat was on.

"Damn it, Betsy, it's almost eight. Where were
you?"

"My client didn't come until six-thirty. I'm sorry."

Before Rick could say anything else Kathy came
tearing down the hall. Betsy dumped her briefcase and
purse on a chair and scooped up their six-year-old daughter.

"I made a picture. You have to come see," Kathy
yelled, fighting to get down as soon as she received a hug
and kiss from her mother.

"Bring it to the kitchen," Betsy answered, lowering
Kathy to the floor and taking off her jacket. Kathy

streaked down the hall toward her bedroom with her long, blond hair flying after her.

"Please don't do this to me again, Betsy," Rick said, when Kathy was far enough away so she wouldn't hear. "I felt like a fool. I was in a meeting with Donovan and three other lawyers and I had to tell them I couldn't participate any longer because I had to pick up my daughter from day care. Something we agreed is your responsibility."

"I'm sorry, Rick. Mom wasn't available and I had to meet this client."

"I have clients too and a position to maintain in my firm. I'm trying to make partner and that's not going to happen if I get a reputation as someone who can't be relied on."

"For Christ's sake, Rick. How many times have I asked you to do this? She's your daughter, too. Donovan understands you have a child. These things happen."

Kathy rushed into the kitchen and they stopped arguing.

"This is the picture, Mom," Kathy said, thrusting forward a large piece of drawing paper. Betsy scrutinized the picture while Kathy looked up at her expectantly. She was adorable in her tiny jeans and striped, long-sleeve shirt.

"Why Kathy Tannenbaum," Betsy said, holding the picture at arm's length, "this is the most fantastic picture of an elephant I have ever seen."

"It's a cow, Mom."

"A cow with a trunk?"

"That's the tail."

"Oh. You're sure it's not an elephant?"

"Stop teasing," Kathy said seriously.

Betsy laughed and returned the picture with a hug

and kiss. "You are the greatest artist since Leonardo da Vinci. Greater even. Now let me get dinner ready."

Kathy ran back to her room. Betsy put a frying pan on the stove and took out a tomato and some lettuce for a salad.

"Who is this big client?" Rick asked.

Betsy didn't want to tell Rick, especially since Darius wanted his visit kept secret. But she felt she owed Rick the information.

"This is very confidential. Will you promise not to breathe a word if I tell you?"

"Sure."

"Martin Darius retained me, tonight," she said, breaking into a huge grin.

"Martin Darius?" Rick answered incredulously. "Why would he hire you? Parish, Marquette and Reeves handles his legal work."

"Apparently he thinks I'm also capable of represent-. ing him," Betsy answered, trying not to show how much Rick's reaction hurt her.

"You don't have a business practice."

"I don't think it's a business matter."

"Then what is it?"

"He didn't say."

"What's Darius like?"

Betsy thought about the question. What was Darius like?

"Spooky," Betsy answered just as Kathy hurtled back into the kitchen. "He likes to be mysterious and he wants you to know how powerful he is."

"What are you cooking, Mom?"

"Roast, little girl," Betsy said, picking up Kathy and nibbling her neck until she squealed. "Now, buzz off or I'll never get dinner ready."

Betsy lowered Kathy to the floor. "Do you want to

stay for dinner?" she asked Rick. He looked uncomfortable and checked his watch.

"Thanks, but I've got to get back to the office."

"All right. Thanks, again, for picking up Kathy. I do know how busy you are and I appreciate the help."

"Yeah, well . . . Sorry I jumped down your throat. It's just . . ."

"I know," Betsy said.

Rick looked like he was going to say something but went to the closet instead and got his raincoat.

"Good luck with Darius," Rick told her as he was leaving. Betsy shut the door behind him. She had heard the hint of jealousy in his voice and regretted telling Rick about her new client. She should have known better than to say anything that would let him know how well she was doing.

" 'But it takes time to make a raft, even when one is as industrious and untiring as the Tin Woodman, and when night came the work was not done. So they found a cozy place under the trees where they slept well until the morning; and Dorothy dreamed of the Emerald City, and of the good Wizard of Oz, who would soon send her back to her own home again.'

"And now," Betsy said, closing the book and laying it on Kathy's bed, "it's time for my little wizard to hit the hay."

"Can't you read one more chapter?" Kathy begged.

"No, I cannot read another chapter," Betsy said, giving Kathy a hug. "I already read you one more than you were entitled to. Enough is enough."

"You're mean, Mommy," Kathy said, with a smile Betsy could not see because her cheek was against Kathy's baby-soft hair.

"That's tough. You're stuck with the world's meanest mommy and there's nothing you can do about it." Betsy kissed Kathy's forehead, then sat up. "Now get to bed. I'll see you in the morning."

"Night, Mom."

Kathy rolled onto her side and wrestled Oliver, an oversized, stuffed skunk, into position against her chest.

"Night, hon."

Betsy closed the door of Kathy's room behind her and went into the kitchen to wash the dishes. Although she would never admit it to her feminist friends, Betsy loved washing dishes. It was perfect therapy. A lawyer's day was littered with stressful situations and insoluble problems. Washing dishes was a finite task that Betsy could do perfectly every time she tried. Instant gratification from a job well done, over and over again. And Betsy needed some instant gratification after being with Rick.

She knew why he was so angry. Rick had been a superstar in law school and Donovan, Chastain and Mills had lured him to their two-hundred-lawyer sweatshop with a large salary and glowing promises of a fast track to a partnership. The firm had worked him like a dog, constantly holding the partnership just out of reach. When he was passed over last year, just as her career was starting to take off, it had been a crushing blow to his ego. Their ten-year-old marriage had not been able to withstand the strain.

Two months ago, when Rick told her he was leaving, Betsy was stunned. She knew they had problems, but she'd never imagined that he would walk out. Betsy had searched her memory for a clue to Rick's jealousy. Had he changed or was he always so self-centered? Betsy had trouble believing that Rick's love was too fragile to withstand her success, but she was not willing to give up her career to appease his ego. Why should she? The way she saw it, it was a matter of Rick accepting her as an equal. If he couldn't do that then she could never stay married to him. If he loved her, it should not be such a hard thing to do. She was proud of his achievements. Why couldn't he be proud of hers?

Betsy poured herself a glass of milk and turned off the light. The kitchen joined the rest of the house in soothing darkness. Betsy carried her glass to the kitchen table and slumped into a chair. She took a sip and gazed sleepily out the window. Many of the houses in the neighborhood were dark. A streetlight cast a pale glow over a corner of the front yard. It was so quiet with Rick gone and Kathy asleep. No traffic sounds outside, no television on. None of the little noises people make shuffling around a house.

Betsy had handled enough divorces to know that many estranged husbands would never have done what Rick had done for her tonight. He had done it for Kathy, because he loved her. And Kathy loved Rick. The separation was very hard on their daughter. There were times, like now, when the house was quiet and Betsy was alone, that she missed Rick. She was not certain she loved him anymore, but she remembered how good it had been. Sleeping alone was the hardest thing. She missed the lovemaking, but she missed the cuddling and the pillow talk more. Sometimes she thought they might get back together. Tonight, before Rick left, she was certain that there was something he wanted to tell her. What was he about to say? And if he said he wanted her back, what would she say? After all, he was the one who had walked out on ten years of marriage, a child, their life together. They were a family and Rick's actions told her that meant nothing to him.

The night Rick walked out, alone in bed, when she

couldn't cry anymore, Betsy had rolled on her side and stared at their wedding picture. Rick was grinning. He had told her he had never been so happy. She had been so filled with joy, she was afraid she could not hold all of it. How could a feeling like that disappear?

Chapter Four

I

"Late night?" Wayne Turner's secretary asked, trying, unsuccessfully, to conceal a grin.

"It shows, huh?"

"Only to those who know how perky you usually look."

The night before, Turner, Senator Raymond Colby's administrative assistant, had gotten stinking drunk celebrating the senator's nomination to the Supreme Court. This morning he was paying for his sins, but he didn't mind. He was happy for the old gent, who had done so much for him. His only regret was that Colby had not run for President. He would have made a great one.

Turner was five feet nine and slender. He had a narrow face, high cheekbones, close-cropped, kinky black hair that was graying at the temples and brown skin a few shades darker than his tan suit. Turner weighed about what he had when he first met Colby. He hadn't lost his intensity, but the scowl that used to be a permanent feature had wilted over the years. Turner hung his jacket on a hook behind the door, lit his fourth Winston of the day and sat behind his cluttered desk. Framed in the window at his back was the shining, white dome of the Capitol.

Turner shuffled through his messages. Many were from reporters who wanted the inside scoop on Colby's nomination. Some were from a.a.s for other senators who were probably calling about Colby's crime bill. A few were from partners in prestigious Washington law firms, confirmation that Turner need not be worried about what he would do after the senator became Chief Justice. Washington power brokers were always interested in someone who had the ear of a powerful man. Turner would do all right, but he would miss working with the senator.

The last message in the stack caught Turner's eye. It was from Nancy Gordon, one of the few people whose call he would have returned yesterday afternoon if he had made it back to the office. Turner assumed she was calling about the nomination. There was a Hunter's Point, New York, number on the message slip.

"It's Wayne," he said when he heard the familiar voice at the other end. "How you doin'?"

"He's surfaced," Gordon answered without any preliminaries. It took Turner a few seconds to catch on, then he felt sick.

"Where?"

"Portland, Oregon."

"How do you know?"

She told him. When she was through, Turner asked, "What are you going to do?"

"There's a flight to Portland leaving in two hours."

"Why do you think he started again?"

"I'm surprised he held out for so long," Gordon answered.

"When did you get the letter?"

"Yesterday, around four. I just came on shift."

"You know about the senator?"

"Heard it on the news."

"Do you think there's a connection? The timing, I mean. It seems odd it would be so soon after the President made the announcement."

"There could be a connection. I don't know. And I don't want to jump to conclusions."

"Have you called Frank?" Turner asked.

"Not yet."

"Do it. Let him know."

"All right."

"Shit. This is the absolute, worst possible time for this to happen."

"You're worried about the senator?"

"Of course."

"What about the women?" Gordon asked coldly.

"Don't lay that trip on me, Nancy. You know damn well I care about the women, but Colby is my best friend. Can you keep him out of it?"

"I will if I can."

Turner was sweating. The plastic receiver was uncomfortable against his ear.

"What will you do when you find him?" he asked nervously. Gordon did not answer immediately. Turner could hear her breathing deeply.

"Nancy?"

"I'll do what I have to."

Turner knew what that was. If Nancy Gordon found the man who had haunted their dreams for the past ten years, she would kill him. The civilized side of Wayne Turner wanted to tell Gordon that she should not take the law into her own hands. But there was a primitive side of Wayne Turner that kept him from saying it, because everyone, including the senator, would be better off if the man Homicide Detective Nancy Gordon was stalking died.

2

The microwave buzzed. Alan Page backed into the kitchen, keeping one eye on the television. The CBS anchorman was talking about the date that had been set for Raymond Colby's confirmation hearing. Colby would give the Supreme Court a solid conservative majority and that was good news, if you were a prosecutor.

Alan took his TV dinner out of the microwave, giving the food the briefest of glances. He was thirty-seven, with close-cropped black hair, a face that still bore the scars of acne and a sense of purpose that made most people nervous. His rail-thin body suggested an interest in distance running. In fact, Alan was thin because he had no use for food and ate the bare minimum that would keep him going. It was worse now that he was divorced. On a good day, breakfast was instant coffee, lunch a sandwich and more black coffee and dinner a pizza.

A reporter was interviewing someone who knew Colby when he was c.e.o. of Marlin Steel. Alan used the remote to jack up the volume. From what he was hearing, there was nothing standing in the way of Colby's confirmation as Chief Justice of the United States. The doorbell rang just as the Colby story ended. Alan hoped it wasn't business. There was a Bogart classic on at nine that he'd been looking forward to all day.

The woman standing on Alan's doorstep held a briefcase over her head to shield herself from the rain. A small, tan valise stood beside her. A taxi was waiting at the curb, its wipers swinging back and forth and its head-light beams cutting through the torrent.

"Alan Page?"

He nodded. The woman flipped open a leather case she was clutching in her free hand and showed Alan her badge.

"Nancy Gordon. I'm a homicide detective with the Hunter's Point P.D. in Hunter's Point, New York. Can I come in?"

"Of course," he said, stepping back. Gordon signaled the taxi, then ducked inside. She held the briefcase at arm's length, shook off the water on the welcome mat, then pulled in the valise.

"Let me take your coat," Alan said. "Can I get you something to drink?"

"Hot coffee, please," Gordon answered as she handed him her raincoat.

"What's a detective from New York doing in Port-land, Oregon?" Alan asked as he hung the coat in the hall closet.

"Does the phrase 'Gone, But Not Forgotten' mean anything to you, Mr. Page?"

Alan stood perfectly still for a second, then turned around. "That information hasn't been released to the public. How do you know about it?"

"I know more than you can imagine about 'Gone, But Not Forgotten,' Mr. Page. I know what the note means. I know about the black rose. I also know who took your missing women."

Alan needed a moment to think.

"Please sit down and I'll get your coffee," he told Gordon.

The apartment was small. The living room and kitchen were one space divided by a counter. Gordon chose an armchair near the television and waited patiently while Alan mixed water from a tea kettle with Folger's instant. He handed the cup to the detective, turned off the set, then sat opposite her on the couch. Gordon was tall with an athlete's body. Alan guessed she was in her mid-thirties. Her blond hair was cut short. She was attractive without working at it. The most striking thing about the detective was her utter seriousness. Her dress was severe, her eyes were cold, her mouth was sealed in a straight line and her body was rigid, like an animal prepared to defend itself.

Gordon leaned forward slightly. "Think of the most repulsive criminals, Mr. Page. Think of Bundy, Manson, Dahmer. The man leaving these notes is smarter and far more dangerous than any of them, because they're all dead or in prison. The man you're after is the man who got away."

"You know who he is?" Alan asked.

Gordon nodded. "I've been waiting for him to surface for ten years."

Gordon paused. She looked into the steam rising from her cup. Then she looked back at Alan.

"This man is cunning, Mr. Page, and he's different. He's not human, the way we think of human. I knew he wouldn't be able to control himself forever and I was right. Now he's surfaced and I can catch him, but I need your help."

"If you can clear this up, you've got all the help you want. But I'm still confused about who you are and what you're talking about."

"Of course. I'm sorry. I've been involved with this case so long, I forget other people don't know what happened. And you'll need to know it all or you won't understand. Do you have the time, Mr. Page? Can I tell you now? I don't think we can wait, even until morning. Not while he's still out there, free."

"If you're not too tired."

Gordon stared into Alan's eyes with an intensity that forced him to look away.

"I'm always tired, Mr. Page. There was a time when I couldn't sleep without pills. I'm over that, but the nightmares haven't stopped and I still don't sleep well. I won't until he's caught."

Alan did not know what to say. Gordon looked down. She drank more coffee. Then she told Alan Page about Hunter's Point.

Part Two

HUNTER'S POINT

Chapter Five

I

The sprawling, two-story colonial was in the middle of a cul-de-sac, set well back from the street. A large, well-tended lawn created a wide buffer zone between the house and those on either side. A red Ferrari was parked in the driveway in front of a three-car garage.

Nancy Gordon knew it was going to be bad as soon as she saw the stunned expressions on the faces of the neighbors, who huddled just outside the police barriers. They were shocked by the presence of police cars and a morgue wagon in the quiet confines of The Meadows, where the houses started at half a million and crime was simply not permitted. She knew it was going to be really bad when she saw the grim faces of the two homicide detectives who were talking in low tones on the lawn near the front door.

Nancy parked her Ford behind a marked car and squeezed through the sawhorses. Frank Grimsbo and Wayne Turner stopped their conversation when they saw her. She was dressed in jeans and a T-shirt. The call had come while she was sprawled in front of the TV in a ratty nightgown, sipping a cheap white wine and watching the Mets smoke the Dodgers. The clothes were the first thing she could find and the last thing she thought about.

"Newman said there's a body this time," she said excitedly.

"Two."

"How can we be sure it's him?" Nancy asked.

"The note and the rose were on the floor near the woman," Grimsbo answered. He was a big man with a beer gut and thinning black hair who wore cheap plaid jackets and polyester slacks.

"It's him all right," said Turner, a skinny black man with close-cropped hair and a permanent scowl who was in his second year in night law school. "The first cop on the scene was smart enough to figure out what was going on. He called me right away. Michaels did the note and the crime scene before anyone else was let in."

"That was a break. Who's the second victim?"

"Melody Lake," Grimsbo answered. "She's six years old, Nancy."

"Oh, fuck." The excitement she felt at finally getting a body disappeared instantly. "Did he . . . Was there anything done to her?"

Turner shook his head. "She wasn't molested."

"And the woman?"

"Sandra Lake. The mother. Death by strangulation. She was beaten pretty badly, too, but there's no evidence of sexual activity. Course, she hasn't been autopsied."

"Do we have a witness?"

"I don't know," Grimsbo answered. "We have uniforms talking to the neighbors, but nothing yet. Husband found the bodies and called it in to 911 about eight-fifteen. He says he didn't see anyone, so the killer must have left way before the husband got home. We got a cul-

de-sac here and it leads into Sparrow Lane, the only road
out of the development. The husband would have seen
someone coming in or out."

"Who's talked to him?"

"I did, for a few minutes," Turner answered. "And
the first cops on the scene, of course. He was too bent out
of shape to make any sense. You know him, Nancy."

"I do?"

"It's Peter Lake."

"The attorney?"

Grimsbo nodded. "He defended Daley."

Nancy frowned and tried to remember what she
could about Peter Lake. She had not done much in the
Daley investigation. All she recalled about the defense
attorney were his good looks and efficient manner. She
was on the stand less than a half hour.

"I better go in," Nancy said.

The entryway was huge. A small chandelier hung
overhead. A sunken living room was directly in front of
her. The room was spotless. She could see a small man-
made lake out back through a large picture window. Stra-
tegically placed around the room, most probably by an
interior decorator, were bleached oak tables with granite
tops, chairs and a sofa in pastel shades and macramé wall
hangings. It looked more like a showroom than a place
where people lived.

A wide staircase was off to the left. A polished wood
banister followed the curve of the stairs to the second
floor. The posts supporting the banister were closely
spaced. Through the spaces, halfway up the stairs, Nancy
could see a small lump covered by a blanket. She turned
away.

Lab technicians were dusting for prints, taking photographs and collecting evidence. Bruce Styles, the dep-

uty medical examiner, was standing with his back to her in the middle of the entryway between a uniformed officer and one of his assistants.

"You finished?" Nancy asked.

The doctor nodded and stepped aside. The woman was facedown on the white shag carpet. She was wearing a white cotton dress. It looked well suited for the heat. Her feet were bare. The woman's head was turned away. Blood matted her long brown hair. Nancy guessed she had been brought down by a blow to the head, and Styles confirmed her suspicion.

"I figure she was running for the door and he got her from behind. She could have been partly conscious or completely out when he strangled her."

Nancy walked around the body so she could see the woman's face. She was sorry she looked. If the woman had been attractive, there was no way to tell now. Nancy took a couple of deep breaths.

"What about the little girl?" she asked.

"Neck broken," Styles answered. "It would have been quick and painless."

"We think she was a witness to the mother's murder," Turner said. "Probably heard her screaming and came down the steps."

"Where's the husband?" Nancy asked.

"Down the hall in the den," Turner said.

"No sense putting it off."

Peter Lake slumped in a chair. Someone had given him a glass of scotch, but the glass was still more than half full. He looked up when Nancy entered the den and she could see he had been crying. Even so, he was a striking man, tall with a trim, athletic build. Lake's styled, gold-blond hair, his pale blue eyes and sharp, clean-shaven features were what won over the women on his juries.

"Mr. Lake, do you remember me?" Nancy asked.

Lake looked confused.

"I'm a homicide detective. My name is Nancy Gordon. You cross-examined me in the Daley case."

"Of course. I'm sorry. I don't handle many criminal cases anymore."

"How are you feeling?" Nancy asked, sitting across from Lake.

"I'm numb."

"I know what you're going through . . ." Nancy started, but Lake's head jerked up.

"How could you? They're dead. My family is dead."

Lake covered his eyes with his hands and wept. His shoulders trembled.

"I do know how you feel," Nancy said softly. "A year ago my fiancé was murdered. The only good thing that came out of it was that I learned how victims really feel, and sometimes I can even help them get through the worst of it."

Lake looked up. He wiped his eyes. "I'm sorry," he said. "It's just so hard. They meant everything to me. And Melody . . . How could someone do that to a little girl? She couldn't hurt anybody. She was just a little girl."

"Mr. Lake, four women have disappeared in Hunter's Point in the past few months. A black rose and a note, identical to the ones you found, were left at each home. I know how much you're grieving, but we have to act fast. This is the first time we have actually found a victim. That could mean you surprised the killer before he had time to take your wife away. Anything you can tell us would be deeply appreciated and may help us catch this man before he kills again."

"I don't know anything. Believe me, I've thought

about it. I was working late on a case. I called to let Sandy know. I didn't see anything unusual when I drove up. Then I . . . I'm really not too clear on what I did after I . . . I know I sat down on the bottom step."

Lake paused. He breathed deeply, trying to keep from crying again. His lip trembled. He took a sip of his scotch.

"This is very hard for me, Detective. I want to help, but . . . Really, this is very hard."

Nancy stood up and placed a hand on Lake's shoulder. He began to weep again.

"I'm going to leave my card. I want you to call me if I can do anything for you. Anything. If you remember something, no matter how insignificant you may believe it to be, call me. Please."

"I will. I'll be better in the morning and I'll . . . It's just . . ."

"It's all right. Oh, one other thing. The media will be after you. They won't respect your privacy. Please don't talk to them. There are many aspects of this case we are not going to release to the public. We keep back facts to help us eliminate phony confessions and to identify the real killer. It's very important that you keep what you know to yourself."

"I won't talk to the press. I don't want to see anyone."

"Okay," Nancy said kindly. "And you're going to be all right. Not one hundred percent, and not for a long time, but you'll deal with your grief. It won't be easy. I'm still not healed, but I'm better, and you'll be better too. Remember what I said about calling. Not the police business. You know, if you just want to talk."

Lake nodded. When Nancy left the den, he was sprawled in the chair, his head back and his eyes closed.

2

Hunter's Point was a commuter suburb with a population of 110,000, a small downtown riddled with trendy boutiques and upscale restaurants, a branch of the State University, and a lot of shopping centers. There were no slums in Hunter's Point, but there were clusters of Cape Cods and garden apartments on the fringe of the downtown area that housed students and families unable to afford the high-priced developments like The Meadows, where the commuting lawyers, doctors and businessmen lived.

Police headquarters was a dull, square building on the outskirts of town. It sat in the middle of a flat, black-topped parking lot surrounded by a chain link fence. The lot was filled with police cars, unmarked vehicles and tow trucks.

The rose killer task force was housed in an old storage area in the back of the building. There were no windows, and the fluorescent lights were annoyingly bright. A watercooler was squeezed between two chest-high filing cabinets. A low wood table stood on rickety legs against a cream-colored wall. On the table sat a coffee maker, four coffee mugs, a sugar bowl and a brown plastic cup filled with several packets of artificial creamer. Four gunmetal-gray, government-issue desks were grouped in the center of the room. Bulletin boards with pictures of the victims and information about the crimes covered two walls.

Nancy Gordon hunched over her reports on the Lake murders. The flickering fluorescents were starting to give her a headache. She closed her eyes, leaned back and pinched her lids. When she opened her eyes, she was staring at the photographs of Samantha Reardon and Patricia Cross that Turner had tacked to the wall. The photos had been supplied by their husbands. Samantha on the deck of a sailboat. A tall woman, the wind blowing her flowing brown hair behind her, a smile of genuine happiness brightening her face. Pat in shorts and a halter top on a beach in Oahu, very slender, too thin, actually. Her friends said she was overly conscious of her figure. Except for Reardon, who had been a nurse, none of the women had ever held a meaningful job, and Reardon stopped working soon after her marriage. They were happy housewives living in luxury, spending their time at golf and bridge. Their idea of contributing to the community was raising money for charity at country club functions. Where were these women now? Were they dead? Had they died quickly, or slowly, in agony? How had they held up? How much of their dignity were they able to retain?

The phone rang. "Gordon," she answered.

"There's a Mr. Lake at the front desk," the receptionist said. Nancy straightened up. Less than seventy-two hours had passed since her visit to the crime scene.

"I'll be right out," Gordon said, dropping her pen on a stack of police reports.

Inside the front door of the police station was a small lobby furnished with cheap chairs upholstered in imitation leather and outfitted with chrome armrests. The lobby was separated from the rest of the building by a counter with a sliding glass window and a door with an electronic lock. Lake was seated in one of the chairs. He was dressed in a dark suit and solid maroon tie. His hair was carefully combed. The only evidence of his personal tragedy was red-rimmed eyes that suggested a lack of sleep and a lot of mourning. Nancy hit the button next to the receptionist's desk and opened the door.

"I wasn't certain you'd be here," Lake said. "I hope you don't mind my showing up without calling."

"No. Come on in. I'll find us a place to talk."

Lake followed Nancy down a hall that reminded him of a school corridor. They walked on worn green linoleum that buckled in places, past unpainted brown wood doors. Chipped flakes of green paint fell from spots on the walls. Nancy opened the door to one of the interrogation rooms and stood aside for Lake. The room was covered with white, soundproof tiles.

"Have a seat," Nancy said, motioning toward one of the plastic chairs that stood on either side of a long wooden table. "I'll grab us some coffee. How do you take yours?"

"Black," Lake answered.

When Nancy returned with two Styrofoam cups, Lake was sitting at the table with his hands in his lap.

"How are you feeling?" she asked.

"I'm very tired, and depressed. I tried going to work today, but I couldn't concentrate. I keep thinking about Melody."

Lake stopped. He took a deep breath. "Look, I'll get to the point. I can't work, and I have a feeling I'm not going to be able to work for quite a while. I sat down with the papers on a real estate closing this morning and it seemed so . . . It just didn't mean anything to me.

"I have two associates who can keep my practice going until I'm able to cope, if that ever happens. But now all I want to do is find out who killed Sandy and Melody. It's all I can think about."

"Mr. Lake, it's all I can think about too. And I'm not alone. I'm going to tell you some things. This is highly confidential. I'll need your promise to keep it confidential."

Lake nodded.

"There were four disappearances before your wife and daughter were killed. None of those women has been found. It took us a while to catch on, because there were no bodies. At first, we treated them like missing persons. But a note with 'Gone, But Not Forgotten' and a black rose was left at each crime scene, so after the second one we knew what we were dealing with. The chief has put together a task force to work on the cases. . . ."

"I'm sure you're working very hard," Lake interrupted. "I didn't mean to be critical. What I want to do is help. I want to volunteer to be part of the task force."

"That's out of the question, Mr. Lake. You aren't a police officer. It also wouldn't be advisable. You're too emotionally involved to be objective."

"Lawyers are trained to be objective. And I can add something to the investigation—the unique insight into the criminal mind that I developed as a defense attorney. Defense attorneys learn things about the way criminals think that the police never know, because we have the criminal's confidence. My clients know they can tell me anything, no matter how horrible, and I will respect their privacy. You see criminals when their false face is on. I see them the way they really are."

"Mr. Lake, police officers get a real good look at the criminal mind—too good. We see these guys on the street, in their homes. You see them cleaned up, in your office, a long way from their victims and after they've had time to rationalize what they've done and cook up a sob story or a defense. But none of that matters, because you simply cannot work on this case. As much as I appreciate the offer, my superiors wouldn't allow it."

"I know it sounds strange, but I really do think I could contribute. I'm very smart."

Nancy shook her head. "There's another good reason you shouldn't get involved in this investigation—it would mean reliving the death of your wife and daughter every day, instead of getting on with your life. We have their autopsy photos lying around, their pictures posted on the wall. Do you want that?"

"I have their pictures all over my house and office, Detective Gordon. And there isn't a minute I don't think about them."

Nancy sighed. "I know," she said, "but you have to stop thinking about them that way or it will kill you."

Lake paused. "Tell me about your fiancé," he said quietly. "How . . . how did you stop thinking about him?"

"I never did. I think about Ed all the time. Especially at night, when I'm alone. I don't want to forget him and you won't want to forget Sandy and Melody.

"Ed was a cop. A drunk shot him. He was trying to calm down a domestic dispute. It was two weeks before our wedding date. At first I felt just like you do. I couldn't work. I could barely make it out of bed. I . . . I was racked with guilt, which is ridiculous. I kept on thinking there was something I could have done, insisted he stay home that day, I don't know. I wasn't really making much sense.

"But it got better, Mr. Lake. Not all better, not even mostly better. You just get to a point where you face the fact that a lot of the pain comes from feeling sorry for yourself, for what you've lost. Then you realize that you have to start living for yourself. You have to go on and keep the memories of the good times. If you don't, then whoever killed your little girl and your wife will have won. They will have killed you too."

Nancy reached across the table and put her hand on Peter Lake's arm.

"We'll get him, Mr. Lake. You have so much to deal

with, you don't want to get involved with this too. Let us handle it. We'll get him, I promise."

Lake stood up. "Thank you, Detective Gordon."

"Nancy. Call me Nancy. And give me a call anytime you want to talk."

3

A week later, Hunter's Point Chief of Police John O'Malley entered the task force office. He was usually in shirtsleeves with his tie askew and his top button open. This morning, O'Malley wore the navy blue suit he saved for Rotary Club speeches and meetings with the city council.

The chief had the broad shoulders and thick chest of a middleweight boxer. His nose had been broken by a fleeing burglar when he worked in New York's South Bronx. His receding red hair revealed an old scar, a memento of one of many gang fights he had been in as a youth in Brooklyn. O'Malley would have stayed in New York City if a heart attack hadn't forced him to pursue police work in a less stressful environment.

Walking behind O'Malley was a huge man dressed in a tan summer-weight suit. Nancy guessed that the suit was custom-tailored, because it fit perfectly, even though the man was oddly oversized, like a serious bodybuilder.

"This is Dr. Mark Klien," O'Malley said. "He's a psychiatrist who practices in Manhattan, and an expert on serial killers. Dr. Klien was consulted in the Son of Sam case, the Atlanta child murders, Bundy. He's worked with VICAP. I met him a few years ago when I was with the NYPD and working a serial case. He was very helpful.

Dr. Klien's seen a full set of reports on these disappearances and the deaths of Melody and Sandra Lake.

"Dr. Klien," O'Malley said, pointing to each member of the task force in turn, "this is Nancy Gordon, Frank Grimsbo, Wayne Turner and Glen Michaels. They've been on this case since it started."

Dr. Klien was so massive, he filled the entrance to the office. When he stepped into the room to shake hands, someone else followed him in. O'Malley looked uncomfortable.

"Before Dr. Klien gets started, I want to explain why Mr. Lake is here. Yesterday the mayor and I met. He explained that Mr. Lake was volunteering to assist the task force in finding the killer of his wife and daughter."

Nancy Gordon and Frank Grimsbo exchanged worried glances. Wayne Turner's mouth opened and he stared at O'Malley. O'Malley flushed angrily, stared back and continued.

"The mayor feels that Mr. Lake brings a unique insight into the criminal mind, developed as a defense attorney, that will give us a fresh perspective on the case."

"I hope I'll be of use," Peter Lake said, smiling apologetically. "I know I'm not a trained policeman, so I'll try to keep out of the way."

"Dr. Klien has a busy schedule," O'Malley said, ignoring Lake. "He has to take a two-fifty shuttle back to the city, so I'm going to let him take over."

Lake took a seat behind everyone in the back of the room. Frank Grimsbo shook his head slowly. Wayne Turner folded his arms across his chest and stared accusingly at O'Malley. Nancy frowned. Only Glen Michaels, the chubby, balding criminologist O'Malley had assigned to do the forensic work for the task force, seemed uninterested in Lake. He was riveted on Mark Klien, who went to the front of the room and stood before a wall covered with victim information.

"I hope what I have to say is of some use to you," Klien said, talking without notes. "One disadvantage a small department like Hunter's Point has in these cases is its inexperience with crimes of this type. Although even larger departments are usually at a loss, since serial killers, for all the suffering they cause and all the publicity they receive, are, fortunately, rare birds. Now that the FBI has established the Violent Crime Apprehension Program in Quantico, small departments, like yours, can forward a description of your case to VICAP and learn if any similar murders have taken place in other parts of the country. VICAP uses a computer program to list violent crimes and their descriptions throughout the country and can hook you up with other police agencies where similar crimes may have occurred, so you can coordinate your investigation.

"What I want to do today is give you a profile of the serial killer in order to dispel any stereotypes you may have and list some common factors you can look for. The FBI has identified two separate categories: the disorganized asocial and the organized nonsocial. Let's discuss the latter type first. The organized nonsocial is a sexual psychopath and, like any psychopath, he is unable to empathize, to feel pity or caring for others. His victims are simply objects he uses as he wishes to serve his own perverted needs. Venting his anger is one of these needs, whether through mutilation or debasing the victim. The Boston Strangler, for example, placed his victims in a position so that the first sight anyone had of them as they entered the room was to see them with their legs spread apart. Another killer mailed the foot of his victim to her parents in order to expand the pain and misery he had already caused."

"Excuse me, Dr. Klien," Wayne Turner said. "Is it possible that our killer is leaving the notes to torment the husbands?"

"That's a good possibility. The cruelty in torturing a victim's loved ones, and thereby creating more victims, would be very attractive to a sexual psychopath, since he is unaffected by any moral code and has no sense of remorse. He is capable of any act. Preserving body parts and eating them is not unusual, and having sex with the corpse of a victim is even less rare. Lucas decapitated one of his victims and had oral sex with the head for a week until the odor became so extreme he had to dispose of it."

"Is that the type of crazy bastard we're dealing with here?" Grimsbo asked.

"Not 'crazy,' Detective. In spite of the extremes of their behavior, these people are not legally insane. They are well aware of what is morally and legally right and wrong. The terrifying thing is that they do not learn from their experiences, so neither treatment nor imprisonment is likely to alter their behavior. In fact, because of the compulsiveness associated with these sexual acts, it is most likely that they will kill again."

"What does the black rose mean?" Nancy asked.

"I don't know, but fantasy and compulsion are very much a part of these killers' actions, and the rose could be part of the killer's fantasy. Prior to the killing, they fantasize about it in great detail, planning very specifically what they will do. This increases their level of excitement or tension so that ultimately their act is one of compulsion. When the murder is completed there is a sense of relief until the tension builds up again, starting the cycle anew. Son of Sam talked of the great relief he felt after each killing, but he also demonstrated his faulty judgment when he said he did not know why his victims struggled so much, since he was only going to kill them, not rape them.

"Since fantasy is so much involved in their behavior, these killers often take a specific body part or item of clothing with them. They use it to relive the act. This heavy use of fantasy also results in the crimes being very well planned. The Hillside Strangler not only brought a weapon, he brought plastic bags to help him dispose of the bodies. This could account for the absence of forensic evidence at your crime scenes. I would guess that your killer is very knowledgeable in the area of police investigation. Am I correct that an analysis of the notes and the roses have yielded no clues, and that the crime scenes haven't turned up so much as a fiber or hair that's been of use?"

"That's pretty much true," answered Glen Michaels. "We did get a print from the Lake note, but it turned out to be the wife's. All the other notes were spotless and there was nothing unusual about the paper or the ink. So far, the lab hasn't picked up a thing we can use."

"I'm not surprised," Klien said. "There is a peculiar interest among these men with police and police work. Some of them have even been involved on the fringes of law enforcement. Bundy attended FBI lectures and Bianchi was in security work and in the police reserve. That means they may be aware of the steps they must take to avoid detection. Their interest in police work may also lie in a need to know how close the police are to catching them.

"Let's talk about the victims. Usually they're accidental, in that the killer simply drives around until he fixes on someone. Prostitutes make easy victims, because they'll get in a car or even allow themselves to be tied up. The victim is generally not from the killer's home turf and is usually a stranger, which makes apprehension much more difficult."

"Do you see that as being true in our case?" Nancy asked. "I mean, these women all fit a pattern. They're married to professionals, they don't have regular jobs, and except for Mrs. Lake they were all childless. They're also from the same town. Doesn't that show advance planning? That he's looking for a particular victim who fits into his fantasy, rather than grabbing women at random?"

"You're right. These victims don't seem to fit the usual pattern of random selection. It's pretty clear that your killer is stalking a particular type of woman in a particular area, which suggests he may live in Hunter's Point."

"What I don't understand is how he gets to them," Wayne Turner said. "We're dealing with educated women. They live in upscale neighborhoods where the residents are suspicious of strangers. Yet there's no sign of a struggle at any home but the Lakes', and, even there, the crime scene was relatively undisturbed."

Klien smiled. "You've brought us to one of the major misconceptions about serial killers, Detective Turner. In the movies they're portrayed as monsters, but in real life they fit into the community and do not look suspicious. Typically, they're bright, personable, even good-looking men. Bundy, the I-5 Bandit, the Hillside Strangler, Cortez—they're all respectable-looking men. So our killer is probably someone these women would let into their home without fear."

"Didn't you say there were two types of serial killers?" Grimsbo asked.

"Yes. There's also the disorganized asocial killer, but in this case we're not dealing with someone who fits that category. That's unfortunate, because they're easier to catch. They're psychotic loners who relate quite poorly to others and don't have the charm or ability to melt into the community. Their acts are impulsive and the weapon is usually whatever is at hand. The body is often mangled or blood-smeared and they frequently get blood all over themselves. The crime scenes can be very gruesome. They're also not mobile, like the organized nonsocials. Their homicides often take place close to their homes and they often return to the scene of the crime, not to check up on the investigation, but to further mutilate the body or relive the killing. Rarely do they penetrate the body sexually. They usually masturbate on it or in the immediate area, which can be helpful, now that we have workable DNA testing. But your boy is much too clever to be a disorganized asocial."

"Why haven't we found the bodies?" Turner asked.

"He's obviously hiding them, like the Green River Killer. Chief O'Malley tells me there's a lot of farmland and forest in this area. Someday a hiker is going to stumble on a mass grave and you'll have your bodies."

"What will they look like, Dr. Klien?" Nancy asked.

"It won't be pretty. We're dealing with a sexual sadist. If he has his victim isolated and he has time . . . You see, these men are expressing their rage toward their women victims. The mutilation and murder increases their sexual stimulation. In some instances, where the killer is usually impotent, the violence makes sex possible. The fantasy and the torture are the foreplay, Detective. The killing is the penetration. Some of these men ejaculate automatically at the moment they kill."

"Jesus," Grimsbo muttered. "And you say these guys aren't crazy."

"I said they weren't crazy, but I didn't say they were human. Personally, I see the man you're looking for as less than human. Somewhere along the way, some of the things that make us human were lost, either because of genetics or environment or . . . Well," Klien shrugged, "it really doesn't matter, does it, because he's beyond hope and must be stopped. Otherwise he'll go on and on and on, as long as there are women out there for him to feed on."

4

Nancy Gordon, Wayne Turner, Frank Grimsbo and Glen Michaels were waiting in O'Malley's office when he returned from dropping Dr. Klien at the airport.

"I sort of expected this," he said, when he saw them.

"Then please explain to us what the fuck is going on," Turner demanded.

"There's no way to sugarcoat it," O'Malley said. "I argued with the mayor and lost, period. We're stuck with Lake."

"You're shitting me," Grimsbo said.

"No, Frank, I'm not shitting you. I'm telling you the facts of political life."

"The guy's a potential suspect," Grimsbo said.

"Let's get this on the table, boys and girls, because I might be able to dump him, if it's true."

"I don't think it is, John," Nancy said. "I've met with him a few times and he's pretty broken up about losing his wife and kid."

"Yeah," Turner countered, "but he says he didn't see anyone coming from the house. Where did the killer go? There's only one road out of that development from the cul-de-sac."

"The neighbors didn't see anyone either," Nancy said.

"No one saw anyone at the scene of any of the disappearances, Wayne," said Glen Michaels.

"What I want to know is what a civilian is doing on a police investigation," Grimsbo said.

O'Malley sighed. "Lake's fixed politically. He's known as a criminal lawyer because he won that insanity defense for that fruitcake Daley. But the guy's specialty is real estate law and he's made a few million at it, some of which he has contributed to the mayor's campaign chest. He's also a major contributor to the governor and he serves on some land use planning council in Albany. The bottom line is, the governor called the mayor yesterday, who then called me to explain how Lake's experience as a criminal lawyer will be invaluable in the investigation and how lucky we are to have him on our team. The press is already on the mayor's ass for keeping the disappearances quiet until the Lake murders forced his hand. He's desperate for results and he's not going to buck a request from the governor or a major campaign contributor."

"I don't trust him," Turner said. "I had a case with Lake a few years back. We served a warrant on this guy and found a kilo of coke in his room. There was a pregnant woman at the house with no record. She swore the coke was hers and the guy was doing her a favor by letting her stay in his room while she was expecting. The defendant beat the case and the d.a. didn't even bother to indict the chick. I could never prove it, but I heard rumors that Lake paid the woman to perjure herself."

"Anyone else heard anything like that?" O'Malley asked.

Michaels shook his head. "He's cross-examined me two or three times. My impression is that he's very bright. He did an excellent job in a case involving blood-spatter evidence. Really had me going up there."

"I've heard he's a smart guy," Grimsbo said, "but I've heard those rumors about the fix too, and a few of the lawyers I know don't like Lake's ethics. He's still a suspect, even if he's a long shot, and I just don't like the idea of a citizen working on something this sensitive."

"Look, I agree with you, Frank," O'Malley said. "It stinks. But it doesn't matter. Until I can convince the mayor otherwise, Lake stays. Just try to keep him out from under our feet. Give him lots of busy work, make him read all the reports. If something comes up you don't want him to see, or there's trouble, come to me. Any questions?"

Turner muttered something about the mayor and Grimsbo shook his head in disgust. O'Malley ignored them.

"Okay, get outta here and back to work. You all heard Klien. We have to stop this psycho fast."

5

Nancy Gordon's stomach growled. She guessed it was a little after six. Her watch said it was almost seven. She had been writing reports and lost track of time. On the way out of the station, she walked by the task force office and noticed the lights were still on. Peter Lake was in shirtsleeves, his feet up on the corner of the desk. Near his elbow were a large stack of reports and a yellow pad. He was making notes as he read.

"You're not going to solve this case in one night," Nancy said quietly. Lake looked around, startled. Then he grinned sheepishly.

"I always work this hard. I'm compulsive."

Nancy walked over to Lake's desk. "What are you doing?"

"Reading about the Reardon and Escalante disappearances. I had an idea. Do you have time?"

"I was going to eat. Want to join me? Nothing special. There's an all-night coffee shop over on Oak."

Lake looked at the stack of reports and the clock.

"Sure," he said, swinging his legs off the desk and grabbing his jacket. "I didn't realize how late it was."

"I was caught up in something too. If my stomach hadn't yelled at me, I'd still be at my desk."

"You must like your work."

"Sometimes."

"How did you get into it?"

"You mean, what's a nice girl like me doing in a job like this?"

"That never occurred to me."

"That I was a nice girl?"

Lake laughed. "No. That you're not suited for police work."

Nancy checked out at the front desk and followed Lake outside. After sundown Hunter's Point was a ghost town, except for a few spots that catered to the college crowd. Nancy could see the marquee of the Hunter's Point Cinema and the neon signs outside a couple of bars. Most of the stores were shuttered for the night. The coffee shop was only a block and a half from the station. An oasis of light in a desert of darkness.

"Here we are," Nancy said, holding open the door of Chang's Cafe. There was a counter, but Nancy led Lake to a booth. Chang's wife brought them menus and water.

"The soup and the pies are good and the rest of the menu is edible. Don't look for anything resembling Chinese. Mr. Chang cooks Italian, Greek and whatever else strikes his fancy."

"You're not from Hunter's Point originally, are you?" Lake asked, after they ordered.

"How could you tell?"

"You don't have the accent. I'm a transplanted westerner myself. Let's see. I'd guess Montana."

"Idaho," Nancy said. "My parents still live there. They're farmers. My brother is a high school teacher in Boise. Me, I didn't love Idaho and I wanted to see the world. Fortunately I run a mean eight hundred meters and the U. offered the best scholarship. So I ended up in Hunter's Point."

"Not exactly Paris," Lake commented.

"Not exactly," Nancy said with a smile. "But it *was* New York, and without the scholarship there was no way I could afford college. By the time I realized New York City and Hunter's Point, New York, were worlds apart I was enjoying myself too much to care."

"And the police work?"

"My major was Criminal Justice. When I graduated, the Hunter's Point P.D. needed a woman to fill its affirmative action quota."

Nancy shrugged and looked at Lake, as if expecting a challenge.

"I bet you made detective on merit," he said.

"Damn straight," Nancy answered proudly, just as Mrs. Chang arrived with their soup.

"How did you end up here?" Nancy asked, as she waited for her minestrone to cool.

"I'm from Colorado," Lake said, smiling. "I went to Colorado State undergraduate, then I served a hitch in the Marines. There was a guy in the judge advocate's corps who went to law school here and suggested I apply. I met Sandy at the U."

Lake paused and his smile disappeared. He looked

down at his plate. The action had an unnatural quality to
it, as if he suddenly realized that a smile would be inap-
propriate when he was discussing his dead wife. Nancy
looked at Lake oddly.

"I'm sorry," he apologized. "I keep thinking about
her."

"That's okay. There's nothing wrong with remembering."

"I don't like myself when I'm maudlin. I've always
been a person in control. The murders have made me
realize that nothing is predictable or permanent."

"If it's taken you this long to figure that out, you're
lucky."

"Yeah. A successful career, a great wife and kid.
They blind you to the way the world really is, don't they?
Then someone takes that away from you in a second and
. . . and you see . . ."

"You see how lucky you were to have what you had,
while it lasted, Peter. Most people never have in their
lifetime what you and I had for a little while."

Lake looked down at the tabletop.

"At the station you said you had an idea," Nancy
said, to break his mood.

"It's probably just playing detective," he answered,
"but something struck me when I was going through the
reports. The day Gloria Escalante disappeared, a florist's
truck was delivering in the area. A woman would open
the door to a man delivering flowers. She would be excited and wouldn't be thinking. He could take the woman
away in the back of his truck. And there's the rose. Someone who works in a florist's would have access to roses."

"Not bad, Peter," Nancy said, unable to hide her ad-
miration. "You might make a good detective after all. The
deliveryman was Henry Waters. He's got a minor record

for indecent exposure and he's one of our suspects. You probably haven't gotten to Wayne's report yet. He's been doing a background check on Waters."

Lake flushed. "I guess you were way ahead of me."

"Peter, did Sandy have any connection with Evergreen Florists?"

"Is that where Waters works?"

Nancy nodded.

"I don't think so. But I can look at our receipts and the checkbook to see if she ever ordered anything from them. I'm pretty certain I never did."

Their dinner arrived and they ate in silence for a few minutes. Nancy's spaghetti was delicious, but she noted that Lake just picked at his food.

"Do you feel like talking about Sandy?" Nancy asked. "We're trying to cross-reference the activities of the victims. See if they belonged to the same clubs, subscribed to the same magazines. Anything that gives us a common denominator."

"Frank asked me to do that the night of the murder. I've been working on it. We were members of the Delmar Country Club, the Hunter's Point Athletic Club, the Racquet Club. I've got a list of our credit cards, subscriptions, everything I can think of. I'll complete it by the end of the week. Is Waters your only suspect?"

"There are others, but nothing solid. I'm talking about known sex offenders, not anyone we've linked to any of the crimes." Nancy paused. "I had an ulterior motive for asking you to eat with me. I'm going to be totally honest with you. You shouldn't be involved in this investigation. You have pull with the mayor, so you're here, but everyone on the task force resents the way you forced yourself on us."

"Including you?"

"No. But that's only because I understand what's

driving you. What you don't understand is how self-destructive your behavior is. You're obsessed with this case because you think immersing yourself in detective work will help you escape from reality. But you're stuck in the real world. Eventually you'll have to come to terms with it, and the sooner you do that the better. You've got a good practice. You can build a new life. Don't put off coming to grips with what's happened by continuing to work on the murders."

Nancy was watching Lake as she spoke. He never took his eyes off her. When she was finished speaking he leaned forward.

"Thank you for your honesty. I know my intrusion into the task force is resented and I'm glad you told me how everyone feels. I'm not worried about my practice. My associates will keep it going without me and I've made so much money that I could live nicely without it. What matters to me is catching this killer before he hurts someone else."

Lake reached across the table and covered Nancy's hand with his.

"It also matters to me that you're concerned. I appreciate that."

Lake stroked Nancy's hand as he spoke. It was a sensual touch, clearly a come-on, and Nancy was struck by the inappropriateness of his action, even if Lake was not.

"I'm concerned for you as a person who is the victim of a horrible crime," Nancy said firmly, as she slid her hand out from under Lake's. "I am also concerned that you might do something that would jeopardize our investigation. Please think about what I've said, Peter."

"I will," Lake assured her.

Nancy started to open her purse but Lake stopped her.

"Dinner's on me," he smiled.

"I always pay my own way," Nancy answered, laying the exact amount of her dinner on top of the check and putting a dollar tip under her coffee cup. She slipped out of the booth and started toward the door.

Peter placed his money next to hers and followed her outside.

"Can I give you a lift home?" he asked.

"My car's in the lot."

"Mine too. I'll walk you back."

They walked in silence until they reached the police station. The lot was dimly lit. Patches were in shadow. Nancy's car was toward the back of the station where the windows were dark.

"It could have happened someplace like this," Lake mused as they walked.

"What?"

"The women," Lake said. "Walking alone at night in a deserted parking lot. It would be so easy to approach them. Didn't Bundy do that? Wear a false cast to elicit sympathy. They would be in the killer's trunk in a minute and it would all be over for them."

Nancy felt a chill. There was no one in the lot but the two of them. They entered an unlit area. She turned her head so she could see Lake. He was watching her, thoughtfully. Nancy stopped at her car.

"That's why I wanted to walk with you," Lake continued. "No woman is safe until he's caught."

"Think about what I said, Peter."

"Good night, Nancy. I think we work well together. Thanks again for your concern."

Nancy backed her Ford out of its space and drove off. She could see Lake watching her in the rearview mirror.

6

Nancy stood in the dark and pumped iron, following the routine she and Ed had worked out. Now she was doing curls, with the maximum weight she could manage. Her forearm arced toward her shoulder, slowly, steadily, as she muscled up the right dumbbell, then the left. Sweat stained her tank top. The veins stood out on her neck.

Something was definitely wrong. Lake had been coming on to her. When Ed died, she had lost all interest in sex for months. It had hurt just to see couples walking hand in hand. But when Lake held her hand, he had stroked it, the way you would caress a lover's hand. When he said he thought they worked well together, it was definitely a proposition.

Nancy finished her curls. She lowered the weights to the floor and took a few deep breaths. It was almost six. She had been up since four-thirty, because a nightmare woke her and she couldn't get back to sleep.

Frank had considered Lake a suspect and she had disagreed. Now she was beginning to wonder. She remembered what Dr. Klien said. Lake was bright and personable. It would have been easy for him to gain the confidence of the victims. They were the type of women he met every day at his clubs, and he was the type of man the victims encountered at theirs.

The organized nonsocial was a psychopath who could not feel pity or care for others. The type of person who would have to fake emotions. Had Lake been caught off guard in the coffee shop between remembering his first meeting with Sandra Lake and making the appropriate reaction to that memory? There had been a brief moment when Lake's features had been devoid of emotion.

Klien also said that these killers were interested in

police work. Lake, an experienced criminal defense attorney, would know all about police procedure. Nancy dropped to the floor and did fifty push-ups. What was normally an easy set was difficult. She couldn't focus. Her head filled with a vision of Lake, alone in the shadows of the parking lot, waiting. How did he know about Bundy's fake cast? Dr. Klien had not mentioned it.

After the weights, she and Ed would run a six-mile loop through the neighborhood. Ed was stronger than Nancy, but she was the faster runner. On Sundays, they raced the loop. The loser cooked breakfast. The winner decided when and how they made love. Nancy could not touch the weights or run the loop for two months after the shooting.

One hundred crunches. Up, down, up, down. Her stomach tight as a drumhead. Her thoughts in the dark, in the parking lot with Lake. Should she tell Frank and Wayne? Was she just imagining it? Would her suspicions sidetrack the investigation and let the real killer escape?

It was six-fifteen. The weights were in a small room next to the bedroom. The sun was starting its ascent over the wealthy suburbs to the east. Nancy stripped off her panties and top and dropped them in the hamper. She had put on weight after Ed died. Except for a month when she was recovering from a hamstring pull in her sophomore year, it was the first time since junior high that she had not worked out regularly. The weight was off now and she could see the ridged muscles of her stomach and the cords that twisted along her legs. Hot water loosened her up. She shampooed her hair. All the time, she was thinking about Peter Lake.

Why were there no bodies found before? Why were the Lake murders different from the others? Sandra Lake had apparently been killed quickly, suddenly. Why? And why would Peter have killed her? Had she discovered something that would link him to the other murders and confronted him with the evidence? And that still left the hardest question of all, was Lake such a monster that he would kill his own daughter to cover his crimes?

As she dressed, Nancy tried to find one concrete fact that she could present to the other detectives. One piece of evidence that linked Peter to the crimes. She came up dry. For the moment, she'd have to keep her feelings to herself.

7

Frank Grimsbo ran a forearm across his forehead, staining the sleeve of his madras jacket with sweat. He was wearing a short-sleeve, white shirt and brown polyester pants, and had jerked his paisley print tie to half mast after unbuttoning his top button. The heat was killing him, and all he could think about was cold beer.

Herbert Solomon answered the door on the third ring. Wearily, Grimsbo held up his shield and identified himself.

"This is about the Lakes, right?" asked Solomon, a stocky man of medium height who sported a well-groomed beard and was dressed in loose green-and-red-checked Bermuda shorts and a yellow T-shirt.

"That's right, Mr. Solomon. My partner and I are canvassing the neighborhood."

"I already spoke to a policeman on the evening it happened."

"I know, sir. I'm a detective on the special task force that's investigating all of the killings, and I wanted to go into a little more detail with you."

"Have there been other murders? I thought these women just disappeared."

"That's right, but we're assuming the worst."

"Come on in out of the heat. Can I get you a beer, or can't you drink on duty?"

Grimsbo grinned. "A beer would be great."

"Wait in there and I'll grab one for you," Solomon said, pointing to a small front room. Grimsbo pulled his shirt away from his body as he walked toward the den. Thank God they were canvassing in The Meadows, where everyone had air-conditioning.

"I hope this is cold enough for you," Solomon said, handing Grimsbo a chilled Budweiser. Grimsbo placed the cold bottle against his forehead and closed his eyes. Then he took a sip.

"Boy, that hits the spot. I wish they could think up a way to air-condition the outside."

Solomon laughed.

"You an accountant?"

"A c.p.a."

"I figured," Grimsbo said, pointing his beer at two large bookcases filled with books about tax and accounting. A desk stood in front of the only window in the room. A computer and printer sat in the center of the desk next to a phone. The window looked out at Sparrow Lane across a wide front lawn.

"Well," Grimsbo said, after taking another swig from the bottle, "let me ask you a few questions and get out of your hair. Were you around the night Mrs. Lake and her daughter were murdered?"

Solomon stopped smiling and nodded. "Poor bastard."

"You know Peter Lake?"

"Sure. Neighbors and all. We have a home-owners committee in The Meadows. Pete and I were on it. We

played doubles together in the tennis tournament. Marge
—that's my wife—she and Sandy were good friends."

"Is your wife home?"

"She's at the club, playing golf. I didn't feel like it in
this heat."

Grimsbo put down the beer and took a pad and pen
out of his inside jacket pocket.

"About what time did you get home on the night it
happened?"

"It had to be about six."

"Did you see anything unusual that night?"

"Not a thing. I was in the dining room until we finished dinner. The dining room looks out into the back
yard. Then I was in the living room for a few minutes. It's
in the back of the house too. After that I was in here
working on the computer with the blinds drawn."

"Okay," Grimsbo said, reluctantly ready to wrap up
the interview and trudge back out into the heat.

"One thing I forgot about when the officer talked to
me the night of the murder. There was so much excitement and Marge was hysterical. I did see Pete come
home."

"Oh, yeah? When was that?"

"I can get pretty close there. The Yankees played a
day game and I caught the score on 'Headline Sports.'
CNN runs the sports scores twenty after and ten to the
hour. I went into the den right after the score, so figure
seven twenty-two or so. I saw Pete's Ferrari when I
closed the blinds."

"He was heading home?"

"Right."

"And you're certain about the time."

"Twenty after the hour, every hour. So it had to be
about then, give or take a minute."

"Did you notice a florist's truck at any time that night, near The Meadows or in it?"

Solomon thought for a second. "There was a TV repairman at the Osgoods'. That's the only unusual vehicle I saw."

Grimsbo levered himself out of his seat and extended his hand. "Thanks for the beer."

Wayne Turner was leaning against the car, looking so cool in his tan suit that it pissed Grimsbo off.

"Any luck?" Turner asked, as he pushed off the car.

"Nada. Oh, Solomon, the last guy I talked to, saw Lake driving home past his house about seven-twenty. Other than that, I don't have a thing that wasn't in the uniforms' reports."

"I struck out too, but I'm not surprised. You get a development like The Meadows, you get houses with land. They're not leaning over each other. Less chance anyone will see what's going on at the neighbor's. And with heat like this, everyone's either inside with the air-conditioning on or out at their country club."

"So what do we do now?"

"Head back in."

"You get a hit on a florist truck?" Grimsbo asked, when he had the car started.

"There was a cable TV repairman at the Osgoods', but no florist."

"Yeah, I got the TV guy too. What do you think of Waters?"

"I don't think anything, Frank. You seen him?"

Grimsbo shook his head.

"Our killer's got to be high IQ, right? Waters is a zero. Skinny, pimple-faced kid. He's got this little wisp of a beard. If he's not retarded, he's not far from it.

Dropped out of school in the tenth grade. He was eighteen. Worked as a gas station attendant and a box boy at Safeway. He lost that job when he was arrested for jacking off outside the window of a sixteen-year-old neighbor girl. The girl's father beat the crap out of him."

"He sounds pretty pathetic," Grimsbo observed.

"The guy's got no life. He lives with his mother. She's in her late sixties and in poor health. I followed him for a few days. He's a robot. Every day it's the same routine. He leaves work and walks to the One Way Inn, this bar that's halfway to his house. Orders two beers, nurses 'em, doesn't say a word to anyone but the bartender. Forty-five minutes after he goes in, he leaves, walks straight home and spends the evening watching TV with his mother. I talked to his boss and his neighbors. If he's got any friends, no one knows who they are. He's held this delivery boy job with Evergreen Florists longer than any of his other jobs."

"You writing him off?"

"He's a weeny-waver. A little twisted, sure, but I don't make him for our killer. He's not smart enough to be our boy. We don't have anything with Waters."

"We don't have anything, period."

Glen Michaels walked into the task force office just as Grimsbo and Turner were finishing the reports on their interviews in The Meadows.

"Whatcha got?" Grimsbo asked. He had shucked his jacket and parked himself next to a small fan.

"Nothing at all," Michaels said. "It's like the guy was never there. I just finished all the lab work. Every print matches up to the victims, Lake or one of the neighbors. There's nothing to do a DNA test on. No unusual hairs, no fibers, no semen. This is one smart cookie, gentlemen."

"You think he knows police procedure?" Turner asked.

"I have to believe it. I've never seen so many clean crime scenes."

"Anyway," Michaels said, heading for the door, "I'm out of here. This heat is boiling my blood."

Turner turned to Grimsbo. "This perp is starting to piss me off. Nobody's that good. He leaves no prints, no hairs, no one sees him. Christ, we've got a development full of people and no one reports an unusual occurrence. No strangers lurking around, not a single odd car. How does he get in and out?"

Grimsbo didn't answer. He was frowning. He levered himself out of his chair and walked over to the cabinet where they kept the master file on the case.

"What's up?" Turner asked.

"Just something . . . Yeah, here it is."

Grimsbo pulled a report out of the file and showed it to Turner. It was the one-page report of the dispatcher who had taken the 911 call from Peter Lake.

"You see it?" Grimsbo asked.

Turner read the report a few times and shook his head.

"The time," Grimsbo said. "Lake called in the 911 at eight-fifteen."

"Yeah? So?"

"Solomon said he saw Lake driving by at seven-twenty. He was certain he'd just heard the sports scores. CNN gives them at twenty after."

"And the bodies were in the hall," Turner said, suddenly catching on.

"How long does it take to park the car, open the door? Let's give Lake the benefit of the doubt and assume Solomon is a little off. He's still gonna be inside by seven-thirty."

"Shit," Turner said softly.

"Am I right, Wayne?" Grimsbo asked.

"I don't know, Frank. If it was your wife and kid . . . I mean, you'd be in shock."

"Sure, the guy's knocked out. He said he sat down on the stairs for a while. You know, gathering himself. But for forty-five minutes? Uh-uh. Something doesn't wash. I think he spent the time cleaning up the crime scene."

"What's the motive? Jesus, Frank, you saw her face. Why would he do that to his own wife?"

"You know why. She knew something, she found something, and she made the mistake of telling Lake. Think about it, Wayne. If Lake killed them it would explain the absence of clues at the crime scene. There wouldn't be any strange cars in the neighborhood or prints that didn't match the Lakes or the neighbors."

"I don't know . . ."

"Yes you do. He killed that little girl. His own little girl."

"Christ, Frank, Lake's a successful lawyer. His wife was beautiful."

"You heard Klien. The guy we're looking for is a monster, but no one's gonna see that. He's smooth, handsome, the type of guy these women would let in their house without a second thought. It could be a successful lawyer with a beautiful wife. It could be anyone who isn't wired right and is working in some psycho world of his own where this all makes sense."

Turner paced around the room while Grimsbo waited quietly. Finally Turner sat down and picked up a picture of Melody Lake.

"We aren't going to do anything stupid, Frank. If Lake is our killer, he is one devious motherfucker. One hint that we're on to him and he'll figure a way to cover this up."

"So, what's the next step? We can't bring him in and sweat him and we know there's nothing connecting Lake to the other crime scenes."

"These women weren't picked at random. If he's the killer, they've all got to be connected to Lake somehow. We have to reinterview the husbands, go back over the reports and recheck our lists with Lake in mind. If we're right, there's going to be something there."

The two men sat silently for a moment, figuring the angles.

"None of this goes in a report," Turner said. "Lake could stumble across it when he's here."

"Right," Grimsbo answered. "I'd better take Solomon's interview with me."

"When do we tell Nancy and the chief?"

"When we have something solid. Lake's very smart and he's got political connections. If he's the one, I don't want him beating this, I want him nailed."

8

Nancy Gordon was deep in a dreamless sleep when the phone rang. She jerked up in bed, flailing for a moment, before she realized what was happening. The phone rang again before she found it in the dark.

"Detective Gordon?" the man on the phone asked.

"Speaking," Nancy said, as she tried to orient herself.

"This is Jeff Spears. I'm a patrolman. Fifteen minutes ago we received a complaint about a man sitting in a car on the corner of Bethesda and Champagne. Seems he's been parked there for three successive nights. One of the neighbors got worried.

"Anyway, Officer DeMuniz and I talked to the guy. He identified himself as Peter Lake. He claims he's working on the task force that's looking into the murders of those women. He gave me your name."

"What time is it?" Nancy asked. The last thing she wanted to do was turn on the light and scorch her eyeballs.

"One-thirty. Sorry about waking you," Spears said apologetically.

"No, that's okay," she answered as she located the digital clock and confirmed the time. "Is Lake there?"

"Right beside me."

Nancy took a deep breath. "Put him on."

Nancy heard Spears talking to someone. She swung her legs over the side of the bed, sat up and rubbed her eyes.

"Nancy?" Lake asked.

"What's going on?"

"Do you want me to explain with the officer standing here?"

"What I want is to go back to bed. Now, what's this about you sitting in a parked car in the middle of the night for three straight nights?"

"It's Waters. I was staking out his house."

"Oh, fuck. I don't believe this. You were staking him out? Like some goddamn movie? Peter, I want you at Chang's in twenty minutes."

"But . . ."

"Twenty minutes. This is too stupid for words. And put Spears back on."

Nancy heard Lake calling to the officer. She closed her eyes and turned on the bedside lamp. Then she raised her lids slowly. The light burned and her eyes watered.

"Detective Gordon?"

"Yeah. Look, Spears, he's okay. He is working on the task force. But that was heads-up work," she added, since he sounded young and eager and the compliment would mean something.

"It sounded suspicious. And, with the murders . . ."

"No, you did the right thing. But I don't want you to mention this to anyone. We don't want what we're doing getting around."

"No problem."

"Thanks for calling."

Nancy hung up. She felt awful, but she had to find out what Lake was up to.

Lake was waiting for her in a booth when Nancy arrived at Chang's. The little cafe stayed open all night for cops, truckers and an occasional college student. It was a safe place to meet. There was a cup of coffee in front of Lake. Nancy told the waitress to make it two.

"Why don't you clue me in on what you thought you were doing, Peter," Nancy said when the waitress left.

"I'm sorry if I was out of line. But I'm certain Waters is the killer. I've been tailing him for three days. Believe me, I did a great job. He has no idea he was followed."

"Peter, this isn't how things are done. You don't go running off with some half-baked idea you picked up from 'Magnum, P.I.' The task force is a team. You have to run your ideas by everyone before you make a move.

"More important, you don't know the first thing about surveillance. Look how easily you were spotted by the neighbor. If Waters saw you, and it spooked him, he might go to ground and we'd lose him forever. And, if he is the killer, you could have been in danger. Whoever killed your wife and daughter has no conscience and he has no compunction about taking a human life. Remember that."

"I guess I was foolish."

"There's no 'guess' about it."

"You're right. I apologize. I never thought about blowing the case or the danger. All I thought about was . . ."

Lake paused and looked down at the table.

"I know you want him, Peter. We all do. But if you don't do this right, you'll ruin the case."

Lake nodded thoughtfully. "You've gone out of your way to help me, Nancy, and I appreciate it. I'm finally starting to cope with losing Sandy and Melody and you're one of the reasons."

Lake smiled at her. Nancy did not return the smile. She watched Lake carefully.

"I've decided to go back to work. This little incident tonight has convinced me I'm not very valuable to the investigation. I thought I could really help, but that was ego and desperation. I'm not a cop and I was crazy to think I could do more than you're doing."

"Good. I'm glad to hear you say that. It's a healthy sign."

"That doesn't mean I'm going to abandon the case altogether. I'd like copies of all the police reports sent to my office. I still might spot something you miss or offer a different perspective. But I'll stop haunting the station house."

"I can have the reports sent, if O'Malley says it's okay. But you'll have to keep them strictly to yourself. Not even your associates should see them."

"Of course. You know, you've really taken good care

of me," Lake said, smiling again. "Do you think we could have dinner sometime? Just get together? Nothing to do with the case."

"We'll see," she said uneasily.

Lake checked his watch. "Hey, we'd better get going. We're going to be dead tired in the morning. I'm paying this time, no arguments."

Nancy slid out of the booth and said good-bye. It was late and she'd had little sleep, but she was wide-awake. There was no question about it now. With his wife dead less than three weeks, Peter Lake was coming on to her. And that wasn't the only thing bothering her. Nancy wanted to know the real reason Peter Lake was tailing Henry Waters.

9

"Dr. Escalante," Wayne Turner said to a heavy-set, dark-complected man with the sad eyes and weary air of someone who has given up hope, "I'm one of the detectives working on your wife's disappearance."

"Is Gloria dead?" Escalante asked, expecting the worst.

They were sitting in the doctor's office at the Way-side Clinic, a modern, two-story building located at the far end of the Wayside Mall. Escalante was one of several doctors, physical therapists and health care specialists who made up the staff of the clinic. His specialty was cardiology and he had privileges at Hunter's Point Hospital. Everyone spoke highly of Dr. Escalante's skills. They also thought he was one hell of a nice guy who was unfailingly cheerful. Or, at least, he had been until a month and a half ago, when he came home to his Tudor-style house in West Hunter's Point and found a note and a black rose.

"I'm afraid we have no more information about your wife. We assume she's alive, until we learn otherwise."

"Then why are you here?"

"I have a few questions that may help us with the case."

Turner read off the names of the other missing women and their spouses, including the Lakes. As he read the names, Turner placed photographs of the victims and their husbands faceup on Escalante's desk.

"Do you or your wife know any of these people in any capacity whatsoever, Doctor?" Turner asked.

Escalante studied the photographs carefully. He picked up one of them.

"This is Simon and Samantha Reardon, isn't it?"

Turner nodded.

"He's a neurosurgeon. I've seen the Reardons at a few Medical Association functions. A few years ago, he spoke at a seminar I attended. I don't recall the topic."

"That's good. Were you friendly with the Reardons?"

Escalante laughed harshly. "People with my skin color don't travel in the same social circles as the Reardons, Detective. I don't suppose you were permitted to interview the esteemed doctor at the Delmar Country Club."

Wayne nodded.

"Yeah. Well, that's the type of guy Simon Reardon is . . ."

Escalante suddenly remembered why Turner was interested in Samantha Reardon and his wife.

"I'm sorry. I should be more charitable. Simon is probably going through the same hell I am."

"Probably. Any of the others ring a bell?"

Escalante started to shake his head, then stopped.

"This one is a lawyer, isn't he?" he asked, pointing at Peter Lake's photograph.

"Yes, he is," Turner answered, trying to hide his excitement.

"It didn't hit me until now. What a coincidence."

"What's that?"

"Gloria was chosen for jury duty six months ago. She sat on one of Lake's cases. I remember because she said she was glad it wasn't a medical malpractice or she would have been excused. It didn't matter though. The lawyers settled the case halfway through, so she didn't vote on it."

"You're certain it was Peter Lake's case?"

"I met her after court. We were going to dinner. I saw him."

"Okay. That's a big help. Anyone else look familiar?" Turner asked, although, at this point, he really didn't care.

"It's Lake, Chief," Frank Grimsbo told O'Malley. "We're certain."

"Are we talking hard evidence?" O'Malley asked.

"Not yet. But there's too much circumstantial to look the other way," Wayne Turner answered.

"How do you two feel about this?" O'Malley asked Glen Michaels and Nancy Gordon.

"It makes sense," Michaels responded. "I'm going back over the evidence in all of the cases tomorrow to see if I have anything I can tie to Lake."

O'Malley turned toward Nancy. She looked grim.

"I'd reached the same conclusion for other reasons, Chief. I don't know how we can nail him, but I'm certain he's our man. I talked to Dr. Klien this morning and ran Lake's profile by him. He said it's possible. A lot of sociopaths aren't serial killers. They're successful businessmen or politicians or lawyers. Think of the advantage you have in those professions if you don't have a conscience to slow you down. In the past few days, I've been talking to people who know Lake. They all say he's charming, but none of them would turn their back on him. He's supposed to have the ethics of a shark and enough savvy to stay just this side of the line. There have been several Bar complaints, but none that was successful. A few malpractice suits. I talked to the lawyers who represented the plaintiffs. He skated on every one of them."

"There's a big difference between being a sleazy lawyer and killing six people, including your own daughter," O'Malley said. "Why would he endanger himself by getting so close to the investigation?"

"So he can see what we've got," Grimsbo said.

"I think there's more to it, Chief," Nancy said. "He's up to something."

Nancy told O'Malley about Lake's stakeout.

"That doesn't make sense," Turner said. "Waters isn't really a suspect. He just happened to be around the Escalante house the day she disappeared. There's no connection between Waters and any other victim."

"But there is a connection between Lake and every victim," Grimsbo cut in.

"Let's hear it," O'Malley said.

"Okay. We have Gloria Escalante sitting on one of his juries. He and the Reardons belong to the Delmar Country Club. Patricia Cross and Sandra Lake were in the Junior League. Anne Hazelton's husband is an attorney. He says they've been to Bar Association functions the Lakes attended."

"Some of those connections are pretty tenuous."

"What are the odds on one person being linked to all six victims?" Turner asked.

"Hunter's Point isn't that big a place."

"Chief," Nancy said, "he's been coming on to me."

"What?"

"It's sexual. He's interested. He's let me know."

Nancy recounted the way Lake acted during their two meetings at Chang's.

O'Malley frowned. "I don't know, Nancy."

"His wife died less than a month ago. It's not normal."

"You're attractive. He's trying to get over his grief. Maybe he and Mrs. Lake didn't get along that well. Did you find any of that when you talked to the neighbors?"

Grimsbo shook his head. "No gossip about the Lakes. They were a normal couple according to the people I talked to."

"Same here," Turner said.

"Doesn't that undercut your theory?"

"Dr. Klien said a serial killer can have a wife and family, or a normal relationship with a girlfriend," Nancy answered.

"Look at the Lake murders," Turner offered. "We know from one of his associates, who was working late, that Lake was at his office until shortly before seven. The neighbor sees him driving toward his house at seven-twenty, maybe a little after. There's no 911 call until forty-five minutes later. What's he doing inside with the dead bodies? If they're dead, that is."

"We think he came in and his wife confronted him with something she'd found that connected him to the disappearances."

"But they weren't news. No one knew about them," O'Malley said.

"Oh, shit," Michaels swore.

"What?"

"The note. It was the only one with prints on it."

"So?" Grimsbo asked.

"The other notes had no fingerprints on them, but

the note next to Sandra Lake's body had her prints on it. According to the autopsy report, Sandra Lake died instantly or, at least, she was unconscious as soon as she was hit on the back of the head. When did she touch the note?"

"I still don't . . ."

"She finds the note or the rose or both. She asks Lake what they are. He knows the story will break in the paper eventually. No matter what he tells her now, she'll know he's the rose killer. So he panics, kills her and leaves the rose and the note next to the body to make us think the same person who's taken the other women also killed his wife. And that explains why only Lake's note has a print and why it's Sandra Lake's print," Michaels said. "She was holding it before she was killed."

"That also explains why no one saw any strange vehicles going in or out of The Meadows."

O'Malley leaned back in his chair. He looked troubled.

"You've got me believing this," he said. "But theories aren't proof. If it's Lake, how do we prove it with evidence that's admissible in court?"

Before anyone could answer, the door to O'Malley's office opened.

"Sorry to interrupt, Chief, but we just got a 911 that's connected to those women who disappeared. Do you have a suspect named Waters?"

"What's up?" Grimsbo asked.

"The caller said he talked with a guy named Henry Waters at the One Way Inn and Waters said he had a woman in his basement."

"Did the caller give a name?"

The officer shook his head. "Said he didn't want to get involved, but he kept thinking about the little kid who was murdered and his conscience wouldn't leave him alone."

"When did this conversation at the bar take place?" Nancy asked.

"A few days ago."

"Did Waters describe the woman or give any details?"

"Waters told him the woman had red hair."

"Patricia Cross," Turner said.

"This is Lake's doing," Nancy said. "It's too much of a coincidence."

"I'm with Nancy," Turner said. "Waters just doesn't figure."

"Can we take the chance?" Michaels asked. "With Lake, all we have is some deductive reasoning. We know Waters was around the Escalante residence near the time she disappeared and he has a sex offender record."

"I want you four out there pronto," O'Malley ordered. "I'd rather be wrong than sit here talking when we might be able to save one of those women."

Henry Waters lived in an older section of Hunter's Point. Oak trees shaded the wide streets. High hedges gave the residents privacy. Most of the homes and lawns were well kept up, but Waters's house, a corner plot, was starting to come apart. The gutters were clogged. One of the steps leading up to the shaded front porch was broken. The lawn was overgrown and full of weeds.

The sun was starting to set when Nancy Gordon followed Wayne Turner and Frank Grimsbo along the slate walk toward Henry Waters's front door. Michaels waited in the car in case he was needed to process a crime scene. Three uniformed officers were stationed behind the house in an alley that divided the large block. Two

officers preceded the detectives up the walk and positioned themselves, guns drawn but concealed, on either
side of the front door.

"We take it easy and we are polite," Turner cautioned. "I want his consent or the search and seizure
issues could get sticky."

Everyone nodded. No one cracked a joke about Turner and law school, as they might have under other circumstances. Nancy looked back at the high grass in the
front yard. The house was weather-beaten. The brown
paint was chipping. A window screen was hanging by one
screw outside the front window. Nancy peeked through a
crack between a drawn shade and the windowsill. No one
was in the front room. They could hear a television playing somewhere toward the back of the house.

"He'll be less fearful if he sees a woman," Nancy
said. Grimsbo nodded and Nancy pressed the doorbell.
She wore a jacket to conceal her holster. There had been
some respite from the heat during the day, but it was still
warm. She could feel a trickle of sweat work its way down
her side.

Nancy rang the bell a second time and the volume of
the TV lowered. She saw a vague shape moving down the
hall through the semi-opaque curtain that covered the
glassed upper half of the front door. When the door
opened, Nancy pulled back the screen door and smiled.
The gangly, loose-limbed man did not smile back. He was
dressed in jeans and a stained T-shirt. His long, greasy
hair was unkempt. Waters's dull eyes fixed first on Nancy,
then on the uniformed officers. His brow furrowed, as if
he were working on a calculus problem. Nancy flashed
her badge.

"Mr. Waters, I'm Nancy Gordon, a detective with
the Hunter's Point P.D."

"I didn't do nothin'," Waters said defensively.

"I'm certain that's true," Nancy answered in a firm but friendly tone, "but we received some information we'd like to check out. Would you mind if we came in?"

"Who is it?" a frail female voice called from the rear of the house.

"That's my mom," Waters explained. "She's sick."

"I'm sorry. We'll try not to disturb her."

"Why do you have to upset her? She's sick," Waters said, his anxiety growing.

"You misunderstood me, Mr. Waters. We are *not* going to bother your mother. We only want to look around. May we do that? We won't be long."

"I ain't done nothin'," Waters repeated, his eyes shifting anxiously from Grimsbo to Turner, then to the uniformed officers. "Talk to Miss Cummings. She's my p.o. She'll tell you."

"We did talk to your probation officer and she gave you a very good report. She said you cooperated with her completely. We'd like your cooperation too. You don't want us to have to wait here while one of the officers gets a search warrant, do you?"

"Why do you have to search my house?" Waters asked angrily. The officers tensed. "Why the hell can't you leave me be? I ain't looked at that girl no more. I'm workin' steady. Miss Cummings can tell you."

"There's no need to get upset," Nancy answered calmly. "The sooner we look around, the sooner we'll be out of your hair."

Waters thought this over. "What do you want to see?" he asked.

"The basement."

"There ain't nothin' in the basement," Waters said, seeming genuinely puzzled.

"Then we won't be here long," Nancy assured him.

Waters snorted. "The basement. You can see all the

basement you want. Ain't nothin' but spiders in the basement."

Waters pointed down a dark hall that led past the stairs toward the rear of the house.

"Why don't you come with us, Mr. Waters. You can show us around."

The hall was dark, but there was a light in the kitchen. Nancy saw a sink filled with dirty dishes and the remains of two TV dinners on a Formica-topped table. The kitchen floor was stained and dirty. There was a solid wood door under the staircase next to the entrance to the kitchen. Waters opened it. Then his eyes widened and he stepped back. Nancy pushed past him. The smell was so strong it knocked her back a step.

"Stay with Mr. Waters," Nancy told the officers. She took a deep breath and flicked the switch at the head of the stairs. There was nothing unusual at the bottom of the wooden steps. Nancy held her gun with one hand and the rickety railing with the other. The smell of death grew stronger as she descended the stairs. Grimsbo and Turner followed. No one spoke.

Halfway down, Nancy crouched and scanned the basement. The only light came from a bare bulb hanging from the ceiling. She could see a furnace in one corner. Odd pieces of furniture, most with a broken look, were stashed against a wall surrounded by cartons of newspapers and old magazines. A back door opened into a concrete well at the back of the house near the alley. Most of the corner near the door was in shadow, but Nancy could make out a human foot and a pool of blood.

"Fuck," she whispered, sucking air.

Grimsbo edged past her. Nancy followed close behind. She knew nothing in the basement could hurt her, but she was having trouble catching her breath. Turner aimed a flashlight at the corner and flicked it on.

"Jesus," he managed in a strangled voice.

The naked woman was sprawled on the cold concrete, swimming in blood and surrounded by an overpowering fecal smell. She had not been "killed" or "murdered." She had been defiled and dehumanized. Nancy could see patches of charred flesh where the skin was not stained with blood or feces. The woman's intestines had burst through a gaping hole in her abdomen. They reminded Nancy of a string of bloated sausages. She turned her head aside.

"Bring Waters down here," Grimsbo bellowed. Nancy could see the tendons in his neck stretching. His eyes bulged.

"You don't lay one hand on him, Frank," Turner managed between gasps.

Nancy grabbed Grimsbo's massive forearm. "Wayne's right. I'm handling this. Back off."

A uniform hustled Waters down the steps. When Waters saw the body, he turned white and fell to his knees. He was mouthing words, but no sound came out.

Nancy closed her eyes and gathered herself. The body wasn't there. The smell wasn't in the air. She knelt next to Waters.

"Why, Henry?" she asked softly.

Waters looked at her. His face crumpled and he bleated like a wounded animal.

"Why?" Nancy repeated.

"Oh, no. Oh, no," Waters cried, holding his head in his hands. The head snapped back and forth with each denial, his long hair trailing behind.

"Then who did this? She's here, Henry. In your basement."

Waters gaped at Nancy, his mouth wide open.

"I'm going to give you your rights. You've heard them before, haven't you?" Nancy asked, but it was clear

Waters was in no condition to discuss constitutional rights. His head hung backward and he was making an inhuman baying noise.

"Take him to the station," she ordered the officer who was standing behind Waters. "If you, or anyone else, asks this man one question, you'll be scrubbing toilet bowls in public rest rooms. Is that understood? He hasn't been Mirandized. I want him in an interrogation room with a two-man guard inside and another man outside. No one, including the chief, is to talk to him. I'll call from here to brief O'Malley. And send Michaels in. Tell him to call for a full forensic team. Post a guard on the stairs. No one else comes down here unless Glen says it's okay. I don't want this crime scene fucked up."

Grimsbo and Turner had drawn closer to the body, making certain to stay outside the circle of blood that surrounded it. Grimsbo was taking short, deep breaths. Turner willed himself to look at the woman's face. It was Patricia Cross, but barely. The killer's savage attack had not been limited to the victim's body.

The young uniformed officer was also riveted on the body. That is why he was slow to react when Waters leaped up. Nancy was half-turned and saw the action from the corner of her eye. By the time she turned back, the cop was sprawled on the floor and Waters was bolting up the stairs, screaming for his mother.

The officer who was watching the cellar door heard Waters's scream. He stepped in front of the entrance to the basement, gun drawn, as Waters barreled into him.

"Don't shoot!" Nancy screamed just as the gun exploded. The officer stumbled backward, crashing into the wall opposite the cellar door. The shot plowed through Waters's heart and he tumbled down the stairs, cracking his head on the cement floor. Waters never felt the impact. He was dead by then.

10

"It was on the late news. I can't believe you caught him," Nancy Gordon heard Peter Lake say. She was alone in the task force office, writing reports. Nancy swiveled her chair. Lake stood in the doorway of the office. He wore pressed jeans and a maroon and blue rugby shirt. His styled hair was neatly combed. He looked happy and excited. There was no indication that he was thinking of Sandra or Melody Lake. No sign of grief.

"How did you crack it?" Lake asked, sitting in the chair opposite Nancy.

"An anonymous tip, Peter. Nothing fancy."

"That's terrific."

"It looks like you were right."

Lake shrugged his shoulders, stifling a smile.

"Say," Lake asked sheepishly, "you didn't tell anyone about my stakeout, did you?"

"That's our little secret."

"Thanks. I feel like a fool, going off on my own like that. You were right. If Waters caught on, he probably would have killed me."

"You must feel relieved, knowing Sandy's and Melody's killer has been caught," Nancy said, watching for a reaction.

Lake suddenly looked somber.

"It's as if an enormous weight was taken off my shoulders. Maybe now my life can go back to normal."

"You know, Peter," Nancy said casually, "there was a time when I tossed around the possibility that you might be the killer."

"Why?" Peter asked, shocked.

"You were never a serious suspect, but there were a few inconsistencies in your story."

"Like what?"

"The time, for instance. You didn't call 911 until eight-fifteen, but a neighbor saw you driving toward your house around seven-twenty. I couldn't figure out why it took you so long to call the police."

"You've got to be kidding."

Nancy shrugged.

"I was a suspect because of this time thing?"

"What were you doing for almost an hour?"

"Jesus, Nancy, I don't remember. I was in a daze. I mean, I might have blacked out for a bit."

"You never mentioned that."

Lake stared at Nancy, openmouthed.

"Am I still a suspect? Are you interrogating me?"

Nancy shook her head. "The case is closed, Peter. The chief is going to hold a press conference in the morning. There were three black roses and another one of those notes on a shelf in the basement. And, of course, there was poor Patricia Cross."

"But you don't believe it? You honestly think I could have . . . ?"

"Relax, Peter," Nancy answered, closing her eyes. "I'm real tired and not thinking straight. It's been one very long day."

"I can't relax. I mean, I really like you and I thought you liked me. It's a shock to find out you seriously thought I could do something . . . something like what was done to that woman."

Nancy opened her eyes. Lake looked distant, like he was visualizing Patricia Cross's eviscerated body. But he had not been to the crime scene or read an autopsy report. The media had not been told the condition of Patricia Cross's body.

"I said you were never a serious suspect and I meant it," Nancy lied with a forced smile. "If you were, I would have told Turner and Grimsbo about the stakeout, wouldn't I?"

"I guess."

"Well, I didn't and you can't be a suspect anymore, what with Waters dead, can you?"

Lake shook his head.

"Look," Nancy told him, "I'm really whacked out. I have one more report to write and I'm gone. Why don't you go home too, and start getting on with your life."

Lake stood. "That's good advice. I'm going to take it. And I want to thank you for everything you've done for me. I don't know how I would have gotten through this without you."

Lake stuck out his hand. Nancy stared at it for a second. Was this the hand that ripped the life out of Patricia Cross and Sandra and Melody Lake or was she crazy? Nancy shook Lake's hand. He held hers a moment longer than necessary, then released it after a brief squeeze.

"When things get back to normal for both of us, I'd like to take you to dinner," Lake said.

"Call me," Nancy answered, her stomach churning. It took every ounce of control to keep the smile on her face.

Lake left the room and Nancy stopped smiling. Waters was too good to be true. She did not believe he was responsible for the carnage in his basement. Lake had to know about the alley and the back door. With Waters at work and the mother an invalid, it would have been simple to drive behind the house without being seen, put the body in the basement and butcher it there. Lake was the anonymous caller, she was certain of it. But she had no proof. And O'Malley would soon tell the world that Henry Waters was a serial killer and the case of the missing women was closed.

Part Three

CLEAR AND CONVINCING EVIDENCE

Chapter Six

"And that's what happened, Mr. Page," Nancy Gordon said. "The case was closed. Henry Waters was officially named as the rose killer. Shortly after, Peter Lake disappeared. His house was sold. He closed his bank accounts. His associates were handed a thriving business. And Peter was never heard from again."

Page looked confused. "Maybe I'm missing something. Your case against Lake was purely circumstantial. Unless there was more evidence, I don't understand why you're so certain Peter Lake killed those women and framed Waters."

Gordon took a newspaper clipping and a photograph of a man leaving a motel room out of her briefcase and laid them side by side.

"Do you recognize this man?" she asked, pointing to the photograph. Page leaned over and picked it up.

"This is Martin Darius."

"Look carefully at this newspaper picture of Peter Lake and tell me what you think."

Page studied the two pictures. He imagined Lake with a beard and Darius without one. He tried to judge the size of the two men and compare builds.

"They could be the same person," he said.

"They are the same person. And the man who is murdering your women is the same man who murdered the women in Hunter's Point. We never released the color of the rose or the contents of the notes. Whoever is killing your women has information known only by the members of the Hunter's Point task force and the killer."

Gordon took a fingerprint card from the briefcase and handed it to Page.

"These are Lake's fingerprints. Compare them to Darius's. You must have some on file."

"How did you find Lake here?" Page asked.

Gordon took a sheet of stationery out of her briefcase and laid it on the coffee table next to the photograph.

"I've had it dusted for prints," she said. "There aren't any."

Page picked up the letter. It had been written on a word processor. The stationery looked cheap, probably the type sold in hundreds of chain stores and impossible to trace. The note read: "Women in Portland, Oregon are 'Gone, But Not Forgotten.'" The first letters of each word were capitalized like those in the notes found in the homes of the victims.

"I received this yesterday. The envelope was postmarked from Portland. The photograph of Darius and an *Oregonian* profile of him were inside. I knew it was Lake the minute I saw the picture. The envelope also contained a clipping about you, Mr. Page, your address and a ticket for a United Airlines flight. No one met me at the airport, so I came to see you."

"What do you suggest we do, Detective Gordon? We certainly can't bring Darius in for questioning with what you've given me."

"No!" Gordon said, alarmed. "Don't spook him. You have to stay away from Martin Darius until your case is airtight. You have no idea how clever he is."

Page was startled by Gordon's desperation.

"We know our business, Detective," he assured her.

"You don't know Peter Lake. You've never dealt with anyone like him."

"You said that before."

"You must believe me."

"Is there something else you aren't telling me?"

Gordon started to say something, then she shook her head.

"I'm exhausted, Mr. Page. I need to rest. You don't know what this is like for me. To have Lake surface after all these years. If you had seen what he did to Patricia Cross . . ."

There was a long pause and Page said nothing.

"I need a place to stay," Gordon said abruptly. "Can you suggest a motel? Someplace quiet."

"There's the Lakeview. We keep out-of-town witnesses there. I can drive you."

"No, don't. I'll take a cab. Can you call one for me?"

"Sure. My phone book is in my bedroom. I'll be right out."

"I'll leave you the fingerprint card, the photograph and the newspaper clipping. I have copies," Gordon said as she gathered up the note.

"You're certain you don't want me to drive you? It's no trouble."

Gordon shook her head. Page went into the bedroom and called for a cab. When he returned to the living room, Gordon was slumped on the couch, her eyes closed.

"They'll be here in ten minutes," he said.

Gordon's eyes snapped open. She looked startled, as if she had drifted off for a few minutes and had been scared awake.

"It's been a long day," the detective said. She looked embarrassed.

"Jet lag," Page said to make conversation. "I hope you're right about Darius."

"I am right," Gordon answered, her features rigid. "I am one hundred percent right. You believe that, Mr. Page. The lives of a lot of women depend on it."

Chapter Seven

I

Something was definitely wrong with Gordon's story. It was like a book with a great plot and a flat ending. And there were inconsistencies. The way Gordon told it, she, Grimsbo and Turner were dedicated detectives. If they were convinced Lake murdered six women and framed Waters, how could they simply let the case go? And why would Lake suddenly leave a thriving practice and disappear, if he thought he was in the clear? Had he ever followed up on his romantic interest in Gordon? She hadn't mentioned any contact after the night of Waters's arrest. Finally, there was the question Page had forgotten to ask. What about the women? Gordon had not told him what happened to the missing women.

While he waited for someone in the Hunter's Point Detective Bureau to pick up the phone, Page listed these points on a yellow legal pad. Rolling black storm clouds were coming in from the west. Page was awfully tired of the rain. Maybe these clouds would give him a break and float across the city before dropping their load. Maybe they would leave a space for the sun to shine through when they left.

"Roy Lenzer."

Page laid his pen down on the pad.

"Detective Lenzer, I'm Alan Page, the Multnomah County district attorney. That's in Portland, Oregon."

"What can I do for you?" Lenzer asked cordially.

"Do you have a detective in your department named Nancy Gordon?"

"Sure, but she's on vacation. Won't be back for a week or so."

"Can you describe her?"

Lenzer's description matched the woman who had visited Page's apartment.

"Is there something I can help you with?" he asked.

"Maybe. We have an odd situation here. Three women have disappeared. In each case, we found a note in the bedroom pinned down by a rose. Detective Gordon told me she was involved with an identical case in Hunter's Point, approximately ten years ago."

"It seems to me I heard something about the case, but I've only been on the force for five years. Moved here from Indiana. So I wouldn't be much help."

"What about Frank Grimsbo or Wayne Turner? They were the other detectives."

"There's no Grimsbo or Turner in the department now."

Page heard a rumble of thunder and looked out the window. A flag on the building across the way was snapping back and forth. It looked like it might rip off the pole.

"I don't suppose there's any chance I can get a copy of the file. The guy who was eventually arrested was Henry Waters . . ."

"W-A-T-E-R-S?"

"Right. He was shot resisting. I think there were six dead women. One of them was named Patricia Cross. Then there was Melody Lake, a young girl, and Sandra Lake, her mother. I don't remember the names of the others."

"If this happened ten years ago, the file is in storage. I'll get on it and let you know when I find it. What's your address and phone number?"

Page was telling them to Lenzer when Randy Highsmith, the chief criminal deputy, opened the door for William Tobias, the chief of police, and Ross Barrow, the detective in charge of the black rose case. Page motioned them into seats, then hung up.

"We may have a break in the case of the missing women," Page said. He started relating Gordon's version of the Hunter's Point case.

"Before the body was found at Waters's house, the chief suspect was Peter Lake, a husband of one of the victims," Page concluded. "There was enough circumstantial evidence to raise the possibility that Lake framed Waters. Shortly after the case was officially closed, Lake disappeared.

"Two days ago, Gordon received an anonymous note with the words 'Women in Portland, Oregon are "Gone, But Not Forgotten."' The first letter in each word was capitalized, just the way our boy does it. Enclosed was a photograph of Martin Darius leaving a motel room. Martin Darius may be Peter Lake. Gordon thinks he's our killer."

"I know Martin Darius," Tobias said incredulously.

"Everyone knows Darius," Page said, "but how much do we know about him?"

Page pushed the photograph of Darius and the newspaper with Lake's picture across the desk. Barrow, Tobias and Highsmith huddled over them.

"Boy," Highsmith said, shaking his head.

"I don't know, Al," Tobias said. "The news photo isn't that clear."

"Gordon left me Lake's prints for comparison. Can you run them, Ross?"

Barrow nodded and took the print card from Page.

"I'm having a hard time buying this," Tobias said. "I'd like to talk to your detective."

"Let me call her in. I'd like you to hear her tell the story," Page said, not revealing his doubts, because he wanted them to have an open mind when they heard Gordon.

Page dialed the number for the Lakeview Motel. He asked to be connected with Gordon's room, then leaned back while the desk clerk rang it.

"She's not? Well, this is very important. Do you know when she left? I see. Okay, tell her to call Alan Page as soon as she gets back."

Page left his number and hung up. "She checked in last night around one, but she's not in now. It's possible she's having breakfast."

"What do you want to do, Al?" Highsmith asked.

"I'd like a twenty-four-hour surveillance on Darius, in case Gordon is right."

"I can do that," Barrow said.

"Make sure you use good people, Ross. I don't want Darius to suspect we're watching him.

"Randy, run a background check on Darius. I want his life story as quickly as you can get it."

Highsmith nodded.

"As soon as Gordon calls, I'll get back to you."

Highsmith led Tobias and Barrow out of the office and closed the door. Page thought of dialing the Lakeview again, but it was too soon after the first call. He swiveled toward the window. It was pouring.

Why hadn't he spotted the flaws in Gordon's story last night? Was it Gordon? She seemed barely in control, on edge, as if electrical charges were coursing through her. He could not take his eyes off her when she talked. It was not a physical attraction. Something else drew him to her. Her passion, her desperation. Now that she was out of sight, he could think more clearly. When she was near him, she created a disturbance in the field, like the lightning flashing over the river.

2

Betsy scanned the restaurant for single women as she followed the hostess between a row of tables. She noticed a tall, athletic woman wearing a bright yellow blouse and a navy blue suit seated in a booth against the wall. As Betsy drew near, the woman stood up.

"You must be Nora Sloane," Betsy said as they shook hands. Sloane's complexion was pale. So were her blue eyes. She wore her chestnut-colored hair short. Betsy noticed a few gray streaks, but she guessed they were about the same age.

"Thank you for meeting me, Mrs. Tannenbaum."

"It's Betsy and you're a good saleswoman. When you called this morning and mentioned a free lunch, you hooked me."

Sloane laughed. "I'm glad you're this easy, because a free lunch is about all you're going to get out of me. I'm writing this article on spec. I got the idea when I covered your suit against the anti-abortion protestors for the *Arizona Republic*."

"You're from Phoenix?"

"New York, originally. My husband got a job in

Phoenix. We separated a year after we moved. I was never crazy about Arizona, especially with my ex living there, and I fell in love with Portland while I was covering your case. So, a month ago I quit my job and moved. I'm living on savings and looking for a job and I decided now was as good a time as any to write this article. I ran the idea by Gloria Douglas, an editor at *Pacific West* magazine, and she's definitely interested. But she wants to see a draft of the article before she commits."

"What exactly will the article cover?"

"Women litigators. And I want to use you and your cases as the centerpiece."

"I hope you're not going to make too much of me."

"Hey, don't get bashful on me," Sloane said with a laugh. "Until recently, women attorneys were relegated to the probate department or handled divorces. Stuff that was acceptable as 'woman's work.' My whole point is that you're at the vanguard of a new generation of women who are trying murder cases and getting million-dollar verdicts in civil cases. Areas that have traditionally been male-dominated."

"It sounds interesting."

"I'm glad you think so, because people want to read about you. You're really the hook for the article."

"What will I have to do?"

"Not much. Mostly, it will be talking to me about Hammermill and your other cases. On occasion, I may want to tag along when you go to court."

"That sounds okay. Actually, I think talking through my cases might help me put them in perspective. I was so close to what was happening when they were going on."

The waiter arrived. Sloane ordered a Caesar salad and a glass of white wine. Betsy ordered yellowfin tuna on pasta, but passed on the wine.

"What did you want to do today?" Betsy asked, as soon as the waiter left.

"I thought we'd go over some background material. I read the piece in *Time*, but I felt it was superficial. It didn't tell me what made you the way you are today. For instance, were you a leader in high school?"

Betsy laughed. "God, no. I was so shy. A real gawk."

Sloane smiled. "I can understand that. You were tall, right? I had the same problem."

"I towered over everyone. In elementary school, I walked around with my eyes down and my shoulders hunched, wishing I could disappear. In junior high, it got worse, because I had these Coke-bottle glasses and braces. I looked like Frankenstein."

"When did you start to feel self-confident?"

"I don't know if I ever feel that way. I mean, I know I do a good job, but I always worry I'm not doing enough. But I guess it was my senior year in high school that I started believing in myself. I was near the top of my class, the braces were gone, my folks got me contacts and boys started noticing me. By the time I graduated Berkeley I was much more outgoing."

"You met your husband in law school, didn't you?"

Betsy nodded. "We're separated, now."

"Oh. I'm sorry."

Betsy shrugged. "I really don't want to talk about my personal life. Will that be necessary?"

"Not if you don't want to. I'm not writing this for the *Enquirer*."

"Okay, because I don't want to discuss Rick."

"I understand you one hundred percent. I went through the same thing in Phoenix. I know how difficult it can be. So, let's move on to something else."

The waiter arrived with their food and Sloane asked

Betsy some more questions about her childhood while they ate.

"You didn't go into private practice right out of law school, did you?" Sloane asked after the waiter cleared their plates.

"No."

"Why not? You've done so well at it."

"That's been all luck," Betsy answered, blushing slightly. "I never thought of going out on my own, back then. My law school grades were all right, but not good enough for a big firm. I worked for the attorney general doing environmental law for four years. I liked the job, but I quit when I became pregnant with Kathy."

"How old is she?"

"Six."

"How did you get back into law?"

"I was bored sitting home when Kathy started pre-school. Rick and I talked it over and we decided I would practice out of our home, so I would be there for Kathy. Margaret McKinnon, a friend of mine from law school, let me use her conference room to meet clients. I didn't have much of a caseload. A few court-appointed misdemeanors, some simple divorces. Just enough to keep me busy.

"Then Margaret offered me a windowless office about the size of a broom closet, rent free, in exchange for twenty hours of free legal work each month. I agonized over that, but Rick said it was okay. He thought it would be good for me to get out of the house, as long as I kept my caseload low enough to pick up Kathy at day care and stay home with her if she got sick. You know, still be a mom. Anyway, it worked out fine and I started picking up some felonies and a few contested divorces that paid better."

"The Peterson case was your big break, right?"

"Yeah. One day I was sitting around without much to

do and the clerk who assigns court-appointed cases asked me if I'd represent Grace Peterson. I didn't know much about the battered woman's syndrome, but I remembered seeing Dr. Lenore Walker on a TV talk show. She's the expert in this area. The court authorized the money and Lenore came out from Denver and evaluated Grace. It was pretty horrible, what her husband did. I'd led a sheltered life, I guess. No one where I grew up did things like that."

"No one you knew about."

Betsy nodded sadly. "No one I knew about. Anyway, the case attracted a lot of publicity. We had the support of some women's groups and the press was behind us. After the acquittal, my business really picked up. Then Andrea hired me because of the verdict in Grace's case."

The waiter arrived with their coffee. Sloane looked at her watch. "You said you had a one-thirty appointment, didn't you?"

Betsy glanced at her own watch. "Is it one-ten already? I really got wrapped up in this."

"Good. I was hoping you'd be as excited about the project as I am."

"I am. Why don't you call me and we can talk again soon?"

"Great. I'll do that. And thanks for taking the time. I really appreciate it."

3

Randy Highsmith shook the rain off his umbrella and laid it on the floor under the dashboard as Alan Page drove out of the parking garage. The umbrella hadn't helped

much in the gusting rain and Highsmith was cold and
wet.

Highsmith was slightly overweight, studious-looking,
a staunch conservative and the best prosecutor in the office, Page included. While earning a law degree from
Georgetown he'd fallen in love with Patty Archer, a con-
gressional aide. He then fell in love with Portland when
he traveled there to meet Patty's family. When her con-
gressman decided not to run for reelection, the newly-
weds moved west, where Patty opened a political
consulting firm and Randy was snapped up by the office
of the Multnomah County district attorney.

"Tell me about Darius," Page said as they got on the
freeway.

"He moved to Portland eight years ago. He had
money to start with and borrowed on his assets. Darius
made his name, and increased his fortune, by gambling
on the revitalization of downtown Portland. His first big
success was the Couch Street Boutique. He bought a
block of dilapidated buildings for a song, converted them
to an indoor mall, then changed the area surrounding the
boutique into the trendiest section in Portland by leasing
renovated buildings to upscale shops and restaurants at
low rents. As business increased, so did the rents. The
upper floors of a lot of the buildings were converted to
condos. That's been his pattern. Buy up all the buildings
in a slum area, set up a core attraction, then build around
it. Recently he's branched out into suburban malls, apartment complexes, and so on.

"Two years ago, Darius married Lisa Ryder, the
daughter of Oregon Supreme Court justice Victor Ryder.
Ryder's old firm, Parish, Marquette and Reeves, handles
his legal work. I talked to a few friends over there in
confidence. Darius is brilliant and unscrupulous. Half the

firm's energy is spent keeping him honest. The other half is spent defending lawsuits when they fail."

"What's 'unscrupulous' mean? Law violations, ethics, what?"

"Nothing illegal. But he has his own set of rules and a total disregard for the feelings of others. For instance, earlier this year he bought up a street of historically significant houses over in the Northwest, so he could tear them down and build town houses. There were several citizen groups up in arms. They got a temporary injunction and were trying to get the houses landmark status. A smart young lawyer at Parish, Marquette convinced the judge to drop the injunction. Darius moved bulldozers in at night and leveled the block before anyone knew what was going on."

"A guy like that must have done something illegal."

"The closest I've got is a rumor that he's friendly with Manuel Ochoa, a Mexican businessman who the D.E.A. thinks is laundering money for a South American drug cartel. Ochoa may be lending Darius money for a big project downstate that was risky enough to scare off some of the banks."

"What about his past?" Page asked as they drove into the parking lot of the Lakeview Motel.

"Doesn't have one, which makes sense if he's Lake."

"Did you check newspaper stories, profiles?"

"I did better than that. I spoke to the *Oregonian*'s top business reporter. Darius does not give interviews about his private life. For all anyone knows, he was born eight years ago."

Page pulled into a parking spot in front of the motel office. The dashboard clock read five twenty-six.

"Stay here. I'll see if Gordon's back."

"Okay. But there's one other thing you should

know." Page waited with the car door half-open. "We've got a link between our missing women and Darius."

Page closed the door. Highsmith smiled.

"I saved the best for last. Tom Reiser, the husband of Wendy Reiser, works for Parish, Marquette. He's the lawyer who convinced the judge to drop the injunction. Last Christmas, the Reisers attended a party at the Darius estate. This summer, they were invited to a bash to celebrate the opening of a mall, two weeks before the disappearances started. Reiser has had numerous business dealings with Darius.

"Larry Farrar's accounting firm has Darius Construction for a client. He and Laura Farrar were at the party for the mall opening too. He's done a lot of work for Darius.

"Finally, there's Victoria Miller. Her husband, Russell, works for Brand, Gates and Valcroft. That's the advertising firm that represents Darius Construction. Russell was just put in charge of the account. They've been on Darius's yacht and to his house. They were also at the mall opening party."

"That's unbelievable. Look, I want a list of the women at that party. We've got to alert Bill Tobias and Barrow."

"I already have. They're putting a second team on Darius."

"Good work. Gordon could be the key to wrapping this up."

Highsmith watched Page duck into the manager's office. A chubby man in a plaid shirt was standing behind the counter. Page showed the manager his i.d. and asked him a question. Highsmith saw the manager shake his head. Page said something else. The manager disappeared into a back room and reappeared in a raincoat. He grabbed a key from a hook on the wall. Page followed the manager outside and gestured to Highsmith.

Highsmith slammed the car door and raced under the protection afforded by the second-floor landing. Gordon's room was around the side of the motel on the ground floor. He arrived just as the manager knocked on the door and called out Gordon's name. There was no answer. A window faced into the parking lot. The green drapes were closed. There was a "Do Not Disturb" sign hanging from the doorknob.

"Miss Gordon," the manager called again. They waited a minute and he shrugged. "She hasn't been in all day, as far as I know."

"Okay," Page said, "let us in."

The manager opened the door with his key and stood aside. The room was dark, but someone had left the bathroom light on and it cast a pale glow over the empty motel room. Page flipped the light switch and looked around the room. The bed was undisturbed. Gordon's tan valise lay open on a baggage stand next to the dresser. Page walked into the bathroom. A toothbrush, a tube of toothpaste and makeup were set out on the bathroom counter. Page pulled back the shower curtain. A bottle of shampoo rested on a ledge. Page stepped out of the bathroom.

"She unpacked in here. There's a shampoo bottle in the bathtub. It's not a motel sample. Looks like she was planning to take a shower."

"Someone interrupted her," Highsmith said, pointing at a half-opened dresser drawer. Some of Gordon's clothes lay in it, while others remained in the valise.

"She had a briefcase with her when we talked at my place. Do you see it?"

The two men searched the room, but they did not find the briefcase.

"Look at this," Highsmith said. He was standing next to the night table. Page looked at a notepad with the motel logo that was next to the phone.

"Looks like directions. An address."

"Let's not touch it. I want a lab tech to dust the room. Treat it as a crime scene, until we know better."

"There's no sign of a struggle."

"There wasn't any at the homes of the missing women, either."

Highsmith nodded. "I'll call from the manager's office, in case there are prints on the phone."

"Do you have any idea where this is?" Page asked, as he reread the notes on the pad.

Highsmith's brow furrowed for a moment, then he frowned.

"As a matter of fact, I do. Remember I told you about the houses Darius bulldozed? This sounds like the address."

"What's there now?"

"A block-wide empty lot. As soon as the neighbors saw what Darius did, they went nuts. There have been protests, lawsuits. Darius went ahead with construction anyway and had three units built, but someone torched them. Construction's been halted ever since."

"I don't like this. How would anyone know where Gordon was? I'm the one who suggested the Lakeview."

"She could have phoned someone."

"No. I asked the manager. There weren't any outgoing calls. Besides, she doesn't know anyone in Portland. That's why she came to my place. She assumed the person who sent her the anonymous letter would meet her at the airport, but no one showed. A clipping about me and my address were in with the note. If she knew anyone else, she would have spent the night with them."

"Then someone must have followed her from the airport to your place and from your place here."

"That's possible."

"What if that person waited until she was in the room, then phoned Gordon and asked her to come to the construction site."

"Or came here and talked Gordon into going with him or took her by force."

"Gordon's a detective," Highsmith said. "I mean, you'd think she would have enough sense to be careful."

Page thought about Gordon. Her edge, the tension in her body.

"She's driven, Randy. Gordon told me she stayed a cop so she could track down Lake. She's been on this case for ten years and she dreams about it. Gordon's smart, but she might not be smart where this case is concerned."

The building site was larger than Page imagined. The houses Darius had destroyed were built along a bluff overlooking the Columbia River. The land included a steep wooded hill that angled down toward the water. A high, chain link fence surrounded the property. A "Darius Construction—Absolutely No Trespassing" sign was fastened to the fence. Page and Highsmith huddled under their umbrellas, the collars of their raincoats turned up around their cheeks, and studied the padlock on the gate. The moon was full, but storm clouds scudded across it with great frequency. The heavy rain made the night as dark as it would have been with no moon.

"What do you think?" Highsmith asked.

"Let's walk along the fence to see if there's another entrance. There's no sign she came in here."

"These are new shoes," Highsmith complained.

Page started off along the periphery without answering. The ground had been stripped bare of grass during construction. Page felt the mud oozing around his shoes. He peered through the fence as he walked, occasionally shining his flashlight inside the site. Most of the land was empty and flat where the bulldozers had done their work. At one point, he saw a shack. At another, his beam highlighted broken and burned timbers that had once been the framework of a Darius town house.

"Al, bring your light here," Highsmith shouted. He had walked ahead and was pointing at a section of fence that had been sheared through and folded back. Page ran over. He paused just before he reached Highsmith. A gust of cold wind struck his face. Page turned away for a second and clutched his collar closer to his neck.

"Look at this," Page said. He was standing under an ancient oak tree pointing the flashlight beam toward the ground. Tire tracks had gouged out the mud where they were standing. The canopy formed by the leaves covered the tracks. Page and Highsmith followed them away from the fence.

"Someone drove off the road across the field in this mud," Page said.

"Not necessarily tonight, though."

The tracks stopped at the street and disappeared. The rain would have washed away the mud from the asphalt.

"I think the driver backed up to the fence, Al. There's no sign that he turned around."

"Why back up? Why drive over to the fence at all and risk getting stuck in the mud?"

"What's in the back of a car?"

Page nodded, imagining Nancy Gordon folded in the confined space of a car trunk.

"Let's go," he said, heading back toward the hole in

the fence. In his heart, Page knew she was down there, buried in the soft earth.

Highsmith followed him through. As he ducked, he snagged his coat on a jagged piece of wire. By the time he freed himself, Page was well ahead, obscured by the darkness, only the wavering beam of the flashlight showing his location.

"Do you see any tracks?" Highsmith asked when he caught up.

"Look out!" Page cried, grabbing Highsmith by his coat. Highsmith pulled up. Page shone his light down. They were on the edge of a deep pit that had been gouged out of the earth for a foundation. Muddy walls sloped down toward the bottom, which was lost in darkness. Suddenly the moon appeared, bathing the bottom of the pit in a pale glow. The uneven surface cast shadows over rocks and mounds of dirt.

"I'm going down," Page said, as he went over the rim. He edged along the wall of the pit sideways, leaning into the slope and digging in with the sides of his shoes. Halfway down, he slipped to one knee and slid along the smooth mud, stopping his descent by grabbing a protruding root. The root had been severed by a bulldozer blade. The end came free of the mud, but Page slowed enough to dig in and stop his slide.

"You okay?" Highsmith called into the wind.

"Yeah. Randy, get down here. Someone's been digging recently."

Highsmith swore, then started edging down the slope. When he reached the bottom, Page was wandering slowly over the muddy ground, studying everything that entered the beam of his flashlight. The ground looked as if it had been turned over recently. He examined it as closely as he could in the dark.

The wind died suddenly and Page thought he heard

a sound. Something slithering in the shadows just out of
his line of sight. He tensed, trying to hear above the
wind, peering helplessly into the darkness. When he convinced himself he was the victim of his imagination, he
turned around and shone the light near the base of a steel
girder. Page straightened suddenly and took a step back,
catching his heel on a timber half-concealed in the mud.
He stumbled and the flashlight fell, its beam fanning out
over the rain-soaked earth, catching something white in
the light. A rock or a paper cup. Page knelt quickly and
recovered the flashlight. He walked over to the object
and squatted next to it. His breath caught in his chest.
Protruding from the earth was a human hand.

The sun was just coming up when they dug the last body
out of the ground. The horizon took on a scarlet tinge as
two officers lifted the corpse onto a stretcher. Around
them, other officers walked slowly over the muddy floor
of the construction site in search of more graves, but the
area had been scoured so thoroughly that no one expected to find one.

A prowl car perched on the edge of the pit. The door
on the driver's side was open. Alan Page sat in the front
seat with one foot on the ground, holding a paper cup
filled with scalding, black coffee, trying not to think about
Nancy Gordon and thinking of nothing else.

Page rested his head against the back of the seat. As
the darkness retreated, the river began taking on dimen-
sion. Page watched the flat black ribbon turn liquid and
turbulent in the red dawn. He believed Nancy Gordon
was in the pit, buried under layers of mud. He wondered
if there was something he could have done to save her.
He imagined Gordon's frustration and rage when she
died at the hands of the man she had sworn to stop.

The rain had ended shortly after the first police car arrived. Ross Barrow took charge of the crime scene, after consulting with the lab techs about the best way to handle the evidence. Floodlights shone down on the workers from the rim of the pit. Designated search areas were fenced off with yellow tape. Sawhorses had been erected as barriers against the curious. As soon as Page was certain Barrow could get along without him, he and Highsmith had grabbed a quick dinner at a local restaurant. By the time they returned, Barrow had positively identified Wendy Reiser's body and an officer had located a second grave.

Through the windshield, Page watched Randy Highsmith trudge toward the car. He had been in the pit observing while Page took a break.

"That's the last one," Highsmith said.

"What have we got?"

"Four bodies and positive i.d.s on Laura Farrar, Wendy Reiser and Victoria Miller."

"Were they killed like Patricia Cross?"

"I didn't look that closely, Al. To tell the truth, I almost lost it. Dr. Gregg is down there. She can give you the straight scoop when she comes up."

Page nodded. He was used to dealing with the dead, but that didn't mean he liked looking at a corpse any more than Highsmith.

"What about the fourth woman?" Page asked hesitantly. "Does she match my description of Nancy Gordon?"

"It's not a woman, Al."

"What!"

"It's an adult male, also naked, and his face and fingertips were burned away with acid. We'll be lucky to identify him."

Page saw Ross Barrow slogging through the mud and got out of the car.

"You're not stopping, Ross?"

"There's nothing more down there. You can look if you want."

"I was sure that Gordon . . . It doesn't make sense. She wrote the address."

"Maybe she met someone here and left with them," Barrow suggested.

"We didn't find any footprints," Highsmith reminded him. "She may not have found a way in."

"Did you find anything down there that'll help us figure out who did this?"

"Not a thing, Al. I'm guessing all four were killed elsewhere and transported here."

"Why's that?"

"Some of the bodies are missing organs. We haven't found them or any pieces of bone or excess flesh. No one could clean the area that thoroughly."

"Do you think we have enough to arrest Darius?" Page asked Highsmith.

"Not without Gordon or some solid evidence from Hunter's Point."

"What if we don't find her?" Page asked anxiously.

"In a pinch, you could swear to what she told you. We might get a warrant out of a judge with that. She's a cop. She'd be reliable. But, I don't know. With something like this, we shouldn't rush."

"And we don't really have a solid connection between Darius and the victims," Barrow added. "Finding them at a site owned by Darius Construction doesn't mean a thing. Especially when it's deserted and anyone could have gotten in."

"Do we know if Darius is Lake?" Page asked Barrow.

"Yeah. The prints match."

"Well, that's something," Highsmith said. "If we can get a match between those tire tracks and one of Darius's cars . . ."

"And if we can find Nancy Gordon," Page said, staring into the pit. He desperately wanted Gordon to be alive, but he had been in the business of violent death and lost hopes too long to grasp at straws.

Chapter Eight

I

"Detective Lenzer, this is Alan Page from Portland, Oregon. We talked the other day."

"Right. I was going to call you. That file you asked for is missing. We switched to computers seven years ago, but I did a search anyway. When I couldn't find it listed, I had a secretary go through the old files in storage. There's no file card and no file."

"Did someone check it out?"

"If they did, they didn't follow procedure. You're supposed to fill in a log sheet in case someone else needs the file, and there's no log entry."

"Could Detective Gordon have checked it out? She had a fingerprint card with her. It probably came from the file."

"The file isn't with her stuff in the office and it's against departmental policy to take files home unless you log them out. There's no record showing anyone logged it out. Besides, if there were six dead women it would be the highest victim count we've ever had here. We're probably talking about a file that would take up an entire shelf. Maybe more. Why would she be lugging around something that big? Hell, you'd need a couple of suitcases to get it home."

Page thought that over. "You're certain it's not in storage and just misplaced?"

"The file's not in storage, believe me. The person who looked for it did a real thorough job and I even went down there for a while."

Page was silent for a moment. He decided to tell Lenzer everything.

"Detective Lenzer, I'm pretty sure Nancy Gordon's in danger. She may even be dead."

"What?"

"I met her for the first time two nights ago and she told me about the Hunter's Point murders. She was convinced the man who committed them is living in Portland under a different name, committing similar crimes here.

"Gordon left my apartment a little after midnight and took a cab to a motel. Shortly after checking in, she left in a hurry. We found an address on a pad in her motel room. It's a construction site. We searched it and discovered the bodies of three missing Portland women and an unidentified man. They were tortured to death. We have no idea where Gordon is, and I'm thinking she was right about your killer being in Portland."

"Jesus. I like Nancy. She's a little intense, but she's a very good cop."

"The key to this case could be in the Hunter's Point files. She may have brought them home. I would suggest searching her house."

"I'll do anything I can to help."

Page told Lenzer to call him anytime, gave him his home number, then hung up. Lenzer had characterized Gordon as intense and Page had to agree. She was also dedicated. Ten years on the trail and still burning with that fire. Page had been like that once, but the years were getting to him. Tina's affair and the divorce had sucked him dry emotionally, but he had been losing ground even before her infidelity took over his life. Fighting for the office of district attorney had been great. Every day was exciting. Then he woke up one morning with the responsibilities of the job and the fear that he might not be able to fulfill them. He had mastered those fears through hard work, and he had mastered the job, but the thrill was gone. The days were all getting to be the same, and he was starting to think about what he would be doing ten years down the road.

The intercom buzzed and Page hit the com button.

"There's a man on line three with information about one of the women who was killed at the construction site," his secretary said. "I think you should talk to him."

"Okay. What's his name?"

"Ramon Gutierrez. He's the clerk at the Hacienda Motel in Vancouver, Washington."

Page hit the button for line three and talked to Ramon Gutierrez for five minutes. When he was done, he called Ross Barrow, then headed down the hall to Randy Highsmith's office. Fifteen minutes later, Barrow picked up Highsmith and Page on the corner and they headed for Vancouver.

2

"Can I watch TV?" Kathy asked.

"Did you have enough pizza?"

"I'm stuffed."

Betsy felt guilty about dinner, but she had put in an

exhausting day in court and didn't have the energy to cook.

"Is Daddy going to come home tonight?" Kathy asked, looking up at Betsy expectantly.

"No," Betsy answered, hoping Kathy would not ask her anymore about Rick. She had explained the separation to Kathy a number of times, but Kathy would not accept the fact that Rick was most probably never going to live with them again.

Kathy looked worried. "Why won't Daddy stay with us?"

Betsy picked up Kathy and carried her to the living room couch.

"Who's your best friend?"

"Melanie."

"Remember the fight you two had, last week?"

"Yeah."

"Well, Daddy and I had an argument too. It's a serious one. Just like the one you had with your best friend."

Kathy looked confused. Betsy held Kathy on her lap and kissed the top of her head.

"Melanie and me made up. Are you and Daddy going to make up?"

"Maybe. I don't know right now. Meanwhile, Daddy is living someplace else."

"Is Daddy mad at you because he had to pick me up at day care?"

"What made you ask that?"

"He was awful mad the other day and I heard you arguing about me."

"No, honey," Betsy said, hugging Kathy tight to her. "This doesn't have anything to do with you. It's just us. We're mad at each other."

"Why?" Kathy asked. Her jaw was quivering.

"Don't cry, honey."

"I want Daddy," she said, sobbing into Betsy's shoulder. "I don't want him to go away."

"He won't go away. He'll always be your daddy, Kathy. He loves you."

Suddenly Kathy pushed away from Betsy and wriggled off her lap.

"It's your fault for working," she yelled.

Betsy was shocked. "Who told you that?"

"Daddy. You should stay home with me like Melanie's mom."

"Daddy works," Betsy said, trying to stay calm. "He works more than I do."

"Men are supposed to work. You're supposed to take care of me."

Betsy wished Rick was here so she could smash him with her fists.

"Who stayed home with you when you had the flu?" Betsy asked.

Kathy thought for a moment. "You, Mommy," she answered, looking up at Betsy.

"And when you hurt your knee at school, who came to take you home?"

Kathy looked down at the floor.

"What do you want to be when you grow up?"

"An actress or a doctor."

"That's work, honey. Doctors and actresses work just like lawyers. If you stayed home all day, you couldn't do that work."

Kathy stopped crying. Betsy picked her up again.

"I work because it's fun. I also take care of you. That's more fun. I love you much more than I like my work. It's no contest. But I don't want to stay home all day doing nothing while you're at school. It would be boring, don't you think?"

Kathy thought about that.

"Will you make up with Daddy, like I did with Melanie?"

"I'm not sure, honey. But either way, you'll see plenty of Daddy. He still loves you very much and he'll always be your dad.

"Now, why don't you watch a little TV and I'll clean up, then I'll read you another chapter of *The Wizard of Oz.*"

"I don't feel like TV, tonight."

"Do you want to help me in the kitchen?"

Kathy shrugged.

"How about a hot chocolate? I could make one while we're cleaning the dishes."

"Okay," Kathy said without much enthusiasm. Betsy followed her daughter into the kitchen. She was too small to have to carry the heavy burden of her parents' problems, but she was going to anyway. That was the way it worked and there was nothing Betsy could do about it.

After they were finished in the kitchen, Betsy read Kathy two chapters of *The Wizard of Oz*, then put her to bed. It was almost nine o'clock. Betsy looked at the TV listings and was about to turn on the set when the phone rang. She walked into the kitchen and picked up on the third ring.

"Betsy Tannenbaum?" a man asked.

"Speaking."

"This is Martin Darius. The police are at my home with a search warrant. I want you over here immediately."

A high brick wall surrounded the Darius estate. A policeman in a squad car was parked next to a black wrought-iron gate. As Betsy turned the Subaru into the driveway, the policeman got out of his car and walked over to her window.

"I'm afraid you can't go in, ma'am."

"I'm Mr. Darius's attorney," Betsy said, holding her Bar card out the window. The officer examined the card for a second, then returned it to her.

"My orders are to keep everyone out."

"I can assure you that doesn't include Mr. Darius's attorney."

"Ma'am, there's a search being conducted. You'd be in the way."

"I'm here because of the search. A warrant to search doesn't give the police the right to bar people from the place being searched. You have a walkie-talkie in your car. Why don't you call the detective in charge and ask him if I can come in."

The officer's patronizing smile was replaced by a Clint Eastwood stare, but he walked back to his car and used the walkie-talkie. He returned less than a minute later, and he did not look happy.

"Detective Barrow says you can go in."

"Thank you," Betsy answered politely. As she drove off, she could see the cop glaring at her in the rearview mirror.

After seeing the old-fashioned brick wall and the ornate scrollwork on the wrought-iron gate, Betsy assumed Darius would live in a sedate, colonial mansion, but she found herself staring at a collection of glass and steel fashioned into sharp angles and delicate curves that had nothing to do with the nineteenth century. She parked next to a squad car near the end of a curved driveway. A bridge covered by a blue awning connected the driveway with the front door. Betsy looked down through a glass roof as she walked along the bridge and saw several officers standing around the edge of an indoor pool.

A policeman was waiting for her at the front door. He guided her down a short set of stairs into a cavernous living room. Darius was standing under a giant abstract painting in vivid reds and garish greens. Beside him was a slender woman in a black dress. Her shiny black hair cascaded over her shoulders and her tan spoke of a recent vacation in the tropics. She was stunningly beautiful.

The man standing next to Darius was not. He had a beer gut and a face that would be more at home in a sports bar than a condo in the Bahamas. He was dressed in an unpressed brown suit and white shirt. His tie was askew and his raincoat was draped unceremoniously over the back of a snow-white sofa.

Before Betsy could say anything, Darius thrust a rolled-up paper at her.

"Is this a valid warrant? I'm not going to permit an invasion of my privacy until you've looked at the damn thing."

"I'm Ross Barrow, Ms. Tannenbaum," said the man in the brown suit. "This warrant's been signed by Judge Reese. The sooner you tell your client we can go through with this, the sooner we'll be out of here. I could have started already, but I waited for you to make certain Mr. Darius had representation during the search."

If Darius was a black dope dealer instead of a prominent white socialite and businessman, Betsy knew the house would have been a shambles by the time she arrived. Somebody had ordered Barrow to go very slowly with this case.

"The warrant seems okay, but I'd like to see the affidavit," Betsy said, asking for the document the police prepare to convince a judge that there is probable cause for the issuance of a warrant to search someone's house.

The affidavit would contain the factual basis for the suspicion that somewhere in the Darius mansion was evidence of a crime.

"Sorry, the affidavit's been sealed."

"Can you at least tell me why you're searching? I mean, what are the charges?"

"There aren't any charges yet."

"Let's not play games, Detective. You don't roust someone like Martin Darius without a reason."

"You're going to have to ask District Attorney Page about the case, Ms. Tannenbaum. I've been told to refer all inquiries to him."

"Where can I reach him?"

"I'm afraid I don't know that. He's probably home, but I'm not authorized to give out that number."

"What kind of bullshit is this?" Darius asked angrily.

"Calm down, Mr. Darius," Betsy said. "The warrant is legal and he can search. There's nothing we can do now. If it turns out that the affidavit is faulty, we'll be able to suppress any evidence they find."

"Evidence of what?" Darius demanded. "They refuse to tell me what they're looking for."

"Martin," the woman in black said, laying a hand on his forearm, "let them search. Please. I want them out of here, and they're not going to leave until they're through."

Darius pulled his arm away. "Search the damn house," he told Barrow angrily, "but you'd better get yourself a good lawyer, because I'm going to sue your ass all over this state."

Detective Barrow walked away, the insults bouncing ineffectively off his broad back. Just as he reached the steps leading out of the living room, a gray-haired man in a windbreaker entered the house.

"The tread on the BMW matches and there's a black

Ferrari in the garage," Betsy heard him say. Barrow motioned to two uniforms who were standing in the entryway. They followed him back to Darius.

"Mr. Darius, I'm placing you under arrest for the murders of Wendy Reiser, Laura Farrar and Victoria Miller."

The color drained from Darius's face and the woman's hand flew to her mouth, as if she was going to be sick.

"You have the right to remain silent . . ." Barrow said, reading from a laminated card he had taken from his wallet.

"What the fuck is this?" Darius exploded.

"What is he talking about?" the woman asked Betsy.

"I have to inform you of these rights, Mr. Darius."

"I think we're entitled to an explanation, Detective Barrow," Betsy said.

"No, ma'am, you're not," Barrow responded. Then he finished reading Darius his *Miranda* rights.

"Now, Mr. Darius," Barrow went on, "I'm going to have to handcuff you. This is procedure. We do it with everyone we arrest."

"You're not handcuffing anyone," Darius said, taking a step back.

"Mr. Darius, don't resist," Betsy said. "You can't do that, even if the arrest is illegal. Go with him. Just don't say a thing.

"Detective Barrow, I want to accompany Mr. Darius to the station."

"That won't be possible. I assume you don't want him questioned, so we'll book him in as soon as we get downtown. I wouldn't go down to the jail until tomorrow morning. I can't guarantee when he'll finish the booking process."

"What's my bail?" Darius demanded.

"There isn't any for murder, Mr. Darius," Barrow answered calmly. "Ms. Tannenbaum can ask for a bail hearing."

"What's he saying?" the woman asked in disbelief.

"May I talk with Mr. Darius for a moment in private?" Betsy asked.

Barrow nodded. "You can go over there," he said, pointing to a corner of the living room away from the windows. Betsy led Darius to the corner. The woman tried to follow, but Barrow told her she could not join them.

"What's this about no bail? I'm not sitting in some jail with a bunch of drug dealers and pimps."

"There's no automatic bail for murder or treason, Mr. Darius. It's in the Constitution. But there is a way to get a judge to set bail. I'll schedule a bail hearing as soon as possible and I'll see you first thing in the morning."

"I don't believe this."

"Believe it and listen to me. Anything you tell anyone will be used to convict you. I don't want you talking to a soul. Not the cops, not a cell mate. No one. There are snitches at the jail who'll trade you to beat their case and every guard will repeat every word you say to the d.a."

"Goddamn it, Tannenbaum. You get me out of this fast. I paid you to protect me. I'm not going to rot in jail."

Betsy saw Detective Barrow motion the two officers toward them.

"Remember, not a word," she said as Barrow reached them.

"Hands behind you, please," said one of the uniforms. Darius complied and the officer snapped on the cuffs. The woman watched in wide-eyed disbelief.

"I'll expect you first thing in the morning," Darius said as they led him away.

"I'll be there."

Betsy felt a hand on her arm.

"Mrs. Tannenbaum . . . ?"

"It's Betsy."

"I'm Martin's wife, Lisa. What's happening? Why are they taking Martin away?"

Lisa Darius looked bewildered, but Betsy did not see any tears. She seemed more like a hostess whose party has been a stunning flop, than a wife whose husband had just been arrested for mass murder.

"You know as much as I do, Lisa. Did the police mention anything about why they were at your home?"

"They said . . . I can't believe what they said. They asked us about the three women who were found at Martin's construction site."

"That's right," Betsy said, suddenly remembering why the names Barrow had spoken sounded so familiar.

"Martin couldn't have had anything to do with that. We know the Millers. They were out on our yacht this summer. This has to be a mistake."

"Mrs. Darius?"

Betsy and Lisa Darius looked toward the living room stairs. A black detective dressed in jeans and a black and red Portland Trail Blazers jacket was walking toward them.

"We're going to seize your BMW. May I have your key, please?" he asked politely, handing her a yellow carbon of a property receipt.

"Our car? Can they do this?" Lisa asked Betsy.

"The warrant mentioned cars."

"Oh, God. Where will this end?"

"I'm afraid my men are going to have to search your house," the detective told her apologetically. "We'll try to be neat and put everything back that we don't take. If you like, you can come along with us."

"I can't. Just be quick, please. I want you out of my house."

The detective was embarrassed. He looked down at the carpet as he walked off. Barrow had taken his raincoat with him, but there was a damp spot on the sofa where it had lain. Lisa Darius looked at the spot with distaste and sat as far from it as she could. Betsy sat next to her.

"How long is Martin going to be in jail?"

"That depends. The State has the burden of convincing the court that it's got a damn good case, if it wants to hold Martin without bail. I'll ask for an immediate hearing. If the State can't meet its burden, he'll be out quickly. If they meet it, he won't get out at all, unless we get a not guilty verdict."

"This is unbelievable."

"Lisa," Betsy asked cautiously, "did you have any idea something like this might happen?"

"What do you mean?"

"It's been my experience that the police usually don't act unless they have a pretty good case. They make mistakes, of course, but that's rarer than you'd think from the way they're portrayed on television. And your husband's no street punk. I can't imagine Alan Page rousting someone of Martin's stature in the community without some pretty strong evidence. Especially on a charge like this."

Lisa stared openmouthed at Betsy for a moment.

"Are you suggesting . . . ? I thought you were Martin's lawyer. If you don't believe him, you have no business handling his case. I don't know why he hired you, anyway. Daddy says Oscar Montoya and Matthew Reynolds are the best criminal lawyers in Oregon. He could have had either one of them."

"A lawyer who only thinks what her client wants her to think isn't doing her job," Betsy said calmly. "If there's something you know about these charges, I have to know it, so I can defend Martin properly."

"Well, there isn't," Lisa answered, looking away from Betsy. "The whole thing is outrageous."

Betsy decided not to push. "Do you have anyone who can stay with you?" she asked.

"I'll be fine by myself."

"This will get rough, Lisa. The press will be hounding you night and day, and living in a spotlight is much worse than most people imagine. Do you have an answering machine you can use to screen your calls?"

Lisa nodded.

"Good. Put it on and don't take any calls from the media. Since we don't have any idea of the case against Martin, we don't know what can hurt him. For instance, where Martin was on a certain date might be crucial. If you tell the press he wasn't with you on that date, it could destroy an alibi. So don't say anything. If a reporter does get through to you, refer her to me. And never talk to the police or someone from the d.a.'s office. There's a privilege for husband-wife communications and you have a right to refuse to talk to anyone. Do you understand?"

"Yes. I'll be okay. And I'm sorry I said that. About how Martin could have gotten someone better. I'm just . . ."

"No need to apologize or explain. This must be very difficult for you."

"You don't have to stay with me."

"I'll stay until the search is finished. I want to see what they're taking. It might tell us why they think Martin's involved. I heard one officer tell Barrow they matched the tread on the BMW to something. That means they've placed Martin's car somewhere. Maybe the crime scene."

"So what? He drives to his construction sites all the time. This whole thing is ridiculous."

"We'll see soon enough," Betsy said, but she was worried. Lisa Darius may have been shocked and surprised by her husband's arrest, but Betsy knew Martin Darius was not. No one gives a $58,000 retainer to a lawyer in anticipation of being arrested for shoplifting. That was the type of retainer a good lawyer received for representing someone on a murder charge.

Chapter Nine

―――――

"It's a pleasure to meet you, Mrs. Tannenbaum," Alan Page said when Betsy was seated across his desk from him. "Randy Highsmith was very impressed with the way you handled the Hammermill case. He had nothing but nice things to say about you. That's really high praise, because Randy hates to lose."

"I think Randy might not have brought the charges if he knew how brutal Andrea's husband was."

"That's being charitable. Let's face it. Randy thought he'd run over you. You taught him a good lesson. Losing 'Hammermill' will make Randy a better prosecutor. But you're not here to talk about old business, are you? You're here to talk about Martin Darius."

"Detective Barrow must have called you at home at the phone number he wouldn't give me."

"Ross Barrow's a good cop who knows how to follow orders."

"Do you want to tell me why you've arrested my client?"

"I think he murdered the four people we found buried at his construction site."

"That's obvious, Mr. Page . . ."

"Why don't you call me Al?"

"I'd be glad to. And you may call me Betsy. Now that we're on a first-name basis, how about telling me why you searched Martin's house and arrested him?"

Page smiled. " 'Fraid I can't do that."

"Won't, you mean."

"Betsy, you know you're not entitled to discovery of our police reports until I've filed an indictment."

"You're going to have to tell the judge what you've got at the bail hearing."

"True. But that's not scheduled yet and there's no indictment, so I'm going to stick to the letter of the discovery statutes."

Betsy leaned back in her chair and smiled sweetly.

"You must not have much confidence in your case, Al."

Page laughed to cover his surprise that Betsy had seen through him so easily.

"I've got plenty of confidence in our case," he lied. "But I also have a healthy respect for your abilities. I won't make Randy's mistake of underestimating you. I must confess, though, that with your commitment to feminism I was surprised when Ross told me you were defending Darius."

"What does feminism have to do with my representation of Martin Darius?"

"Hasn't he told you what he's done?"

"Martin Darius has no idea why you're holding him and neither do I."

Page looked at her for a moment, then made a decision.

"I guess it's not fair leaving you completely in the dark, so I'll tell you that we plan to indict your client for the kidnapping, torture and murder of three women and one man."

Page took a color photo of Wendy Reiser's body out
of a manila envelope and handed it to Betsy. She
blanched. The picture had been taken right after the
body had been dug up. The naked woman was sprawled
in the mud. Betsy could see the incisions on her stomach
and the cuts and burn marks on her legs. She could also
see Wendy Reiser's face clearly. Even in death, she
seemed to be suffering.

"That's what Martin Darius does to women, Betsy,
and this may not be the first time he's done it. We have
pretty solid information that ten years ago a man named
Peter Lake murdered six women in Hunter's Point, New
York, in much the same way these victims were murdered. We also have conclusive proof that Peter Lake and
Martin Darius are the same person. You might want to
ask your client about that.

"One other thing. There's another missing woman.
This is a one-time offer: If she's alive and Darius tells us
where she is, we might be able to deal."

The jail elevator opened onto a narrow concrete hallway
painted in yellow and brown pastels. Across from the elevator were three solid doors. Betsy used the key the
guard had given her when she checked in at the visitor's
desk. The middle door opened into a tiny room. In front
of her was a wall divided in half by a narrow ledge. Below
the ledge was concrete; above, a slab of bulletproof glass.
Betsy placed her legal pad on the ledge, sat down on an
uncomfortable metal folding chair and picked up the receiver on the phone that was attached to the wall to her
left.

On the other side of the glass, Martin Darius lifted
his receiver. He was dressed in an orange jumpsuit, but

he still looked as imposing as he had in her office. His hair and beard were combed and he sat erect and at ease. Darius leaned forward until he was almost touching the glass. His eyes looked a little wild, but that was the only sign of discontent.

"When is the bail hearing scheduled?" Darius asked.

"It isn't."

"I told you I wanted out of here. You should have scheduled the hearing first thing this morning."

"This isn't going to work. I'm an attorney, not a gofer. If you want someone to order around I'll refer you to a maid service."

Darius stared at Betsy for a moment, then flashed an icy smile of concession.

"Sorry. Twelve hours in this place doesn't help your disposition."

"I met with Alan Page, the district attorney, this morning. He had some interesting things to tell me. He also showed me the crime scene photographs. The three women were tortured, Martin. I've seen a lot of cruelty, but nothing like this. The killer didn't just end their lives, he slaughtered them. Tore them open . . ."

Betsy stopped, as the memory of what she'd seen took her breath away. Darius watched her. She waited for him to say something. When he didn't, she asked:

"Does any of this sound familiar?"

"I didn't kill those women."

"I didn't ask you if you killed them. I asked if anything about the crimes sounded familiar."

Darius studied Betsy. She didn't like the way he made her feel like a lab specimen.

"Why are you interrogating me?" Darius asked. "You work for me, not the d.a."

"Mr. Darius, I decide whom I work for and right now I'm not so sure I want to work for you."

"Page said something, didn't he. He played with your head."

"Who is Peter Lake?"

Betsy expected a reaction, but not the one she got. The look of icy calm deserted Darius. His lip trembled. He looked, suddenly, like a man on the verge of tears.

"So Page knows about Hunter's Point."

"You haven't been honest with me, Mr. Darius."

"Is that what this is all about?" Darius asked, pointing at the bulletproof glass. "Is that why you didn't ask for a contact visit? Are you afraid to be locked in with me? Afraid I'll . . ."

Darius stopped. He put his head in his hands.

"I don't think I'm the right person to represent you," Betsy told him.

"Why?" Darius asked, his voice filled with pain. "Because Page claims I raped and murdered those women? Did you refuse to represent Andrea Hammermill when the district attorney said she murdered her husband?"

"Andrea Hammermill was the victim of a husband who beat her constantly during her marriage."

"But she killed him, Betsy. I did *not* murder those women. I swear it. I did *not* kill anyone in Hunter's Point. I was Peter Lake, but, do you know who Peter Lake was? Did Page tell you that? Does he even know?

"Peter Lake was married to the most wonderful woman in the world. He was the father of a perfect child. A little girl who never hurt anyone. And his wife and daughter were murdered by a madman named Henry Waters for an insane reason Peter could never fathom.

"Peter was a lawyer. He made money hand over fist. He lived in a magnificent house and drove a fancy car, but all that money and everything he owned couldn't make him forget the wife and daughter who'd been taken from him. So he ran away. He assumed a new identity and started a new life, because his old life was impossible to bear."

Darius stopped talking. There were tears in his eyes. Betsy did not know what to think. Moments ago, she was convinced Darius was a monster. Now, seeing his pain, she wasn't so sure.

"I'll make you a deal, Betsy," Darius said, his voice barely above a whisper. "If you reach the point where you don't believe I'm innocent, you can walk away from my case with my blessing, and you can keep your retainer."

Betsy did not know what to say. Those pictures. She couldn't stop wondering how the women felt in those first, long moments of terror, knowing that the best that could ever happen to them in the rest of their lives was a death that would bring an end to their pain.

"It's all right," Darius said, "I know how you feel. You only saw the pictures. I saw the dead bodies of my wife and my child. And I still see them, Betsy."

Betsy felt ill. She took a deep breath. She could not stay in the narrow room any longer. She needed air. And she needed to find out a lot more about Peter Lake and what happened in Hunter's Point.

"Are you okay?" Darius asked.

"No, I'm not. I'm very confused."

"I know you are. Page laid a heavy trip on you. They said I'd be arraigned tomorrow. You get a good night's sleep and tell me what you've decided to do, then."

Betsy nodded.

"Two things, though," Darius said, looking directly at Betsy.

"What's that?"

"If you decide to keep me as a client, you've got to fight like hell for me."

"And the other thing?"

"From now on, I want every visit to be a contact visit. No more glass cage. I don't want my lawyer treating me like a zoo animal."

Chapter Ten

As soon as Rita Cohen opened the door wide enough, Kathy squeezed through and raced into the kitchen.

"You didn't buy that bubble-gum-flavored cereal again, did you, Mom?" Betsy asked.

"She's a little kid, Betsy. Who could stand that healthy stuff you feed her all the time? Let her live."

"That's what I'm trying to do. If it was up to you, she'd be on an all-cholesterol diet."

"When I was growing up, we didn't know from cholesterol. We ate what made us happy, not the same stuff you feed horses. And look at me. Seventy-four and still going strong."

Betsy hugged her mother and gave her a kiss on the forehead. Rita was only five feet four, so Betsy had to bend down to do it. Betsy's dad never topped five feet nine. No one could figure where Betsy got her height.

"How come there's no school?" Rita asked.

"It's another teacher planning day. I forgot to read the flyer they sent home, so I didn't know until yesterday evening, when Kathy mentioned it."

"You have time for a cup of coffee?" Rita asked.

Betsy looked at her watch. It was only seven-twenty. They would not let her into the jail to see Darius until eight.

"Sure," she said, dropping the backpack with Kathy's things on a chair and following her mother into the living room. The television was already on, tuned to a morning talk show.

"Don't let her watch too much TV," Betsy said, sitting down on the couch. "I packed some books and games for her."

"A little television isn't going to kill her any more than that cereal."

Betsy laughed. "One day with you undoes all the good habits I've instilled in a year. You're an absolute menace."

"Nonsense," Rita answered gruffly, pouring two cups of coffee from the pot she had prepared in expectation of Betsy's visit. "So, what are you doing this morning that's so important you had to abandon that lovely angel to such an ogre?"

"You've heard of Martin Darius?"

"Certainly."

"I'm representing him."

"What did he do?"

"The d.a. thinks Darius raped and killed the three women they found at his construction site. He also thinks Darius tortured and killed six women in Hunter's Point, New York, ten years ago."

"Oh, my God! Is he guilty?"

"I don't know. Darius swears he's innocent."

"And you believe him?"

Betsy shook her head. "It's too early to say."

"He's a rich man, Betsy. The police wouldn't arrest someone that important without proof."

"If I took the State's word for everything, Andrea Hammermill and Grace Peterson would be in prison today."

Rita looked concerned. "Should you be representing

a man who rapes and tortures women after all the work you've done for women's rights?"

"We don't know that he tortured anyone, Mom, and that feminist label is something the press stuck on me. I want to work for women's rights, but I'm not just a woman's lawyer. This case will help me be seen as more than one-dimensional. It could make my career. And, more important, Darius may be innocent. The d.a. won't tell me why he thinks Darius is guilty. That makes me very suspicious. If he had the goods on Darius he'd be confident enough to tell me what he's got."

"I just don't want to see you get hurt."

"I won't get hurt, Mom, because I'll do a good job. I learned something when I won Grace's case. I have a talent. I'm a very good trial attorney. I have a knack for talking to jurors. I'm damned good at cross-examination. If I win this case, people across the country are going to know how good I am, and that's why I want this case so badly. But I'm going to need your help."

"What do you mean?"

"The case is going to go on for at least a year. The trial could last for months. With the State asking for the death penalty, I'm going to have to fight every step of the way, and the case is extremely complicated. It's going to take all my time. We're talking about events that occurred ten years ago. I've got to find out everything there is to know about Hunter's Point, Darius's background. That means I'll be working long hours and weekends and I'm going to need help with Kathy. Someone has to pick her up from day care, if I'm tied up in court, make her dinner . . ."

"What about Rick?"

"I can't ask him. You know why."

"No, I don't know why. He's Kathy's father. He's also your husband. He should be your biggest fan."

"Well, he's not. He's never accepted the fact that I'm a real lawyer with a successful practice."

"What did he think you'd be doing when you hung out your shingle?"

"I think he thought it was going to be a cute hobby like stamp collecting, something to keep me occupied when I wasn't cooking dinner or cleaning."

"Well, he is the man of the house. Men like to feel they're in charge. And here you are, getting all the headlines and talking on the television."

"Look, Mom, I don't want to discuss Rick. Do you mind? I just get angry."

"All right, I won't discuss him and, of course, I'll help."

"I don't know how I'd make it without you, Mom."

Rita blushed and waved a hand at Betsy. "That's what mothers are for."

"Granny," Kathy yelled from the kitchen, "I can't find the chocolate syrup."

"Why would she want chocolate syrup at seven-thirty in the morning?" Betsy asked menacingly.

"None of your business," Rita answered imperiously. "I'm coming, sweetheart. It's too high up. You can't reach it."

"I've got to go," Betsy said, with a resigned shake of the head. "And please keep the TV to a minimum."

"We're only reading Shakespeare and studying algebra this morning," Rita answered as she disappeared into the kitchen.

Reggie Stewart was waiting for Betsy on a bench near the visitor's desk at the jail. Stewart had worked at several unsatisfying jobs before discovering a talent for investigation. He was a slender six-footer with shaggy brown hair and bright blue eyes who was most comfortable in plaid flannel shirts, cowboy boots and jeans. Stewart had an odd way of looking at events and a sarcastic air that put off some people. Betsy appreciated the way he used his imagination and his knack for making people trust him. These attributes proved invaluable in the Hammermill and Peterson cases, where the best evidence of abuse came from the victims' relatives and would have remained buried under layers of hate and family pride if it was not for Reggie's persuasiveness and persistence.

"Ready, Chief?" Stewart asked, smiling as he unwound from the bench.

"Always," Betsy answered with a smile.

Stewart had filled out visitor's forms for both of them. A guard sat behind a glass window in a control room. Betsy pushed the forms and their i.d. through a slot in the window and asked for a contact visit with Martin Darius. As soon as the guard told them it was set, she and Reggie emptied the metal objects from their pockets, took off their watches and jewelry and walked through the metal detector. The guard checked Betsy's briefcase, then called for the elevator. When it came, Betsy inserted the key for the seventh floor in a lock and turned it. The elevator rode up to seven and the doors opened on the same narrow hall Betsy had stepped into the day before. This time, she walked to the far end and waited in front of a thick metal door with an equally thick piece of glass in the upper half. Through the glass, she could see the two seventh-floor contact rooms. They were both empty.

"Darius is going to be a demanding client," Betsy told Stewart as they waited for the guard. "He's used to being in charge, he's very bright and he's under tremendous pressure."

"Gottcha."

"Today, we listen. The arraignment isn't until nine,

so we have an hour. I want to get his version of what happened in Hunter's Point. If we're not done by nine, you can finish up later."

"What's he facing?"

Betsy pulled a copy of the indictment from her briefcase.

"This don't look good, Chief," Stewart said after reading the charges. "Who's 'John Doe'?"

"The man. The police have no idea who he is. His face and fingertips were disfigured with acid and the killer even smashed his teeth with a hammer to try and prevent an i.d. from his dental records."

Stewart grimaced. "This is one set of crime scene photos I'm not lookin' forward to seeing."

"They're the worst, Reg. Look at them before breakfast. I almost lost mine."

"How do you dope it out?"

"You mean, do I think Darius did it?" Betsy shook her head. "I'm not sure. Page is convinced, but either Darius put on a great performance for me yesterday, or he's not guilty."

"So we have a real whodunit?"

"Maybe."

Out of their sight, a heavy lock opened with a loud snap. Betsy craned her neck and saw Darius precede the guard into the narrow space in front of the two contact rooms. When her client was locked in one of them, the guard let Betsy and Stewart into the contact area, then secured the door to the hall where they had been waiting. After locking them in with Darius, the guard left the contact visiting area by the door through which he had entered.

The contact room was small. Most of the space in it was taken up by a large circular table and three plastic chairs. Darius was sitting in one of them. He did not stand up when Betsy entered.

"I see you brought a bodyguard," Darius said, studying Stewart carefully.

"Martin Darius meet Reggie Stewart, my investigator."

"You're only using one?" Darius asked, ignoring Reggie's outstretched hand. Stewart pulled his hand back slowly.

"Reggie is very good. I wouldn't have won 'Hammermill' without him. If I think you need more investigators, you'll get them. Here's a copy of the indictment."

Darius took the paper and read it.

"Page is charging you under several theories in the death of each person: personally killing a human being during the commission of the felony crime of kidnapping; torture killing; more than one victim. If he gets a conviction on any theory of Aggravated Murder, we go into a second, or penalty, phase of the trial. That's a second trial on the issue of punishment.

"In the penalty phase, the State has to convince the jurors that you committed the murder deliberately, that the victim's provocation, if any, did not mitigate the killing and that there's a probability that you'll be dangerous in the future. If the jurors answer 'yes' unanimously to these three questions, you'll be sentenced to death, unless there is some mitigating circumstance that convinces any juror that you should not get a death sentence.

"If any juror votes 'no' on any question, the jurors then decide on whether you get life without parole or life with a thirty-year minimum sentence. Any questions, so far?"

"Yes, Tannenbaum," Darius said, looking at her with an amused smile. "Why are you wasting your time on an explanation of the penalty phase? I did not kidnap, torture or kill these women. I expect you to explain that to our jury."

"What about Hunter's Point?" Betsy asked. "That's going to play a huge part in your trial."

"A man named Henry Waters was the killer. He was shot trying to escape arrest. They found the body of one of his victims disemboweled in his basement. Everyone knew Waters was guilty and the case was closed."

"Then why is Page convinced you killed the Hunter's Point women?"

"I have no idea. I was a victim, for God's sake. I told you. Waters killed Sandy and Melody. I was part of the task force that investigated the killings."

"How did that happen?" Betsy asked, surprised.

"I volunteered. I was an excellent lawyer and I did a lot of criminal defense when I started out. I felt I could provide a unique insight into the criminal mind. The mayor agreed."

"Why didn't you set up a law practice in Oregon?"

Darius stopped smiling. "Why is that important?"

"It looks like you're trying to hide. So does dyeing your hair black."

"My wife and child were murdered, Tannenbaum. I found their bodies. Those deaths were part of my old life. When I moved here, it was my chance to start over. I didn't want to see my old face in the mirror, because I would remember how Sandy and Melody looked beside me in old photographs. I didn't want to work at the same job, because there were too many associations between that job and my old life."

Darius leaned forward. He rested his elbows on the table and supported his head on his lean fingers, massaging his forehead, as if he was trying to wipe away painful memories.

"I'm sorry if that sounds crazy, but I was a little

crazy for a while. I'd been so happy. Then that maniac . . ."

Darius closed his eyes. Stewart studied him carefully. Betsy was right. Either the guy was a great actor or
he was innocent.

"We'll need the old files from Hunter's Point," Betsy
told Stewart. "You'll probably have to go back there to
talk to the detectives who worked the case. Page's theory
falls apart if Martin didn't kill the Hunter's Point
women."

Stewart nodded, then he leaned toward Darius.

"Who are your enemies, Mr. Darius? Who hates you
enough to frame you for these murders?"

Darius shrugged. "I've made lots of enemies. There
are those fools who are tying up the project where the
bodies were found."

"Mr. Darius," Stewart said patiently, "with all due
respect, you're not seriously suggesting a group dedicated
to preserving historic buildings is responsible for framing
you, are you?"

"They torched three of my condos."

"You don't see a difference between setting fire to an
inanimate object and torturing three women to death?
We're looking for a monster here, Mr. Darius. Who do
you know who has no conscience, no compassion, who
thinks people are no more valuable than bugs and hates
your guts?"

Betsy did not expect Darius to put up with Stewart's
insolence, but he surprised her. Instead of getting mad,
he leaned back in his chair, his brow furrowing in frustration as he tried to think of an answer to Stewart's question.

"What I say doesn't leave here, right?"

"Reggie is our agent. The attorney-client privilege
applies to anything you tell him."

"Okay. One name comes to mind. There's a project in Southern Oregon I couldn't fund. The banks didn't trust my judgment. So I went to Manuel Ochoa. He's a man who doesn't do much but has lots of money. I never asked where it came from, but I've heard rumors."

"Are we talking Colombians, Mr. Darius? Cocaine, tar heroin?" Reggie asked.

"I don't know and I didn't want to. I asked for the money, he gave me the money. There were terms I agreed to that I'll have trouble meeting if I stay in jail. If Darius Construction defaults, Ochoa will make a lot of money."

"And druggies would snuff a woman or two without thinking twice," Stewart added.

"Does Ochoa know about Hunter's Point?" Betsy asked suddenly. "We're not just looking for a psychopath. We're looking for a psychopath with intimate knowledge of your secret past."

"Good point," Stewart said. "Who knew about Hunter's Point besides you?"

Darius suddenly looked ill. He rested his elbows on the table again and let his head fall heavily into his open palms.

"That's the question I've been asking myself, Tannenbaum, ever since I realized I was being framed. But it's a question I can't answer. I've never told anyone in Portland about Hunter's Point. Never. But the person who's framing me knows all about it, and I just don't know how that's possible."

"Coffee, black," Betsy told her secretary as she flew through the front door, "and get me a turkey, bacon and swiss from the Heathman Pub."

Betsy tossed her attaché case on her desk and took a

brief look at the mail and messages Ann had stacked in
the center of the blotter. Betsy tossed the junk mail in the
wastebasket, placed the important letters in her in-box
and decided that none of the callers needed to be phoned
immediately.

"The sandwich will be ready in fifteen minutes,"
Ann said as she put a cup of coffee on Betsy's desk.

"Great."

"How did the arraignment go?"

"A zoo. The courthouse was swarming with reporters. It was worse than 'Hammermill.'"

Ann left. Betsy sipped some coffee, then punched
out the phone number of Dr. Raymond Keene, a former
state medical examiner who was now in private practice.
When a defense attorney needed someone to check the
m.e.'s results, they went to Dr. Keene.

"What ya got for me, Betsy?"

"Hi, Ray. I've got the Darius case."

"No kidding."

"No kidding. Three women and one man. All brutally tortured. I want to know everything about how they
died and what was done to them before they died."

"Who did the autopsies?"

"Susan Gregg."

"She's competent. Is there some special reason you
want her findings checked?"

"It's not so much her findings. The d.a. thinks Darius did this before, ten years ago, in Hunter's Point, New
York. Six women were murdered there, as far as I can
tell. There was a suspect in that case who was killed resisting arrest. Page doesn't believe the suspect was the
murderer. When we get the Hunter's Point autopsy reports, I want you to compare the cases to see if there is a
similar m.o."

"Sounds interesting. Did Page clear it?"

"I asked him after the arraignment."

"I'll call Sue and see if I can get over to the morgue this afternoon."

"The quicker the better."

"You want me to perform another autopsy or just review her report?"

"Do everything you can think of. At this point, I have no idea what might be important."

"What lab tests has Sue done?"

"I don't know."

"Probably not as many as she should. I'll check it out. The budget pressures don't encourage a lot of lab work."

"We don't have to worry about a budget. Darius will go top dollar."

"That's what I like to hear. I'll call as soon as I have something to tell you. Give 'em hell."

"I will, Ray."

Betsy hung up the phone.

"Are you ready for lunch?" Nora Sloane asked hesitantly from the office doorway. Betsy looked up, startled.

"Your receptionist wasn't in. I waited for a few minutes."

"Oh, I'm sorry, Nora. We did have a lunch date, didn't we?"

"For noon."

"I apologize. I forgot all about it. I just picked up a new case that's taking all my time."

"Martin Darius. I know. It's the headline in the *Oregonian*."

"I'm afraid today isn't good for lunch. I'm really swamped. Can we do it another day?"

"No problem. In fact, I was sure you'd want to cancel. I was going to call, but . . . Betsy," Sloane said excitedly, "could I tag along on this case, sit in on conferences, talk to your investigator? It's a fantastic opportunity to see how you work on a high profile case."

"I don't know . . ."

"I wouldn't say anything, of course. I'd keep your confidences. I only want to be a fly on the wall."

Sloane seemed so excited, Betsy did not want to turn her down, but a leak about defense strategy could be devastating. The front door opened and Ann appeared in the doorway carrying a brown paper bag. Sloane looked over her shoulder.

"Sorry," Ann said, backing away. Betsy motioned her to stop.

"I'll talk to Darius," Betsy said. "He'll have to give his okay. Then I'll think about it. I won't do anything that could endanger a client's case."

"I understand perfectly," Sloane said. "I'll call in a few days to see what you decide."

"Sorry about lunch."

"Oh, no. That's okay. And thank you."

There was a van with a CBS logo and another from ABC in Betsy's driveway when she pulled in.

"Who are they, Mom?" Kathy asked, as two beautifully dressed blondes with perfect features approached the car. The women held microphones and were followed by muscular men armed with portable television cameras.

"Monica Blake, CBS, Mrs. Tannenbaum," the shorter woman said as Betsy pushed open the door. Blake stepped back awkwardly and the other woman took advantage of the break.

"How do you explain a woman who is known for her strong feminist views defending a man who is alleged to have kidnapped, raped, tortured and killed three women?"

Betsy flushed. She turned abruptly and glared at the reporter from ABC, ignoring the microphone thrust in her face.

"First, I don't have to explain anything. The State does. Second, I'm an attorney. One of the things I do is defend people—male or female—who have been accused of a crime. Sometimes these people are unjustly accused, because the State makes a mistake. Martin Darius is innocent and I am proud to be representing him against these false accusations."

"What if they're not false?" asked the CBS reporter. "How can you sleep nights, knowing what he did to these women?"

"I suggest you read the Constitution, Ms. Blake. Mr. Darius is presumed innocent. Now, I have dinner to make and a little girl to take care of. I won't answer any questions at my house. I consider this an invasion of my privacy. If you want to talk to me, call my office for an appointment. Please don't come to my house again."

Betsy walked around the car and opened Kathy's door. She jumped out, looking over her shoulder at the cameras as Betsy dragged her toward the house. The two reporters continued to shout questions at her back.

"Are we gonna be on TV?" Kathy asked, as Betsy slammed the door.

Chapter Eleven

I

Alan Page was trapped in a car, careening downhill through traffic at breakneck speed on a winding turnpike, brakes screeching, tires smoking, twisting the wheel furiously to avoid an inevitable collision. When he sat up in bed, he was inches from the burning headlights of a massive semi. Sweat glued his flannel pajamas to his damp skin and he could feel the thunderous pounding of his heart. Page gulped down lungfuls of air, still uncertain where he was and half-expecting to die in a fireball of lacerated steel and shattered glass.

"Jesus," he gasped when he was oriented. The clock read four fifty-eight, an hour and a half before the alarm would go off, four and a half hours before the bail hearing. He fell back onto his pillow, anxious and sure sleep was impossible, haunted by the question that had hounded him since the arrest of Martin Darius. Had he moved too soon? Was there "clear and convincing" evidence that Martin Darius was a murderer?

Ross Barrow and Randy Highsmith had argued against searching Darius's house, even after hearing what

168

Gutierrez had to say. They wanted to wait until Nancy Gordon was found and they had a stronger case, but he had overridden them and instructed Barrow to make an arrest if the tire tracks at the scene matched the treads on Darius's car. Now, he wondered if Barrow and Highsmith hadn't been right all along. He had counted on finding Nancy Gordon for the bail hearing, but even with three detectives working around the clock, they were striking out.

If he could not sleep, he could rest. Page closed his eyes and saw Nancy Gordon. He had thought of the detective constantly since learning that her body was not in the pit. If she was alive, she would have gotten in touch with him as soon as she learned of Darius's arrest. If she was alive, she would have returned to the Lakeview. Was she dead, a look of unimaginable suffering on her face? Darius knew the answer to Page's questions, but the law forbade Alan to talk to him.

Page would need all of his energy in court, but the fear in his belly would not let him rest. He decided he would shower, shave, eat breakfast, then dress in his best suit and a crisp, starched shirt, fresh from the laundry. A shower and a big breakfast would make him feel human. Then he would drive to the courthouse and try to convince the Honorable Patrick Norwood, judge of the Multnomah County Circuit Court, that Martin Darius was a serial killer.

2

Martin Darius slept peacefully and felt well rested when he awoke with the other inmates of the Multnomah County Jail. Betsy Tannenbaum had arranged to have his hair cut by his barber, and the watch commander was permitting him an extra shower before court. Only a breakfast of sticky pancakes soaked in gluey, jailhouse syrup spoiled his mood. Darius used the acidic taste of the jail coffee to cut the sweetness and ate them anyway, because he knew it would be a long day in court.

Betsy had exchanged a full wardrobe for the clothes in which Darius was arrested. When Darius met her in the interview room before court, he was attired in a double-breasted, chalk-striped, dark wool suit, a cotton broadcloth shirt and a navy blue, woven silk tie with white pinpoint dots. Betsy wore a single-breasted jacket and matching skirt of black and white, windowpane plaid and a white silk blouse with a wide collar. When they walked down the courthouse corridor in the glare of the television lights, they would look like a couple you might see on "Lifestyles of the Rich and Famous," rather than a suspected mass murderer and his mouthpiece.

"How are you feeling?" Darius asked.

"Fine."

"Good. I want you at your best today. Jail is interesting, if you treat it as an educational experience, but I'm ready to graduate."

"I'm glad to see you're keeping your sense of humor."

Darius shrugged. "I have faith in you, Tannenbaum. That's why I hired you. You're the best. You won't let me down."

The praise made Betsy feel good. She basked in it and believed what Darius told her. She was the best. That was why Darius chose her over Matthew Reynolds, Oscar Montoya and the other established criminal defense lawyers.

"Who's our judge?" Darius asked.

"Pat Norwood."

"What's he like?"

"He's a crusty old codger who's nearing retirement. He looks like a troll and acts like an ogre in court. He's no legal scholar, either. But he is completely impartial. Norwood's rude and impatient with the prosecution and the defense and he won't be buffaloed by Alan Page or the press. If Page doesn't meet his burden of proof on the bail issue, Norwood will do the right thing."

"Do you think the State will meet its burden?" Darius asked.

"No, Martin, I don't think they will."

Darius smiled. "That's what I wanted to hear." Then the smile faded as he changed the subject. "Is Lisa going to be in court?"

"Of course. I talked to her yesterday."

"Looks like you're having more luck getting in touch with my wife than I am."

"Lisa's staying with her father. She didn't feel comfortable alone in the house."

"That's funny," Darius said, flashing Betsy a chilly smile. "I called His Honor last night and he told me she wasn't home."

"She may have been out."

"Right. The next time you talk to my wife, please ask her to visit me, will you?"

"Sure. Oh, before I forget, there's a woman named Nora Sloane who's writing an article about women defense attorneys. She wants to follow me through your case. If I let her, there's a chance she might learn defense strategy or attorney-client confidences. I told her I had to ask your permission before I let her get involved. Do you have any objections to her tagging along?"

Darius considered the question for a moment, then shook his head.

"I don't mind. Besides"—he grinned—"you'll have

more incentive to do a great job for me if someone is writing about you."

"I never thought of it that way."

"That's why I'm a millionaire, Tannenbaum. I always figure the angles."

3

There were several new courtrooms outfitted with state-of-the-art video equipment and computer technology that Patrick L. Norwood could have commandeered because of his senior status, but Judge Norwood preferred the courtroom where he had ruled with an iron fist for twenty years. It had high ceilings, grand marble columns and a hand-carved wooden dais. It was an old-fashioned court-room, perfect for a man with the judicial temperament of a nineteenth-century hanging judge.

The courtroom was filled to capacity for the Martin Darius bail hearing. Those who were too late to find a seat stood in line in the hall. Spectators had to pass through a metal detector before entering the courtroom and there were extra security guards inside, because of death threats.

Harvey Cobb, an elderly black man, called the court to order. He had been Norwood's bailiff from the day the judge was appointed. Norwood came out of his chambers through a door behind the bench. Short and squat, he was ugly as sin, but his toadlike face was crowned by a full head of beautiful snowy white hair.

"Be seated," Cobb said. Betsy took her place beside Martin Darius and glanced briefly at Alan Page, who was sitting next to Randy Highsmith.

"Call your first witness, Mr. Page," Norwood ordered.

"The State calls Ross Barrow, Your Honor."

Harvey Cobb had Detective Barrow raise his right hand and swear to tell the truth. Barrow sat in the witness box and Page established his credentials as a homicide investigator.

"Detective Barrow, sometime in mid-August did you become aware of a series of unusual disappearances?"

"Yes, I did. In August a detective from our missing persons bureau told me that a woman named Laura Farrar was reported missing by her husband, Larry Farrar. Larry told the detective that . . ."

"Objection, hearsay," Betsy said, standing.

"No," Norwood ruled. "This is a bail hearing, not a trial. I'm going to permit the State some leeway. If you need to examine some of these witnesses, you can subpoena them. Let's move on, Mr. Page."

Page nodded at Barrow, who continued with his account of the investigation.

"Farrar told the detective that he had come home from work on August tenth, about eight o'clock. His house looked perfectly normal, but his wife was missing. None of her clothes was missing or her makeup. In fact, nothing was missing from the house, as far as he could tell. The only unusual circumstance was a rose and a note Mr. Farrar found on his wife's pillow."

"Was there anything odd about the rose?"

"Yes, sir. A lab report on the rose indicates that it had been dyed black."

"What did the note say?"

" 'Gone, But Not Forgotten.' "

Page handed a document and a photograph to the judge's clerk.

"This is a photocopy of the Farrar note and a photo-

graph of the rose, Your Honor. The originals are still at
the lab. I talked about this with Mrs. Tannenbaum and
she's willing to stipulate to the introduction of these and
other copies, solely for purposes of this hearing."

"Is that so?" Norwood asked Betsy. She nodded.

"The exhibits will be received."

"Did the detective from missing persons tell you
about a second disappearance in mid-September?"

"Yes, sir. Wendy Reiser, the wife of Thomas Reiser,
was reported missing by her husband under identical circumstances."

"Nothing disturbed in the house or missing?"

"Correct."

"Did Mr. Reiser find a black rose and a note on his
wife's pillow?"

"He did."

Page introduced a photocopy of the Reiser note and
a photograph of the Reiser rose.

"What did the lab say about the second note and
rose?"

"They are identical to the note and rose found at the
Farrar house."

"Finally, Detective, did you learn about a third, recent disappearance?"

"Yes, sir. Russell Miller reported his wife, Victoria,
missing under circumstances that were identical to the
other cases. Note and rose on the pillow. Nothing disturbed or missing in the house."

"Several days ago, did you learn where the women
were?"

Barrow nodded gravely. "The three women and an
unidentified male were found buried in a construction
site owned by Darius Construction."

"Who owns Darius Construction?"

"Martin Darius, the defendant."

"Was the gate to the site locked?"

"Yes, sir."

"Was a gaping hole located in the fence near the area where the bodies were found?"

"Yes, sir."

"Were tire tracks located near that hole?"

"They were."

"On the evening Mr. Darius was arrested, did you execute a search warrant at his residence?"

"Yes, sir."

"Did you locate any vehicles during the search?"

"We located a station wagon, a BMW and a black Ferrari."

"Move to introduce exhibits ten to twenty-three, which are photographs of the construction site, the hole in the fence, the tire tracks, the burial site and the bodies being removed from it, and the vehicles."

"No objection," Betsy said.

"Received."

"Was a cast made of the tire tracks?"

"It was. The tracks at the site match the tread on the BMW we found at Darius's house."

"Was the trunk of the BMW examined for trace evidence, such as hairs and fibers, that might have belonged to any of the victims?"

"Yes, sir. None was found."

"Did the lab report explain why?"

"The trunk had been recently vacuumed and cleaned."

"How old was the BMW?"

"A year old."

"Not a brand-new car?"

"No, sir."

"Detective Barrow, are you aware of any connections between the defendant and the murdered women?"

"I am. Yes. Mr. Reiser works for the law firm that represents Darius Construction. He and his wife met the defendant at a party Mr. Darius threw this summer to celebrate the opening of a new mall."

"How soon before the disappearance of the first woman, Laura Farrar, was this party?"

"Approximately three weeks."

"Were Mr. and Mrs. Farrar at that party?"

"They were. Mr. Farrar works for the accounting firm that Mr. Darius uses."

"And Russell and Victoria Miller?"

"They were at the party too, but they have closer ties with the defendant. Mr. Miller was just put in charge of the Darius Construction account at Brand, Gates and Valcroft, the advertising agency. They also socialized with Mr. and Mrs. Darius."

Page checked his notes, conferred with Randy Highsmith, then said, "Your witness, Mrs. Tannenbaum."

Betsy looked at a legal pad on which she had listed several points she wanted to bring out through Barrow. She selected several police reports from the discovery she received from the district attorney.

"Good morning, Detective Barrow. Teams of criminalists from the Oregon State Crime Lab went through the houses of all three women, did they not?"

"That's true."

"Isn't it also true that none of these fine scientists found a single piece of physical evidence connecting Martin Darius to the homes of Laura Farrar, Victoria Miller or Wendy Reiser?"

"The person who murdered these women is very clever. He knows how to clean up a crime scene."

"Your Honor," Betsy said calmly, "will you please direct Detective Barrow to listen to the questions I ask him and respond to those questions? I'm sure Mr. Page will try to explain the problems with his case during argument."

Judge Norwood glared at Betsy. "I don't need an editorial from you, Mrs. Tannenbaum. Just make your objections." Then Norwood swiveled toward the witness. "And you've testified enough times to know you only answer what you're asked. Save the clever answers. They don't impress me."

"So, Detective Barrow, what's your answer? Was a single shred of physical evidence linking my client to any victim found at any of the homes of the missing women?"

"No."

"How about on the bodies?"

"We found the tire tracks."

"Your Honor?" Betsy asked.

"Detective Barrow, were there tire tracks on the body of any of those women?" the judge asked sarcastically.

Barrow looked embarrassed. "Sorry, Your Honor."

"Are you catching on, Detective?" Judge Norwood asked.

"There was no physical evidence at the burial site connecting the defendant with any of the women," Detective Barrow answered.

"A dead man was also found at the burial site?"

"Yes."

"Who is he?"

"We don't know."

"So there's nothing connecting this man to Martin Darius?"

"We don't know that. Until we find out who he is, we can't investigate his possible connection with your client."

Betsy was going to object but decided to let the remark pass. If Barrow kept fencing, he'd keep pissing off the judge.

"You told the judge about the tire tracks you found near the fence. Don't you think you should tell him about the interview you had with Rudy Doschman?"

"I interviewed him. What about it?"

"Do you have your report of that interview?" Betsy asked, as she walked toward the witness stand.

"Not with me."

"Why don't you take my copy and read this paragraph?" Betsy said, handing the detective a police report she had found in the discovery material. Barrow read the report and looked up.

"Mr. Doschman is a foreman with Darius Construction who was working on the site where the bodies were found?" Betsy asked.

"Yes."

"He told you Mr. Darius visited the site on many occasions, did he not?"

"Yes."

"In his BMW?"

"Yes."

"He also explained that the hole in the fence was there for some time?"

"Yes."

"In fact, it may have been the way the arsonists who burned down some of Mr. Darius's town houses entered the site several weeks ago?"

"It could be."

"There is no evidence connecting Mr. Darius to the roses or the notes?"

Barrow looked like he was going to say something, but he choked it back and shook his head.

"And you stand by that statement, even though of-

ficers of the Portland Police Bureau made a thorough
search, pursuant to a warrant, of Mr. Darius's home."

"We found nothing connecting him to the roses or
the notes," Barrow answered tersely.

"No murder weapons either?"

"No."

"Nothing in the trunk of the BMW connecting him
to the crimes?"

"No."

Betsy turned to Darius. "Anything else you want me
to ask?"

Darius smiled. "You're doing just fine, Tannenbaum."

"No further questions."

Barrow hoisted himself out of the witness box and
walked quickly to the back of the courtroom as Page
called his next witness.

"Dr. Susan Gregg," Page said. An attractive woman
in her early forties with salt-and-pepper hair, wearing a
conservative gray suit, took the witness stand.

"Will counsel stipulate to Dr. Gregg's qualifications
for purposes of this hearing?" Page asked Betsy.

"We assume Dr. Gregg is well known to the court,"
Betsy said, "so, for purposes of this hearing only, we stipulate that Dr. Gregg is the state medical examiner and
qualified to give opinions on cause of death."

"Thank you," Page said to Betsy. "Dr. Gregg, were
you called to a construction site owned by Darius Construction, earlier this week, to examine the remains of
four individuals who were found buried there?"

"I was."

"And you conducted the autopsies of all four victims?"

"Yes."

"What is an autopsy, Dr. Gregg?"

"It's an examination of a body after death to determine, among other things, cause of death."

"Will you explain what your autopsy involved?"

"Certainly. I examined the bodies carefully for serious injuries, natural diseases and other natural causes of death."

"Did any of the victims die a natural death?"

"No."

"What injuries did you observe?"

"All four individuals had numerous burns and cutting injuries on various parts of their bodies. Three of the male's fingers had been severed. There was evidence of sharp cuts on the women's breasts. The nipples on the women had been mutilated, as had the genitalia of the man and the women. Do you want me to go into detail?"

"That won't be necessary for this hearing. How did the three women die?"

"Their abdomens had been deeply cut, resulting in serious injuries to their bowel and abdominal viscera."

"When a person is disemboweled, do they die quickly?"

"No. A person can stay alive for some time in this condition."

"Can you give the court a rough estimate?"

Gregg shrugged. "It's hard to say. Two to four hours. Eventually they die from shock and loss of blood."

"And that was the cause of death of these women?"

"Yes."

"And the male?"

"He suffered a fatal gunshot wound to the back of his head."

"Did you order laboratory tests?"

"Yes. I had the blood tested for alcohol. The results were negative for all of the victims. I ordered a urine screen for drugs of abuse. This involves testing the urine for the presence of five drugs: cocaine, morphine, marijuana, amphetamine and PCP. Our results were all negative."

Page studied his notes and conferred with Highsmith before turning the witness over to Betsy. She reread a portion of the autopsy report and frowned.

"Dr. Gregg, I'm confused by some remarks you made on page four of your report. Were the women raped?"

"That's hard to say. I found bruises and tears around the genitalia and rectum. Tearing that would indicate invasion by a foreign object."

"Did you test for semen?"

"I did not find any traces of seminal fluid."

"So you can't say conclusively that the women were raped?"

"I can only say there was penetration and violent injury. There was no evidence of male ejaculation."

"Did you draw a conclusion concerning whether the women were murdered at the construction site?"

"I believe they were killed elsewhere."

"Why?"

"There would have been a large amount of blood at the murder scene because of their massive cutting injuries. There were also organs removed from two of the women."

"Would the rain obscure traces of their blood?"

"No. They were buried. The rain would have washed away the blood on the surface, but we should have found larger quantities under the bodies in the graves."

"So you believe the women were killed someplace else and transported to the site?"

"Yes."

"If they were transported in the trunk of a BMW, could you erase all traces of blood from the trunk?"

"Objection," Page said. "Dr. Gregg is not qualified to answer that question. She is a medical doctor, not a forensic chemist."

"I'll let her answer, if she can," the judge ruled.

"I'm afraid that's outside my area of expertise," the doctor answered.

"The male was not disemboweled?"

"No."

"Nothing further."

Alan Page stood. He looked a little unsure of himself.

"Your Honor, I'm going to call myself as a witness. Mr. Highsmith will examine."

"Objection, Your Honor. It's unethical for an attorney to testify as a witness in a case he's trying."

"That might be true in a trial before a jury, Your Honor," Page replied, "but the court is not going to have any trouble deciding my credibility as a witness, if that comes into question, simply because I'm also arguing the State's position."

Norwood looked troubled. "This is unusual. Why do you have to testify?"

"What's he up to?" Darius whispered in Betsy's ear.

Betsy shook her head. She was studying Page. He looked ill at ease and grim. Something was troubling the district attorney.

"Your Honor, I'm in possession of evidence you must hear if you are going to make a reasoned decision on the issue of bail. Unless I testify, you'll be without the most important evidence we have that Martin Darius is the man who killed Laura Farrar, Wendy Reiser and Victoria Miller."

"I'm confused, Mr. Page," Norwood said testily.

"How can you have this evidence? Were you an eyewitness?" Norwood shook his head. "I don't get it."

Page cleared his throat. "Your Honor, there is a witness. Her name is Nancy Gordon." Darius took a deep breath and leaned forward intently. "Ten years ago, an identical series of murders occurred in Hunter's Point, New York. The day before we found the bodies, Detective Gordon told me about those murders and why she believed Martin Darius committed them."

"Then call Detective Gordon," Norwood said.

"I can't. She's missing and she may be dead. She checked into a motel room after leaving me. I called her several times starting around eight, eight-thirty, the next morning. I think something happened to her shortly after she checked in. It looks like she was unpacking when something interrupted her. All of her possessions were in the room, but she hasn't come back for them. I have a team of detectives looking for her, but we've had no luck so far."

"Your Honor," Betsy said, "if Mr. Page is going to testify about this woman's statements to prove my client murdered some women ten years ago, it will be pure hearsay. I know the court is giving Mr. Page leeway, but Mr. Darius has state and federal constitutional rights to confront the witnesses against him."

Norwood nodded. "That's true, Mrs. Tannenbaum. I'll tell you, Mr. Page, this bothers me. Isn't there another witness from Hunter's Point you can call who can testify about these other crimes?"

"Not on such short notice. I know the names of the other detectives who worked on the case, but they don't work for the Hunter's Point police anymore and I haven't traced them."

Norwood leaned back and almost disappeared from view. Betsy was dying to know what the missing detective had told Page, but she had to keep the testimony out if it was the ammunition Page needed to keep Martin Darius in jail.

"It's eleven-fifteen, folks," Norwood said. "We'll adjourn until one-thirty. I'll hear legal argument then."

Norwood stood up and walked out of the courtroom. Harvey Cobb rapped the gavel and everyone stood.

"Now I know why Page thinks I killed those women," Darius whispered to Betsy. "When can we talk?"

"I'll come up to the jail right now."

Betsy turned to one of the guards. "Can you put Mr. Darius in the interview room? I want to talk to him."

"Sure, Mrs. Tannenbaum. We're gonna wait for the court to clear before taking him up. You can ride with us in the jail elevator if you want."

"Thanks, I will."

The guard handcuffed Darius. Betsy glanced toward the back of the courtroom. Lisa Darius was standing near the door, talking to Nora Sloane. Lisa glanced toward Betsy. Betsy smiled. Lisa did not smile back, but she did nod toward her. Betsy raised a hand to let Lisa know she would be right with her. Lisa said something to Sloane. Sloane smiled and patted Lisa's shoulder, then left the courtroom.

"I'm going to talk to Lisa for a moment," Betsy told Darius. Lisa was waiting just inside the door, looking nervously through the glass at the waiting reporters.

"That woman said she's working with you on an article for *Pacific West*," Lisa said.

"That's right. She's going to tag along while I try Martin's case to see how I work."

"She said she'd like to talk to me. What should I do?"

"Nora seems responsible, but you make up your own mind. How are you holding up?"

"This is terrible. The reporters won't leave me alone. When I moved to Daddy's house I had to sneak out of the estate through the woods so they wouldn't know where I was going."

"I'm sorry, Lisa. This isn't going to get any easier for you."

Lisa hesitated, then she asked, "Will the judge let Martin out on bail?"

"There's a good chance he'll have to. The State's evidence has been pretty weak, so far."

Lisa looked worried.

"Is something troubling you?"

"No," Lisa answered too quickly.

"If you know anything about this case, please tell me. I don't want any surprises."

"It's the reporters, they've really gotten to me," Lisa said, but Betsy knew she was lying.

"We're ready," the guard told Betsy.

"I've got to talk to Martin. He wants you to visit him."

Lisa nodded, but her thoughts seemed far away.

"Who is Nancy Gordon?" Betsy asked Darius. They were sitting next to each other in the narrow confines of the courthouse jail visiting room.

"One of the detectives on the task force. I met her the night Sandy and Melody died. She interviewed me at the house. Gordon was engaged to another cop, but he was killed a few weeks before the wedding. She was still grieving when I joined the task force and she tried to help me deal with my grief.

"Nancy and I were thrown together on several occasions. I didn't realize it, but she took my friendliness as something else and, well . . ." Darius looked into Betsy's eyes. Their knees were almost touching. His head bent toward her. "I was vulnerable. We both were. You can't understand what it feels like to lose someone you love like that, until it happens to you.

"I became convinced Waters was the rose killer and I did a stupid thing. Without telling anyone, I started following him. I even staked out his house, hoping I'd catch him in the act." Darius smiled sheepishly. "I made a mess of things and almost blew the investigation. I was so obvious, a neighbor called the police to complain about this strange man who was camped outside their house. The police came. I felt like an idiot. Nancy bailed me out. We met at a restaurant near the police station and she let me have it.

"By the time we'd finished eating, it was late. I offered to drive her home because her car was in for repairs. We'd both had a few beers. I don't even remember who started it. The bottom line is, we ended up in bed."

Darius looked down at his hands, as if he was ashamed. Then he shook his head.

"It was a stupid thing to do. I should have known she would take it too seriously. I mean, it was good for us to have someone to spend the night with. We were both so lonely. But she thought I loved her, and I didn't. It was too soon after Sandy. When I didn't want to continue the relationship, she grew bitter. Fortunately Waters was caught soon after that and my involvement with the task force ended, so there was no reason for us to see each other. Only, Nancy couldn't let go. She called me at home and at the office. She wanted to meet and talk about us. I told her there was no 'us,' but it was hard for her to accept."

"Did she accept it?"

Darius nodded. "She stopped calling, but I knew she was bitter. What I can't understand is how she could possibly think I killed Sandy and Melody."

"If the judge lets Page testify," Betsy said, "we'll soon find out."

Chapter Twelve

"Let me tell you how I see it, Mrs. Tannenbaum," Judge Norwood said. "I know what the Constitution says about confronting the witnesses and I'm not saying you don't have a point, but this is a bail hearing and the issues are different at trial. What Mr. Page is trying to do is convince me he's got so much evidence a guilty verdict at the trial is almost a sure thing. He thinks some of this trial evidence is going to come from this missing detective or from someone else in New York. I'm going to let him tell me what the evidence is, but I'm also going to take into account that he doesn't have his witness and may not be able to produce her, or these other detectives, at trial. So, I'll decide what weight to give to this testimony, but I'm going to let it in. If you don't like my ruling, I don't blame you. I might be wrong. That's why we have appeals courts. But, right now, Mr. Page can testify."

Betsy had already made her objections for the record, so she said nothing more when Alan Page was sworn in.

"Mr. Page," Randy Highsmith asked, "the evening before the bodies of Victoria Miller, Wendy Reiser, Laura Farrar and an unknown male were unearthed at a construction site owned by the defendant, did a woman visit you at your residence?"

"Yes."

"Who was this woman?"

"Nancy Gordon, a detective with the Hunter's Point Police Department in New York."

"At the time of Detective Gordon's visit were the details surrounding the disappearances of the three Portland women widely known?"

"To the contrary, Mr. Highsmith. The police and the district attorney's office weren't certain of the status of the missing women, so we were treating them as missing persons cases. No one in the press knew of the links between the cases and the husbands were cooperating with us by not divulging details of the disappearances."

"What were the links you spoke of?"

"The black roses and the notes that said 'Gone, But Not Forgotten.' "

"What did Detective Gordon say that led you to believe she had information that could be useful in solving the mystery surrounding these disappearances?"

"She knew about the notes and the roses."

"Where did she say she had acquired this knowledge?"

"Ten years ago in Hunter's Point, when an almost identical series of disappearances occurred."

"What was her connection with the Hunter's Point case?"

"She was a member of a task force assigned to that case."

"How did Detective Gordon learn about our disappearances and the similarities between the cases?"

"She told me she received an anonymous note that led her to believe that the person who was responsible for the Hunter's Point murders was living in Portland."

"Who was this person?"

"She knew him as Peter Lake."

"Did she give some background information on Peter Lake?"

"She did. He was a successful lawyer in Hunter's Point. He was married to Sandra Lake and they had a six-year-old daughter, Melody. The wife and child were murdered and a 'Gone, But Not Forgotten' note and black rose were found on the floor near the mother's body. Lake had a lot of political clout and the mayor of Hunter's Point ordered the police chief to put him on the task force. Lake soon became the primary suspect, though he was not aware of that fact."

"Have the prints of Peter Lake been compared to the fingerprints of Martin Darius?"

"Yes."

"With what results?"

"Martin Darius and Peter Lake are the same person."

Highsmith handed the clerk two fingerprint cards and a report from a fingerprint expert and introduced them into evidence.

"Mr. Page, did Detective Gordon tell you why she believed the defendant murdered the Hunter's Point women?"

"She did."

"Tell the court what she told you."

"Peter Lake had a connection to each of the women who disappeared in Hunter's Point. Gloria Escalante sat on one of Lake's juries. Samantha Reardon belonged to the same country club as the Lakes. Anne Hazelton's husband was an attorney and the Lakes and Hazeltons had been to some of the same Bar Association functions. Patricia Cross and Sandra Lake, Peter's wife, were both in the Junior League.

"Detective Gordon met Lake the evening Sandra and Melody Lake were murdered. This was the first time a body was discovered. In all the other cases, when the women disappeared, the note and rose were found on the woman's pillow in her bedroom. None of these notes had fingerprints on them. The note found at Lake's house had Sandra Lake's prints on it. The detectives believed that Sandra Lake discovered the note and was killed by her husband so she would not connect him to the disappearances when the notes were made public. They also believed Melody saw her mother killed and was murdered because she was a witness."

"Was there a problem with the time that Peter Lake reported the murders to the police?"

"Yes. Peter Lake told the police that he discovered the bodies right after he entered the house, that he sat down on the steps for a while, in shock, then called 911. The 911 call came in at eight-fifteen, but a neighbor, who lived near the Lakes, saw Peter Lake arrive home shortly after seven-twenty. The task force members believed it took Lake fifty-five minutes to report the murders because the victims were alive when Lake got home."

"Was there anything else that implicated Lake?"

"A man named Henry Waters worked for a florist. His truck was seen near the Escalante house on the day she disappeared. Waters had a sex offender record as a Peeping Tom. The body of Patricia Cross was found in the basement of Waters's house. She was disemboweled, just like the three Portland women.

"Waters was never really a suspect, but Lake didn't know that. Waters was borderline retarded and had no history of violence. There wasn't any connection between him and any other victim. Without telling anyone, Lake staked out Waters's house and followed him for days before the body of Patricia Cross was discovered."

"What led the police to Waters's house?"

"An anonymous male caller, who was never identified. The task force members believed Lake brought Cross to Waters's house, murdered her in the basement, then made the phone call to the police."

"Why wasn't Lake prosecuted in Hunter's Point?"

"Waters was killed during his arrest. The police chief and the mayor made a public statement labeling Waters as the rose killer. There were no more murders and the cases were closed."

"Why did Detective Gordon come to Portland?"

"When she learned about the Portland notes and roses, she knew the same person had to be responsible for the Hunter's Point and Portland crimes, because the color of the rose and the contents of the notes were never made public in Hunter's Point."

"Where did Detective Gordon go after she left your residence?"

"The Lakeview Motel. The manager said she checked in about twenty minutes after leaving my place."

"Have you seen or talked to Detective Gordon since she left your residence?"

"No. She's disappeared."

"Have you searched her room at the motel?"

Page nodded. "It looked like she was in the midst of unpacking when something happened. When she was at my place, she had an attaché case with a lot of material relating to the case. It was missing. We also found the address of the construction site where the bodies were found on a pad next to the phone."

"What conclusion do you draw from that?"

"Someone called her with the address."

"What do you believe happened then?"

"Well, she had no car. We've checked all of the taxi

companies. None of them picked her up from the Lakeview. I believe the person who called her picked her up."

"No further questions, Your Honor."

Betsy smiled at Page, but he did not smile back. He looked grim and sat stiffly, back straight, with his hands folded in his lap.

"Mr. Page, there was a lengthy investigation in Hunter's Point, wasn't there?"

"That's what Detective Gordon said."

"I assume you've read the police reports from that investigation."

"No, I haven't," Page answered, shifting uncomfortably on his seat.

"Why is that?"

"I don't have them."

"Have you ordered them from Hunter's Point?"

"No."

Betsy's brow furrowed. "If you're planning on having Detective Gordon testify, you'll have to produce her reports."

"I know that."

"Is there a reason you haven't ordered them?"

Page colored. "They've been misplaced."

"Excuse me?"

"The Hunter's Point police are looking for them. The reports were supposed to be in a storage area, but they aren't. We think Detective Gordon may know where they are, because she gave me some items—including Peter Lake's fingerprint card—we assume came from the file."

Betsy decided to switch to another topic.

"On direct examination, you repeatedly said, 'The task force members believed . . .' Have you talked to these task force members?"

"No, other than Detective Gordon."

"Do you even know where they are?"

"I just learned that Frank Grimsbo is the head of security at Marlin Steel."

"Where is his office located?"

"Albany, New York."

Betsy made a note.

"You haven't talked to Grimsbo?"

"No."

"What are the names of the other detectives?"

"Besides Gordon and Grimsbo, there was a criminalist named Glen Michaels and another detective named Wayne Turner."

Betsy wrote down the names. When she looked up Page was stone-faced.

"Mr. Page, isn't it true that you have no support for the story your mysterious visitor told you?"

"Other than what the detective said, no."

"What detective?"

"Nancy Gordon."

"This was the first time you saw this woman, correct?"

Page nodded.

"Have you ever seen a photograph of Nancy Gordon?"

"No."

"So you can't say that the person who introduced herself as Detective Nancy Gordon is really Nancy Gordon, can you?"

"A Nancy Gordon works for the Hunter's Point Police Department."

"I don't doubt that. But we don't know that she is the person who visited you, do we?"

"No."

"There's also no proof that this woman is dead or even a victim of foul play, is there?"

"She's missing."

"Was there blood found in her room?"

"No."

"Or signs of a struggle?"

"No," Page answered grudgingly.

"Were there any witnesses to the murders of Melody and Sandra Lake?"

"Your client may have witnessed the killings," Page answered defiantly.

"You have nothing but theories propounded by your mystery woman to support that position."

"That's true."

"Isn't it also true that the chief of police and the mayor of Hunter's Point officially declared Henry Waters to be the murderer of all the women?"

"Yes."

"That would include Sandra and Melody Lake?"

"Yes."

"Which would make Mr. Lake—Mr. Darius—a victim, wouldn't it?"

Page did not answer and Betsy did not force him to.

"Mr. Page, there were six victims in Hunter's Point, including a six-year-old girl. Can you think of any reason why a responsible public official would close a case like that and publicly declare an individual to be the killer, if there was any possibility that the murderer was still at large?"

"Maybe the officials wanted to allay the fears of the community."

"You mean the public announcement might be part of a ruse to make the killer lower his guard while the investigation continued?"

"Exactly."

"But the investigation didn't continue, did it?"

"Not according to Detective Gordon."

"And the murders stopped after Mr. Waters was killed, didn't they?"

"Yes."

Betsy paused and looked directly at Judge Norwood.

"No further questions, Your Honor."

"Mr. Highsmith?" Judge Norwood asked.

"I have nothing further of Mr. Page."

"You can step down, Mr. Page."

Page stood slowly. Betsy thought he looked tired and defeated. She took satisfaction in this. Betsy did not enjoy humiliating Page—he seemed a decent sort—but Page deserved any pain she inflicted. It was clear he had arrested Martin Darius on the flimsiest evidence, made him spend several days in jail and slandered him. A public defeat was a small price to pay for that kind of callous disregard of his public duty.

"Any other witnesses?" the judge asked.

"Yes, Your Honor. Two, both brief," Highsmith answered.

"Proceed."

"The State calls Ira White."

A chubby man in an ill-fitting brown suit hurried forward from the back of the courtroom. He smiled nervously as he was sworn. Betsy guessed he was in his early thirties.

"Mr. White, what do you do for a living?" Randy Highsmith asked.

"I'm a salesman for Finletter Tools."

"Where is your home office?"

"Phoenix, Arizona, but my territory is Oregon, Montana, Washington, Idaho and parts of Northern California, near the Oregon border."

"Where were you at two p.m. on October eleventh of this year?"

The date rang a bell. Betsy checked the police reports. Victoria Miller was reported missing that evening.

"In my room at the Hacienda Motel," White said.

"Where is that motel located?"

"It's in Vancouver, Washington."

"Why were you in your room?"

"I just checked in. I had a meeting scheduled for three and I wanted to unpack, take a shower and change out of my traveling clothes."

"Do you remember your room number?"

"Well, you showed me a copy of the ledger, if that's what you mean."

Highsmith nodded.

"It was 102."

"Where is that located in relation to the manager's office?"

"Right next to it on the ground floor."

"Mr. White, at approximately two p.m. did you hear anything in the room next to yours?"

"Yeah. There was a woman yelling and crying."

"Tell the judge about that."

"Okay," White said, shifting so he could look up at Judge Norwood. "I didn't hear anything until I got out of the shower. That's because the water was running. As soon as I turned it off, I heard a shriek, like someone was in pain. It startled me. The walls in that motel aren't thick. The woman was begging not to be hurt and she was crying, sobbing. It was hard to hear the words, but I'd catch a few. I could hear her crying, though."

"How long did this go on?"

"Not long."

"Did you ever see the man or the woman in the next room?"

"I saw the woman. I was thinking of calling the manager, but everything quieted down. Like I said, it didn't last long. Anyway, I dressed for my appointment and I left around two-thirty. She was coming out at the same time."

"The woman in the next room?"

White nodded.

"Do you remember what she looked like?"

"Oh, yeah. Very attractive. Blonde. Good figure."

Highsmith crossed over to the witness and showed him a photograph.

"Does this woman look familiar?"

White looked at the photograph. "That's her."

"How certain of that are you?"

"Absolutely positive."

"Your Honor," Highsmith said, "I offer State's exhibit thirty-five, a photograph of Victoria Miller."

"No objection," Betsy said.

"No further questions," Highsmith said.

"I don't have any questions for Mr. White," Betsy told the judge.

"You're excused, Mr. White," Judge Norwood told the witness.

"State calls Ramon Gutierrez."

A neatly-dressed, dark-skinned young man with a pencil-thin mustache took the stand.

"Where do you work, sir?" Randy Highsmith asked.

"The Hacienda Motel."

"That's in Vancouver?"

"Yes."

"What's your job there?"

"I'm the day clerk."

"What are you doing in the evenings?"

"I'm in college at Portland State."

"What's your field of study?"

"Premed."

"So you're working your way through?" Highsmith asked with a smile.

"Yes."

"That sounds tough."

"It isn't easy."

"Mr. Gutierrez, were you working at the Hacienda on October eleventh of this year?"

"Yes."

"Describe the layout of the motel."

"It's two stories. There's a landing that goes around the building on the second floor. The office is at the north end on the ground floor, then we have the rooms."

"How are the rooms numbered on the ground floor?"

"The room next to the office is 102. The one next to that is 103 and so on."

"Have you brought the check-in sheet for October eleventh?"

"Yes," Gutierrez said, handing the deputy district attorney a large, dull-yellow ledger page.

"Who was checked into Room 102 that afternoon?"

"Ira White from Phoenix, Arizona."

Highsmith turned his back to the witness and looked at Martin Darius.

"Who was checked into Room 103?"

"An Elizabeth McGovern from Seattle."

"Did you check in Ms. McGovern?"

"Yes."

"At what time?"

"A little after noon."

"I am handing the witness State's exhibit thirty-five. Do you recognize that woman?"

"That's Ms. McGovern."

"You're certain?"

"Yeah. She was a looker," Gutierrez said sadly.

"Then, I saw her picture in the *Oregonian*. I knew her right away."

"To what picture are you referring?"

"The picture of the murdered women. Only it said her name was Victoria Miller."

"Did you call the district attorney's office as soon as you read the paper?"

"Right away. I talked with Mr. Page."

"Why did you call?"

"It said she disappeared that night, the eleventh, so I thought the police might want to know about the guy I saw."

"What guy?"

"The one who was in the room with her."

"You saw a man in the room with Mrs. Miller?"

"Well, not in the room. But, I saw him go in and come out. He'd been there before."

"With Mrs. Miller?"

"Yes. Like once or twice a week. She would register and he would come later." Gutierrez shook his head. "What I couldn't figure out is, if he wanted to sneak around, why did he drive that car?"

"What car?"

"This fantastic black Ferrari."

Highsmith searched for a photograph among the exhibits on the clerk's desk, then handed it to the witness.

"I'm handing you State's exhibit nineteen, which is a photograph of Martin Darius's black Ferrari and I ask you if it looks like the car driven by the man who went into the room with Mrs. Miller?"

"I know it's the car."

"How do you know?"

Gutierrez pointed at the defense table. "That's Martin Darius, right?"

"Yes, Mr. Gutierrez."

"He's the guy."

"Why didn't you tell me about Victoria Miller?" Betsy asked Martin Darius as soon as they were alone in the visiting room.

"Calm down," Darius said patiently.

"Don't you tell me to calm down," Betsy responded, infuriated by her client's icy composure. "Damn it, Martin, I'm your lawyer. Don't you think I would find it interesting that you were screwing one of the victims, and beat her up, the day she disappeared?"

"I didn't beat up Vicky. I told her I didn't want to see her anymore and she became hysterical. She attacked me and I had to control her. Besides, what does my fucking Vicky have to do with getting bail?"

Betsy shook her head. "This could sink you, Martin. I know Norwood. He's straight-laced. Real old-fashioned. The guy's been married to the same woman for forty years and goes to church on Sunday. If you'd told me, I could have softened the impact."

Darius shrugged. "I'm sorry," he said, without meaning it.

"Were you having sex with Laura Farrar or Wendy Reiser?"

"I hardly knew them."

"What about this party for the mall?"

"There were hundreds of people there. I don't even remember talking to Farrar or Reiser."

Betsy leaned back in her seat. She felt very uncomfortable alone with Darius in the narrow confines of the visiting room.

"Where did you go after you left the Hacienda Motel?"

Darius smiled sheepishly. "To a meeting at Brand, Gates and Valcroft with Russ Miller and the other people working on the advertising for Darius Construction. I'd just seen to it that Russ was put in charge of the account. I guess that won't work anymore."

"You are one cold son-of-a-bitch, Martin. You screw Miller's wife, then throw him a bone. Now you're joking about her when she's been murdered. Dr. Gregg said she could have been alive for hours, sliced open, in the most godawful pain. Do you know how much she must have suffered before she died?"

"No, Tannenbaum, I don't know how much she suffered," Darius said, the smile leaving his face, "because I didn't kill her. So how about spreading a little of your sympathy in my direction? I'm the one who's being framed. I'm the one who wakes up every morning to this jail stench and has to eat the slop that passes for food."

Betsy glared at Darius and stood up. "Guard!" she shouted, pounding on the door. "I've had enough of you for today, Martin."

"Suit yourself."

The guard bent down to put the key in the lock.

"The next time we talk, I want the truth about everything. And that includes Hunter's Point."

The door opened. As Darius watched her walk away, the thinnest smile creased his lips.

Chapter Thirteen

―

I

International Exports was on the twenty-second floor of the First Interstate Bank Tower in a small suite of offices tucked away in a corner next to an insurance company. A middle-aged Hispanic woman looked up from her word processor when Reggie Stewart opened the door. She looked surprised, as if visitors were an uncommon sight.

Moments later, Stewart was seated across the desk from Manuel Ochoa, a well-dressed, heavy-set Mexican with a swarthy complexion and a bushy, salt-and-pepper mustache.

"This business with Martin is so terrible. Your district attorney must be insane to arrest someone so prominent. Certainly there is no evidence against him?" Ochoa said as he offered Stewart a slender cigarillo.

Stewart raised his hand, declining the smoke.

"Frankly, we don't know what Alan Page has. He's playing his cards close to the vest. That's why I'm talking to people who know Mr. Darius. We're trying to figure out what in the world Page is thinking."

Ochoa shook his head sympathetically. "I'll do anything I can to help, Mr. Stewart."

"Why don't you explain your relationship to Darius."

"We are business partners. He wanted to build a shopping mall near Medford and the banks would not finance it, so he came to me."

"How's the venture going?"

"Not well, I'm afraid. Martin has been having trouble lately. There is the unfortunate business with the site where the bodies were discovered. He has a lot of money tied up in the town house project. His debts are mounting. Our venture has also been stalled."

"How serious is Darius's financial situation?"

Ochoa blew a stream of smoke at the ceiling. "Serious. I am concerned for my investment, but, of course, I am protected."

"If Mr. Darius stays in jail or is convicted, what will happen to his business?"

"I can't say. Martin is the genius behind his firm, but he does have competent men working for him."

"How friendly are you with Mr. Darius?"

Ochoa took a long drag on his cigarillo.

"Until recently, you could say we were friends, but not close friends. Business acquaintances would be more accurate. I have had Martin to my home, we socialized occasionally. However, business pressures have strained our relationship."

Stewart laid photographs of the three women and a sheet of paper with the dates of their disappearances on the blotter.

"Were you with Mr. Darius on any of these dates?"

"I don't believe so."

"What about the photographs? Have you ever seen Mr. Darius with any of these women?"

Ochoa studied the photos, then shook his head. "No,

but I have seen Martin with other women." Stewart took out a pad. "I have a large house and I live alone. I enjoy getting together with friends. Some of these friends are attractive, single women."

"Do you want to spell this out for me, Mr. Ochoa?"

Ochoa laughed. "Martin likes young women, but he is always discreet. I have guest bedrooms for my friends."

"Did Mr. Darius use drugs?"

Ochoa eyed Stewart curiously. "What does that have to do with your case, Mr. Stewart?"

"I need to know everything I can about my client. You never know what's important."

"I have no knowledge of drugs and," Ochoa said, looking at his Rolex, "I'm afraid I have another appointment."

"Thanks for taking the time to see me."

"It was my pleasure. If I can be of further help to Martin, let me know. And wish him the best for me."

2

Nora Sloane was waiting for Betsy on a bench outside the courthouse elevator.

"Did you talk to Mr. Darius?"

"Martin says you can tag along."

"Great!"

"Let's meet after court and I'll set up some ground rules."

"Okay. Do you know how Judge Norwood is going to rule?"

"No. His secretary just said to be here at two."

Betsy turned the corner. Judge Norwood's court was

at the far end of the hall. Most of the people in the corridor were congregating outside the courtroom door. Television crews were grouped around the entrance and a guard was checking people through the metal detector. Betsy flashed her Bar card at the guard. He stood aside. Betsy and Sloane cut behind him and went into the courtroom without having to go through the metal detector.

Martin Darius and Alan Page were in court. Betsy slid into the chair next to Darius and took her files and a pad out of her attaché case.

"Have you seen Lisa?" he asked.

Betsy scanned the packed courtroom. "I told my secretary to call her, but she's not here yet."

"What's he going to do, Tannenbaum?"

Darius was trying to sound casual, but there was an edge to his voice.

"We'll soon find out," Betsy said as Harvey Cobb rapped the gavel.

Judge Norwood strode out of his chambers. He was clutching several sheets of yellow, lined paper. Norwood was a shoot-from-the-hip guy. If he'd taken the time to write out the reasons for his decision, he was expecting it to be appealed.

"This is a very troubling case," the judge said without preliminaries. "Someone brutally tortured and murdered four innocent people. That person should not be roaming our streets. On the other hand, we have a presumption in this country that a person is innocent until proven guilty. We also have a guarantee of bail in our Constitution, which can be denied a defendant in a murder case only on a showing by the State that there is clear and convincing evidence of guilt.

"Mr. Page, you proved these people were murdered.

You proved they were buried at a site owned and visited by Mr. Darius. You proved Mr. Darius knew the three women victims. You also proved he was having an affair with one of them and may have beaten her the day she disappeared. What you have not shown, by clear and convincing evidence, is a connection between the defendant and the murders.

"No one saw Mr. Darius kill these people. There is no scientific evidence connecting him to any of the bodies or the homes from which they disappeared. You have matched the tires on the BMW to the tracks left at the murder site, but Mr. Darius visited that site frequently. Granted, it is suspicious that the tracks led up to the hole in the fence, but that's not enough, especially when there is no evidence connecting the BMW with any victim.

"Now I know you'll tell me that Mr. Darius destroyed the evidence by cleaning the trunk of his car, and that looks suspicious. But the standard I must use to deny bail is clear and convincing evidence, and the absence of evidence, no matter how suspicious the circumstances, is not a substitute for evidence.

"Really, Mr. Page, the crux of your case is the information given to you by this Gordon woman. But she wasn't here to be cross-examined by Mrs. Tannenbaum. Why isn't she here? We don't know. Is it because of foul play or because she made up the story she told you and is smart enough to avoid committing perjury?

"Even if I accept what you say, Mr. Darius is guilty of the Hunter's Point murders only if we accept Detective Gordon's theory. This Henry Waters fellow was named by the Hunter's Point police as the killer. If Waters is the killer, then Mr. Darius was a victim of the man."

Judge Norwood paused to take a sip of water. Betsy

choked back a victory grin. She glanced to her left. Alan Page was sitting stiffly, eyes straight ahead.

"Bail will be set in the sum of one million dollars. Mr. Darius may be released if he posts ten percent."

"Your Honor," Page exclaimed, leaping to his feet.

"This won't help you, Mr. Page. I've made up my mind. Personally, I'm surprised to see you force this hearing with such a skimpy case."

Judge Norwood turned his back on the prosecutor and walked off the bench.

"I knew I did the right thing hiring you, Tannenbaum," Darius exclaimed. "How long will it take to get me out of here?"

"As long as it takes you to post the bail and the jail to process you."

"Then call Terry Stark, my accountant at Darius Construction. He's waiting to hear from you. Tell him the amount he has to post and tell him to get it down here immediately."

Nora Sloane watched Betsy field questions from the press, then walked with her toward the elevators.

"You must feel great," Sloane said.

Betsy was tempted to feed Sloane the same upbeat line she had given to the reporters, but she liked Nora and felt she could confide in her.

"Not really."

"Why is that?"

"I admit, winning gives me a rush, but Norwood is right. Page's case was very skimpy. Anyone would have won this hearing. If this is the best Page can do, he won't get his case to a jury.

"Also, I don't know who Martin Darius is. If he's a husband and father who found his wife and child brutally murdered, then I did something good today. But what if he really murdered the women in the pit?"

"You think he's guilty?"

"I didn't say that. Martin insists he's innocent and I haven't seen anything to convince me otherwise. What I mean is, I still don't know for certain what happened here or in Hunter's Point."

"If you knew for certain that Darius was the rose killer, would you still represent him?"

"We have a system in America. It's not perfect, but it's worked for two hundred years and it depends on giving a fair trial to every person who goes through the courts, no matter what they've done. Once you start discriminating, for any reason, the system breaks down. The real test of the system is when it deals with a Bundy or a Manson, someone everyone fears and despises. If you can try that person fairly, then you send a message that we are a nation of law."

"Can you imagine a case you wouldn't take?" Sloane asked. "A client you might find so repulsive that your conscience would not let you represent him?"

"That's the question you confront when you choose to practice criminal law. If you can't represent that client, you don't belong in the business."

Betsy checked her watch. "Look, Nora, that's going to have to be it for today. I've got to make certain Martin's bail is posted, and my mother's watching Kathy, so I've got to leave the office a little early."

"Kathy is your daughter?"

Betsy smiled.

"I'd like to meet her."

"I'll introduce you to Kathy soon. My mom, too. You'll like them. Maybe I'll have you over for dinner."

"Great," Sloane said.

3

"Lisa Darius is waiting for you in your office," Ann said as soon as Betsy walked in. "I hope you don't mind. She's very upset about something and she was afraid to sit in the waiting room."

"That's okay. Does she know Martin's going to be released on bail?"

"Yes. I asked her how the judge ruled when she came in and she said you won."

"I didn't see her in court."

"I called her about the court appearance as soon as you told me to."

"I'm sure you did. Look, call Terry Stark at Darius Construction," Betsy said, writing down the name and phone number. "I told him how to post the bail a few days ago. He'll need a cashier's check for one hundred thousand. If there are any problems, buzz me."

Betsy did not recognize Lisa at first. She wore tight jeans, a blue turtleneck and a multicolored ski sweater. Her long hair was pulled back in a French braid, her emerald eyes were red from crying.

"Lisa, are you all right?"

"I never thought they'd let him out. I'm so scared."

"Of Martin? Why?"

Lisa put her hands to her face. "He's so cruel. No one knows how cruel. In public, he's charming. And sometimes he's just as charming with me when we're alone. He surprises me with flowers, jewelry. When he wants to, he treats me like a queen and I forget what he's really like inside. Oh God, Betsy, I think he killed those women."

Betsy was stunned. Lisa started to cry.

"Do you want some water?" Betsy asked.

Lisa shook her head. "Just give me a moment."

They sat quietly while Lisa caught her breath. Outside, a winter sun was shining and the air was so crisp and brittle, it seemed you could crack it into a million pieces. When Lisa spoke, her words came in a rush.

"I understand what Andrea Hammermill went through. Taking it, because you don't want anyone to know how bad it is and because there are good times and . . . and you love him."

Lisa sobbed. Her shoulders shook. Betsy wanted to comfort Lisa, but not as much as she wanted to learn what Darius had done to her to put her in this state, so she sat stiffly, waiting for Lisa to regain her composure.

"I do love him and I hate him and I'm scared of him," Lisa said hopelessly. "But this . . . If he . . ."

"Wife-beating is very common, Lisa. Serial murder isn't. Why do you think Martin may have killed these women?"

"It's more than beatings. There's a perverted side to . . . to what he does. His sexual needs . . . One time . . . This is very hard for me."

"Take your time."

"He wanted sex. We'd been to a party. I was tired. I told him. He insisted. We had an argument. No. That's not true. He never argues. He . . . he . . ."

Lisa closed her eyes. Her hands were clenched in her lap. Her body was rigid. When she spoke, she kept her eyes shut.

"He told me very calmly that I would have sex with him. I was getting angrier and angrier. The way he was speaking, it's the way you talk to a very small child or someone who's retarded. It enraged me. And the more I screamed, the calmer he became.

"Finally he said, 'Take off your clothes,' the way you'd command a dog to roll over. I told him to go to hell. The next thing I knew, I was on the floor. He hit me in the stomach. I lost my air. I was helpless.

"When I started to breathe, I looked up. Martin was smiling. He ordered me to take my clothes off again in that same voice. I shook my head. I couldn't talk yet, but I was damned if I was going to give in. He knelt down, grabbed my nipple through my blouse and squeezed. I almost blacked out from the pain. I was crying now and thrashing around on the floor. He did it to my other nipple, and I couldn't stand it. The horrible thing was how methodical he was. There was no passion in it. And he had the tiniest smile on his face, as if he was enjoying himself immensely but didn't want anyone to know.

"I was on the verge of passing out when he stopped. I sprawled on the floor, exhausted. I knew I couldn't fight him anymore. The next time he ordered me to, I took off my clothes."

"Did he rape you?" Betsy asked. She felt queasy.

Lisa shook her head. "That was the worst thing. He looked at me for a moment. There was a smile of satisfaction on his face I will never forget. Then he told me that I must always submit to him when he wanted sex and that I would be punished anytime I disobeyed him. He told me to get on all fours. I thought he was going to take me from behind. Instead, he made me crawl across the floor like a dog.

"We have a clothes closet in our bedroom. He opened the door and made me go in, naked. He said I would have to stay there without making a sound until he let me out. He told me I would be severely punished if I made any sound."

Lisa started sobbing again.

"He kept me in the closet all weekend without food. He put in some toilet paper and a bucket to . . . to use if I . . . I was so hungry and so scared.

"He told me that he would open the door when he was ready and I would immediately have sex with him or I would go back. When he opened the door I just crawled out and . . . and did anything he wanted. When he was through with me, he led me into the bathroom and bathed me, as if I was a baby. There were clothes laid out on the bed. Evening clothes. And a bracelet. It must have cost a fortune. Diamonds, rubies, gold. It was my reward for obedience. When I was dressed, he took me to a restaurant for a lavish dinner. All evening, he treated me like a queen.

"I was certain he would want me again when we got home. It's all I thought about at dinner. I had to force myself to eat, because I was nauseous thinking of what was coming but I was afraid he would do something to me if I didn't eat. Then when we got home he just went to sleep and he didn't touch me for a week."

"Did he ever do anything like that to you again?"

"No," Lisa said, hanging her head. "He didn't have to. I learned my lesson. If he said he wanted sex, I did what he wanted. And I received my rewards. And no one knew, until now, what I've been going through."

"Did you ever think of leaving him?" Betsy asked.

"He . . . he told me if I told anyone the things he did, or tried to run away, he would kill me. If you heard the way he said it, so calm, so detached . . . I knew he'd do it. I knew."

Lisa took deep breaths until she was back in control.

"There's something else," Lisa said. Betsy noticed a shopping bag lying next to Lisa's chair. Lisa leaned over and took a scrapbook out of it and placed it in her lap.

"I was certain Martin was having an affair. He never said anything and I never saw him with anyone, but I knew. One day I decided to search his things while he was at work to see if I could find proof. Instead, I found this."

Lisa tapped the cover of the scrapbook, then handed it across to Betsy. Betsy placed the book in the center of her blotter. The cover was a faded brown with a gold trim. Betsy opened the scrapbook. On the first page, under a plastic sheet, were clippings about the Hunter's Point case from the Hunter's Point paper, the New York *Times, Newsday* and other papers. Betsy flipped through some of the other pages without reading the articles. They were all about the Hunter's Point case.

"Did you ever ask Martin about this?" Betsy asked.

"No. I was too scared. I put it back. But I did do something. I hired a private detective to follow Martin and to find out about Hunter's Point."

"What's the detective's name?"

"Sam Oberhurst."

"Do you have an address and phone number where I can reach him?"

"I've got a phone number."

"No address?"

"I got his name from a friend who used him in her divorce. She gave me the number. It's an answering machine. We met at a restaurant."

"Where did you send your checks?"

"I always paid him in cash."

"Give me your friend's name and I'll have my investigator contact her if it's necessary."

"Her name is Peggy Fulton. Her divorce attorney was Gary Telford. He's the one who gave her the name. I'd rather you didn't go to her, unless you have to."

"The lawyer's better," Betsy said as she pulled a sheet of paper out of her drawer and filled in several blanks. "This is a release of information form giving me or my investigator the right to see Oberhurst's files."

While Lisa read the form, Betsy told Ann to have Reggie Stewart come to her office immediately. Lisa signed the release and handed it back to Betsy.

"What did Oberhurst tell you?"

"He was certain Martin was cheating, but he didn't have a name yet."

"And Hunter's Point?"

"He told me he hadn't started working on that aspect of the investigation."

Lisa's story had affected Betsy deeply. The thought of Darius treating his wife like an animal disgusted her and Lisa's description made Betsy physically ill. But it did not mean Darius was a murderer, and she was still his attorney.

"Why did you come to me, Lisa?"

"I don't know. I'm so confused by everything. You seemed so understanding at the house and I knew how hard you fought for Andrea Hammermill and the Peterson woman. I hoped you could tell me what to do."

"Do you plan to tell the district attorney what you've told me or to give him this book?"

Lisa looked startled. "No. Why would I do that?"

"To hurt Martin."

"No. I don't want to . . . I still love him. Or, I . . . Mrs. Tannenbaum, if Martin did those things . . . If he tortured and killed those women, I have to know."

Betsy leaned forward and looked directly into Lisa's moist green eyes.

"I'm Martin's lawyer, Lisa. My professional loyalty lies with him, even if he is guilty."

Lisa looked shocked. "You'd continue to defend him, even if he did that?"

Betsy nodded. "But he may not have, Lisa, and what you've told me could be very important. If Oberhurst was following Martin on a date when one of those women disappeared, he could provide Martin with an alibi. Page is going to argue that the same man killed all three women, and he probably did. All I have to do is show Martin didn't kill one of the victims and the d.a.'s case disappears."

"I hadn't thought of that."

"When is the last time you talked to Oberhurst?"

"A few weeks ago. I left a few messages on his machine, but he didn't return my calls."

"I'll have my investigator contact Oberhurst. Can I hold on to the scrapbook?"

Lisa nodded. Betsy walked around the desk and laid a hand on Lisa's shoulder.

"Thank you for confiding in me. I know how hard it must have been."

"I had to tell someone," Lisa whispered. "I've kept it in so long."

"I have a friend who might help you. Alice Knowland. She's very nice and very compassionate. I've sent other women with similar problems to her and she's helped some of them."

"What is she, a doctor?"

"A psychiatrist. But don't let that scare you off. Psychiatrist is just a fancy title for a good listener with experience in helping troubled people. She might be good for you. You could go to her a few times, then stop if she isn't helping. Think it over and give me a call."

"I will," Lisa said, standing. "And thank you for listening."

"You're not alone, Lisa. Remember that."

Betsy put her arms around Lisa and hugged her.

"Martin will be home late tonight. Will you stay with him?" Betsy asked.

"I can't. I'm living with my father until I decide what to do."

"Okay."

"Don't tell Martin I came, please."

"I won't if I can help it. He is my client, but I don't want to hurt you."

Lisa wiped her eyes and left. Betsy was drained. She pictured Lisa, hungry and terrified, cowering in the closet in the dark with the smell of her own urine and feces. Betsy's stomach rolled. She walked out of the office and down the hall to the rest room and ran some cold water in the sink. She splashed her face with the running water, then cupped her hands and drank.

She remembered the questions Nora and the reporters had asked. How could she sleep if she saved Martin Darius, knowing what she knew about him? What would a man who treated his wife like a dog do to a woman he did not know, if she fell under his power? Would he do what the rose killer had done to his victims? Was Martin the killer?

Betsy remembered the scrapbook and dried her face, then returned to her office. She was halfway through the scrapbook when Reggie Stewart walked in.

"Congratulations on the bail hearing."

"Pull a chair next to me. I've got something that might break Martin's case."

"Excellent."

"Lisa Darius was just here. She suspected Martin might be cheating on her, so she hired an investigator to tail him. Have you heard of a p.i. named Sam Oberhurst?"

Stewart thought for a moment, then shook his head.

"The name sounds vaguely familiar, but I'm sure we've never met."

"Here's his phone number and a release from Lisa. Oberhurst has an answering machine. If you can't get through to him, try a divorce attorney named Gary Telford. Lisa got the name from one of his clients. Tell Gary you're working for me. We know each other. Find out if Oberhurst was tailing Darius on a date when any of the women disappeared. He could be Martin's alibi."

"I'll get right on it."

Betsy pointed to the scrapbook. "Lisa found this in Martin's things when she was looking for evidence of the affair. It's filled with clippings from the Hunter's Point case."

Stewart looked over Betsy's shoulder as Betsy turned the pages. Most of the stories concerned the disappearances. There were several stories about the murders of Sandra and Melody Lake. A section was devoted to the discovery of the disemboweled body of Patricia Cross in Henry Waters's basement and Waters's death. Betsy turned to the final section of the scrapbook and stopped cold.

"My God, there were survivors."

"What? I thought all the women were murdered."

"No. Look here. It says Gloria Escalante, Samantha Reardon and Anne Hazelton were found alive in an old farmhouse."

"Where?"

"It doesn't give any other information. Wait a minute. No, there's nothing else. According to the article, the women declined to be interviewed."

"I don't get it. Didn't Darius tell you about this?"

"Not a word."

"Page?"

"He always referred to them as if they were dead."

"Maybe Page doesn't know," Stewart said.

"How is that possible?"

"What if Gordon didn't tell him?"

"Why wouldn't she? And why wouldn't Martin tell me? Something's not right, Reg. None of this makes sense. Gordon and Martin don't mention the survivors. The Hunter's Point files have disappeared. I don't like it."

"I know you love a mystery, Betsy, but I see this as our big break. The survivors will know who kidnapped and tortured them. If it wasn't Darius, we're home free."

"Maybe Martin didn't mention the survivors because he knew they'd identify him."

"There's only one way to find out," Stewart said. "Have Ann book me on an early flight to Hunter's Point."

"I want you to go to Albany, New York, first. Frank Grimsbo, one of the other detectives on the task force, is head of security at Marlin Steel. His office is in Albany."

"You got it."

Betsy buzzed Ann and told her what to do. When she got off the intercom, Stewart asked:

"What about the p.i.?"

"I'll run down Oberhurst. I want you on that flight, first thing. There's something weird about this case, Reg, and I'm betting that the answers we need are in Hunter's Point."

4

Alan Page left the courtroom in a daze. He barely heard the reporters' questions and answered them mechanically. Randy Highsmith told him not to take the loss personally, and assured him that it wasn't his fault that they couldn't find Nancy Gordon, but Highsmith and Barrow had warned him that he was making a mistake by rushing to arrest Darius. Even after they learned about the incident at the Hacienda Motel, the detective and the deputy district attorney wanted to move slowly. Page had overruled them. Now he was paying the price.

Page left work as soon as he could. There was an elevator in the rear of the district attorney's office that went to the basement. He took it and dodged across the street to the parking garage, hoping no one would see him and ask him about his public humiliation.

Page poured his first scotch as soon as he took off his raincoat. He drank it quickly, refilled his glass and carried it into the bedroom. Why was he screwing up like this? He hadn't been thinking straight since Tina left him. This was the first time his ragged thought processes had gotten him in trouble, but it had been only a matter of time. He wasn't sleeping, he wasn't eating right, he couldn't concentrate. Now, he was haunted by the ghost of a woman he had known for all of two hours.

Page settled down in front of his television in an alcoholic haze. The old movie he was watching was one he had seen many times before. He let the black and white images float across the screen without seeing them. Did he order the arrest of Martin Darius to protect Nancy Gordon? Did he think he could keep them apart and rescue her? What sense did that make? What sense did anything in his life make?

5

Martin Darius parked his Ferrari in front of his house. It was cold. The mist pressed against him when he stepped out of the car. After a week in jail, the chill, damp air felt good. Darius crossed over the bridge. The lights were out. He could barely see the placid pool water through the glass roof. The rest of the house was also dark. He opened the front door and punched in the code that turned off the alarm.

Lisa was probably hiding from him at her father's house. He didn't care. After a week crowded in with unwashed, frightened men in the stale air of the county correctional facility, a night alone would be a pleasure. He would relish the quiet and bask in the luxury of soaping off the sour jail smell that had seeped into his pores.

There was a bar in the living room, and Darius fixed himself a drink. He flipped on the outside lights and watched the rain fall on the lawn through the picture window. He hated jail. He hated taking orders from fools and living with idiots. When he was practicing criminal law in Hunter's Point, he'd had only contempt for his clients. They were losers who were not equipped to succeed in the world, so they dealt with their problems through stealing or violence. A superior man controlled his environment and bent the will of others to him.

To Darius's way of thinking, there was only one reason to tolerate inferior minds. Someone had to do menial labor. Martin wondered what the world would be like if it was ruled by the strong, with the menial work done by a slave class selected from docile, mentally inferior men and women. The men could do the heavy work. The inferior women could be bred for beauty.

It was cold in the house. Darius shivered. He thought about the women. Docile women, bred for beauty and subservience. They would make excellent pets. He imagined his female slaves instantly submitting to his commands. Of course, there would be disobedient slaves who would not do as they were told. Such women would have to be chastised.

Darius grew hard thinking about the women. It would have been easy to give in to the fantasy, to open his fly and relieve the delicious feeling of tension. But giving in would be a sign of weakness, so he opened his eyes and breathed deeply. The inferior man lived only in his fantasies, because he lacked willpower and imagination. The superior man made his fantasies a reality.

Darius took another sip, then placed the cool glass to his forehead. He had given his dilemma a lot of thought while he was locked up in jail. He was certain he knew what was coming next. He was free. The newspapers had printed Judge Norwood's opinion that the evidence was not strong enough to convict him. That meant someone else would have to die.

Darius looked at his watch. It was almost ten. Lisa would be up. Getting through to her was the problem. At the jail only collect calls were permitted. Justice Ryder had refused every one he made. Darius dialed the judge's number.

"Ryder residence," a deep voice answered after three rings.

"Please put my wife on the phone, Judge."

"She doesn't want to talk to you, Martin."

"I want to hear that from her lips."

"I'm afraid that's not possible."

"I'm out now and I don't have to put up with your interference. Lisa is my wife. If she says she doesn't want to talk to me, I'll accept that, but I want to hear it from her."

"Let me talk to him, Dad," Lisa said in the background. The judge must have covered the receiver, because Darius could hear only a muffled argument. Then Lisa was on the phone.

"I don't want you to call me, Martin."

She sounded shaky. Darius imagined her trembling.

"Judge Norwood let me out because he didn't believe I was guilty, Lisa."

"He . . . he doesn't know everything I know."

"Lisa . . ."

"I don't want to see you."

"Are you afraid?"

"Yes."

"Good. Stay afraid. There's something going on here you know nothing about." Darius heard an intake of breath and the judge asked Lisa if he was threatening her. "I don't want you to come home. It's too dangerous for you. But I don't want you staying at your father's house, either. There isn't anywhere in Portland you'll be safe."

"What are you talking about?"

"I want you to go away somewhere until I tell you to come back. If you're afraid of me, don't tell me where you go. I'll get in touch with you through your father."

"I don't understand. Why should I be afraid?"

Darius closed his eyes. "I can't tell you and you don't want to know. Believe me when I say you are in great danger."

"What kind of danger?"

Lisa sounded panicky. Justice Ryder snatched the phone from her hand. "That's it, Darius. Get off this phone or I'll call Judge Norwood personally and have you thrown back in jail."

"I'm trying to save Lisa's life and you're endangering it. It's imperative that . . ."

Ryder slammed the phone down. Darius listened to the dial tone. Ryder had always been a pompous ass. Now his bullheadedness could cost Lisa her life. If Darius explained why, the judge would never believe him. Hell, he'd use what Darius said to put him on Death Row. Darius wished he could talk over his problem with Betsy Tannenbaum. She was very bright and she might come up with a solution, but he couldn't go to her either. She'd honor the attorney-client privilege, but she would drop him as a client and he needed her.

Darius had not seen the moon all the time he was in

jail. He looked for it now, but it was obscured by clouds.
He wondered what phase the moon was in. He hoped it
was not full. That brought out the crazies. He should
know. Martin shivered, but not from the cold. Right now,
he was the only one who was not in danger, but that
could change at any moment. Darius did not want to admit it, but he was afraid.

Part Four

THE DEVIL'S
BARGAIN

Chapter Fourteen

I

Gary Telford had the smile and bright eyes of a young man, but his flabby body and receding hairline made him look middle-aged. He shared a suite of offices with six other lawyers in one of the thirty-story glass boxes that had sprung up in downtown Portland during the past twenty years. Telford's office had a view of the Willamette River. On clear days he could see several mountains in the Cascade range, including majestic Mount Hood and Mount St. Helens, an active volcano that had erupted in the early eighties. Today, low-lying clouds owned the sky and it was hard to see the east side of the river in the fog.

"Thanks for seeing me," Betsy said as they shook hands.

"It's been too long," Gary said warmly. "Besides, I'm dying to know how I'm connected with this Darius business."

"When you represented Peggy Fulton in her divorce, did you use a p.i. named Sam Oberhurst?"

Telford stopped smiling. "Why do you want to know?"

"Lisa Darius suspected her husband was having an affair. She asked your client for advice and Peggy gave her Oberhurst's name. He was tailing Darius. I was hoping Oberhurst was conducting surveillance when one of the women disappeared and can give Darius an alibi."

"If Lisa Darius employed Oberhurst, why do you need to talk to me?"

"She doesn't have his address. Just a phone number. I've called it several times, but all I get is an answering machine. He hasn't returned my calls. I was hoping you'd have his office address."

Telford considered this information for a moment. He looked uncomfortable. "I don't think Oberhurst has an office."

"What's he do, work out of his home?"

"I guess. We always met here."

"What about bills? Where did you send his checks?"

"Cash. He wanted cash. Up front."

"Sounds a little unusual."

"Yeah. Well, he's a little unusual." Telford paused. "Look, I'll try to help you find Oberhurst, but there's something you need to know. Some of the stuff he does isn't on the up-and-up. You follow me?"

"I'm not sure I do."

Telford leaned forward conspiratorially. "Say you want to find out what someone says when they think the conversation is private, you hire Oberhurst. See what I mean?"

"Electronics?"

Telford nodded. "Phones, rooms. He hinted he's not above a little b. and e. And the guy's got a record for it. I think he did penitentiary time down south somewhere for burglary."

"Sounds pretty unsavory."

"Yeah. I didn't like him. I only used him that one time and I'm sorry I did."

"Why?"

Telford tapped his fingers on his desk. Betsy let him decide what he wanted to say.

"Can we keep this confidential?"

Betsy nodded.

"What Peg wanted . . . Well, she was a little hysterical. Didn't take the divorce well. Anyway, I was sort of like a middleman with this. She said she wanted someone to do something, a private investigator who wouldn't ask too many questions. I hooked them up and paid him his money. I never really used him to work on the case.

"Anyway, someone beat up Mark Fulton about a week or so after I introduced Oberhurst to Peg. It was pretty bad from what I hear. The police thought it was a robbery."

"Why do you think different?"

"Oberhurst tried to shake me down. He came to my office a week after the beating. Showed me a newspaper article about it. He said he could keep me out of it for two thousand bucks.

"I told him to take a hike. I didn't know a goddamn thing about it. For all I knew, he could have been making the whole thing up. I mean, he reads the article, figures he can touch me for two grand and I won't squawk because the amount's not worth the risk."

"Weren't you afraid?"

"Damn straight. He's a big guy. He even looks like a gangster. He has a broken nose, talks tough. The whole bit. Only, I figured he was testing me. If I'd given in, he would have kept coming back. Besides, I didn't do anything wrong. Like I said, I only hooked them up."

"How do I get to Oberhurst?" Betsy asked.

"I got his name from Steve Wong at a party. Try him. Say I told you to call."

Telford thumbed through a lawyer's directory and wrote Wong's number on the back of a business card.

"Thanks."

"Glad I could help. And be careful with Oberhurst, he's bad news."

2

Betsy ate lunch at Zen, then shopped at Saks Fifth Avenue for a suit. It was one-fifteen when she returned to her office. There were several phone messages in her slot and two dozen red roses on her desk. Her first thought was that they were from Rick, and the idea made her heart pound. Rick sent her flowers when they were dating and on Valentine's Day. It was something he would do if he wanted to come home.

"Who are these from?" she asked Ann.

"I don't know. They were just delivered. There's a card."

Betsy put down her phone messages. A small envelope was taped to the vase. Her fingers trembled as she pried open the flap of the envelope and pulled out a small white card that said:

> For man's best friend, his lawyer.
> You did a bang-up job,
> **A VERY GRATEFUL CLIENT**
> Martin

Betsy put down the card. Her excitement turned sour.

"They're from Darius," she told Ann, hoping her disappointment didn't show.

"How thoughtful."

Betsy said nothing. She had wished so hard that the flowers were from Rick. Betsy debated with herself for a moment, then dialed his number.

"Mr. Tannenbaum's office," Rick's secretary said.

"Julie, this is Betsy. Is Rick in?"

"I'm sorry, Mrs. Tannenbaum, he's out of the office all day. Should I tell him you called?"

"No, thanks. That's okay."

The line went dead. Betsy held the receiver for a moment, then hung up. What would she have said if Rick had taken the call? Would she have risked humiliation and told him she wanted to get together? What would Rick have said? Betsy closed her eyes and took a few deep breaths to calm her heart. To distract herself, she looked through her phone messages. Most could be put off, but one was from Dr. Keene. When Betsy was back in control, she dialed his number.

"Sue did a good job, Betsy," the pathologist said, when they finally got down to business, "but I've got something for you."

"Let me get a pad. Okay, shoot."

"A medical examiner always collects urine samples from the body to screen for drugs. Most labs only do a d.a.u., which screens for five drugs of abuse to see if the victim used morphine, cocaine, amphetamines and so on. That's what Sue did. I had my lab do a urine screen for other substances. We came up with strong positive barbiturate readings for the women. I retested the blood. Every one of these ladies showed pentobarbital levels that were off scale."

"What does that mean?"

"Pentobarbital is not a common drug of abuse, which is why the lab didn't find it. It's an anesthetic."

"I don't follow."

"It's used in hospitals to anesthetize patients. This is not a drug these women would take themselves. Someone gave it to them. Now, this is where it gets strange, Betsy. These women all had three to four milligrams percent of pentobarbital in their blood. That's a very high level. In fact, it's a fatal level."

"What are you telling me?"

"I'm telling you that the three women died from an overdose of pentobarbital, not from their wounds."

"But they were tortured."

"They were mutilated, all right. I saw burn marks that were probably from cigarettes and electrical wires, there were cuts made with razor blades, the breasts were mutilated and there's evidence that objects had been inserted into their anus. But there's a chance the women were unconscious when these injuries were inflicted. Microscopic sections from around the wounds showed an early repair process. This tells me death occurred about twelve to twenty-four hours after the wounds were inflicted."

Betsy was quiet for a moment. When she spoke she sounded confused. "That doesn't make sense, Ray. What possible benefit is there in torturing someone who's unconscious?"

"Beats me. That's your problem. I'm just a sawbones."

"What about the man?"

"Here we have a different story. First, there's no pentobarbital. None. Second, there is evidence of repair around several wounds, indicating that he was tortured over a period of time. Death was sometime later from a gunshot wound, just like Sue said."

"How could Dr. Gregg have been fooled about the cause of death of the women?"

"Easy. You see a person cut from crotch to chest, the heart torn out, the intestines hanging out, you assume that's what killed 'em. I would have thought the same, if I hadn't found pentobarbital."

"You've given me a king-size headache, Ray."

"Take two aspirin and call me in the morning."

"Very funny."

"I'm glad I could bring some joy into your life."

They hung up, but Betsy kept staring at her notes. She doodled on the pad. The drawings made as much sense as what Dr. Keene had just told her.

3

Reggie Stewart's cross-country flight arrived late at JFK, so he had to sprint through the terminal to catch the connecting, upstate flight. He felt ragged by the time the plane landed at Albany County Airport. After checking into a motel near the airport, Stewart ate a hot meal, took a shower, and exchanged his cowboy boots, jeans and a flannel shirt for a navy blue suit, a white shirt and a tie with narrow red and yellow stripes. He was feeling human again by the time he parked his rental car in the lot of Marlin Steel's corporate headquarters, fifteen minutes before his scheduled appointment with Frank Grimsbo.

"Thanks for seeing me on such short notice," Stewart said, as soon as the secretary left him alone with the chief of security.

"Curiosity got the better of me," Grimsbo answered with an easy smile. "I couldn't figure out what a private investigator from Portland, Oregon, would want with me." Grimsbo gestured toward his wet bar. "Can I get you a drink?"

"Bourbon, neat," Stewart said, as he looked out the window at a breathtaking view of the Hudson River.

Grimsbo's office was furnished with an eight-foot rosewood desk and rosewood credenza. Old English hunting scenes hung from the walls. The couch and chairs were black leather. It was a far cry from the stuffy, converted storage area he had shared with the task force members in Hunter's Point. Like his surroundings, Grimsbo had also changed. He drove a Mercedes instead of a beat-up Chevy and he'd long since lost his taste for polyester. His conservative, gray pinstripe suits were custom-tailored to conceal what was left of a beer belly that had been dramatically reduced by dieting and exercise. He had also lost most of his hair, but he had gained in every other way. If old acquaintances thought he missed his days as a homicide detective, they were mistaken.

"So, what brings you from Portland, Oregon, to Albany?" Grimsbo asked as he handed Stewart his drink.

"I work for a lawyer named Betsy Tannenbaum. She's representing a prominent businessman who's been charged with murder."

"So you told my secretary when you called. What's that have to do with me?"

"You used to work for the Hunter's Point Police Department, didn't you?"

"I haven't had anything to do with Hunter's Point P.D. for nine years."

"I'm interested in discussing a case you worked on ten years ago. The rose killer."

Grimsbo had been raising his glass to his lips, but he stopped abruptly.

"Why are you interested in the rose killer? He's ancient history."

"Bear with me and I'll explain in a minute."

Grimsbo shook his head. "That's a hard case to forget."

"Tell me about it."

Grimsbo tilted his head back and closed his eyes, as if he was trying to picture the events. He sipped his scotch.

"We started getting reports of missing women. No signs of a struggle, nothing missing at the crime scenes, but there was always a rose and a note that said 'Gone, But Not Forgotten' left on the women's pillows. Then a mother and her six-year-old daughter were murdered. The husband found the bodies. There was a rose and a note next to the woman.

"A neighbor had seen a florist truck at the house of one of the victims, or maybe it was near the house. It's been some time now, so I may not have my facts exactly right. Anyway, we figured out who the deliveryman was. It was a guy named Henry Waters. He had a sex offender record. Then an anonymous caller said he was talking to Waters at a bar and Waters told him he had a woman in his basement. Sure enough, we found one of the missing women."

Grimsbo shook his head. "Man, that was a sight. You wouldn't believe what that bastard did to her. I wanted to kill him right there, and I would have, but fate took over and the son-of-a-bitch tried to escape. Another cop shot him and that was that."

"Was Peter Lake the husband who found the two bodies? The mother and daughter?"

"Right. Lake."

"Are you satisfied that the deliveryman was the killer?"

"Definitely. Hell, they found some of the roses and a note. And, of course, there was the body. Yeah, we got the right man."

"There was a task force assigned to investigate the case, wasn't there?"

Grimsbo nodded.

"Was Nancy Gordon a member of the task force?"

"Sure."

"Mr. Grimsbo . . ."

"Frank."

"Frank, my client is Peter Lake. He moved to Portland about eight years ago and changed his name to Martin Darius. He's a very successful developer. Very respected. About three months ago, women started disappearing in Portland. Roses and notes identical to those left in the Hunter's Point case were found on the pillows of the missing women. About two weeks ago the bodies of the missing women and a man were found buried at a construction site owned by Martin Darius. Nancy Gordon told our district attorney that Darius—Lake—killed them."

Grimsbo shook his head. "Nancy always had a bee in her bonnet about Lake."

"But you don't agree with her?"

"No. Like I said, Waters was the killer. I have no doubt about that. Now, we did think Lake might be the killer for a while. There was circumstantial evidence pointing that way, and I even had bad feelings about the guy. But it was only circumstantial evidence and the case against Waters was solid."

"What about Lake leaving Hunter's Point?"

"Can't blame him. If my wife and kid were brutally murdered, I wouldn't want to be reminded of them every day. Leaving town, starting over—sounds like the smart thing to do."

"Did the other investigators agree that Lake was innocent?"

"Everyone but Nancy."

"Was there any evidence that cleared Lake?"

"Like what?"

"Did he have an alibi for the time of any of the disappearances."

"I can't recall anything like that. Of course, it's been some time. Why don't you check the file? I'm sure Hunter's Point still has it."

"The files are missing."

"How did that happen?"

"We don't know." Stewart paused. "What kind of a person is Gordon?"

Grimsbo sipped his scotch and swiveled toward the window. It was comfortable in Grimsbo's office, but there was a thin coating of snow on the ground outside the picture window and the leafless trees were swaying under the attack of a chill wind.

"Nancy is a driven woman. That case got to all of us, but it affected her the most. It came right after she lost her fiancé. Another cop. Killed in the line of duty shortly before her wedding. Really tragic. I think that unbalanced her for a while. Then the women started disappearing and she submerged herself in the case.

"Now I'm not saying she isn't a fine detective. She is. But she lost her objectivity in that one case."

Stewart nodded and made some notes.

"How many women disappeared in Hunter's Point?"

"Four."

"And one was found in Waters's basement?"

"Right."

"What happened to the other women?"

"They were found in some old farmhouse out in the

country, if I remember correctly. I wasn't involved with that. Got stuck back at the station writing reports."

"How were they found?"

"Pardon?"

"Wasn't Waters shot almost as soon as the body was found in the basement?"

Grimsbo nodded.

"So, who told you where the other women were?"

Grimsbo paused, thinking. Then he shook his head.

"You know, I honestly can't remember. It could have been his mother. Waters was living with his mother. Or he might have written something down. I just don't recall."

"Did any of the survivors positively i.d. Waters as the killer?"

"They may have. Like I said, I didn't question any of them. They were pretty messed up, if I remember. Barely alive. Tortured. They went right to the hospital."

"Can you think of any reason why Nancy Gordon wouldn't tell our d.a. there were survivors?"

"She didn't?"

"I don't think so."

"Hell, I don't know. Why don't you ask her?"

"We can't. She's disappeared."

"What?" Grimsbo looked alarmed.

"Gordon showed up at the home of Alan Page, our d.a., late one night and told him about the Hunter's Point case. Then she checked into a motel. When Page called her the next morning, she was gone. Her clothing was still in the room, but she wasn't there."

"Have they looked for her?" Grimsbo asked anxiously.

"Oh, yeah. She's Page's whole case. He lost the bail hearing when he couldn't produce her."

"I don't know what to say. Did she return to Hunter's Point?"

"No. They thought she was on vacation. She never told anyone she was coming to Portland, and they haven't heard from her."

"Jesus, I hope nothing serious happened. Maybe she took off somewhere. Didn't you say Hunter's Point P.D. thought she was on vacation?"

"If she was going on vacation she wouldn't leave her clothes and makeup."

"Yeah." Grimsbo looked solemn. He shook his head. Stewart watched Grimsbo. The security chief was very upset.

"Is there anything else I can do for you, Mr. Stewart? I'm afraid I have some work to do," Grimsbo asked.

"No, you've been a big help." Stewart laid his and Betsy's business cards on Grimsbo's desk. "If you remember anything about the case that might help our client, please call me."

"I will."

"Oh, there is one other thing. I want to talk with all the members of the Hunter's Point task force. Do you know where I can find Glen Michaels and Wayne Turner?"

"I haven't heard from Michaels in years, but Wayne will be easy to find in about two weeks."

"Oh?"

"All you gotta do is turn on your TV. He's Senator Colby's administrative assistant. He should be sitting right next to him during the confirmation hearings."

Stewart scribbled this information into his notebook, thanked Grimsbo and left. As soon as the door closed behind Stewart, Grimsbo went back to his desk and dialed a Washington, D.C., phone number. Wayne Turner answered on the first ring.

Chapter Fifteen

I

Reggie Stewart eased himself into a seat across the desk from Dr. Pedro Escalante. The cardiologist had put on weight over the past ten years. His curly black hair was mostly gray. He was still cheerful with patients, but his good humor was not second nature to him anymore.

They were meeting in the cardiologist's office in the Wayside Clinic. A diploma from Brown University and another from Tufts Medical School hung on one wall. Beneath the diplomas was a child's crayon drawing of a stick-figure girl standing next to a yellow flower that was almost as tall as she was. A rainbow stretched from one side of the picture to the other.

"That your daughter?" Stewart asked. A photograph of Gloria Escalante holding a little girl on her lap stood on one corner of the doctor's desk. Stewart figured the child for the artist and asked about her as a way of easing into a conversation that was certain to evoke painful memories.

"Our adopted daughter," Escalante replied sadly. "Gloria lost the ability to conceive after her ordeal."

Stewart nodded because he could not think of a single thing to say.

"I'm afraid you've wasted your trip, if it was made solely to talk to my wife. We have tried our best to put the past behind us."

"I appreciate why Mrs. Escalante wouldn't want to talk to me, but this is literally a matter of life and death. We have the death penalty in Oregon and there's no doubt that my client will receive it, if he's convicted."

Dr. Escalante's features hardened. "Mr. Stewart, if your client treated those women the way my wife was treated, the death penalty would be insufficient punishment."

"You knew my client as Peter Lake, Dr. Escalante. His wife and daughter were killed by Henry Waters. He suffered the same anguish you suffered. We're talking about a frame-up of the worst kind, and your wife may have information that can prove an innocent man is being prosecuted."

Escalante looked down at his desk. "Our position is firm, Mr. Stewart. My wife will not discuss what happened to her with anyone. It has taken ten years to put the past behind her and we are going to keep it behind her. However, I may be of some help to you. There are answers to questions I may be able to give you."

"Any help will be appreciated."

"I don't want you to think her hard, Mr. Stewart. We did consider your request for an interview most seriously, but it would be too much for Gloria. She is very strong. Very strong. Otherwise she would not have survived. But as strong as she is, it is only within the past few years that she has been anything like the woman she used to be. Since your call, the nightmares have returned."

"Believe me, I would never subject your wife to . . ."

"No, no. I understand why you're here. I don't blame you. I just want you to understand why I can't permit her to relive what happened."

"Dr. Escalante, the main reason I wanted to talk to your wife was to find out if she saw the face of the man who kidnapped her."

"If that's why you came, I'm afraid I must disappoint you. She was taken from behind. Chloroform was used. During her captivity, she was forced to wear a leather hood with no eyelets whenever . . . whenever her captor . . . when he came."

"She never saw his face?"

"Never."

"What about the other women? Did any of them see him?"

"I don't know."

"Do you know where I can find Ann Hazelton or Samantha Reardon?"

"Ann Hazelton committed suicide six months after she was freed. Reardon was in a mental hospital for some time. She had a complete breakdown. Simon Reardon, Samantha's husband, divorced her," Escalante said with obvious distaste. "He moved away years ago. He's a neurosurgeon. You can probably locate him through the American Medical Association. He might know where Mrs. Reardon is living."

"That's very helpful," Stewart said as he wrote the information in his notebook.

"You could ask the other investigator. He may have located her."

"Pardon?"

"There was another investigator. I wouldn't let him speak to Gloria either. He came during the summer."

"The disappearances didn't start until August."

"No, this would have been May, early June. Somewhere in there."

"What did he look like?"

"He was a big man. I thought he might have played football or boxed, because he had a broken nose."

"That doesn't sound like anyone from the d.a.'s office. But they wouldn't have been involved that early. Do you remember his name or where he was from?"

"He was from Portland and I have his card." The doctor opened the top drawer of his desk and pulled out a white business card. "Samuel Oberhurst," he said, handing the card to Stewart. The card had Oberhurst's name and a phone number, but no address. The number was the one Betsy had given him.

"Dr. Escalante, what happened to your wife and the other women after they were kidnapped?"

Escalante took a deep breath. Stewart could see his pain even after all these years.

"My wife told me that there were three women with her. They were kept in an old farmhouse. She isn't clear where the house was situated, because she was unconscious when he brought her there and she was in shock when she left. Almost dead from starvation. It was a miracle."

Escalante paused. He ran his tongue across his lips and breathed deeply, again.

"The women were kept naked in stalls. They were chained at the ankles. Whenever he would come, he was masked and he would make them put on the hoods. Then he . . . he would torture them." Escalante closed his eyes and shook his head, as if trying to clear it of images too painful to behold. "I have never asked her to tell me what he did, but I have seen my wife's medical records."

Escalante paused again.

"I don't need that information, Doctor. It's not necessary."

"Thank you."

"The important thing is the identification. If your wife can remember anything about her captor that would help us to prove he was not Peter Lake."

"I understand. I'll ask her, but I'm certain she won't be able to help you."

Dr. Escalante shook hands with Stewart and showed him out. Then he returned to his office and picked up the photograph of his wife and child.

2

Betsy had a trial scheduled to start Friday in a divorce case and she was putting the file in her attaché case to bring home when Ann told her Reggie Stewart was on the line.

"How was your trip?" Betsy asked.

"Just fine, but I'm not accomplishing much. There's something weird about this business and it's getting weirder by the minute."

"Go on."

"I can't put my finger on what's wrong, but I know I'm getting the runaround about the case when no one should have any reason to lie to me."

"What are they lying about?"

"That's just it. I have no idea. But I know something's up."

"Tell me what you've learned so far," Betsy said, and Stewart recounted his conversations with Frank Grimsbo and Dr. Escalante.

"After I left Escalante, I spent some time at the public library going over newspaper accounts of the case. I figured there would be interviews with the victims, the cops. Nothing. John O'Malley, the chief of police, was the mayor's spokesman. He said Waters did it. Case closed. The surviving women were hospitalized immediately. Reardon was institutionalized. Escalante wouldn't talk to reporters. Ditto Hazelton. A few weeks of this and interest fades. On to other stories. But you read the news reports and you read O'Malley's statements, and you still don't know what happened to those women.

"Then I talked to Roy Lenzer, a detective with Hunter's Point P.D. He's the guy who's trying to run down the case files for Page. He knows Gordon is missing. He searched her house for the files. No luck. Someone carted off all of the files in the case. I mean, we're talking a full shelf of case reports, photographs. But why? Why take a shelf-load of paper in a ten-year-old case? What was in those files?"

"Reg, did Oberhurst visit the police?"

"I asked Lenzer about that. Gave Grimsbo a call, too. As far as I can tell, Oberhurst never talked to anyone after he talked to Dr. Escalante. Which doesn't make sense. If he was investigating the case for Lisa Darius, the police would be his first stop."

"Not necessarily," Betsy said. Then she told her investigator about her meetings with Gary Telford.

"I have a very bad feeling about this, Reg. Let me run something by you. Say you're an unscrupulous investigator. An ex-con who works on the edge. Someone who's not averse to a little blackmail. The wife of a prominent businessman hires you because she thinks her husband is having an affair. She also gives you a scrapbook containing clippings about an old murder case.

"Let's suppose that this crooked p.i. flies to Hunter's Point and talks to Dr. Escalante. He's no help, but he does tell the investigator enough information so he can track down Samantha Reardon, the only other surviving victim. What if Oberhurst found Reardon and she positively identified Peter Lake as the man who kidnapped and tortured her?"

"And Oberhurst returned to Portland and what?" Stewart said. "Blackmailed a serial killer? You'd have to be nuts."

"Who's the John Doe, Reg?"

The line was quiet for a moment, then Stewart said, "Oh, shit."

"Exactly. We know Oberhurst lied to Lisa. He told her he hadn't started investigating the Hunter's Point case, but he was in Hunter's Point. And he's disappeared. I talked to every lawyer I could find who's employed him. No contact. He doesn't return calls. The John Doe is Oberhurst's size and build. What do you want to bet the corpse has a broken nose?"

"No bets. What are you going to do?"

"There's nothing we can do. Darius is our client. We're his agents. This is all confidential."

"Even if he killed the guy?"

"Even if he killed the guy."

Betsy heard a sharp intake of air, then Stewart said: "You're the boss. What do you want me to do next?"

"Have you tried to set up a meeting with Wayne Turner?"

"No go. His secretary says he's too busy, because of the confirmation hearings."

"Damn. Gordon, Turner, Grimsbo. They all know something. What about the police chief? What was his name?"

"O'Malley. Lenzer says he retired to Florida about nine years ago."

"Okay," Betsy said with a trace of desperation.

"Keep trying to find Samantha Reardon. She's our best bet."

"I'll do it for you, Betsy. If it was someone else . . . I gotta tell you, I usually don't give a fuck, but I'm starting to. I don't like this case."

"That makes two of us. I just don't know what to do about it. We're not even certain I'm right. I have to find that out, first."

"If you are, what then?"

"I have no idea."

3

Betsy put Kathy to sleep at nine and changed into a flannel nightgown. After brewing a pot of coffee, Betsy spread out the papers in Friday's divorce case on the dining room table. The coffee was waking her up, but her mind wandered to the Darius case. Was Darius guilty? Betsy could not stop thinking about the question she had put to Alan Page during her cross-examination: With six victims, including a six-year-old girl, why would the mayor and chief of police of Hunter's Point close the case if there was any possibility that Peter Lake, or anyone else, was really the murderer? It made no sense.

Betsy pushed aside the documents in the divorce and pulled a yellow pad in front of her. She listed what she knew about the Darius case. The list stretched for three pages. Betsy came to the information she had learned from Stewart that afternoon. A thought occurred to her. She frowned.

Betsy knew Samuel Oberhurst was not above blackmail. He'd tried it on Gary Telford. If Martin Darius was the rose killer, Darius would have no compunction about killing Oberhurst if the investigator tried to blackmail him. But Betsy's assumption that John Doe was Samuel Oberhurst made sense only if Samantha Reardon identified Martin Darius as the rose killer. And that's where the difficulty lay. The police would have questioned Reardon when they rescued her. If the task force suspected that Peter Lake, not Henry Waters, was the kidnapper, they would have shown Reardon a photograph of Lake. If she identified Lake as her kidnapper, why would the mayor and the police chief announce that Waters was the killer? Why would the case be closed?

Dr. Escalante said that Reardon was institutionalized. Maybe she couldn't be interviewed immediately. But she would have been interviewed at some point. Grimsbo told Reggie that Nancy Gordon was obsessed with the case and never believed Waters was the killer. So, Betsy thought, let's assume that Reardon did identify Lake as the killer at some point. Why wouldn't Gordon, or someone, have reopened the case?

Maybe Reardon wasn't asked until Oberhurst talked to her. But wouldn't she have read about Henry Waters and known the police had accused the wrong man? She could have been so traumatized that she wanted to forget everything that happened to her, even if it meant letting Lake go free. But if that was true, why tell Oberhurst that Lake was her kidnapper?

Betsy sighed. She was missing something. She stood up and carried her coffee cup into the living room. The Sunday New York *Times* was sitting in a wicker basket next to her favorite chair. She sat down and decided to look through it. Sometimes the best way to figure out a problem was to forget about it for a while. She had read the Book Review, the Magazine and the Arts section, but she still hadn't read the Week in Review.

Betsy skimmed an article about the fighting in the

Ukraine and another about the resumption of hostilities
between North and South Korea. Death was everywhere.

Betsy turned the page and started reading a profile
of Raymond Colby. Betsy knew Colby would be confirmed and it upset her. There was no more diversity of
opinion on the Court. Wealthy white males with identical
backgrounds and identical thoughts dominated it. Men
with no concept of what it was like to be poor or helpless,
who had been nominated by Republican Presidents for
no reason other than their willingness to put the interests
of the wealthy and big government ahead of individual
rights. Colby was no different. Harvard Law, c.e.o. of
Marlin Steel, governor of New York, then a member of
the United States Senate for the last nine years. Betsy
read a summary of Colby's accomplishments as a governor and senator and a prediction of the way he would
vote on several cases that were before the Supreme
Court, then skimmed another article about the economy.
When she was finished with the paper, she went back to
the dining room.

The divorce case was a mess. Betsy's client and her
husband didn't have children and they had agreed to split
almost all of their property, but they were willing to go to
the mat over a cheap landscape they had bought from a
sidewalk artist in Paris on their honeymoon. Going to
court over the silly painting was costing them both ten
times its value, but they were adamant. Obviously it was
not the painting that was fueling their rage. It was a case
like this that made Betsy want to enter a nunnery. But,
she sighed to herself, it was also cases like this that paid
her overhead. She started reading the divorce petition,
then remembered something she had read in the article
about Raymond Colby.

Betsy put the petition down. The idea had come so
fast that it made her a little dizzy. She walked back to the

living room and reread Colby's biography. There it was. He had been a United States senator for nine years. Hunter's Point Chief of Police John O'Malley retired to Florida nine years ago. Frank Grimsbo had been with Marlin Steel, Colby's old company, for nine years. And Wayne Turner was the senator's administrative assistant.

The heat was on in the house, but Betsy felt like she was hugging a block of ice. She went back to the dining room and reread her list of important facts in the Darius case. It was all there. You just had to look at the facts in a certain way and it made perfect sense. Martin Darius was the rose killer. The Hunter's Point police knew that when they announced that Henry Waters was the murderer and closed the case. Now Betsy knew how Peter Lake could walk away from Hunter's Point with the blood of all those innocent people on his hands. What she could not imagine was why the governor of New York State would conspire with the police force and mayor of Hunter's Point to set free a mass murderer.

Chapter Sixteen

I

The sun was shining, but the temperature was a little below freezing. Betsy hung up her overcoat. Her cheeks hurt from the cold. She rubbed her hands together and asked Ann to bring her a cup of coffee. By the time Ann set a steaming mug on her coaster, Betsy was dialing Washington, D.C.

"Senator Colby's office."

"I'd like to speak to Wayne Turner, please."

"I'll connect you to his secretary."

Betsy picked up the mug. Her hand was trembling. She wanted to sound confident, but she was scared to death.

"Can I help you?" a pleasant female voice asked.

"My name is Betsy Tannenbaum. I'm an attorney in Portland, Oregon. I'd like to speak to Mr. Turner."

"Mr. Turner is very busy with the confirmation hearings. If you leave me your number, he'll call you when he gets the chance."

Betsy knew Turner would never return her call. There was only one way to force him to get on the phone.

Betsy was convinced she knew what had happened in Hunter's Point and she would have to gamble she was right.

"This can't wait. Let Mr. Turner know that Peter Lake's attorney is on the phone." Then Betsy told the secretary to tell Turner something else. The secretary made her repeat the message. "If Mr. Turner won't talk to me, tell him I'm sure the press will."

Turner's secretary put Betsy on hold. Betsy closed her eyes and tried a meditation technique she had learned in a YWCA yoga class. It didn't work, and she jumped when Turner came on the line.

"Who is this?" he barked.

"I told your secretary, Mr. Turner. My name is Betsy Tannenbaum and I'm Martin Darius's attorney. You knew him as Peter Lake when he lived in Hunter's Point. I want to talk to Senator Colby immediately."

"The senator is extremely busy with the confirmation hearings, Ms. Tannenbaum. Can't this wait until they're over?"

"I'm not going to wait until the senator is safely on the Court, Mr. Turner. If he won't speak to me, I'll be forced to go to the press."

"Damn it, if you spread any irresponsible . . ."

"Calm down, Mr. Turner. If you thought about this at all, you'd know it would hurt my client to go to the papers. I'll only do it as a last resort. But I won't be put off."

"If you know about Lake, if you know about the senator, why are you doing this?" Turner pleaded.

Betsy paused. Turner had asked a good question. Why was she keeping what she knew to herself? Why hadn't she confided in Reggie Stewart? Why was she willing to fly across the country for the answer to her questions?

"This is for me, Mr. Turner. I have to know what kind of man I'm representing. I have to know the truth. I must meet with Senator Colby. I can fly to Washington tomorrow."

Turner was silent for a few seconds. Betsy looked out the window. In the office across the street, two men in shirtsleeves were discussing a blueprint. On the floor above them, a group of secretaries were working away on word processors. Toward the top of the office building, Betsy could see the sky reflected in the glass wall. Green-tinted clouds scudded across a green-tinted sky.

"I'll talk to Senator Colby and call you back," Turner said.

"I'm not a threat, Mr. Turner. I'm not out to wreck the senator's appointment. Tell him that."

Turner hung up and Betsy exhaled. She was not used to threatening United States senators or dealing with cases that could destroy the reputations of prominent public figures. Then she thought about the Hammermill and Peterson cases. Twice she had shouldered the burden of saving a human life. There was no greater responsibility than that. Colby was just a man, even if he was a United States senator, and he might be the reason Martin Darius was free to murder three innocent women in Portland.

"Nora Sloane is on one," Ann said over the intercom.

Betsy's divorce client was supposed to meet her at the courthouse at eight forty-five and it was eight-ten. Betsy wanted to concentrate on the issues in the divorce, but she decided she could spare Sloane a minute.

"Sorry to bother you," Sloane said apologetically. "Remember I talked to you about interviewing your mother and Kathy? Do you suppose I could do that this weekend?"

"I might be out of town. My mom will probably

watch Kathy, so you could talk to them together. Mom will get a kick out of being interviewed. I'll talk to her and get back to you. What's your number?"

"Why don't I call you? I'm going to be in and out."

"Okay. I've got court in half an hour. I should be done by noon. Call me this afternoon."

Betsy checked her watch. She had twenty minutes to prepare for court and no more time to spend thinking about Martin Darius.

2

Reggie Stewart found Ben Singer, the attorney who handled Samantha Reardon's divorce, by going through the court records. Singer had not heard from Reardon in years, but he did have an address near the campus.

Most of the houses around the University were older, single-family dwellings surrounded by well-kept lawns and shaded by oak and elm trees, but there was a pocket of apartments and boardinghouses that catered to students located several blocks behind the campus near the freeway. Stewart turned into a parking lot that ran the length of a dull-gray garden apartment complex. It had snowed the night before. Stewart stepped over a drift onto the shoveled sidewalk in front of the manager's office. A woman in her early forties dressed in heavy slacks and a green wool sweater answered the door. She was holding a cigarette. Her face was flushed. There were curlers in her strawberry-red hair.

"My name is Reggie Stewart. I'm looking for the apartment manager."

"We're full," the woman answered brusquely.

Stewart handed the woman his card. She stuck her cigarette in her mouth and examined it.

"Are you the manager?" Stewart asked. The woman nodded.

"I'm trying to find Samantha Reardon. This was the last address I had for her."

"What do you want with her?" the woman asked suspiciously.

"She may have information that could clear a client who used to live in Hunter's Point."

"Then you're out of luck. She's not here."

"Do you know when she'll be back?"

"Beats me. She's been gone since the summer." The manager looked at the card again. "The other investigator was from Portland too. I remember, because you two are the only people I ever met from Oregon."

"Was this guy big with a broken nose?"

"Right. You know him?"

"Not personally. When did he show up?"

"It was hot. That's all I remember. Reardon left the next day. Paid a month's rent in advance. She said she didn't know how long she'd be gone. Then, about a week later, she came back and moved out."

"Did she store anything with you?"

"Nah. The apartment's furnished and she hardly had anything of her own." The manager shook her head. "I was up there once to fix a leak in the sink. Not a picture on the wall, not one knickknack on a table. The place looked just like it did when she moved in. Spooky."

"You ever talk to her?"

"Oh, sure. I'd see her from time to time. But it was mostly 'good morning' or 'how's it going' on my part and not much from her. She kept to herself."

"Did she have a job?"

"Yeah. She worked somewhere. I think she was a

secretary or receptionist. Something like that. Might have
been for a doctor. Yeah, a doctor, and she was a bookkeeper. That was it. She looked like a bookkeeper, too.
Real mousy. She didn't take care of herself. She had a
nice figure if you looked hard. Tall, athletic. But she always dressed like an old maid. It looked to me like she
was trying to scare men off, if you know what I mean."

"You wouldn't happen to have a picture of her?"

"Where would I get a picture? Like I said, I don't
even think she had any pictures in her place. Weird. Everyone has pictures, knickknacks, things to remind you of
the good times."

"Some people don't want to think about the past,"
Stewart said.

The manager took a drag on her cigarette and nodded in agreement. "She like that? Bad memories?"

"The worst," Stewart said. "The very worst."

3

"Let me help you with the dishes," Rita said. They had
left them after dinner, so they could watch one of Kathy's
favorite television shows with her, before Betsy put her to
bed.

"Before I forget," Betsy said as she piled up the
bread plates, "a woman named Nora Sloane may call you.
I gave her your number. She's the one who's writing the
article for *Pacific West.*"

"Oh?"

"She wants to interview you and Kathy for background."

"Interview me?" Rita preened.

"Yeah, Mom. It's your chance at immortality."

"*You're* my immortality, honey, but I'm available if she calls," Rita said. "Who better to give her the inside story than your mother?"

"That's what I'm afraid of."

Betsy rinsed the plates and cups and Rita put them in the dishwasher.

"Do you have some time before you go home? I want to ask you about something."

"Sure."

"You want coffee or tea?"

"Coffee will be fine."

Betsy poured two cups and they carried them into the living room.

"It's the Darius case," Betsy said. "I don't know what to do. I keep on thinking about those women, what they went through. What if he killed them, Mom?"

"Aren't you always telling me that your client's guilt or innocence doesn't matter? You're his lawyer."

"I know. And that is what I always say. And I believe it. Plus I'm going to need the money I'm making on the case, if Rick and I . . . if we divorce. And the prestige. Even if I lose, I'll still be known as Martin Darius's attorney. This case is putting me in the major leagues. If I dropped out, I'd get a reputation as someone who couldn't handle the pressure of a big case."

"But you're worried about getting him off?"

"That's it, Mom. I know I can get him off. Page doesn't have the goods. Judge Norwood told him as much at the bail hearing. But I know things Page doesn't and I . . ."

Betsy shook her head. She was visibly shaken.

"Someone is going to represent Martin Darius," Rita said calmly. "If you don't do it, another lawyer will. I listen to what you say about giving everyone, even killers and drug pushers, a fair trial. It's hard for me to accept. A

man who would do that to a woman. To anyone. You want
to spit on them. But you aren't defending that person.
Isn't that what you tell me? You're preserving a good system."

"That's the theory, but what if you feel sick inside?
What if you can't sleep because you know you're going to
free someone who . . . Mom, he did this same thing in
Hunter's Point. I'm certain of it. And, if I get him off,
who's next? I keep thinking about what those women
went through. Alone, helpless, stripped of their dignity."

Rita reached across the space between them and
took her daughter's hand.

"I'm so proud of what you've done with your life.
When I was a girl I never thought about being a lawyer.
That's an important job. You're important. You do important things. Things other people don't have the courage to
do. But there's a price. Do you think the President sleeps
well? And judges? Generals? So, you're finding out about
the bad side of responsibility. With those battered
women, it was easy. You were on God's side. Now, God is
against you. But you have to do your job even if you
suffer. You have to stick with it and not take the easy way
out."

Suddenly Betsy was crying. Rita moved over and
threw her arms around her daughter.

"I'm a mess, Mom. I loved Rick so much. I gave him
everything and he walked out on me. If he was here to
help me . . . I can't do it alone."

"Yes, you can. You're strong. No one could do what
you've done without being strong."

"Why don't I see it that way? I feel empty, used up."

"It's hard to see yourself the way others see you. You
know you're not perfect, so you emphasize your weaknesses. But you've got plenty of strengths, believe me."

Rita paused. She looked distant for a moment, then she looked at Betsy.

"I'm going to tell you something no other living soul knows. The night your father passed away, I almost took my own life."

"Mom!"

"I sat in our bedroom, after you were asleep, and I took out pills from our bathroom cabinet. I must have looked at those pills for an hour, but I couldn't do it. You wouldn't let me. The thought of you. How I would miss seeing you grow up. How I would never know what you did with your life. Not taking those pills was the smartest thing I ever did, because I got to see you the way you are now. And I am so proud of you."

"What if I'm not proud of myself? What if I'm only in this for the money or the reputation? What if I'm helping a man who is truly evil to escape punishment, so he can be free to cause unbearable pain and suffering to other innocent people?"

"I don't know what to say to you," Rita answered. "I don't know all the facts, so I can't put myself in your place. But I trust you and I know you'll do the right thing."

Betsy wiped at her eyes. "I'm sorry I laid this on you, but you're the only one I can let my hair down with now that Rick's walked out."

"I'm glad to know I'm good for something." Rita smiled back. Betsy hugged her. It had been good to cry, it had been good to talk out what she had been holding inside, but Betsy didn't feel she was any closer to an answer.

Chapter Seventeen

On Sunday afternoon Raymond Colby stood in front of the fireplace in his den waiting for the lawyer from Portland to arrive. A servant had built a fire. Colby held his hands out to catch the heat and dispel a chill that had very little to do with the icy rain that was keeping his neighbors off the streets of Georgetown.

The front door opened and closed. That would be Wayne Turner with Betsy Tannenbaum. Colby straightened his suit coat. What did Tannenbaum want? That was really the question. Was she someone with whom he could reason? Did she have a price? Turner didn't think Lake's attorney knew everything, but she knew enough to ruin his chance of being confirmed. Perhaps she would come over to their side once she knew the facts. After all, going public would not only destroy Raymond Colby, it would destroy her client.

The door to the den opened and Wayne Turner stood aside. Colby sized up his visitor. Betsy Tannenbaum was attractive, but Colby could see she was not a woman who traded on her looks. She was dressed in a severe black suit with a cream-colored blouse. All business, a little nervous, he guessed, feeling somewhat out of her league, yet willing to confront a powerful man on his own turf.

Colby smiled and held out his hand. Her handshake was firm. She was not afraid to look Colby in the eye or to look him over much the way he had scrutinized her.

"How was your flight?" Colby asked.

"Fine." Betsy looked around the cozy room. There were three high-backed armchairs drawn up in front of the fireplace. Colby motioned toward them.

"Can I get you something to take off the chill?"

"A cup of coffee, please."

"Nothing stronger?"

"No, thank you."

Betsy took the chair closest to the window. Colby sat in the center chair. Wayne Turner poured coffee from a silver urn a servant had set up on an antique, walnut side table. Betsy stared into the fire. She had barely noticed the weather on the ride from the airport. Now that she was inside, she shivered in a delayed reaction to the tension of the preceding hours. Wayne Turner handed Betsy a delicate china cup and saucer covered with finely-drawn roses. The flowers were a pale pink and the stems a tracery of gold.

"How can I help you, Mrs. Tannenbaum?"

"I know what you did ten years ago in Hunter's Point, Senator. I want to know why."

"And what did I do?"

"You corrupted the Hunter's Point task force, you destroyed police files, and you engineered a cover-up to protect a monstrous serial killer who revels in torturing women."

Colby nodded sadly. "Part of what you say is true, but not all of it. No one on the task force was corrupt."

"I know about the payoffs," Betsy answered curtly.

"What do you think you know?"

Betsy flushed. She had been spurred on by the coincidences, the improbabilities, to the only possible solution, but she did not want to sound like she was bragging. On the other hand, letting Colby know how she figured it out would make him see that she could not be fooled.

"I know that a senator's term is six years," Betsy answered, "and that you are in the middle of your second term. That means you've been a United States senator for nine years. Nine years ago, Frank Grimsbo left a low-paying job on an obscure, small city police force to assume a high-paying job at Marlin Steel, your old company. Nine years ago, John O'Malley, the police chief of that police force, retired to Florida. Wayne Turner, another member of the rose killer task force, is your administrative assistant. I asked myself how three members of the same small city police force could suddenly do so well, and why they would all do so well the year you decided to run for the United States Senate. The answer was obvious. They had been paid off to keep a secret and for destroying the files of the rose killer investigation."

Colby nodded. "Excellent deductions, but only partly correct. There were rewards, but no bribes. Frank Grimsbo earned his position as head of security after I helped him get a job on the security force. Chief O'Malley had a heart attack and was forced to retire. I'm a very wealthy man. Wayne told me John was having financial problems and I helped him out. And Wayne was working his way through law school when the kidnappings and murders occurred. He graduated two years later and I helped him get a job in Washington, but it was not on my staff. Wayne didn't come on board until a year before my first term ended. By then he had established an excellent reputation on the Hill. When Larry Merrill, my a.a., went back into law practice in Manhattan, I asked Wayne if he would take his place. So, you see, the explanations for these events are less sinister than you supposed."

"But I'm right about the records."

"Chief O'Malley took care of that."

"And the pardon?"

Colby looked very old all of a sudden.

"Everyone has something in their life they wish they could undo. I think about Hunter's Point all the time, but I can't see how it could have ended differently."

"How could you have done it, Senator? The man's not human. You had to know he would do this again, somewhere, sometime."

Colby turned his face toward her, but he was not seeing Betsy. He looked completely lost, like a man who has just been told that he has an incurable illness.

"We knew, God forgive us. We knew, but we had no choice."

Part Five

HUNTER'S POINT

Chapter Eighteen

I

Nancy Gordon heard a tinkle of glass when Peter Lake broke the lower left pane in the back door so he could reach between the jagged shards and open it from the inside. Nancy heard the rusty hinges squeak. She shifted under the covers and trained her eyes on the doorway, straining to see in the dark.

Two hours earlier, Nancy had been alone in the task force office when Lake appeared to tell her he had heard about the shooting of Henry Waters on the late news. As planned, Nancy told Lake she had suspected him of being the rose killer because of the gap between the time he had been seen driving home and the call to 911 and his stakeout of Waters's home. Lake had been alarmed, but Nancy assured him that she was satisfied that Waters was the murderer and had kept her suspicions to herself. Then she had yawned and told Lake she was heading home. Since then Nancy had been in bed, waiting.

Black slacks, a black ski mask and a black turtleneck helped Lake blend into the darkness. There was an ugly snub-nosed revolver in his hand. Nancy did not hear him cross the living room. One second, her bedroom doorway was empty, then Lake filled it. When he snapped on the light, Nancy sat up in bed, feigning surprise. Lake removed the ski mask.

"You knew, didn't you, Nancy?" She gaped at him, as if the visit was unexpected. "I really do like you, but I can't take the chance you'll reopen the case."

Nancy looked at the revolver. "You can't believe you'll get away with murdering a cop."

"I don't have much choice. You're far too intelligent. Eventually you would have realized Waters was innocent. Then you would have kept after me. You might even have dug up enough evidence to convince a jury."

Lake walked around the side of the bed. "Place your hands on top of the sheet and take it off slowly," he said, gesturing with the gun. Nancy was sleeping under a single light sheet because of the heat. She pulled away the sheet slowly, careful to gather it up near her right hip so Lake would not see the outline of the gun that was hidden there. Nancy was wearing bikini panties and a T-shirt. The T-shirt had bunched up beneath her breasts, revealing her rigid stomach muscles. Nancy heard a quiet intake of breath.

"Very nice," Lake said. "Remove the shirt."

Nancy forced herself to look at him wide-eyed.

"I'm not going to rape you," Lake assured her. "It's not that I don't want to. I've fantasized about playing with you quite a lot, Nancy. You're so different from the others. They're all so soft, cows really, and so easy to train. But you're hard. I'm certain you would resist. It would be very enjoyable. But I want the authorities to believe that Henry Waters is the rose killer, so you'll die during a burglary."

Nancy looked at Lake with disgust. "How could you kill your wife and daughter?"

"You can't think I planned that. I loved them, Nancy. But Sandy found a note and a rose I was planning to use the next day. I'm not proud of myself. I panicked. I couldn't think of a single explanation I could make to Sandy once the notes became public knowledge. She would have gone to the police and it would have been over for me."

"What's your excuse for killing Melody? She was a baby."

Lake shook his head. He looked genuinely distraught.

"Do you think that was easy?" Lake's jaw trembled. There was a tear in the corner of one eye. "Sandy screamed. I got to her before she could do it again, but Melody heard her. She was standing on the stairs, looking through the bars on the banister. I held her and hugged her while I tried to think of some way to spare her, but there wasn't a way, so I made it painless. It was the hardest thing I've ever done."

"Let me help you, Peter. They'll never find you guilty. I'll talk to the district attorney. We'll work out an insanity plea."

Lake smiled sadly. He shook his head with regret. "It would never fly, Nancy. No one would ever let me off that easy. Think about what I did to Pat. Think about the others. Besides, I'm not crazy. If you knew why I did it, you'd understand."

"Tell me. I want to understand."

"Sorry. No time. Besides, it won't make any difference to you. You're going to die."

"Please, Peter. I have to know. There has to be a reason for a plan this brilliant."

Lake smiled condescendingly. "Don't do this. It's not becoming. What's the purpose in stalling?"

"You can rape me first. Tie me up. You want to, don't

you? I'd be helpless," she begged, sliding her right hand under the sheet.

"Don't debase yourself, Nancy. I thought you had more class than the others."

Lake saw Nancy's hand move. His face clouded. "What's that?"

Nancy went for the gun. Lake brought the revolver down hard on her cheek. Bone cracked. She went blind for a second. Her closet door slammed open. Lake froze as Wayne Turner came out of the closet. Turner fired and hit Lake in the shoulder. Lake's gun dropped to the floor just as Frank Grimsbo hurtled through the bedroom door, tackling Lake into the wall.

"Stay down," Turner yelled at Nancy. He scrambled across the bed, knocking the wind out of her. Lake was pinned to the wall and Grimsbo was smashing him in the face.

"Stop, Frank!" Turner yelled. He kept his gun trained on Lake with one hand and tried to restrain Grimsbo's arm with the other. Grimsbo delivered one more clubbing blow that bounced Lake's head off the wall. Lake's head lolled sideways. A damp patch spread across the black fabric that covered his right shoulder as blood seeped from his wound.

"Get his gun," Turner said. "It's next to the bed. And check on Nancy."

Grimsbo stood up. He was shaking.

"I'm okay," Nancy said. Her cheek was numb and she could barely see out of her left eye.

Grimsbo picked up Lake's gun. He stood over Lake and his breathing increased.

"Cuff him," Turner ordered. Grimsbo stood there, the gun rising like something with a life of its own.

"Don't fuck around, Frank," Turner said. "Just put the cuffs on."

"Why?" Grimsbo asked. "He could have been shot twice when he attacked Nancy. You hit him in the shoulder when you came out of the closet and I fired the fatal shot when this piece of shit spun toward me, and, as fate would have it, caught him between the eyes."

"It didn't happen that way, because I know it didn't," Turner said evenly.

"And what? You'd turn me in and testify at my murder trial? You'd send me to Attica for the rest of my life because I exterminated this scumbag?"

"No one would know, Wayne," Nancy said quietly. "I'd back Frank."

Turner looked at Nancy. She was watching Lake with a look of pure hatred.

"I don't believe this. You're cops. What you want to do is murder."

"Not in this case, Wayne," Nancy said. "You have to take the life of a human being to commit murder. Lake isn't human. I don't know what he is, but he's not human. A human being doesn't murder his own child. He doesn't strip a woman naked, then slice her open from groin to chest, pull out her intestines and let her die a slow death. I can't even imagine what he's done to the missing women." Nancy shuddered. "I don't want to guess."

Lake was listening to the argument. He did not move his head, but his eyes focused on each speaker as his fate was debated. He saw Turner waiver. Nancy got off the bed and stood next to Grimsbo.

"He'll get out someday, Wayne," she said. "He'll convince the Parole Board to release him or he'll convince a jury he was insane and the hospital will let him out when he is miraculously cured. Do you want to wake up some morning and read about a woman who was kidnapped in Salt Lake City or Minneapolis and the note that was left on her pillow telling her husband she was 'Gone, But Not Forgotten'?"

Turner's arm fell to his side. His lips were dry. His gut was in a knot.

"It'll be me, Wayne," Grimsbo said, pulling out his service revolver and handing Nancy Lake's weapon. "You can leave the room if you want. You can even remember it like it happened the way I said, because that's the way it will really have happened, if we all agree."

"Jesus," Turner said to himself. One hand was knotted into a fist, and the one holding the gun was squeezed so tight the metal cut into his palm.

"You can't kill me," Lake gasped, the pain from his wound making it hard for him to speak.

"Shut the fuck up," Grimsbo said, "or I'll do you now."

"They're not dead," Lake managed, squeezing his eyes shut as a wave of nausea swept over him. "The other women are still alive. Kill me and they'll die. Kill me and you kill them all."

2

Governor Raymond Colby ducked under the rotating helicopter blades and ran toward the waiting police car. Larry Merrill, the governor's administrative assistant, leaped out after the governor and followed him across the runway. A stocky, red-haired man and a slender black man were standing next to the police car. The redhead opened the back door for Colby.

"John O'Malley, Governor. I'm the Hunter's Point police chief. This is Detective Wayne Turner. He's going to brief you. We have a very bad situation here."

Governor Colby sat in the rear seat of the police car and Turner slid in beside him. When Merrill was in the front, O'Malley started toward Nancy Gordon's house.

"I don't know how much you've been told, Governor."

"Start from the beginning, Detective Turner. I want to make certain I don't miss anything."

"Women have been disappearing in Hunter's Point. All married to professionals, childless. No sign of a struggle. With the first woman, we assumed we were dealing with a missing persons case. The only oddity was a note on the woman's pillow that said 'Gone, But Not Forgotten,' pinned down by a rose that had been dyed black. We figured the wife left it. Then the second woman disappeared and we found an identical rose and note.

"After the fourth disappearance, all with notes and black roses, Sandra and Melody Lake were murdered. Sandra was the wife of Peter Lake, whom I believe you know. Melody was his daughter."

"That was tragic," Colby said. "Pete's been a supporter of mine for some time. I appointed him to a board last fall."

"He killed them, Governor. He murdered his wife and daughter in cold blood. Then he framed a man named Henry Waters by bringing one of the kidnapped women to Waters's house, disemboweling her in Waters's basement, planting some roses and one of the notes in Waters's house and calling the police anonymously."

It was four a.m. and pitch-black in the car, but Turner saw Colby blanch as the car passed under a streetlight.

"Peter Lake killed Sandy and Melody?"

"Yes, sir."

"I find that hard to believe."

"What I'm going to tell you now is known only to

Chief O'Malley, Detectives Frank Grimsbo and Nancy Gordon and me. The chief created a task force to deal with the disappearances. It consists of Gordon, Grimsbo and me, plus a forensic expert. We suspected Lake might be our killer, even after we found Patricia Cross's body at Waters's house, so we set him up. Gordon told Lake she suspected him but had kept the incriminating evidence to herself. Lake panicked, as we'd hoped he would. He broke into Gordon's house to kill her. She tricked him into admitting the killings. We wired her house and we have his confession on tape. Grimsbo and I were hiding and heard it all. We arrested Lake."

"Then what's the problem?" Merrill asked.

"Three of the women are still alive. Barely. Lake's been keeping them on a starvation diet—he only feeds them once a week. He won't tell us when he fed them last or where they are unless the governor gives him a full pardon."

"What?" Merrill asked incredulously. "The governor's not going to pardon a mass murderer."

"Can't you find them?" Colby asked. "They must be in property Lake owns. Have you searched them all?"

"Lake's made a good deal of money over the years. He has vast real estate holdings. Most of them aren't in his name. We don't have the manpower or time to find and search them all before the women starve."

"Then I'll promise to pardon Peter. After he tells us where he's holding the women, you can arrest him. A contract entered into under duress won't stand up."

Merrill looked uncomfortable. "I'm afraid it might, Ray. When I was with the U.S. attorney, we gave immunity to a contract killer for the mob in exchange for testimony against a higher-up. He said he was present when the hit was ordered, but he was in Las Vegas on the day the body was found. We checked out his story. He was registered at Caesars Palace. Several honest witnesses saw him eating at the casino. We gave him his deal, he testified, the higher-up was convicted, he walked. Then we found out he did the hit, but he did it at fifteen minutes before midnight, then flew to Vegas.

"We were furious. We rearrested him and indicted him for murder, but the judge threw out the indictment. He ruled that everything the defendant told us was true. We just didn't ask the right questions. I researched the hell out of the law on plea agreements trying to get the appellate court to rule for us. No luck. Contract principles apply, but so does due process. If both sides enter into the agreement in good faith and the defendant performs, the courts are going to enforce the agreement. If you go into this with your eyes open, Ray, I think the pardon will stick."

"Then I have no choice."

"Yes, you do," Merrill insisted. "You tell him no deal. You can't pardon a serial killer and expect to be reelected. It's political suicide."

"Damn it, Larry," Colby snapped, "how do you think people would react if they found out I let three women die to win an election?"

Raymond Colby opened the door to Nancy Gordon's bedroom. Frank Grimsbo was seated next to the door, holding his weapon, his eyes on the prisoner. The shades were drawn and the bed was still unmade. Peter Lake was handcuffed to a chair. His back was to the window. No one had treated the cuts on Lake's face and the blood had dried, making him look like a badly defeated fighter. Lake should have been scared. Instead, he looked like he was in charge of the situation.

"Thanks for coming, Ray."

"What's going on, Pete? This is crazy. You murdered Sandy and Melody?"

"I had to, Ray. I explained that to the police. You know I wouldn't have killed them if I had a choice."

"That sweet little girl. How can you live with yourself?"

Lake shrugged his shoulders. "That's really beside the point, Ray. I'm not going to prison, and you're going to see to that."

"It's out of my hands, Pete. You killed three people. You're morally responsible for Waters's death. I can't do anything for you."

Lake smiled. "Then why are you here?"

"To ask you to tell the police where you're keeping the other women."

"No can do, Ray. My life depends on keeping the cops in the dark."

"You'd let three innocent women die?"

Lake shrugged. "Three dead, six dead. They can't punish me anymore after the first life sentence. I don't envy you, Ray. Believe me when I say that I wish I didn't have to put an old friend, whom I admire deeply, in this position. But I won't tell you where the women are if I don't get my pardon. And, believe me, every minute counts. Those women are mighty hungry and mighty thirsty by now. I can't guarantee how much longer they'll last without food and water."

Colby sat on the bed across from Lake. He bent forward, his forearms resting on his knees and his hands clasped in front of him.

"I do consider myself your friend, Pete. I still can't believe what I'm hearing. As a friend, I beg you to save those women. I promise I'll intercede on your behalf with the authorities. Maybe a plea to manslaughter can be worked out."

Lake shook his head. "No prison. Not one day. I
know what happens in jail to a man who's raped a
woman. I wouldn't last a week."

"You're expecting a miracle, Pete. How can I let you
go free?"

"Look, Ray, I'll make this simple for you. I walk or
the women die. There's no other alternative, and you're
using up valuable time jawing with me."

Colby hunched his shoulders. He stared at the floor.
Lake's smile widened.

"What are your terms?" Colby asked.

"I want a pardon for every crime I committed in
New York State and immunity from prosecution for every
conceivable crime the authorities can think up in the future. I want the pardon in writing and I want a videotape
of you signing it. I want the original of the tape and the
pardon given to a lawyer I'll choose.

"I want immunity from prosecution in federal
court . . ."

"I can't guarantee that. I have no authority to . . ."

"Call the U.S. attorney or the attorney general. Call
the President. This is non-negotiable. I'm not going to get
hit with a federal charge for violation of civil rights."

"I'll see what I can do."

"That's all I ask. But if you don't do what I want, the
women die.

"There's one other thing. I want a guarantee that the
State of New York will pay any civil judgments if I get
sued by the survivors or Cross's husband. I'm not going
to lose any money over this. Attorney fees, too."

Lake's last remark helped the governor see Lake for
what he was. The handsome, urbane young man with
whom he had dined and played golf was the disguise
worn by a monster. Colby felt rage replacing the numb-
ness he'd experienced since learning Lake's true nature.

Colby stood. "I have to know how much time those
women have, so I can tell the attorney general how
quickly we must act."

"I'm not going to tell you, Ray. You're not getting
any information from me until I have what I want. But,"
Lake said with a smile, "I will tell you to hurry."

3

The police cars and ambulances bounced along the unpaved back road, their sirens blaring in hopes that the
captive women would hear them and take heart. There
were three ambulances, each with a team of doctors and
nurses. Governor Colby and Larry Merrill were riding
with Chief O'Malley and Wayne Turner. Frank Grimsbo
was driving another police car with Nancy Gordon riding
shotgun. In the back of that car was Herb Carstairs, an
attorney Lake had retained. A videotape of Governor
Colby signing a pardon and a copy of the pardon with an
addendum signed by the United States attorney rested in
Carstairs's safe. Next to Carstairs, in leg irons and handcuffs, sat Peter Lake, who seemed indifferent to the high-
speed ride.

The cavalcade rounded a curve in the country road
and Nancy saw the farmhouse. It looked deserted. The
front yard was overgrown and the paint was peeling. To
the right of the house, across a dusty strip of yard, was a
dilapidated barn.

Nancy was out and ·running as soon as the car
stopped. She raced up the steps of the house and kicked
in the front door. Medics and doctors raced after her.
Lake had said the women were in the basement. Nancy
found the basement door and threw it open. A stench of

urine, excrement and unwashed bodies hit her and she gagged. Then she took a deep breath and yelled, "Police. You're safe," as she started down the stairs, two at a time, stopping her headlong rush the moment she saw what was in the basement.

Nancy felt like someone had punched a hole through her chest and torn out her heart. Later it occurred to her that her reaction must have been similar to the reactions of the servicemen who liberated the Nazi concentration camps. The basement windows were painted black and the only light came from bare bulbs that hung from the ceiling. A section of the basement was divided by plywood walls into six small stalls. Three of the stalls were empty. All of the stalls were covered with straw and outfitted with dirty mattresses. A videotape camera sat on a tripod outside each of the three occupied stalls. In addition to the mattress, each stall contained a cheap clock, a plastic water bottle with a plastic straw, and a dog food dish. The water bottles looked empty. Nancy could see the remains of some kind of gruel in the dishes.

Toward the rear of the basement was an open area. In it was a mattress covered with a sheet and a large table. Nancy could not make out all of the instruments on the table, but one of them was definitely a cattle prod.

Nancy stepped aside as the doctors rushed past her. She stared at the three survivors. The women were naked. Their feet were chained to the wall at the ankles. The chain extended just far enough to reach the water bottle and dog food dish. The women in the first two stalls lay on their side on their mattress. Their eyes seemed to be floating in the sockets. Nancy could see their ribs. There were burn marks and bruises everywhere. The woman in the third stall was Samantha Reardon. She huddled against the wall, her face expressionless, staring blankly at her rescuers.

Nancy walked slowly to the bottom of the stairs. She recognized Ann Hazelton only from her red hair. Her legs were drawn up to her chest in a fetal position and she was whimpering pitifully. Ann's husband had furnished a photograph of her standing on the eighteenth hole of their country club golf course, a smile on her face and a yellow ribbon holding back her long red hair.

Gloria Escalante was in the second stall. There was no expression on her face, but Nancy saw tears in her eyes as a doctor bent next to her to check her vital signs and a policeman went to work on her shackles.

Nancy began to shake. Wayne Turner walked up behind her and put his hands on her arms.

"Come on," he said gently, "we're just in the way."

Nancy let herself be led up the stairs into the light. Governor Colby had glanced into the basement for a moment, then backed out of the farmhouse into the fresh air. His skin was gray and he was sitting on one of the steps that led up to the porch, looking like he did not have the strength to stand.

Nancy looked across the yard. She spotted the car holding Lake. Frank Grimsbo was standing guard outside it. Lake's attorney had wandered off to smoke. Nancy walked past the governor. He asked her if the women were all right, but she did not answer. Wayne Turner walked beside her. "Let it be, Nancy," he said. Nancy ignored him.

Frank Grimsbo looked up expectantly. "They're all alive," Turner said. Nancy bent down and looked at Lake. The back window was open a crack, so the prisoner could breathe in the stifling heat. Lake turned toward Nancy. He was rested and at peace, knowing he would soon be free.

Lake smirked, goading her with his eyes but saying nothing. If he expected Nancy to rage at him, he was

mistaken. Her face was blank, but her eyes bored into
Lake. "It's not over," she said. Then she stood up and
walked toward a stand of trees on the side of the house
away from the barn. With her back to the farmhouse, all
she could see was beauty. There was cool shade under
the greenery. The smell of grass and wildflowers. A bird
sang. The horror Nancy felt when she saw the captive
women was gone. Her anger was gone. She knew the
future and was not afraid of it. No woman would ever
have to fear Peter Lake again, because Peter Lake was a
dead man.

4

Nancy Gordon wore a black jogging outfit, her white
Nikes were coated with black shoe polish, and her short
hair was held back by a navy blue head band, making her
impossible to see in the dim light of the quarter moon
that hung over The Meadows. Her car was parked on a
quiet side street. Nancy locked it and loped through a
back yard. She was strung tight and conscious of every
sound. A dog barked, but the houses on either side stayed
dark.

Until Peter Lake came into her life, Nancy Gordon
had never hated another human being. She wasn't even
certain she hated Lake. What she felt went beyond hate.
From the moment she saw those women in the farmhouse
basement, Nancy knew Lake had to be removed, the
same way vermin were removed.

Nancy was a cop, sworn to uphold the law. She respected the law. But this situation was so far outside normal human experience that she did not feel everyday laws
applied. No one could do what Peter Lake had done to

those women and walk away. She could not be expected
to wait day after day for the newspaper that brought news
of the next disappearance. She knew the minute Lake's
body was found she would be a prime suspect. God
knows, she did not want to spend the rest of her life in
prison, but there was no alternative. If she was caught, so
be it. If she killed Lake and walked away, it was God's
will. She could live with the consequences of her act. She
could not live with the consequences of letting Peter
Lake go free.

Nancy circled behind Lake's two-story colonial by
skirting the man-made lake. The houses on either side of
Lake's were dark, but there were lights on in his living
room. Nancy glanced at her digital watch. It was three-
thirty a.m. Lake should be asleep. Nancy knew the security system in the house was equipped with automatic
timers for the lights and decided to gamble that that was
why the living room was lit.

Nancy crouched down and ran across the back yard.
When she reached the house, she pressed herself against
the side wall. She was holding a .38 Ed had seized from a
drug dealer two years ago. Ed never reported the seizure
and the gun could not be traced to her.

Nancy crept around to the front door. She had studied the crime scene photographs earlier that evening.
Mentally, she walked herself through Lake's house, remembering as much as she could about the layout from
her only visit. She had learned Lake's alarm code during
the murder investigation. The alarm panel was to the
right of the door. She would have to disarm it quickly.

The street in front of Lake's house was deserted.
Nancy had taken Sandra Lake's keys from an evidence
locker at the police station. She turned the front door key
in the lock, then took out a penlight. Nancy grasped the
doorknob with her free hand, took a deep breath, and

pushed it open. The alarm emitted a screeching sound. She trained the penlight on the keyboard and punched in the code. The sound stopped. Nancy swung around and held her gun out. Nothing. She exhaled, switched off the penlight and straightened.

A quick tour of the ground floor confirmed Nancy's guess about the lights in the living room. After making certain no one was downstairs, Nancy edged up the stairs, her gun leading the way. The second floor was dark. The first room on the left was Lake's bedroom. When she came level with the landing, she saw his door was closed.

Nancy approached the door slowly, walking carefully even though the carpet muffled her footfalls. She paused next to the door and walked through the shooting in her head. Ease open the door, switch on the light, then shoot into Lake until the gun was empty. She breathed in and exhaled as she opened the door, an inch at a time.

Her eyes adjusted to the dark. She could see the outline of the king-size bed that dominated the room. Nancy cleared her mind of hate and all other feelings. She removed herself from the action. She was not killing a person. She was shooting into an object. Just like target practice. Nancy slipped into the room, hit the switch and aimed.

Part Six

AVENGING ANGEL

Chapter Nineteen

"The bed was empty," Wayne Turner told Betsy. "Lake was gone. He started planning his disappearance the day after he murdered his wife and daughter. All but one of his bank accounts had been emptied the day after the murder and several of his real estate holdings had been sold. His lawyer was handling the sale of his house. Carstairs said he didn't know where Lake was. No one could compel him to tell, anyway, because of the attorney-client privilege. We assumed that Carstairs had instructions to send the money he collected to accounts in Switzerland or the Caymans."

"Chief O'Malley called me immediately," Senator Colby said. "I was sick. Signing Lake's pardon was the most difficult thing I've ever done, but I couldn't think of anything else to do. I couldn't let those women die. When O'Malley told me Lake had disappeared all I could think of was the innocent victims he might claim because of me."

"Why didn't you go public?" Betsy asked. "You could have let everyone know who Lake was and what he'd done."

"Only a few people knew Lake was the rose killer and we were sworn to silence by the terms of the pardon."

"Once the women were free, why didn't you say to hell with him and go public anyway?"

Colby looked into the fire. His voice sounded hollow when he answered.

"We discussed the possibility, but we were afraid. Lake said he would take revenge by killing someone if we breached our agreement with him."

"Going public would have destroyed the senator's career," Wayne Turner added, "and none of us wanted that. Only a handful of people knew about the pardon or Lake's guilt. O'Malley, Gordon, Grimsbo, me, the U.S. attorney, the attorney general, Carstairs, Merrill and the senator. We never even told the mayor. We knew how courageous Ray had been to sign the pardon. We didn't want him to suffer for it. So we took a vow to protect Ray and we've kept it."

"And you just forgot about Lake?"

"We never forgot, Mrs. Tannenbaum," Colby told her. "I used contacts in the Albany Police and the FBI to hunt for Lake. Nancy Gordon dedicated her life to tracking him down. He was too clever for us."

"Now that you know about the pardon, what are you planning to do?" Turner asked.

"I don't know."

"If the pardon, and these new murders, become public knowledge, Senator Colby cannot be confirmed. He'd lose the support of the law-and-order conservatives on the Judiciary Committee and the liberals will crucify him. This would be the answer to their prayers."

"I realize that."

"Going public can't help your client, either."

"Wayne," Colby said, "Mrs. Tannenbaum is going to have to make up her own mind about what to do with what she knows. We can't pressure her. God knows, she's under enough pressure as it is.

"But," Colby said, turning to Betsy, "I do have a question for you. I have the impression that you deduced the existence of the pardon."

"That's right. I asked myself how Lake could have walked away from Hunter's Point. A pardon was the only answer and only the governor of New York could issue a pardon. You could keep the existence of a pardon from the public, but the members of the task force would have to know about it and they're the ones who were rewarded. It was the only answer that made sense."

"Lake doesn't know you're here, does he?"

Betsy hesitated, then said, "No."

"And you haven't asked him to confirm your guess, have you?"

Betsy shook her head.

"Why?"

"Do you remember the conflicting emotions you felt when Lake asked you to pardon him? Imagine how I feel, Senator. I'm a very good attorney. I have the skills to free my client. He maintains his innocence, but my investigation turned up evidence that made me question his word. Until today, I didn't know for certain if Martin was lying. I didn't want to confront him until I knew the truth."

"Now that you know, what will you do?"

"I haven't worked that out yet. If it was any other case, I wouldn't care. I'd do my job and defend my client. But this isn't any case. This is . . ."

Betsy paused. What could she say that everyone in the room did not know firsthand.

"I don't envy you, Mrs. Tannenbaum," the senator said. "I really believe I had no choice. That is the only reason I've been able to live with what I did, even though I regret what I did every time I think of the pardon. You can walk away from Lake."

"Then I'd be walking away from my responsibilities, wouldn't I?"

"Responsibilities," Colby repeated. "Why do we take them on? Why do we burden ourselves with problems that tear us apart? Whenever I think of Lake I wish I hadn't gone into public life. Then I think of some of the good I've been able to do."

The senator paused. After a moment he stood up and held out his hand. "It's been a pleasure meeting you, Mrs. Tannenbaum. I mean that."

"Thank you for your candor, Senator."

"Wayne can drive you back to your hotel."

Wayne Turner followed Betsy out of the room. Colby sank back down into the armchair. He felt old and used up. He wanted to stay in front of the fire forever and forget the responsibilities about which he had just spoken. He thought about Betsy Tannenbaum's responsibility to her client and her responsibilities as a member of the human race. How would she live with herself if Lake was acquitted? He would haunt her for the rest of her life, the way Lake haunted him.

Colby wondered if the pardon would become public. If it did, he would be finished in public life. The President would withdraw his nomination and he would never be reelected. Strangely, he was not concerned. He had no control over Betsy Tannenbaum. His fate rested with the decisions she made.

Chapter Twenty

―――――――

I

"Dr. Simon Reardon?"

"Yes."

"My name is Reginald Stewart. I'm a private investigator. I work for Betsy Tannenbaum, an attorney in Portland, Oregon."

"I don't know anyone in Portland."

Dr. Reardon sounded annoyed. Stewart thought he detected a slight British accent.

"This is about Hunter's Point and your ex-wife, Dr. Reardon. That's where I'm calling from. I hope you'll give me a few minutes to explain."

"I have no interest in discussing Samantha."

"Please hear me out. Do you remember Peter Lake?"

"Mr. Stewart, there is nothing about those days I can ever forget."

"Three women were kidnapped in Portland recently. A black rose and a note that said 'Gone, But Not Forgotten' were left at each scene. The women's bodies were dug up recently on property belonging to Peter Lake. He's been charged with the homicides."

"I thought the Hunter's Point police caught the murderer. Wasn't he some retarded deliveryman? A sex offender?"

"The Multnomah County d.a. thinks the Hunter's Point police made a mistake. I'm trying to find the Hunter's Point survivors. Ann Hazelton is dead. Gloria Escalante won't talk to me. Mrs. Reardon is my last hope."

"It's not Mrs. Reardon and hasn't been for some time," the doctor said with distaste, "and I have no idea how you can find Samantha. I moved to Minneapolis to get away from her. We haven't spoken in years. The last I heard, she was still living in Hunter's Point."

"You're divorced?"

Reardon laughed harshly. "Mr. Stewart, this was more than a simple divorce. Samantha tried to kill me."

"What?"

"She's a sick woman. I wouldn't waste my time on her. You can't trust anything she says."

"Was this entirely a result of the kidnapping?"

"Undoubtedly her torture and captivity exacerbated the condition, but my wife was always unbalanced. Unfortunately I was too much in love with her to notice until we were married. I kept rationalizing and excusing . . ." Reardon took a deep breath. "I'm sorry. She does that to me. Even after all these years."

"Dr. Reardon, I don't want to make you uncomfortable, but Mr. Lake is facing a death sentence and I need to know as much about Hunter's Point as I can."

"Can't the police tell you what you want to know?"

"No, sir. The files are missing."

"That's strange."

"Yes, it is. Believe me, if I had those files I wouldn't be bothering you. I'm sure it's painful having me dig up this period in your life, but this is literally a matter of life and death. Our d.a. has a bee in his bonnet about Mr. Lake. Peter was a victim, just like you, and he needs your help."

Reardon sighed. "Go ahead. Ask your questions."

"Thank you, sir. Can you tell me about Mrs. Reardon, or whatever she calls herself now?"

"I have no idea what her name is. She still called herself Reardon when I left Hunter's Point."

"When was that?"

"About eight years ago. As soon as the divorce was final."

"What happened between you and your wife?"

"She was a surgical nurse at University Hospital. Very beautiful, very wanton. Sex was what she was best at," Reardon said bitterly. "I was so caught up in her body that I was oblivious to what was going on around me. The most obvious problem was the stealing. She was arrested for shoplifting twice. Our lawyer kept the cases out of court and I paid off the stores. She was totally without remorse. Treated the incidents like jokes, once she was in the clear.

"Then there was the spending. I was making good money, but we were in debt up to our ears. She drained my savings accounts, charged our credit cards to the limit. It took me four years after the divorce to get back on my feet. And you couldn't reason with her. I showed her the bills and drew up a budget. She'd get me in bed and I'd forget what I'd told her, or she'd throw a tantrum or lock me out of the bedroom. It was the worst three years of my life.

"Then she was kidnapped and tortured and she got

worse. Whatever slender string kept her tethered to reality snapped during the time she was a prisoner. I can't even describe what she was like after that. They kept her hospitalized for almost a year. She rarely spoke. She wouldn't let men near her.

"I should have known better, but I took her home after she was released. I felt guilty because of what had happened. I know I couldn't have protected her—I was at the hospital when she was kidnapped—but, still, you can see how . . ."

"That's very common, that feeling."

"Oh, I know. But knowing something intellectually and dealing with it emotionally are two different things. I wish I had been wiser."

"What happened after she came home?"

"She wouldn't share a bedroom with me. When I was home, she would stay in her room. I have no idea what she did when I was at work. When she did speak, she was clearly irrational. She insisted that the man who kidnapped her was still at large. I showed her the newspaper articles about Waters's arrest and the shooting, but she said he wasn't the man. She wanted a gun for protection. Of course I refused. She started accusing me of being in a conspiracy with the police. Then she tried to kill me. She stabbed me with a kitchen knife when I came home from the hospital. Fortunately a colleague was with me. She stabbed him too, but he hit Samantha and stunned her. We wrestled her to the floor. She was writhing and screeching about . . . She said I was trying to kill her . . . It was very hard for me. I had to commit her. Then I decided to get out."

"I don't blame you. It looks like you went above and beyond the call."

"Yes, I did. But I still feel bad about deserting her, even though I know I had no choice."

"You said you committed her. Which hospital was that?"

"St. Jude's. It's a private psychiatric hospital near Hunter's Point. I moved and cut off contact with her completely. I know she was there for several years, but I believe she was released."

"Did Samantha try to contact you after she was released?"

"No. I dreaded the possibility, but it never happened."

"Would you happen to have a photo of Samantha? There weren't any in the newspaper accounts."

"When I moved to Minnesota, I threw them away, along with everything else that might remind me of Samantha."

"Thank you for your time, Doctor. I'll try St. Jude's. Maybe they have a line on your ex-wife."

"One other thing, Mr. Stewart. If you find Samantha, please don't tell her you talked with me or tell her where I am."

2

Randy Highsmith drove straight to the district attorney's office from the airport. He was feeling the effects of jet lag and wouldn't have minded going home, but he knew how badly Page wanted to hear what he had found out in Hunter's Point.

"It's not good, Al," Highsmith said as soon as they were sitting down. "I was a day behind Darius's investigator everywhere I went, so he knows what we know."

"Which is?"

"Nancy Gordon wasn't straight with you. Frank

Grimsbo and Wayne Turner told me only Gordon considered Lake a serious suspect. She was fixated on him and
never accepted Waters as the rose killer, but everyone
else did.

"There's something else she didn't tell us. Three of
the Hunter's Point women didn't die. Hazelton, Escalante and Reardon were found alive in an old farmhouse.
And, before you ask, Hazelton is dead, I haven't located
Reardon and Escalante never saw the face of the man
who abducted her."

"Why did she let me think all the Hunter's Point
women were murdered?"

"I have no idea. All I know is that our case against
Martin Darius is turning to shit."

"It doesn't make sense," Page said, more to himself
than to Highsmith. "Waters is dead. If he was the rose
killer, who murdered the women we found at the construction site? It had to be someone who knew details
about the Hunter's Point case that only the police knew.
That description only fits one person, Martin Darius."

"There is one other person it fits, Al," Highsmith
said.

"Who?"

"Nancy Gordon."

"Are you crazy? She's a cop."

"What if she's crazy? What if she did it to frame
Darius? Think about it. Would you have considered Darius a suspect if she didn't tell you he was Lake?"

"You're forgetting the anonymous letter that told her
that the killer was in Portland."

"How do we know she didn't write it herself?"

"I don't believe it."

"Well, believe it or not, our case is disappearing. Oh,
and there's a new wrinkle. A Portland private investigator

named Sam Oberhurst was looking into the Hunter's Point murders about a month before the first Portland disappearance."

"Whom did he represent?"

"He didn't say and he didn't tell anyone why he was asking about the case, but I'm going to ask him. I have his phone number and I'll get the address through the phone company."

"Have they had any luck with the files?"

"None at all."

Page closed his eyes and rested his head against the back of his chair.

"I'm going to look like a fool, Randy. We'll have to dismiss. I should have listened to you and Ross. We never had a case. It was all in my head."

"Don't fold yet, Al. This p.i. could know something."

Page shook his head. He had aged since his divorce. His energy had deserted him. For a while this case had recharged him, but Darius was slipping away and he would soon be a laughingstock in the legal community.

"We're going to lose this one, Randy. I can feel it. Gordon was all we had and now it looks like we never had her."

3

"Hi, Mom," Betsy said, putting down her suitcase and hugging Rita Cohen.

"How was your flight? Have you had anything to eat?"

"The flight was fine and I ate on the plane."

"That's not food. You want me to fix you something?"

"Thanks, but I'm not hungry," Betsy said as she hung up her coat. "How was Kathy?"

"So-so. Rick took her to the movies on Saturday."

"How is he?" Betsy asked, hoping she sounded disinterested.

"The louse wouldn't look me in the eye the whole time he was here. He couldn't wait to escape."

"You weren't rude to him?"

"I didn't give him the time of day," Rita answered, pointing her nose in the air. Then she shook her head.

"Poor kid. Kathy was all excited when she left with him, but she was down in the dumps as soon as he dropped her off. She moped around, picked at her food at dinner."

"Did anything else happen while I was gone?" Betsy asked, hoping there had been some good news.

"Nora Sloane came by, Sunday evening," Rita said, smiling mischievously. "I told all."

"What did she ask about?"

"Your childhood, your cases. She was very good with Kathy."

"She seems like a nice woman. I hope her article sells. She's certainly working hard enough on it."

"Oh, before I forget, when you go to school, talk to Mrs. Kramer. Kathy was in a fight with another little girl and she's been disruptive in class."

"I'll see her this afternoon," Betsy said. She sounded defeated. Kathy was usually an angel at school. You didn't have to be Sigmund Freud to see what was happening.

"Cheer up," Rita told her. "She's a good kid. She's just going through a rough time. Look, you've got an hour before school lets out. Have some coffee cake. I'll make you a cup of decaf and you can tell me about your trip."

Betsy glanced at her watch and decided to give in.

Eating cake was a surefire way of dealing with depression.

"Okay. I am hungry, I guess. You fix everything. I want to change."

"Now you're talking," Rita said with a smile. "And, for your information, Kathy won the fight. She told me."

Chapter Twenty-one

When Betsy Tannenbaum was a very little girl, she would not go to sleep until her mother showed her that there were no monsters in her closet or under her bed. The stage passed quickly. Betsy stopped believing in monsters. Then she met Martin Darius. What made Darius so terrifying was his dissimilarity to the slavering, fanged deformities that lurked in the shadows in her room. Give one hundred people the autopsy photographs and not one of them would believe that the elegantly-dressed gentleman standing in the doorway to Betsy's office was capable of cutting off Wendy Reiser's nipples or using a cattle prod to torture Victoria Miller. Even knowing what she knew, Betsy had to force herself to make the connection. But Betsy did know, and the shining winter sun could not keep her from feeling as frightened as the very little girl who used to listen for monsters in the dark.

"Sit down Mr. Darius," Betsy said.

"We're back to Mr. Darius, are we? This must be serious."

Betsy did not smile. Darius looked at her quizzically, but took a seat without making any more remarks.

"I'm resigning as your attorney."

"I thought we agreed that you'd only do that if you

believed I was guilty of murdering Farrar, Reiser and Miller."

"I firmly believe you killed them. I know everything about Hunter's Point."

"What's everything?"

"I spent the weekend in Washington, D.C., talking to Senator Colby."

Darius nodded appreciatively. "I'm impressed. You unraveled the whole Hunter's Point affair in no time at all."

"I don't give a damn for your flattery, Darius. You lied to me from day one. There are some lawyers who don't care whom they represent as long as the fee is large enough. I'm not one of them. Have your new attorney call me so I can get rid of your file. I don't want anything in my office that reminds me of you."

"My, aren't we self-righteous. You're sure you know everything, aren't you?"

"I know enough to distrust anything you tell me."

"I'm a little disappointed, Tannenbaum. You worked your way through this puzzle part of the way, then shut down that brilliant mind of yours just as you came to the part that needs solving."

"What are you talking about?"

"I'm talking about having faith in your client. I'm talking about not walking away from someone who desperately needs your help. I am *not* guilty of killing Reiser, Farrar and Miller. If you don't prove I'm innocent, the real killer is going to walk away, just the way I did in Hunter's Point."

"You admit you're guilty of those atrocities in Hunter's Point?"

Darius shrugged. "How can I deny it, now that you've talked to Colby?"

"How could you do it? Animals don't treat other animals like that."

Darius looked amused. "Do I fascinate you, Tannenbaum?"

"No, Mr. Darius, you disgust me."

"Then why ask me about Hunter's Point?"

"I want to know why you thought you had the right to walk into someone else's life and turn the rest of their days on Earth into Hell. I want to understand how you could destroy the lives of those poor women so casually."

Darius stopped smiling. "There was nothing casual about what I did."

"What I can't understand is how a mind like yours or Speck's or Bundy's works. What could possibly make you feel so badly about yourself that you can only keep going by dehumanizing women?"

"Don't compare me to Bundy or Speck. They were pathetic failures. Thoroughly inadequate personalities. I'm neither insane nor inadequate. I was a successful attorney in Hunter's Point and a successful businessman here."

"Then why did you do it?"

Darius hesitated. He seemed to be in a debate with himself. "Am I still covered by the attorney-client privilege?" Betsy nodded. "Anything I tell you is between us?" Betsy nodded again. "Because I'd like to tell you. You have a superior mind and a female viewpoint. Your reactions would be informative."

Betsy knew she should throw Darius out of her office and her life, but her fascination with him paralyzed her intellect. When she remained silent, Darius settled back in his chair.

"I was conducting an experiment, Tannenbaum. I wanted to know what it felt like to be God. I don't remember the exact moment the idea for the experiment germinated. I do remember a trip Sandy and I took to Barbados. Lying on the beach, I thought about how perfect my life was. There was my job, which provided me with more money than I ever dreamed of, and there was Sandy, still sexy as all get-out, even after bearing my lovely Melody. My Sandy, so willing to please, so mindless. I'd married her for her body and never checked under the hood until it was too late."

Darius shook his head wistfully.

"Perfect is boring, Tannenbaum. Sex with the same woman, day after day, no matter how beautiful and skilled she is, is boring. I've always had an intense fantasy life and I wondered what it would be like if my fantasy world was real. Would my life be different? Would I discover what I was searching for? I decided to find out what would happen if I brought my fantasy world to life.

"It took me months to find the farmhouse. I couldn't trust workmen, so I built the stalls myself. Then I selected the women. I chose only worthless women. Women who lived off their husbands like parasites. Beautiful, spoiled women who used their looks to entice a man into marriage, then drained him of his wealth and self-respect. These women were born again in my little dungeon. Their stall became their world and I became their sun, moon, wind and rain."

Betsy remembered Colby's description of the women he had seen. Their hollow eyes, the protruding ribs. She remembered the vacant stares on the faces of the dead women in the photographs.

"I admit I was cruel to them, but I had to dehumanize them so they could be molded in the image I chose. When I appeared, I wore a mask and I made them wear leather masks with no eyeholes. Once a week I doled out rations scientifically calculated to keep them on the brink of starvation. I limited the hours they could sleep.

"Did Colby mention the clocks and the videotape machines? Did you wonder what they were for? It was my crowning touch. I had a wife and child and a job, so I could only be with my subjects for short periods each week, but I wanted total control, omniscience, even when I was gone. So I rigged the videotapes to run when I wasn't there and I gave the women commands to perform. They had to watch the clock. Every hour, at set times, they would bow to the camera and perform dog tricks, rolling over, squatting, masturbating. Whatever I commanded. I reviewed the tapes and I punished deviations firmly."

Darius had an enraptured look on his face. His eyes were fixed on a scene no sane person could imagine. Betsy felt she would shatter if she moved.

"I changed them from demanding cows to obedient puppies. They were mine completely. I bathed them. They ate like dogs from a doggy bowl. They were forbidden to speak unless I told them to, and the only time I let them was to beg me for punishment and thank me for pain. In the end they would do anything to escape the pain. They pleaded to drink my urine and kissed my foot when I let them."

Darius's face was so tight Betsy thought his skin might rip. A wave of nausea made her stomach roll.

"Some of the women resisted, but they soon learned that there can be no negotiations with a god. Others obeyed immediately. Cross, for instance. She was no challenge at all. A perfect cow. As docile and unimaginative as a lump of clay. That's why I chose her for my sacrifice."

Before Darius started speaking, Betsy assumed there was nothing he could say that she would not be able to handle, but she did not want to hear any more.

"Did your experiment bring you peace?" Betsy

asked to stop Darius from talking about the women. Her breathing was ragged and she felt light-headed. Darius snapped out of his trance.

"The experiment brought me the most exquisite pleasure, Tannenbaum. The moments I shared with those women were the finest moments in my life. But Sandy found the note and it had to end. There was too much danger of being caught. Then I was caught, and then I was free, and that freedom was exhilarating."

"When was the next time you repeated the experiment, Martin?" Betsy asked coldly.

"Never. I wanted to, but I learn from experience. I had one lucky break and I was not going to risk life in prison or the death penalty."

Betsy stared at Darius with contempt.

"I want you out of my office. I don't ever want to see you again."

"You can't quit, Tannenbaum. I need you."

"Hire Oscar Montoya or Matthew Reynolds."

"Oscar Montoya and Matthew Reynolds are good lawyers, but they aren't women. I'm banking that no jury will believe that an ardent feminist would represent a man who treated a woman the way the murderer treated Reiser, Farrar and Miller. In a close case, you're my edge."

"Then you just lost your edge, Darius. You're the most vile person I've ever known. I don't ever want to see you again, let alone defend you."

"You're reneging on our deal. I told you, I did not murder Farrar, Reiser or Vicky Miller. Someone is framing me. If I'm convicted, this case will be closed and you'll be responsible for the killer's next victim and the one after that."

"Do you think I'll believe anything you say after what you just told me, after all your lies?"

"Listen, Tannenbaum," Darius said, leaning across the desk and pinning Betsy with an intense stare, "I did not kill those women. I'm being set up by someone and I'm pretty certain I know who she is."

"She?"

"Only Nancy Gordon knows enough about this case to frame me. Vicky, Reiser, those women would never have suspected her. She's female. She'd flash her badge. They'd let her in easy. That's why there were no signs of a struggle at the crime scenes. They probably went with her willingly and didn't know what was happening until it was too late."

"No woman would do what was done to those women."

"Don't be naive. She's been obsessed with me since Hunter's Point. She's probably insane."

Betsy remembered what she had learned about Nancy Gordon. The woman had tried to murder Darius in Hunter's Point. She had dedicated her life to finding him. But, to frame him like this? From what she knew, it was more likely that Gordon would have walked up to Darius and shot him.

"I don't buy it."

"You know Vicky left the Hacienda Motel at two-thirty. I was with Russell Miller and several other people at the advertising agency until almost five."

"Who can alibi you after .you left the ad agency?"

"Unfortunately, no one."

"I'm not going to do it. You stand for everything in life I find repulsive. Even if you didn't kill the women in Portland, you did commit those inhuman crimes in Hunter's Point."

"And you are going to be responsible for murdering the next victim in Portland. Think about it, Tannenbaum. There's no case against me now. That means another woman will have to die to supply the evidence the State can use to convict me."

That evening Kathy snuggled close to Betsy, her attention riveted on a cartoon special. Betsy kissed the top of her daughter's head and wondered how this peaceful scene could coexist with a reality where women, curled up in the dark, waited for a torturer to bring them unbearable pain? How could she meet with a man like Martin Darius at work and watch Disney with her daughter at home without losing her sanity? How could Peter Lake spend the morning as the horror god of a warped fantasy and the evening playing with his own little girl?

Betsy wished there was only one reality: the one where she and Rick sat watching Disney with Kathy squirreled between them. The one she thought was reality before Rick walked out on her and she met Martin Darius.

Betsy had always been able to separate herself from her work. Before Darius, her criminal clients were more pathetic than frightening. She represented shoplifters, drunk drivers, petty thieves and scared juveniles. She was still friendly with the two women she had saved from homicide charges. Even when she brought her work home with her, she saw it as something that was only temporarily in her house. Darius was in Betsy's soul. He had changed her. She no longer believed she was safe. And much worse, she knew Kathy was not safe either.

Chapter Twenty-two

I

St. Jude's looked more like an exclusive private school than a mental hospital. A high, ivy-covered wall stretched back into deep woods. The administration building, once the home of millionaire Alvin Piercy, was red brick, with recessed windows and gothic arches. Piercy, a devout Catholic, died a bachelor in 1916 and left his fortune to the church. In 1923 the mansion was converted into a retreat for priests in need of counseling. In 1953 a small, modern psychiatric hospital was constructed behind the house, which became the home of St. Jude's administration. From the gate, Reggie Stewart could see the administration building through the graceful limbs of the snow-covered trees that were scattered across the grounds. In the fall, the lawn would be a carpet of green and the tree limbs would be graced with leaves of gold and red.

Dr. Margaret Flint's office was at the end of a long corridor on the second floor. The window faced away from the hospital and toward the woods. Dr. Flint was an angular, horse-faced woman with shoulder-length gray hair.

"Thank you for seeing me," Stewart said.

Dr. Flint responded with an engaging smile that softened her homely features. She took Stewart's hand in a firm grip, then motioned him into one of two armchairs that were set up around a coffee table.

"I've often wondered what became of Samantha Reardon. She was such an unusual case. Unfortunately there was no follow-up, once she was released."

"Why is that?"

"Her husband refused to pay after the divorce and it wasn't covered by insurance. In any event, I doubt Samantha would have permitted me to pry into her affairs after she gained her freedom. She hated everything associated with the hospital."

"What can you tell me about Mrs. Reardon?"

"Normally I wouldn't tell you a thing, because of patient-doctor confidentiality rules, but your phone call raised the possibility that she may be a danger to others, and that takes precedence over those rules in certain circumstances."

"She may be involved in a series of murders in Portland."

"So you said. Is there a connection between the murders and her captivity in Hunter's Point?" Dr. Flint asked.

"Yes. How did you know?"

"I'll tell you in a moment. Please bear with me. I need to know the background of your request for information."

"A man named Peter Lake was the husband of one of the Hunter's Point victims and the father of another. He moved to Portland eight years ago so he could start a new life. Someone is duplicating the Hunter's Point m.o. in

Portland. Are you familiar with the way the Hunter's Point women were treated?"

"Of course. I was Samantha's treating psychiatrist. I had full access to the police reports."

"Dr. Flint, would Reardon be capable of subjecting other women to the torture she experienced in order to frame my client?"

"A good question. Not many women could go through torture, then subject another woman to that same experience, but Samantha Reardon was in no way normal. We all have personalities that are thoroughly ingrained. Our personalities are usually very difficult, if not impossible, to change. People with personality disorders have maladaptive personalities. The signs they present vary with the disorder.

"Prior to her horrible victimization, Samantha Reardon had what we call a borderline personality, which lies between a neurosis and a psychosis. At times she would exhibit psychotic behavior, but generally she would be seen as neurotic. She demonstrated perverse sexual interests, antisocial behavior, such as passing bad checks or shoplifting, anxiety, and strong self-centeredness. Her relationship with her ex-husband typifies this kind of behavior. There were periods of intense sexuality, frequent instability, and he found her impossible to reason with and totally self-centered. When she was caught stealing, she showed no interest in the charges, no remorse. She used sex to distract Dr. Reardon and gain favors from him. She destroyed his finances without regard to the long-term consequences for both of them. When Samantha was kidnapped and tortured she became psychotic. She is probably still in that state.

"Samantha saw St. Jude's as an extension of her captivity. I was the only doctor to whom she related, probably because I was the only female on the staff. Samantha

Reardon hates and distrusts all men. She was convinced that the Hunter's Point mayor, the police chief, the governor, even, at times, the President of the United States —all men—were conspiring to protect the man who tortured her."

"So," Stewart interjected, "it's possible she would act on these fantasies if she located the man she believed was responsible for her captivity?"

"Most certainly. When she was here, she spoke of nothing but revenge. She saw herself as an avenging angel arrayed against the forces of darkness. She hated her captor, but she is a danger to any man, because she sees them all as oppressors."

"But the women? How could she bring herself to torture those women after what she went through?"

"Samantha would see any means that furthered her ends as acceptable means, Mr. Stewart. If she had to sacrifice some women in the process of attaining her goal, in her eyes that would be a small price to pay for her revenge."

2

Rick was sitting in the waiting room when Betsy arrived at work. He seemed subdued.

"I know I'm not expected, but I wanted to talk. Are you busy?"

"Come in," Betsy told him. She was still angry with him for telling Kathy that her career was to blame for their separation.

"How's Kathy?" Rick asked, as he followed her into her office.

"There's an easy way to find out."

"Don't be like that. Actually, one of the reasons I stopped by is to ask if she can sleep over. I just moved into a new apartment and it has a guest room."

Betsy wanted to say no, because it would hurt Rick, but she knew how much Kathy missed her father.

"Fine."

"Thanks. I'll pick her up tomorrow, after work."

"What else did you want to talk about?"

Rick was uncomfortable. He looked down at the desktop.

"I . . . Betsy, this is very hard for me. The partnership, my job . . ." Rick paused. "I'm not doing this very well." He took a deep breath. "What I'm trying to say is that my life is in turmoil right now. I'm under so much pressure that I'm not thinking straight. This time by myself, it's given me some distance, some perspective. I guess what I'm saying is, don't give up on me. Don't close me out. . . ."

"I never wanted to do that, Rick. You're the one who closed me out."

"When I left, I said some things about how I felt about you that I didn't mean."

"When you're certain how you feel, tell me, Rick. But I can't promise how I'm going to feel. You hurt me very badly."

"I know," he said quietly. "Look, this merger I'm working on, it's got me tied up night and day, but I think everything will be under control in a month. I've got some time off in December and Kathy has Christmas vacation, so she wouldn't miss school. I thought maybe the three of us could go somewhere where we could be by ourselves."

Betsy's breath caught in her chest. She didn't know what to say.

Rick stood up. "I know I sprang this on you without

any warning. You don't have to answer me right away. We have time. Just promise me you'll think about it."

"I will."

"Good. And thanks for letting me see Kathy."

"You're her father," Betsy said.

Betsy opened the office door before Rick could say anything else. Nora Sloane was standing next to Ann's desk.

"Do you have a minute?" Sloane asked.

"Rick was just leaving," Betsy answered.

Sloane stared at Rick for a second.

"Are you Mr. Tannenbaum?"

"Yes."

"This is Nora Sloane," Betsy said. "She's working on an article about women litigators for *Pacific West* magazine."

"Your wife has been a wonderful help."

Rick smiled politely. "I'll pick up Kathy around six and take her to dinner," he told Betsy. "Don't forget to pack her school things. Nice meeting you, Ms. Sloane."

"Wait," Betsy said. "I don't have the address and phone number at your new place."

Rick gave them to her and Betsy wrote them down. Then Rick left.

"The reason I dropped in is to see if we can schedule some time to discuss the Hammermill case and your strategy in the Darius case," Sloane said.

"I hope this won't upset your plans, Nora, but I'm getting off Martin's case."

"Why?"

"Personal reasons I can't discuss with you."

"I don't understand."

"There's a conflict. Ethical problems are involved. I can't put it any other way without violating the attorney-client privilege."

Nora rubbed her forehead. She looked distracted.

"I'm sorry if this affects the article," Betsy said. "There isn't anything I can do about what happened."

"That's all right," Nora replied, quickly regaining her composure. "The Darius case isn't essential to the article."

Betsy opened her appointment book. "As soon as I'm officially off Martin's case, I'll have plenty of free time. Why don't we tentatively schedule a meeting for lunch next Wednesday?"

"That sounds fine. See you then."

The door closed and Betsy looked at the work on her desk. They were cases she'd had to put off because of Martin Darius. Betsy pulled the top case off a pile, but she did not open the file. She thought about Rick. He seemed different. Less self-assured. If he wanted to come back, would she let him?

The buzzer rang. Reggie Stewart was calling from Hunter's Point.

"How's tricks?" Stewart asked.

"Not so good, Reg. I'm off the case."

"Did Darius fire you?"

"No, it's the other way around."

"Why?"

"I found out Darius did kill the women in Hunter's Point."

"How?"

"I can't tell you."

"Jesus, Betsy, you can trust me."

"I know I can, but I'm not going to explain this, so don't press me."

"Well, I'm a little concerned. There's a possibility Darius is being framed. It turns out Samantha Reardon is a very weird lady. I talked to Simon Reardon, her ex. He's a neurosurgeon and she was one of his surgical

nurses. He became infatuated with her and the next thing
he knows, they're married and he's on the verge of bankruptcy. She's shoplifting like crazy, running up his credit
cards, and his lawyers are rushing around covering up the
lady's indiscretions. Then Darius kidnaps and tortures
her and she really goes over the edge. I met with Dr.
Flint, her shrink at St. Jude's. That's where she was committed after she tried to kill Reardon."

"What?"

"She knifed him and a friend he brought home. They
subdued her and she spent the next few years in a padded cell insisting that the man who kidnapped her was
still at large and she was the victim of a conspiracy."

"She was, Reg. The authorities covered up for Darius. I can't fill you in on the details, but Samantha may
not have been completely crazy."

"She may have been right about the cover-up *and*
insane. Dr. Flint thought she was mad as a hatter. Reardon was an abused child. Her father ran away when she
was two and her mother was a hopeless drunk. She
learned morals from a street gang she ran with. She has a
juvenile record for robbery and assault. That was a stab-
bing, too. She was smart enough to get through high
school without doing any real work. Her I.Q.'s been
tested at 146, which is a hell of a lot higher than mine,
but her school performance was lousy.

"There was an early marriage to Max Felix, a manager at a department store where she was working. I
called him and he tells the same story Dr. Reardon does.
She must be a great lay. Her first husband says he
couldn't see up from down while she was cleaning out his
bank account and charging him into debt. The marriage
only lasted a year.

"Next stop was a community college, then nursing
school, then the good doctor. Dr. Flint says Reardon had

a personality disorder—borderline personality—to begin with, and the stress from the torture and captivity made her psychotic. She was obsessed with avenging herself on her captor."

Betsy felt a queasy sensation in the pit of her stomach.

"Did you ask Dr. Flint if she would be capable of subjecting other women to the kind of torture she endured just to frame Darius?"

"According to Dr. Flint, it wouldn't bother her one bit to slice up those ladies, if that's what it took to accomplish her plan."

"It's so hard to believe, Reg. A woman doing those things to other women."

"It makes sense, though, Betsy. Think about it. Oberhurst interviews Reardon and shows her a photo of Darius; Reardon recognizes Darius and follows Oberhurst to Portland; she reads about the hassle Darius is having at the construction site and figures it's the ideal place to bury Oberhurst after she kills him; later, she adds the other bodies."

"I don't know, Reg. It still makes more sense for Darius to have killed them."

"What do you want me to do?"

"Try to get a picture of her. There weren't any in the newspaper accounts."

"I'm way ahead of you. I'm going to look at her college yearbook. She went to the State University in Hunter's Point, so that should be easy."

Stewart hung up, leaving Betsy very confused. Moments before, she was certain Darius had killed the Portland women. But if Reggie's suspicions were right, Darius was being framed, and everyone was being manipulated by a very intelligent and dangerous woman.

3

Randy Highsmith and Ross Barrow took I-84 down the Columbia River Gorge until they came to the turnoff for the scenic highway. Stark cliffs rose up on either side of the wide river. Waterfalls could occasionally be seen through breaks in the trees. The view was breathtaking, but Barrow was too busy trying to see through the slashing rain to enjoy it. The gusting winds that funneled down the gorge pushed the unmarked car sideways. Barrow fought the wheel and kept the car from skidding as he took the exit.

They were in country. National forest, farmland. The trees provided some protection from the rain, but Barrow still had to lean forward and squint to catch the occasional street signs.

"There," Randy Highsmith shouted, pointing to a mailbox with the address stuck on in cheap, iridescent numerals. Barrow turned the car sharply and the back wheels slid sideways on the gravel. The house Samuel Oberhurst was renting was supposed to be a quarter mile up this unpaved road. The rental agent had described it as a bungalow, but it was only a step up from a shack. Except for the privacy the surrounding countryside provided, Highsmith could not see a thing to recommend it. The house was square with a peaked roof. It may once have been painted red, but the weather had turned it rust-colored. A beat-up Pontiac was parked out front. No one had cut the grass in weeks. Cinder blocks served as front steps. There were two empty beer cans next to the steps and an empty pack of cigarettes wedged into a crack between two of the blocks.

Barrow pulled the car as close to the front door as he could and Highsmith jumped out, ducking his head, as if that would somehow protect him from the rain. He pounded on the door, waited, then pounded again.

"I'm going around the side," he yelled to Barrow. The detective cut the motor and followed him. The curtains on the front windows were closed. Highsmith and Barrow walked through the wet grass on the east side of the house and discovered that there were no windows on that side and the shades were down in the windows at the back. Barrow peered through a small window on the west side.

"Looks like a fucking sty in there," Barrow said.

"No one's home, that's for sure."

"What about the car?"

Highsmith shrugged. "Let's try the front door."

Water dripped off Highsmith's face and he could barely see through his glasses. The front door was not locked. Barrow let them in. Highsmith took off his glasses and dried the lenses with his handkerchief. Barrow turned on a light.

"Jesus!"

Highsmith put on his glasses. A television stood on a low stand under the front window. Across from it was a second-hand sofa. The upholstery was torn in spots, stuffing was coming out and it sagged. A full suit of men's clothes had been thrown on the sofa. Highsmith saw a jacket, underwear, a pair of pants. Next to the TV, fitted into the corner, was an old gray, stand-up filing cabinet. All the drawers were out and papers had been thrown around the room. Highsmith was suddenly distracted from the chaos in the front room. He sniffed the air.

"What's that smell?"

Barrow did not answer. He was concentrating on a heavy chair that lay on its side in the center of the room. As he edged around it, he could see bloodstains on the chair and the ground around it. Scraps of heavy tape that could have been used to secure a man's legs stuck out from the sides of the chair legs. On a table a few feet from the chair was a kitchen knife encrusted with blood.

"How's your stomach?" Barrow asked. "We've got a crime scene here and I don't want your breakfast all over it."

"I've been in crime scenes before, Ross. I was at the pit, remember?"

"I guess you were. Well, take a gander at this."

There was a plastic soup bowl next to the knife. Highsmith looked in it and turned green. The soup bowl contained three severed fingers.

"John Doe," Barrow said softly.

Highsmith walked around the chair so he could see the seat. It was covered with blood. He felt queasy. In addition to the three fingers, Doe's genitals had been missing and Randy did not want to be the one who found them.

"I'm not certain who has jurisdiction here," Barrow said as he walked around the chair. "Call the state police."

Highsmith nodded. He looked for a phone. There was none in the front room. There were two rooms in the back of the house. One was a bathroom. Highsmith opened the other slowly, afraid of what he might find. There was barely enough room in the bedroom for a single bed, a dresser and an end table. The phone was on the end table.

"Hey, Ross, look at this."

Barrow came into the room. Highsmith pointed to an answering machine that was connected to the phone. A red light was flashing, indicating there were messages on the machine. Highsmith skimmed through a few messages before stopping at one.

"Mr. Oberhurst, this is Betsy Tannenbaum. This is

the third time I've called and I'd appreciate it if you would call me at my office. The number is 555-1763. It's urgent that you contact me. I have a release from Lisa Darius giving you permission to discuss her case. Please call anytime. I have an answering service that can reach me at home, if you call after hours or on a weekend."

The machine beeped. Highsmith and Barrow looked at each other.

"Oberhurst is hired by Lisa Darius, then he's tortured and his body ends up in the pit at Darius's construction site," Barrow said.

"Why did Lisa Darius hire him?"

Barrow looked through the door at the open filing cabinet.

"I wonder if that was what Darius was looking for—his wife's file."

"Hold it, Ross. We don't know Darius did this."

"Randy, say Darius found out what was in his wife's file and it was something that could hurt him. I mean, if he did this, tortured Oberhurst, cut off his fingers and dick, it was because that file had something in it that was dynamite. Maybe something that could prove Darius is the rose killer."

"What are you getting . . . Oh, shit. Lisa Darius. He couldn't get at her before, because he's been in jail since we discovered the bodies."

Barrow grabbed the phone and started dialing.

4

The Oregon Supreme Court sits in Salem, the state capital, fifty miles south of Portland. The hour commute was the only thing Victor Ryder disliked about being a Supreme Court justice. After all the years of seven-day work weeks and sixteen-hour days he had spent in private practice, the more leisurely pace of work at the court was a relief.

Justice Ryder was a widower who lived alone behind a high evergreen hedge in a three-story, brown and white Tudor house in the Portland Heights section of the West Hills. The view of Portland and Mount Hood from the brick patio in the rear of the house was spectacular.

Ryder unlocked the front door and called out for Lisa. The heat was on in the house. So were the lights. He heard voices coming from the living room. He called out to Lisa again, but she did not answer. The voices he heard came from the television, but no one was watching it. Ryder switched off the set.

At the bottom of the stairs, Ryder called out again. There was still no answer. If Lisa had gone out, why was the set on? He headed down the hall to the kitchen. Lisa knew her father always snacked as soon as he got in the door, so she left notes on the refrigerator. The refrigerator door was covered with recipes and cartoons, affixed to the smooth surface with magnets, but there was no note. There were two coffee cups on the kitchen table, and the remains of a piece of coffee cake on a cake dish.

"Must have gone off with a friend," Ryder said to himself, but he was still bothered by the TV. He cut a piece of coffee cake and took a bite, then he walked to Lisa's room. There was nothing out of place, nothing that aroused his suspicion. Still, Justice Ryder felt very uneasy. He was about to go to his room to change when he heard the doorbell. Two men were huddled under an umbrella on the front steps.

"Justice Ryder? I'm Randy Highsmith with the Multnomah County district attorney's office. This is

Detective Ross Barrow, Portland Police. Is your daughter in?"

"Is this about Martin?"

"Yes, sir."

"Lisa's been staying with me, but she's not here now."

"When did you see her last?"

"At breakfast. Why?"

"We have some questions we wanted to ask her. Do you know where she can be reached?"

"I'm afraid not. She didn't leave a note and I just got in."

"Could she be with a friend?" Highsmith asked casually, so Ryder would not see his concern.

"I really don't know."

Ryder remembered the TV and frowned.

"Is something wrong, sir?" Barrow asked, keeping his tone neutral.

"No. Not really. It's just that there were two coffee cups on the kitchen table, so I thought she was entertaining a friend. They'd been eating a piece of coffee cake, too. But the TV was on."

"I don't understand," Barrow said.

"It was on when I came home. I couldn't figure out why she'd leave it running if she was talking with a friend in the kitchen or leaving the house."

"Is it normal for her to go out without leaving a note?" Barrow asked.

"She hasn't lived at home for some time and she's been staying in the house at night since Martin got out. But she knows I worry about her."

"Is there something you're not telling us, sir?"

Justice Ryder hesitated.

"Lisa's been very frightened since Martin was released. She talked about leaving the state until he's back behind bars."

"Wouldn't she have told you where she was going?"

"I assume so." Ryder paused, as if he just remembered something. "Martin called Lisa the night he was released. He said there was nowhere in Portland she would be safe. Maybe he called again and she panicked."

"Was he threatening her?" Barrow asked.

"I thought so, but Lisa wasn't certain. It was an odd conversation. I only heard Lisa's end of it and what she told me he said."

Highsmith handed the judge his business card. "Please ask Mrs. Darius to give me a ring the minute you hear from her. It's important."

"Certainly."

Barrow and Highsmith shook hands with the judge and left.

"I don't like this," Barrow said as soon as the front door closed. "It's too much like the other crime scenes. Especially the TV. She'd have turned that off if she was going out with a friend."

"There was no note or rose."

"Yeah, but Darius isn't stupid. If he's got his wife, he's not going to broadcast the fact. He could have changed his m.o. to put us off the track. Any suggestions?"

"None at all, unless you think we've got enough to pick up Darius."

"We don't."

"Then we wait, and hope Lisa Darius is out with a friend."

Part Seven

GONE, BUT NOT FORGOTTEN

Chapter Twenty-three

I

Betsy heard a car pull into the carport and looked out the kitchen window.

"It's Daddy!" Kathy yelled. She had been waiting in the living room all afternoon, giving only half-hearted attention to the television, since Betsy told her she was going to Rick's for the weekend.

"Get your things," Betsy told Kathy as she opened the door.

"They're all here, Mom," Kathy said, pointing to her backpack, book bag, small valise and Oliver, the stuffed skunk.

The door opened and Kathy jumped into Rick's arms.

"How you doin', Tiger?" Rick asked with a laugh.

"I packed myself," Kathy said, pointing at her things.

"Did you pack your toothbrush?" Betsy asked suddenly.

"Uh oh," Kathy said.

"I thought so. Run and get it right now, young lady."

Rick put Kathy down and she raced down the hall for the bathroom.

"She's very excited," Betsy told Rick. He looked uncomfortable.

"I thought I'd take her to the Spaghetti Factory."

"She likes that."

They stood without talking for a moment.

"You look good, Bets."

"You should see how I look when I haven't had to spend the day in Judge Spencer's court," Betsy joked self-consciously, sidestepping the compliment. Rick started to say something, but Kathy was back with her toothbrush and the moment passed.

"See you Monday," Betsy said, giving Kathy a big hug and kiss. Rick gathered up everything but Oliver. Betsy watched from the doorway until they drove away.

2

Alan Page looked up from his desk. Randy Highsmith and Ross Barrow were standing in the doorway. He glanced at his watch. It was six twenty-five.

"I just got off the phone with Justice Ryder. She's still missing," Barrow said.

Page put down his pen.

"What can we do? There's not a shred of evidence pointing toward Darius," Page said. He looked pale and sounded exhausted and defeated.

"We have a motive, Al," Barrow said. "Lisa Darius is the only person who can connect Martin to Sam Oberhurst. He couldn't get to her when he was in jail. I say we have at least probable cause. No sooner is he out than she's missing."

"And there was that phone call," Highsmith added.

"Ryder can't be certain there was a threat. The call can even be interpreted as a warning to Lisa to be careful of someone else." Page shook his head. "I'm not making the same mistake twice. Unless I'm certain we have probable cause, I'm not asking for a search warrant."

"Don't get gun-shy, Al," Highsmith warned. "We're talking about a life here."

"I know that," Page answered angrily. "But where do we search? His house? He's not going to be stupid enough to keep her there. Some property he owns? Which one? I'm as frustrated as you are, but we have to be patient."

Highsmith was about to say something when the intercom buzzed.

"I know you didn't want to be disturbed," his secretary said, "but Nancy Gordon is on the line."

Page felt cold. Highsmith and Barrow straightened. Page put the call on the speaker phone.

"Detective Gordon?"

"I'm sorry I disappeared on you, Mr. Page," a woman said. Page tried to remember what Gordon sounded like. He remembered a throaty quality to her voice, but their connection was bad and the woman's voice was distorted.

"Where are you?"

"I can't tell you that now," Gordon said. Page thought she sounded sluggish and uncertain.

"Have you read the news? Do you know Darius is out, because we didn't have your testimony at his bail hearing?"

"It couldn't be helped. You'll understand everything in a while."

"I'd like to understand it now, Detective. We have a situation here. Darius's wife has disappeared."

"I know. That's why I'm calling. I know where she is and you have to act quickly."

3

Darius Construction was in trouble. When Darius was arrested, the company was on the verge of bringing in two lucrative projects. Both jobs were now with other construction companies and no new projects would appear while Darius was under indictment. Darius had been counting on the income the projects would generate to help him with the company's financial problems. Without the new income, bankruptcy was a real possibility.

Darius spent the day closeted with his accountant, his attorney and his vice presidents working on a plan to save the company, but he had trouble keeping his mind on business. He needed Betsy Tannenbaum, and she had dropped him. At first he'd wanted her to represent him simply because he thought a feminist attorney would give him an edge with the jury. Then Betsy won the bail hearing and convinced him that she had the skills to save him. Their recent meeting had increased his respect. Tannenbaum was tough. Most women would have been too frightened to confront him alone. They would have brought a man for protection. Darius believed Betsy would never break under the pressure of a trial and he knew she would fight to the end for a client in whom she believed.

When the meeting ended at six p.m. Darius drove home. He punched in the alarm code for his gate and it swung open with a metallic creak. Darius glanced in the rearview mirror. He saw the gleam of headlights as a car drove past the gate, then the driveway turned and he lost his angle.

Darius entered the house through the garage and deactivated the alarm. The house was cool and quiet. While Lisa was living with him, there was always an undercurrent of noise in the background. Darius was learning to live without the murmur of kitchen appliances, the muted chatter from the television and the sounds Lisa made passing from room to room.

The living room looked sterile when he turned on the light. Darius took off his jacket and tie and poured himself a scotch. He wondered if there was a way to talk Betsy into coming back. Her anger was evident, but anger could cool. It was her fear that was keeping Betsy from him. He could not blame her for thinking him a monster after what she learned from Colby. Normally a woman's fear would excite Darius, but Betsy's fear was driving her from him and he could not think of a way to allay it.

Darius draped his tie and jacket over his arm and walked upstairs to his bedroom. He had barely eaten all day and his stomach growled. He switched on the bedroom light and set his glass on his dresser. As he turned toward the closet, a flash of color caught his eye. There was a black rose on his pillow. Beneath the rose was a sheet of stationery. Darius stared at the note. His stomach turned. He spun toward the doorway, but there was no one there. He strained for the slightest noise but heard only the normal house sounds.

Darius kept a gun in his dresser. He took it out. His heart was beating wildly. How could someone get into his house without setting off the alarm? Only he and Lisa knew the alarm code and . . . Darius froze. His mind made the logical jump and he headed for the basement, switching on the house lights as he went.

Darius paused at the top of the cellar stairs, knowing what he would see when he turned on the light. He heard the first siren when he was halfway down. He thought about going back, but he had to know. A police car skidded to a halt in front of the house as Darius reached the bottom of the stairs. He put his gun down, because he did not want to risk being shot. Besides, he would not need it. There was no one in the house with him. He knew that when he saw the way the body was arranged.

Lisa Darius lay on her back in the center of the basement. She was naked. Her stomach had been sliced open and her entrails poked through a gaping, blood-soaked hole. The body of Patricia Cross had been left in Henry Waters's basement in exactly this way.

4

As soon as Rick and Kathy drove away, Betsy went back to the kitchen and fixed herself something to eat. She had toyed with the idea of going out for dinner or calling a friend, but the idea of spending a quiet night alone was too appealing.

When she was finished with dinner, Betsy went into the living room and glanced at the television listings. Nothing looked interesting, so she settled into an easy chair with an Updike novel. She was just starting to get into it when the phone rang. Betsy sighed and ran into the kitchen to answer it.

"Mrs. Tannenbaum?"

"Yes."

"This is Alan Page." He sounded angry. "I'm at Martin Darius's estate. We've rearrested him."

"On what grounds?"

"He just murdered his wife."

"My God! What happened?"

"Your client gutted Lisa Darius in his basement."

"Oh, no."

"You did her a real favor when you convinced Norwood to release Darius on bail," Page said bitterly. "Your client wants to talk to you."

"Do you believe me now, Tannenbaum?" Darius asked. "Do you see what's going on?"

"Don't say anything. The police are listening, Martin. I'll see you in the morning."

"Then you're sticking with me?"

"I didn't say that."

"You've got to. Ask yourself how the police found out about Lisa and you'll know I'm innocent."

Was Darius really innocent? It didn't make sense that he would kill his wife and leave her body to decompose in his own basement. Betsy thought over what she knew about the Hunter's Point case. Betsy imagined Henry Waters answering the door, Nancy Gordon walking down the steps to Waters's basement, the shocked look on Waters's face when he saw Patricia Cross sprawled in her own blood, disemboweled. It was Patricia Cross all over again. Darius had asked her to find out how the police knew Lisa Darius was in his basement. She tried to remember how the police had found out about Patricia Cross.

"Put Page back on," she told Darius.

"I don't want anyone talking to Darius," she told the district attorney.

"I wouldn't think of it," Page replied rudely.

"You're wasting your anger on me, Alan. I knew Lisa Darius better than you did. This hurts, believe me."

Page was silent for a moment. He sounded subdued when he spoke.

"You're right. I had no business biting your head off. I'm as mad at myself for screwing up at the bail hearing as I am at you for doing such a good job. But he's staying in this time. Norwood won't make another mistake."

"Alan, how did you know you'd find Lisa's body in the basement?"

Betsy held her breath while Page decided if he would answer.

"Ah, you'll find out anyway. It was a tip."

"Who told you?"

"I can't tell you that, now."

A tip, just like the anonymous tip that led the Hunter's Point police to Henry Waters's basement. Betsy hung up the phone. Her doubts about Darius's guilt were starting to grow. Martin Darius had murdered the women in Hunter's Point, but was he innocent of the Portland murders?

Chapter Twenty-four

I

The door to the jail interview room opened and Darius walked in. He was dressed in the shirt and suit pants he had been wearing when he was arrested. His eyes were bloodshot and he seemed less self-assured than he looked during their other meetings.

"I knew you'd be here, Tannenbaum," Darius said, trying to appear calm but sounding a little desperate.

"I don't want to be. I'm required to represent you until another attorney relieves me of my obligation."

"You can't leave me in the lurch."

"I haven't changed my mind, Martin. I meant everything I said the other day."

"Even though you know I'm innocent?"

"I don't know that for certain. And even if you are innocent, it doesn't change what you did in Hunter's Point."

Darius leaned forward slightly and locked his eyes on hers.

"You do know I'm innocent, unless you think I'm

stupid enough to murder my wife in my basement, then call Alan Page and tell him where to find the corpse."

Darius was right, of course. The case against him was too pat and the timing of this new killing too opportune. Doubts had kept Betsy up for most of the night, but they had not changed the way she felt about Darius.

"We'll be going up to court in a few minutes. Page will arraign you on a complaint charging you with Lisa's murder. He'll ask for a no-bail hold and ask Norwood to revoke your bail on the other charges. I can't see any way of convincing the judge to let you out on bail."

"Tell the judge what we know about Gordon. Tell him I'm being framed."

"We have no proof of that."

"So this is how it's going to be. I guess I figured you wrong, Tannenbaum. What happened to your high-blown sense of ethics? Your oath as an attorney? You're going to throw this one, aren't you, because you can't stand me?"

Betsy flushed with anger. "I'm not throwing a goddamn thing. I shouldn't even be here. What I am doing is letting you know the facts of life. Judge Norwood took a big chance letting you out. When he sees the pictures of Lisa spread-eagled in your basement with her guts pulled through her abdominal wall, he is not going to feel like letting you out again."

"The State calls Victor Ryder, Your Honor," Alan Page said, turning toward the rear of the room to watch the courtly justice walk past the spectators and through the bar of the court. Ryder was six feet three with a full head of snow-white hair. He walked with a slight limp from a wound he had received in World War Two. Ryder kept his back rigid, scrupulously avoiding eye contact with

Martin Darius, as if he was afraid of the rage that might overpower him if he set eyes on the man.

"For the record," Page said as soon as Ryder was sworn, "you are a justice of the Oregon Supreme Court and the father of Lisa Darius?"

"Yes," Ryder answered, his voice cracking slightly.

"Your daughter was married to the defendant, was she not?"

"Yes, sir."

"When Mr. Darius was arrested, did your daughter move in with you?"

"She did."

"While Lisa was staying at your home, did her husband phone her?"

"Repeatedly, Mr. Page. He phoned from jail several times each evening."

"Is it true that inmates can only make collect calls?"

"Yes. All his calls were collect."

"Did your daughter accept the calls?"

"She instructed me to refuse them."

"To the best of your knowledge, did your daughter speak to the defendant while he was incarcerated?"

"She may have, once or twice immediately after his arrest. Once she moved in with me, she stopped."

"What was your daughter's attitude toward her husband?"

"She was scared to death of him."

"Did this fear increase or decrease when Mr. Darius was released on bail?"

"It increased. She was terrified he would come for her."

"Did the defendant phone Lisa Darius after his release on bail?"

"Yes, sir. The first evening."

"Did you hear the conversation?"

"Snatches of it."

"Did you hear the defendant make any threats?"

"I believe he told her she would not be safe in Portland."

"When you say you believe he said this, what do you mean?"

"Lisa told me he said it. I was standing at Lisa's shoulder and could hear some of what he said."

"Do you know if Mrs. Darius believed the defendant meant this as a threat?"

"She was confused. She told me she wasn't certain what he meant. He seemed to be implying Lisa was in danger from someone else, but that didn't make sense. I took it that he was threatening her indirectly, so no blame could be placed on him."

"Justice Ryder, when was the last time you saw your daughter alive?"

For a brief moment the judge lost his composure. He sipped from a cup of water before answering.

"We had breakfast together between seven and seven-thirty a.m. Then I drove to Salem."

"When did you return home?"

"Around six in the evening."

"Was your daughter home?"

"No."

"Did you see anything in the house that alarmed you?"

"The television was on, but no one was home. The sound was high enough so Lisa should have heard it and turned it off before she left."

"Was there evidence that she'd had a visitor?"

"There were two coffee cups in the kitchen and some coffee cake was out, as if she'd been talking to someone."

"Did your daughter leave a note telling where she was going?"

"No."

"Nothing further."

"Your witness, Mrs. Tannenbaum," Judge Norwood said.

"He's lying," Darius whispered. "I never threatened Lisa. I was warning her."

"He's not lying, Martin. He's saying what he honestly believes happened. If I push him, he'll just harden his position."

"Bullshit. I've seen you take witnesses apart. Ryder is a pompous asshole. You can make him look like a fool."

Betsy took a deep breath, because she did not want to lose her temper. Then she leaned over to Darius and spoke quietly.

"Do you want me to push Justice Ryder until he breaks down, Martin? Do you really think it will help you get bail if I cause one of the most respected judges in the state, and the father of a young woman who has been brutally murdered, to crack up in open court in front of one of his colleagues?"

Darius started to say something, then shut up and turned away from Betsy.

"No questions, Your Honor," Betsy said.

"Our next witness is Detective Richard Kassel," Page told the judge.

Richard Kassel sauntered down the aisle. He was dressed in a brown tweed sports coat, tan slacks, a white shirt and a bright yellow print tie. His shoes were polished and his black hair was styled. He had the smug look of a person who took himself too seriously.

"Detective Kassel, how are you employed?"

"I'm a detective with the Portland Police Bureau."

"Did you arrest the defendant yesterday evening?"

"Yes, sir."

"Tell the judge how that came about."

Kassel swiveled toward the judge.

"Detective Rittner and I received a call over the police radio. Based on that communication, I entered the grounds. The door to the defendant's house was locked. We identified ourselves as police and demanded that the defendant open the door. He complied. Detective Rittner and I secured the defendant and waited for the other cars to arrive, as we had been ordered to do."

"Did other officers arrive soon after?"

Kassel nodded. "About fifteen minutes after we arrived, you and Detective Barrow arrived, followed by several others."

Betsy's brow furrowed. She checked something she had written during Justice Ryder's testimony. Then she made some notes on her pad.

"Did you discover the body?" Page asked.

"No, sir. Our instructions were to stay with the defendant. The body was discovered by other officers."

"Did you give Mr. Darius his *Miranda* warnings?"

"Yes, sir."

"Did Mr. Darius make any statements?"

"Other than to ask to call his lawyer, no."

"Your witness, Mrs. Tannenbaum."

Betsy looked unsure of herself. She asked the judge for a minute and pretended to look through a police report while she worked through her thoughts.

"Detective Kassel," Betsy asked cautiously, "who told you to enter the Darius estate and arrest Mr. Darius?"

"Detective Barrow."

"Did he say why you were to arrest Mr. Darius?"

"Yes, ma'am. He said there was a tip that the defendant had killed his wife and her body was in his basement."

"Did Detective Barrow tell you who gave him the tip?"

"I didn't ask."

"How was Mr. Darius dressed when he opened the door for you?"

"He was wearing a white shirt and pants."

"Mr. Darius, please stand up."

Darius stood.

"Are these the pants?"

Detective Kassel took a second to look at Darius. "Yeah. Those are the ones we arrested him in."

"And this is the white shirt?"

"Yes."

"It's in the same condition as when you arrested him?"

"Yes."

"There's no blood on this shirt, is there?"

Kassel paused, then answered, "No, ma'am."

"Did you view the body of Lisa Darius at any point?"

"Yes."

"When it was still in the basement?"

"Yes."

"Mrs. Darius was disemboweled, was she not?"

"Yes."

"There was blood all over that basement, wasn't there?"

"Yes," Kassel answered grudgingly.

"The gate to the Darius estate is locked. How did you get in?"

"Detective Barrow had the combination."

"How is it that you arrived at the Darius estate so far ahead of Detective Barrow, Mr. Page and the other officers?" Betsy asked with an easy smile that disguised the tension she was feeling. She would know if her suspicions were correct after a few more questions.

"We were parked outside it."

"Was that by chance?"

"No, ma'am. We had the defendant under surveillance."

"How long had you had him under surveillance?"

"We've been surveilling him for quite a while. Back before his first arrest."

"Just you and Detective Rittner?"

"Oh, no. There were three teams. We switched off. You can't do that twenty-four hours."

"Of course not. When did your shift start on the day you arrested Mr. Darius?"

"Around three in the afternoon."

"Where did you start?"

"Outside his office."

"I assume you took over for another surveillance team?"

"Right. Detectives Padovici and Kristol."

"When had they started?"

"Around five in the morning."

"Where did they start?"

"The defendant's house."

"Why did the other team start so early?"

"The defendant gets up around five-thirty and leaves for work around six-thirty. By getting there at five, we kept him covered when he left his place."

"Is that what Kristol and Padovici did?"

"Yeah."

"I suppose they followed Mr. Darius to work?"

"That's what they said."

"Anything unusual happen that day, according to the detectives?"

"No. He went right to work. I don't think he ever left his office. Detective Padovici said it looked like he sent out for sandwiches at lunchtime. Around six a bunch of guys in suits left. I think they were having a meeting."

"When Mr. Darius left, you followed him home?"

"Right."

"Was he ever out of your sight?"

"No, ma'am."

"How long after Mr. Darius arrived home did you receive the instructions from Detective Barrow to enter the Darius estate and arrest Mr. Darius?"

"Not long."

"Give me your best guess."

"Uh, about fifteen, twenty minutes."

Betsy paused. She felt sick about asking the next series of questions, but her sense of duty, and the possibility that the answers could prove her client innocent, overcame her revulsion at the prospect of Martin Darius walking free.

"Did you ever see Mr. Darius with Lisa Darius that day?"

"No, ma'am."

"What about Padovici and Kristol? Did they say they saw Mr. Darius with his wife?"

Kassel frowned, as if he suddenly realized where Betsy's questions were leading. Betsy looked to her left and saw Alan Page in an animated discussion with Randy Highsmith.

"I can't recall," he answered hesitantly.

"I assume you wrote a daily surveillance log listing any unusual occurrences?"

"Yes."

"And the other members of the surveillance team also kept logs?"

"Yes."

"Where are the logs?"

"Detective Barrow has them."

Betsy stood. "Your Honor, I would like the logs produced and Detectives Kristol and Padovici made available for questioning. Justice Ryder testified that he last saw his daughter at seven-thirty a.m. Detective Kassel says Padovici and Kristol reported that Mr. Darius left his estate at six-thirty and went directly to work. If neither team saw Mr. Darius with his wife during the day, when did he kill her? We can produce the people who were with Mr. Darius yesterday. They'll say he was in his office from about seven a.m. until a little after six p.m."

Judge Norwood looked troubled. Alan Page leaped to his feet.

"This is nonsense, Judge. The surveillance was on Darius, not his wife. The body was in the basement. Mr. Darius was with the body."

"Your Honor," Betsy said, "Mr. Darius could not have killed his wife before he got home, and he was only home for a short time when Detective Kassel arrived. The person who disemboweled Lisa Darius would have blood all over him. There was no blood on my client. Look at his white shirt and his pants.

"I suggest that Mr. Darius is being set up. Someone was at Justice Ryder's house having coffee with Lisa Darius during the day. It wasn't the defendant. Lisa Darius left the house without turning off the television. That's because she was forced to leave. That person took her to the estate and murdered her in the basement, then phoned in the anonymous tip that led the police to the body."

"That's absurd," Page said. "Who is this mysterious person? I suppose you'll suggest the mystery man also butchered the four people we found at your client's construction site."

"Your Honor," Betsy said, "ask yourself who knew the body of Lisa Darius was in Mr. Darius's basement. Only the killer or someone who saw the murder. Is Mr. Page suggesting that Mr. Darius found his wife alive in his home, butchered her in the fifteen minutes or so between the time Detective Kassel lost sight of him and the time Detective Kassel arrested him, got no blood on his white shirt while disemboweling her and was such a good citizen that he reported himself to the police so they could arrest him for murder?"

Judge Norwood looked troubled. Betsy and Alan Page watched him intently.

"Mrs. Tannenbaum," the judge said, "your theory depends on Mr. Darius leaving his estate at six-thirty and being in his office all day."

"Yes, Your Honor."

The judge turned to Alan Page. "I'm keeping Mr. Darius in jail over the weekend. I want you to give copies of the logs to Mrs. Tannenbaum and I want the detectives here Monday morning. I'll tell you, Mr. Page, this business has me seriously concerned. You better have a good explanation for me. Right now, I can't see how this man killed his wife."

2

"Goddamn it, Ross, how did this slip by you?"

"I'm sorry, Al. I don't review the log entries every day."

"If Darius didn't go near Justice Ryder's house, we have trouble, Al," Randy Highsmith said.

"The surveillance teams must have screwed up," Page insisted. "She was there. She got into the basement somehow. Didn't you tell me there were paths through the woods? The surveillance teams weren't watching Lisa. She could have used the paths to sneak onto the estate while the teams were tailing Darius."

"Why would she go to the estate if she was terrified of Darius?" Highsmith asked.

"He could have sweet-talked her over the phone," Page said. "They were man and wife."

"Then why sneak in?" Highsmith asked. "Why not drive through the front gate and up to the front door? It's her house. It makes no sense for her to sneak in if she was going back willingly."

"Maybe the press has been hounding her and she wanted to avoid reporters."

"I don't buy that."

"There's got to be a logical explanation," Page answered, frustrated by the seeming impossibility of the situation.

"There are a few other things that are nagging at me, Al," Highsmith told his boss.

"Let's hear them," Page said.

"How did Nancy Gordon know where to find the body? Tannenbaum's right. Darius couldn't have killed Lisa at night, because she was alive in the morning. He couldn't have killed her off the estate. We had him under surveillance every minute during the day. If Darius did it, he killed her in the house. There aren't windows in the basement. How would anyone else know what was going on? There are problems with the case, Al. We have to face them."

3

"How was the meeting?"

"Don't ask," Raymond Colby told his wife. "My head's like putty. Help me with this tie. I'm all thumbs."

"Here. Let me," Ellen said, untying the Windsor knot.

"Can you fix me a drink? I'll be in the den. I want to watch the late news."

Ellen pecked her husband on the cheek and walked toward the liquor cabinet. "Why don't you just go to bed?"

"Bruce Smith made some dumb comment on the highway bill. Wayne insists I hear it. It should be on toward the top of the news. Besides, I'm too wound up to go right to sleep."

Colby went into the den and turned on the news. Ellen came in and handed the senator his drink.

"If this doesn't relax you, we'll think of something that will," she said mischievously.

Colby smiled. "What makes you think I have the energy for that kind of hanky-panky?"

"A man who can't rise to the occasion shouldn't be on the Supreme Court."

Colby laughed. "You've become a pervert in your old age."

"And about time, too."

They both laughed, then Colby suddenly sobered. He pointed the remote control at the screen and turned up the volume.

". . . a startling new development in the case against millionaire builder Martin Darius, who is accused of the torture-murder of three women and one man in Portland, Oregon. A week ago Darius was released on bail when trial judge Patrick Norwood ruled that there was insufficient evidence to hold him. Yesterday evening, Darius was rearrested when police found the body of his wife, Lisa Darius, in the basement of the Darius mansion. A police spokesman said she had been tortured and killed in a manner similar to the other victims.

"Today, in a court hearing, Betsy Tannenbaum, Darius's attorney, argued that Darius was the victim of a frame-up after it was revealed that police surveillance teams followed Darius all day on the day his wife was murdered and never saw him with his wife. The hearing will resume Monday.

"On a less serious note, Mayor Clinton Vance is reported to have . . ."

Colby turned off the set and closed his eyes.

"What's wrong?" Ellen asked.

"How would you feel if I was not confirmed by the Senate?"

"That's not possible."

Colby heard the uncertainty in his wife's voice. He was so tired. "I have to make a decision. It concerns something I did when I was governor of New York. A secret that I thought would stay buried forever."

"What kind of secret?" Ellen asked hesitantly.

Colby opened his eyes. He saw his wife's concern and took her hand.

"Not a secret about us, love. It concerns something I did ten years ago. A decision I had to make. A decision I would make again."

"I don't understand."

"I'll explain everything, then you tell me what I should do."

Chapter Twenty-five

I

Alan Page looked at the illuminated digital display on his alarm clock as he groped for the phone in the dark. It was four-fifteen.

"Is this Alan Page, the district attorney for Multnomah County?" a man asked.

"It is, and I'll still be d.a. when the sun's up."

"Sorry about that, but we have a three-hour time difference here and my flight leaves in thirty minutes."

"Who is this?" Page asked, awake enough to be annoyed.

"My name is Wayne Turner. I'm Senator Raymond Colby's administrative assistant. I used to be a detective with the Hunter's Point Police Department. Nancy Gordon and I are good friends."

Page swung his legs over the side of the bed and sat up.

"You've got my attention. What's this about?"

"I'll be at the Sheraton Airport Hotel by ten, your time. Senator Colby wants me to brief you."

"This concerns Darius?"

"We knew him as Peter Lake. The senator wants you fully informed about certain matters you may not know."

"Such as?"

"Not over the phone, Mr. Page."

"Is this going to help my case against Darius?"

"My information will make a conviction certain."

"Can you give me a clue about what you're going to say?"

"Not over the phone," Turner repeated, "and not to anyone but you."

"Randy Highsmith is my chief criminal deputy. You talked to him. Can I bring him along?"

"Let me make myself clear, Mr. Page. Senator Colby is going as far out on a limb for you as someone in public life can go. My job is to see that the limb doesn't get sawed off. When Mr. Highsmith called, I gave him the runaround. You're going to hear the things I did not want Mr. Highsmith to know. This is not by my choosing. It's the senator who insisted I fly to Portland. It's my job to do what he wants, but I'm going to protect him as much as I am able. So there will be no witnesses, no notes and you can expect to be patted down for a wire. You can also be assured that what you hear will be worth any inconvenience you suffered by being awakened before dawn. Now, I've got to make my flight, if you still want me to."

"Come on down, Mr. Turner. I'll respect your wishes. See you at ten."

Page hung up and sat in the dark, wide-awake. What would Turner tell him? What possible connection was there between the President's nominee to the United States Supreme Court and Martin Darius? Whatever it was, Turner thought it would guarantee Darius's conviction, and that was what mattered. Darius would pay. Since the first bail hearing, the case seemed to be slipping away from him. Not even Lisa Darius's tragic death had given the prosecution substance. Maybe Turner's information would save him.

Wayne Turner opened the door and let Alan Page into his hotel room. Turner was impeccably dressed in a three-piece suit. Page's suit was wrinkled, his shoes unpolished. If anyone looked like he had just flown three thousand miles, it was Page.

"Let's get the striptease out of the way," Turner said when the door was closed. Page took off his jacket. Turner patted him down expertly.

"Satisfied?" Page asked.

"Not one bit, Mr. Page. If I had my druthers, I'd be back in D.C. You want some coffee?"

"Coffee would be nice."

There was a thermos on a coffee table and the remains of a sandwich. Turner poured for both of them.

"Before I tell you a damn thing, we have to have some ground rules. There is an excellent chance that Senator Colby will not be confirmed if what I tell you is made public. I want your word that you will not call the senator or me as a witness in any court proceeding or make what I tell you available to anyone else—even members of your staff—unless it is absolutely necessary to secure the conviction of Martin Darius."

"Mr. Turner, I respect the senator. I want to see him on the Court. The fact that he's willing to risk his nomination to give me this information reinforces the feelings I've had about his worth to this country. Believe me, I will do nothing to jeopardize his chances, if I can help it. But I want you to know, up front, this prosecution is in a lot of trouble. If I had to bet, I'd pick Martin Darius to walk, based on what I've got now."

2

Kathy insisted on eating at the Spaghetti Factory again. There was the usual forty-five-minute wait and the service was slow. They were not back in Rick's apartment until after nine. Kathy was pooped, but she was so excited she did not want to go to bed. Rick spent half an hour reading to her. He was surprised how much he enjoyed reading to his daughter. That was something Betsy usually did. He enjoyed dinner too. In fact, he had enjoyed all the time they spent together.

The doorbell rang. Rick checked his watch. Who would be calling at nine forty-five? Rick looked through the peephole. It took him a moment to remember the woman who was standing in the hall.

"Miss Sloane, isn't it?" Rick asked, when the door was open.

"You have a good memory."

"What can I do for you?"

Sloane looked embarrassed. "I really shouldn't intrude like this, but I remembered your address. You told Betsy before you left the office. I was in the neighborhood. I know it's late, but I was going to arrange a meeting with you for background for my article, anyway, so I thought I'd take a chance. If you're busy, I can come some other time."

"Actually, that would be best. I've got Kathy with me and she just went to sleep. I don't want to disturb her, and I'm pretty beat myself."

"Say no more, Mr. Tannenbaum. Could we meet later in the week?"

"Do you really want to talk to me? Betsy and I are separated, you know."

"I do know, but I would like to talk to you about her.

She's a remarkable woman and your view of her would be very informative."

"I'm not sure I want to discuss our marriage for publication."

"Will you think it over?"

Rick hesitated, then said, "Sure. Call me at the office."

"Thank you, Mr. Tannenbaum. Do you have a card?"

Rick patted his pockets and remembered his wallet was in the bedroom.

"Step in for a minute. I'll get you one."

Rick turned his back on Nora Sloane and started into the apartment. Nora was taller than Rick. She glided behind him and looped her left arm around his neck while she drew the knife out of her deep coat pocket with her right hand. Rick felt himself jerked up on his toes when Sloane leaned back and tilted his chin up. He did not feel anything when the knife slashed across his throat, because his body went into shock. There was a jolt when the knife slid into his back, then another jolt. Rick tried to struggle, but he lost control of his body. Blood spurted from his neck. He viewed the red fountain like a tourist staring at a landmark. The room wavered. Rick felt his energy drain out of him along with the blood that drenched the floor. Nora Sloane released her hold and Rick slid to the carpet. She closed the apartment door quietly and looked around. There was a living room at the end of the hall. Sloane walked through it, down another hall and stopped at the first door. She pushed it open gently and stared at Kathy. The darling little girl was asleep. She looked lovely.

Chapter Twenty-six

Betsy was finishing breakfast when the doorbell rang. A light rain had been falling all morning and it was hard to see Nora Sloane through the streaked pane in the kitchen window. She was standing on the welcome mat holding an umbrella in one hand and a large shopping bag in the other. Betsy carried her coffee cup to the front door. Nora smiled when it opened.

"Can I come in?" Sloane asked.

"Sure," Betsy said, stepping aside. Sloane leaned her umbrella against the wall in the entryway and unbuttoned her raincoat. She was wearing tight-fitting jeans, a light blue work shirt and a dark blue sweater.

"Can we sit down?" Nora asked, gesturing toward the living room. Betsy was confused by this morning visit, but she sat down on the couch. Nora sat in an armchair across from her and took a gun out of the shopping bag. The coffee cup slipped from Betsy's fingers and shattered when it struck the marble tabletop. A dark brown puddle formed around the shards.

"I'm sorry I frightened you," Sloane said calmly.

Betsy stared at the gun.

"Don't let this bother you," Sloane said. "I wouldn't hurt you. I like you. I'm just not certain how you'll react when I explain why I'm here, and I want to be certain you don't do anything foolish. You won't do anything rash, will you?"

"No."

"Good. Now, listen carefully to me. Martin Darius must not be freed. On Monday, before the hearing starts, you will ask to use Judge Norwood's jury room to speak in private with your client. There's a door that opens into the corridor. When I knock on the door, you'll let me in."

"Then what?"

"That's none of your concern."

"Why should I do this for you?"

Nora reached into the shopping bag and pulled out Oliver. She handed the stuffed animal to Betsy.

"I have Kathy. She's a sweet child. She'll be fine, if you do what I tell you."

"How . . . how did you get Kathy? Rick didn't call me."

"Rick's dead." Betsy gaped at Nora, not certain she had heard her correctly. "He hurt you. Men are like that. Martin is the worst example. Making us act like dogs, forcing us to fuck each other, mounting us as if we were inanimate objects, cartoon women, so he could live out his fantasies. But other men do the same thing in different ways. Like Rick. He used you, then discarded you."

"Oh, God!" Betsy wept, stunned and only half-believing what Sloane said. "He's not dead."

"I did it for you, Betsy."

"No, Nora. He didn't deserve this."

Sloane's features hardened. "They all deserve to die, Betsy. All of them."

"You're Samantha Reardon, aren't you?"

Reardon nodded.

"I don't understand. After what you went through, how could you kill those women?"

"That was hard, Betsy. I made certain they didn't suffer. I only marked them when they were anesthetized. If there was another way, I would have chosen it."

Of course, Betsy thought, if Reardon kidnapped the women to frame Martin Darius, it would be easier to deal with them if they were unconscious. A nurse who assisted in surgery would know all about anesthetics like pentobarbital.

Reardon smiled warmly, reversed the gun and held it out to Betsy.

"Don't be afraid. I said I wouldn't hurt you. Take it. I want you to see how much I trust you."

Betsy half-reached, then stopped.

"Go on," Reardon urged her. "Do as I say. I know you won't shoot me. I'm the only one who knows where Kathy is. If I was killed, no one would be able to find her. She'd starve to death. That's a cruel and horrible way to die. I know. I almost died from starvation."

Betsy took the gun. It was cold to the touch and heavy. She had the power to kill Reardon, but she felt utterly helpless.

"If I do what you say, you'll give me Kathy unharmed?"

"Kathy is my insurance policy, just as I was Peter Lake's. Nancy Gordon told me all about the governor's pardon. I've learned so much from Martin Darius. I can't wait to thank him, in person."

Reardon sat quietly for a while. She did not move. Betsy tried to stay just as still, but it was impossible. She shifted on the couch. The seconds passed. Reardon looked as if she was having trouble framing her thoughts. When she spoke, she looked into Betsy's eyes with an expression of deep concern and addressed Betsy the way a teacher addresses a prize pupil when she wants to make certain that the student understands a key point.

"You have to see Darius for what he is to understand what I'm doing. He is the Devil. Not just a bad person, but pure evil. Ordinary measures wouldn't have worked. Who would believe me? I've been committed twice. When I tried to tell people in Hunter's Point, no one would listen. Now I know why. I always suspected there were others working with Martin. Nancy Gordon confirmed that. She told me all about the conspiracy to free Martin and blame Henry Waters. Only the Devil would have so much power. Think of it. The governor, the mayor, policemen. Only Gordon resisted. And she was the only woman."

Reardon watched Betsy intently. "I'll bet you'll be tempted to call the police as soon as I leave. You mustn't do that. They might catch me. I'll never tell where Kathy is if I'm caught. You must be especially strong when the police tell you Rick is dead and Kathy has been kidnapped. Don't weaken and give me away."

Reardon smiled coldly.

"You must not put your faith in the police. You must not believe that they can break me. I can assure you that nothing the police can do to me compares to what Martin did, and Martin never broke me. Oh, he thought he did. He thought I was submitting, but only my body submitted. My mind stayed strong and focused.

"At night I could hear the others whimpering. I never whimpered. I folded my hate inside me and kept it safe and warm. Then I waited. When they told me Waters was the one, I knew they were lying. I knew Martin had done something to them to make them lie. The Devil can do that—twist people, change them around like clay figures—but he didn't change me."

"Is Kathy warm?" Betsy asked. "She can get sick if she's in a damp place."

"Kathy is warm, Betsy. I'm not a monster like Darius. I'm not inhuman or insensitive. I need Kathy to be safe. I don't want to harm her."

Betsy did not hate Reardon. Reardon was insane. It was Darius she hated. Darius knew exactly what he was doing in Hunter's Point when he created Reardon by stripping her of her humanity. Betsy handed the gun to Reardon.

"Take it. I don't want it."

"Thank you, Betsy. I'm pleased to see you trust me as much as I trust you."

"What you're doing is wrong. Kathy is a baby. She never did anything to you."

"I know. I feel badly about taking her, but I couldn't think of any other way to force you to help me. You have such high principles. I was upset when you told me you were dropping Darius as a client. I counted on you to get me close to him. But I admired you for refusing to represent him. So many lawyers would have continued for the money. I helped you with your marital problems so you'd see how much I respect you."

Reardon stood up. "I've got to go. Please don't worry. Kathy's safe and warm. Do what I told you and she'll be back with you soon."

"Can you have Kathy call me? She'll be frightened. It would help her if she heard my voice."

"I'm sure you're sincere, Betsy, but you might try to have my calls traced. I can't take that chance."

"Then give this to her," Betsy said, handing Oliver to Reardon. "It will make her feel safe."

Reardon took the stuffed animal. Tears streaked down Betsy's face.

"She's all I have. Please don't hurt her."

Reardon closed the door without answering. Betsy ran into the kitchen and watched her walk up the driveway, back straight, unwavering. At that moment, Betsy suddenly knew how the husbands felt when they came home to find only notes that read "Gone, But Not Forgotten."

Betsy wandered back to the living room. It was still dark, though a sliver of light was starting to show on the fringe of the hills. Betsy slumped on the couch, exhausted by the effort it took to keep her emotions at bay, unable to think and in shock. She wanted to mourn Rick, but all she could think about was Kathy. Until Kathy was safe, her heart would have no time to ache for Rick.

Betsy tried not to think of the women in the autopsy photographs, she tried to block her memory of the picture Darius had painted of his dehumanized prisoners, but she could not stop herself from seeing Kathy, her little girl, frantic and defenseless, curled up in the dark, terrified of every sound.

Time passed in a blur. The rain stopped and the sky changed from dark to light without her noticing. The pool of cold coffee had spread between the fragments of the broken cup and across the top of the coffee table. Betsy walked into the kitchen. There was a roll of paper towels under the sink. She tore some off the roll, found a small paper bag and grabbed a large sponge. Doing something helped. Moving helped.

Betsy picked up the pieces of the cup and put them in the paper bag. She sponged off the tabletop and used the paper towels to wipe it down. As she worked, she thought about help. The police were out. She could not control them. Betsy believed Samantha Reardon. If Reardon thought Betsy betrayed her, she would kill Kathy. If the police arrested her, she would never tell where she was holding Kathy.

Betsy put the wet towels into the bag, carried the bag into the kitchen and put it in the garbage. Finding Kathy was the only thing she cared about. Reggie Stewart was an expert at finding people and she could control him, because Reggie worked for her. More important, he was sensitive. He would put finding Kathy ahead of arresting Samantha Reardon. Betsy would have to act quickly. It was only a matter of time before someone discovered Rick's body and the police investigation started.

Reggie Stewart's flight from Hunter's Point landed in Portland after midnight, and Betsy's call aroused him from a sound sleep. He had wanted to go back to bed, but Betsy sounded so upset and cryptic on the phone, he was concerned. Stewart smiled when Betsy opened the door, but his smile faded as soon as he saw Betsy's face.

"What's up, Chief?"

Betsy did not answer Stewart until they were seated in the living room. She looked like she was barely under control.

"You were right. Samantha Reardon killed the people at the construction site."

"How do you know that?"

"She told me, this morning. She . . ."

Betsy closed her eyes and took a deep breath. Her shoulders started to shake. She put a hand over her eyes. Betsy did not want to cry. Stewart knelt next to her. He touched her, gently.

"What's happening, Betsy? Tell me. I'm your friend. If I can help you, I will."

"She killed Rick," Betsy sobbed, collapsing into Reggie's arms.

Stewart held her close and let her cry.

"Have you told the police?"

"I can't, Reggie. She has Kathy hidden somewhere. The police don't know Rick is dead. If they arrest Samantha, she won't tell where she has Kathy hidden and she'll starve to death. That's why I need you. You have to find Kathy."

"You don't want me, Betsy. You want the cops and the FBI. They're much better equipped to find Kathy than I am. They have computers, manpower . . ."

"I believe Samantha when she says Kathy will die if she learns I went to the police. Reardon has already murdered the four people at the site, Lisa Darius and Rick."

"How do you know Reardon so well?"

"The day after Darius hired me, a woman calling herself Nora Sloane phoned me. She said she wanted to meet me for lunch to discuss an article she was writing about women defense attorneys. She wanted to use my cases as the centerpiece. I was flattered. When Darius was arrested, she was already my friend. When she asked if she could tag along while I worked up Martin's case, I agreed."

"Reardon?"

"Yes."

"Why did she kill Rick?"

"She said she killed Rick because he left me."

"If she killed Rick because he hurt you, why hurt you more by kidnapping Kathy?"

Betsy decided not to tell Stewart about Reardon's instructions. She trusted her investigator, but she was afraid Stewart would warn the police if he learned of Reardon's plan to get into the jury room with Darius.

"After I found out Martin killed the women in Hunter's Point, I told him I wouldn't represent him, and I told Reardon I was dropping Martin as a client. She was very upset. I think she wants to be able to control the case. With Kathy as a prisoner, she can force me to do things that will ensure Martin's conviction. If you don't find Kathy, I'll have to do what she says."

Stewart walked back and forth, thinking. Betsy wiped her eyes. Talking to someone helped.

"What do you know about Reardon?" Stewart asked. "Have you seen her car? Has she mentioned anything about where she lives? When you met for lunch did she pay with a credit card?"

"I've been trying to think about those things, but I really don't know anything about her. I've never seen her drive, but I'm certain she has a car. She had to transport the bodies to the construction site, my house is out of the way and she's attended all of Darius's court appearances."

"What about where she's living? Has she mentioned a long ride to town, how beautiful the view is in the country? Do you have her phone number?"

"She's never talked much about herself, now that I think about it. We've always talked about me or Darius or the battered women cases and never about her. I don't think I ever asked her where she lives. The one time I asked for her phone number, she said she would call me, and I didn't press her. I do remember that she paid for the lunch with cash. I don't think I've ever seen a piece of i.d."

"Okay. Let's hit this from another angle. Darius chose an isolated farmhouse so no one would see him bringing the women there and to cut the chances that anyone would stumble onto the women while he was away. Sloane doesn't have the problem of a wife and job, she could stay with the women most of the time, but she came to court when Darius had appearances and she met with you a number of times. I'm betting she's living in a rural area that's near enough to Portland so she can come to town, then get back, easily. The house probably has a basement so she can keep her prisoners out of sight. She'd also have to have electricity . . ."

"I asked if she'd let Kathy phone me. She said she wouldn't because she was worried I might trace her calls. She must have a phone," Betsy said.

"Good. That's the way to think. Utilities, a phone, garbage service. And she's a single woman. I have contacts at Portland General Electric and the phone company who can check to see if a Nora Sloane or Samantha Reardon started phone service or electricity around the time Reardon came to Portland. I've got a buddy at the Motor Vehicle Division who can run her names to see if we can get her address off a license application.

"She probably rented the house. I bet she set everything up the first time she was in Portland, so it would be ready when she moved back, but she probably didn't start the services until she came here the second time.

"I'll call Reardon's landlady in Hunter's Point and try to get the exact date she followed Oberhurst and the date she returned to Portland. Then I'll check real estate listings for rural houses with basements for rent in the tri-county area for the first time she was in Portland. I'll see how many were rented by a single woman . . ."

"Why not purchased? It would be safer. She wouldn't have to worry about the owner coming to the house to collect the rent or check on its condition."

"Yeah. She'd think of that. But I had the impression she didn't have a lot of money. She was renting in Hunter's Point and she had a low-paying job. I'm guessing she's renting. I'll cross-check what we find about the utilities with the rentals."

"How long will that take?"

The look of excitement on Stewart's face faded.

"That's the problem with using me instead of the police, Betsy. It's going to take a while. We can hire people to do some of the work, like checking the real estate ads, then I can follow up, but this is all very time-consuming and we could miss her altogether. She may have said she was married and her husband was coming later. She may have found a house in the city that suited her purposes. She may have rented under one name and taken the phone and utilities under another. Fake i.d. is pretty easy to come by.

"Even if I've doped this out correctly, it's a weekend. I don't know how many of my contacts I can get through to and when they can get into their offices to do the work."

Betsy looked defeated. "We don't have a lot of time. I don't know how well she's taking care of Kathy or what Reardon will do to her, if she decides she doesn't need me."

"Maybe you should reconsider. The police and the FBI can be discreet."

"No," Betsy said emphatically. "She said Kathy would die if I told them. There would be too many people involved. There's no way I could be certain she wouldn't learn about the investigation. Besides, in her twisted way, I think Reardon likes me. As long as she doesn't see me as an enemy, there's always the hope she won't harm Kathy."

The rest of the day was so bad, Betsy had no idea how she would get through a second one. It was hard to believe that only a few hours had passed since Samantha Reardon's visit. Betsy wandered into Kathy's room and sat on her bed. *The Wizard of Oz* lay on its side on Kathy's bookshelf. They had four more chapters to read.

Was it possible that Kathy would never learn about Dorothy's safe return home? Betsy curled up on the bed, her cheek on Kathy's pillow, and hugged herself. She could smell Kathy's freshness on the pillow, she remembered the softness of her skin. Kathy, who was so precious, so good, was now in a place as distant as Oz where Betsy could not protect her.

The house was chilly. Betsy had forgotten to turn on the heat. Eventually the cold made her uncomfortable. Betsy sat up. She felt old and wasted, chilled to the bone by the icy air, as if her blood had been drained from her, leaving her too weak to cope with the horror that had invaded her life.

The thermostat was in the hall. Betsy adjusted it and listened to the rumble of the furnace starting up. She drifted aimlessly from room to room. The silence overwhelmed her. It was rare for her to be completely alone. Since Kathy's birth, she had always been surrounded by sound. Now she could hear every raindrop fall, the creak of timbers, water dripping in the kitchen sink, the wind. So much silence, so many signs of loneliness.

Betsy saw the liquor cabinet, but rejected the idea of numbing herself. She had to think, even if each thought was painful. Liquor was a trap. There was going to be a lot of pain in her future and she had to get used to it.

Betsy brewed a cup of tea and turned on the television for company. She had no idea what show she was watching, but the sound of laughter and applause made her feel less alone. How was she going to get through the night, if getting through the day was so unbearable?

Betsy thought about calling her mother but rejected the idea. Rick's body would be discovered soon and Rita would learn that Kathy was missing. She decided to spare her mother suffering for as long as possible.

Stewart called at four to check on Betsy. He had

talked to his contacts at the utility companies and the phone companies and had hired several investigators he trusted to scour the real estate ads for the relevant time period. Stewart insisted on coming by with Chinese take-out. Betsy knew he was doing it so she would not be alone. She was too tired to tell him not to come and she appreciated the company when he arrived.

Stewart left at six-thirty. An hour later, Betsy heard a car pull into her carport. She hurried to the door, hoping, irrationally, that her visitor was Samantha Reardon bringing Kathy home. A police car was parked in one side of the carport. A uniformed officer was driving. Ross Barrow got out of the passenger side. He looked troubled. Betsy's heart beat wildly, certain he was here to tell her about Rick's murder.

"Hello, Detective," she said, trying to sound nonchalant.

"Can we step inside, Ms. Tannenbaum?" Barrow asked.

"Is this about Martin's case?"

Barrow sighed. He had been breaking the news of violent death to relatives for longer than he cared to remember. There was no easy way to do it.

"Why don't we go inside?"

Betsy led Barrow into the house. The other officer followed.

"This is Greg Saunders," Barrow said. Saunders nodded.

"Do you want some coffee?"

"Not right now, thank you. Can we sit down?"

Betsy walked into the living room. When they were seated, Barrow asked, "Where were you last night and today?"

"Why do you want to know?"

"I have an important reason for asking."

"I was home."

"You didn't go out? No one visited you?"

"No," Betsy answered, afraid to mention Reggie Stewart.

"You're married, aren't you?"

Betsy looked at Barrow for a moment, then looked down at her lap.

"My husband and I are separated. Kathy, our daughter, is staying with him for a few days. I've been taking advantage of the peace and quiet to sleep late, catch up on some reading. What's this all about?"

"Where are Mr. Tannenbaum and your daughter staying?" Barrow asked, ignoring her question.

"Rick just rented a new apartment. I have the address written down. But why are you asking?"

Betsy looked back and forth between Barrow and Saunders. Saunders would not meet her eye.

"Has something happened to Rick and Kathy?"

"Ms. Tannenbaum, this isn't easy for me. Especially since I know you. The door to your husband's apartment was open. A neighbor found him."

"Found Rick? How? What are you talking about?"

Barrow looked Betsy over carefully.

"Do you want some brandy or something? Are you gonna be okay."

"Oh, God," Betsy said, letting her head drop into her hands, so her face was covered.

"The neighbor has already identified Mr. Tannenbaum, so you'll be spared that."

"How did he . . . ?"

"He was murdered. We need you to come to the apartment. There are some questions only you can answer. You don't have to worry, the body's been removed."

Betsy suddenly jerked upright. "Where's Kathy?"

"We don't know, Ms. Tannenbaum. That's why we need you to come with us."

Most of the lab technicians were gone by the time Betsy arrived at Rick's apartment. Two officers were smoking in the hall outside his door. Betsy heard them laughing when the elevator doors opened. They looked guilty when they saw her step out. One of them held his cigarette at his side as if he was trying to hide evidence.

The door to Rick's apartment opened into a narrow hall. At the end of the hall, the apartment fanned out into a large living room with high windows. The lights were on in the hall. Betsy saw the blood immediately. It had dried into a large brown stain. Rick had died there. She looked up quickly and followed Barrow as he stepped over the spot.

"In here," he said, gesturing toward the guest room. Betsy walked into the room. She saw Kathy's book bag. Dirty jeans and a green, striped long-sleeve shirt lay crumpled on the floor in a corner. On the ride over, Betsy wondered if she could fake crying when the time came. She need not have worried.

"They're Kathy's," she managed. "She was so proud, because she packed everything herself."

There was a commotion at the front door. Alan Page tore into the apartment and went directly to Betsy.

"I just heard. Are you okay?"

Betsy nodded. Gone was the self-confidence Page had seen in court. Betsy looked like she could break into a million pieces at any moment. He took her hands and gave them a gentle squeeze.

"We'll get your daughter back. I'm putting everything we've got into this. I'll call in the FBI. We'll find out who has her."

"Thank you, Alan," Betsy answered dully.

"Are you through with her, Ross?"

Barrow nodded.

Page led Betsy out of the room and into a small den. He made Betsy sit down and he sat opposite her.

"Can I do anything for you, Betsy?"

Page was concerned by Betsy's pallor. Betsy took a deep breath and shut her eyes. She was used to thinking of Alan Page as a stone-hard adversary. Page's show of concern disarmed her.

"I'm sorry," Betsy said. "I just can't seem to focus."

"Don't apologize. You're not made of iron. Do you want to rest? We can talk about this later."

"No. Go ahead."

"Okay. Has anyone contacted you about Kathy?"

Betsy shook her head. Page looked troubled. It didn't make sense. Rick Tannenbaum had probably been killed the day before. If the person who took Kathy was after ransom he'd have called Betsy by now.

"This wasn't a robbery, Betsy. Rick's wallet was full of money. He had on a valuable watch. Can you think of anyone with a reason to hurt Rick?"

Betsy shook her head. It was hard lying to Alan, but she had to do it.

"He had no enemies?" Page asked. "Personal, business, someone in his firm, someone he bested in court?"

"No one comes to mind. Rick didn't get into court. He does contracts, mergers. I never heard him say anything about personal problems with anyone in his firm."

"I don't want to hurt you," Page said, "but Ross told me you and Rick were separated. What happened? Was he drinking, using drugs, was there another woman?"

"It was nothing like that, Alan. It was . . . He . . . he desperately wanted to be a partner at Donovan, Chastain and Mills and it looked like they weren't going to let him. And . . . and he was terribly jealous of my success." Tears welled up in Betsy's eyes. "Making partner meant so much to him. He couldn't see that I didn't care. That I loved him."

Betsy could not go on. Her shoulders shook with each sob. It all sounded so stupid. To break up a marriage over something like that. To leave your wife and daughter for a name on a letterhead.

"I'll be sending you home with an officer," Page said quietly. "I want to set up a command post in your house. Until we learn otherwise, we're treating Kathy's disappearance as a kidnapping. I want your permission to put a tap on your home and office phones, in case the person who has Kathy calls. We'll cut off any call from a client as soon as we know it's not the kidnapper. I'll have the office tapes erased."

"Okay."

"We haven't released Rick's identity yet and we aren't going to let the media know Kathy's missing until we have to, but we'll probably have to give out Rick's name in the morning. You're going to be hounded by the press."

"I understand."

"Do you want me to call someone to stay with you?"

There was no longer a reason to keep Kathy's disappearance from Rita. Betsy needed her more than ever.

"I'd like my mother to stay with me."

"Of course. I can have an officer drive her to your house."

"That won't be necessary. May I use the phone?"

Page nodded. "One other thing. I'll explain what happened to Judge Norwood. He'll set over the Darius hearing."

Betsy's heart leaped. She had forgotten about the hearing. How would Reardon react, if it was set over?

Reardon was holding Kathy because of the hearing. The longer it was put off, the greater was the danger that Reardon would harm Kathy.

"I'm going to work, Alan. I'll go crazy if I just sit at home."

Page looked at her oddly. "You won't want to tackle anything as complex as Darius's case now. You'll be too distracted to do a competent job. I want Darius more than I've ever wanted anyone, but I'd never take advantage of a situation like this. Believe me, Betsy. We'll talk about his case after the funeral."

The funeral. Betsy hadn't even thought about a funeral. Her brother had taken care of her father's funeral. What did you do? Whom did you contact?

Page saw how confused Betsy looked and took her hand. She had never noticed his eyes before. Everything else about the district attorney, from his lean build to the angles that made up his face, were so hard, but his eyes were soft blue.

"You look like you're about to fold up," Page said. "I'm going to send you home. Try to get some sleep, even if you have to take something. You'll need all your strength. And don't give up hope. You have my word. I'll do everything in my power to get back your little girl."

Chapter Twenty-seven

I

"Tannenbaum was killed Friday evening," Ross Barrow said as he uncapped a Styrofoam cup filled with black coffee. Randy Highsmith pulled a jelly doughnut out of a bag Barrow had placed on Alan Page's desk. It was still dark. Through the window behind Page, a river of headlights flowed across the bridges spanning the Willamette River as the Monday morning commuters drove into downtown Portland.

"Three days without a call," Page muttered to himself, fully aware of the implications. "Anything last night at Betsy's house?" he asked Barrow.

"A lot of condolence calls, but no kidnapper."

"How do you figure it?" Page asked Highsmith.

"First possibility, it's a kidnapping, but the kidnapper hasn't gotten in touch with Betsy for some reason known only to him."

"The kid could be dead," Barrow offered. "He wants to hold her for ransom, but fucks up and kills her."

"Yeah," Highsmith said. "Or, possibility number two, he has Kathy and he's not interested in ransom."

"That's the possibility I don't even want to consider," Page said.

"Do we have anything new, Ross?" Highsmith asked.

Barrow shook his head. "No one saw anyone leaving the apartment house with a little girl. The murder weapon is missing. We're still waiting on results from the lab."

Page sighed. He'd had very little sleep in the past few days and he was exhausted.

"The only good thing to come out of this mess is the extra time it's bought with Darius," Page said. "What was in the surveillance logs?"

"Nothing that helps us," Barrow answered. "Padovici and Kristol were on Darius from the moment he left his estate at six forty-three a.m. I talked to Justice Ryder again. He's positive he was eating breakfast with Lisa Darius at seven-thirty. The teams were on Darius constantly. Besides, Darius met with people all day, in his office. I've had every member of his staff and visitors interviewed twice. If they're covering for him, they're doing a great job."

"There has to be an answer," Page said. "Has the team we've got searching for Gordon turned up anything?"

"Nada, Al," Barrow answered. "No one's seen her since she checked into that motel."

"We know she's alive," Page said, his tone echoing his frustration. "She made that damn call. Why won't she show herself?"

"We have to start facing the fact that Gordon may have lied to you," Highsmith said. "Darius may have been a victim in Hunter's Point. Waters may have been the killer."

Page wished he could let Highsmith and Barrow

know what Wayne Turner had told him. Then they would know Gordon was telling the truth.

"Remember I suggested Gordon might be our killer, Al," Highsmith continued. "I think we'd better start considering her very seriously. I can't see any way she could have known we would find Lisa Darius in the basement, unless she put her there.

"What if she visited Lisa and convinced her to help her break into Martin's house to find evidence to convict him. They go through the woods. Lisa knows how to turn off the alarms. Martin Darius is at work all day and the house is deserted. She kills Lisa to frame Darius, waits until she sees him come home, then calls you. The only flaw in the plan is that Gordon doesn't know about the surveillance teams."

"Nancy Gordon did not kill those women," Page insisted. "Darius killed them, and he's not beating this case."

"I'm not saying Darius isn't guilty. I'm saying this case makes less and less sense every time I look at it."

Alan Page checked his watch. It was ten-thirty in Washington, D.C.

"This is going nowhere. I want to attend Rick Tannenbaum's funeral, and, believe it or not, I have some work to do that has nothing to do with Martin Darius or Rick Tannenbaum's murder. Let me know about any developments immediately."

"You want me to leave a doughnut?" Barrow asked.

"Sure. Why not? I should have at least one good thing happen to me today. Now get out and let me work."

Ross Barrow handed Alan a maple bar and followed Highsmith into the hall. As soon as the office door closed, Page dialed Senator Colby's office and asked for Wayne Turner.

"Mr. Page, what can I do for you?" Turner asked. Page could hear the tension in the administrative assistant's voice.

"I've been thinking about the senator's information all weekend. My situation is desperate. Even my own staff is starting to doubt Darius's guilt. We know Darius killed three women in Hunter's Point, including his wife and daughter, but the judge is starting to see him as an innocent victim and me as his persecutor. If Darius is released, I have no doubt he'll kill again. I don't see I have any choice but to ask the senator to testify about the pardon."

The line was silent for a moment. When Wayne Turner spoke, he sounded resigned.

"I was expecting your call. I'd do the same thing in your shoes. Darius has to be stopped. But I think there might be a way to protect the senator. Betsy Tannenbaum seems like a responsible person."

"She is, but I wouldn't count on her staying on the Darius case. Someone murdered her husband on Friday and kidnapped her little girl."

"My God! Is she okay?"

"She's trying to keep herself together. The husband's funeral is this afternoon."

"That might complicate matters. I was hoping we could convince her to tell Judge Norwood about the pardon in camera. That way he could use the information to deny bail without the public finding out about it."

"I don't know," Page said hesitantly. "You run into all sorts of constitutional problems if you try to bar the press. Besides, Darius would have to give his okay. I can't imagine him not trying to pull down Senator Colby with him."

"Take a shot at it, will you? The senator and I have

been talking this out. We might be able to weather the storm, but we don't want to, if we don't have to."

2

Storm clouds cast somber shadows over the mourners as the graveside service began. Then a light rain started to fall. Rick's father opened an umbrella over Betsy. Cold drops blew under it. Betsy did not feel them. She tried to pay attention to the eulogies, but her mind kept wandering to Kathy. She was grateful for the concern everyone had shown for her daughter, but every mention of Kathy drove a knife into her heart. When the rabbi closed his prayer book and the mourners began to drift away, Betsy stayed by the grave.

"Let her have some private time with him," Betsy heard Rita tell Rick's parents. Rick's father pressed the umbrella into her hand.

The cemetery spread across low, rolling hills. The headstones near Rick's grave were weathered, but well cared for. An oak tree would provide shade in the summer. Betsy stared at Rick's grave. What was left of her husband's body was covered by the earth. His spirit had flown. The future they might have had together would be a mystery forever. The finality terrified her.

"Betsy."

She looked up. Samantha Reardon was standing beside her. She wore a black raincoat and a wide-brimmed hat that left her face in shadow. Betsy looked around for help. Most of the mourners were walking quickly toward their cars to get out of the rain. Her brother was walking with the rabbi. Rita was talking to two of her friends.

Rick's family was huddled together, looking away from the grave.

"The hearing was supposed to be today."

"It's the funeral. I couldn't . . ."

"There will be no stalling, Betsy. I was counting on you and you let me down. I went to the courthouse and you weren't there."

"It's Rick's funeral."

"Your husband is dead, Betsy. Your daughter is still alive."

Betsy saw it would be useless to try and reason with Reardon. Her face was void of compassion. Her eyes were dead.

"I can call the judge," Betsy said. "I'll do it."

"You'd better, Betsy. I was so upset when I heard the hearing was delayed that I forgot to feed Kathy."

"Oh, please," Betsy pleaded.

"You've upset me, Betsy. When you upset me, I will punish Kathy. One meal a day is all she'll get until you've done as I say. There will be just enough water and just enough food so she can last. The same diet I received in Hunter's Point. Kathy will suffer because you disobeyed me. Every tear she sheds will be shed because of you. I'll be checking with the court. I better hear that a date has been set for the hearing."

Reardon walked away. Betsy took a few steps after her, then stopped.

"You forgot your umbrella," Alan Page said.

Betsy turned and stared at him blankly. The umbrella had slipped from her hand while Reardon was talking to her. Page held it over them.

"How are you holding up?" Page asked.

Betsy shook her head, not trusting herself to talk.

"You'll get through this. You're tough, Betsy."

"Thank you, Alan. I appreciate everything you've done for me."

It was hard dealing with grief in a house full of strangers. The FBI agents and the police tried to be unobtrusive, but there was no way to be alone without hiding in her bedroom. Page had been wonderful. He had arrived with the first invasion on Saturday night and stayed until dawn. On Sunday, Page returned with sandwiches. The simple, humanitarian gesture made her cry.

"Why don't you go home. Get out of this rain," Page suggested.

They turned away from the grave. Page covered them with the umbrella as they walked up the hill toward Rita Cohen.

"Alan," Betsy said, stopping suddenly, "can we hold the hearing for Darius tomorrow?"

Page looked surprised by the request. "I don't know Judge Norwood's calendar, but why do you want to go to court tomorrow?"

Betsy scrambled for a rational explanation for her request.

"I can't stand sitting in the house. I don't think the kidnapper will call, if he hasn't called by now. If . . . if this is a kidnapping for ransom, we have to give the kidnapper a chance to contact me. He may have guessed you'd tap the phones. If I'm at the courthouse, in a crowd, he might try to approach me."

Page tried to think of a reason to dissuade Betsy, but she made sense. There had been no attempt to phone or write Betsy at her home or office. He was beginning to accept the possibility that Kathy was dead, but he did not want to tell Betsy. Going along with her would give Betsy some hope. Right now, that was all he could do for her.

"Okay. I'll set it up as soon as I can. Tomorrow, if the judge can do it."

Betsy looked down at the grass. If Judge Norwood scheduled the hearing, Kathy might be home tomorrow. Page laid his hand on her shoulder. He handed the umbrella to Rita, who had walked down the hill to meet them.

"Let's go home," Rita said. Rick's family closed around her and followed her to the car. Page watched her walk away. The rain pelted down on him.

Chapter Twenty-eight

I

Reggie Stewart sat in his modest apartment staring at the lists spread across the kitchen table. Stewart did not feel good about what he was doing. He was an excellent investigator, but cross-checking hundreds of names on dozens of lists required manpower, and could be done a thousand times more efficiently by the FBI or the police.

Stewart was also concerned that he was obstructing justice. He knew the name of Kathy's kidnapper and he was concealing this information. If Kathy died, he would always wonder if the police could have saved her. Stewart liked and respected Betsy, but she was not thinking straight. He understood her concerns about the way the police and FBI might act, but he did not agree with her. He had half-decided to go to Alan Page if he did not come up with something quickly.

Stewart took a sip of coffee and started through the lists again. They were from real estate offices, utilities companies, phone companies. Some of them had cost him, but he had not considered the price. So far, there

z

380

were no listings for a Samantha Reardon or a Nora
Sloane, but Stewart knew it wouldn't be that easy.

On his second trip through a list of new Washington
County phone subscribers Stewart stopped at Dr. Samuel
Felix. Samantha Reardon's first husband was named Max
Felix. Stewart cross-checked the other lists and found that
a Mrs. Samuel Felix had rented a Washington County
home the week Oberhurst returned to Portland from
Hunter's Point. Stewart called Pangborn Realty as soon as
their office opened. The saleswoman who handled the
deal remembered Mrs. Felix. She was a tall, athletic
woman with short brown hair. A friendly lady who confided that she was not completely happy with moving
from upstate New York, where her husband practiced
neurosurgery.

Stewart called Betsy, but Ann told him she was on
her way to court on the Darius case. Stewart realized the
opportunity this presented. Reardon attended all the
court hearings in the Darius case. She would probably
attend this one and leave Kathy alone.

The house was at the end of a dirt road. It was white,
with a porch and a weather vane, a happy house that was
the least likely suspect to conceal suffering inside. Reggie
Stewart circled around the house through the woods. He
saw tire tracks in the front yard but no car. The door to
the small, unattached garage was open and the garage
was empty. The curtains were closed on most of the windows, but were open on the front window. There were no
lights on inside. Stewart spent twenty minutes watching
for any movement in the front room and saw none. If
Samantha Reardon lived in this house, she was not there
now.

Stewart darted across the yard and ducked into a

concrete well at the side of the house. Six steps led down
to a basement door. The basement windows were blacked
out with paint. If Reardon was duplicating Darius, Kathy
would be in the basement. The painted windows reinforced that belief.

Stewart tried the basement door. It was locked. The
lock did not look sturdy, and Stewart thought he could
kick in the door. He backed up two steps and braced his
arms against the sides of the concrete well, then reared
back and snapped his foot against the door. The wood
broke and the door gave a little. Stewart braced himself
again and swung his leg against the damaged part of the
door. It gave with a loud crack.

The basement was cloaked in darkness and Stewart
could see inside only as far as the sunlight penetrated. He
edged inside and was greeted by stale air and a foul odor.
Stewart pulled a flashlight out of his coat pocket and
played the beam around the room. Against the wall on his
right were homemade shelves of unpainted wood holding
a coil of hose, some cracked orange pots and miscellane-
ous gardening tools. A child's sled, some broken furniture
and several lawn chairs were piled in the middle of the
floor in front of the furnace. The odor seemed to emanate
from the corner across from the door where the darkness
was thickest. Stewart crossed the basement cautiously,
maneuvering around objects, alert for any noise.

The flashlight beam found an open sleeping bag.
Stewart knelt next to it. He saw encrusted blood where a
head would lie and smelled a faint odor of urine and feces. Another open bag lay a few feet farther into the darkness. Stewart was moving toward it when he saw the
third bag and the body sprawled across it.

2

The night before the hearing, Betsy was so preoccupied with Kathy that she forgot about Martin Darius. Now he was all she could think about. Samantha Reardon was forcing Betsy to choose between Kathy's life and the life of a man who did not deserve to live. The choice was simple, but it was not easy. As sick and twisted as he was, Darius was still a human being. When Betsy let Samantha Reardon into the jury room, she had no illusions about what would happen. If Martin Darius died, she would be an accomplice to murder.

Newspaper reporters surrounded Betsy as soon as she stepped off the elevator. She turned her head to avoid the glaring lights of the television cameras and the microphones as she hurried down the corridor toward Judge Norwood's courtroom. The reporters asked the same questions about Rick's murder and Kathy's disappearance over and over. Betsy answered none of them.

Betsy spotted Samantha Reardon as soon as she entered the packed courtroom. She walked past her quickly and hurried down the aisle to her seat. Darius was already at the counsel table. Two guards sat directly behind him and several others were spread through the courtroom.

Alan Page was just putting his file on the table when Betsy walked through the spectators. He caught Betsy as she entered the bar of the court.

"Are you certain you want to go through with this?"

Betsy nodded.

"Okay. Then there's something we have to discuss with Judge Norwood. I told him we would want to meet in his chambers before court started."

Betsy looked puzzled. "Should Darius be there?"

"No. This is between you, me and Norwood. I'm not letting Randy come in with us."

"I don't understand."

Page leaned close to Betsy and whispered, "I know Senator Colby pardoned Darius. The senator sent his a.a. to see me."

"Wayne Turner?"

Page nodded. "You know how the senator's confirmation hearing will be affected if news of the pardon is made public. Will you meet with the judge in chambers or are you going to insist we do this in open court?"

Betsy considered the situation quickly. Darius was watching her.

"I'm going to have to tell Darius. I can't agree to anything unless he consents."

"Can you wait until we meet with the judge?"

"All right."

Page went back to his table and Betsy sat next to Darius.

"What was that about?"

"Page wants us to meet with the judge in chambers."

"About what?"

"He's being mysterious."

"I don't want anything going on behind my back."

"Let me handle this, Martin."

Darius looked like he was going to balk for a moment. Then he said, "Okay. I trust you. You haven't let me down, so far."

Betsy started to stand up. Darius put a hand on her forearm.

"I heard about your husband and daughter. I'm sorry."

"Thank you, Martin," Betsy answered coldly.

"I mean it. I know what you think of me, but I do have feelings and I respect you."

Betsy did not know what to say. Before the hour was up, she would cause the death of the man who was trying to console her.

"Look, if the kidnapper wants money, I can help," Darius said. "Whatever he wants, I'll cover it."

Betsy felt her heart contract. She managed to thank Darius, then pulled away.

Judge Norwood stood when Betsy walked into his chambers. He looked concerned.

"Sit down, Mrs. Tannenbaum. Can I get you anything?"

"I'm fine, Judge."

"Do they have any news about Mrs. Tannenbaum's daughter, Al?"

"Nothing new, Judge."

Norwood shook his head. "I'm terribly sorry. Al, you tell your people to interrupt if they have to talk to you."

"I will."

The judge turned to Betsy.

"And, if you want to stop the hearing, if you aren't feeling well, anything at all, just tell me. I'll set over the hearing on my own motion, so your client won't be prejudiced."

"Thank you, Judge. Everyone is being so kind. But I want to go through with the hearing. Mr. Darius has been in jail for several days and he needs to know if he is going to be released."

"Very well. Now tell me why you wanted this meeting, Al."

"Betsy and I are aware of information about the Hunter's Point incident that is known to very few people. One of those people is Senator Raymond Colby."

"The President's nominee to the Court?" Norwood asked incredulously.

Page nodded. "He was the governor of New York

when the murders occurred in Hunter's Point. His information could affect your decision on bail, but it would badly damage Senator Colby's chances of being nominated."

"I'm confused. Are you saying Senator Colby is mixed up in the Hunter's Point murders?"

"Yes, sir," Page answered.

"And you agree, Mrs. Tannenbaum?"

"Yes."

"What is this information?"

"Before Mr. Page tells you," Betsy said, "I want to object to you hearing any of this testimony. If this information is used against Mr. Darius in any way, it will violate the due process guarantees of the United States Constitution and an agreement between Mr. Darius, the State of New York and the federal government. I think we need to hash this out in much greater detail before you call your witness."

"An agreement Darius made with those parties can't bind Oregon," Page said.

"I think it would."

"You two are getting way ahead of me. What type of agreement are we dealing with here?"

"A pardon, Judge," Page said. "Colby pardoned Darius when he was governor of New York."

"For what?"

"I'd prefer the contents of the pardon were not revealed until you decide the threshold question of admissibility," Betsy said.

"This is getting extremely complicated," Judge Norwood said. "Mrs. Tannenbaum, why don't we have the guards take Mr. Darius back to jail. It's obvious to me that this is going to take some time."

Betsy's stomach churned. She felt like she might collapse.

"I'd like to confer with Mr. Darius in private. Can I use your jury room?"

"Certainly."

Betsy walked out of the judge's chambers. She felt light-headed as she told the guards that Judge Norwood was letting her confer with Darius in the jury room. One of the guards went into the judge's chambers to check with Norwood. He came out a minute later and the guards escorted Darius into the room. Betsy looked toward the rear of the courtroom, just as Reardon walked into the hall.

A guard stationed himself outside the door to the courtroom. Another guard was in front of the door that opened into the hall. Betsy shut the door to the jury room behind them and turned the lock. A table long enough to accommodate twelve chairs filled the center of the large room. There was a narrow rest room in one corner and a sink, countertop and cabinet filled with plastic coffee cups and dishes against one wall. The other wall held a bulletin board covered with announcements and cartoons about judges and jurors.

Darius sat down at one end of the table. He was still dressed in the clothes he was wearing when he was arrested. The pants were rumpled and his shirt was wrinkled. He was not wearing a tie and he had jail-issue sandals on his feet.

Betsy stood at the edge of the table trying not to look at the door to the corridor.

"What's going on?" Darius asked.

"Page knows about the pardon. Colby told him."

"That son-of-a-bitch."

"Page wants to have the judge take Colby's testimony in secret, so the senator's chances of being confirmed won't be affected."

"Fuck him. If he tries to screw me, I'll take him down. They can't use that pardon anyway, can they?"

"I don't know. It's a very complicated legal issue."

There was a knock on the hall door. Darius noticed the way Betsy jerked her head around.

"Are you expecting someone?" he asked suspiciously.

Betsy opened the door without answering. Reardon was standing behind a guard. She was holding a black Gladstone bag.

"This lady says you're expecting her," the guard said.

"That's true," Betsy answered.

Darius stood up. He stared at Reardon. His eyes widened. Reardon looked into those eyes.

"Don't . . ." Darius started. Reardon shot the guard in the temple. His head exploded, spraying flesh and bone over her raincoat. Betsy stared. The guard crumpled to the floor. Reardon pushed Betsy aside, dropped the bag and locked the hallway door.

"Sit down," she commanded, pointing the gun at Darius. Darius backed away and sat in the chair at the end of the table. Reardon turned to Betsy.

"Take a chair on the other side from me, away from Darius, and fold your hands on the table. If you move, Kathy dies."

Darius stared at Betsy. "You planned this?"

"Shut up, Martin," Reardon said. Her eyes were wide. She looked manic. "Dogs don't talk. If you utter a sound without my asking, you'll suffer pain like you've never known."

Darius kept his mouth shut and his eyes riveted on Reardon.

"You made me an expert on pain, Martin. Soon you'll see how well I learned. My only regret is that I won't have those private moments with you that you shared with me. Those days alone together when you made me plead for pain. I remember each minute we shared. If we had time, I would make you relive every one of them."

Reardon picked up the black bag and placed it on the table.

"I have a question for you, Martin. It's a simple question. One you should have no trouble answering. I give you permission to answer it, if you can. Considering the time we spent together, it should be a breeze. What's my name?"

Someone pounded on the hall door. "Open up! Police."

Reardon half-turned toward the door, but kept her eyes on Darius.

"Get away or I'll kill everyone in here. I've got Betsy Tannenbaum and Martin Darius. If I hear anyone at the door, they die. You know I mean it."

There was a scraping at the door to the courtroom. Reardon fired a shot through the top of the door. Betsy heard several screams.

"Get away from the doors or everyone dies," Reardon yelled.

"We've backed off!" someone shouted from the hall.

Reardon pointed her gun at Betsy. "Talk to them. Tell them about Kathy. Tell them she'll die if they try to come in here. Tell them you'll be safe if they do as I say."

Betsy was shaking.

"Can I stand up?" she managed.

Reardon nodded. Betsy walked to the courtroom door.

"Alan!" she shouted, fighting to keep her voice from breaking.

"Are you okay?" Page shouted back.

"Please keep everyone away. The woman in here was one of the women Darius kidnapped in Hunter's

Point. She's hidden Kathy and she's not feeding her. If you capture her, she won't tell me where she's holding Kathy and she'll starve to death. Please keep everyone away."

"All right. Don't worry."

"In the hall, too," Reardon commanded.

"She wants everyone away from the hall door, too. Please. Do as she says. She won't hesitate to kill us."

Reardon turned her attention back to Darius. "You've had time to think. Answer the question, if you can. What's my name?"

Darius shook his head and Reardon smiled in a way that made Betsy feel cold.

"I knew you wouldn't know, Martin. We were never people to you. We were meat. Fantasy figures."

Betsy could hear people moving around in the courtroom and the corridor. Reardon opened the bag. She took out a hypodermic. Betsy could see surgical implements lying on trays.

"My name is Samantha Reardon, Martin. You're going to remember it when I'm through. I want you to know something else about me. Before you kidnapped me and ruined my life, I was a surgical nurse. Surgical nurses learn how to mend broken bodies. They see parts of the body maimed and twisted and they see what a surgeon has to do to relieve the pain injuries cause. Can you see how that information might be useful to a person who wanted to cause pain?"

Darius knew better than to answer. Reardon smiled.

"Very good, Martin. You're a fast learner. You didn't speak. Of course, you invented this game. I remember what happened the first time you asked me a question after telling me that dogs don't speak and I was foolish enough to answer. I'm sorry I don't have a cattle prod handy, Martin. The pain is exquisite."

Reardon laid a scalpel on the tabletop. Betsy felt sick. She sucked air. Reardon ignored her. She moved down the table closer to Darius.

"I have to get to work. I can't expect those fools to wait forever. After a while, they'll decide to try something stupid.

"You probably think I'm going to kill you. You're wrong. Death is a gift, Martin. It is an end to suffering. I want you to suffer as long as possible. I want you to suffer for the rest of your life.

"The first thing I'm going to do is shoot you in both kneecaps. The pain from this injury will be excruciating and it will cripple you sufficiently to prevent you from being a physical threat to me. I will then ease your pain by administering an anesthetic."

Reardon held up the hypodermic.

"Once you're unconscious, I'm going to operate on you. I'm going to work on your spinal cord, the tendons and ligaments that enable you to move your arms and legs. When you wake up, you'll be totally paralyzed. But that won't be all, Martin. That won't be the worst part."

A glow suffused Reardon's features. She looked enraptured.

"I'm also going to put out your eyes, so you won't be able to see. I'm going to cut out your tongue, so you won't be able to talk. I'm going to make you deaf. The only thing I'm going to leave intact will be your mind.

"Think about your future, Martin. You're relatively young. You're in good shape. A healthy specimen. With life support, you'll stay alive thirty, forty years, locked in the perpetual darkness of your mind.

"Do you know why they call prisons penitentiaries?"

Darius did not respond. Reardon chuckled.

"Can't fool you, can I. It's a place for penitence. A place for those who have wronged others to think about their sins. Your mind will become your penitentiary and you'll be locked in it, unable to escape, for the rest of your life."

Reardon positioned herself in front of Darius and aimed at his right knee.

"You in there. This is William Tobias, the police chief. I'd like to talk to you."

Reardon turned her head and Darius moved with uncanny speed. His left foot shot up, catching Reardon's wrist. The gun flew across the table. Betsy watched it skid toward her as Reardon staggered backward.

Betsy's hand closed on the gun as Darius grabbed Reardon's wrist to shake loose the hypodermic. Reardon lashed out with her foot and kicked Darius in the shin. She jabbed the fingers of her free hand at his eyes. Darius moved his head and the blow caught him on the cheek. Reardon leaped forward and sank her teeth into Darius's throat. He screamed. They smashed against the wall. Darius held tight to the hand holding the needle. He grabbed Reardon's hair with his free hand and tried to pull her off. Betsy saw Darius turn white from pain. Reardon struggled to free the hypodermic. Darius let go of Reardon's hair and smashed his fist into her head several times. Reardon's grip loosened and Darius pulled away. The flesh around his throat was ragged and covered with blood. Darius grabbed Reardon's hair, held her head away from him and smashed his forehead against her nose, stunning her. Reardon's legs gave way. Darius snapped her wrist and the syringe fell to the floor. He moved behind Reardon, wrapping an arm around her neck.

"No!" Betsy screamed. "Don't kill her. She's the only one who knows where Kathy is."

Darius paused. Reardon was limp. He was holding

her off the ground so only her toes were touching. His choke hold was cutting off her air.

"Please, Martin," Betsy begged.

"Why should I help you?" Darius yelled. "You set me up."

"I had to. She would have killed Kathy."

"Then Kathy's death will be a fitting punishment."

"Please, Martin," Betsy begged. "She's my little girl."

"You should have thought of that when you decided to fuck me over," Darius said, tightening his hold.

Betsy raised the gun and aimed it at Darius.

"Martin, I will shoot you dead if you don't put her down. I swear it. I'll keep shooting you until the gun is empty."

Darius looked across Reardon's shoulder. Betsy locked eyes with him. He calculated the odds, then he relaxed his grip and Reardon collapsed on the floor. Darius moved away from Reardon. Betsy reached behind her.

"I'm opening the door. Don't shoot. Everything is all right."

Betsy opened the door to the courtroom. Darius sat down at the table with his hands in plain view. Two armed policemen entered first. She gave one of them the gun. The other officer handcuffed Reardon. Betsy collapsed on one of the chairs. Several policemen entered from the hall. The jury room was suddenly filled with people. Two officers lifted Reardon off the floor and sat her in a chair opposite Betsy. She was still struggling for air. Alan Page sat next to Betsy.

"Are you all right?" he asked.

Betsy nodded mechanically. Her attention was riveted on Reardon.

"Samantha, where is Kathy?"

Reardon lifted her head slowly. "Kathy is dead."

Betsy turned pale. Her lips trembled as she tried to hold herself together. Reardon looked at Alan Page.

"Unless you do exactly what I say."

"I'm listening."

"I want what Peter Lake got. I want a pardon for everything. The cop in the hall, the women, the kidnappings. I want the United States attorney to guarantee no federal prosecution. I want the governor here personally. We'll videotape the signing. I'll walk. Just like Lake. Complete freedom."

"If you get your pardon will you tell us where you're holding Kathy Tannenbaum?"

Reardon nodded. "And Nancy Gordon."

"She's alive?" Page asked.

"Of course. Nancy is the only one who continued to track Martin. She's the only one who believed me. I wouldn't kill her. And there's something else."

"I'm listening."

"I can give you the proof to convict Martin Darius of murder."

Darius sat rigidly at the far end of the table.

"What proof is that?" Page asked.

Reardon turned toward Darius. She smiled.

"You think you've won, Martin. You think no one will believe me. A jury will believe a crazy woman if she has proof to back up her testimony. If she has photographs."

Darius shifted a little in his seat.

"Photographs of what?" Page asked.

Reardon spoke to Page, but she stared at Darius.

"He wore a mask. A leather mask. He made us wear masks too. Leather masks that covered our eyes. But there was one time, for a brief moment, when I saw his face. Just a moment, but long enough.

"Last summer, a private investigator named Samuel

Oberhurst showed me pictures of Martin. As soon as I saw the pictures I knew he was the one. There was the beard, the dark hair, he was older, but I knew. I flew to Portland and I began to follow Martin. I was with him everywhere and I kept a photographic record of what I saw.

"The week I arrived, Martin threw a party to celebrate the opening of a new mall. I mixed with the guests and selected several women to use as evidence against Martin. One of the women was his mistress, Victoria Miller. I sent a picture of Martin leaving their room at the Hacienda Motel to Nancy Gordon to lure her to Portland.

"The evening after I gathered Victoria, I followed Martin. He drove into the country to Oberhurst's house. I watched for hours while Martin tortured Oberhurst. When Martin took his body to the construction site, I was there. I took pictures. Most of them did not come out, because it was night and there was a lot of rain, but there's one excellent photograph of Martin lifting the body out of the trunk of his car. The trunk light illuminated everything."

Page looked across the table at Darius. Darius met Page's stare without blinking. Page turned back to Reardon.

"You'll get your pardon. We'll go to my office. It will take a while to firm up everything. Will Kathy and Nancy Gordon be all right?"

Sloane nodded. Then she smiled at Betsy.

"You didn't have to worry. I lied about starving Kathy. I fed her before I came here, then I put her to sleep. I gave Kathy her stuffed animal, too, and made certain she was nice and warm. I like you, Betsy. You know I wouldn't hurt you, if I didn't have to."

Page was about to tell two of the officers to take

Reardon to his office when Ross Barrow rushed into the room.

"We know where the girl is. She's all right. Tannenbaum's investigator found her in Washington County."

3

The woman the medics carried out of the dark basement looked nothing like the athletic woman who told Alan Page about Hunter's Point. Nancy Gordon was emaciated, her cheeks sunken, her hair unkempt. Kathy, on the other hand, looked like an angel. When Stewart found her, she was in a drugged sleep, lying on a sleeping bag, hugging Oliver. The doctors let Betsy touch Kathy's forehead and kiss her cheek, then they rushed her to the hospital.

In the living room, Ross Barrow took a statement from an excited Reggie Stewart while Randy Highsmith looked at photographs of Martin Darius that had been found during a search of the house. In one of the photos, the trunk light clearly showed Darius lifting the dead body of Samuel Oberhurst out of the trunk of Martin Darius's car.

Alan Page stepped out onto the porch. Betsy Tannenbaum was standing by the railing. It was cold. Page could see the mist formed by her breath.

"Are you feeling better, now that Kathy's safe?" Page asked.

"The doctors think Kathy will be fine physically, but I'm worried about psychological damage. She must have been terrified. And I'm frightened of what Reardon will do if she's ever released."

"You don't have to worry about that. She's going to be locked up forever."

"How can you be sure of that?"

"I'm having her civilly committed. I would have done that even if I was forced to give her a pardon. The pardon wouldn't have prevented me from committing her to a mental hospital if she's mentally ill and dangerous. Reardon has a documented history of mental illness and hospital commitments. I spoke to the people at the State Hospital. There will have to be a hearing, of course. She'll have a lawyer. I'm certain there will be some tricky legal issues. But the bottom line is that Samantha Reardon is insane and she will never see the light of day again."

"And Darius?"

"I'm dismissing all of the counts except the one for killing John Doe. With the picture of Darius with Oberhurst's body and the evidence about the murders in Hunter's Point, I think I can get the death penalty."

Betsy stared at the front yard. The ambulances were gone, but there were still several police cars. Betsy wrapped her arms around herself and shivered.

"A part of me doesn't believe you'll get Darius. Reardon swears he's the Devil. Maybe he is."

"Even the Devil would need a great lawyer with the case we have."

"Darius will get the best, Al. He's got enough money to hire anyone he wants."

"Not anyone," Page said, looking at her, "and not the best."

Betsy blushed.

"It's too cold to stand out here," Page said. "Do you want me to drive you to the hospital?"

Betsy followed Page off the porch. Page held open the door for her. She got in. He started the engine. Betsy looked back toward Kathy's prison. Such a charming place. To look at it, no one would ever guess what went on in the basement. No one would guess about Reardon, either. Or Darius. The real monsters did not look like monsters, and they were out there, stalking.

Epilogue

At eleven-thirty on a sultry summer morning, Raymond Francis Colby placed his left hand on a Bible held by the chief deputy clerk of the United States Supreme Court, raised his right hand and repeated this oath, after Associate Justice Laura Healy:

"I, Raymond Francis Colby, do solemnly swear that I will administer justice without respect to persons, and do equal right to the poor and to the rich, and that I will faithfully and impartially discharge and perform all the duties incumbent on me as Chief Justice of the United States according to the best of my abilities and understanding, agreeably to the Constitution and laws of the United States. So help me God."

"Is she a judge too, Mommy?" Kathy Tannenbaum asked.

"Yes," Betsy whispered.

Kathy turned back to the ceremony. She was wearing a new, blue dress Betsy bought for their trip to Washington. Her hair smelled of flowers and sunshine, as only the freshly shampooed hair of a little girl can smell. No one looking at Kathy would guess the ordeal she had undergone.

The invitation to Senator Colby's investiture arrived

a week after the Senate confirmed his appointment to the Court. The Lake pardon had been the nation's hottest news story for weeks. Speculation ran rampant that Colby would not withstand the revelation that he had set free the rose killer. Then Gloria Escalante publicly praised Colby for saving her life and Alan Page commended the senator's bravery in making the pardon public while still unconfirmed. The final vote for confirmation had been wider than anticipated.

"I think he's going to make a good justice," Alan Page said, as they left the Court's chambers and headed toward the conference room, where the reception for the justices and their guests was being held.

"I don't like Colby's politics," Betsy answered, "but I like the man."

"What's wrong with his politics?" Page deadpanned. Betsy smiled.

A buffet had been set up at one end of the room. There was a courtyard with a fountain outside a set of French windows. Betsy filled a plate for Kathy and found a chair for her to sit on near the fountain, then Betsy went back inside for her own food.

"She looks great," Page told her.

"Kathy's a trouper," Betsy answered proudly. "The investiture came at a good time, too. Kathy's therapist thought a change of scenery would be beneficial. And we're going home by way of Disneyland. Ever since I told her, she's been on cloud nine."

"Good. She's lucky. You too."

Betsy stacked some cold cuts and fresh fruit on her plate and followed Page back toward the courtyard.

"How are you doing with Darius?" Betsy asked.

"Don't worry. Oscar Montoya is making a lot of noise about the pardon, but we'll get it into evidence."

"What's your theory?"

"We believe Oberhurst was blackmailing Darius about the Hunter's Point murders. The pardon is relevant to prove Darius committed them."

"If you don't get the death penalty, you have to lock him up forever, Alan. You have no idea what Darius is like."

"Oh, I think I do," Alan answered smugly.

"No, you don't. You only think you do. I know things about Darius—things he told me in confidence—that would change you forever. Take my word for it: Martin Darius must never leave prison. Never."

"Okay, Betsy. Take it easy. I'm not underestimating him."

Betsy had been so intense that she did not notice Justice Colby until he spoke. Wayne Turner was standing beside the new Chief Justice.

"I'm glad you came," Colby told Betsy.

"I was flattered you invited me."

"You're Alan Page," Colby said.

"Yes, sir."

"For you and Betsy, I will always be Ray. You have no idea how much your statement meant to my confirmation. I hope you can come to the party I'm throwing tonight at my home. It will give us a chance to talk. I'd like to get to know you two better."

Colby and Turner walked off and Betsy led Page into the courtyard, where they found Kathy talking to a woman with crutches.

"Nancy," Alan Page said. "I didn't know you'd be here."

"I wouldn't have missed the senator's swearing-in," she said with a smile.

"Have you met Betsy Tannenbaum, Kathy's mother?"

"No," Gordon said, extending her hand. "It's a pleasure. This is one tough kid," she added, ruffling Kathy's hair.

"I'm so pleased to meet you," Betsy said. "I tried to see you at the hospital, but the doctors wouldn't let me. Then you flew back to Hunter's Point. Did you get my note?"

"Yeah. I'm sorry I didn't write back. I've always been a lousy correspondent. Kathy tells me you're going to Disneyland after you leave Washington. I'm jealous."

"You can come too," Kathy said.

Gordon laughed. "I'd love to, but I have to work. Will you write me and tell me all about your trip?"

"Sure," Kathy said earnestly. "Mom, can I have more cake?"

"Certainly. Alan, will you show Kathy where the cake is?"

Alan and Kathy walked off and Betsy sat down beside Gordon.

"Kathy looks great," Gordon said. "How's she doing?"

"The doctors say she's fine physically and the psychiatrist she's seeing says she's going to be okay."

"I'm glad to hear that. I was worried about how she'd come out of it. Reardon treated her pretty well most of the time, but there were some grim moments."

"Kathy told me how you kept up her spirits. The psychiatrist thinks that having you there really helped."

Gordon smiled. "The truth is, she's the one who kept up my spirits. She's one brave little girl."

"How are you feeling?"

"Better each day. I can't wait to get rid of these," Gordon said, pointing at her crutches. Then she stopped smiling. "You're Martin Darius's attorney, aren't you?"

"Was. Oscar Montoya is representing him now."

"How did that happen?"

"After I spoke to Senator Colby and learned what he did to the Hunter's Point women I didn't want him as a client, and he didn't want me as his lawyer when he realized I helped Samantha Reardon get to him."

"What's going to happen to Darius?"

"He tortured Oberhurst. I saw the autopsy photographs. They turned my stomach. Alan Page is certain he'll get the death penalty when the jury sees the photos and hears what happened in Hunter's Point."

"What do you think will happen?"

Betsy recalled the smug look on Alan's face when he talked about how certain he was that he could convict Darius, and she felt uneasy.

"I'm not as certain as Alan. He doesn't know Martin like we do."

"Except for Gloria Escalante and Samantha Reardon, no one knows Darius like we do."

Darius had told Betsy, "The experiment brought me the most exquisite pleasure," when he described his kingdom of darkness. There was no sign of remorse or compassion for the pain his victims had suffered. Betsy knew Darius would repeat his experiment if he thought he could get away with it, and she wondered if Darius had any plans for her now that he knew Betsy had betrayed him.

"You're worried he'll get out, aren't you?" Gordon asked.

"Yes."

"Worried about what he might do to you and Kathy?"

Betsy nodded. Gordon looked directly into Betsy's eyes.

"Senator Colby has contacts at the FBI. They're monitoring the case and they'll keep a close watch on

Darius. I'll be told if there's even a possibility that Darius
will leave prison."

"What would you do if that happened?" Betsy asked.

When Gordon spoke, her voice was low and firm
and Betsy knew she could trust anything Gordon promised.

"You don't have to worry about Martin Darius,
Betsy. He'll never hurt you or Kathy. If Darius sets one
foot out of prison, I'll make certain he never hurts anyone
again."

Kathy ran up with a plate piled high with cake.

"Alan said I could have as much as I wanted," she
told Betsy.

"Alan is as bad as Granny," Betsy answered.

"Give the kid a break." Page laughed and sat next to
Betsy. Then he asked her, "Do you ever daydream about
arguing here?"

"Every lawyer does."

"What about you, Kathy?" Page asked. "Would you
like to come here as a lawyer and argue in front of the
United States Supreme Court?"

Kathy looked over at Nancy Gordon, her features
composed and very serious.

"I don't want to be a lawyer," she said. "I want to be
a detective."

WILD JUSTICE

Revenge is a kind of wild justice.
——Francis Bacon

Acknowledgments

Many generous people helped me research and write *Wild Justice*. My thanks to Janet Billups; Ted Falk; Drs. Nathan and Karen Selden; Claudia Gravett; Dr. Jay Mead; Dr. Don Girard; Marlys Pierson; Rabbi Emanuel Rose; Carole Byrum; Debi Wilkinson; Maggie Frost; Brian Hawke; the Honorable Susan Svetkey and the equally honorable Larry Matasar; Joseph, Eleonore, Judy, and Jerry Margolin; Helen and Norman Stamm; Dr. Roy Magnusson; Dr. Edward Grossenbacher; Dr. Michael Palmer; Drs. Rob and Carol Unitan; Dr. Stanley Abrams; and Jerry Elshire.

Special thanks go to my tireless and relentless editor, Dan Conaway. Every reader who enjoys reading *Wild Justice* should also thank him. And thanks also to Bob Spizer for his useful insights.

I also want to thank Jean Naggar for finding me a home at HarperCollins and, as always, thank you to everyone else at Jean V. Naggar Literary Agency: You are the best.

And finally to Doreen, Daniel and Ami, thanks for putting up with me.

Part I

Cardoni's Hand

1

A lightning flash illuminated the Learjet that waited on the runway of the private airstrip moments before a thunderclap startled Dr. Clifford Grant. Grant scanned the darkness for signs of life, but there were no other cars in the lot and no one moving on the tarmac. When he checked his watch his hand trembled. It was 11:35. Breach's man was five minutes late. The surgeon stared at the glove compartment. A sip from his flask would steady his nerves, but he knew where that would lead. He had to be thinking clearly when they brought the money.

Large drops fell with increasing speed. Grant turned on his wipers at the same moment a huge fist rapped on his passenger door. The doctor jerked back and stared. For an instant he thought the rain was distorting his vision; but the man glaring at him through the window was really that big, a monster with a massive, shaved skull and a black knee-length leather coat.

"Open the door," the giant commanded, his voice harsh and frightening.

Grant obeyed instantly. A chill wind blew a fine spray into the car.

"Where is it?"

"In the trunk," Grant said, the words catching in his throat as he jerked his thumb backward. The man tossed an attaché case into the car and slammed the door shut. Water beaded the smooth sides of the brief-case and made the brass locks glisten. The money! Grant wondered how much the recipient was going to pay for the heart, if he and his partner were receiving a quarter of a million dollars.

Two rapid thumps brought Grant around. The giant was pounding on the trunk. He had forgotten to pop the release. As Grant reached for the latch another lightning flash lit the view through his rear window—and the cars that had appeared from nowhere. Without thinking, he floored the accelerator and cranked the wheel. The giant dove away with amazing agility as the sedan careened across the asphalt, leaving the smell of burning rubber. Grant was vaguely aware of the screech of metal on metal as he blasted past one of the police cars and took out part of a chain-link fence. Shots were fired, glass shattered and the car tipped briefly on two wheels before righting itself and speeding into the night.

The next thing Clifford Grant remembered clearly was banging frantically on his partner's back door. A light came on, a curtain moved and his partner glared at him in disbelief before opening the door.

"What are you doing here?"

"The police," Grant gasped. "A raid."

"At the airfield?"

"Let me in, for God's sake. I've got to get in."

Grant stumbled inside.

"Is that the money?"

Grant nodded and staggered to a seat at the kitchen table.

"Let me have it."

The doctor pushed the briefcase across the table. It opened with a clatter of latches, revealing stacks of soiled and crumpled hundred-dollar bills bound by rubber bands. The lid slammed shut.

"What happened?"

"Wait. Got to. . . catch my breath."

"Of course. And relax. You're safe now."

Grant hunched over, his head between his knees.

"I didn't make the delivery."

"What!"

"One of Breach's men put the money on the front seat. The heart was in the trunk. He was about to open it when I saw police cars. I panicked. I ran."

"And the heart is . . . ?"

"Still in the trunk."

"Are you telling me that you stiffed Martin Breach?"

"We'll call him," Grant said. "We'll explain what happened."

A harsh laugh answered him. "Clifford, you don't *explain* something like this to Breach. Do you understand what you've done?"

"You have nothing to worry about," Grant answered bitterly. "Martin has no idea who you are. I'm the one who has to worry. We'll just have to return the money. We didn't do anything wrong. The police were there."

"You're certain he doesn't know who I am?"

"I never mentioned your name."

Grant's head dropped into his hands and he began to tremble. "He'll come after me. Oh, God."

"You don't know that for sure," his partner answered in a soothing tone. "You're just frightened. Your imagination is running wild."

The shaking grew worse. "I don't know what to do."

Strong fingers kneaded the tense muscles of Grant's neck and shoulders.

"The first thing you've got to do is get hold of yourself."

The hands felt so comforting. It was what Grant needed, the touch and concern of another human being.

"Breach won't bother you, Clifford. Trust me, I'll take care of everything."

Grant looked up hopefully.

"I know some people," the voice assured him calmly.

"People who can talk to Breach?"

"Yes. So relax."

Grant's head fell forward from relief and fatigue. The adrenaline that had powered him through the past hour was wearing off.

"You're still tense. What you need is a drink. Some ice-cold Chivas. What do you say?"

The true extent of Grant's terror could be measured by the fact that he had not even thought of taking a drink since he saw the police through his rear window. Suddenly every cell in his body screamed for alcohol. The fingers lifted; a cupboard door closed; Grant heard the friendly clink of ice bouncing against glass. Then a drink was in his hand. He gulped a quarter of the contents and felt the burn. Grant closed his eyes and raised the cold glass to his feverish forehead.

"There, there," his partner said as a hand slapped smartly against the base of Grant's neck. Grant jerked upright, confused by the sharp sting of the ice pick as it passed through his brain stem with textbook precision.

The doctor's head hit the tabletop with a thud. Grant's partner smiled with satisfaction. Grant had to die. Even thinking about returning a quarter of a million dollars was ridiculous. What to do with the heart, though? The surgeon sighed. The procedure to remove it had been performed flawlessly, but it was all for nothing. Now the organ would have to be cut up, pureed and disposed of as soon as Grant took its place in the trunk.

2

The deputy district attorney had asked three questions of Darryl Powers, the arresting officer, before Amanda Jaffe realized that the first question had been improper. She leaped to her feet.

"Objection, hearsay."

Judge Robard looked perplexed. "How could Mr. Dart's question possibly be hearsay, Ms. Jaffe?"

"Not that one, Your Honor. I believe it was . . . let's see. Yes. Two questions before."

Judge Robard looked as though he were in great pain.

"If you thought that question was hearsay, why didn't you object to it when it was asked?"

Amanda felt fires ignite in her cheeks.

"I didn't realize it was hearsay until just now."

The judge shook his head sadly and cast his eyes skyward, as if asking the Lord why he had to be plagued with such incompetence.

"Overruled. Proceed, Mr. Dart."

It took Amanda a moment to remember that "overruled" meant she had lost. She collapsed in her seat. By then, Dart had asked another killer question. Welcome to the real world, a tiny voice whispered in her head. She had earned an A in Evidence at one of the nation's top law schools and had written a note on hearsay for the law review, but she could not think fast enough to make a timely objection in court. Now the judge was certain that she was a moron, and only God knew what the jury thought of her.

Amanda felt a hand patting her forearm. "Don't feel bad, girlfriend," LaTricia Sweet said. "You're doin' fine."

Great, Amanda thought. I'm screwing up so badly that my client feels she has to console me.

"And were you dressed as you are now, Officer Powers?" Rodney Dart continued.

"No, sir. I was dressed in civilian clothes, because this was an undercover operation."

"Thank you, Officer. Please tell the jury what happened next."

"I asked the defendant how much it would cost to have her engage in the sex acts she had suggested. The defendant said that she had her crib in the motel across the street and would feel more comfortable discussing business there. I drove to the motel lot and followed the defendant into room one-oh-seven."

"What occurred inside the motel room?"

"I asked the defendant to explain the price of the various sex acts, and she mentioned rates ranging from fifty dollars to two hundred dollars for something she described as 'a night of ecstasy.'"

"What exactly was this 'night of ecstasy,' Officer Powers?"

"Quite honestly, Mr. Dart, it was too complicated to remember, and I couldn't take out my notebook at that time because I was undercover."

Darryl Powers had baby blue eyes, wavy blond hair and the type of smile Amanda had seen only in a

toothpaste commercial. He had even blushed when
he answered the "night of ecstasy" question. Two of
the female jurors looked as if they were about to leap
the railing of the jury box and tear off pieces of his
clothing.

Amanda grew more despondent as Powers continued to explain the circumstances leading up to La-
Tricia's arrest for prostitution. Her cross examination
was pathetic. When she was through, Rodney Dart
said, "The State rests." Then he turned toward
Amanda, his back to the jury, and smirked. Amanda
thought about giving Dart the finger, but she was too
depressed to defend herself. What she really wanted
to do was finish her first trial, go home, and commit
seppuku. Besides, Dart had every right to smirk. He
was riding roughshod over her.

Officer Powers smiled at the jury as he left the
stand. All five of the women jurors smiled back.

"Any witnesses, Ms. Jaffe?" Judge Robard asked,
but Amanda did not hear him. She was thinking
about the previous afternoon when the senior partner in her law firm, her father, Frank Jaffe, had given
her LaTricia's case and told her to be ready to try it
in the morning.

"*How can I possibly try my first case without interviewing any of the witnesses or doing any investigation?*"
Amanda had asked in horror.

"*Believe me,*" *Frank Jaffe had replied,* "*with LaTricia as
your client, the less you know, the better off you are.*"

Amanda had read over the file in State v. Sweet *four
times before marching down the hall to her father's office,
planting herself in front of his desk and waving it in his
face.*

"*What am I supposed to do with this?*" *she'd demanded
angrily.*

"Put on a vigorous defense," Frank had answered.

"How? There's only one witness, a sworn officer of the law. He's going to testify that our client promised to do things to him for money that I'll bet ninety-five percent of humanity has never heard of."

"LaTricia can take care of herself."

"Dad, get real. She has thirteen priors for crimes like prostitution, prohibited touching and lewd behavior. Who is going to take her word over the cop's?"

Frank had shrugged. "It's a funny world, Amanda."

"I can't try a case this way," Amanda had insisted.

"Of course you can. Trust me. And trust LaTricia. Everything will work out just fine if you go with the flow."

Judge Robard cleared his throat, then repeated himself.

"Ms. Jaffe, any witnesses?"

"Uh, yes, Your Honor."

The skirt of her black Donna Karan power suit rode up her long legs as Amanda stood. She wanted to tug it down, but she was afraid that everyone in court would see her, so she stood before the court with her thighs partially exposed and color rising in her cheeks.

"The defense calls LaTricia Sweet."

Before leaving her seat to cross to the witness box, LaTricia leaned over and whispered in Amanda's ear.

"Don't worry about nothin', honey. After I swear to tell the whole truth, you ask me what I do for a living, what I said to that police and why I said it. Then sit back and let me do my thing."

Before Amanda could reply, LaTricia sashayed across the room. Her bust and butt were so huge that Amanda was afraid that they would rip her tight red sweater and black leather mini skirt. A blond-orange wig, slightly askew, sat atop her head. Amanda com-

pared her client to the radiant Darryl Powers and
moaned inwardly.

Since she had no plan, Amanda decided to follow
her client's instructions.

"Ms. Sweet," she asked after LaTricia was sworn,
"what do you do for a living?"

"I walk the streets of Portland and sell my body,
Ms. Jaffe."

Amanda blinked. The confession was a surprise,
but she was relieved that her client was not lying under oath.

"Can you tell the jury what happened on the
evening of August third of last year?"

"Yes, ma'am."

LaTricia composed herself and turned toward the
jury.

"On August third I was working on Martin Luther
King Boulevard when Officer Powers drove by."

"Did you know that he was a policeman?"

"Yes, I did."

"You did?"

"Oh, yes. I've seen Officer Powers run a game on
several of my friends."

"Then why did you . . . Uh, what happened next?"

LaTricia straightened her skirt and cleared her
throat.

"Officer Powers asked me if I would have sex with
him. Now, I knew what he was trying to do. I've seen
him arrest my friends, like I said. But I knew he
couldn't arrest me if I didn't mention money. So I told
him that I had a room in the motel across the street
and I would feel more comfortable discussing our
mutual interests there. Officer Powers asked me what
those interests might be, and I described a few things
that seemed to perk him up. At least I thought they

did, because his face got all red and I noticed that
something more than his temperature was rising."

Two of the jurors glanced at each other.

"What happened then?" Amanda asked.

LaTricia looked at the jurors, then down at her lap.

"Officer Powers parked in the motel lot and we
went to my crib. Once we was inside I . . . This is a little embarrassing for me, Ms. Jaffe, but I know I got to
tell the truth."

"Just take your time, Ms. Sweet," Amanda advised her. LaTricia nodded, took a deep breath and
continued.

"Like I said, I'd seen Officer Powers around and I
thought that he was about the sweetest thing I ever
did see, so young and shy. All those friends of mine
he'd busted said he was polite and treated them like
ladies. Not like the other police. And, well. . . "

"Yes?"

LaTricia cast her eyes down. When she spoke, her
voice was barely audible.

"The truth is, I fell in love with Officer Powers and
I confessed my love as soon as I shut the door to my
room."

The jurors leaned forward. Someone in the back of
the room giggled.

"I know that sounds crazy," LaTricia said, direct-
ing her comment to the spectators, "and I know Officer Powers didn't say nothin' 'bout my confession
when he was on the stand. I don't know if he left that
out because he was embarrassed or because he didn't
want to embarrass me. He's such a gentleman."

LaTricia squared her shoulders and turned back to
the jury.

"Soon as we was alone I came clean and told him
that I knew that he was a policeman. Then I told him

that I knew that I was just an old whore, used up by life, but that I had never felt about any man the way I felt about him. Officer Powers, he blushed and looked like he wanted to be anywhere but with me, and I can understand that. He probably has himself a fine white woman, someone foxy. But I told him that all I wanted was one night of love with him and that he could take me to jail when it was over, because one night of his sweet love would be worth an eternity of jail."

A tear trickled down LaTricia's cheek. She paused, drew a handkerchief from her purse, dabbed at the tear, then said, " 'Scuse me," to the jurors.

"Do you want some water, Ms. Sweet?" asked Amanda, who had been swept up in the drama of the moment. Rodney Dart leaped to his feet.

"Objection, Your Honor. This is too much."

"Oh, I don't 'spect you to believe any of this, Mr. DA. An old bag like me trying to find love with a man half her age. But can't I dream?"

"Your Honor," Dart begged.

"The defendant is entitled to put on a defense, Mr. Dart," Judge Robard answered in a tone that let the jurors know that he wasn't buying LaTricia's act, but several of the jurors were casting angry glances at the prosecutor.

"Ain't much more to say," LaTricia concluded. "I gambled for love and I lost. I'm ready to take what fate has in store. But I want you to know that I never wanted money from that man. All I wanted was love."

Frank Jaffe, the senior partner in Jaffe, Katz, Lehane and Brindisi, was a big man with a ruddy complexion and black curly hair that was streaked with gray. His nose had been broken twice in his youth, and he looked more like a teamster or a stevedore than an attorney. Frank was in his office dictating a letter when Amanda walked in waving the *Sweet* file.

"How could you do this to me?"

Frank grinned. "You won, didn't you?"

"That's beside the point."

"Ernie Katz was in the back of the courtroom. He said you weren't totally awful."

"You sent Ernie to watch me be humiliated?"

"He also said that you looked scared to death."

"I was, and giving me this insane case didn't help."

"You'd have been scared no matter what case you tried first. When I tried my first case I spent the whole trial trying to remember the words you say when you want to introduce a piece of evidence. I never did get it right."

"Thank you for sharing."

"Hey, I lost my first trial. I knew you'd have a fighting chance with LaTricia as your client no matter how badly you screwed up. I've been representing her for years, and she usually comes out okay. Ernie said the jury was back in twenty minutes."

"Twenty-two," Amanda answered with a grudging smile. "I have to admit winning was a rush."

Frank laughed. "Ernie also said that your closing argument was a doozy. Especially the part where you told the jury that you had scoured the statutes of the state of Oregon and had been unable to find love defined as a crime."

Amanda grinned. It had been a great line. Then she stopped smiling.

"I still think you're a bastard."

"You're a warrior now, kiddo. The whole office is waiting at Scarletti's to celebrate."

"Oh, shit, they're just going to razz me. Besides, I didn't do much. LaTricia won the case with her cockamamie story."

"Hey, trial lawyers should never be humble. Crow about your victories and blame your defeats on biased judges, ignorant juries, and the tricks of fascist prosecutors. As of now, you're the only lawyer in this office who's never lost a case."

Until she found a place of her own, Amanda was living with Frank in the green, steep-roofed East Lake Victorian where she had grown up. Amanda had not been home, except for summers and holiday visits, since she'd started college, nine years ago. Staying in the second-floor bedroom where she had spent her childhood felt strange after so many years of independence. The room was filled with mementos of her youth: diplomas from high school and college, shelves loaded down with swimming trophies and medals, framed newspaper clippings detailing her athletic feats.

Amanda was exhausted and a little drunk when she climbed into bed at ten, but she was too upset to sleep. Frank had had no business throwing her into court unprepared in the same way he'd thrown her into the pool at the YMCA when she was three to teach her how to swim. Then, at Scarletti's, Frank had embarrassed the hell out of her by giving a speech that compared her victory in court to her surprise win her freshman year at the state high school swimming championships. She wanted her father to stop thinking of her as his little girl and to realize that she was a grown woman who had earned credentials that could open any door in the legal community.

Amanda had forgotten how controlling Frank could be. His assumption that he always knew what was best for her was infuriating. Tonight was not the first time she'd wondered if she had made a mistake by joining Frank's firm instead of going to one of the many San Francisco firms that had courted her or applying for a clerkship at the United States Supreme Court, as Judge Madison had advised.

Amanda stared at the shadows on the bedroom ceiling and asked herself why she had come back to Portland, but she knew the answer. Ever since she had been old enough to understand what her father did, she had been steeped in, and seduced by, the mystery and adventure of criminal law, and no one was better at criminal defense than Frank Jaffe. As a little girl, she had watched her father charm juries and confound hostile witnesses. He had held her in his arms at news conferences and discussed his strategy with her at the kitchen table over hot chocolate. While her law school classmates talked about the money they would make, she thought about the innocents she would save.

Amanda turned on her side. Her eyes had grown used to the dark. She studied the symbols of her successes that Frank had assembled. Frank had lived a lost childhood through her. She knew he loved her and wanted what was best for her. What she wanted was the chance to decide for herself what was best.

3

Mary Sandowski burst through the operating room doors. As the nurse rushed along the crowded hospital corridor, she ducked her head to hide the tears that coursed down her cheeks. Moments later Dr. Vincent Cardoni slammed through the same doors and ran after her. When the powerfully built surgeon caught up with Sandowski, he grabbed the slender woman's elbow and spun her toward him.

"You incompetent cow."

Visitors, patients and hospital personnel stopped to stare at the outraged physician and the woman he was berating.

"I tried to tell you. . . ."

"You switched the cups, you moron."

"No. You—"

Cardoni shoved her against the wall and leaned forward until his face was inches from the cowering nurse. The pupils in his bloodshot eyes were dilated, and the tendons in his neck swelled.

"Don't you ever contradict me."

"Vincent, what do you think you're doing?"

Cardoni pivoted. A tall woman with caramel-

colored hair and an athletic figure was bearing down
on him. She was wearing a loose brown dress and a
white doctor's smock. The cold eyes she fixed on the
surgeon were the color of jade.

Cardoni turned his rage on the newcomer.

"This is not your business, Justine."

The woman stopped a few paces from Cardoni
and stood her ground.

"Take your hands off her or I'll have you up before
the Board of Medical Examiners. I don't think you
can stand another complaint, and there will be plenty
of witnesses this time."

"Is there a problem, Dr. Castle?"

Justine glanced at the broad-shouldered man in
green OR scrubs who now stood beside her. The
white letters on his black plastic name tag identified
him as Anthony Fiori.

"There's no problem, because Dr. Cardoni is going
to leave," Justine said, returning her gaze to Cardoni.
A pulse throbbed in the surgeon's temple and every
muscle in his body tensed, but he suddenly noticed
the crowd that had gathered, and he released
Sandowski's elbow. Justine stepped closer to Cardoni and studied his eyes.

"My God," she said in a low tone that was still
loud enough to carry beyond them. "Are you on
something? Were you operating on drugs?"

Cardoni's fists knotted. For a moment it appeared
that he would strike Justine. Then he spun and
stalked away, shouldering through the onlookers.
Sandowski sagged against the wall. Fiori caught her.

"Are you okay?" he asked gently.

She nodded as she wept.

"Let's get you someplace less public," Justine said,
taking Sandowski's arm and leading her down a side

hall and into a call room where the residents sacked out. Justine eased the shaken nurse onto a narrow metal-frame bed that stood against one wall, and sat beside her. Fiori fetched a cup of water.

"What happened?" Justine asked once Sandowski regained her composure.

"He said I switched the cups, but I didn't. He filled the syringe without looking."

"Slow down. I'm not following you."

Sandowski took a deep breath.

"That's better. Just relax."

"Dr. Cardoni was performing a carpal tunnel release. You anesthetize the hand with lidocaine before you operate."

Justine nodded.

"Then you irrigate the wound with hydrogen peroxide before suturing it."

Justine nodded again.

"The lidocaine and the hydrogen peroxide were in two cups. Dr. Cardoni insisted on filling the syringe himself. He didn't look."

"He injected the patient with hydrogen peroxide instead of the lidocaine?" Justine asked incredulously.

"I tried to tell him that he had it wrong, but he told me to shut up. Then Mrs. Manion, the patient, started complaining that it was stinging, so he injected her again and she started to scream."

"I don't believe this," Justine said, shaking her head in disgust. "How could he possibly mistake lidocaine for hydrogen peroxide? One of them is clear and the other has bubbles in it. It's like confusing Champagne and water."

"I really tried to tell him, but he wouldn't let me. I

don't know what would have happened if Dr. Metzler hadn't stopped him. It wasn't my fault. I swear I didn't mix up the cups."

"Do you want to report this? I'll back you up."

Sandowski looked startled. "No, no. I don't have to, do I?"

"It's your decision."

Sandowski's eyes were wide with fear. "You're not going to report it, are you?"

"Not if you don't want me to," Justine answered soothingly.

Sandowski's head dropped, and she started to cry again. "I hate him. You don't know what he's like," Sandowski sobbed.

"Oh, yes, I do," she said. "I'm married to that bastard."

Fiori looked surprised.

"We're separated," Justine said forcefully.

She handed Sandowski a tissue. "Why don't you go home for the rest of the day?" Justine suggested. "We'll clear everything with the head nurse."

Sandowski nodded, and Fiori used the phone to make arrangements for the nurse to leave.

"Something's got to be done about him," Justine said as soon as Sandowski was out of the call room.

"Were you serious when you accused Cardoni of operating on drugs?"

Justine looked at Fiori. She was flushed.

"He can't get through the day without cocaine. He's a malpractice case waiting to happen. I know he's going to kill someone if something isn't done, but I can't say a word. He's an established surgeon. I'm only a resident. I'm also suing him for divorce. No one would take me seriously."

"I see what you mean," Fiori answered thoughtfully. "It puts you in a tough spot. Especially if Nurse Sandowski won't report him."

"I can't ask her to. She's scared to death."

Fiori nodded.

"Thank you for stepping in when you did, by the way. I don't know what Vincent would have done if you hadn't been there."

Fiori smiled. "You looked like you were handling yourself okay."

"Thanks anyway."

"Hey, we lowly residents need to stick together." Fiori saw the time on a wall clock. "Oops, got to run or I'll be late for a date with a fatty tumor in Lumps and Bumps."

The handsome resident took off down the corridor with a purposeful stride. Justine Castle watched him until he disappeared around a corner.

4

Martin Breach's sandy hair was thinning, his drab brown eyes were watery and he had the pale complexion of someone who rarely went outside during the day. He also had dreadful taste in clothes. Breach wore orange or green slacks with garish jackets and loud ties that were unfashionably wide. His outfits made him look silly, but Breach didn't care. By the time his enemies realized that they had underestimated him, they were frequently dead.

Breach had started in the trenches breaking legs for Benny Dee, but he was too intelligent to stay a leg breaker for long. Now Breach ran the most efficient and ruthless criminal organization in the Pacific Northwest. No one knew where to find Benny Dee.

Martin's right-hand man, Art Prochaska, was a giant with thick lips, a broad nose and pencil-thin eyebrows. Rumor had it that in his days as a collector for the mob he had used his huge head to stun debtors as effectively as an electric charge from a Taser. Prochaska had none of Breach's smarts, but he shared his taste for violence. When Martin climbed the ladder of crime, he pulled along the only person in the world he trusted.

Prochaska limped through the door of Breach's office in the rear of the Jungle Club and settled himself across the desk from his boss. He had injured himself when he hit the pavement at the airfield diving to avoid Clifford Grant's car. The office was tiny, and the furniture was rickety and secondhand. Pictures of naked women and a calendar from a motor oil company decorated the paper-thin walls. Raucous music from the strip club made it difficult to hear. Breach wanted the club to look run-down so that the IRS could not get a true picture of the money that flowed through it.

"So?" Breach asked.

"Grant's gone. We checked his place and the hospital. No one's seen him since he split during the raid."

Breach was very quiet. To someone who did not know, he seemed relaxed, but Prochaska was aware that a rage of monumental proportions was building.

"This is bad, Arty. I'm out a quarter of a million bucks, I'm out my profit and my reputation has taken a hit because of that quack."

"If he hadn't taken off with the heart, we'd have been arrested."

Breach stared at Prochaska long enough to make the giant look down.

"Where is he?"

"No one knows. Eugene and me searched his apartment. We didn't find squat. I got the feeling someone had tossed it before we did, but I couldn't say for sure."

"The cops?"

"No, the place was too neat."

"The partner?"

"Maybe."

"Who is he, Arty?"

Prochaska answered hesitantly. He always hated to tell Breach bad news. "I got one possible lead. My friend at the phone company gave me Grant's records. He made a few calls to a number in the West Hills. The phone belongs to Dr. Vincent Cardoni."

"Is he a surgeon?"

"Yeah, and he works at St. Francis Medical Center."

Breach's eyes narrowed. Clifford Grant had privileges at St. Francis.

"The lady across the way from his apartment said that Grant didn't get many visitors, but she saw a woman up there and a man, maybe two. Anyway, the woman was a knockout, so the neighbor kidded Grant about her. She says he got all nervous. He said she was an associate from work named Justine Castle."

"So what?"

"She's a doctor, a surgeon, and that ain't all. Castle is married to Vincent Cardoni."

Breach thought for a moment while Prochaska shifted nervously in his seat.

"Do you think the cops have Grant?" Breach asked.

"Our people in the Bureau say no."

"Do a background check on those two, Arty."

"I'm doin' it already."

"I want Grant, I want his partner and I want my money back. And once I've got all three, I'm going to get me a replacement for the heart I lost."

5

Dr. Carleton Swindell, the hospital administrator for St. Francis Medical Center, won his bid on
the computer bridge game, then checked his watch.
He'd kept his appointment waiting for twenty minutes. Swindell's thin lips drew into a satisfied smile.
Stewing was probably more accurate, if he knew Dr.
Cardoni. Well, that was too bad. It would do Cardoni
good to learn a little humility.

Swindell clicked his mouse. The bridge game disappeared and was replaced by a screen saver showing Einstein and Leonardo da Vinci playing
tennis—another game at which Swindell excelled.
The hospital administrator went into his private
washroom and adjusted his bow tie in the mirror. He
believed himself to be a handsome man, still as dapper at forty-five in his tweed sports jacket, blue Oxford shirt and sharply creased slacks as he had been
at Yale. His blond hair was growing a bit thin in
places and he needed his gold wire-rimmed glasses
for reading, but he sculled every morning on the
Willamette, so his weight was the same as it had been
during his university days.

Carleton returned to his office and glanced at his watch again. Twenty-five minutes. Cardoni would be boiling, he thought with satisfaction. Oh, well, no need to overdo it. He leaned forward and buzzed his secretary.

"Please send in Dr. Cardoni, Charlotte."

Swindell composed himself and waited for the explosion. He was not disappointed. Charlotte opened his office door wide and pressed against it. Cardoni charged in. The scene reminded Swindell of a bull-fight he'd seen in Barcelona. Charlotte was the matador, the door her cape, and the bull. . . He had to fight to suppress a smile.

"I've been out there half an hour," Cardoni said.

"I'm sorry, Vincent. I was on an important long-distance call," the administrator replied calmly. If Cardoni had seen the unlit lines on Charlotte's phone, he'd know that Swindell was lying, but Swindell bet he wouldn't call him on it. "Have a seat."

"What's this about?" Cardoni demanded.

Swindell leaned back and made a steeple of his fingers. "I've had a disturbing report about you."

Cardoni glared. The administrator noted the surgeon's flushed pallor, his disheveled hair and unkempt clothes. Cardoni was clearly on the edge. Maybe the rumors of drug use were true.

"Did you accost a nurse in a public corridor yesterday?"

"Accost?" Cardoni mocked. "What does that mean, Carleton?"

"You know very well, Vincent," Swindell answered evenly. "Did you accost Mary Sandowski?"

"Who told you that?"

"That's confidential. Well?"

Cardoni smirked. "No, Carleton, I did not accost her. What I did was ream her out."

"I see. And you, um, reamed her out in front of patients and staff at this hospital?"

"I have no idea who was around. The dumb bitch fucked up during an operation. I should have gotten her fired."

"I'd appreciate a little less profanity, Vincent. Also, you should know that more than one person has informed me that you were responsible for the mistake in the OR. Injecting your patient with hydrogen peroxide instead of lidocaine, I believe."

"After that moron switched the cups."

Carleton tapped his fingertips together and studied Cardoni before replying.

"You know, Vincent, this isn't the first complaint of. . . well, to put it bluntly, incompetence that's been made against you."

Every muscle in the surgeon's body went rigid.

"I want to be frank," Swindell continued. "If Mrs. Manion were to file a malpractice case against you, it would make three complaints." Swindell shook his head sadly. "I don't want to take action, but I have a duty to this hospital."

"None of those charges has any foundation. I've consulted my attorney."

"That may be, but there's a lot of talk. Rumors of drug use, for instance."

"So you've been chatting with Justine."

"I can't reveal my sources." Swindell looked at Cardoni sympathetically. "You know, there are wonderful programs for doctors in trouble," he said in a man-to-man tone. "They're all confidential. Charlotte can give you a list when you leave."

"She really got to you, didn't she, Carleton? Did you know that Justine's filed for divorce? She'd do anything to blacken my reputation."

"You seem to have a number of court cases going on. Wasn't there something last year involving an assault?"

"Where is this going?"

"Going? Well, that depends on what I find out after my investigation is complete. I invited you here so you could tell me your side of the story."

Cardoni stood. "You've heard it. If there's nothing more, I've got things to do."

"There's nothing more for now. Thank you for dropping by."

Cardoni turned his back on the administrator and stalked out without shutting the door. Swindell sat motionless.

"Did you want this closed?" Charlotte asked.

Swindell nodded, then swiveled his chair until he was looking out at the lights of Portland. Cardoni was crude and disrespectful, but the problem he presented could be dealt with. Swindell's lips twisted into a smile of anticipation. It would be a pleasure taking the arrogant surgeon down a peg or two.

Vincent Cardoni waited for his connection beneath a freeway off-ramp. Thick concrete pilings straddled the narrow street. There was a vacant lot across the way, and a plumbing supply warehouse was the nearest building. At ten in the evening the area was deserted.

Cardoni was still in a rage as a result of his meeting with Carleton Swindell. Cardoni never called the administrator "Doctor." The wimp may have trained as a surgeon, but he couldn't cut it. Now he was an administrator who got his rocks off by making life difficult for the real doctors. What really burned Cardoni was the prick's refusal to say whether it was Sandowski or Justine who had informed on him. Cardoni was leaning toward Justine. The nurse was too afraid of him, and it would be just like his bitch wife to use Swindell to put on the pressure so that she would have leverage in the divorce proceedings.

Headlights at the far end of the block flashed on and off, and Cardoni got out of his car. Moments later Lloyd Krause pulled under the off-ramp. Lloyd was six-two and a fat 250 pounds. His long, dirty hair reached the shoulders of his black leather jacket, and there were grease stains on his worn jeans. Cardoni could smell him as soon as he climbed out of his car.

"Hey, man, got your page," Krause said.

"I appreciate the speed."

"You're a valued customer, Doc. So, what can I do you for?"

"I'll take an eight ball, Lloyd."

"My pleasure," Krause answered. He walked to his trunk, popped the lid and rummaged around. When he stood up he was holding a Ziploc bag filled with two and a half grams of white powder, which Cardoni pocketed.

"Two fifty, my man, and I'll be on my way."

"I came straight from the hospital, so I don't have the cash with me. I'll get it to you tomorrow."

The dealer's easy smile vanished.

"Then you'll get the snow tomorrow," he said.

Cardoni had expected this. "Where do you want me to meet you?" he asked, making no move to return the cocaine.

Krause held out his hand, palm up. "The Baggie," he demanded.

"Look, Lloyd," Cardoni answered casually, "we've been friends for almost a year. Why make this hard?"

"You know the rules, Doc. No dough, no snow."

"I'm going to pay you tomorrow, but I'm using this cocaine tonight. Let's not damage a good relationship."

Lloyd's hand plunged into his pocket. When it came out, he was holding a switchblade.

"That's a scary knife," Cardoni said without a trace of fear.

"The coke, and no more fucking around."

Cardoni sighed. "I'm certain you're experienced with that knife."

"That is fucking correct."

"But you might want to ask yourself one question before you try to use it."

"This isn't *Jeopardy*. Give me the coke."

"Think for a moment, Lloyd. You're bigger than me and you're younger than me and you have a knife, but I don't look worried, do I?"

Doubt flickered in the dealer's eyes, and he took a quick look around.

"No, no, Lloyd, that's not it. We're all alone, just the two of us. I wanted it that way because I thought you might act like this."

"Look, I don't want to hurt you. Just give me the dope."

"You're not going to hurt me, and I'm not returning the eight ball. I know that for a fact. You better figure out why, quickly, before something bad happens."

"What the fuck are you talking about?"

"It's a secret, Lloyd. Something I know that you don't. Something I know about what happened the last time someone pulled a knife on me."

Cardoni noticed that the dealer had not moved closer, and he noted a tremor in Krause's hand.

"There's a lot about me that you don't know, Lloyd."

He looked directly into his connection's eyes.

"Have you ever killed a man? Have you? With your bare hands?"

Krause took a step back.

"Fear the unknown, Lloyd. What you don't know can kill you."

"Are you threatening me?" Krause asked with false bravado.

Cardoni shook his head slowly.

"You don't get it, do you? We're all alone here. If something happens, no one can help you."

Cardoni straightened to his full height, moving sideways to give the dealer a smaller target.

"I honor my debts, and I will pay you tomorrow."

The dealer hesitated. Cardoni's cold eyes bored into him. Krause licked his lips. The doctor got in his car, and Krause made no move to stop him.

"It's three hundred tomorrow," Lloyd said, his voice shaky.

"Of course, for the inconvenience."

"You better fucking bring it."

"No problem, Lloyd." Cardoni started the car. "You have a good evening."

Cardoni drove off, waving casually, the way he might after finishing a friendly round of golf.

6

Mary Sandowski's eyes opened. Wherever she was, it was pitch black and a blanket of warm, muggy air pressed down on her. Mary wondered if you could feel the touch of air in a dream but was too tired to figure out the answer, so she closed her eyes and dozed off.

Time passed. Her eyes opened again, and Mary willed herself out of the fog. She tried to sit up. Restraints cut into her forehead, ankles and wrists and anchored her in place. She panicked, she struggled, but she soon gave up. Lying in the dark, in the silence, she could hear her heart *tap-tap-tapping*.

"Where am I?" she asked out loud. Her voice echoed in the darkness. Mary took deep breaths until she was calm enough to take stock. She knew that she was naked because she could feel the air on her body. There was a sheet under her, and under the sheet was a firm padded surface. She might be on a gurney or an examining table like the ones at the hospital. A hospital! She must be in a hospital. That had to be it.

"Hello! Is anybody here?" Mary shouted. A nurse would hear her. Someone would come in and tell her why she was in the hospital . . . if she was in a hospital. It dawned on Mary that the air smelled slightly foul. Missing was the antiseptic odor she associated with St. Francis.

A door opened. She heard the click of a switch, and a flash of light blinded her. Mary closed her eyes in self-defense. The door closed.

"I see the patient is awake," a friendly voice said. It sounded vaguely familiar. Mary opened her eyes slowly, squinting into the light of the bare bulb that dangled directly overhead.

"I hope you're rested. We have a lot to do."

"Where am I?" Mary asked.

There was no answer. Mary heard the sound of shoes moving across the floor. She strained to see the person who was standing at the foot of the table.

"What's wrong with me? Why am I here?"

A shape moved between Mary and the lightbulb. She saw a section of a green hospital gown that surgeons wore when they operated. Mary's heart lurched. A needle pricked a vein in her forearm.

"What are you doing?" Mary asked anxiously.

"Just giving you a little something that will heighten your sensitivity to pain."

"What?" Mary asked, not certain she had understood correctly.

Suddenly Mary's throat constricted. She became aware of a warm feeling. Every nerve in her body began to tingle. She heaved for breath and began to sweat. Her pores exuded the smell of fear. Suddenly the sheet beneath her was damp and rough to the touch, and the air that caressed her naked body felt like sandpaper.

Without a word, a hand slid across her left breast. It felt unbearably cold, like dry ice.

"Please," she begged, "tell me what's happening."

A thumb caressed her nipple, and she felt fear so intense that it raised her body a fraction of an inch from the table.

"Good," the voice remarked. "Very good."

The hand slid away. There was complete quiet. Mary bit her lip and tried to stop shaking.

"Talk to me, please," she pleaded. "Am I sick?" Mary heard the unmistakable metallic ping of surgical instruments touching accidentally. "Are you going to operate?"

The doctor did not answer her.

"I'm Mary Sandowski. I'm a nurse. If you tell me what you're going to do, I'll understand, I won't be afraid."

"Really?"

The doctor chuckled and moved to Mary's side. She saw light dancing off the smooth steel of a scalpel blade. Now she was babbling with fear, but the doctor still refused to answer her question and began to hum a tune.

"Why are you doing this?" Mary sobbed.

For the first time the doctor seemed interested in something she had said. There was a pause while the surgeon contemplated her question. Then the doctor leaned closer and whispered.

"I'm doing this because I want to, Mary. Because I can."

7

Amanda Jaffe executed a flip turn and felt her foot slip on the tiles as she somersaulted off the pool wall. The bad turn made her shimmy as she headed into the final lap of her 800-meter freestyle, and she had to fight the water to get her body right. Amanda was on the edge of exhaustion, but she dug in for a final sprint. When she saw the far wall through the churning water, she gritted her teeth for one last, great effort, lunged forward and collapsed against the side of the pool. A clock hung on the wall in front of her. Amanda pulled her goggles onto her forehead. As soon as she saw her time, she groaned. It was nowhere near the time she had registered five years ago in the finals of the PAC-10 championships.

Amanda tugged off her swim cap and shook out her long black hair. She cut an imposing figure, with shoulders that were broad and muscular from years of competitive swimming. When her breathing leveled, Amanda checked the clock again, noting that her recovery time was also a hell of a lot slower than it had been when she was twenty-one. For a brief moment she thought about working out a little longer, but she knew she'd had it. She hoisted herself out of the pool and headed for the Jacuzzi, where she would soak until the pain in her tired muscles disappeared.

When she was dressed, Amanda went to the reception desk at the Y and stood in line to swap her key for her membership card. She had noticed the woman ahead of her when she was showering. She had the hard, muscled physique of someone who works out with weights and runs long distances, and her looks were as impressive as her body. The woman got her card from the clerk and walked toward an equally striking man in a blue warm-up suit. They made quite a couple. The man looked athletic. He had a dark complexion and blue eyes, and his black hair fell across his forehead in a boyish tangle.

Amanda frowned. There was something familiar about the woman's companion, but she couldn't remember where she'd seen him before. Then he smiled and she knew.

"Tony?"

The man turned.

"I'm Amanda Jaffe."

Tony Fiori's face lit up.

"My God, Amanda, of course! How many years has it been?"

"Eight, nine," Amanda answered. "When did you get back to Portland?"

"About a year ago. I'm a doctor. I'm doing my residency at St. Francis."

"That's great!"

"What are you up to?"

"I'm a lawyer."

"Not medical malpractice, I hope?"

Amanda laughed. "No, I'm with my dad's firm."

"Hey, I'm forgetting my manners." Tony turned to
the woman. "Amanda Jaffe, Justine Castle. Justine's a
friend from the hospital, another overworked and
underpaid resident. Amanda and I went to high
school together, and her father and mine used to be
law partners."

Justine had watched quietly while Amanda and
Tony spoke. Now she smiled and extended a hand. It
was cool to the touch, and her grip was strong.
Amanda thought that her smile was forced.

Tony looked at his watch. "We've got to get back
to St. Francis," he said. "It was great seeing you.
Maybe we can get together for lunch sometime."

"That would be terrific. Nice meeting you, Justine."

Justine nodded, and she and Tony walked down
to the parking lot. Amanda had parked on the street.
She smiled as she headed to her car. Tony had always
been a hunk, but she could only fantasize about him
in high school when she was a geeky freshman and
he was a godlike senior. Then the difference in their
ages had been huge. It didn't seem so great now.
Maybe she would ask him out for coffee.

Amanda laughed. If he accepted, her social life
would improve 100 percent. The only man her age at
the firm was married, and she spent most of her
working hours out of the office at the law library,
which was not heavily populated by swinging sin-
gles. She had bar-hopped a few times with two girlfriends she knew from high school, but she didn't
like the forced gaiety. In truth, she found dating
painful. Most of the men she'd gone out with hadn't
held her interest for long. Her only serious affair had
been with a fellow law student. It had ended when a
Wall Street firm hired him and she accepted a clerk-

ship on the United States Court of Appeals for the Ninth Circuit, which sat in San Francisco. Todd had made their continuing relationship conditional upon Amanda staying in New York and sacrificing the clerkship. Amanda had decided to sacrifice Todd instead and had never regretted the decision.

Though she didn't miss Todd, she did miss being with someone. Amanda had fond memories of buying the Sunday *New York Times* at one A.M. and reading it at breakfast over toasted bagels and hot coffee. She liked morning sex and studying with someone warm and friendly nearby. Amanda wasn't going to give up her identity for any man, but there were times when it was nice having a man around. She wondered if Tony and Justine were more than friends. She wondered if Tony would say yes to a cup of coffee.

8

The weather in Portland was cold and wet, and Bobby Vasquez was tired and cranky. The wiry vice cop had spent the last two weeks trying to gain the confidence of a low-level junkie whose brother was connected in a big way to some very serious offenders. The junkie was sly and suspicious, and Vasquez was beginning to think that he was wasting his time. He was writing a report about their last meeting when the receptionist buzzed him.

"There's a weird call on line one."

"Give it to someone else."

Vasquez still had on the stained jeans, torn flannel shirt and red-and-black Portland Trailblazers T-shirt that he'd been wearing for two straight days. They smelled and he smelled, and he wanted nothing more out of life than a shower, a six-pack and tonight's Blazer telecast.

"You're the only one in," the receptionist said.

"Then get a number, Sherri, I'm busy."

"Detective Vasquez, I've got a strange feeling about this. The person is disguising his or her voice with some kind of electronic equipment."

Sherri had just started, and she treated every new

case as if it was the next O.J. Vasquez decided that it would be easier to take the call than argue with her, and it would definitely be more fun than writing the report. He picked up the phone.

"This is Detective Vasquez. Who am I speaking to?"

"Listen to me, I won't repeat myself," the caller said through a device that produced an eerily inhuman monotone. "Dr. Vincent Cardoni, a surgeon at St. Francis Medical Center, recently purchased two kilos of cocaine from Martin Breach. Cardoni is hiding the cocaine in a mountain cabin. He is going to sell it to two men from Seattle within the week."

"Where is this cabin?"

The caller told Vasquez the location.

"This is very interesting," Vasquez was saying when the line went dead. He gazed at the receiver, then stared into space. The mystery snitch had said the magic word. Vasquez could care less about some junkie doctor. Martin Breach was another matter.

The closest they had come to indicting Breach was two years ago when Mickey Parks, a cop on loan from a southern Oregon police department, infiltrated Breach's organization. Vasquez had been Parks's control, and they had grown close. A week before Breach was going to be arrested, Parks disappeared. Over the next month, the vice and narcotics squad received untraceable packages containing the policeman's body parts. Everyone knew that Breach had killed Parks, knowing that he was a cop, but there was not a shred of evidence connecting Breach to the murder. Breach had cracked jokes during his interrogation while the detectives, including Vasquez, looked on helplessly.

Vasquez swiveled his chair and imagined a doctor

in handcuffs slumped forward in an interrogation room, his tie undone, his shirt rumpled, sweat beading his forehead. A doctor in those circumstances would be very vulnerable. Draw a few pictures for him of the downside of spending time in the company of deranged bikers, honkie-hating homeboys and slavering queers and the doctor would drink gasoline to avoid prison. It wouldn't take much effort to convince a terrified physician that ratting out Martin Breach was easier than guzzling premium unleaded.

Vasquez swiveled again and confronted the first problem he foresaw. To arrest the doctor Vasquez needed evidence. The cocaine would do it, but how was he going to find Cardoni's stash? The courts had ruled that the phone tip of an anonymous informant was not a sufficient basis for securing a search warrant. If the informant would not give his name, he could be a liar with a grudge or a prankster. Information provided by an anonymous informant had to be corroborated before a judge would consider it. Vasquez could not get a warrant to search the cabin unless he could present some proof that the cocaine was inside. That was not going to be easy, but nailing Breach was worth the effort.

9

The gravel in the nearly empty parking lot of the Rebel Tavern crunched under the tires of Bobby Vasquez's dull green Camaro. Two Harleys and a dust-coated pickup truck were parked on either side of the entrance. Vasquez checked the rear and found Art Prochaska's cherry red Cadillac parked under the barren limbs of the lot's only tree.

At night, the Rebel Tavern looked like a scene from a postapocalyptic sci-fi flick. Bearded, unwashed bodies clad in leather and decorated with terrifying tattoos stood four deep at the bar, eardrum-busting music made speech impossible and blood flowed at the slightest excuse. But at three on a Friday afternoon the cruel sun spotlighted the tavern's fading paint job and the jukebox was turned low enough for the hung-over to bear.

Vasquez entered the tavern and waited while his eyes adjusted to the dark. His investigation was not going well. Vincent Cardoni was under investigation by the Board of Medical Examiners, and his behavior at St. Francis Medical Center was becoming increasingly erratic and violent; there were even rumors about cocaine use. But none of this information provided probable cause to search Cardoni's mountain cabin for two kilos of cocaine. Vasquez was desperate, so he had set up this meeting with Art Prochaska, who had been busted by the DEA recently. Vasquez would have to help Prochaska with his federal beef if he wanted information, a prospect he found as appealing as a prostate examination, but it was starting to look as though Breach's enforcer might be his only hope.

Prochaska was nursing a scotch at the bar. While Vasquez bought a bottle of beer, Prochaska went to the men's room. Vasquez followed a moment later. As soon as the door closed, Prochaska locked it and slammed Vasquez face forward into the wall. Vasquez could not stand the feel of Prochaska's hands on him, but he expected the frisk and stifled his impulse to smash his beer bottle into the gangster's face. When the pat-down was finished, Prochaska stepped back and told Vasquez to turn around. The vice cop was standing close enough to smell the garlic on Prochaska's breath.

"Long time, Art."

"If I never saw you, it wouldn't be too long, Vasquez," Prochaska answered in a voice that sounded like a car driving over crushed gravel.

Vasquez took a sip of his beer and leaned back against the bathroom wall. "I hear you're under indictment for possession with intent to distribute. I want to help you with the feds."

Prochaska laughed. "You born again?"

"Don't be so cynical. I've been known to help bigger turds than you when it worked to my advantage."

"Why don't you quit wasting my time and tell me what you want?"

"I need some information about Dr. Vincent Cardoni, a surgeon at St. Francis."

"Don't know him."

"Look, Art, you know I'm not wired. This is between us. I'm just trying to corroborate some information I received."

"How can I help you if I don't know this guy?"

"By telling me if Martin Breach sold him two kilos of cocaine."

Prochaska moved very quickly for a man his size. Before Vasquez could react, Prochaska pinned him to the wall and pressed his forearm against Vasquez's windpipe. The beer bottle crashed to the floor. Prochaska tilted Vasquez's chin up, so he was forced to stare into the hit man's eyes.

"I should crush your throat and kick you to death for even suggesting that I rat out my best friend."

Vasquez tried to struggle, but Prochaska had a hundred pounds on him. Panic made him twitch as he consumed the last of his air, but Prochaska confined him like a straitjacket. Just as Vasquez became light-headed, Prochaska eased off and stepped back. Vasquez sagged against the wall and gulped in the urine-scented air. Prochaska smiled wickedly.

"That's how easy it is," he said. Then he was gone.

10

An hour later Bobby Vasquez turned onto the two-lane highway that led into the mountains near Cedar City. The highway gained altitude quickly. Low-hanging clouds shrouded the tops of high green foothills, and the air was heavy with the threat of snow. On the north side of the highway, through a break in the towering evergreens, the cold, clear water of a runoff rushed downhill over large gray stones polished smooth by the constant torrent. On the south side, the highway ran beside a river that boiled with white water in some spots and crept along with lazy indifference in others.

While Mickey Parks had been undercover, Vasquez was the only person Parks could talk to without fear of giving himself away. He'd confided his fears and hopes to Vasquez as if Bobby were a priest in a confessional, and Vasquez had grown to like and admire the naïve, dedicated cop. Parks's death hit Vasquez hard. Prochaska's refusal to corroborate his tip did not dissuade Vasquez from going after his killers. It made him only more determined to bring down Breach.

A narrow dirt driveway led from the highway to

the cabin. The weak light from the setting sun was
cut off by thick rows of towering evergreens and the
driveway was covered with dark shadows. At the
end of a quarter mile the headlights settled on a modern home of rough cedar with high picture windows
and a wide deck along the north and west sides. A
stone chimney was part of the east side of the house
and rose above the peaked shake roof. Vasquez wondered how much Cardoni's "cabin" cost. Even before
his divorce, the best Vasquez had been able to afford
had been a house half its size.

Vasquez parked the car so that it was pointing
back toward the road. He pulled on latex gloves and
walked toward the cabin. Crime was almost nonexis-
tent in this mountain community and the house did
not have an alarm. Once he stepped inside he would
be committing a felony, but Vasquez had to know if
Cardoni really had two kilos hidden in this house. If
he found the stash, he would leave and figure out a
way to get a warrant. He could even tail Cardoni and
try to catch him selling. The main thing was to find
out if he was on a wild-goose chase.

Vasquez turned his collar up against the chill and
worked his way around the house, trying the exterior
doors before resorting to forced entry. He got lucky
when he turned the knob of a small door in the rear
of the garage and it opened. Vasquez turned on the
garage lights and searched. The garage had an un-
used feel to it. No tools hung from the walls; Vasquez
saw no gardening equipment or junk lying about. He
also found no cocaine, but he did find a key for the
house hanging on a hook. A moment later Vasquez
was standing in a downstairs hall at the foot of a
flight of stairs.

At the top of the stairs was a living room with a

wall of glass that provided a panoramic view of the
forest. Something moved on the periphery of his vision, and Vasquez went for his gun, stopping when
he realized that he'd seen a deer bounding into the
woods. Vasquez exhaled and turned on the lights. He
had no fear of being discovered. Cardoni's nearest
neighbors were half a mile away.

The living room was sparsely furnished; the furniture was cheap and looked out of place in such an ex-
pensive home. It occurred to Vasquez that there was
no dust or dirt anywhere, as if the living room had
been cleaned recently. There were plastic plates and
cups in the cupboards, a few mismatched utensils in
the drawers. A pottery mug half filled with cold coffee sat on the drain board next to the sink. Vasquez
also noted a coffeepot still holding a small amount of
coffee. He touched the pot. It was cold.

The master bedroom had the same unlived-in
feel. Vasquez saw an empty bookcase, a wooden
straight-back chair and a cheap mattress that rested
on the floor. There were no sheets on the mattress,
but there were several dried brown spots that looked
like blood. Vasquez searched the closets and the connecting bathroom. Then he moved on to the other
rooms on the main floor. The more Vasquez
searched, the more uneasy he felt. He had never seen
such a tidily desolate home. Aside from the coffee
cup and the coffeepot, there were no signs of life
anywhere.

When Vasquez finished with the main floor he
headed downstairs to the basement. There were four
rooms, one of which was padlocked. Vasquez
searched the other rooms. All were empty and devoid
of dust or dirt.

Vasquez returned to the padlocked door. He had a set of lock picks with him and was soon inside a long and narrow room with walls and floor of unpainted gray concrete. A faint unpleasant odor permeated the air. Vasquez looked around. A sink was in one corner and a refrigerator in another. Between them, in the center of the room, was an operating table. Hanging from the padded tabletop were leather straps that could be used to secure a person's arms, legs and head. A metal tray that would hold surgical implements during an operation was completely empty.

The detective studied the floor around the operating table more closely and spotted several bloodstains. Vasquez knelt to get a better look at the blood and caught sight of something under the table. It was a scalpel. Vasquez picked it up gingerly and examined it closely. Flecks of dried blood covered the blade and the handle. He laid it carefully on the tray, then turned his attention to the refrigerator.

Vasquez grasped the handle. The door caught briefly, then popped free. The detective blinked hard, then released the handle as if his fingers had been burned. The refrigerator door slammed shut, and Vasquez fought the urge to bolt from the room. He took a deep breath and opened the door again. On the top shelf were two glass jars with screw-on tops labeled VIASPAN. The jars were full of a clear liquid with a faint yellow tinge. Vasquez spotted a plastic bag filled with a white powder on the bottom shelf. Not two kilos' worth. Nowhere near that amount. Days later the state crime lab would report that the powder was indeed cocaine. By that time, Vasquez would have trouble remembering that cocaine was even involved in the case against Dr. Vincent Cardoni. What Bobby Vasquez would remember for the rest of his life were the dead eyes that stared at him from the two severed heads that sat on the middle shelf.

11

Milton County sheriff Clark Mills, a sleepy-eyed man with shaggy brown hair and a thick mustache, struggled valiantly to maintain his composure when Vasquez showed him the severed heads. Both belonged to white women. One head was oval in shape and covered with blond hair that was stiff and stringy from the extreme cold. It leaned against the interior wall of the refrigerator like a prop in a horror film. The second head was covered with brunette hair and leaned against the first. The eyes in both skulls had rolled back so far that the pupils had almost disappeared. The skin looked like a pale rubber compound created by a special-effects wizard and was ragged and uneven where the neck had been severed from the body.

Jake Mullins, Mills's deputy, had blinked furiously for a few seconds before backing out of the room. The person who seemed the least affected by the horror in the refrigerator was Fred Scofield, the Milton County district attorney. Scofield, a heavy man tottering on the brink of obesity, had been in Vietnam and was a big-city DA before burning out and moving to the peace and seclusion of the mountain community of Cedar City.

"What should we do, Fred?" the sheriff asked.

Scofield was chewing on an unlit cigar and staring dispassionately at the heads. He turned his back to the refrigerator and addressed the shaken lawman.

"I think we should clear out of here so we don't mess up the crime scene. Then you should get on the horn and have the state police send a forensic team up here ASAP."

They collected the deputy, whose complexion was as pale as the heads in the refrigerator. While Sheriff Mills phoned the state police and the deputy collapsed on the living room couch, Scofield led Bobby Vasquez outside onto the deck and lit up his cigar. The temperature was in the low thirties, but the cold country air was a welcome relief after the close, fetid smell in the makeshift operating room.

"What brought you to this house of horrors, Detective?"

Vasquez had worked on his story while waiting for the police, and he had it down pat. He figured he could get it past anyone if he could get it by the flinty district attorney.

"I've been investigating an anonymous tip that a doctor named Vincent Cardoni was planning to sell two kilos of cocaine he had purchased from Martin Breach, a major narcotics dealer."

"I know who Breach is," Scofield said.

"The cocaine was supposed to be hidden in this house."

"I assume you corroborated this tip before barging into Dr. Cardoni's domicile?"

There was not much of a moon, but Scofield could

see Vasquez's eyes in the light from the living room. He watched them carefully while Vasquez answered his question. The vice cop's gaze never wavered.

"Art Prochaska, Breach's lieutenant, was arrested recently by the DEA. I leaned on him, and he agreed to talk about Cardoni if I helped him with his federal case and kept him out of this one."

"But you're not keeping him out of it."

"No, sir. Not now. We're talking serial murders. That changes a lot of things."

Scofield nodded, but Vasquez thought he saw a glimmer of skepticism in the older man's features.

"Prochaska confirmed that Cardoni had been buying small, personal-use quantities from one of Breach's dealers until a few weeks ago, when he suddenly asked for two kilos. Cardoni checked out, so Breach sold him the dope. Prochaska told me that the doctor had a buyer and the sale was going down today."

Scofield's jaw dropped and he almost lost his cigar.

"You mean Cardoni and his buyer could be on their way here right now?"

"I don't think so. I think we missed the sale. I searched everywhere. The only cocaine I found was the small amount in the refrigerator."

Scofield puffed on his cigar thoughtfully. "We just met, Detective. The only thing I know about you is that you're a sworn officer of the law. But I do know a thing or two about Martin Breach and Art Prochaska. Frankly, I am having a hard time believing that Prochaska would give any police officer the time of day, much less discuss Martin Breach's business."

"That's what happened, Mr. Scofield."

"Prochaska is going to deny everything."

"Probably, but it will be my word against his."

"The word of an experienced police officer against that of a scumbag dope dealer," Scofield reflected, nodding thoughtfully.

"Exactly."

Scofield did not look like he was buying anything Vasquez was selling.

"Why didn't you put all of this information in an affidavit and present it to a judge, who could give you a warrant to search Dr. Cardoni's home?"

"There wasn't time. Besides, I didn't need a warrant. I had exigent circumstances here," Vasquez said, naming one of the exceptions to the rule that searches must be conducted with a warrant. "Prochaska said that the sale was going down today, but he didn't know when it was going down. I figured that I might miss the sale if I took the time to get a warrant. As it turned out, I missed it anyway."

"Why didn't you bring backup or call ahead to Sheriff Mills or the state police?"

"I should have done all those things," Vasquez said, looking properly chagrined. "It was bad judgment on my part to handle this alone."

Scofield looked off into the forest. The only sound was the occasional rustle of leaves in the wind. He puffed on his cigar. Then he broke the silence.

"I guess you know that I'll be prosecuting this mess right here in Cedar City and you're gonna be my star witness."

Vasquez nodded.

"Do you want to add to anything you've told me or correct anything you've said?"

"No, sir."

"All right, then, that's it. And I hope it is what happened, because this whole case will go down the toilet if I can't convince Judge Brody that he can rely on your word."

12

Sean McCarthy came to the crime scene because of an inquiry by Bobby Vasquez, who remembered that Cardoni had recently assaulted a nurse who had disappeared. McCarthy was forty-seven, meticulously dressed and as pale and cadaverous as the corpses that were the subject of his homicide investigations. The detective's red hair was spotted with gray, the freckles that dotted his alabaster skin were dull pink and his eyes were rimmed with dark circles.

Detective McCarthy stood inches from the open refrigerator and gazed at the severed heads thoughtfully while Vasquez and Scofield looked on. Then he took out a stack of snapshots and raised a Polaroid to eye level. He studied it, then he studied the heads. McCarthy had shown none of the revulsion or shock expressed by the other officers who viewed the remains. Instead, his lips creased, forming a smile that was as enigmatic as it was out of place. When he was satisfied he closed the refrigerator door.

"Those fucking heads don't bother you?" Vasquez asked.

McCarthy did not answer the question. He glanced

at the forensic experts who were photographing and measuring the basement room.

"Let's get out of here so these gentlemen can work undisturbed."

McCarthy led Vasquez and Scofield upstairs and onto the deck. Vasquez was exhausted and wanted only to sleep. Scofield seemed edgy. McCarthy gazed at the morning sky for a moment, then held up one of the Polaroids so that Vasquez and Scofield could see it.

"One of the victims is Mary Sandowski. I don't know the identity of the other one."

McCarthy was about to continue when a deputy emerged from one of the hiking trails that led into the forest.

"Sheriff," he called to Mills, who was conferring with two men at the side of the house. "We found something."

"Ah," McCarthy said, "I've been expecting this."

"Expecting what?" Vasquez asked, but the homicide detective set off after Mills and the deputies without answering. Vasquez looked at Scofield, who shrugged and followed the lanky detective into the woods. The men marched silently along a narrow trail. The sound of their footsteps was dulled by the thick dark soil. A loamy scent mixed with the smell of pine. A sign announced that the men were entering national forest; a quarter of a mile later, the trail bent right and they were suddenly in a clearing. A shovel was sticking out of a pile of dirt in the middle of the field.

"It looked like the earth had been turned recently," the deputy explained, "so I got a shovel and came back out here."

He stepped aside so that the other men could see

his discovery. Vasquez walked over to the narrow hole that the deputy had dug. At the bottom was a human arm.

Dr. Sally Grace, an assistant medical examiner, arrived shortly before the last of nine bodies was exhumed from the damp ground. All of the corpses were naked. Two were headless females. Of the remaining corpses, four were female, three were male and all but one appeared to be young. After a cursory examination, Grace informed the law enforcement officials gathered around her that, with the exception of the middle-aged male, all of the victims showed evidence of torture. Furthermore, Grace told them, one of the headless females had been ripped open from the breastbone to the abdomen and was missing her heart, and one of the males and another female had midline cuts from the area beneath the sternum to the pubic bone and were missing kidneys.

While Dr. Grace talked, Vasquez studied the corpses. All of the victims seemed pathetically frail and defenseless. Their rib cages showed. Their shoulder blades looked sharp and visible under their translucent skin, more like wire hangers than bones. Vasquez wanted to do something to comfort the dead, like brushing off the clumps of dirt that clung to their pale skin or laying a blanket over them to keep them warm, but none of that would help now.

When Dr. Grace finished her briefing, McCarthy wandered up and down the row of corpses. Vasquez watched him work. McCarthy gave eight of the bodies a cursory examination, but he squatted next to the seemingly untouched middle-aged male and withdrew another Polaroid from his jacket pocket. Mc-

Carthy glanced back and forth between the photograph and the corpse, then spent a few moments in deep thought. When he stood up he summoned the medical examiner. Vasquez could not hear what the detective said, but he watched Dr. Grace squat next to the corpse and examine the back of its neck. She beckoned McCarthy and he squatted next to her, nodding as she pointed to an area of the neck and gestured with her hands.

"Thank you, Dr. Grace," McCarthy said to the medical examiner. He stood up.

"Want to fill us in, Detective?" Scofield asked, making it clear that he did not appreciate mysterious behavior in a fellow investigator.

McCarthy started back toward the cabin. "About a month ago, a detective from Montreal contacted me with information about an ailing Canadian millionaire who was negotiating with Martin Breach to secure a heart on the black market. Do you know who Breach is?"

Scofield and Vasquez nodded.

"We've long suspected that Breach has a small but lucrative sideline: the sale of human organs on the black market to wealthy individuals who are unwilling to wait for a donor. We also suspected that the organs are frequently obtained from unwilling donors. The investigation in Canada included wiretaps. Dr. Clifford Grant was mentioned several times. He was a surgeon at St. Francis Medical Center." McCarthy showed them the photograph he had examined earlier, then nodded back toward the bodies. "He's the middle-aged victim who bore no marks of torture."

Scofield and Vasquez examined the picture, and they walked in silence for a while. When Scofield returned the photo the homicide detective continued.

"We put Grant under twenty-four-hour surveillance as soon as we learned he was going to be involved in harvesting the heart. A few evenings after we received the tip, Grant was observed picking up a cooler from a locker at the bus station and placing it in the trunk of his car. If the cooler contained the heart, Grant could not have been the person who harvested it. You've only got a leeway of four to six hours between removing a heart and transplanting it into the body of the new recipient, and Grant was under constant surveillance. That meant that Grant had a partner."

"Cardoni," Vasquez said.

"Possibly."

Scofield lit a cigar and took a few puffs. The smoke curled up and spread out until it disappeared.

"I was one of several officers who followed Grant to a private airfield. We observed Art Prochaska, Martin Breach's lieutenant, place an attaché case in Grant's car. Grant spotted us and took off before giving Prochaska the cooler. A few days later his car was discovered at the long-term parking lot at the airport."

"And now we've found Grant and the operating room where the organs were harvested," Vasquez said.

"And since we found Grant here," Scofield added, "it's not much of a stretch to say that Grant's partner probably killed him."

They walked in silence for a few moments. As they came in sight of the cabin, Vasquez put out his hand to stop McCarthy.

"I want to ask you a favor," he said. "I want Breach, and I want Cardoni. I want to be part of this investigation. It was my case to begin with. I don't want to be cut out. What about it?"

McCarthy nodded thoughtfully.

"Let me talk to some people. I'll see what I can do."

13

Frank Jaffe was an excellent storyteller. Amanda's favorite tale was the account of her miraculous birth, which Frank told her for the first time on her fifth birthday during a visit to Beth Israel cemetery. It was terribly cold that afternoon, but Amanda didn't notice the raw wind or the stark gray and threatening sky, so intense was her concentration on the grave of Samantha Jaffe, born September 3, 1953, died March 10, 1974. The headstone was small because Frank had not been able to afford elegance when he purchased it. The grave lay beneath the swaying leafless branches of an ancient maple tree, third in from a narrow road that roamed through the graveyard. Frank had gazed with sad eyes at the headstone. Then he had looked down on his little girl. Amanda was all that was good in the world and the reason that Frank persevered. In his mid-twenties Frank had been tall and strong, but a single father who worked all day and struggled in law school each night needed more than strength and youth to keep from folding.

"You were born on March the tenth," Frank had begun, "coincidentally the very same day as today, at three-oh-eight in the afternoon, which is almost the time it is now, in the year nineteen hundred and seventy-four."

"At three-oh-eight in the afternoon?"

"Three-oh-eight on the dot," Frank assured her. "Your mother was lying in a wide bed on soft white sheets. . . ."

"How did she look?"

"She was smiling a wonderful smile because she knew you were about to be born, and that smile made her look like an angel—the most beautiful of angels. Except, of course, she didn't have wings yet."

"Did she get wings?"

"Certainly. It was part of the bargain, but the angel and your mother did not make their bargain right away, so your mother had to wait for her wings."

"When did the angel come?"

"She appeared in the hospital in your mother's room just as you were about to be born. Now, angels are usually invisible, but your mother could see this angel."

"Only my mother?"

"Only your mother. And that was because she was so like an angel herself."

"What did the angel say?"

"'Samantha,' she said, in a voice that sounded like a light rain falling, 'God is very lonely in heaven and he wants you to visit.' 'Thank God for me,' your mother said, 'but I am about to bring a wonderful baby girl into the world, so I must stay with her.' 'God will be very sad to hear that,' the angel replied. 'It can't be helped,' your mother told the angel. 'My little girl is the most precious little girl in the world, and I love her to bits. I would be very sad myself if I couldn't be with her always.'"

"What happened then?"

"The angel flew back to heaven and told God what your mother had said. As you can imagine, God was very sad. He even cried a few tears. But God is very smart and an idea occurred to him, so he sent the angel back to earth."

"Did the angel tell Mother God's idea?"

"She certainly did. 'Would you come and visit God in heaven if you could be with your little girl always?' she asked. 'Of course,' your mother answered. She was a wonderful person and never liked to see anyone sad. 'God has an idea,' the angel told your mother. 'If you will come with me right now, God will put your soul in your little girl, right next to her heart. Then you will be with her always. It will even be better than the way other mothers are with their children. You'll be with her everywhere she goes, even if she is at school or on the playground or on a trip.' 'How wonderful,' Samantha said, and she shook hands with the angel to seal the bargain."

"Then what happened?"

"A miraculous thing. As you know, you can't get to heaven unless you die, so your mother died, but she didn't die until the second that you opened your mouth and took your first breath. When your mouth was its widest, the soul of Samantha Jaffe jumped right inside of you and went straight to a spot next to your heart."

"Which is where she is today?"

"Which is where she is every minute of every day," Frank had answered, giving Amanda's hand a gentle squeeze.

Amanda remembered the story of her miraculous birth every time she and Frank made their birthday pilgrimage to the cemetery. For years Amanda really believed that Samantha lived next to her heart. As a small girl, at night, snug in her bed, she talked to Samantha about the things daughters confide to their mothers. As a teenager, it became a ritual before she mounted the blocks in each swim meet for Amanda to press her fist against her heart and silently ask her mother for strength.

Frank had never remarried, and an older Amanda wondered if her father really believed that Samantha dwelt with them. She had asked him once why he never married again. Frank told her that he had come close twice but had backed out in the end because neither woman could make him forget the love of his life. This saddened Amanda, because she wanted her father to be happy, but Frank always seemed at peace with himself, and she guessed that someone as strong as Frank would have married again if he had fallen in love.

Frank's sacrifice, if it was one, also impressed upon Amanda the power of true love. The emotion was not something to be trifled with, and she did not give herself easily. Love was very serious business. It was, as she learned from her father's example, something that could truly last forever.

Frank and Amanda had been lucky. A hard rain had fallen on the morning of March tenth, but it quit a little after noon and never resumed. The sun had even come out for a while when they were visiting Samantha's grave. As usual, Frank and Amanda were silent after leaving the cemetery. March tenth was always a hard day for both of them, and they used the drive home as a time to think.

A Porsche was idling in their driveway. As soon as

Frank pulled next to it, the door to the Porsche opened and Vincent Cardoni started toward them wearing loose-fitting sweatpants and a faded UCLA sweatshirt. He was six-two and well muscled, with long black hair combed back from a high forehead. Cardoni's jaw was square and his nose classically Roman, but his complexion was washed out and his cheeks were sunken, as if he was not eating properly. A hard edge showed in the doctor's eyes, and anger forced his lips into a tight line.

"There are cops at my house," Cardoni said as soon as Frank's door was open.

"It's a bit cold out here, Vince," Frank said with a friendly smile. "Why don't we talk inside?"

"Did you hear me, Frank? I said cops. More than one. I counted three cars. They were looking in the bushes around my house. The door was open. They were inside."

"If they're in your house, the damage is done. We'll need to discuss this calmly if I'm going to repair it."

"I want those motherfuckers out of my house, now!"

Frank's face darkened when Cardoni swore. "I don't believe I've ever introduced you to my daughter. Amanda is a fine attorney. She's just finished a clerkship at the Ninth Circuit Court of Appeals. That's a very prestigious job. Now she's lowered herself and is working in my firm. Amanda, this is Dr. Vincent Cardoni. He's a surgeon at St. Francis."

Cardoni stared at Amanda as if seeing her for the first time.

"Pleased to meet you, Dr. Cardoni," Amanda said, extending her hand.

Cardoni gripped her hand hard, and his eyes

stayed on hers for a brief moment before sliding down her body. Amanda felt the heat rise in her cheeks. She released Cardoni's hand. His eyes held hers for a moment, then shifted back to her father.

"Let's go inside," Cardoni said in a tone that made the words sound more like an order than the acceptance of an invitation. Frank led the way, and the doctor followed. Amanda hung back to allow a bit of distance between her and Frank's client. Inside, Frank turned on the lights and escorted Cardoni into the living room, where he indicated a couch.

"Tell me what's going on," Frank said when they were all seated.

"I have no idea. I was out for a run in Forest Park. When I drove back, I saw cops swarming over my yard and my house. I didn't stop to ask them why." He paused for a moment. "This can't have anything to do with the scrape you got me out of last year, can it?"

"Doubtful. The case was dismissed with prejudice."

"Then what's going on?"

"No use speculating. What's your phone number at home?"

Cardoni looked puzzled.

"I'm going straight to the horse's mouth. The police are probably still at your house. I'll ask the man in charge what's going on."

Cardoni rattled off his number, and Frank left the room. Amanda did not like being left alone with Cardoni, but he showed no interest in her. He fidgeted, then stood and began to pace around the living room, glancing briefly at the artwork and fingering curios. Cardoni walked behind Amanda and stopped moving. She waited for Cardoni to move again, but he did not. When she could not stand the stillness any longer, Amanda turned sideways on the sofa so she could see the surgeon. He was standing behind her, his eyes on the painting across the room from him. If he had been watching her, there was no way Amanda could prove it.

"We're going to drive over to your house, Vince," Frank said as he reentered the living room.

"Did they tell you what's going on?"

"No. I spoke with Sean McCarthy, the detective in charge. He wouldn't answer any of my questions. Vince, Sean is a homicide detective."

"Homicide?"

Frank nodded, watching Cardoni for his reaction. "Sean is a sharp cookie, very sharp. He said he wants to talk to you. When I hemmed and hawed, he threatened to get an arrest warrant."

"You're kidding."

"He sounded very serious. Is there something we need to worry about? I don't like walking a client into a meeting with a homicide detective when I'm not fully prepared."

Cardoni shook his head.

"Okay, then. Listen up. I have lost damn few cases, but when a client of mine has been convicted it is usually his mouth that's done him in. Do not speak unless I give you the okay, and when you do respond to questions, listen to what you're asked. Do not volunteer anything. Do you have that straight?"

Cardoni nodded.

"Then let's go."

Frank turned to Amanda. "I'll ride with Vincent. You follow in our car."

* * *

On the ride to Cardoni's house, Amanda decided that she did not like Frank's client. She didn't appreciate the way he had moved his eyes over her when Frank had introduced her. It was unnerving to be examined so clinically, without lust or friendliness. The speed with which the doctor had switched off his anger while he studied her was also unsettling. However, Amanda's concerns about the doctor were quickly forgotten in the excitement of being included by Frank in what might be a murder investigation.

Since joining Jaffe, Katz, Lehane and Brindisi, Amanda, like most first-year associates, had been given the jobs no one else wanted to do. She liked legal research, so she had not resented her time in the law library. But she really wanted to try cases, and the bigger the stakes, the better. She wasn't certain if Frank had asked her along because he wanted her involved in Cardoni's case or because he might need a ride home. She didn't care. Either way, she would be in at the start of a murder case.

Cardoni lived in a sprawling yellow-and-white Dutch Colonial on half an acre of land shaded by beech, oak and cottonwood. When Amanda drove up she saw black-jacketed PPB officers scouring the grounds. Police cars were blocking the garage, so Cardoni parked his Porsche in the street and Amanda parked behind him. Sean McCarthy was waiting for them at the front door.

"Frank," McCarthy said with a smile.

"Good to see you again, Sean. This is Dr. Cardoni, and this is my daughter, Amanda. She's an attorney with my firm."

McCarthy nodded to Amanda and extended a hand toward Cardoni, which the surgeon ignored. McCarthy seemed unconcerned about the rebuke.

"I apologize for the intrusion, Doctor. I've given strict orders to my men to respect your property. If there's any damage, please notify me and I'll see that you're compensated."

"Cut the bullshit and get your men out of my house," Cardoni responded angrily.

"I can understand why you're upset," the detective answered politely. "I'd be too if I found strangers prowling through my home." McCarthy withdrew a document from his jacket and handed it to Frank. "However, we do have court authorization to search. All I can promise is that we'll be out of your hair as soon as possible."

"Is that legal?" Cardoni asked.

"I'm afraid so," Frank answered after reading the search warrant.

"You have a very pleasant den. Why don't we go in there and talk? It will be warmer, and we won't be in the way of my men. That will speed up the search."

Cardoni glared at the detective. Frank placed a hand on his arm and said, "Let's get this over with, Vince."

McCarthy led them down a hall and into a comfortable wood-paneled den where several other men waited. McCarthy introduced them.

"Frank, this is Bobby Vasquez. This is the Milton County sheriff, Clark Mills. And this is Fred Scofield, the Milton County district attorney. Gentlemen, this is Dr. Vincent Cardoni and his attorneys, Frank and Amanda Jaffe. Dr. Cardoni, why don't you have a chair?"

"Thanks for inviting me to sit down in my own home," Cardoni replied. Amanda heard the edge in his voice but wasn't certain if it came from anger, fear or both.

"What's going on here, Sean?" Frank asked.

"I'll answer you in a minute. First I'd like to ask your client a few questions."

"Go ahead," Frank said to McCarthy. Then he turned to Cardoni and told him to wait to answer each question until after they consulted.

"Dr. Cardoni, do you know Dr. Clifford Grant? I believe he also practices at St. Francis."

Cardoni and Frank leaned toward each other and had a whispered conversation.

"I know who Dr. Grant is," Cardoni said when they were through. "I've even spoken to him a few times. But I don't know him well."

"Do you know a woman named Mary Sandowski?"

Cardoni looked disgusted. He didn't bother consulting with Frank before answering.

"Is this about Sandowski? What happened? Did she swear out a complaint?"

"No, sir. She didn't."

Cardoni waited for more explanation. When it did not come, he answered McCarthy.

"I know her."

"In what capacity?"

"She's a nurse at St. Francis."

"That's it?" Vasquez pressed.

The interruption seemed to annoy McCarthy. Cardoni's eyes swung slowly between the vice cop and McCarthy. Cardoni was so focused and tight that it made Amanda uneasy.

"What's going on here?" the surgeon demanded.

"When was the last time you were at your cabin in Milton County, Dr. Cardoni?" McCarthy asked.

"What the fuck are you talking about? I don't own a cabin in Milton County, and I'm not going to play

this game anymore. Either tell me why you're ran-
sacking my home or get the fuck out."

Frank raised his hand to quiet Cardoni.

"I'm going to instruct my client not to answer any
more questions until you explain the reason for
them," he said.

"Fair enough," McCarthy replied. He walked over
to a television and VCR that sat in a gap between
books in a floor-to-ceiling bookshelf and turned on
the TV. There was a videocassette on top of the VCR.
McCarthy took the cassette out of its case and put it
in the machine.

"We found this cassette in your bedroom, Dr. Cardoni. I'd be interested in your comments on the contents, if your attorney gives you permission to give
them. It appears to have been shot in a basement
room in a house in the mountains in Milton County.
We found several items at the house that bore your
fingerprints. One of the items is a scalpel that looks a
lot like the scalpel you'll see on the tape. By the way,
the cassette has already been dusted for prints, and
yours are on it."

"So what? I have dozens of videocassettes in the
house."

"Vincent, from this point on, I don't want you
talking to anyone but me unless I say it's okay,"
Frank said. "Understood?"

Cardoni nodded, but Amanda could see that he
was upset by the restriction. McCarthy turned on the
set and the VCR. Amanda noticed that none of the
law enforcement officers was looking at the TV; they
were all focused on Cardoni.

A woman's terrified face filled the screen. She was
saying something, but there was no sound on the
tape. The camera panned down her naked body. She

was gaunt, as if she had not eaten in days. The camera focused on her breasts and zoomed in on the woman's left nipple. It was flaccid. A gloved finger moved into view and stimulated the nipple until it became erect. The finger withdrew, and the woman's face filled the screen again. Suddenly her eyes grew impossibly wide and she screamed. Amanda froze. The woman screamed again and again. Then her eyes rolled back in her head and she passed out.

The gloved hand slapped the woman's cheeks until she came around. She began to sob. The camera was still tight on her face, and Amanda could read her lips. They formed the word *please*, and she said it repeatedly as tears streamed down her cheeks.

The camera moved, and the woman's face disappeared from the screen as it panned the surroundings. Amanda saw concrete walls, a sink, and a refrigerator. Then the camera returned to the woman. It pulled back and showed her from a side view. Blood was trickling down her heaving ribs. The camera shifted upward for a shot above the woman. There was a red puddle on her chest. The camera moved in. The nipple was missing.

Amanda's breath caught. She squeezed her eyes shut, and only a great effort of will kept her together. When she was under control, Amanda opened her eyes, making sure that she was not looking at the screen.

All the blood had drained from her father's face, but Cardoni's complexion had not changed. The detective switched off the set. Cardoni turned slowly until he was looking directly at McCarthy.

"Will you please tell me what the fuck that was all about?" he asked in a hard, emotionless voice.

"Recognize the woman?" the detective asked.

Frank regained his composure. He reached out and grabbed Cardoni's forearm. "Not a word." Then he stared at McCarthy. "I thought better of you, Sean. This is a cheap trick, and this interview is at an end."

McCarthy did not look surprised.

"I thought you'd be interested in the type of person you're representing."

Frank stood. He still looked shaky, but his voice was steady.

"I didn't see Dr. Cardoni in that horror movie. I assume you didn't either or you would have shown us a different segment."

"You'll receive full discovery, including a copy of this tape, at the appropriate time."

McCarthy switched his attention to the doctor. "Vincent Cardoni, I must inform you that you have the right to remain silent. Anything you say can and will be used against you in a court of law. You have a right to an attorney. If you cannot afford to retain an attorney, one will be appointed to represent you. Do you understand these rights?"

Cardoni stood up and glared at McCarthy.

"You can kiss my ass," he said slowly and distinctly.

Frank stepped between his client and McCarthy.

"Are you arresting Dr. Cardoni?"

"Sheriff Mills is placing Dr. Cardoni under arrest. Multnomah County may have its own charges in the near future."

"Is Dr. Cardoni charged with the murder of the woman on the tape?" Frank pressed.

Fred Scofield stood up and answered Frank.

"Sheriff Mills will be arresting Dr. Cardoni on the charge of murdering Mary Sandowski and for possession of cocaine, which was found in the doctor's bedroom, but I'll be going to a grand jury very soon to ask for indictments on eight other charges of aggravated murder. I anticipate that Dr. Cardoni will be spending a lot of time in Milton County in the near future."

"I'd like you to step aside, Mr. Jaffe," Sheriff Mills said. "We're going to cuff your client."

Cardoni switched into a fighting stance. Vasquez reached for his weapon. Frank laid his hand on Cardoni's arm.

"Don't resist, Vince. I'll deal with this."

"Then deal with it. I'm not going to jail."

"You have to. If you resist, it will make things worse. It could affect release, and it can be used against you at a trial."

Amanda could see Cardoni processing this information. He relaxed instantly, again amazing Amanda at the speed with which he could change his emotions.

"Can I speak with my client in private for a few moments?" Frank asked.

McCarthy thought about the request, then nodded. "You can do it in here, but I want Dr. Cardoni in handcuffs."

Cardoni's hands were cuffed behind his back, and Sheriff Mills conducted a pat-down search of the prisoner.

"Do you need me?" Amanda asked, trying to sound casual.

"It would be better if Dr. Cardoni and I talked alone. We'll only be a minute."

"No problem," Amanda answered, smiling to mask her disappointment.

"I'm not going to pull any punches," Frank said as

soon as the door closed. "You're in a lot of trouble. Aggravated murder is the most serious crime you can face in Oregon. It carries a potential death sentence."

For the first time Cardoni looked worried.

"Where are they going to take me?"

"Probably to the Cedar City jail."

"How quickly can you get me out?"

"I'm not sure. There is no automatic bail in a murder case, and I don't want to move for a bail hearing until we're in the best position to get you out."

"I'm not some car mechanic who can afford to sit around and collect unemployment. I'm a physician. I have patients scheduled for surgery."

"I know, and I'll try to get the administration at St. Francis involved on your behalf."

"Those bastards won't help me. They've been trying to get rid of me. This will give them their opening. Do you have any idea how long it takes to become a doctor? Do you know how hard I've worked? You've got to keep me out of jail."

"I'm going to do everything I can, but I don't want to lie to you and build up your hopes. Scofield said that they were thinking of adding eight more counts of aggravated murder to the indictment. That could mean that they have eight other bodies. This is not going to be simple, like your assault case.

"Now listen to me. Following my instructions could save your life. I mean that literally. You will be in a police car and then the jail, where they will process you in. Do everything they tell you. Do not resist. But do not, under any circumstances, discuss this case with anyone. I'm talking about cops, DAs and other prisoners, especially other prisoners. You're going to feel isolated and in need of a friend. There are going to be prisoners who will be your

friend. They'll get you to feel comfortable. You'll un-
burden yourself to them. The next time you see your
friend he will be testifying against you in exchange
for having his case dropped. Do you understand
what I just said?"

Cardoni nodded.

"Good. I'll be out to see you tomorrow. Try to
think of people who can vouch for you at a bail hearing, and see if you can figure out why McCarthy
wanted to know if you knew Dr. Clifford Grant."

Frank laid a gentle hand on Cardoni's arm. "One
last thing, Vince. Don't give up hope."

Cardoni looked directly into Frank Jaffe's eyes.
His voice was steady and hard.

"I never give up, Frank, and I never forget, either.
Someone has set me up. That means that someone is
going to pay."

"So," Frank asked Amanda when they were alone
in the car and headed home, "what do you make of
all that?"

Amanda had been very quiet since the videotape
started to roll, and she was subdued when she answered Frank's question.

"The police seem pretty certain that Cardoni is
guilty."

"What do you think?"

Amanda shivered. "I don't like him, Dad."

"Any specific reason, or just your gut?"

"His reactions aren't normal. Have you noticed
that he switches emotions the way you and I switch
TV channels? One second he's in a rage, the next he's
cold as ice."

"Vince isn't Marcus Welby, MD. That's for sure."

"What was the other case you handled for him?"

"An assault. Vince was trying to score some co-caine." Amanda's eyebrows raised. "He was in a bar that doesn't usually cater to members of the medical profession. He also tried to score with someone's girlfriend. When the boyfriend objected, Vince beat him so badly that he had to be taken to the hospital. Fortunately for Vince the man was an ex-con, and no one in that type of bar has decent eyesight or much of a memory when it's the police asking the questions."

The mention of violence made Amanda flash on Mary Sandowski's tearstained face. She felt a little dizzy and squeezed her eyes shut. Frank noticed that Amanda's face was drained of color.

"Are you okay?" he asked.

"I was just thinking about that poor woman."

"I'm sorry you had to see that."

Amanda grew thoughtful. "When I was a little girl, you never took me to court when you tried the really bad cases, did you?"

"You were too young."

"You didn't even do it when I was in high school. I remember asking you about the Fong case and the one where the two girls were tortured, but you never seemed to have the time."

"You didn't need to hear about stuff like that at that age."

"You always did shelter me when I was growing up."

"You think it was easy for me raising a little girl by myself?" Frank answered defensively. "I always tried to figure out what your mother would have done, and I could never see Samantha letting me take an eleven-year-old to a rape trial."

"No, I don't suppose she would have," Amanda answered with a brief smile. Then she thought about the videotape again and grew somber.

"I guess it doesn't get much worse than what I just saw," she said.

"No, it doesn't."

"I never really understood what you did, until now. I mean I knew intellectually, but . . . "

"There's nothing intellectual about criminal law, Amanda. There are no ivory towers, just tragedy and human beings at their worst."

"Why do you do it?"

"Good question. Maybe because it is real. I'd be bored silly closing real-estate deals or drawing up contracts. And every once in a while you do make a difference in some poor bastard's life. I've represented a lot of very bad people, but I've also freed two people from prison who were sentenced to death for crimes they didn't commit, and I've kept people out of jail who didn't deserve to be there. I guess you can say that I spend a lot of my time in the shit, but every so often I come up with a pearl, and that makes the bad stuff worthwhile."

"You don't have to take every case, though. You can turn some away."

Frank glanced at his daughter. "Like this one, you mean?"

"What if he's guilty?"

"We don't know that."

"What if you knew beyond any doubt that Cardoni tortured that woman? How could you help a person who could do what we saw on that tape?"

Frank sighed. "That's the question every criminal lawyer asks at some point in his or her career. I expect you'll be mulling it over while we work on this case. Those who decide they can't do it switch to some more refined type of law."

"Are there enough pearls to justify working for someone like Cardoni?"

"Do you remember the McNab boy?"

"Vaguely. I was in junior high school, wasn't I?"

Frank nodded. "I fought that case and fought that case. He was convicted in the first trial. I cried after the verdict because I knew he was innocent. I wasn't experienced in handling death cases. I truly believed that the verdict was my fault. Guilt drove me, and I didn't stop until I'd won the appeal and a new trial.

"The jury hung at the retrial. I couldn't sleep, I lost weight and I charged every moment that poor boy spent in jail to my soul. Then my investigator talked to Mario Rossi's mother."

"The snitch?"

Frank nodded. "Rossi's testimony kept Terry Mc-Nab on death row for four years, but he confessed to his mother that he lied to get a deal for himself. When Rossi recanted, the prosecutor had to dismiss."

Frank was silent for a moment. Amanda saw the color rise in his cheeks and his eyes water. When he spoke again, Amanda heard his voice catch.

"I can still remember that afternoon. We ended the hearing around four, and Terry's father and mother and I had to wait another hour for Terry to be processed out of jail. Terry looked stunned when he stepped outside. It was February and the sun had gone down, but the air was clear and crisp. When he stood on the steps of the jail Terry looked up at the stars. He just stood there, looking up. Then he took a deep breath.

"My plane didn't leave until the morning, so I was

staying at a motel on the edge of town. Terry's folks invited me to dinner, but I begged off. I knew they were just being polite and that the family would much rather be alone. Besides, I was wrecked. I'd left everything in the courtroom."

Frank paused again.

"Do you know the thing I remember most about that day? It was the way I felt when I entered my motel room. I hadn't been alone until then, and the enormousness of what I had done had not sunk in. Four and a half years of fighting to do the right thing, the lost sleep, the tears and the frustration . . . I closed the door behind me and I stood in the middle of my motel room. I suddenly understood that it was over: I had won, and Terry would never have to spend another moment caged up.

"Amanda, I swear my soul rose out of my body at that moment. I closed my eyes and tilted my head back and felt my soul rise right up to the ceiling. It was only a moment, and then I was back on earth, but that feeling made every moment of those horrible four years worthwhile. You don't get that feeling doing anything else."

Amanda remembered how she had felt when she heard "Not guilty" in LaTricia Sweet's case. It had been so heady to win, especially when she hadn't thought she would. Then Amanda remembered what she had seen on the tape, and she realized that there was no comparison between LaTricia Sweet's case and the murder of Mary Sandowski. LaTricia wasn't hurting anyone but herself. No one had to fear her after she was set free. It would be totally different to help free the person who tortured Mary Sandowski.

Amanda had no doubt that her father meant what he had said. What she didn't know was whether she believed that the chance to save a few deserving people would ever be enough compensation for representing a monster who could coldly and cruelly cut the nipple off a screaming human being.

14

Bobby Vasquez parked in his assigned spot in the lot of his low-rent garden apartment. On one side of the complex was the interstate and on the other a strip mall. Truth was, between the IRS and his child support payments, this was the best he could afford. There were two rows of mailboxes near the parking spot. Vasquez collected his mail and thumbed through it while he climbed the stairs to his second-floor apartment. Ads and bills. What did he expect? Who would write him?

Vasquez opened his door and flipped on the light. The furniture in the living room was secondhand and covered by a thin layer of dust. Sections of a three-day-old *Oregonian* littered the floor, the threadbare couch and one end of a low plywood coffee table. Each weekend Vasquez vowed to clean up, but he made an effort only when the dirt and debris overwhelmed him. He was rarely home, anyway. Undercover work kept him out at odd hours. When he wasn't working he kept company with Yvette Stewart, a cocktail waitress at the cop bar where he did his serious drinking. His wife had left him because he was never around, and he had continued the tradition after moving to this shithole.

Vasquez tossed his mail onto the coffee table and walked into the kitchen. There was nothing in the refrigerator but a six-pack, a carton of spoiled milk and a half-eaten loaf of stale bread. Vasquez didn't care. He was too exhausted to be hungry, anyway. Too exhausted to sleep, too.

Vasquez flopped onto the couch, popped the top on a beer can and flipped channels until he found ESPN. He closed his eyes and ran the cold can across his forehead. Everything was going just fine so far. Cardoni was in jail, and everyone seemed to have bought his story about the search. It felt good on those rare occasions when things went right for a change. Another thing that cheered Vasquez was Cardoni's claim that he did not own the Milton County house. Something like that was easy to check.

Vasquez turned off the set and pushed himself off the couch. He crumpled the sections of the newspaper and the beer can and threw them in the trash. Then he dragged himself into the bathroom. While he brushed his teeth he savored the fact that Dr. Vincent Cardoni was spending the first of what would be an endless number of days behind bars.

15

Frank Jaffe sat in a back booth in Stokely's Café on Jefferson Street in Cedar City and finished his apple pie while reading the final page of the police reports Fred Scofield had given him earlier that morning. The café had always been an oasis for Frank, his father and other weary hunters exhausted from hours of trudging through thick underbrush with nothing to show for their efforts but scratches, running noses and tales about the giant bucks that got away. It was the first place Frank had ordered a cup of coffee and sipped a beer. When Amanda was old enough, Frank had taught her how to shoot and introduced her to the wonders of Stokely's chicken-fried steak and hot apple pie.

Frank finished his coffee and paid the check. The Milton County jail was three blocks away on Jefferson in a modern annex behind the county courthouse, and Frank set off in that direction. In the days of Frank's youth, the population of Cedar City hovered around thirteen hundred and Jefferson had been the only paved street, but developers had ruined the town. Family-owned hardware and grocery stores were dying a slow death as national chains moved in; there was a mall with a multiplex cinema at the east end of town; Stokely's was forced to include caffè latte on its menu in order to survive; and the three-story red-brick courthouse on Jefferson was one of the few buildings that was more than thirty years old.

After checking in with the deputy at the reception desk, Frank was led to the attorney visiting room. A few moments later the thick metal door opened and Vincent Cardoni was brought in. The surgeon was dressed in an orange jail-issue jumpsuit, and there were dark circles under his eyes. As soon as the guard locked them in, Cardoni glared at Frank.

"Where the hell have you been? I thought you were coming first thing this morning."

"I met with Fred Scofield first," Frank answered calmly. "He gave me some discovery that I needed to read through before we met."

Frank placed a stack of police reports on the cheap wooden table that separated them.

"This set is for you. I thought we could go over some of it before the bail hearing."

Frank handed Cardoni a copy of the criminal complaint.

"There are two counts against you now. The first involves the cocaine that the cops found in your bedroom." Frank paused. "The other is a charge of aggravated murder for killing Mary Sandowski, the woman on the tape."

"I didn't—"

Frank cut him off. "Sandowski was found on property about twenty-five miles from here. More corpses were buried a short distance from the cabin where they discovered two severed heads. Most of the victims were tortured."

"I don't care what happened at that cabin. I didn't do it."

"Your word alone isn't going to be enough to win this case. Scofield has several witnesses who will testify that you attacked Mary Sandowski in the hallway of St. Francis."

Cardoni looked exasperated. He addressed Frank the way he might talk to a not-too-bright child.

"Haven't I made myself clear, Frank? I do not own a house in Milton County, and I do not know a thing about these murders."

"What about the videocassette? McCarthy says your prints are on it."

"That's easy. The person who planted it obviously stole it from my house, taped over what was on it and returned it."

"And the cocaine they found in your bedroom?"

The question surprised Cardoni. He colored and broke eye contact with Jaffe.

"Well?" Frank asked.

"It's mine."

"I thought you were going to get help after I got you out of that last scrape."

"Don't preach at me, Frank."

"Do you hear me preaching?"

"What? Now you're disappointed in me? Fuck that. You're my lawyer, not a priest or a shrink, so let's get back to these bullshit charges. What else do the cops have?"

"Your prints are on a scalpel with Sandowski's blood on it. They were also on a half-filled coffee mug that was found next to the kitchen sink."

Suddenly Cardoni looked interested.

"What kind of coffee mug?"

"It's in here someplace."

Frank shuffled through the stack of police reports until he found what he was after. He gave two photocopied sheets to Cardoni. One showed the mug sitting on the kitchen counter, and the other was a close-up. Cardoni looked up triumphantly.

"Justine bought this mug for me in one of those boutiques on Twenty-third Street when we were dating. It was in my office at St. Francis until it disappeared a few weeks ago. I thought one of the cleaning people stole it."

"What about the scalpel?"

"I'm a surgeon, Frank! I handle scalpels every day. It's obvious. Someone is framing me."

Frank thought about that possibility. He thumbed through the police reports.

"This whole thing started with Bobby Vasquez, the cop with the mustache who watched the tape with us. He got a tip that you purchased two kilos of cocaine from Martin Breach and were storing them in a cabin you owned in the mountains near Cedar City. Vasquez claims that an informant corroborated the tip. He went to the cabin to search and found the severed heads in a refrigerator in the makeshift operating room we saw on the tape."

"Who gave Vasquez the tip?" Cardoni asked.

"It was anonymous."

"Really? How convenient."

A thought occurred to Frank.

"Does Martin Breach supply your cocaine?"

"I said I didn't want to talk about the blow."

"I have a reason for asking. Do you buy from Breach?"

"No, but the guy I buy from might. I don't know his source."

Frank made some notes on a yellow pad.

"Let's talk about Clifford Grant."

Cardoni looked confused. "What's this about Grant? That cop asked me about him at the house."

Frank told Cardoni about the investigation into Breach's black-market organ sales, the tip from the police in Montreal and the failed raid at the private airport.

"It looks like the organs were being removed at the Milton County house, but the police are certain that Grant didn't harvest the heart. They think he had a partner."

"And they think the partner is me?" Cardoni asked calmly.

Frank nodded.

"Well, they're wrong."

"If they are, someone went to a hell of a lot of trouble to frame you. Who hates you enough to do that, Vince?"

Before Cardoni could answer, the door opened and the guard entered carrying a plastic clothing bag. Frank looked at his watch. It was nine-forty.

"We've only got twenty minutes until the bail hearing. I brought a suit, shirt and tie for you from your house. Put them on and I'll meet you in court. Read through the discovery carefully. You're a very bright guy, Vince. Help me figure this out."

The bail hearing in *State v. Cardoni* was held on the second floor of the county courthouse in the pre–World War I courtroom of the Honorable Patrick Brody. Frank and his client sat at one counsel table and Scofield at another. Beyond the bar of the court were rows of hard wooden benches for spectators. Most days a few retirees and a sprinkling of interested parties were the only visitors, but the benches were packed for the hearing. Vans with network logos on their sides and satellite dishes on their roofs jammed the street in front of the courthouse; parking, which was usually a breeze, was impossible to find, as were accommodations at any motel within twenty miles. The combination of mass murder, black-market organ sales, torture and a handsome physician who had already been dubbed Dr. Death by the tabloids had lured reporters from all over the United States and several foreign countries to Cedar City.

While he waited for Fred Scofield to call his first witness, Frank glanced around the courtroom and spotted Art Prochaska watching the proceedings from a seat near the window at the back. Frank had represented several of Martin Breach's "employees," but never Prochaska. Nonetheless, Frank recognized him instantly and wondered what he was doing at the hearing.

Judge Brody rapped his gavel, and Scofield called Sean McCarthy to lay out the case against Cardoni. Then the prosecutor put on several forensic experts before calling his final witness.

A woman crossed the courtroom and took the witness stand. She was beautifully dressed in a pale gray pantsuit, a green cashmere turtleneck and pearl earrings. The woman's caramel hair fell gently across her shoulders. Her jade-colored eyes flicked toward Cardoni for a second, then she ignored him. Frank had never seen her before, but his client obviously had, because he stiffened and stared angrily.

"Could you please state your name for the record?" the bailiff asked.

"Dr. Justine Castle," she replied in a firm voice that carried easily to all corners of the courtroom.

"How are you employed, Dr. Castle?"

"I'm a physician, and I'm currently in a residency program in general surgery at St. Francis Medical Center in Portland."

"Where did you attend college and medical school?"

"I received a BS in chemistry at Dartmouth and a master's in biochemistry from Cornell, and I attended medical school at Jefferson in Philadelphia."

"Did you work between college and medical school?"

"Yes. I spent two years working as a research chemist for a pharmaceutical firm in Denver, Colorado."

"What is your relationship to the defendant, Vincent Cardoni?"

"He is my husband," Justine answered tersely.

"Were you living together at the time of his arrest on the present charges?"

Justine turned toward Cardoni and stared directly at him.

"No. I moved out after he beat me."

There was a stir in the crowd, and Judge Brody called for order as Frank stood.

"Objection, Your Honor. This is not relevant to the issue before the court, which is whether there is strong proof of my client's guilt of the murders in Milton County."

"Overruled."

"Can you tell Judge Brody the circumstances of this beating?" Scofield continued.

Justine's voice did not waver and she did not flinch when she answered.

"It occurred during a rape. Vincent wanted me to have sex with him. He was using cocaine and I refused. He pounded me with his fists until I submitted. Afterward he beat me some more for sport. I moved out that night."

"And when was this?"

"Two months ago."

Judge Brody was old-fashioned. He had been married to the same woman for forty years, and his weekly attendance at church was not for show. His expression reflected the way he felt about men who abused women. Frank saw his chances of obtaining bail fading with each word Justine Castle spoke.

"You mentioned drug use. Is the defendant addicted to drugs?"

"My husband is a cocaine addict."

"Does this affect his judgment?"

"His behavior has become increasingly erratic during our marriage."

"Did you recently witness erratic behavior on the part of your husband during an incident involving a nurse at St. Francis Medical Center named Mary Sandowski?"

"Yes, I did."

"Please tell Judge Brody what you saw."

When Justine finished recounting Cardoni's assault on Sandowski, Scofield changed the subject.

"Dr. Castle, do you have any reason to believe that the defendant would be a flight risk if he is released on bail?"

"Yes, I do."

"Please explain to the judge why you believe the defendant might flee."

"I have filed for divorce. My divorce attorney has been trying to locate my husband's assets. Almost immediately after I filed, my husband tried to withdraw large sums of money from our joint accounts

and our investment accounts. We were able to anticipate some of these moves, but he still sent a lot of this
money to offshore accounts. We also believe that he
has accounts in Switzerland. These accounts would
provide him with enough money to live in luxury if
he was to flee the country."

The cords in Cardoni's neck were tight with anger.
He leaned his head toward Frank without taking his
eyes off Justine.

"You asked me who would want to set me up,"
Cardoni whispered. "You're looking at her. The bitch
has access to my office at the hospital, and she has
keys to my house. It would have been easy for Justine
to steal the coffee mug, the scalpel and the videocassette. And Justine knew Grant."

"You're suggesting that Justine was Grant's partner?"

"She's a surgeon, Frank. Harvesting those organs
would be a piece of cake."

"What about murder? Do you think she's capable
of that?"

"As capable as she is of lying under oath. I never
raped Justine and I don't have any offshore accounts.
Her whole testimony is a lie."

"**W**hat happened?" Amanda asked as soon as Frank
walked through the door to her office.

"Bail denied," her father answered. He looked exhausted. "I wasn't surprised. Cardoni couldn't come
up with a single character witness, and Scofield's
case is very strong."

"How did Cardoni take the judge's decision?"

"Not well," Frank answered without elaborating.
He had no desire to relive Cardoni's tirade, which

was peppered with threats against Justine Castle and every member of every branch of government that was involved in his prosecution.

"Where do you go from here?"

"I'm already working on a motion to suppress, but I don't have much hope that I'll win."

"Let me take a crack at it," Amanda asked eagerly.

Frank hesitated. Amanda took a breath and plunged in.

"Why did you ask me to come to work for you, Dad? Were you being charitable?"

Frank was taken aback by the question. "You know that's not it."

"I know I don't need charity. I was law review at one of the top schools in the country, and I just finished clerking for a federal appeals court. I can get any job I want, and I'm going to start looking if you don't give me some responsibility."

Frank looked angry and started to say something, but Amanda pressed her case.

"Look, Dad, I might be a neophyte in a trial court, but I'm a sixth-degree black belt when it comes to legal research. You tell me where you could get someone better to work on this motion."

Frank hesitated. Then he threw his head back and laughed.

"You're damn lucky you're my daughter. If any other associate talked to me like that, I'd kick their ass into the center of Broadway."

Amanda grinned but held her tongue. One thing she knew from watching tons of appellate arguments was that you shut up when you'd won.

"Come down to my office for the file," Frank said. An idea occurred to him. "Since you're so anxious to get your hands dirty, why don't you keep Herb

Cross company when he interviews Justine Castle,
Cardoni's wife? She killed us at the bail hearing. Her
testimony at a sentencing hearing could send Cardoni to death row."

"Is Castle a doctor?"

"Yes. Why?"

"And she's very attractive?"

"A knockout."

"I've met her."

Every weekday morning Carleton Swindell rowed the Willamette, then showered at his athletic club. His hair was still a tad damp when he entered the anteroom of his office at seven-thirty sharp a few days after Vincent Cardoni's bail hearing. As soon as the hospital administrator walked in the door, Sean McCarthy stood up and displayed his badge.

"I hope you don't mind my waiting in here, Dr. Swindell," McCarthy said while Swindell inspected his identification. "There wasn't anyone around."

"No problem, Detective. My secretary doesn't get in until eight."

McCarthy followed Swindell into the administrator's office. Diplomas from several prestigious universities, including a medical degree and a master's in public health from Emory University, were prominently displayed next to photographs of Swindell posing with President Clinton, Oregon's two senators and several other dignitaries. A tennis trophy and two plaques for rowing victories graced a credenza under a large picture window with a view of downtown Portland, the Willamette River and three snow-capped mountains. McCarthy did not see any family photographs.

"I don't have any overdue parking tickets, do I?"

"I wish it were that simple. I assume you know that one of the doctors at your hospital has been charged with murder."

Swindell's smile disappeared. "Vincent Cardoni." He shook his head. "It's unbelievable. The whole hospital's been talking about nothing else."

"So you were surprised by the arrest."

Swindell looked thoughtful. "Why don't you sit down?" he said as he walked around his desk. When he was seated, Swindell swiveled toward his view, leaned back and steepled his fingers.

"You asked if I'm surprised. The type of crime—a mass serial killing—of course that shocks me. How could it not? But Dr. Cardoni has been a problem for this hospital since we hired him."

"Oh?"

Swindell looked pensive.

"Your visit presents me with a problem. I'm not certain I can discuss Dr. Cardoni with you. Confidentiality and all that."

McCarthy took a document out of his inside jacket pocket and held it out across the desk.

"I had a judge issue a subpoena before I came. It's for Dr. Cardoni's records."

"Yes, well, I'm sure it's in order. I'll have to have our attorneys review it. I'll expedite the matter, of course."

"Thank you."

"Shocking. The whole business." Swindell hesitated. "May I speak off the record?"

"Of course."

"Now, I don't have proof of anything I'm going to tell you. It's what I believe you call deep background."

McCarthy nodded, amused by the TV cop lingo.

"A week or so ago, Dr. Cardoni attacked Mary Sandowski, one of our nurses." Swindell shook his head. "I read that she was one of the poor souls you found in that mountain graveyard."

McCarthy nodded again.

"He's a violent man, Detective. Last year he was arrested for assault, and I've had complaints of abusive behavior from our staff. And there are rumors of drug use." Swindell looked grim. "We've never substantiated the rumors, but I've got a gut feeling that there is something to them."

"Another doctor who worked here was found in the graveyard."

"Ah, Clifford." Swindell sighed. "You know, of course, that he was in danger of losing his privileges here?"

"No, I didn't."

"Drinking," Swindell confided. "The man was a hopeless alcoholic."

"Did Cardoni know Clifford Grant?"

"I assume so. Dr. Grant was supervising Justine Castle's residency until we convinced him to take a leave of absence. Dr. Castle is married to Vincent."

"Interesting. Is there anything else that would tie Grant to Cardoni?"

"Not that I can think of right now."

McCarthy stood. "Thank you, Dr. Swindell. Your information has been very helpful. And thank you for expediting the subpoena."

Swindell smiled at the detective and said, "My pleasure."

As soon as McCarthy was out of the office, Swindell phoned Records. He wanted to make sure that the police received anything on Cardoni as soon as possible. It was the least he could do to thank them for taking care of a very annoying problem.

Walter Stoops made a living scrambling after personal injury clients and pleading out drunk drivers. Three years earlier Stoops had been suspended from the practice of law for six months for misusing client funds. Late last year the thinnest of technicalities had enabled him to avoid a count of money laundering when a Mexican drug ring was busted.

Stoops practiced out of an office on the top floor of a run-down, three-story building near the freeway. The cramped reception area was barely big enough to accommodate the desk of the secretary/receptionist, a young woman with stringy brown hair and too much makeup. She looked up uncertainly when Bobby Vasquez stepped through the door. He guessed that Stoops did not have many clients.

"Could you please tell Mr. Stoops that Detective Robert Vasquez would like to talk to him?"

He flashed his badge and dropped into a chair beside a small table covered with year-old issues of *People* and *Sports Illustrated.* The young woman hurried through a door to her left, returned a moment later and showed Vasquez into an office not much larger than the reception room. Seated behind a scarred wooden desk was a fat man in a threadbare brown suit wearing tortoiseshell glasses with thick lenses. His sparse hair was combed sideways across the top of his head, and the collar of his white shirt was frayed.

Stoops flashed Vasquez a nervous smile. "Maggie says you're with the police."

"Yes, I am, Mr. Stoops. I'd like to ask you a few questions in connection with an investigation that I'm conducting. Mind if I sit?"

"No, please," Stoops said, pointing to an empty chair. "But if this is about one of my clients, I may not be able to help you, you understand," he said, trying hard to sound nonchalant.

"Sure. Just stop me if there's a problem," Vasquez answered with a smile as he pulled a stack of papers out of a briefcase he was carrying. "Are you familiar with Northwest Realty, an Oregon corporation?"

Stoops's brow furrowed for a moment. Then a light went on.

"Northwest Realty. Sure. What about it?"

"You're listed as the corporate agent. Would you mind telling me a little about the company?"

Stoops suddenly looked concerned. "I'm not certain I can do that. Attorney-client confidence, you know."

"I don't see the problem, Mr. Stoops." Vasquez thumbed through the printouts. "For instance, it's public record that you purchased a three-acre lot in Milton County in 1990 for the company. Your name is on the deed."

"Well, yeah."

"Have you purchased any other property for the corporation?"

"Uh, no, just that one. Can you tell me what this is about?"

"What other things have you done for Northwest Realty besides buying the land in Milton County?"

Stoops twisted nervously in his chair. "I'm very

uncomfortable discussing a client's business. I don't think I can continue unless you explain why you're asking these questions."

"That's fair," Vasquez answered cordially. He pulled two photographs out of his briefcase and tossed them on the blotter. The photos were upside-down for Stoops. He leaned forward, not yet processing what he was seeing. He reached out gingerly and rotated the snapshots. Then his face lost all color. Vasquez pointed to the photograph on the right.

"These heads were found in a refrigerator in the basement of the house you bought for Northwest Realty."

Stoops's mouth worked, but no sound came out. Vasquez pointed at the other photo.

"This is a picture of a graveyard we found. It's a short distance from the house. There are nine corpses. Two of them were decapitated. All of these people were probably tortured in the basement room where we found the heads."

"Jesus" was all Stoops managed. He was sweating profusely. "Why the fuck didn't you warn me?"

"I didn't know if that was necessary. I thought you might have seen these bodies before."

Stoops's eyes widened, and he bolted upright. "Wait a second here. Wait one second. I read about this in the paper this morning. Oh, no. Now wait a minute. You can't come into my office and show me pictures like these."

"Let me ask you again: What can you tell me about Northwest Realty?"

The lawyer sank back in his chair. He pulled a handkerchief out of his pocket and mopped his brow.

"I've got a heart condition. Did you know that?"

Stoops glanced at the photographs again, then
pulled his eyes away. "What did you think you were
doing?"

Vasquez leaned forward. "Let's not play games,
Walter. I usually work narcotics. I know all about
your arrangement with Javier Moreno. You're a fucking crook who got lucky. You owe one to the criminal
justice system, and I'm here to collect. Talk to me,
now, or I'll bring you in as an accessory to murder."

Stoops looked shocked. "You can't think . . . Hey,
this is bullshit."

Vasquez stood up and took out his handcuffs.
"Walter Stoops, the law requires me to advise you
that you have a right to remain silent. Anything you
say—"

Stoops held out his hands, palms out. "Wait, wait.
I wasn't involved in that," he said, pointing toward
the photographs. "I don't know a thing about these
murders. I overreacted, that's all. It was a shock seeing those heads. I'm gonna see the goddamn things
in my sleep." Stoops wiped his brow again. "Go
ahead and ask your questions."

Vasquez sat down, but he set the handcuffs on the
desk where Stoops could see them.

"Who owns the Milton County property?"

"I can't tell you."

Vasquez reached for the cuffs.

"You don't understand," Stoops said desperately.
"I don't know who owns it. The guy contacted me by
mail. I can't even say it's a guy. It could be a woman.
The deal was that I was supposed to find rural property with a house on it. It had to be isolated. There
was a whole list of conditions. I would have said no,
but . . . Well, to be honest, I was in trouble with the
IRS, and I was suspended for a while from practice,

so there was hardly any money coming in. And, well, the price was right and there didn't seem to be anything wrong with what the buyer was asking. It was just a real-estate transaction."

"Where did the corporation come in?"

"That was the buyer's idea. I was supposed to set one up and use it to buy the property. The deal was I would get cashier's checks, money orders and stuff like that to set up the corporation. Then I would send pictures and descriptions of properties I thought would work to a box number. When the client found a place he wanted, the corporation would buy it. It sounded peculiar, but it didn't sound illegal. That was the only transaction I was ever involved with for Northwest Realty. After I bought the land I never heard from the guy again."

"Does the name Dr. Vincent Cardoni mean anything to you?"

"Just from the morning paper."

"Would you have any objection to my seeing your file on Northwest Realty?"

"No, not now."

Stoops stood up and opened a gray metal filing cabinet that stood in one corner of his office. He handed a file to Vasquez and sat down. Vasquez thumbed through the documents. The only thing that interested him were photocopies of cashier's checks and money orders, all in amounts less than ten thousand dollars, that added up to almost three hundred thousand dollars. The significance of the amount of each money order was obvious to anyone who dealt with drug dealers. Selling dope was easy; using the cash you got for it was the hard part. The Bank Secrecy Act required banks to report cash transactions of $10,000 or more and to keep records of individuals who engaged in such transactions. In order to avoid this problem drug dealers structured their cash transactions in amounts less than $10,000.

"Can I get a copy of the file?" he asked.

"I can't give you copies of the correspondence, but I can give you everything else."

Vasquez could have pressured him for copies of the few letters in the file, but there was nothing in them of use. All of the letters of instruction were unsigned and written on a computer. He settled for the rest of the file.

Vasquez sat in the waiting room while Stoops's secretary brought the material down the hall to a copier. He was disappointed. He had counted on Stoops to link Cardoni to the land, but it looked as though Cardoni had covered his tracks. It probably didn't matter. There was overwhelming evidence against the surgeon. There were the items with his prints that had been found in the cabin and the videocassette that had been found in his house in Portland. Once the jury saw that videotape, Cardoni was dead. Still, Vasquez thought, it would have been nice to have another piece of evidence tying him to the killing ground.

17

Seven years ago a white grocery clerk had mistakenly accused Herb Cross, an African-American, of robbing a convenience store. Cross hired Frank Jaffe to represent him. When Frank's investigator failed to find witnesses to support Cross's alibi, Frank's client took matters into his own hands and used his contacts to track down the real robber. Frank was so impressed that he offered his client a job.

"I'll ask the questions," Cross instructed Amanda as they walked down the fifth-floor corridor of St. Francis Medical Center toward the conference room in the Department of Surgery where Justine Castle was waiting. "You listen and take notes. If there's something you think I haven't covered, chime in when I'm through. Our object today is to get as much information as possible from Dr. Castle, so let her talk. And don't defend Cardoni, no matter what she says. We want to see how she feels and what she knows. We're not here to convert her to our cause."

Cross got no argument out of Amanda. She had never interviewed a witness before and was relieved that Herb would be doing the questioning.

The windowless conference room was narrow and stuffy, and the air was permeated by the faint smell of sweat. A flickering fluorescent light fixture hung above shelves of medical books and journals. Justine Castle was sitting on one side of a conference table sipping a cup of black coffee. She had been in surgery for a good part of the afternoon, and Amanda thought that she looked worn out. Her hair was swept back in a ponytail, and she was not wearing makeup.

"I'm Herb Cross, Frank Jaffe's investigator. We spoke on the phone. This is Amanda Jaffe. She's an attorney with the firm."

"We met at the Y," Amanda reminded Castle, who showed no sign of recognition. "You were with Tony Fiori."

"Oh, yes," Castle answered dismissively. "Tony's high school friend."

The cold response surprised Amanda, but she did not show it.

"I want to thank you for seeing us, Dr. Castle," Herb said.

"I only agreed to see you to be polite, Mr. Cross. Nothing I say will help your client. Our divorce is not amicable, and I find Vincent repulsive."

"Yet you married him," Cross said. "You must have seen something good in him."

Justine smiled ruefully. "Vincent can be charming when he's not coked up."

Amanda and Cross sat opposite Dr. Castle. Amanda took out a pad and prepared to take notes.

"You've read the newspaper account of the murders in Milton County," Herb began. "Had Dr. Cardoni ever said or done anything that made you suspect that he was killing these people?"

"Mr. Cross, if I had any idea that my husband had done something like that, I would have called the police immediately."

"Do you think he's capable of this type of violence?"

"Vincent is a violent man," she answered without hesitation. "I assume you know about my testimony in court."

"You testified that he beat you and raped you."

"It's not a far stretch from rape and assault to murder."

"The murders in Milton County were not acts of passion," Cross said. "They were well-thought-out acts of sadism."

"Vincent is a sadist, Mr. Cross. The rape was very methodical. The beating was not administered in some sort of insane rage. Vincent looked very satisfied with himself when he was through."

"Dr. Cardoni denies raping or beating you."

"Of course he does. You don't expect him to admit it, do you?"

"Did you report the rape to the police or seek medical assistance?"

Justine looked disgusted. "You mean, can I prove Vincent raped me?"

"It's my job to check the facts in a case."

"Let's not kid each other, Mr. Cross. It's your job to trick me into saying something that will help Vincent escape the punishment he deserves. But to answer your question, no, I did not report the rape or seek medical assistance. So it's Vincent's word against mine. That possibility does not intimidate me in the least."

"Dr. Castle, did you know that your husband owned a home in Milton County?"

"The police asked me about that. If he does own
that place, he never told me."

"Your divorce lawyer never ran across a reference
to it or property owned by Northwest Realty when
you were trying to discover Dr. Cardoni's assets?"

"No."

"Did you know Dr. Clifford Grant?"

Justine's anger faded away and was replaced by a
weary sadness.

"Poor Clifford," she said. "He was my attending
until the administration started taking his responsibilities away from him. Not that I can blame them.
He couldn't stop drinking. That's why his wife left,
and that made him drink even more. Then there was
that incident in surgery. He almost killed a four-year-
old boy."

"And yet I get the impression that you liked Dr.
Grant."

Justine shrugged. "He was going through his divorce while he was supervising me. We went out for
dinner every now and then. He trusted me and un-
burdened himself on occasion."

She stopped talking, and her eyes grew distant. "I
can't help wondering if I'm responsible for his death."

"Why would you say that?"

"Vincent and Clifford didn't become friendly until
we were engaged. The papers say that they were harvesting organs for the black market. I wonder if Clifford would have trusted Vincent if I hadn't brought
them together."

"What can you tell us about the incident with
Mary Sandowski?" Cross asked.

"I was there when he attacked her. The poor
woman was speechless with fright. He had her by the
arm and he was screaming at her."

"Do you know why he was so angry?"

"Mary told me that Vincent screwed up during an operation and became furious with her when she tried to warn him. I'm certain she was right."

"Why is that?"

"I saw Vincent's eyes. He was coked to the gills."

"What's your husband's reputation among the other doctors at St. Francis?"

"I can't speak for them. If you want gossip, you might want to talk to Carleton Swindell, the hospital administrator. I do know that the Board of Medical Examiners is looking into several complaints of malpractice that are probably legitimate. If it was up to me I would never let him in an operating room. I think he's a drug addict and an incompetent."

"He's also rich, isn't he?"

Justine raised an eyebrow suspiciously. "What if he is?"

"I don't want to offend you, Dr. Castle, but isn't it true that you'd come away from the divorce with a lot of property and money if your husband is convicted of murder?"

Justine pushed away from the table and stood up.

"Anything I take out of this marriage I've earned, believe me. And now I'm afraid that I have to end this interview. I've been working since early this morning and I need to get some rest."

"**W**hat do you think?" Amanda asked as they headed toward the elevator.

"I think that Dr. Justine Castle is one pissed-off lady."

"Wouldn't you be if you were the victim of rape and assault?"

"Then you believe her?"

Amanda was going to answer when she noticed Tony Fiori walking toward them. He was wearing green surgical scrubs under a white coat that looked as though it had never been washed. Scraps of paper poked out of the jacket's bulging pockets.

"Tony!"

Fiori looked puzzled for a moment. Then he smiled.

"Hey, Amanda. What are you doing up here?"

"We just finished interviewing a witness in a case. This is Herb Cross, our investigator. Herb, this is Dr. Tony Fiori, an old friend from high school."

Herb shook Tony's hand.

"Do you have time for a cup of coffee?" Tony asked Amanda. "I got bumped out of the OR by an emergency and I've still got half an hour before I have to be back."

"I don't know," Amanda said hesitantly, looking at Cross.

"That's fine," the investigator replied.

"You're sure you don't need me?"

"I'm just going back to the office to write my report. We'll catch up later."

"Okay, then. I'll see you at the office."

She turned to Tony. "I can use a caffeine fix. Let's go."

It was raining when Amanda and Tony walked outside. They sprinted across the street to Starbucks, and Amanda found a table while Tony ordered for them.

"One grande skinny caramel latte," he said, placing the drink in front of Amanda.

"That looks like regular coffee," Amanda said, pointing to Tony's cup.

"Hey, I'm a barbarian. What can I say?"

Amanda laughed. "It's strange—we don't see each other for years, and now we bump into each other twice in less than a month."

"It's fate," Tony answered with an easy smile.

"You look like you're working hard."

"Like the proverbial dog. Fortunately, my senior resident is a good guy, so it's not as bad as it could be."

"What are you doing?"

"I've been on the surgical intensive care rotation for two months, but I've been doing elective surgeries for the past two days—hernias, appendectomies. It's two-for-one day today. Let me take out your appendix and I'll remove your spleen for free."

"No, thanks," Amanda answered with a laugh. "I gave at the office."

Tony took a long drink of coffee. "Man, I needed that. I've been at it since six this morning without a break."

"I'm glad I came along."

Tony leaned back and studied Amanda.

"You know what I remember about you?" he asked with a smile. "The swimming. You were so great at the state meet my senior year, and you were only a freshman. Did you keep it up in college?"

"All four years."

"How'd you do?"

"Pretty well. I won the two hundred free in the PAC-Ten my junior and senior years and placed at nationals."

"Impressive. Did you try for the Olympics?"

"Yeah, but I never really had a chance to make the team. There were three or four girls who could kick my butt on my best day. To tell you the truth, I was burnt out by my senior year. I didn't swim at all when I was at law school. I'm just getting back to it now."

"Where did you go to law school?"

"NYU. The last two years I had a clerkship at the Ninth Circuit Court of Appeals in San Francisco. You went to Colgate, right?"

"Only for a year. My dad died and it hit me hard." Tony's eyes grew moist, and he looked down at the table.

Now Amanda remembered. Dominic Fiori had been Frank's law partner. He was raising Tony after a bitter divorce. During winter break of Amanda's sophomore year in high school, Dominic had died in a fire. The sudden death of a parent was bound to be traumatic.

"Anyway, I dropped out for a while and bummed around Europe and South America for a year after that," he continued in a subdued tone. "Then I was a ski instructor in Colorado for a while before I got my act together and went back to school at Boulder. My grades weren't good enough for an American medical school, so I ended up in Peru. I took some tests when I graduated and was accepted at St. Francis for my residency."

"That's a tough road."

Tony shrugged. "I guess," he answered, looking a little embarrassed. "So you were interviewing Justine for your case?" he asked, changing the subject.

"How did you know?"

"I have amazing psychic powers. Also, I read the papers. Your father and Cardoni have been all over the news since they found those heads." Tony was suddenly serious. "You know, I was there when Cardoni had his run-in with Sandowski."

"No, I didn't."

"Did he really decapitate her?"

Amanda's legal training reared its head. "I can't really talk about that."

"Sorry, I didn't mean to be nosy. It's just . . . I knew 'em both." He shook himself, as if trying to clear away an unpleasant image.

Amanda hesitated, then made a decision. "I guess I can tell you. It'll come out at the trial anyway. There's a videotape of Mary Sandowski being killed. Whoever did it operated on her while she was conscious." She shivered. "You're probably used to seeing people in pain, but I've never seen anything like that."

"I haven't seen anything like that either, Amanda. A doctor tries to ease suffering. I'd have been just as upset as you."

Tony glanced up at the clock on the wall. "I'm going to have to get back." He hesitated. "Uh, look," he asked nervously, "do you want to get together sometime? You know, dinner, a movie?"

Amanda flashed a reassuring smile. "Sure. I'd like that."

Tony grinned. "Great. Give me your number."

Amanda took out a business card and wrote her home number on the back. Tony stood up.

"Don't rush off," he told her. "Finish your latte. I'll call soon."

Amanda watched Tony duck into the rain and jog back toward the hospital. She wondered if he'd really call. It would be tough giving up an evening in the li-

brary to go to dinner with a drop-dead gorgeous doctor, but Amanda believed she was woman enough to
make the sacrifice.

"**A**nd she sent us on our way," Herb Cross told
Frank Jaffe as he concluded his account of the Justine
Castle interview.

"What was your opinion of her?" Frank asked.
Cross slouched in the client chair in Frank's office
and stared at the West Hills through the window at
Frank's back while he gathered his thoughts.

"She's very bright and very dangerous. She hates
our client and will do everything she can to put him
on death row if she's called as a witness."

"Cardoni thinks she set him up."

Cross looked surprised. "He thinks Castle is a serial killer?"

"That's what he says. She's a surgeon, she knew
Grant."

Cross looked skeptical.

"I don't buy it either," Frank said, "but we have to
worry about Castle. I need to know if there's some
way to get to her if she testifies. Go to the jail. Talk to
our client. Get as much background on her as you
can, then go after her."

18

Bobby Vasquez found Sean McCarthy neck deep in paperwork when he walked into the squad room and pulled up a chair to the detective's desk.

"Hey, Bobby," McCarthy said. "What have you got?"

"A lot," he answered, opening a file he was carrying. "Cardoni grew up outside of Seattle. His parents were divorced and Cardoni started getting in trouble soon after the split. He was a star wrestler in high school, excellent grades, but he was also arrested for assault. The case never came to trial. I don't know why it was dismissed.

"After high school Cardoni went to Penn State on a wrestling scholarship, but he lost it in his sophomore year when he was arrested for assault."

"Any specifics?"

"I got the police report on that one. It was a bar fight. He really fucked up the other guy. Cardoni went into the army as part of a plea bargain. Charges were dismissed."

"How'd he do in the army?"

"No trouble I could find. He qualified for the wrestling team and trained during his hitch. He also excelled at unarmed combat. After the army, Cardoni went to Hearst College, in Idaho. Good grades, NCAA Division Two nationals as a junior and a senior, then medical school in Wisconsin and a residency at New Hope Hospital in Denver."

"Any trouble in Idaho, Wisconsin or Colorado?"

"Cardoni was the defendant in a malpractice suit in Colorado. The insurance company settled it. I've got rumors of cocaine use, and there were a couple of sexual harassment complaints that went nowhere. After Cardoni finished his residency, he moved to Portland."

"Where does Cardoni's money come from?" McCarthy asked.

"Some of it comes from an inheritance. His folks are dead. I also hear that he's invested wisely."

McCarthy leaned back in his chair and tapped his fingers together thoughtfully.

"If Cardoni is a serial killer, he may have cut his teeth before moving to Portland. Find out if a killing field like the one near the cabin was ever found in Washington, Pennsylvania, Idaho, Wisconsin, Colorado or any other place Cardoni lived."

"Okay."

"And while we're on the subject, did you have any luck tracing the ownership of the Milton County property?"

"None. I went to the banks that cut the cashier's checks, but there was no record of the purchases because they were under ten thousand dollars. Is there anything new on your end?"

"A little. I'm certain that the Milton County cabin is the place where the illegal organs were harvested. Remember those jars in the refrigerator?"

"The ones with Viaspan written on them?"

"Right. Viaspan is a cardiac preservation fluid. Before you cut the heart out of a donor's body, you inject Viaspan into it. It replaces the blood, fills up the vessels and preserves the heart so the metabolic processes don't continue when the heart stops beating. After you remove the heart, you place it in a plastic bag filled with Viaspan. Viaspan would also be used when transplanting other organs."

"Like a kidney?"

"Exactly. We've also identified several of the victims. The decapitated woman without the heart is Jane Scott, a runaway. One of the victims is Kim Bowers, a prostitute who disappeared a year and a half ago, and another is Louise Pierre."

"The Lewis and Clark student who went missing in June?"

McCarthy nodded "One of the males is Rick Elam, a shipping clerk who was reported missing in September. Elam and Pierre were missing kidneys. Now, here is the interesting part. Scott, Elam and Pierre were patients at St. Francis within months of their disappearances."

"No shit! Were any of them a patient of Cardoni?"

"No, but they didn't have to be. All you need to do to find a donor for a heart is to find a person whose blood type is compatible with the recipient's and who is within twenty percent of the recipient's body weight. The heart of a person with type O blood can be given to anyone. All Cardoni or Grant had to do was look at their files."

"Were any of the other victims missing organs?"

McCarthy shook his head sadly. "It looks like Cardoni was just having fun with some of those poor bastards and mixing business with pleasure with the others."

19

Amanda was half an hour late for her date with Tony Fiori when she finally arrived at the YMCA. On the ride over she had worried that he would think she'd stood him up, but he smiled when he saw her.

"I'm sorry," Amanda apologized. "I had a jury out and they came back just before five."

"Did you win?"

Amanda let her grin answer the question.

"It was so great, Tony. Dad put me on the court appointment list so I could get more trial experience, and they appointed me to help this poor woman, Maria Lopez. She's a single mother and she's got these three maniac kids. So she's at Kmart and José, her two-year-old, streaks down the aisle toward these toys, so she stuffs a roll of Scotch tape and a bottle of aspirin in her coat pocket and goes after him. José knows how to run, but he hasn't figured out stopping yet. *Bam*, he goes headfirst into this display counter. Maria is holding José, who is screaming his head off, and trying to comfort Teresa, who's three and is screaming to keep José company, and trying to keep an eye on Miguel, who's four. Naturally she forgets about the tape and the aspirin, and some idiot security officer arrests her for shoplifting."

"How did you get her off?"

"I slam-dunked the security officer. He testified that Maria was looking around 'stealthily' when she 'slipped' the stuff in her pocket. And he said that José didn't take off for a second or so after she 'secreted the goods on her person.' He made Maria sound like some master thief. Then I showed him the videotape from the store's security camera. You should have heard him stammer and stutter after that. Maria was so grateful. She just manages to get by, and she was scared to death of what would happen to her kids if she went to jail."

"Sounds like you did a super job."

"Bet your ass I did," Amanda said, puffing up like a peacock.

"Then you deserve an amazing dinner as a reward."

"Oh? Where are we going?"

"It's a surprise. I'll tell you when we're finished working out."

They swam hard for an hour, and Amanda found that the time went quickly with Tony as her workout partner. She showered, toweled her hair dry and emerged from the locker room moments before Tony came out.

"Tell me where we're going to dinner," she demanded. "I'm famished."

"Great, because it's a very exclusive Italian place I know. Did you drive?"

Amanda nodded.

"Then follow me."

Tony took the freeway, then exited onto the winding streets of a residential neighborhood with which she was unfamiliar. Finally Tony pulled into the driveway of a blue two-story Victorian with white gingerbread trim. A high hedge enclosed a small backyard, and a shaded porch fronted the street.

"Welcome to Papa Fiori's, home of the finest Italian food in Portland," Tony said when Amanda got out of her car.

"You're cooking?"

"*Sì, signorina.*"

Tony opened the front door and flipped on the lights.

"This is lovely," Amanda said as she admired the stained-glass windows above the front door.

"It was the windows that sold me. The place was built in 1912, and those are original."

There was a television, a VCR and a stereo in the living room, but most of the furnishings in the house were in keeping with its age. Tony led Amanda through the dining room. The dining table was polished mahogany, ornate molding created a border for the high ceiling and the cherrywood mantel over the fireplace was decorated with intricately carved cherubs, dragons and devils.

"Is all this original, too?"

"Mostly, yeah. It's all from the general period."

Tony flipped on the kitchen light and pointed to a table near the stove. "Why don't you sit over there while I prepare spaghetti and meatballs alla Fiori. Do you like garlic bread?"

"I love it."

"Then you're in for a treat."

*   *   *

"This was as good as advertised," Amanda said after finishing a second piece of garlic bread. She felt fat and drowsy after consuming too much pasta and two glasses of Chianti.

"Some more wine?"

"Just a little. I've got to drive home."

Tony topped off her glass and watched as Amanda took a sip. She caught him looking and smiled to let him know that she didn't mind. Amanda could not remember spending a more relaxing evening with a man.

They carried their wineglasses into the living room.

"How's work coming?" Tony asked as he lit the logs in the fireplace.

"I'm pretty busy."

"You seem to like what you're doing."

"Yeah, for the most part," she answered wistfully. "I'd like more responsibility."

"You're working on the Cardoni case, aren't you?"

"A little. The motion to suppress is set for Monday, and Dad's got me researching it. And I've gone out with Herb Cross, our investigator, the guy you met at the hospital."

"How's it going?" Tony asked when they were settled on the couch.

"I think we're going to get clobbered at the motion."

"How come?"

"Do you understand what happens at a motion to suppress?"

"I watch *The Practice* when I get a chance."

Amanda took another sip of wine. Her stocking feet were up on Tony's coffee table and she could feel the heat from the fire on her soles. She decided that she wouldn't mind staying like this for a long time.

"Police usually need a warrant when they search a house, but there are exceptions. One of them comes into play when an officer doesn't have time to get a warrant because the evidence he's looking for might be destroyed or moved while he goes to a judge. That's what the cop who searched the cabin is claiming, and we can't find a way of getting around that."

Tony was curled up on the couch beside Amanda. His hair was mussed, and the wine had put a glow in his cheeks. Amanda had a hard time keeping her eyes off him.

"What happens if you lose?" Tony asked.

"The state gets to introduce all of the evidence it took from the mountain cabin and Cardoni's house in Portland, and our case is in big trouble."

"If Cardoni killed all of those people, maybe that isn't such a bad thing."

"That's one way to look at it."

"But really, if he's that cold, that cruel, wouldn't you want him locked away someplace where he couldn't hurt people?"

"That's a question of punishment. It's for a judge to decide. You don't ask for the personal history of everyone you operate on, do you? If you found out a patient was a serial killer, would you refuse to treat him?"

"I guess not." Tony looked at the fire for a moment. "I wonder how a guy like that thinks. I mean, if he did it. Everyone has a dark side, but what he did . . . "

"Some people just aren't made like the rest of us, Tony. I sat in when Dad talked to Albert Small. He's a psychiatrist Dad consults with on tough cases."

"What did he say?"

"The serial killer who murdered the people at the

cabin is called an organized nonsocial. They are very adept at fitting into society and have above-average intelligence, respectable looks and an uncanny ability to tune in to the needs of others, a skill they use to manipulate people and disarm potential victims. They also have active fantasy lives and visualize their crimes in advance. That helps them anticipate errors that could lead to their capture."

"I guess Cardoni fits that profile, right? He's a medical doctor and a good-looking man with above-average intelligence, and he was able to convince a bright woman like Justine Castle to marry him."

"That's true, but there are several differences between the profile and Cardoni. His outrageous behavior attracts attention. He botched operations, used drugs blatantly and made himself generally hated."

"I see what you mean," Tony said thoughtfully. "He sure didn't anticipate errors that could lead to his capture. Leaving that mug and scalpel with his fingerprints at the scene of the murder was really dumb."

"If he left them."

"What do you mean?"

"Cardoni claims that he's being framed. Planting those objects at the scene would be a smart move if Cardoni isn't the killer and the real killer wanted to set him up."

"Do you believe him? Do you think that's what's happening?"

Amanda sighed. "I don't know. We pointed this out to Dr. Small, and he had an alternative explanation. Organized nonsocials are people who have never grown out of the 'me' stage that most children are in until they're socialized. They think only of their own needs and see themselves as the center of the universe. They can't conceive of themselves as ever being wrong, which leads them to have very poor judgment on occasion. Their very belief in their own infallibility leads them to make mistakes. Add cocaine use to an already impaired ability to make sound judgments and you end up with someone who leaves incriminating evidence at a crime scene because he can't conceive of being caught."

Amanda stifled a yawn, then blushed and laughed.

"Oh, my gosh. I'm boring you," Tony said with a grin. "Should I tell you some dirty jokes or juggle?"

Amanda gave him a sleepy smile. "It's not you. I'm just wiped from the workout and my trial."

She yawned again.

Tony laughed. "Time for you to go home. Do you feel awake enough to drive?"

Amanda wondered if Tony would offer his guest bedroom if she answered in the negative and where that might lead. Before she could get too deep into those woods, Tony stood up.

"Let me fix you a cup of espresso," he said. "I make it strong enough to get you to the moon and back without blinking."

Frank was working in the den when Amanda came home a little after eleven. She stuck her head in the door and said, "Hi."

Frank looked up and smiled. "Where've you been?"

"Remember Tony Fiori?"

"Dominic's son?"

"I had dinner with him."

"Really? I haven't seen Tony since . . . It must be at least ten years. How did you two get together?"

"I talked to him at the Y a few weeks ago. Then we bumped into each other at St. Francis after Herb and I interviewed Justine Castle. We had coffee and he asked me out a few days later."

"What was he doing at St. Francis?"

"He's a doctor."

"No kidding."

"Why are you so surprised?"

"He had a tough time after Dom died. I heard he dropped out of school. I'm glad to hear that things have worked out for him. Did you have a good time?"

"Very."

"How'd your trial go?"

Amanda gave Frank a thumbs-up, then told him about the case.

"All right," Frank answered enthusiastically just as the phone rang.

Frank held up his hand and answered it.

"Is this Frank Jaffe?" a man asked.

Amanda looked at him expectantly, hoping that Tony was calling to say good night. Frank said, "This is he," as he shook his head.

"I'm beat, Dad. I'm going to hit the hay," Amanda told him, and headed to her room. Frank waved at her, then returned to the phone.

"What can I do for you?" Frank asked the caller.

"It's what I can do for you."

"Oh?"

"I know something about the Cardoni case. We should talk."

On hot summer nights the Carrington, Vermont, marching band performed concerts in a gazebo on the town square, and you could lie back in the grass, look up at the stars and believe that you were living in a slower, more peaceful time when kids ate ice cream and played tag and adults whiled away the time strolling arm in arm down by Hobart Creek. On those nights the darkness hid the fact that many of the quaint nineteenth-century shops that surrounded the square were out of business or barely hanging on. In daylight there was no way to hide the poverty of the town where Justine Castle had grown up.

As Herb Cross drove to James Knoll's farmhouse, he wondered what Justine's life had been like in this town of trailer parks, taverns and failing mills, and he hoped that the former chief of police could give him the answer. Knoll had seemed excited about the opportunity to talk about police work when Cross phoned him from the police station. He had even offered lunch.

A tall, lanky man with a full head of snow-white hair, leathery skin and bifocals walked down from the porch as soon as Herb parked. Cross shook hands with Knoll.

"Come on inside. My wife fixed us some sandwiches and coffee."

When they were seated at the kitchen table, Knoll studied the investigator.

"Portland to Carrington is a long way to travel."

"Our client is facing the death penalty."

Knoll nodded to indicate that no other explanation was necessary.

"It's been some time since I've thought about Justine Castle." Knoll shook his head. "That was a bad business."

"What happened, exactly? I read a newspaper account, but the details were sketchy."

"We kept it that way. Didn't want a scandal. Gil was dead and there was a young woman's reputation at stake."

Knoll took a bite of his sandwich and a sip of coffee before going on.

"Gil Manning was our star quarterback and star basketball player . . . and a star asshole. 'Course, everyone overlooked the asshole part because he was . . . "

"A star?" Herb smiled.

"Exactly. Justine was the prettiest girl in school, and they were an item starting in their junior year. Justine was our valedictorian. They were a glamorous couple. Homecoming weekend their senior year, Gil won the game with a ninety-yard run in the final minutes. It was all anyone talked about until they announced their engagement.

"Gil was a good high school athlete, but he wasn't good enough for a college athletic scholarship. He didn't have the grades, anyway. Justine could have gone to any college. She was accepted at quite a few, if I recall. Then she got pregnant and that was that. She and Gil were married the day after graduation and they moved in with his parents. That's when the trouble started.

"Gil couldn't handle life after high school. He wasn't important anymore. He always drank a lot, but that was boys-will-be-boys stuff while he was the big man on campus. After high school he was just another town problem when he got tanked up.

"The real trouble began when he started taking out his frustrations on Justine. One night Gil beat her up so bad she lost the baby. I tried to get her to tell the truth about what happened. It was pretty obvious that she hadn't fallen down any stairs. But Gil was at the hospital, hovering over her, real solicitous, and she wouldn't speak against him."

Knoll shook his head sadly. "Justine had always been so pretty and so bright, but the woman I saw at the hospital looked dragged out and used up, and she was only eighteen. It would have given me great pleasure to haul Gil's sorry ass to jail, but we had no case without Justine."

Knoll paused to take a bite from his sandwich.

"Two months later we got a nine-one-one from the Manning place. It was Justine, scared to death. She was gulping air and could hardly speak. I got there about one in the morning. Gil was stretched out by the front door, facedown. She'd killed him with his hunting rifle, one shot, right through the heart. When I got to the farm Justine was sitting at the kitchen table. She was still holding the phone. Dispatch had told her to stay on the line until we got there. I had to pry the receiver out of her hand. She was shaking like a leaf."

"Did she tell you what happened?"

"Oh, yeah. We talked about it once I got her settled down. Gil had insisted she go drinking with him. She didn't want to, but he made a scene. Gil got drunk and nasty at Dave Buck's tavern, and Dave tossed him after he tried to start a fight with some kid from a rival high school. On the way home Gil started blaming her for his life being shit. He said she was a fat pig, claimed she was holding him back." Knoll shook his head. "From what, I could never guess. Then he cracked her on the jaw. There was a bad bruise. We took pictures. He hit her in the eye, too. Then he pushed her out of the car and tried to run her down.

"Justine ran away, and Gil was too tanked to catch her. When he stopped looking she headed home in the dark. By the time she reached the farm she was hysterical and scared to death. She said that she was certain that Gil would kill her when he came home. Gil's folks were visiting their other son in Connecticut, so she was all alone. She grabbed Gil's rifle and sat on the couch in the front room.

"Meanwhile Gil had crashed the car. He wasn't hurt, but the car was totaled. Gil got a ride home from Andy Laidlaw, one of his drinking buddies. Andy told me that Gil admitted trying to run down Justine, but he also said that Gil was real remorseful about what he'd done. When they got to the farm, Andy offered to go inside with Gil, but Gil sent him off. Andy said that Gil was standing in the front yard when he drove away."

"How did Gil end up dead?"

"Justine said she heard the car drive in and thought it was Gil's. She didn't know he had wrecked it. When he came through the door, she told him to leave or she would shoot him. He took a step forward, she fired and that was that."

"How close to town was Justine's parents' house?"

"Closer than the farm, but she said that she was so scared after Gil tried to kill her that she just ran back to the farm without thinking. She didn't want her parents to know, anyway. She was ashamed that the marriage wasn't working."

"Didn't she cool down while she was sitting there with the gun?"

"Didn't have time."

"When did they leave the bar?"

"About eleven o'clock."

"When did she phone in the nine-one-one?"

"About one."

"That means there was probably an hour and a half between the time she ran away from her husband and the time she shot him."

"We knew that, but you have to remember that she ran the four and a half miles from town. It took her close to an hour. During that time, Gil was wrecking the car, going to Andy's house and getting a lift. Justine said that Gil walked in about five to ten minutes after she got home."

"So you figured the shooting was justifiable?"

"I talked it over with the county prosecutor, and he didn't want to go with it," Knoll said, not answering Herb's question. "Justine was a good girl who was stuck with a bad man. Everyone knew it. Everyone knew about the baby, too. There wasn't much sympathy for Gil. The only ones who wanted Justine prosecuted were Gil's parents, but that's to be expected. They claimed that Justine murdered Gil to get the insurance."

Cross raised an eyebrow. "How much was that?"

"About a hundred thousand dollars, if I recollect correctly."

"That's a lot of money for a farm girl."

"That's a lot of money for anyone."

Cross watched Knoll carefully when he asked his next question.

"Did you believe Dr. Castle's story?"

Knoll never broke eye contact. "I never had any reason not to, but then I never pushed much to prove she was lying. It was one of those times when no one wanted me to be much of a detective."

21

The Cardoni case had created big-city parking problems in Cedar City, and Amanda drove around town for fifteen minutes looking for a space. At the courthouse, Amanda went to the head of the line of people waiting for the first available seat in Judge Brody's courtroom and showed her bar card to the guard. Frank was conferring with Cardoni at the defense counsel's table while they waited for the judge to make his entrance. Their client was wearing a charcoal gray business suit, a white silk shirt and a blue tie with narrow yellow stripes. Amanda could understand why someone as sophisticated as Justine Castle would fall for the surgeon. He had rugged good looks and broad shoulders. He also looked dangerous, leaning slightly forward, tense, like a hunted animal.

"You made it," Frank said with a smile.

"I almost didn't. There isn't a place to park in the whole town. I got lucky over by Stokely's."

"Vince, you remember my daughter, Amanda? She helped me research the motion, and I wanted her as second chair in case we're faced with a tricky legal issue."

Cardoni barely acknowledged Amanda. She forced herself to smile at him and took her seat. She was glad that her father was sitting between her and their client.

Amanda had barely gotten her papers out of her attaché case when a door opened behind the dais and the judge entered the courtroom. The bailiff rapped his gavel, and everyone stood until Judge Brody indicated that they could be seated.

"Are you gentlemen ready to proceed?" Brody asked. Scofield nodded from his counsel table.

"Ready for Dr. Cardoni, Your Honor," Frank Jaffe said.

"Opening statement, Mr. Jaffe?"

"A brief one, Your Honor. We are seeking to suppress every piece of evidence gathered at a cabin in Milton County and Dr. Cardoni's home in Multnomah County. The State searched the Milton County house without a warrant, so it bears the burden of convincing the court of the existence of an exception to the state and federal rules requiring government agents to procure a warrant before searching a citizen's home.

"The search of Dr. Cardoni's Portland residence was conducted pursuant to a warrant, but the warrant was issued because of information in an affidavit. We contend that the evidence discussed in the affidavit was obtained during an illegal warrantless search of the Milton County home. If the court agrees, we ask you to suppress the evidence gathered in Portland under the 'fruit of the poisonous tree' doctrine, which I have discussed in the memorandum of law submitted by me in support of this motion."

"Very well. Mr. Scofield, what is your position?"

Scofield rose slowly. He rocked in place as he spoke.

"Well, Judge, Detective Robert Vasquez, a Portland police detective, received an anonymous tip informing him that the defendant was holding two kilos of cocaine in his home up here in Milton County. He'll tell you that he corroborated the tip, then had to act fast because he learned that the sale of the coke was imminent. He rushed up here and searched the house without a warrant because he had established exigent circumstances. As it was, he missed the sale.

"As the court knows, a police officer does not have to stop and get a search warrant if he has reason to believe that stopping to get the warrant will lead to the loss or destruction of the very evidence that he wants to seize. Of course, if the search here in Milton County was okay, there was nothing wrong with using the evidence found in the mountain home as the basis for probable cause in the warrant affidavit for the defendant's Portland house."

"Who's your first witness, Mr. Scofield?" Judge Brody asked.

"The State calls Sherri Watson."

Watson was the receptionist at vice and narcotics who had transferred the anonymous call to Vasquez. After she testified that the call had in fact been phoned in to police headquarters, Scofield called Bobby Vasquez to the stand.

Vasquez was wearing a navy blue sports jacket and tan slacks. Amanda thought he looked nervous when he took the oath. He took a sip of water as he waited for the district attorney's first question.

"Please tell the court the circumstances that led you to search the Milton County cabin without a warrant," Scofield asked after the detective re-counted his background in police work.

"I was at my desk in vice and narcotics writing a police report when the receptionist put through a caller who wanted to report a crime. I was the only one available, so it was chance that I caught the call."

"What did the caller tell you?" Scofield asked.

"The informant said that Dr. Vincent Cardoni was going to sell two kilos of cocaine."

"Did the caller tell you where the defendant was keeping the cocaine?"

"Yes, sir. In a mountain cabin here in Milton County."

"Did you obtain a warrant to search the cabin?"

"No, sir. The caller never identified him- or her-self. The tip was anonymous. I knew I needed corrob-oration before I could go to a judge."

"Did you try to corroborate the call?" Scofield asked.

"Yes, sir. I confronted a known drug dealer who knew the person who had sold Dr. Cardoni the co-caine, and he confirmed that Cardoni was going to sell the two kilos."

"Did your informant know who was buying the two kilos of cocaine from the defendant?"

"No. Just that Dr. Cardoni was selling and that the two kilos were supposedly in the doctor's cabin."

"So he corroborated the anonymous caller's state-ment that the drugs were in Milton County?"

"Yes, sir."

"Now that you had corroboration, why didn't you get a warrant?"

"There wasn't time. I talked to this informant in the afternoon. He said the sale was going down that day. It takes about an hour and a half to drive to the defendant's house from Portland. I was afraid that I would miss the sale if I waited for a judge to issue a warrant."

"Tell the judge what happened when you arrived at the cabin."

"I gained entry to the house. Once I was inside I noticed a padlock on one of the doors on the bottom floor. This made me suspicious, and I concluded that it was probable that the defendant had locked the room to protect his contraband."

"How did you open the lock?"

"With a lock pick I had with me."

"Did you find cocaine in the ground-floor room?"

"Yes, sir," Vasquez answered grimly.

"What else did you find?"

"The severed heads of two Caucasian females."

There was a stir in the courtroom, and Judge Brody rapped his gavel. While order was being restored, Vasquez took a drink of water.

"Can you identify these items, Detective Vasquez?" Scofield asked.

Vasquez took three photographs from the district attorney and identified them as different views of the refrigerator and its contents. Scofield handed the photos to the judge and moved to enter them into evidence for purposes of the hearing. Brody's face drained of color when he saw the pictures. The judge looked at the evidence quickly, then turned the photographs facedown.

"After finding the severed heads, did you call the Milton County Sheriff's Department?"

"Yes, sir."

"What happened then?"

"Representatives of that department, the Oregon State Police, and the Portland Police Bureau arrived at the scene and conducted a thorough examination of the premises."

"Were a number of physical items, including numerous pieces of scientific evidence, seized from the cabin?"

"Yes, sir."

"Your Honor, I am handing you State's exhibit one. It is a list of all the items seized from the cabin. Rather than having Detective Vasquez take up court time, Mr. Jaffe and I have stipulated that this is the evidence that the defendant wishes to suppress."

"Do you so stipulate, Mr. Jaffe?" the judge asked.

"Yes, Your Honor."

"Very well, the stipulation will be accepted and the list will be admitted into evidence. Proceed, Mr. Scofield."

Scofield walked Vasquez through the search of the Portland home, then concluded his questioning.

"Your witness, Mr. Jaffe."

Frank leaned back in his chair and studied the policeman. Vasquez sat quietly, looking very professional.

"Detective Vasquez, how many other officers accompanied you to the cabin when you made the search?"

"None."

Frank looked bewildered. "You expected to meet two or more men who were trafficking in cocaine, did you not?"

"Yes, sir."

"You presumed that they would be dangerous, didn't you?"

"I didn't know."

"Isn't it true that drug dealers often carry guns?"

"Yes."

"Are they frequently violent men?"

"They can be."

"And you went to meet these drug dealers, who were most probably armed, without backup?"

"It was stupid. In retrospect, I guess I should have brought help or called on Sheriff Mills to assist me."

"So you lay your failure to bring backup to stupidity?"

Vasquez nodded. "I should have known better."

"Could there have been another reason why you drove to the cabin alone?"

Vasquez thought for a moment.

"I'm afraid I don't understand the question."

"Well, Detective, if there had been other officers there, they would have witnessed your illegal entry into the cabin and could have testified against you, couldn't they?"

"Objection," Scofield said. "The court will decide if the entry was illegal."

"Sustained," Judge Brody agreed.

"Detective Vasquez, have you read the fingerprint report from the Oregon State Police?"

"Yes, sir."

"Were your prints lifted from the crime scene?"

"No."

"And why is that?"

"I wore latex gloves."

"Why would you do that?"

Vasquez hesitated. He had not anticipated this question.

"I, uh . . . It was a crime scene, Counselor. I didn't want to confuse the forensic experts."

"What confusion could there be? Your prints are on file. It would be very easy to eliminate them."

"I didn't want to cause the lab extra work."

"Or leave incriminating evidence of an illegal break-in?" Frank asked.

"Objection," Scofield said.

"Sustained," Brody said. "Stop throwing mud on this officer's reputation and move on, Mr. Jaffe."

"Yes, Your Honor. Detective Vasquez, you testified that you met the informant who corroborated the anonymous caller on the afternoon of the day you searched the cabin?"

"That's correct."

"As soon as you had your corroboration, you drove to Milton County?"

"Yes. I felt I had to go immediately or risk missing the sale of the cocaine."

"I gather that the informant who corroborated your information was the only witness you talked to that day before heading for Milton County?"

"Right."

"What is the name of the person who corroborated your information on the day of the search?"

"I'm afraid I can't reveal that, Mr. Jaffe. He spoke to me on a guarantee of confidentiality."

"Your Honor, I ask the court to instruct the witness to answer. Otherwise you will be in the position of having one anonymous informant corroborating another."

Brody turned to Vasquez. "Why won't you reveal this man's name?"

"He would be in great danger, Your Honor. He could even be killed."

"I see. Well, I'm not going to risk that, Mr. Jaffe. If you are implying that no such witness exists, I'll just have to judge Detective Vasquez's credibility."

"And I assume that you will suppress all of the evidence if you conclude that the officer is lying?"

"Of course," Brody answered with a scowl, "but you're a far way from establishing that, Mr. Jaffe."

The ghost of a smile played on Frank's lips as he told the court that he had no more questions of the witness.

After a brief redirect examination of Vasquez, Fred Scofield summoned several more police witnesses. Judge Brody called a halt to the proceedings a little before noon, and the spectators rushed for the door. Frank and Fred Scofield walked over to the judge and had a quiet conversation at the bench while Amanda started collecting her papers.

"How do you think your father did?" Cardoni asked.

"I think he scored some points," Amanda answered without looking at the doctor.

Cardoni grew quiet. Amanda finished packing her attaché case.

"You don't like me, do you?"

The question startled Amanda. She forced herself to look at Cardoni. He was slouched in his chair, studying her.

"I don't know you well enough to like you or dislike you, Dr. Cardoni, but I am working very hard to help you."

"That's nice of you, considering the fee I'm paying your firm."

"This has nothing to do with the fee, Doctor. I work hard for all of our clients."

"How hard can you work when you think I killed those people?"

Amanda colored. "My belief in your guilt or innocence has no effect on my professional performance," she answered stiffly.

"Well, it matters to me," Cardoni said just as the guards who were going to escort him to the jail appeared. Cardoni turned away from Amanda and put his hands behind his back. Amanda was relieved that their conversation was over. Frank returned to the table while the guards were securing Cardoni's handcuffs.

"The judge has some matters in other cases at one-thirty," he said to his client. "We should start at two. Fred is resting, so it's our turn to put on witnesses after lunch. I'll see you in court."

The guards led Cardoni away.

"You going to Stokely's?" Frank asked Amanda.

"Where else? Want to join me?"

"Sorry, I can't. I have a lot to do during the lunch hour. Eat a big slice of pie for me."

"You bet," Amanda said. Just as she reached the courtroom door she turned slightly and saw Cardoni watching her. His scrutiny unsettled her, but she forced herself to meet his eyes. For a moment she refused to back down. Then a thought occurred to her. It did not take much courage to confront a prisoner in manacles who was surrounded by guards. Would she have the courage to stare him down if he was loose? The odds were that Cardoni would be convicted, but Frank was very good. What if he won freedom for the surgeon? Would he remember her brazen stare?

Amanda's mouth went dry. She decided that she did not want to antagonize Cardoni; she did not want him thinking about her at all. Amanda broke eye contact and hurried out of the courtroom.

22

"Any witnesses for the defendant, Mr. Jaffe?"

"I do have a witness, Your Honor. He's waiting in the hall. May I get him?"

Amanda watched her father walk up the aisle and into the courthouse corridor and return with a hulking, bald-headed man. Fred Scofield frowned, and Bobby Vasquez turned ash gray.

"Please state your name for the record," the bailiff instructed the witness after swearing him in.

"Arthur Wayne Prochaska."

"Mr. Prochaska, how are you employed?" Frank asked.

"I manage a couple of bars in Portland."

"Would one of those bars be the Rebel Tavern?"

"Yeah."

"Mr. Prochaska," Frank asked, "do you know a police officer named Robert Vasquez?"

"Sure, I know Bobby."

"Can you point him out for the record?"

Prochaska grinned and pointed directly at Vasquez. "He's the good-lookin' fella sitting behind the DA."

"When is the last time you spoke with Officer Vasquez?"

Prochaska looked thoughtful for a moment. "We met at the Rebel the day he found those heads. It was afternoon. I read about them heads in the paper the next day."

"Why did you meet with Officer Vasquez on that day?"

"He asked me to," Prochaska answered with a shrug. "I wasn't doing anything, so I said okay."

"Did Officer Vasquez explain why he wanted to talk to you?"

"Yeah. He said a friend of mine sold some doctor cocaine. I told Bobby I didn't know anything about it. To tell the truth, I was pissed off that he would ask me to rat out a friend."

"Was the doctor he asked you about Vincent Cardoni?"

"Right. That was the guy. Cardoni."

"Did you know Dr. Cardoni?"

"Never heard of him until Bobby showed up."

"Did you tell that to Officer Vasquez?"

"Yeah."

"Did Officer Vasquez try to bribe you?"

"I don't know if you'd call it a bribe. The cops do it all the time. You know, they bust you, then they tell you they'll go easy on you if you'll tell them about someone else."

"And Officer Vasquez tried to bargain with you in that manner?"

"Yeah. I was waiting on charges of possession with intent. He said he'd talk to the feds if I told him about this doctor. Only I couldn't, because I didn't know him."

"Mr. Prochaska, Officer Vasquez has testified under oath about a conversation he alleges occurred on the afternoon of the day that he discovered the heads of the dead women. Was anyone else with you when you spoke with Officer Vasquez?"

"No."

"Officer Vasquez testified that the person he talked to said that Dr. Cardoni purchased two kilos of cocaine from someone the informant knew. Dr. Cardoni allegedly was holding the cocaine in a cabin in Milton County and was going to sell it that afternoon. Do you remember saying anything like that to Officer Vasquez?"

Prochaska laughed. "I think Bobby got caught with his pants down when he broke into the cabin, so he made this stuff up."

"Objection, Your Honor," Scofield said. "Speculation, nonresponsive. I move to strike the answer."

"Objection sustained," Brody said. He looked angry, and his tone was harsh when he ordered Prochaska to confine his answer to the question he had been asked.

"Mr. Prochaska, do you deny that you gave Officer Vasquez information about Dr. Cardoni?"

"Yeah, absolutely. That's why I'm testifying. I don't want no one spreading lies about me."

"Your witness, Mr. Scofield."

Fred Scofield's lips formed a grim smile as he studied Art Prochaska. The dealer's reputation was well known, and he could not wait to get at him.

"Have you ever been convicted of a crime, Mr. Prochaska?" he asked calmly.

"Yeah, several. But none lately."

"Why don't you tell Judge Brody your criminal history?"

"Okay. Let's see. I got a couple of assaults. I was down at the state pen for two years. There's some drug stuff. I was busted a few times, but they didn't prove it except once. I did do a few years on that."

"Mr. Prochaska, you are the right-hand man of Martin Breach, a notorious drug dealer, are you not? His enforcer?"

"Martin is my business partner. I don't know about that other stuff."

"Mr. Breach has a reputation for killing people who inform on him, doesn't he?"

"I never seen it."

"If you admitted that you informed on Mr. Breach, it would put you at some risk, wouldn't it?"

"I would never do something like that. I don't believe in it."

"Not even to save yourself from serving a fifteen-year sentence in a federal penitentiary?"

"No, sir. Besides, those charges are gonna be dropped."

"But you didn't know that when Officer Vasquez talked to you."

"I suspected they might be," Prochaska answered with a smirk.

"Isn't it true that you did corroborate Officer Vasquez's information but are afraid to admit it for fear that Martin Breach will kill you?"

"Vasquez was lying if he says I told him that stuff."

Scofield smiled. "We have only your word for that against the word of an officer of the law, don't we?"

"Hey, I got proof he lied."

Scofield paled. "What proof?"

"Do you think I'm dumb enough to meet a cop

and not protect myself? Bobby and me had our chat
in the men's john, where I got surveillance equipment. I taped the whole conversation."

Scofield turned toward Vasquez. The policeman
looked sick. Frank leaped to his feet, a cassette in his
hand. He had been waiting for this moment.

"I have the tape of the conversation, Your Honor. I
think we should play it and resolve this dispute between the witnesses."

"Objection, Your Honor," Scofield said. His voice
was shaking.

"On what grounds?" Brody asked angrily.

"Uh, if . . . if there is such a tape, it was recorded
surreptitiously. That violates Oregon law."

Brody glared at the district attorney. "Mr. Scofield, your question opened the door for this evidence. And I'll tell you something else: If someone is
lying in my courtroom, I want to know about it. I
don't care if that tape was made by Iraqi terrorists.
We are going to hear it right now. Play the tape, Mr.
Jaffe."

Frank placed the cassette in a boom box that he
had brought with him from Portland. When he hit
the play button, everyone in the court heard a door
slam shut and the sound of a brief struggle. Then
Bobby Vasquez said, "Long time, Art."

The tape spun along. When Prochaska turned
down Vasquez's offer to help him with his federal
charges, Judge Brody's eyes narrowed, and he cast a
withering glance at Vasquez. Then Prochaska told
Vasquez that he did not know Vincent Cardoni and
refused to talk about Martin Breach. By the time the
tape wound to a halt Judge Brody was furious,
Scofield was shell-shocked and Vasquez was staring
at his feet. Vincent Cardoni smiled triumphantly.

"I want Officer Vasquez back on the witness stand immediately," Brody ordered Scofield.

"I believe Officer Vasquez should seek counsel before answering any questions about the tape we've just heard," Scofield said, casting a quick, angry look at the detective.

"Quite right, quite right, Mr. Scofield. Thank you for correcting me. Officer Vasquez better get one hell of a lawyer, because his criminal conduct has forced me to suppress every piece of evidence seized at the house in Milton County and every piece of evidence seized from Dr. Cardoni's home in Portland. I grant this motion regretfully, but I have no choice, Mr. Scofield, because your star witness is a damned liar."

Judge Brody glared at Vasquez.

"Nine people have been slaughtered, Detective. Horribly butchered. I make no pronouncement as to the guilt or innocence of Dr. Cardoni. I haven't heard the evidence in this case. I do know that the person who killed those people is probably going to escape his justly deserved punishment because of you. I hope you can live with that."

Frank stood up to speak. "Your Honor, will you reconsider your decision on bail for Dr. Cardoni? In order for bail to be denied in an aggravated murder case it must appear to the court that the state will be able to prove its case at trial by clear and convincing evidence. Now that the court has suppressed all of the State's evidence, it is unlikely that the case will go to trial. I don't even see how Mr. Scofield can appeal your ruling in good faith. I ask that the court release Dr. Cardoni on his own recognizance.

"I am also putting Mr. Scofield on notice that I am moving against his indictment on the grounds that it was obtained through the submission to the grand jury of illegally obtained evidence and police perjury."

Frank handed the original of his motion, which he had prepared in advance of the hearing, to Judge Brody and gave a copy to the district attorney. As soon as Brody finished skimming the new motion his head dropped. When he raised it, his eyes blazed with anger.

"You have tied my hands with your unprofessional conduct, Mr. Scofield. I have no idea how Vasquez took you in. Your preparation for this motion to suppress borders on the criminal. You won your motion to deny bail by promising that you would produce all sorts of evidence against Dr. Cardoni. Now you can't present any of it.

"Your motion to release Dr. Cardoni on his own recognizance is granted, Mr. Jaffe. I will take the motion to dismiss under advisement. Mr. Scofield, you have thirty days to file a notice of appeal from any of my rulings or they will become final. Court is in recess."

Judge Brody fled to his chambers.

"Thank you, Frank," Cardoni told Amanda's father. Then he looked at her. "And thank you, Amanda. I know you think I'm guilty, but Frank's told me how hard you've worked for me, and I appreciate it."

Amanda was surprised at how sincere Cardoni sounded, but it didn't change her opinion. What had just happened frightened her. Frank was a magician in the courtroom, but his latest trick could have horrifying consequences.

Reporters mobbed Frank in the corridor outside the courtroom. Amanda forgot her misgivings as she was caught up in the action. Some of the reporters directed their questions to her, and it dawned on Amanda that she was a celebrity, if only for the length of a sound bite. After the furor died down, father and daughter walked to Stokely's to eat dinner. Frank was uncharacteristically quiet after a victory of this magnitude.

"What happens to Cardoni now?" Amanda asked.

"He'll be processed out of jail, Herb will drive him home and he'll try to put his life back together."

"So it's over?"

"It should be. Art Prochaska's testimony was the legal equivalent of a nuclear weapon. There isn't any evidence left for the State to use."

"How long have you known about Prochaska?"

"He called Friday evening."

"So you knew we'd win all along."

"There's no such thing as a sure thing, but this is as close as I've ever gotten." Frank noticed the look on Amanda's face and added, "I hope you're not upset that I didn't tell you about Art."

"No, that's okay," Amanda answered, but she was upset. They walked in silence for half a block. Then Amanda's thoughts shifted to Cardoni.

"I know I should be excited because we won, but I just . . . I think he killed those people, Dad."

"I don't feel so good about this one myself," Frank admitted.

"If he's guilty, they can't try him, can they?"

"Nope. I did too good a job. Vincent's free and clear."

"What if he does it again?"

Frank put his arm around Amanda's shoulders. His closeness was comforting, but it could not make

her forget the videotape or the still pictures of the
nine corpses.

"About three years after I started out I second-
chaired a terrible case with Phil Lomax. Two young
children and their baby-sitter were murdered during
a home burglary. The crime was brutal. The defendant was a very bad actor. Totally unrepentant, cruel,
with a long history of prior vicious assaults. The DA
was certain she had the right man, but the evidence
was paper thin. We fought our guts out, and the
chances of conviction were about fifty-fifty by the
end of the trial.

"After the jury went out, Phil and I went to one
bar to wait and the DA and her staff went to another.
The jury came back four hours later with a guilty verdict. About a month later I bumped into one of the
DA's investigators. He told me that Phil and I had
been the subject of discussion while the prosecutor
and her assistants were waiting for the verdict. They
thought that we were very ethical lawyers who had
fought hard but had also fought clean. They respected us as people and they had come to the conclusion that we'd sleep better with a conviction than
an acquittal. They were right. I was actually relieved
that we had lost, even though I gave one hundred
and ten percent for our client."

"Do you feel bad now?"

"Do you hear me bragging about our victory,
Amanda? As a professional, I'm proud that I did my
job. As an officer of the court, I feel good about exposing perjury by someone who is sworn to protect
us and uphold the Constitution. What Vasquez did
was inexcusable. But I'm also a human being and I'm
worried. So I pray that Vincent Cardoni is an innocent man who has been wrongly accused. If he's

guilty, I pray that this experience has frightened him so much that he won't hurt anyone else."

Frank gave Amanda's hand a squeeze.

"This is not an easy business, Amanda. It's not easy at all."

23

Martin Breach was hunkered down over a slab of ribs when Art Prochaska walked into the restaurant. He motioned Prochaska into a chair with a hand stained with barbecue sauce.

"You want a plate?" Breach asked. His mouth was stuffed with meat, and the question was barely intelligible.

"Yeah."

Breach waved. A waiter appeared immediately.

"The deluxe combo and another pitcher of beer," Breach said. The waiter scurried away.

"So?" Breach asked.

"Cardoni is out."

"Good work. I was worried that puke would cut a deal with the DA if he went down." Breach ripped a chunk of meat off a long bone. A sloppy scarlet ring of sauce circled Breach's mouth. "Now I want my money. Put Eugene and Ed Gordon on Cardoni. The first chance they get, I want him snatched."

Prochaska nodded. Breach handed Prochaska a fat rib. The enforcer started to protest, but Breach insisted.

"Take it, Arty. I'll get one of yours when your order comes."

Breach wiped his face with a napkin, then reached for another rib.

"I want Cardoni in good enough condition to chat," he told Prochaska between bites. "No brain damage. Tell the two of 'em. If Cardoni is too fucked up to tell me where my money is, I'll take it out on them."

24

There was a message from Herb Cross on the answering machine when Frank and Amanda arrived home from Cedar City. Frank shucked his jacket and tie, fixed himself a glass of scotch and dialed a number in Vermont.

"What's up?" Frank asked when he was connected to Cross's hotel room.

"I may be on to something."

"Oh?"

Frank listened quietly while Herb told him what he had learned during his meeting with James Knoll.

"It doesn't sound like there's anything we can use," Frank said when Herb was through. "Evidence that Dr. Castle shot an abusive husband in self-defense when she was in her teens isn't going to be admissible to prove that she kidnapped and tortured people."

"I'd agree if that was all I found. Gil Manning was insured for one hundred thousand dollars. When the police cleared Castle, the insurance company paid off. She used the money to pay her tuition at Dartmouth. In her senior year she married a wealthy

classmate, and they moved to Denver after graduation. Eight months later Castle's husband was dead."

"You're shitting me."

"It was a one-car accident. He was heavily intoxi-
cated. He was also heavily insured and he had a fat
trust fund. Castle inherited the money from the trust
fund and she received the insurance money."

"Now that is interesting."

"I phoned the dead husband's parents in Chicago.
They swear that their son was never more than a social drinker. They pressed for an investigation, but
the cops told them that they were satisfied that their
son's death was an accident. Castle's in-laws think
that Justine was a gold digger. They were opposed to
the marriage."

"Was there any evidence of foul play?"

"I haven't looked into the accident yet. Do you
want me to go to Denver?"

"No, come home."

"I think I'm on to something with this, Frank. I
think we should pursue it."

"That's not necessary. I won the motion to suppress. Cardoni is free and it's unlikely he'll be prosecuted."

"What! How did that happen?"

"If you've got a few minutes, I'll tell you."

25

Granite cherubs and gargoyles peered down on passersby from the ornate stone scrollwork that graced the façade of the Stockman Building, a fourteen-story edifice that had been erected in the center of downtown Portland shortly after World War I. The law firm of Jaffe, Katz, Lehane and Brindisi leased the eighth floor. Frank Jaffe's spacious corner office was decorated with antiques. He sat behind a partner's desk that he had picked up for a song at an auction. Currier and Ives prints graced one wall, and a nineteenth-century oil of the Columbia Gorge, which Frank had discovered at another auction, hung across from him over a comfortable sofa. The only jarring note was the computer monitor that sat on the edge of Frank's desk.

Vincent Cardoni showed no interest in the décor of Frank's office. The physician's attention was riveted on his attorney, and he shifted anxiously as Frank explained Fred Scofield's latest legal maneuver.

"So you're saying we have to go back to court?"

"Yes. Judge Brody has set the hearing for next Wednesday."

"What kind of bullshit is this? We won, didn't we?"

"Scofield moved to reopen the motion to suppress. He has a new theory, inevitable discovery."

"What's that mean?"

"It comes out of *Nix v. Williams*, a United States Supreme Court opinion. Around Christmas of 1968 a ten-year-old girl disappeared from a YMCA building in Des Moines, Iowa. Shortly after she disappeared, Robert Anthony Williams was seen leaving the YMCA carrying a large bundle wrapped in a blanket. A young boy who helped Williams open his car door saw two skinny white legs under the blanket.

"The next day Williams's car was found a hundred and sixty miles east of Des Moines in Davenport, Iowa. Later clothing belonging to the child and a blanket similar to the one Williams carried from the Y were found in a rest stop between Des Moines and Davenport. The police concluded that Williams had left the girl's body between Des Moines and the rest stop.

"The police used two hundred volunteers to conduct a large-scale search in an attempt to find the body of the victim. Meanwhile, Williams surrendered to the police in Davenport and contacted an attorney in Des Moines. Two Des Moines detectives drove to Davenport, picked up Williams and drove him back to Des Moines. During the trip, one of the detectives told Williams that snow might cover the little girl, making it impossible to find her body. Then he said that the girl's parents were entitled to a Christian burial for the little girl who had been snatched away from them on Christmas Eve. Later in the ride, Williams told the detectives how to find the body.

"Before trial, Williams's attorney moved to suppress evidence of the condition of the body on the ground that its discovery was the fruit of Williams's statements and those statements were the product of an interrogation that was illegal because it had been conducted out of the presence of his attorney.

"I'm not going to bore you with all the ins and outs of the appeals that eventually brought the case to the United States Supreme Court twice. What you need to know is that the justices adopted the inevitable-discovery rule. They concluded that the evidence supported a finding that the search party would inevitably have discovered the body of the little girl even if Williams had not led the police to it. Then the Court ruled that evidence that would normally be excluded because of police misconduct is still admissible if it would have been discovered inevitably."

"How does that help Scofield?"

"The cabin is on private land, but the graveyard is on a trail that goes through national forest land. Scofield is arguing that the graveyard was so obvious that Vasquez, a hiker, a forest ranger, somebody would inevitably have discovered it, giving a judge grounds to issue a search warrant for the cabin."

Cardoni laughed. "That's bullshit. Vasquez never went back there and there wasn't anyone near the cabin until Vasquez called the cops."

"You're right, Vince. The argument is total horseshit, but Brody might jump on this with both feet. There's an election coming up. Word is that Brody is going to run for one more term, then retire. If he lost the election, he would be humiliated. Granting Scofield's motion would get him off the hook for the most unpopular decision that he's ever made. Most Milton County voters don't understand the subtleties of search-and-seizure law. All they know is that Brody let you out and that the cops think you're Jack the Ripper's meaner cousin."

"Even if that tub of lard does rule for Scofield, you'd win on appeal, wouldn't you?"

"I'm pretty sure I would. The problem is that Brody will put you back in jail pending trial."

Cardoni's toe tapped rapidly.

"I pay you to anticipate things like this."

"Well, I didn't. Hell, Vince, there's no way I could."

Cardoni glared at Frank. He was rigid with anger.

"I am not going back to jail because some fat-ass judge wants to win an election. Either you handle this or I will."

Eugene Pritchard and Ed Gordon were intelligent muscle whom Martin Breach used when
more than simple violence was needed. Pritchard
had been a professional fighter with a decent record
until he was busted smuggling cocaine into the country after a fight in Mexico. Gordon was an ex-marine.
He had been dishonorably discharged for assaulting
an officer.

At eight o'clock on the day that Frank Jaffe told
Cardoni about Scofield's motion to reopen, Pritchard
and Gordon were debating the pros and cons of a
home invasion when Cardoni's car drove out of his
garage. They followed without lights until Cardoni
turned onto a major thoroughfare. Then they stayed a
few cars behind the doctor and tried to guess where
he was headed. After a while it got confusing. Cardoni seemed to be wandering aimlessly. He cruised
the streets of downtown Portland for a while, then
headed out of town along Burnside. Several miles
later Cardoni turned onto Skyline Boulevard and followed it past the cemetery until he reached a bumpy
dirt track that ended abruptly at Forest Park, a vast
wooded area.

Gordon turned off the headlights and followed at a safe distance. Cardoni got out of his car and started off along a narrow trail with a flashlight in hand.

"What's he doing out here?" Pritchard asked.

"Maybe he's got a few more bodies stashed in the woods."

Pritchard shook his head. "He is one sick fuck."

"Don't make disparaging remarks about someone who's making our job so easy. We'll take him here. It's isolated and there are no witnesses."

Pritchard grabbed a flashlight and they set off after Cardoni.

The Wildwood Trail runs for more than twenty miles through Portland's park system. The part of this trail Cardoni was walking led into the deep central section of Forest Park, far from roads or houses. Even though Pritchard was in the middle of a big city, he felt that he was standing in the dark heart of an unexplored jungle. Gordon had hiked and camped in the army, but Pritchard was a city boy who preferred watching TV and drinking in bars to trekking through the forest primeval. He definitely did not like wandering through the woods in the dark.

Following the faint glow of the doctor's flashlight was easy, and Pritchard kept his off. The rotting corpse of a tree felled by the violent storms of winter blocked part of the trail, and Gordon tripped over a root. He swore under his breath and squinted, trying to make out the floor of the forest in the dark. Pritchard turned his head and told his partner to shut up and watch where he was going. When he looked forward he could not find Cardoni's light. The men froze. The only sounds they heard were the swish of tree branches and the scratch of tiny claws in the underbrush.

Then Pritchard heard a crack, a grunt and a second sharp blow. He spun toward the sound and turned on his flashlight. Gordon was down and blood was pooling under him. Pritchard felt for a pulse. Gordon was breathing, but he was not moving.

"It's spooky in the woods at night."

Cardoni was behind him. Pritchard pulled his gun and spun around.

"Do you feel like Hansel and Gretel all alone in the forest of the wicked witch?"

"You can stop with the games, " Pritchard said, fighting hard to keep the fear out of his voice.

"You're the one who's been playing hide-and-seek all week, or didn't you think I'd notice?" Cardoni answered from a new location. Pritchard had not heard him move. He aimed his flashlight at Cardoni's voice. The beam cut between a western hemlock and a red cedar, but it did not find the surgeon.

"Let's cut the shit," Pritchard shouted into the darkness. He waited for an answer, but none came. Pritchard turned slowly in a circle, pointing his gun and the flashlight at the trees. A twig snapped and he almost fired. Two tree limbs rubbed together and he jumped sideways off the trail.

"That's enough, goddamn it. Get out here," Pritchard yelled, but he heard only the sound of his own labored breathing. He began backing down the trail toward the car, shifting the gun back and forth across the path every time he heard a sound. The muscles in his shoulders and arms ached from tension. His heel caught on a tree root. Pritchard flailed his arms to arrest his fall, and the gun flew from his hand. He landed hard on the packed earth and rolled toward the gun. He expected to feel a knife blade slice into his body or a club smash across his back as he groped for his weapon, but the only sounds he heard were those he made.

Pritchard could not find the gun, and he was too vulnerable on his hands and knees. He got to his feet and spun in place, keeping the flashlight in front of him to use as a weapon. Something hard smashed into Pritchard's right kneecap. His leg gave out and he toppled sideways. As he fell, Cardoni broke his right shoulder. Pritchard's eyes squeezed shut involuntarily from the intense pain and he almost blacked out. When he opened them Cardoni was standing over him, tapping a tire iron against the palm of his hand.

"Hi," the surgeon said. "How you doing?"

Pritchard was in too much pain to answer. Cardoni added to his pain by breaking his left kneecap.

"Rule number one: Remove your opponent's legs."

Cardoni walked around Pritchard slowly. He was sprawled on his back, gritting his teeth and fighting to stay conscious.

"A blow to the kneecap ranks as one of life's most painful experiences. It rivals a thrust to the genital area. Shall we make a comparison test?"

Cardoni's foot flashed. Boxers are used to pain, but this was pain on a new level. Pritchard made no effort to stifle his scream.

"I bet that smarts. In fact, I know it does. Doctors know every place on the human body that can cause suffering."

Pritchard wanted to say something brave in response to Cardoni's taunts, but he was weak with fear. If Cardoni wanted to inflict more pain, he knew he would be helpless to stop him.

"Do you know where you are, little man?"

When Pritchard did not answer, Cardoni gave his

right kneecap a casual tap. Pritchard arched his back
as if electricity had shot through him.

"You're in the House of Pain, and I run the estab-
lishment. There's one rule in the House of Pain: Anything I say goes. Disobedience is punished swiftly.
Now, here's my first question. It's an easy one.
What's your name?"

"Fuck you—" Pritchard started, but the sentence
was cut short by a scream when Cardoni gripped his
left wrist and extended his arm out at an awkward
angle, forcing Pritchard to roll onto his injured knees.

"The hand is a marvelous creation designed by
God to do the most wonderful things," Cardoni said.
"I use my hand to wield instruments that save lives. I
bet you use yours to pick your nose and beat off."

Pritchard tried to struggle, but Cardoni brought
him to heel with a small amount of pressure on his
wrist. Then the surgeon gripped the man's index finger tightly. He tried to resist, but Cardoni had no
trouble prying it out straight.

"There are twenty-seven bones in the hand. That
gives me twenty-seven opportunities to inflict excruciating pain on you."

Cardoni tightened his grip on Pritchard's index
finger.

"The bones of the fingers and thumb are called
phalanges. A single phalange is the length of bone
from one knuckle to the next. There are three phalanges in your index finger." Cardoni bent the index
finger backward. "All of them are going to be broken
if you don't become more cooperative."

Pritchard screamed.

"Now, what is your name? Even a moron like you
should be able to answer that question."

Cardoni applied pressure.

"Gene, Gene Pritchard," he gasped.

"Good boy."

Pritchard lunged suddenly. Cardoni backed away and jerked hard on his wrist. Pritchard's feet splayed out and he howled like a dog. Cardoni snapped Pritchard's index finger. As the bone cracked, the man sagged, almost passing out.

"The next time you decide to pick on someone, make sure you're man enough for the job," Cardoni said as he pried Pritchard's pinkie away from his fist.

"Now, Gene, who sent you to follow me?"

Pritchard hesitated for a second and paid for it. The last time he remembered crying was when he was eight. Tears trickled down his cheeks.

"Martin Breach," Pritchard gasped without having to be asked again.

"That's a very good boy. And what does Martin want you to do besides tail me?"

"We're . . . supposed to . . . bring you . . . to him."

"Dead or alive?"

"Alive, in good condition."

"Why?"

"The money he paid for the heart. He wants it back."

Cardoni studied Pritchard for what seemed like an eternity to the crippled enforcer. Then he released Pritchard's hand, backed into the shadows and disappeared without another word.

Bobby Vasquez knocked an empty bottle of whiskey into two empty beer bottles as he rolled onto his side. The three bottles crashed to the floor, and the sound of breaking glass brought Vasquez partway out of his drunken stupor. He opened his eyes and blinked. His first thought was, What time is it? Then, What day? Then he wondered why he cared. Since his suspension every day had been shit.

Vasquez struggled into a sitting position, squeezed his eyes shut against the light and waited for the throbbing to subside. After his humiliation and destruction at the motion to suppress, action had been swift. Vasquez had been placed on suspension, and Internal Affairs was conducting an investigation. Milton County would probably indict him for perjury, obstruction of justice and any other crime they could stick him with. The union lawyer represented him in front of Internal Affairs, but he had to foot the bill for his criminal lawyer, and that would probably wipe out his savings. If he was convicted or thrown off the force, he could kiss his pension goodbye.

Vasquez looked for something to drink. All the

bottles he could see were empty. He lurched to his feet and stumbled into the kitchen. He smelled. He had not shaved in days. He didn't care. He wasn't going to see anyone, and no one was going to see him. Yvette had called, but he had been drunk and insulted her. She did not call again. So much for true love. There had been calls from some of his cop friends, but he let the machine take them. What could he say? He had no excuses. He'd just gotten caught up in the thing. First there'd been his desire to avenge Mickey Parks. Then he'd found the heads, and he'd wanted Cardoni so badly that he had broken the law. To make matters worse, it was Breach's man who had brought him down. Now he was probably going to go to jail, and a man who had butchered nine human beings was walking free.

Vasquez went through the kitchen cabinets until he located the only liquor bottle left with something in it. He tilted it up and sucked down all of the remaining whiskey as his last thought echoed in his head. He would be in jail soon, and Cardoni would be free. His life was over, and Cardoni's would continue. The psycho fuck would kill again, and Vasquez would be responsible for each new death. Why go on? Why face disgrace and jail? He was starting to believe that the answer to his problems was a single shot through his brain when an alternative suddenly occurred to him. The brain in question did not have to be his own. If he was really willing to end his life, he could do anything he wanted to do. It was like having a terminal disease. No one could punish you worse than you were going to be punished. There was no threat that could deter you. The rules no longer applied. If he killed himself, Cardoni would still be free to cause untold suffering. If he killed Cardoni, he would be a hero to some and his conscience would be clear.

Art Prochaska entered Martin Breach's office in the Jungle Club and yelled, "Ed and Eugene are in the hospital," so that Breach could hear him over the blaring heavy metal music to which a buxom ecdysiast named Miss Honey Bush was disrobing.

"What happened?"

"Cardoni surprised them."

"Both of them?" Martin Breach asked in disbelief.

Prochaska nodded. "They're in pretty bad shape."

"Motherfucker!" Breach screamed as he leaped up from behind his desk and started pacing. When he stopped, he leaned forward on his knuckles and glared across the desk at his enforcer. Breach's fists were clamped so tightly that his knuckles were white.

"You take care of this personally. When I'm through with Cardoni he's going to beg to tell me where he's hiding my money."

29

The phone was ringing. Amanda sat up in bed and groped for it in the dark.

"Frank, I'm in trouble."

It was Vincent Cardoni, and he sounded desperate.

"This is Amanda Jaffe, Dr. Cardoni."

"Put your father on."

"He's in California taking depositions. If you give me a number where he can reach you, I'll have him call tomorrow."

"Tomorrow will be too late. There's something that I have to show him right away."

"The best I can do is give my father your message."

"No, you don't understand. It's about the murders."

"What about them?"

Amanda heard heavy breathing as Cardoni whispered into the telephone.

"I know who committed them. I'm at the cabin in Milton County. Get up here, right away."

"The cabin? I don't—"

"You're my lawyer, goddamn it. I pay your firm to represent me, and I need you up here. This is about my case."

Amanda hesitated. Frank would never refuse to help a client who sounded this desperate. If she didn't go, how could she explain her inaction to her father? How could she practice criminal law if she would not help a client because he frightened her? Criminal lawyers represented rapists, murderers and psychopaths every day. They were all frightening people.

"I'll leave right away."

The line went dead, and Amanda instantly regretted telling Cardoni she would meet him. It was midnight, and it would take her a little over an hour to drive to the cabin. That meant that she would be alone with Cardoni in the middle of nowhere in the middle of the night. Her stomach churned. Amanda remembered what had happened in that cabin. She saw Mary Sandowski's face drained of all color and all hope. What if Cardoni had done those things? What if he wanted to do them to her?

Amanda went downstairs to the den. Frank liked guns, and he'd had her on a pistol range as soon as she was old enough to hold one. Amanda enjoyed target practice and knew her way around weapons. Frank kept a .38 snubnose in the lower drawer of his desk. Amanda loaded it and slipped it in her jacket pocket. She had never shot a handgun off a range. She'd heard and read that shooting a person was totally different from shooting at a metal cutout, but she was not going to meet Vincent Cardoni in the woods after midnight without protection.

The temperature was in the thirties, so Amanda had thrown her ski jacket over jeans and a dark blue turtleneck. The rain started shortly before one and changed to snow near the pass. Amanda had four-wheel drive, so she was not worried, but she was still relieved when the snow fell away to a light rain. She was within eyesight of the turnoff to the cabin when a car suddenly swept out of the narrow dirt road and sped past her. Amanda thought she recognized the driver in the brief moment when the two cars were side by side. Then the taillights of the other car faded in her rearview mirror.

As soon as her headlights illuminated the house Amanda was certain that something was wrong. The lights were on in the living room and the front door was wide open. The wind had picked up and was blowing sheets of rain slantwise into the house. Common sense told her that she should turn the car around and speed toward safety, but she knew her father wouldn't turn tail and run. Amanda sucked in a deep breath, took her gun out of her pocket and walked toward the cabin.

The first thing that Amanda noticed when she entered the house was the blood that dampened the planks of the hardwood floor in the living room. The stain was not large, but it was wide enough to let her know that something bad had happened in the room.

"Dr. Cardoni," Amanda called in a trembling voice. There was no response. She scanned the large front room cautiously and saw nothing else that was odd. The other lights on the main floor were off, but the lights were on in the stairwell that led to the bottom-floor operating room. A blood trail led toward the stairs.

Amanda eased down the stairway, the .38 leading the way. The door to the operating room was wide open. Amanda edged along the wall. She stopped opposite the entrance to the horror chamber and stood in the door frame, her heart hammering in her chest.

It took a moment for Amanda to understand what she was seeing. The operating table was covered with a fresh white sheet. Drops of blood radiated outward from one large stain that covered the middle of the sheet. In the center of the stain was a severed hand.

Amanda bolted up the stairs and through the door. She covered the space between the house and her car in a flash and dove inside. The ignition would not catch. Amanda panicked. She looked toward the house while she fumbled with the key, half expecting to see an apparition streaking toward her, blood pumping from its severed limb.

The engine started. The car burned rubber. Amanda was shaking. She was cold. Terror forced her to drive faster, never slowing even when the road curved or the car went airborne after bouncing out of a pothole. She stared in the rearview mirror and almost fainted with relief when she did not see headlights bearing down on her. She brought her eyes forward and spotted the highway. The car careened onto it, and she drove as fast as she could for five minutes before her heart rate slowed and she started to think about what she would do next.

Amanda parked in front of the cabin and waited for the sheriff's deputies to pull in before getting out of her car. Fred Scofield had ridden from Cedar City to the cabin with her. He got out of the passenger side and turned up his collar against the wind, which had turned fierce while Amanda was giving her statement at the sheriff's office. The DA gestured through the storm toward the still-open front door.

"Are you sure you want to go back in there?" Scofield asked solicitously.

"I'm fine," Amanda answered with more confidence than she really felt.

"Let's go, then."

Clark Mills and four deputies fought their way through the gusts of snow and entered the cabin. Amanda and Scofield followed the policemen inside. Amanda surveyed the brightly lit front room. As far as she could see, except for a dusting of snow just inside the front door, everything was as she had left it.

Scofield looked over his shoulder at the front yard. "It's too bad that the snow waited until after that car drove off. We might have gotten some tracks." He looked back at Amanda. "How certain are you that the driver was Art Prochaska?"

"My window was streaked with rain, the interior of the other car was dark and it went by very fast. All I had was a momentary impression. I don't know if I could swear that it was Prochaska in court. But I think the man I saw was bald and his head was unusually large."

"This floor is clear," Sheriff Mills said to Amanda and Scofield after his deputies completed a sweep. "We're going downstairs. You can wait up here if you like, Miss Jaffe."

"Let's go."

Amanda hung back and let the sheriff, the DA and two armed deputies precede her down the stairs. When she reached the lower hall, she saw that the door to the operating room was still open and the lights inside were still on.

"Everyone but Clark please wait in the hall," Scofield said before entering the room. The men who crammed the narrow hallway blocked Amanda's view. She edged along the wall behind them until she found a spot where she could see between two of the deputies.

The hand still sat in the center of the operating table. Drained of blood, it looked chalky white. Scofield and Mills approached it cautiously, as if afraid that it might spring from the table and grab them. They leaned over it and stared intently. The amputated hand was large and a man's, judging from the hair on the back. Scofield lowered his head until he could make out the letters on a ring that covered part of one finger. Vincent Cardoni had graduated from the medical school in Wisconsin whose name was engraved on the ring.

Amanda crossed the Multnomah County line a little after four in the morning and, without a second thought, headed toward Tony Fiori's house. The house was dark when she parked in Tony's driveway at four-thirty. She walked onto the porch and rang the doorbell. A light went on after the third ring, and Amanda heard faint footsteps coming down the stairs. A moment later Tony peered through the glass panel in the front door. Then he opened the door a crack.

"What are you doing here?" Tony asked uncomfortably, and she knew instantly that she'd made a big mistake. Over Tony's shoulder, Amanda saw a woman wrapped in a silk dressing gown descending the stairs. The gown parted to reveal bare legs. Amanda looked from the woman to Tony. Then she backed away from the door.

"I'm sorry . . . I—I didn't know," Amanda stuttered, turning to go.

"Wait," Tony said. "What's wrong?"

But Amanda was already opening the door of her car. As she backed out she saw Tony staring at her. Then the woman was beside him in the doorway, and Amanda got a second look at her. While she was finding Vincent Cardoni's severed hand in the cabin in Milton County, Tony Fiori had been spending the night with Justine Castle.

30

Amanda spotted her father coming off the 9:35 P.M. plane from LA before he saw her in the crowd at the gate. He looked agitated, and his head swung back and forth as he searched for her. Amanda stepped forward, and Frank threw a bear hug on his daughter. Then he held her at arm's length.

"Are you okay?"

"I'm fine, Dad. I was never in any danger. How was your flight?"

"Damn the flight. You don't know how upset I've been."

"Well, you shouldn't have been upset. I told you I was fine this morning."

They started moving with the crowd toward the baggage claim. Now that he saw that Amanda was in one piece, Frank's face darkened.

"What were you thinking, meeting Cardoni in that place in the middle of the night?"

"I was thinking of what you would have done. I even brought your thirty-eight with me."

"You're not serious, are you? Did you think Car-

doni would stand in front of you and let you shoot
him?"

"No, Dad, I thought he was a client in trouble.
Don't tell me that you would have stayed in bed with
your covers over your head and told Vincent to come
to your office in the morning. He sounded desperate.
He said he knew who murdered the victims at the
cabin. It looks like he may have been right."

Amanda had given Frank a capsule version of her
Milton County adventure early Friday morning. He
had wanted to fly straight home, but Amanda convinced him to finish his deposition. As they waited
for Frank's luggage Amanda told him everything
that had happened at the cabin.

"Do they know yet if the hand is Cardoni's?"
Frank asked as he hefted his bags and headed toward
the parking garage.

Amanda nodded. "Mr. Scofield called me at work.
The prints match."

"Jesus." Frank sounded subdued. "You must have
been scared out of your wits."

"If I could move as fast in the pool as I moved
when I ran out of the cabin, I'd have Olympic gold on
my wall."

That got a grudging smile out of Frank.

"What about the body?" he asked.

"They're digging up the property, but they hadn't
found a thing when Scofield called."

Frank and Amanda walked for a while without
talking. He loaded his bags in the trunk, and
Amanda started the car. On the way back to town
Frank told his daughter about the deposition and
asked about the office. When they were halfway
home on the freeway, he asked Amanda twice about

a research project he'd given her before getting an answer.

"Is something besides what happened at the cabin bothering you?"

"What?"

"I asked if something else is worrying you besides what happened to Cardoni."

"What makes you think that?" Amanda asked warily.

"I'm your father. I know you. Do you want to tell me what's wrong?"

"Nothing."

"You forget who you're trying to con. Some of the best liars in the state have tried to fool me."

Amanda sighed. "I feel like such a fool."

"And what's made you feel that way?"

"Not what, who. Last night the police let me go around three in the morning. I was still upset, and it was dark when I got back to Portland. I just didn't want to be alone, so I drove to Tony's house."

Amanda colored. It was so embarrassing. Frank waited patiently while she collected herself.

"He wasn't by himself. He . . . There was a woman with him."

Frank felt his heart tighten.

"It was Justine Castle. I . . . I ran off without talking to him. I shouldn't have. It was immature. We just went out a few times and we never . . . We weren't intimate. It's academic now, anyway. Tony was just accepted into a residency program in New York and he's not even going to be here."

"How do you know that?"

Amanda's color deepened.

"I called him to apologize." Amanda sighed. "I

really liked him, Dad. I guess I'm just disappointed," she said in a way that broke Frank's heart.

"Tony might not be the best person for you to get serious with."

Amanda turned toward Frank for a moment before bringing her eyes back to the road.

"You don't like Tony?"

"Did he tell you that he was seeing Justine Castle at the same time he was seeing you?"

"We weren't serious. He never even made a pass at me. If he was seeing Justine, that was his business. He didn't lead me on. I . . . I just got my hopes up. Anyway, like I said, it's all over. Tony is going to New York."

31

The first thing that Bobby Vasquez noticed when Sheriff Mills ushered him into the long, narrow interrogation room was the hand. It had been printed and cleaned up, then placed in a large jar, where it floated in preservative that gave the skin a faint yellow cast. The jar was at one end of a long table in front of Fred Scofield. Scofield was in shirtsleeves, his collar undone and his tie yanked down away from his fleshy neck. It was warm in the room, but Sean McCarthy was still wearing a suit jacket and his tie was knotted. To McCarthy's right was a guy named Ron Hutchins from Internal Affairs who dressed like a mortician and sported a goatee. Sheriff Mills was in uniform.

Scofield pointed at the hand. "What do you think, Bobby?"

"Ugly mother," Vasquez answered. "Whose is it?"

"Don't you know?" Scofield asked.

"What is this, Twenty Questions?"

"Sit down, Bobby," McCarthy said in a kind, non-threatening way.

Vasquez slouched onto an unoccupied chair. The sheriff sat behind Hutchins's shoulder. They were all facing him now. The theory was that he would feel overwhelmed, but he didn't feel anything at all.

"How are you doing?" McCarthy asked with real concern.

"As well as anyone whose career has been ruined and who's facing bankruptcy and jail," Vasquez responded with a weary smile.

The homicide detective smiled back. "I'm glad to see you've kept your sense of humor."

"It's the only thing I still own, *amigo*."

"Where's your lawyer?" Scofield asked.

"He charges by the hour, and I don't need him. I know how to plead the Fifth if I have to."

"Fair enough," Scofield said.

"You want something to drink?" McCarthy asked. "Coke, a cup of coffee?"

Vasquez laughed. "Who's playing the bad cop?"

McCarthy grinned. "There isn't any bad cop, Bobby. Besides, how are we going to con you? You already know all the tricks."

"I'm not thirsty." Vasquez turned his attention back to the hand. "You still haven't told me who this belongs to."

"This is the right hand of Dr. Vincent Cardoni," McCarthy said, watching closely for his reaction. "We found it in the basement of the Milton County cabin."

"You're kidding!"

McCarthy thought that Vasquez's surprise was genuine.

"Dr. Death himself," Scofield answered. "The prints check out."

"Where's the rest of him?"

"We don't know."

"Poetic justice."

"I call it cold-blooded murder," Scofield responded. "We have the rule of law here, Bobby. Guilt is decided at a trial. You remember, a jury of your peers and all that shit?"

"You think I did this?" Vasquez asked, pointing at the jar and its ghoulish resident.

"You're a suspect," McCarthy answered.

"Mind telling me why?" Vasquez asked. He leaned back in his chair, trying to look cool, but McCarthy could read the tension in his neck and shoulders.

"You had a real hard-on for Cardoni. You screwed up your career to get him. Then Prochaska shot you down and Cardoni walked."

"What? I'm gonna kill everyone who beats one of my cases?"

"You wanted this guy bad enough to burglarize his house and lie under oath."

Vasquez looked down. "I'm not sorry Cardoni is dead, and I'm not sorry he was chopped up. I hope the sick son-of-a-bitch suffered. But I wouldn't do it that way, Sean. Not torture."

"Where were you on Thursday night and Friday morning?" Scofield asked.

"Home, by myself. And no, I don't have anyone who can vouch for me. And yes, I could have driven to the cabin, killed Cardoni and returned unnoticed."

McCarthy studied Vasquez closely. He had means, motive and opportunity, just like they say in the detective movies, but would Vasquez saw off a man's hand for revenge? There McCarthy was undecided. And if they could not decide, they were left where they started, with suspects but no grounds for an arrest. Art Prochaska denied murdering the physician and even had an alibi. Prochaska's lawyer had faxed over a list of five witnesses who would swear that they were playing poker with Prochaska from six P.M. on Thursday night until four A.M. Friday morning. The problem with the alibi was that all five witnesses worked for Martin Breach.

"What's your next question?" Vasquez asked.

"We don't have any for now," Scofield answered.

"Then let me ask you one. Why are you so certain that Cardoni is dead?"

McCarthy cocked his head to one side, and Scofield and Mills exchanged glances.

Vasquez studied the hand. "You've moved to re-open the motion to suppress, right, Fred?"

Scofield nodded.

"What's the chance that Judge Brody will grant the motion and reverse the decision to suppress?"

"Fifty-fifty."

"If you win, Cardoni goes back to jail. What are your chances at trial?"

"If I get to trial with what we found in the cabin and his house in Portland, I'll send him to death row."

Vasquez nodded. "There's a rumor that Martin Breach has a contract out on Cardoni because he thinks Cardoni was Clifford Grant's partner and stiffed him on the deal at the airport."

"We've heard the rumor. Where is this going?"

"Can a doctor amputate his own hand?" Vasquez asked.

"What?" Sheriff Mills exclaimed.

"You think Cardoni chopped off his own hand?" McCarthy asked simultaneously.

"He's got a contract out on him placed by the most relentless son of a bitch I've ever dealt with. If he es-capes Breach's hit men, he's looking at a stay on death row. The only way the law and Martin Breach will stop looking for Cardoni is if they believe that he's dead."

"That's ridiculous," Mills said.

"Is it, Sheriff?" Vasquez paused and looked at the hand again. "There are animals that will gnaw off their own limb to get out of a trap. Think about that."

Part II

⟡

Ghost Lake

32

At eight o'clock on a blustery Friday evening, Amanda Jaffe parked on the deserted street in front of the Multnomah County courthouse, showed her bar card to the guard and took the elevator to the third floor. Two weeks ago it had taken only one hour for the jury to find Timothy Dooling guilty of a horrible crime. The same jury had been out two and a half days deciding whether Dooling would live or die. What did that mean? She would soon find out.

In the five years she had been working in her father's firm, the county courthouse had become Amanda's second home. During the day its corridors and courtrooms hummed with drama, high and low. Every so often there was even a little comedy. At night, absent the hustle and bustle, Amanda could hear the tap of her heels on the marble floor.

As Amanda approached Judge Campbell's courtroom, she remembered the mob of reporters that had filled the Milton County courthouse during *State v. Cardoni,* her first death penalty case. The sad truth was that death penalty cases had become so common that Dooling's case merited the attention of only the *Oregonian* reporter with the courthouse beat.

This was not the first time that Amanda had thought about Vincent Cardoni during the four years that had passed since his mysterious disappearance. The case had made her wonder whether she really wanted to practice criminal law. She stayed on the fence for two months. Then her legal arguments helped win the dismissal of unwarranted rape charges against a dirt-poor honor student who now attended an excellent college on scholarship instead of rotting in a cell for a crime he did not commit. The student's case convinced Amanda that she could do a lot of good as a defense attorney. It also helped her understand that every defendant was not like the deranged surgeon, although her present client came pretty close.

Amanda paused at the courtroom door and watched Timothy Dooling through the glass. He was sitting in his chair at the counsel table, shackled and watched by two armed guards. It seemed absurd that anyone would be wary of a slip of a man barely out of his teens who tipped the scale at 140 pounds, but Amanda knew the guards had good reason to keep a careful watch on her client. The slight build, the wavy blond hair and the engaging smile did not fool her, as it had the young girl he had murdered. Even during those times when she felt relaxed in his company, the presence of the jail guards made her feel a lot more comfortable. She liked to think that Tim would never hurt her even if he had the chance, but she knew that was probably wishful thinking. The psychiatric reports and the biography Herb Cross had compiled made it very clear that Dooling was so badly broken that he could never be put together again. From the earliest age, his alcoholic mother had abused him physically. When he was barely out of diapers, one of her boyfriends had sexually assaulted him. Then he'd been abandoned and placed in one foster home after another, where he had been the victim of more sexual and physical abuse. It was not an excuse for the rape and the murder, but it explained why Tim had become a monster. No one in her right mind would argue that Dooling should ever be let out of maximum security, but Amanda had argued that he should be allowed to live. There were good arguments against her position. Mike Greene, the prosecutor, had made all of them.

Dooling turned when Amanda walked in and looked at her expectantly with big blue eyes that begged to be trusted.

"How are you feeling?" Amanda asked as she set down her attaché case and took her seat.

"I don't know. Scared, I guess."

There were times, like now, when Amanda actually felt sorry for Dooling, and other times when she actually liked him. It was the craziest thing, something only another criminal attorney would understand. He was so dependent on her; in all likelihood she was Tim's only friend. How pathetically sad must a man's life be, Amanda thought, when his attorney was the only person in the world who cared about him?

The bailiff rapped his gavel, and the Honorable Mary Campbell entered the courtroom through a door behind her bench. She was a bright, no-nonsense brunette in her early forties with short hair and a shorter temper who ran a tight ship. With Campbell running the show, her client had received a fair trial. That was bad news if the verdict was death.

"Bring in the jury," the judge told the bailiff.

Across the way, Mike Greene looked grim. Amanda knew that he was feeling the tension as much as she was. She found this comforting, because Greene was a seasoned prosecutor. Amanda liked Greene, who had barely heard of her father when he moved to Portland from LA two years ago. It had been hard for Frank Jaffe's daughter to establish her own identity and reputation. Mike was one of the few DAs, lawyers and judges who did not think of her initially as Frank Jaffe's little girl.

When the jurors filed in, Amanda kept her eyes forward. She had long ago quit trying to guess verdicts by studying the expressions on the faces of the jurors.

"What happens now?" Dooling asked nervously, even though Amanda had explained the process to him several times.

"The judge gave the jurors four questions to answer. The questions are set out in the statute that governs sentencing in an aggravated murder case. The jury's answer to each question must be unanimous. If all of the jurors answer all of the questions with yes, the court has to impose a death sentence. If the answer of any juror to any of these questions is no, the judge has to give you life."

A slender, middle-aged woman with gray hair stood up when Judge Campbell asked if the jury had a verdict. This was Vivian Tahan, a CPA with a large accounting firm. Amanda would never have let Tahan on if she'd had a choice, but she had run out of peremptory challenges by the time Tahan was called and she had discovered no reason to ask for her dismissal for prejudice. The fact that the strong-willed Tahan was the foreperson made Amanda very nervous.

Judge Campbell took the verdict forms from the bailiff and read through them. Amanda's eyes were riveted to the stack of paper.

"I'm going to read the questions posed to the jurors and their answers to each," Judge Campbell said. "I note for the record that each juror has signed the verdict form. On the first charge in the indictment, to the first question, 'Was the conduct of the defendant, Timothy Roger Dooling, that caused the death of Mary Elizabeth Blair committed deliberately and with the reasonable expectation that death of the deceased would result?' the jurors have unanimously answered yes."

During the guilt phase, the jury had found that Dooling acted intentionally when he strangled Mary Blair to death. There was a legal distinction between intent and deliberation, but it was the width of a hair. While the yes finding did not surprise Amanda, it still caused her heart to skip a beat.

"On the second question, 'Is there a probability that the defendant, Timothy Roger Dooling, will commit criminal acts of violence that would constitute a continuing threat to society?' the jurors have unanimously answered yes."

There were still no surprises. Timothy Dooling's first violent act occurred in third grade, when he set a dog on fire. They had never stopped, and they had gotten progressively more serious.

The third question asked whether the defendant's action in killing the deceased was an unreasonable response to the provocation, if any, of the deceased. The only time this became an issue in a case was in situations of self-defense or long-term abuse. Dooling's victim had been kidnapped, held hostage for days and systematically raped and murdered. It was no shock that the jurors had unanimously found Dooling's conduct unreasonable.

Amanda and Mike Greene leaned forward when Judge Campbell started to read the last question and the jury's answer to it. Question four was the only important one in most cases. The question, "Should the defendant receive a death sentence?" opened the door for defense counsel to present any argument against death that could be supported by evidence. Amanda had presented witness after witness to attest to the horrors of Timothy Dooling's childhood, and she had argued that the mother who gave him life had handcrafted him from birth to be the monster he had become. If one of the twelve jurors agreed with her arguments, Tim Dooling would live.

"To question four," Judge Campbell said, "the jury has answered no by a vote of three to nine."

Dooling sat stone still. Amanda did not move either. It was only when she saw the prosecutor's head bow that she knew that she had convinced three of the jurors that Dooling's life was worth saving.

"Did we win?" Tim asked her, his eyes wide with disbelief.

"We won."

"Ain't that something." Tim was grinning. "That's the first time I ever won anything in my whole life."

Amanda returned to her loft at ten-thirty, exhausted but ecstatic at having beaten back her first death verdict. The loft was twelve hundred square feet of open space in a converted red-brick warehouse in Portland's Pearl District. The floors were hardwood, the windows were tall and wide and the ceiling was high. There were two art galleries on the ground floor and good restaurants and coffeehouses nearby. She could walk to work in fifteen minutes when the weather was good.

Amanda had filled the loft with furniture and fixtures she loved. A solemn Sally Haley pear in a pewter bowl that cost a month's salary hung across from a bright and cheery abstract painted by an artist she had met in one of the street-level galleries. Amanda had discovered her oak sideboard in an antique store two blocks away, but her dining table had been crafted in a woodworker's studio on the coast. It was made of planks the artisan had salvaged from a fishing vessel that had run aground in Newport during a storm.

Amanda flipped on the lights and threw her jacket onto the couch. She was too excited to go to sleep and too distracted for TV, so she poured herself a glass of milk and put two slices of bread in the toaster before collapsing in her favorite easy chair.

Tim Dooling's case was her first capital murder as lead counsel. The pressure on her during the past nine months had been tremendous. Nothing had prepared her to handle a case where one mistake could result in the death of a client. When the verdict was read Amanda had not experienced the manic surge she'd felt when she won her first PAC-10 swimming title; she had simply felt relieved, as if someone had removed an immense burden from her shoulders.

The toaster dinged, and Amanda dragged herself to her feet. As she crossed the room she suddenly noticed how quiet it was in her loft. Amanda enjoyed her solitude, but there were times, like tonight, when it would have been nice to have someone with whom she could share her triumph. She had dated a few men since moving back to Portland. There had been a six-month affair with a stockbroker that had died a mutually agreeable death and a longer relationship with a lawyer from one of Portland's large firms who had asked her to marry him. Amanda had asked for time to consider the proposal, then realized that she wouldn't have to think at all if he was "the one."

Amanda wouldn't have minded having Frank to crow to, but he was in California with Elsie Davis, a schoolteacher who had been a character witness for a student Frank had defended. While interviewing her, Frank discovered that she had lost her husband to cancer and had stayed single for twelve years because she had never found anyone to take his place. Their cautious friendship had blossomed into a serious relationship, and they were on their first vacation together.

Amanda buttered her toast at the kitchen table. While she sipped her milk she took stock of her life. On the whole she was happy. Her career was going well, she had money in the bank and a place she loved to live in, but she was lonely at times. Two of her girlfriends had married during the past year, and she was beginning to feel isolated. Couples went out with couples. Soon there would be children to occupy their time. Amanda sighed. She didn't feel incomplete without a man. It was more a question of companionship. Just having someone to talk to, who would be around to share her triumphs and help her up when she fell.

33

Andrew Volkov performed his custodial duties at St. Francis Medical Center diligently. Tonight, as he cleaned the floor outside the offices of the Department of Surgery, he moved slowly and deliberately, making certain that his mop covered every inch of the corridor. Volkov was tall, but it was hard to guess his height because he slouched and shuffled as he worked. He rarely spoke and never met the eye of anyone who spoke to him. His own eyes were gray-green, his hair was close-cropped and blond, and he had the broad cheekbones, wide nose and brooding brow of a Slav. Volkov rarely showed any emotion, maintaining a stolid expression that reinforced the impression that he was as much a mule as a man. When told to do something, he obeyed immediately. His superiors had learned quickly to be precise in their instructions because Volkov demonstrated little imagination and followed orders literally.

The offices of the Department of Surgery were quiet and deserted at two A.M. Volkov pushed his cart against the wall and straightened slowly. He rested his mop against the wall, checked the corridor and shuffled toward the door to the next office. He opened it and turned on the light. The office was narrow and not very deep, a windowless cubicle, really, hardly wider than a closet. A gunmetal gray desk took up most of the floor. It was covered with medical journals, textbooks, mail and miscellany. Volkov was under strict instructions never to touch anything on a doctor's desk, but he was supposed to empty the wastebasket under the desk.

Volkov took a duster from his cart and ran it over the shelves of a bookcase that stood against one wall. When he was through dusting, he looked down at the patch of floor that was not covered by the desk, the bookshelves and the two visitor chairs. It was an area so small that it was hardly worth dealing with, but Volkov's boss had instructed him to clean any surface that could be cleaned, so Volkov shuffled outside, emptied the wastebasket, then took his vacuum cleaner off the cart. He plugged it in and ran it back and forth across the floor. When he was satisfied that he had done all he could do, Volkov placed the vacuum cleaner back on the cart.

Volkov reentered the office one last time. He closed and locked the door and drew a pair of latex gloves out of one pocket and a Ziploc bag out of the other. Then he stepped behind the desk and opened the bottom drawer. The coffee mug was right where he had seen it on other nights. Volkov placed the mug in the Ziploc bag, left the office and relocked the door. He placed the bag under a pile of towels along with the gloves. Then he grabbed his mop and began pushing it slowly and deliberately toward the next office.

34

On this moonless Sunday night, even with his high beams on, all Multnomah County sheriff's deputy Oren Bradbury could see through his rain-streaked windshield was the yellow line that divided the two-lane country road and an occasional glimpse of farmland.

"You know this is a bullshit call, don't you?" his partner, Brady Paggett, griped. "The place has been deserted since . . . Hell, I can't remember when."

"It could be kids."

"On a night like this?"

Bradbury shrugged. "We weren't doing anything anyway."

They rode in silence until Paggett pointed toward a rusted mailbox whose post leaned precariously toward the tall grass on the side of the road.

"There it is."

A dilapidated wooden fence bordered the road. Its slats were unpainted. Several had broken loose on one end and dangled from the few nails that were still in place. Bradbury spotted the break in the fence and turned through it. The patrol car bounced along a rutted dirt track. There were tall trees on either side. After a quarter mile the headlights picked up a farmhouse with peeling brown paint and a front yard overgrown with weeds. When they drew closer, the deputies could make out a dim glow through a front window.

"Maybe this isn't a bullshit call," Paggett said.

"What exactly did dispatch say again?" Bradbury asked.

"Someone phoned in to report screams."

"Who?"

"Dispatch couldn't get a name."

"The caller had to be right here. The next neighbor is half a mile down the road. There's no way you'd hear anything if you were driving by, and no one's gonna be walking along the road tonight."

As the patrol car swung into the front yard, its light swept across a dark blue Volvo that was parked at the side of the house.

"Someone's here," Bradbury said just as a person in a hooded jacket and jeans burst through the front door and streaked for the Volvo. Bradbury hit the brakes, and Paggett jumped out of the car with his gun drawn.

"Stop, police!"

The runner skidded to a halt and froze in the police car's headlights.

"Hands in the air," Paggett commanded.

Bradbury drew his weapon and got out, keeping the car between him and the hooded apparition. Paggett squinted to keep the rain out of his eyes.

"Step over to our car, put your hands on the roof and spread your legs."

As soon as the person was in position, Paggett

reached out and pulled back the hood. A cascade of honey brown hair fell across a woman's shoulders. The deputy kept his gun on her as he patted her down. He noticed that her chest was heaving, as if she had run a distance.

"Is anyone else inside?" Paggett asked.

The woman nodded vigorously.

"I . . . I think he's dead," she managed. The words came out in gasps.

"Who's dead?" Paggett demanded.

"I don't know. He's in the basement."

"And who are you?" Paggett asked.

"Dr. Justine Castle. I'm a surgeon at St. Francis."

"All right, Dr. Castle, you can put your hands down." Paggett opened the back door of the police car. "Why don't you get in out of the rain and try to calm down."

Justine sat down in the backseat. Bradbury walked around the car and joined Paggett at the rear passenger door.

"What are you doing here, Dr. Castle?" Paggett asked.

Justine's saturated hair hung along her damp face. Her breathing was still not under control.

"There was a call. He said that he was from St. Francis, that it was about Al Rossiter."

"Who is Rossiter?" Bradbury asked.

"One of the surgeons."

"And who was the caller?"

"I'm not sure. I think he said that his name was Delaney or Delay. I really don't remember. It wasn't someone I knew."

"Okay, go ahead."

"The man said Dr. Rossiter was working on someone who was badly injured and needed my help. He said that it was urgent. He told me to come here and he gave me directions."

"Do you usually drive to the scene of an injury?"

"No, it's definitely not routine. I asked why they didn't send for an ambulance. I said I would meet them at the hospital. That's where all our equipment and staff are. This Delaney or Delay said that he couldn't explain over the phone but that it was a matter of life and death and I would understand when I got here. He said that the man's condition was desperate. Then he hung up."

"Where's everyone else? Where's Dr. Rossiter?" Paggett asked.

Justine shook her head. She looked upset and confused.

"I don't know."

Justine squeezed her eyes shut and took a deep, shuddering breath.

"Are you okay, Dr. Castle?" Paggett asked.

Justine nodded slowly, but she did not look okay.

"Is anyone besides the dead man inside?" Bradbury asked.

"I . . . I don't know. I didn't see anyone. When I saw him . . ." Justine swallowed hard. "I panicked. I ran."

"You stay with Dr. Castle," Bradbury said. He walked toward the farmhouse, his gun at the ready.

Paggett closed the rear door of the patrol car. There were no handles on the inside. Justine was effectively a prisoner, but she made no protest and seemed content to sit with her eyes closed and her head against the back of the seat.

The drops were pounding harder. Paggett put on his hat to keep the rain off. He checked his watch and wondered what was keeping Bradbury. When Oren came out, he looked glassy-eyed and pale.

"You got to see this, Brady. It's horrible."

Paggett and his partner had seen car wreck victims, abused children and other mangled and degraded human beings. It would take a lot to put Oren in this state. He headed for the farmhouse with Bradbury close behind. The first thing that struck him as odd was the cleanliness. Weeds ruled the front yard and the exterior walls were in disrepair, but every inch of the entryway and the front room appeared to have been vacuumed clean. There was no furniture in the entryway and only a cheap coffee table and a straight-back chair in the living room.

"The stairs to the basement are in the kitchen," Bradbury said. "The kitchen lights were on when I came in the house."

"Those must have been the lights we saw when we drove up."

The kitchen was as clean as the other rooms. There was a card table and two straight-back chairs standing on the yellow linoleum floor. Paggett opened one of the cupboards and saw a few plastic plates and cups. A half-filled coffeepot and a coffee mug were on a drain board next to the sink. When Paggett drew closer, he saw that there was still some coffee in the mug.

"The body is down there," Bradbury said, pointing through the open basement door. His voice was shaky.

"What's it look like?"

"Bad, Brady. You'll see."

As Paggett walked down the wooden steps that led to the basement, he noticed the suffocating odor that permeates the air when death has been a visitor.

A bare 40-watt bulb threw dim shadows over the un-painted concrete floor and walls. Paggett could see a mattress next to the furnace. Lying on the mattress was a figure. The light was too dim to make out details, but there was enough light to see that the body was naked and cuffed at the wrists and ankles by manacles that were attached to the wall by lengths of thick chain.

Paggett walked slowly toward the corpse. When he was a few feet away he saw the body clearly for the first time and almost lost it. The deputy blinked, not quite trusting his eyes. The mattress was satu-rated with blood; so much of the body was covered with dried blood that it was very difficult to tell its race. An ear and several digits were missing. Paggett's stomach heaved. He turned away, squeezed his eyes shut and took deep breaths. The smell almost overpowered him, but he struggled to keep his food down.

"Are you okay?" Bradbury asked anxiously.

"Yeah, yeah." Paggett was bent over with his hands on his knees. "Give me a second."

When he was ready, Paggett straightened up and took a closer look at the corpse.

"Holy Jesus," he whispered reverently. Paggett had seen a lot of bad shit in his day, but nothing like this.

The deputy turned away from the body, relieved to have it out of his sight, and surveyed the rest of the basement. At first the dimensions of the room con-fused him. The basement seemed smaller than he ex-pected. Then Paggett realized that a gray concrete wall with a narrow doorway divided the basement in half. He walked through the doorway. Inside a sec-ond room was an operating table. A tray of surgical equipment stood next to the table. Among the tools was a scalpel encrusted with blood. Paggett turned and headed back up the stairs.

"I'm gonna check out the rest of this place. You call it in. We need homicide and forensics."

"What about the woman?"

"After what we saw, I'm not letting her out until we know for sure that she didn't do this guy."

Paggett shook his head again, as if to clear it of the image of what he had just seen. Bradbury left the house. Paggett took a deep breath and started to explore the main floor. After taking a second look at the kitchen and living room, Paggett walked toward the rear of the house and found two empty rooms with closed doors. They had been vacuumed clean.

As he started to climb the stairs to the second floor, something occurred to Paggett. He turned around and went through the main floor again. He was right. There weren't any telephones in the house. The deputy wondered if he would find a phone on the second floor.

He didn't, but the second floor did yield a discovery. In one of the rooms were a bookcase, an armchair and a single bed with a mattress and a pillow. A lamp stood between the bed and the armchair. There was no sheet on the bed and no pillowcase on the pillow. Paggett guessed that the killer had used the bed but had taken the sheet and pillowcase because they might contain trace evidence like hair or semen stains.

Paggett read some of the titles in the bookcase. He found *The Torturer's Handbook, Cleansing the Fatherland: Nazi Medicine and Racial Hygiene,* and *Sweet Surrender: A Sadist's Bible* mixed in with medical texts and other books on torture.

Also in the bookcase was a black three-ring binder. Paggett used his handkerchief to take it out of the bookcase and open it. A computer had generated the pages.

> *Tuesday: Watched from dark as subject revived. 8:17 P.M.: Subject disoriented. Realizes that she is naked and manacled to wall. Struggles for less than minute before commencing to sob. Screams for help commence at 8:20, end 8:25. Watched subject until 9:00. Went upstairs to eat. When kitchen door opened and closed, subject commenced begging. Listened from kitchen while I ate. No fighting spirit, pathetic, subject may provide little new data.*
>
> *Wednesday: Approached subject for first time. Begging, pleading, questions: "Who are you?" "Why are you doing this?" etc. Subject is extremely docile, drew into fetal position at touch. Moved head slightly, but accepted training hood with little struggle. When released from manacles obeyed commands immediately. No challenge.*
>
> *Saturday: After two days without food and with sensory deprivation, subject is weak and lethargic. I am disappointed at lack of resistance. Have decided to commence pain tolerance experiments immediately.*
>
> *8:25: Remove manacles and lead subject to operating table. No resistance, subject obeys command to mount table and submits to restraints. 8:30: hood removed, subject's head secured to table. Begging, pleading. Subject sobs quietly. I have decided to start with the soles of the feet.*

Paggett felt light-headed. He could read no further. Let the DA and the homicide detectives find out what happened to . . . It hit him suddenly. The journal referred to the subject as "she." The corpse in the basement was a male. Paggett flipped through the journal.

There were more entries.

35

It took three rings to drag Amanda out of a deep sleep. The phone rang again, and Amanda groped for the receiver in the dark while reading the bright red 2:13 on her digital clock.

"Miss Jaffe?"

"Yes?" Amanda answered groggily.

"This is Adele at the answering service. I'm sorry to disturb you."

"That's okay."

Amanda swung her legs over the side of the bed and sat up.

"I have a woman on the line. She's calling from the police station. She asked for your father."

"Mr. Jaffe is out of town."

"I know. I told her that you were taking his calls. She said that was okay."

"Did she say what this is about?"

"No. Just that she had to talk to you."

Amanda sighed. The last thing in the world she wanted to do was talk to a drunk driver at two o'clock on Monday morning, but middle-of-the-night calls came with the territory when you practiced criminal law.

"Put her through, Adele."

Adele's voice was replaced by Tony Bennett singing "I Left My Heart in San Francisco." Amanda closed her eyes and rubbed her lids.

"Is this Amanda Jaffe?"

Amanda's eyes opened. She knew that voice.

"This is Justine Castle. We met several years ago."

Amanda felt a chill pass through her.

"You're Vincent Cardoni's wife."

Amanda suddenly flashed on a vision of the doctor descending Tony Fiori's staircase on the evening she had discovered Cardoni's hand. Her hand tightened on the receiver.

"Why are you calling my father at this hour?"

"Something terrible has happened."

Amanda detected a tremor when the doctor spoke.

"I . . . I've been arrested."

This time the tremor was more pronounced, as if Justine was barely holding herself together.

"Where are you calling from?"

"The Justice Center."

"Is anyone with you?"

"Detective DeVore and a deputy district attorney named Mike Greene."

Justine had her attention now. DeVore was homicide, and Mike rarely handled anything but capital cases.

"Are DeVore and Greene listening to this call?" Amanda asked.

"They're in the room."

"Answer my questions yes or no and do not say anything else unless I say it's okay. Do you understand?"

"Yes."

"Have you been arrested for a serious crime?"

"Yes."

"Some type of homicide?"

"Yes."

"I'm coming down. From this point on you are not to speak with anyone but me. Is that clear?"

"Yes, but—"

"Dr. Castle, Alex DeVore and Mike Greene are very nice men, but they are also specialists in sending people to death row. One way they do that is by befriending confused and frightened people who are under tremendous stress. These people trust them because they're so nice. They say things to Mike and Alex that they do not realize are going to be used to crucify them in court.

"Now, I am going to repeat my instructions. Do not—I repeat—do not talk to anyone about this matter except me unless I say it's okay. Do you understand my instructions?"

"Yes."

"Good. Please give Mr. Greene the phone."

"Hi, Amanda," Mike Greene said a moment later.

Amanda was in no mood for small talk.

"Dr. Castle says you've arrested her. Mind telling me what for?"

"Not at all. Two sheriff's deputies caught her fleeing the scene of a homicide."

"Did she confess?"

"Claims she didn't do it."

"But you arrested her anyway?"

"Of course. We always arrest people when we can prove they're guilty."

36

Prior to 1983 the Multnomah County jail was an antiquated, fortresslike edifice constructed of huge granite blocks that was located several miles from the Multnomah County courthouse at Rocky Butte. When the Rocky Butte jail was torn down to make way for the I-205 freeway, the detention center was moved to the fourth through tenth floors of the Justice Center, a sixteen-story, state-of-the-art facility one block from the courthouse in the heart of downtown Portland. In addition to the jail the Justice Center also housed the Portland police central precinct, a branch of the Multnomah County district attorney's office, state parole and probation, the Portland police administrative offices, the state crime laboratory, two circuit courts and two district courts.

Before Amanda could visit Justine Castle she had to check in with a guard on the second floor of the Justice Center and go through the metal detector. The guard led Amanda to the jail elevator and keyed her up to the floor where Justine Castle was being held. When the elevator stopped, Amanda found herself in a narrow, brightly lit hallway. At one end a telephone without a dial was attached to the wall next to a massive steel door. Above the door was a surveillance camera. Amanda used the telephone to summon a guard. A few minutes later a corrections officer opened the door and let Amanda into another narrow corridor. On one side of this hall were three visiting rooms. Amanda could see into each room through a plate of thick glass. The guard opened the heavy metal door of the room nearest the elevators. On the other side of the room was another steel door that opened onto a hall that led to the cells. A black button stuck out from the bottom of an intercom that was recessed into the yellow concrete wall. The guard pointed to it.

"Press that if you need assistance," he said as he closed the door behind him.

Amanda sat on an orange molded plastic chair. She took a legal pad and a pen out of her attaché case and placed them in front of her on a small, round table that was secured to the floor by iron bolts. From experience Amanda knew that it would take a while for the guard to bring Justine to her. While she waited Amanda thought about the last time she'd seen Justine Castle.

Four years ago, finding Justine with Tony Fiori had been a shock, but the incident was ancient history. There hadn't been anything between her and Tony, anyway. She was honest enough to admit that she wished that there had been but realistic enough to know that they had just been friends.

The locks snapped, and a uniformed jail matron led Dr. Castle into the visiting room. Amanda studied her for the changes that time might have wrought. Justine was exhausted, and no one looks chic in an orange jailhouse jumpsuit at three in the morning. Justine's hair, ruined by the rain, was unkempt, but Justine was still beautiful, even under these trying circumstances, and the strength was there, even if it was being sorely tested.

"Thank you for coming," Justine said.

"Dr. Castle—"

"Justine, please."

"My father's in California. He won't be back for a week. If you want another lawyer to represent you, I can give you a list of several excellent attorneys."

"But you're a criminal lawyer, too, aren't you?" Amanda sensed a hint of desperation in the question. "The district attorney told me that you just beat him in a murder case. He thinks you're very good."

"Mr. Greene was being kind. I didn't win the case. My client was found guilty. I just convinced the jury to give him a life sentence instead of a death sentence."

"I read about what your client did to that girl. It can't be easy to convince a jury to save the life of someone like that."

"No, it's not."

"So Mr. Greene wasn't being charitable when he said you were good."

Amanda shrugged, uneasy with the compliment. "I work very hard for my clients."

"Then you're the lawyer I want. And I want you to get me out of here as soon as possible."

"That might not be easy."

"You don't understand. I can't be charged with murder. My reputation will be ruined, my career would be . . . ."

Justine stopped. Amanda could see that she hated to sound needy and desperate.

"This has nothing to do with my ability as a lawyer. It has to do with the way that the law is written. In Oregon every crime except murder has automatic bail. Remember your husband's case? My father had to ask for a bail hearing when the DA objected to release. We'll have to hold a similar hearing for you unless the DA agrees to release you."

"Then get him to agree."

"I'll try. We're meeting as soon as I finish talking to you. But I can't guarantee anything."

Justine leaned forward and focused all of her energy on Amanda. It made Amanda feel uncomfortable, but Justine's stare was so intense that she could not look away.

"Let me make two things clear to you. First, I did not kill anyone. Second, I have been set up."

"By whom?"

"I don't know," Justine answered with obvious frustration, "but I do know that I was lured to that farm, and the police turning up when they did was no coincidence."

Justine told Amanda about the phone call that convinced her to rush to the farmhouse and what happened after she arrived.

"Do you know the victim?"

"I don't think so, but I can't say for sure. I only had a brief look, and his face was so disfigured."

Amanda noticed that Justine's hands were folded in front of her on the table and she was clasping them so tightly that the knuckles were white. If the mental image of the dead man could freak out a surgeon, Amanda was not looking forward to viewing the autopsy pictures and crime scene photos.

"Besides finding you at the scene, can you think of anything that would make the police believe that you killed the man in the basement?"

"No."

"Did you say anything that could be interpreted as a confession?"

Justine looked annoyed. "I told you I didn't kill anyone. The man was dead when I got there."

"Were you arrested at the crime scene?"

"No. The two officers who found me were very polite. Everyone was, Mr. Greene and the detective, too, after I arrived at the Justice Center. They brought me coffee, got me a sandwich. They were very sympathetic. Then they got a call from the crime lab and everything changed. DeVore and the DA went into the hall and talked. When they came back DeVore read me my rights."

"Did they say what had happened?"

"They said that they knew I'd killed that man. They insisted I was lying when I denied it. That's when I called you."

Amanda made a few notes.

"When did you get the call about Dr. Rossiter?"

"Around nine on Sunday night."

"Where were you?"

"At my house."

"Were you alone?"

"Yes."

"Were you with anyone earlier in the day? Someone who can give you an alibi?"

"No. I was away for the weekend. I have a cabin on the coast. It's been hectic at the hospital, and I drove out Friday evening to get away from everyone and watch the storm. I got home shortly before the call."

"You said that was about nine."

Justine nodded.

"Where is the farmhouse located?"

"Out in the country on a two-lane road in the middle of nowhere. I got really concerned when I drove into the front yard. The place looked like it hadn't been lived in for years."

Justine looked unsettled again.

"Go on," Amanda urged.

"You were involved in Vincent's defense, weren't you?"

"I assisted my father."

"And you've been to that cabin in Milton County? You're the one who found Vincent's hand?"

"Yes," Amanda answered softly.

Justine took a deep breath and closed her eyes for a moment.

"It wasn't seeing the body that made me run."

Justine exhaled slowly and gathered herself while Amanda waited patiently.

"The farmhouse basement is divided in two by a cement wall. There is a room on the other side of the wall. When I walked into the room I saw the table."

"What table?" Amanda asked as a sick feeling formed in her stomach.

"An operating table."

Amanda's mouth gaped open. "This sounds like . . ."

Justine nodded. "It was the first thing I thought of. That's why I ran, and that's why I called your father."

Amanda stood up.

"I've got to talk to Mike Greene. He was a DA in Los Angeles when Cardoni was arrested. He wouldn't know about the case."

"Wouldn't DeVore have heard?"

"It wasn't his case, and most of the action was in Milton County."

Amanda rang for the guard, then turned to Justine.

"The worst part of being in jail isn't what they

show you on TV," she said. "It's the boredom. Sitting around all day with nothing to do. I'm going to give you a job that will keep you occupied and help your defense. I want you to write an autobiography for me."

The request seemed to take Justine by surprise.

"Why do you need that?"

"I'm going to be blunt with you. I hope I win this case and you go free, but a good lawyer always prepares for the worst. If you're convicted of aggravated murder, there will be a second phase to your trial: the penalty phase. That's when the jury decides your sentence, and one of the sentences that can be imposed is death. In order to convince a jury to spare you I'll need to get them to see you as a human being, and I do that by telling them the story of your life."

Justine looked uncomfortable.

"If you don't use the biographical information unless I'm convicted, why don't I wait to write it?"

"Justine, I hope I never have to use any of the material you give me, but I know from experience that I can't wait until the last moment to prepare for the penalty phase. The judge usually gives you only a few days between the trial and the penalty phase. There won't be enough time to do a thorough job unless we start now."

"How far back do you want me to go?"

"Start when you were born," Amanda answered with a smile.

The locks snapped, and the door started to open.

"I'll come back this afternoon for the arraignment. While you're waiting, write the bio. You'll thank me for giving you something to take your mind off your troubles."

37

Mike Greene dealt with rapists, killers and criminal defense attorneys all day but always seemed to be in a good mood. He had curly black hair, pale blue eyes and a shaggy mustache. His head was large but did not seem out of proportion because he was six-five with the kind of massive body that compelled males to ask if he had played basketball or football. He had not; he didn't even watch sports on TV. He did play chess and was a rated expert during his days on the chess team at the University of Southern California. Greene's other passion was tenor sax, which he played proficiently enough to be asked to sit in on occasion with a jazz quartet that entertained at local clubs.

Alex DeVore was a dapper little man who always dressed well and looked fresh and alert even at three-thirty in the morning. He had been the lead detective in two cases Amanda had cocounseled with Frank. She remembered him as being low-key and businesslike.

The deputy DA and the detective were sipping coffee from foam cups at DeVore's desk in the homicide bureau when Amanda walked in. A Dunkin' Donuts box with its lid folded back sat in front of them.

"I saved a jelly doughnut and a maple bar for you, just to show that there are no hard feelings over Dooling," Greene told her.

Amanda was hungry and exhausted. "Can I get some coffee?" she asked as she grabbed the maple bar.

"We'll even give you powdered creamer if you'll plead out your client."

"No deal. I don't cop my clients for anything less than a grande caramel latte."

"Damn," Greene answered with a snap of his fingers. "All we've got is industrial-strength caffeinated."

"Then it looks like we'll have to go to the mat."

Greene filled a cup with a sludgy black liquid. Amanda took a sip and grimaced.

"What is this stuff? If I ever find out that you gave it to one of my clients, I'll sue you."

DeVore smiled, and Greene let out a belly laugh.

"We brew this specially for defense attorneys."

Amanda took a big bite out of her maple bar to cut the taste of the coffee.

"What do you say to some form of release for Dr. Castle?"

Greene shook his head. "Can't do it."

"C'mon, Mike. She's a doctor. She has patients to tend to."

"That's regrettable, but you have no idea what's going on here."

"Tell me."

Greene looked at DeVore. The detective nodded. Greene leaned back in his chair.

"Your client's been using the farmhouse as a torture chamber."

Greene waited for Amanda to react. When she didn't, he continued.

"We found a man in the basement." Greene shook his head and the pleasant smile disappeared. "Count yourself lucky that you'll only have to look at the photos. What makes it even more evil is the journal."

"What journal?"

"Your client has kidnapped other victims. The journal is an account of her torture sessions with each of them. She kept them in pain for days. It takes a lot to get to me, but I could not read the journal straight through."

"Is the journal in Dr. Castle's handwriting?"

Greene shook his head. "No, the pages were generated by a computer. Her name's not in it, either. It would have made our job easier if Dr. Castle had signed it, but she didn't."

"So how can you be sure she wrote it?"

"We found a section of the journal in Castle's house when we executed a search warrant, earlier this evening. It contains a graphic description of what she did to the poor bastard we found in the basement. A copy will be included in your discovery. I'd wait a few hours after you eat to read it.

"By the way, the medical examiner's preliminary finding is that our John Doe committed suicide by chewing through the veins in his wrist. When you read the journal entry you'll see why he killed himself. Can you imagine how desperate and how terrified a person has to be to kill himself like that?"

The blood drained from Amanda's face.

"Did anything else at the crime scene connect Dr. Castle to the murder?" she asked quietly.

"You'll get our reports when they're ready."

"Dr. Castle believes that she's been set up."

"Does she have a suspect in mind?" Greene asked skeptically.

"Actually, we both do. You told Justine that the cops came to the farmhouse in response to an anonymous nine-one-one call. The farmhouse is a quarter mile from the road, isn't it? How did this anonymous caller get close enough to hear screams?"

"Good question. I'm sure you'll ask the jury to consider it."

"Come on, Mike. Doesn't this sound like a setup to you? The police just happen to get a call that sends them to a murder scene at the precise moment that the killer rushes out."

"You can argue that, too."

Amanda hesitated before plunging in.

"You've found more victims at the farm, haven't you?"

DeVore had been half listening, but the question got his attention. Mike's eyebrows went up.

"Did you get that from your client?"

"So I'm right."

"How did you know?"

"I'll tell you that if you'll tell me whether you arrested Justine Castle because you found items with her fingerprints in the house."

The detective and the DA exchanged looks again.

"Yes," Greene answered.

"What items?"

"A scalpel with the victim's blood and a mug half filled with coffee."

Amanda controlled her excitement. "Was the mug found in the kitchen?"

"How did you know that?" DeVore asked.

She ignored the question. "Was there anything else with trace evidence on it?"

"We found a surgical gown, cap and booties in a closet in the bedroom. They're at the lab and the technicians are going over them for hair and fibers. Now it's your turn to answer a few questions. How did you know about the other bodies and where we found the mug?"

Amanda took a sip of her coffee while she thought about the best way to answer Greene's question.

"Do you know anything about the Cardoni case?"

Mike Greene looked blank.

"The guy in Milton County with the hand," DeVore said.

Amanda nodded. "This was about four and a half years ago, Mike, before you moved up here. Dr. Vincent Cardoni was a surgeon at St. Francis, and he was married to Justine Castle."

"That's right!" DeVore exclaimed.

"A Portland vice cop named Bobby Vasquez got an anonymous tip that Cardoni was storing cocaine in a home in the mountains in Milton County. He couldn't corroborate the tip, so he broke into the house. Guess what he found?"

DeVore was sitting up, and Amanda could see that he was remembering more and more about the Cardoni case.

"What are you getting at?" the homicide detective asked.

"There was a graveyard in the woods near the house with nine victims. Most of them had been tortured. There was an operating room in the basement and a bloody scalpel with Cardoni's prints on it. Cardoni's prints were also found in the kitchen on a coffee mug. A videotape that showed one of the victims being tortured was found in Cardoni's house. Is this starting to sound familiar?"

"Are you suggesting that Cardoni killed the people at the farmhouse?" Greene asked.

Before she could answer, DeVore said, "He couldn't. Cardoni is dead."

"We don't know that," Amanda said to the detective before turning back to Greene. "Not for sure."

"You guys are going too fast for me," Greene said.

"My father represented Dr. Cardoni. There was a motion to suppress. Vasquez lied under oath to cover up his illegal entry, and Dad proved that he perjured himself. The State lost all its evidence, and Cardoni was released from jail. A week or so later Cardoni called me at home, at night, and said that he had to meet me at the house in Milton County."

"I remember now," DeVore said. "You found it!"

"Found what?" Greene asked.

"Cardoni's right hand. It was on the operating table. Someone cut it off."

"Who?" Greene asked.

"No one knows."

"So it's an unsolved murder?"

"Maybe, maybe not," Amanda said. "Cardoni's body was never found. If he cut off his own hand, it wouldn't be a murder, would it?"

38

By the time Amanda staggered home to her loft it was almost five in the morning. Her eyes were bloodshot, and her head felt as though it were stuffed with cotton. Amanda would have given anything to dive under the covers, but there was too much to do, so she tried to fool her body into believing that she had slept by following her morning routine. She doubted that she would have been able to sleep, anyway. Her head was spinning with ideas for Justine's defense, and the possibility that Vincent Cardoni was back made her skin crawl.

After twenty minutes of calisthenics and an ice-cold shower, Amanda donned one of her dark blue court suits and walked two blocks to a hole-in-the-wall café that had been in the neighborhood since the fifties. It was still pitch black outside, and the raw, biting wind helped her stay awake. So did the flapjack breakfast she ate hunkered down in one of the café's red vinyl booths. As a swimmer, Amanda always stoked up on carbohydrates the night before a big race. Swimming distance and trying cases were a lot alike. You stored up as much energy as you could, then you dove in and kept driving.

During breakfast, Amanda could not stop thinking about Cardoni. What if he was alive? What if he was lurking in the dark, killing again? The idea terrified her, but it also thrilled her. If Cardoni was back from the dead—if Justine was an innocent woman, falsely accused—this case would make her reputation and bring her out of her father's shadow.

The moment that thought intruded Amanda felt guilty. She focused on the torment Cardoni's victims had to have experienced and forced herself to remember what she'd seen on the Mary Sandowski tape, but she could not suppress the excitement she felt when a secret part of her whispered about a future in which she would be as acclaimed and sought after as Frank Jaffe.

Amanda fought down these thoughts. She told herself that she was ambitious but that she also cared more for her clients than she did for success. Saving Justine Castle was her first, and only, priority. Fame might follow, but she knew that it was wrong to take a case for the notoriety it would bring. Still, the idea of her name in headlines was tough to ignore.

Then a disturbing thought occurred to her. Her father would be back from his vacation in a week. What would she do if he tried to grab her case? Could she stop Frank from moving her aside? She was only an associate at Jaffe, Katz, Lehane and Brindisi. Frank was a senior partner. If Frank wanted the Castle case, Amanda could not stop him from taking over. Maybe Justine would insist on Frank's being lead counsel. When Justine phoned from the Justice Center she had asked for Frank Jaffe, not his daughter.

Amanda chastised herself for thinking this way. She was putting her needs ahead of her client's. If Justine wanted her father to represent her, she would

step aside. Right now she shouldn't even be thinking
about anything but getting Justine out of jail.

By six-forty-five Amanda was in the basement of the
Stockman Building looking through the firm's storage area. The files in *State v. Cardoni* filled three
dusty, cobweb-covered cartons. There would have
been many more boxes if the case had gone to trial.
Loading the boxes on a dolly while keeping her suit
clean was not easy, but Amanda managed. As soon
as she rolled the boxes into her office she stripped off
her suit jacket and started piling their contents on
her desk.

Frank's case files were always well organized. One
three-ring binder was for memos discussing legal issues that might be raised in the case. After each
memo there were photocopies of the cases and
statutes that supported each argument. Another
binder contained police reports arranged chronologi-
cally. A third binder held reports generated by the
defense investigation. A fourth binder was set up al-
phabetically for potential witnesses and contained
copies of every report generated by either side that
made any reference to the witness. A typed sheet
with potential direct or cross-examination questions
and areas of investigation that needed to be pursued
preceded the reports. A final binder contained press
clippings about the case.

Amanda opened the binder that had been compiled for the motion to suppress. It contained an inventory of the items found at the Milton County
house. There was also an envelope with photographs
of the crime scene. Amanda spread the photos across
her desk and referred to the report. It took her only a

moment to find the coffee mug and scalpel in the inventory and the photographs that showed where each item had been found in the house. Mike Greene had promised to give Amanda a set of crime scene photographs this afternoon at Justine's arraignment. She was willing to bet that those photographs would be similar to the photos spread across her desk.

At eight o'clock Amanda sent her secretary to the district attorney's office to get the keys to Justine Castle's house so that she could select clothes for Justine's court appearance. At eleven-thirty she wolfed down a sandwich and drank more coffee at her desk. By the time Amanda headed to the Justice Center at one o'clock for Justine's arraignment, she was exhausted but up to speed on Vincent Cardoni's case.

Amanda made it through the glass-vaulted lobby of the Justice Center and up the curving marble stairs to the third floor before someone from KGW-TV called her by name; instantly she became the focus of a mob of shouting reporters. An attractive brunette from KPDX asked Amanda if she was a stand-in for her famous father, and a short, disheveled reporter from the *Oregonian* wanted to know if there was a connection between the murders at the farmhouse and the infamous Cardoni case. Amanda ducked to avoid the mikes and the glare of the TV lights while repeating "No comment" to each question. When the doors of the arraignment court closed behind her, sealing her off from the press, she sighed with relief.

The courtroom was packed. Attorneys sat with their clients. Anxious wives bounced children on their knee, trying desperately to keep them quiet so the guard would not expel them before their husbands were brought out of the holding area. Mothers and fathers held hands, watching nervously for a child who had gone wrong. Girlfriends and gang members shifted in their seats while they enjoyed the excitement of seeing someone they knew in court, just like on TV.

A row of chairs inside the bar of the court was reserved for lawyers from the public defender's office, private attorneys who were waiting for court appointments and retained counsel. Amanda took a seat in this section and waited for Justine's case to be called. Arraignment, a defendant's first court appearance, was the time when the judge informed the accused about the nature of the charges filed against him and his right to counsel. If the defendant was indigent, counsel was appointed at the arraignment. Release decisions were sometimes made. Amanda had been to arraignments many times, and they were all the same. She paid attention to the first few cases because it gave her something to do, but she soon lost interest and glanced back at the spectator section out of boredom.

Amanda was about to return her attention to the front of the room when she sensed someone watching her. She scanned the crowd and was ready to chalk up the incident to her imagination when she noticed a large, muscular man with close-cropped blond hair. The man sat with hunched shoulders and his hands folded tightly in his lap, giving the impression that he was uncomfortable being in court. He wore a flannel shirt buttoned to the neck, khakis and a stained trench coat. Something about him was vaguely familiar, but Amanda had no idea where, or if, she had seen him before.

The door to the hall opened, and Mike Greene

fought his way past the reporters. Once inside, he used his height to scan the room and spotted Amanda. Greene was still dressed in the brown tweed sports coat, rumpled white shirt and gray slacks that he had been wearing at three in the morning.

"I see you went home," Mike said when he was seated beside Amanda.

"I've got on new duds, but I never got to sleep."

"That makes two of us. The sleep part, that is."

Mike handed Amanda a thick manila envelope.

"The complaint, some of the police reports and a set of the crime scene photographs. Don't say I never gave you anything."

"Thanks for not being a hard-ass."

Mike smiled. "It's the least I can do after making you drink that foul sludge the homicide dicks call coffee."

"Have you given any more thought to release?"

"Can't do it. Too many bodies, too much evidence."

"*State v. Justine Elizabeth Castle,*" the bailiff called out.

Mike Greene walked to a long table at which another assistant district attorney sat. Its top was almost obscured by three gray metal tubs filled with case files. While Greene took out Justine's file, Amanda went to the other side of the room. A guard led Justine out of the holding area. Her client had on no makeup, but she looked good in her dark suit and silk shirt.

The arraignment moved swiftly. Amanda entered her name as attorney of record and waived a reading of the complaint. While the judge conferred with his clerk about a date for a bail hearing, Amanda explained what was going on. Justine listened carefully and nodded in the appropriate places, but Amanda had the impression that her client was barely holding herself together.

"Are you okay?" Amanda asked.

"No, but I won't break. You do your best to get me out as fast as you can."

The judge ended Justine's arraignment, and the guard started to lead her away.

"I'm working on your case full time," Amanda told her client. "I won't see you again today, but I'll be by tomorrow. Don't lose faith."

Justine held her head high as she walked through the door that led to the elevator that would transport her back to jail. Amanda wondered if she'd be able to carry herself with that much dignity if she was in Dr. Castle's shoes.

The reporters swarmed around Amanda in the corridor outside the courtroom. She refused to comment and fought through the crowd to the street. The rain had stopped but it was still cold and blustery. Amanda hunched her shoulders and crossed the street to Lownsdale Park, hurrying past the war memorial and the empty benches. While she waited for the light at Fourth and Salmon to change she cast a glance behind her and thought she saw movement near the small red-brick rest room on the edge of the park. The light changed and Amanda crossed the street, heading down Fourth toward her office. She had the sense that someone was behind her. Could one of the reporters be following her? Amanda stopped and turned around. A man in a trench coat ducked into the entrance of the office building across the way. Amanda stared at the entrance. She even walked back up the block a few steps for a better

view. Two women walked out of the building.
Amanda stared at the door they exited, but no one
else came out. Suddenly a wave of fatigue hit her,
and she leaned against a parking meter. She closed
her eyes for a moment and still felt a little dizzy when
she opened them. She chalked up her feeling of being
followed to exhaustion, took a deep breath to clear
her head and walked down Fourth to the Stockman
Building.

39

Mike Greene grew up in Los Angeles, married his high school sweetheart and graduated from the law school at UCLA. Everything was going wonderfully, his life was perfectly on course. Then one day in his fourth year as a prosecutor for the Los Angeles district attorney's office Mike ate a bad burrito for lunch. When court resumed he was too sick to go on, so the judge recessed for the day. Mike thought about calling his wife, Debbie, but he didn't want to worry her, so he rested for an hour and drove home.

Mike walked through the door of his split-level three hours earlier than usual and found Debbie astride his next-door neighbor. He stood in the bedroom doorway, too stunned to speak. While the guilty couple scrambled for their clothes, he turned without a word and left.

Greene moved in with a fellow DA until he found a gloomy furnished apartment. He'd loved his wife so much that he blamed himself for her betrayal. The divorce was over in a flash. Debbie got the house, most of their savings and everything else she wanted because Mike would not fight. After the divorce, Mike tried to concentrate on his job, but he was so depressed that his work suffered. His supervisor recommended a leave of absence. Mike had never been out of California except for his honeymoon in Hawaii and a vacation or two in Mexico. He sold his car and bought a ticket to London.

Six months in Europe, which included a brief fling with a lovely Israeli tourist, gave Mike some perspective. He decided that Debbie's extracurricular sexcapades were not his fault and that it was time to get on with his life. A friend in the Multnomah County district attorney's office set up a job interview. Now Mike lived in a condo near the Broadway Bridge, across the Willamette River from the Rose Garden, where the Trailblazers played.

As Greene walked from the Justice Center to the Multnomah County courthouse after Justine Castle's arraignment, he fantasized about showering, eating a light meal and going to sleep on the flannel sheets of his king-size bed. That dream went up in smoke when he found Sean McCarthy waiting for him in the reception area of the district attorney's office, his nose buried in a book.

"A cop who reads Steinbeck," Greene said. "Can't that get you fired?"

McCarthy looked up, amused. He was just as gaunt as he had been four years before, but his red hair was thinner.

"How you doing, Mike?"

"Dreadful. If I don't get some sleep soon, you're going to be investigating my demise."

McCarthy marked his place in *The Grapes of Wrath* and followed Greene through a waist-high gate and down a narrow hall to Mike's small office. A poster advertising last year's Mount Hood Jazz Festival adorned one wall. It showed a tenor sax superim-

posed on the snow-covered mountain. Mike had sat
in for a set with a local trio during the festival. A
chess set decorated a credenza that ran under
Greene's window. The deputy district attorney was
studying a variation of the king's Indian defense in
his spare time, and the position reached by white after thirteen moves was displayed on the board.

Sean McCarthy took a chair opposite Mike's desk.
Greene closed the door to his office and slumped in
his chair.

"About four years ago a doctor named Vincent
Cardoni was accused of torturing several victims in a
house in Milton County. That was your case, right?"

"It was a Milton County case, but I assisted," Mc-
Carthy answered.

"Frank Jaffe represented Cardoni. His daughter,
Amanda, is representing Justine Castle, Cardoni's ex-
wife, in a case with several similarities to the old
case. Amanda thinks her client has been set up by
Cardoni."

"Cardoni is dead."

"That's what Alex DeVore said, but Amanda says
that no body was ever found."

"That's true."

"So . . . ?"

McCarthy was quiet for a moment. "How similar
are the crime scenes?"

"Amanda says they're almost identical."

"Really. Identical how?"

Greene found the crime scene photographs and
handed them to McCarthy. The detective shuffled
through them slowly. He kept one picture and set the
stack down on Greene's desk.

"What do you think?" the deputy DA asked.

McCarthy turned over the picture he was holding.

It showed the half-filled coffee mug that had been found on the drain board in the farmhouse kitchen.

"Did the lab find Justine Castle's fingerprints on this mug?" McCarthy asked.

Greene nodded. "They were on a scalpel with the blood of one of the victims on it, too."

"That really bothers me."

"Why?"

"We found more or less the same thing in the house in Milton County four years ago. The press knew about the scalpel, but we never told them about the coffee mug."

"What about the motion to suppress?"

"A list of the items seized was submitted, but there was no mention that prints were found on any of them."

"So you think that someone who knew about the mug set up Justine Castle?"

"Or she poured herself some coffee while she was working. A year or so after Cardoni disappeared I had a drink with Frank Jaffe. At one point the conversation turned to the Cardoni case. Frank told me that Justine Castle had given the coffee mug to Cardoni as a present and Cardoni claimed the mug had been stolen from his office at St. Francis. Cardoni thought that Justine Castle had used the mug and the scalpel to set him up."

40

The weather front that had bedeviled Oregon for the past week was attacking again. Sheet after sheet of heavy rain bombarded Amanda's car. Even with the wipers on full, the visibility was so poor that Amanda counted herself lucky when she spotted the gap in the fence that bordered the farm. As soon as she turned onto the driveway the car started hitting puddles and potholes. Rain pounded the roof. Amanda's high beams raked the darkness, illuminating trees and shrubs before spotlighting the yellow crime scene tape that stretched across the door to the farmhouse.

Amanda shut off the engine and sat listening to the rain. She had convinced herself that she would know if Cardoni had created both chambers of horror simply by walking through the farmhouse. Now that she was here, the idea sounded ridiculous. Amanda turned on the interior light and took another look at the pictures that Mike Greene had given her. One showed the graveyard surrounded by trees and far from the boundaries of the property: a place that would be hard to find accidentally. She flipped to the next shot. Three bodies, all showing marks of torture, lay stretched out on a ground sheet. A tarp had been erected over them to keep the corpses as dry as possible. A close-up of a female victim showed the abuse the frail body had taken in the days before she died.

Another set of photographs showed the interior of the farmhouse. Amanda shuffled quickly past the close-ups of the body in the basement. One long look when she first saw the photos had been enough. She reviewed the other pictures before realizing that she was stalling. Amanda grabbed a flashlight and ran through the rain until she reached the overhang that covered the front door. She ripped away the bright yellow tape and walked inside.

Amanda played the beam of her flashlight over the entryway and the living room. They were as bare and sparsely furnished as the house in Milton County had been. Amanda found the bedroom. The police had left the furniture after dusting it for prints and scouring it for trace evidence, but they had taken the books and the journal from the bookcase. Amanda tried to imagine the killer sitting in the armchair and thumbing through the manuals in preparation for the next torture session. What type of monster could coldly plan the ritual degradation of another human being?

Amanda walked back through the living room to the kitchen. Outside, the wind gusted, rattling the shutters and skittering across the roof. Amanda felt a flutter in her stomach when she turned the knob of the basement door and looked into the dark space below. She flicked a light switch, and a bare bulb lit the lower part of the basement stairs. An oil-burning furnace stood in one corner. In another corner a rectangular patch of floor, cleaner than the area surrounding

it, told her where the mattress had lain before forensics had removed it. She saw holes in the wall where
the manacles had been secured; these too had been
moved to the crime lab. Then she noticed the crudely
mortared concrete wall that divided the basement in
half.

The wall looked as if it had been constructed by a
do-it-yourselfer from a how-to book. Amanda descended the stairs and peered through an opening
that led into a dark space where the light from the 40-
watt bulb barely reached. Amanda turned on her
flashlight and shone it through the doorway. The operating table was there. Above it was another bulb.
Amanda pulled the string attached to it, and the light
illuminated a space bare except for the operating
table. Everything else from the room had gone to the
crime lab. Suddenly she flashed on an image of Mary
Sandowski's tearstained face, and a wave of nausea
surged through her. She shut her eyes for a moment
and breathed deeply. There was no way that she
could prove it, but there was absolutely no doubt.
The person who had turned the mountain cabin into
a place of horror had been at work here.

Amanda circled the table. Fingerprint powder
darkened the steel legs. She knelt down and saw a
dark brown fleck. Was that blood? She stared at it for
a moment, then stood up.

A man was standing in the doorway.

41

The man stepped out of the shadows, blocking the only way out. He was wearing a rain-drenched trench coat. Amanda raised the flashlight and retreated.

"I'm not here to hurt you," the man said, raising an empty hand, palm outstretched. "I'm Bobby Vasquez."

It took a moment, then Amanda recognized the intruder. Vasquez's face was fleshy. Rain dripped from his long, unkempt black hair; a bushy mustache covered his upper lip. Under the open raincoat Amanda could see faded jeans, a flannel shirt and a threadbare sports jacket.

"I didn't mean to scare you," Vasquez told her. "I tried to talk to you at the Justice Center, but I couldn't get close with all the reporters."

Vasquez paused. He saw that Amanda was frightened and wary.

"Do you remember me?" he asked.

"The motion to suppress."

"Not exactly my shining hour," Vasquez said grimly. "But I was right about Cardoni. He killed those people in Milton County and he killed these

people, too. You know it, don't you? That's why
you're here."

Amanda forgot her fear. "What makes you think
he's alive?"

"Look at this place. When I read about the graveyard and the operating room, I knew."

"What about the hand? Cardoni was a surgeon.
He wouldn't cut off his hand."

"Cardoni counted on everyone buying into that
notion, that a surgeon would never amputate his
own hand. But most surgeons aren't being hunted by
a maniac like Martin Breach."

"Or facing a death sentence."

"That too. Plus, this guy is flat-out insane."

Amanda shook her head. "I want to believe Cardoni did this. The crime scenes are so alike. But I always come back to the hand. How could he do it?
How could he cut off his own hand?"

"It's not as difficult as you might think. Not for a
doctor, anyway. I asked around. All Cardoni had to
do was tie a tourniquet around his biceps and run an
IV filled with anesthetic into his forearm. That would
put his arm to sleep. He could amputate the hand
without feeling a thing. After the hand was off he
would have covered the stump with a sterile cloth
until the bleeding stopped, then bandaged it and
used more anesthetic to block the pain."

Amanda digested what Vasquez had said, then
made a decision.

"Okay, Mr. Vasquez, I'll level with you. I am here
because of Cardoni."

"I knew it! So tell me, what else was in the police
reports? You're not just here on a hunch."

Amanda hesitated.

"Look, Miss Jaffe, I can help you. Who knows

more about Cardoni than I do? I never believed that he was dead. I still have my file on him. I know Cardoni's life story; I can tell you what the police knew four years ago. You'll need an investigator."

"Our firm has an investigator."

"This will just be another case for him. It's my chance at redemption. Cardoni ruined my life."

"You ruined your own life," Amanda answered curtly.

Vasquez looked down. "You're right. I have to take the blame for what I did. It took me a while to figure that out." Vasquez swung his arm across the operating room. "I take the blame for this, too. If I hadn't screwed up, Cardoni would be in prison and these people would be alive. I've got to make this right." He paused. "Besides, if we prove that Cardoni killed these people, your client goes free."

Vasquez sounded desperate and sincere. Amanda took a final look around the operating room.

"Let's get out of here," she said. "We'll talk upstairs."

Amanda pulled the cord attached to the lightbulb and plunged the makeshift operating room into darkness.

"What can you tell me?" Vasquez asked as they climbed the stairs. "Are there other similarities between the crime scenes?"

"I don't think I should get into that."

"You're right. Sorry. I'm just anxious. You have no idea how I felt when I saw Dr. Castle's name in the paper this morning and read about the operating room. All of a sudden there was hope that this nightmare might finally end."

Amanda turned off the basement light and shut the door behind her.

"Look, Mr. Vasquez, let's be straight here, okay? I heard rumors about you after you were fired. My father heard them, too. If I ask my father to let you work with us on this case, he's going to want to know if you're reliable."

Vasquez looked as though he had been down this road before.

"What do you want to know?" He sighed.

"What did you do after you were kicked off the force?"

"I drank. That's what you're after, right? Being a cop was my whole life. One moment I was and the next I wasn't. I couldn't cope. There's a year and a half in there that's still very blurry. But I came out of it and I stopped drinking on my own. I don't drink anymore, not even a beer. Tell your father that I'm a licensed investigator. It's how I've been earning my living. I'm good at it, and believe it or not, there are still some people on the job who'll talk to me."

"We'll have to see."

"When you're thinking about hiring me, think about this. I've already got a jump on the cops."

"What do you mean?"

"Four years ago I figured I'd nail Cardoni by tying him to the Milton County house. You know, get the deed, show he owned it. Only I couldn't. He was very clever. The property was owned by a corporation, and the corporation was set up by a shady attorney named Walter Stoops, who was hired by someone he never met and paid in cashier's checks. The whole thing turned out to be a dead end, because we couldn't identify the person who purchased the cashier's checks. But it did establish an MO.

"This morning, as soon as I read about the farmhouse, I went through the records for this property. Guess what I found?"

"The land is owned by a corporation and was purchased by a lawyer."

"Bingo. The sale went through two years ago, which would give Cardoni enough time to set up a new identity and prepare for his return to Portland."

"Is the purchaser the same corporation that bought the land in Milton County?"

"No. And the lawyer's different. But the MO's the same."

"What makes you think you'll be able to prove who purchased the property this time?"

"I don't know that I can, but Cardoni screwed up four years ago and we almost got him. I'm hoping he'll screw up again."

42

That night Amanda slept like the dead and through her alarm. It was too late for her morning calisthenics or breakfast, so she took a fast shower and picked up a latte and a piece of coffee cake to go. When she walked into her office at eight-thirty her father was sitting behind her desk reading through the file on Justine Castle. He looked up and smiled. Amanda froze in the doorway.

"Good morning, Amanda."

"You're supposed to be on vacation. What are you doing here?" she asked, fighting to keep the disappointment out of her voice.

"Didn't you think I'd be interested in your latest case?"

"I was sure you would be. That's why I left strict instructions that no one was to tell you about it if you called in."

"No one did."

"Then how did you find out?"

"It's in the California papers. Somebody figured out the connection to the Cardoni case and, presto, we've got another sensation on our hands. Did you check your phone messages?"

"Not yet."

"I glanced through them. If you want to be a media celebrity, 20/20, 60 *Minutes*, Larry King and Geraldo are all standing by."

"You're kidding."

Amanda set her attaché case, the latte and the bag with the coffee cake on the edge of her desk and sat in one of her client chairs.

"Isn't Elsie pissed that you've ruined her vacation?"

"Elsie is a wonderful woman. She ordered me to come back and help you."

"Thanks for the vote of confidence," Amanda answered sarcastically. "I was perfectly able to save Dooling's ass all by myself. What makes you think I'm not competent to represent Justine Castle?"

"Hold on," Frank said, raising a hand defensively. "No one's saying you're incompetent, and don't get huffy on me. You know damn well that it takes two lawyers to handle something this complex."

"Are you going to be lead counsel?" Amanda asked, bracing for the worst.

"I wouldn't think of it."

Amanda tried to hide her surprise, but she must have failed, because Frank's lips twitched as if he was suppressing a grin.

"Justine might want you to be," Amanda said warily. "She asked for you when she was arrested."

"Is she satisfied with you calling the shots?"

"I think so."

"Then let's see how things go. Right now it's your case. Why don't you bring me up to speed?"

Between sips of her latte and bites of her coffee cake, Amanda laid out the details, starting with Justine's late-night phone call. When she told Frank about her visit to the farmhouse she didn't mention her encounter with Vasquez.

"I wish you hadn't gone inside, Amanda," Frank said when she was finished. "It was a sealed crime scene."

"I know, but the forensic experts had gone through it already, and I had to see the place before it changed too much."

Frank leaned back. "What was your impression?"

"It's either the same killer or someone who knows an awful lot about the Cardoni case. I'm sure of it."

Amanda paused a moment to think of how to broach the subject of Vasquez. She decided to plunge in.

"When I was looking over the basement at the farmhouse, Bobby Vasquez showed up."

"The cop who lied at Cardoni's motion?"

Amanda nodded. "He wants to work with us on the case. He's convinced that Cardoni faked his death four years ago and is responsible for the new murders."

"Did you know that Vasquez was one of the leading suspects in Cardoni's disappearance? He was obsessed with Cardoni. The theory is that he went vigilante when the court set him free."

Amanda tried to picture Vasquez as Cardoni's killer.

"It makes no sense for Vasquez to tell me that Cardoni killed the people at the farm if he knows that Cardoni is dead. Why would he follow me to the farmhouse? Why would he offer to work on the case?"

"I don't know and I don't care," Frank snapped.

"You have every right to be angry about what Vasquez did in Cardoni's case. But you shouldn't let that stop you from thinking about what he can do in this one."

"He's dishonest, Amanda. He's a drunk."

"He says that he's not drinking anymore, and he looked sober. I think you should remember why Vasquez lied under oath. He did it because he thought it was the only way to put a very bad person in prison."

"That doesn't excuse what he did."

"I'm not saying it does. I just think you should look at this with an open mind. Vasquez knows everything the police knew about Cardoni, and he's already uncovered some useful information."

"Such as?"

Amanda told Frank about Vasquez's investigation into the ownership of the farm.

"That's nothing Herb or the cops wouldn't have discovered," Frank said dismissively. "I don't know why Vasquez wants to work this case, but I'm not going to associate with a perjurer and a drunk."

Amanda gathered herself. Then she looked directly at her father.

"Either I'm lead counsel or I'm not. If I am, then I choose my team."

Frank wasn't used to being told what to do, and Amanda could see that he didn't like it.

"I'm not sure about Vasquez myself," Amanda added quickly while she had the edge, "but I want the right to decide if he's in or out."

Frank let out the breath he'd been holding.

"Let's talk about this later."

"I want it decided now. Do you think I'm competent to run this defense?"

Frank hesitated.

"Do you, Dad? We've worked together for five

years. You've had a lifetime to evaluate my abilities. If you don't think I can hack it, I'll resign from the firm today."

Frank put his head back and roared with laughter.

"You make me long for the good old days when little girls were courteous to their fathers and studied home economics."

"Screw you," Amanda said, fighting hard but failing to suppress a triumphant grin.

"Where did you learn such language?"

"From you, you old bastard. Now let's get back to Justine's case."

"I'd better before you try to get a raise, too."

Amanda lifted an eyebrow. "Not a bad idea."

"Quit while you're ahead, you ingrate."

Amanda laughed. Then she grew serious. "Were there other suspects in Cardoni's disappearance?"

Frank nodded. "Martin Breach's enforcer, Art Prochaska, the guy you thought you saw driving away from the cabin."

"Of course."

"Breach had a reputation for dismembering people he didn't like, and he had a contract out on Cardoni because he thought Vincent had double-crossed him in a deal involving the black-market sale of organs. The rest of Cardoni may have been in the trunk of Prochaska's car when he passed you."

"That's a pleasant thought."

"You asked."

"Do you know Prochaska well enough so he would talk to you?"

"Why?"

"I'd like to know what he was doing at the cabin on the night I found the hand. If he didn't kill Cardoni, he might tell us."

"Prochaska claimed that he wasn't at the cabin. He had an alibi."

"He's lying, Dad. I couldn't swear in court that it was Prochaska I saw, but he was in that car."

Frank thought for a moment. "Martin always trusted me. I'm certain he told Art to be a witness for Cardoni. Let me see what I can do. I'll let you know what Martin says as soon as I talk to him."

Frank left to work his way through the mail that had piled up while he was away. Amanda wandered out to the front desk, picked up a thick stack of phone messages and returned to her office. Frank hadn't lied about the calls from Geraldo and company, but the message that made her pause wasn't from New York or LA. Amanda tapped the slip against her palm, uncertain whether to call the number or not. She swiveled her chair and stared out the window. The name on the slip aroused mixed emotions. Suddenly Amanda said, "Why not?" and dialed St. Francis Medical Center. She told the operator her caller's name and was put on hold. After a moment the voice of Tony Fiori came on the line.

"Amanda?" he asked hesitantly.

"Long time, Tony," Amanda said evenly. "I didn't know you were in town."

"Yeah. I'm back at St. Francis."

"How was New York?"

"Good. Actually, I was so busy most of the time that I didn't take as much advantage of being there as I should have."

"So, what's up?" Amanda asked, dying to know why he had called but unwilling to ask.

"I was in New Orleans since last Friday and didn't see a paper until this morning. I read about Justine being charged with those killings."

Amanda flashed on a vision of Justine and Tony standing side by side in Fiori's doorway four years ago.

"So that's why you called, because of Justine?" she asked, fighting to mask her disappointment.

"Your name was in the paper, too, Amanda." He paused. "Look, I've got to be in surgery in three minutes, so I don't have much time. I'd like to see you. Could we have dinner?"

Amanda's pulse gave an unexpected flutter.

"I don't know."

"If you don't want to, I'll understand."

"No, it's not that." She did want to see Tony. "I'll be up to my neck in Justine's case for the next few days."

"How about this weekend?"

"Okay."

"I'll make a dinner reservation at the Fish Hatchery for Friday night. Is that okay?"

"Sure."

"See you then."

Amanda hung up the phone. Tony Fiori. Wow! Now here was a blast from the past. Amanda laughed. She'd really acted like a schoolgirl when she found out he'd been sleeping with Justine, but that was years ago and she was a lot tougher now. And she had enjoyed the time they'd spent together. Amanda stared out the window for a moment. Then she smiled. It would be interesting to see how well Tony had aged in four years.

43

The view from Carleton Swindell's office had not changed, but Dr. Swindell's blond hair was thinning, and Sean McCarthy suspected that a facelift had been performed on the hospital administrator of St. Francis Medical Center during the past four years.

"Detective," Swindell said as he rose from behind his desk to extend a hand. The administrator's grip was still strong, and the detective noticed several new rowing plaques and medals had been added to the trophies that graced Swindell's credenza. "I assume you're here about Justine Castle."

McCarthy nodded as he handed Swindell a subpoena for the doctor's records. Swindell examined it briefly. He looked as though he hadn't been sleeping well.

"After that business with Vincent Cardoni I thought I'd seen everything. But this . . ." He shook his head in dismay. "Frankly, Detective, I find it hard to believe that Justine could do the things I read about in the paper."

"She was arrested at the scene of the murders, and we have other evidence connecting her to them."

"Even so." Swindell hesitated. Then he leaned for-

ward. "I followed Cardoni's case. Of course, I only
had access to the media accounts, but these new murders, aren't they similar to the murders Cardoni was
supposed to have committed? The newspaper even
commented on it."

"I'm afraid I can't discuss the evidence."

"Oh, of course. I didn't mean to pry. It's just that,
well, when Cardoni was arrested, no one was
shocked. But Justine . . . We've never had any reason
to suspect that she would be capable of anything like
this. Her record is spotless."

Swindell shifted uncomfortably. "I know this isn't
my area of expertise, but with such bizarre circumstances, wouldn't you suspect that the person who
committed one set of murders also committed the
others?"

"That's a possibility that we're investigating,
along with several others."

The administrator flushed. "Yes, I should have
guessed that."

"Dr. Swindell, the last time we spoke, you mentioned a connection between Dr. Castle and Clifford
Grant."

"He was her attending, her supervisor during her
residency."

"So they would have been close?"

"Professionally, yes."

"Four years ago, would Dr. Castle have had the
skills to harvest a human heart for use in a heart
transplant? If you know."

"I trained as a surgeon before I decided to become
a hospital administrator, so I'm well aware of the
technique," Swindell said with some pride. "Justine
is a highly skilled surgeon. I believe she would have
been able to perform the operation."

McCarthy considered Swindell's answer for a moment. Then he stood. "Thank you, Doctor."

"Feel free to call on me for help anytime."

"We appreciated the way you sped things along the last time I asked for your help. If you could do the same with this subpoena . . . "

Swindell held up his hand. "Say no more. I'll get on it immediately."

44

The reservation at the Fish Hatchery was for eight, but Amanda was intentionally late. When she spotted Tony in the upscale crowd in the lounge at eight-twenty she was pleased to see him casting anxious glances toward the door. He was wearing a dark sports jacket without a tie, a white shirt and gray slacks, and he was every bit as handsome as she remembered. Amanda worked her way through the crush at the bar. Tony saw her and flashed a wide smile. Amanda extended her hand but Tony ignored it, pulling her into a quick bear hug.

"You look great," Tony said enthusiastically. He pushed her back. "God, look at you."

Amanda felt herself flush.

"Our table won't be ready for a few minutes. Do you want a drink?"

"Sure."

Amanda ordered a margarita. The bar was packed, and she and Tony were pushed hip to hip. The contact felt good.

"When did you get back to Portland?" she asked while they waited for the drinks.

"I've been at St. Francis for almost a year."

"Oh," Amanda answered coldly, stung by the fact that he'd taken so long to call her. "I guess you've been busy."

"You've got every right to be mad. It's just that . . . Well, I guess I was embarrassed because of what happened the night you showed up at my house. I didn't know if you'd want to hear from me."

"You have nothing to be embarrassed about," Amanda said, keeping her tone neutral. "I certainly had no right to assume that you would be alone."

"You needed someone to comfort you, and you came to me. When I found out what you'd gone through in the mountains I felt like a complete shit."

"There wasn't any reason for you to feel that way," Amanda said, answering more sharply than she had intended.

Tony looked upset. He took a deep breath.

"We were friends, Amanda. You don't have to sleep with someone to care for them."

The hostess chose that moment to tell them that their table was ready. Amanda was grateful for the interruption and followed her in embarrassed silence. The hostess gave them menus and a wine list. As soon as she left, Tony put down his menu.

"Let me clear the air, okay? Otherwise we're both going to be blushing and mumbling all evening. I'm going to start with Justine. I'd seen her around the hospital, but I never spent much time with her until Cardoni attacked Mary Sandowski. I happened to be passing by when Justine confronted him. I was afraid that he might hit her, so I asked if there was a problem, just to let Cardoni know that Justine wasn't alone. After we calmed down Mary, Justine and I talked. One thing led to another. When I ran into you at the Y, we were already sleeping together."

Tony paused and looked down at the table.

"I don't want you to take this the wrong way. I'm not someone who flits from woman to woman. But Justine and I . . . Well, I don't know any other way to put this. Our sex was recreational. She was going through a hard time, and I was a distraction. I liked her and I think she liked me, but it didn't mean anything."

"Tony . . ."

"Let me finish. You did mean something to me. I've always liked you, even when we were kids. But it was more like a big-brother-little-sister thing then. When I saw you at the Y it was confusing. You weren't a kid anymore. You were a woman. I didn't know how to treat you. After we spent those two evenings together I couldn't stop thinking about you, and I wanted to see you again."

"So what stopped you?"

"I was accepted into one of the best residency programs in the country, and it was in New York. A long-distance romance didn't make any sense. And I had no idea how you felt about me. We'd only dated a few times. You were starting a career." Tony shrugged. "Then you saw me with Justine. The only thing I want to know is how badly I hurt you, because I always hoped that you didn't care enough for me for my leaving to matter."

A welter of emotions confused Amanda. She was thrilled that Tony felt strongly enough about her to bare his soul, but his frontal assault was coming so fast that it didn't give her time to think.

"I don't know how I felt when you left, Tony. It's been years, and a lot has happened in between."

"Maybe that's best," he said. "Maybe we should

just start over and see what happens. Would that be okay? Could you do that?"

Amanda smiled. "I'm here, aren't I?"

"I guess that's right. You didn't shoot me down."

"And I didn't shoot you, either." She smiled. "Not yet, anyway."

The waiter arrived, and Tony seemed grateful for the interruption. Amanda opted for a safe topic of conversation as soon as the waiter left with their orders.

"What are you doing at St. Francis?"

"I've finished my residency and I'm an attending plastic surgeon. I just gave a paper in New Orleans, last Friday, at the annual meeting of the American Society of Plastic and Reconstructive Surgeons," Tony said proudly.

"What was it about?"

"The long-term aesthetic effects of immediate versus delayed breast reconstruction using the pedicled TRAM flap."

"In English, please, for the scientifically impaired."

Tony laughed. "Sorry. It's not that complicated, really. You can do breast reconstruction after a mastectomy in a number of ways. The pedicled TRAM flap involves taking abdominal tissue to use in the reconstruction. You don't have to do the reconstruction at the same time as the mastectomy. You could do it a year later, if you wanted to. But I've concluded that immediate reconstruction looks better, and I talked about the basis for my conclusion. Impressed?" Tony asked, sipping his margarita.

"Not bad for a college dropout," Amanda answered with a smile.

"Now that you know all about pedicled TRAM

flaps, fill me in on what you've been up to. It said in the paper that you just won a death penalty case. Are you specializing in criminal law like your father?"

"Yup. I think I'm genetically programmed for it."

"Do you like representing criminals?"

"I don't know if *like* is the right word. Criminal law is exciting, and I think the work is important. With a case like Justine's I feel I can do some real good."

"How is she holding up?"

"She's a strong woman. But no one really does that well under these circumstances. She's worried about her career and her future. Jail is a lousy place to be even if you're guilty. It's hell if you're innocent."

"So you don't think she's guilty?"

"No, I don't."

"Why?"

Amanda was not certain how much she should reveal about the case to someone who was not involved in Justine's representation. But Tony was very bright, and it would be interesting to see how a non-lawyer saw the case after hearing the facts.

"You have to promise to keep what I tell you to yourself."

"Of course. Doctors have confidentiality restrictions, too."

Amanda laid out what she knew. Tony tensed when she described the similarities between the Milton County and Multnomah County crime scenes, and his brow furrowed when she explained that an anonymous caller had summoned the police to the farmhouse.

"It looks like a setup," Tony concluded when Amanda was done. "I can't believe that the cops don't see it."

"A setup doesn't fit into their scenario. It complicates matters, and the cops like their cases to have simple solutions."

"What about the anonymous call that sent the cops to the farmhouse? How do they explain that?"

"The DA says he doesn't have to explain it, that it's my job to construct a defense for Justine."

"That's bullshit. It's obviously a frame. And you know what I think? It's got to be someone with access to the hospital. Think about it. The scrubs, the cap, the scalpel—all that stuff came from St. Francis, and they aren't something a casual visitor could pick up. You'd have to know when Justine was going to be in surgery, you'd have to have access to the room where Justine discarded her cap and scrubs."

"That means Justine has an enemy at St. Francis," Amanda said. "Do you know anyone who hates her so much he would do something like this?"

Tony thought for a moment, then shook his head.

"The only person I can think of . . . No, it's not possible."

"You're thinking about Vincent Cardoni."

"Yeah, but he's dead."

"We don't know that for sure," Amanda said. "His body was never recovered."

"You think Cardoni is working at St. Francis?"

"I think it's possible. He'd have to have had plastic surgery and he couldn't be working as a doctor. He doesn't have a hand."

"Actually . . ." Tony started, then stopped, lost in thought.

"What?"

Tony looked up. He leaned toward Amanda.

"A hand transplant," he said excitedly. "It's possible to transplant a hand. They tried it for the first time in Ecuador in 1964. The operation failed because the tissue was rejected, but there are new antirejection drugs and advanced surgical techniques that have resulted in several successful hand transplants."

"Of course," Amanda answered, echoing Tony's excitement. "I remember reading about them." She sobered suddenly. "A transplant would be so spectacular that everyone would know about it. The one I remember was front-page news. If Cardoni had a hand transplant in the past four years, we'd have heard."

"Not if it was done clandestinely. Didn't Justine believe that Cardoni had money stashed away in offshore accounts?"

"Yes."

"With enough money, Cardoni could find a doctor who would change his appearance and try a hand transplant. And he doesn't have to be working as a doctor. Maybe he has a prosthesis and is working at some other job."

Tony thought for a moment. "Do you know when the farmhouse was purchased?"

"About two years ago, I think."

Tony leaned forward. He looked intense.

"That's it, then. I'll get someone in personnel at St. Francis to give me a printout of every male employee who was hired in the past two years. Cardoni could change his appearance and his weight. He could also change his height, but I'm betting he didn't. I'll look for white men about six-two who are roughly Cardoni's age."

Tony reached across the table and covered Amanda's hand with his.

"If Cardoni is at St. Francis, I'll track him down. We'll catch him, Amanda."

The waiter arrived with their wine and the first course, and Amanda had a chance to calm down. She ate her salad in silence while she thought about getting Tony involved in Justine's case.

"Maybe I should have our investigator get the personnel records."

"Why?"

"If Cardoni is our killer, you'd be putting yourself in danger by looking for him."

"Your investigator wouldn't have the expertise to spot a really good facial reconstruction. I'd recognize one in an instant. And believe me, I'm not going to take any chances. If I find Cardoni, we'll go straight to the police."

Amanda hesitated.

"Amanda, I like Justine. I don't want to see an innocent person suffer. But I like me, too, and I'm too young to die. I appreciate how dangerous this can be. I'm not going to put myself at risk."

"Promise?"

"Promise."

"You know what?" Tony asked.

"What?"

"I think we should stop talking shop for the rest of our meal."

Amanda smiled. "I agree. What shall we talk about?"

"I just had an idea. Have you seen the new Jackie Chan flick?"

"I haven't seen a movie in ages."

"It's showing at the Broadway Metroplex at ten-thirty. Are you in the mood for some mindless violence?"

"You bet."

Tony smiled. "You're a girl after my own heart."

45

When Bobby Vasquez had called earlier for an appointment, Mary Ann Jager had answered her own phone. Now he knew why: The lawyer's tiny waiting room reeked of failure. There was no receptionist, and the top of the receptionist's desk was bare and covered with a light layer of dust. Vasquez knocked on the doorjamb of an open doorway. A slender woman with short brown hair looked up, startled, from the fashion magazine she was reading.

Vasquez had learned a lot about Jager from the Martindale-Hubbell Law Directory listing of attorneys' résumés and the file of complaints against Jager that he had obtained through the Oregon state bar. She had gone to work for a midsized firm for a decent salary after graduating high in her law school class. There were no problems until shortly before her divorce, when a client complained about irregularities in her trust account and rumors of substance abuse began to circulate. Jager was suspended from the practice of law for a year and fired from her firm. When she could practice again, she opened her own office. Jager's history was very similar to that of Walter Stoops, and Vasquez wondered if Cardoni found his lawyers by studying complaints filed against members of the bar.

"Ms. Jager? I'm Bobby Vasquez. I called earlier."

The lawyer stood up quickly, walked around her desk and extended a damp hand. Vasquez noticed a slight tremor.

"I hope you weren't waiting outside long," Jager said nervously. "My receptionist is out with that flu that's going around."

Bobby smiled sympathetically, though he was certain that there was no receptionist—and very little business, to judge from the empty state of Jager's in-box and her bare desktop.

"I'm interested in contacting the owner of some land you purchased approximately two years ago for Intercontinental Properties, a corporation you formed," Vasquez said when they were seated.

Jager frowned. "That was a farm, right?"

Vasquez nodded, breathing a silent prayer of thanks that he had beaten the police to Jager and that she did not know that the land she had purchased had been turned into a slaughterhouse.

"I'd like to help you, but I have no idea who owns the property. The owner contacted me by mail. I was paid to form Intercontinental Properties for the sole purpose of buying the land. My retainer and the money for the property were paid in cashier's checks. I forwarded the title to a post office box in California."

"If you could give me the owner's name, I can try to trace him."

"I don't have a name. There was no signature on my instructions."

"This all sounds very mysterious."

"It is, but it's completely legal."

"Of course."

Vasquez paused, then acted like a man who has just gotten an idea.

"Could I see your file? Maybe there's a clue to the owner's identity in it."

"I don't know if I can do that. The information in the file is privileged."

Vasquez leaned forward and lowered his voice, even though he and the lawyer were alone.

"Ms. Jager, my client is very intent on negotiating for this property. He has authorized me to compensate you for your time and for reasonable copying costs. I don't see where a problem would arise. Most of the information is public record anyway."

The mention of money got Jager's attention.

"I charge one hundred and fifty dollars an hour."

"That sounds reasonable."

Jager hesitated, and Vasquez knew that she was desperate for more money. He hoped that she didn't go crazy on him. Until the Jaffes hired him, he was fronting his expenses.

"My copying costs are rather high. I would need another fifty dollars to cover them."

"That's fine."

Vasquez slid two hundred dollars across the desk.

"May I see the file?"

Jager rotated her chair and retrieved a manila folder from a cabinet behind her desk. Inside, Vasquez found copies of documents he'd seen in the Multnomah County file. He asked for copies of only the checks. Jager was gone for a few minutes. When she returned, she handed a stack of photocopies to Vasquez.

"What's so important about this farm?" Jager

asked. "You're the second person who's been interested in it. Is someone going to build a subdivision?"

"Someone else asked about this property?"

"Yeah, about a week ago."

Vasquez put the photocopies away and dug a photograph of Cardoni out of his attaché case.

"Was this the man?"

Jager studied the photograph for a moment. Then she shook her head.

"The man who came in was blond and looked different. More like a Russian."

"How tall was he?"

"Over six feet."

"Did he say why he wanted to buy the property?"

"No. He was more interested in how it was purchased."

"Can you tell me any more about him?"

"No. He just showed up and asked about the farm."

"Did you show him the file?"

"Yes."

Vasquez was stumped. Who else would be interested in the farm?

"If this guy shows up again, try to get some more information about him."

"How will I let you know?"

Vasquez gave Jager his business card and another fifty.

Ten minutes later Vasquez was on the phone with Amanda Jaffe.

"Have you had a chance to talk to your father about me?" Vasquez asked anxiously.

"I'm lead counsel on Dr. Castle's case, so it's my decision."

"Look, I know you're worried, but I'm good and I've already got a jump on the cops."

Vasquez eagerly related what he had learned during his meeting with Mary Ann Jager. Amanda only half listened until Vasquez told her that someone else had been asking about the property.

"Do you think he was just interested in buying the farm?" Amanda asked.

"I don't know. I showed Jager a photograph of Cardoni. The person who came to the office was his height, but Jager said that he looked different."

"If he's alive, Cardoni may have had plastic surgery."

"If he's alive, I'll find him. It doesn't matter what he looks like."

Vasquez's determination pushed Amanda toward a decision. Frank might not trust Vasquez, but she did. He had a burning desire to get Vincent Cardoni, and you could not buy that kind of drive.

"Mr. Vasquez, I think you can help Dr. Castle. I want you to work for me."

"You won't regret this. What do you want me to do?"

"Serial killers refine their techniques. Our murderer has used a unique MO twice. I want you to see if he's used it before. Start searching for unsolved murders involving mass graves. Maybe you'll find another property purchased in a similar way. Maybe we'll get lucky and Cardoni has made a mistake that will let us nail him."

46

Mike Greene had asked Fred Scofield to send him a copy of the Milton County file in the Cardoni prosecution shortly after Justine Castle's arrest. It arrived on Monday afternoon. Greene was reading the file when Sean McCarthy walked into his office a little after five. The homicide detective looked depressed. He dropped a sheaf of police reports on Greene's desk and lowered himself into a chair.

"Jesus, you look terrible," Greene said. "You want some coffee?"

McCarthy dismissed the offer with a despondent wave.

"We have a real problem, Mike. Everything we've got so far makes me believe that the person who committed the murders in Milton County also committed the murders at the farm. Both properties were purchased at the behest of an anonymous buyer through dummy corporations set up by a lawyer who's been in deep trouble with the bar. The crime scenes are so similar that it can't be a coincidence."

Greene looked confused. "Why is that a problem?"

"If Dr. Castle murdered the victims at the farm, we screwed everything up four years ago."

"Then we'll make everything right."

"That might not be so easy. If we can't prove Cardoni's dead, the Jaffes will argue that he's returned to frame Castle. They can call Fred Scofield and Sheriff Mills as witnesses to testify that they were convinced that Cardoni murdered the victims in Milton County. Hell, Mike, they can call me and I'd have to swear that I was certain that Cardoni did it."

Greene thought about that. He pointed at the papers that were strewn across his desk.

"The evidence against Cardoni was pretty convincing."

"And there was none implicating Dr. Castle."

Greene was lost in thought for a moment. When he turned his attention back to McCarthy he looked concerned.

"Have you been able to identify the victims at the farm? Are any of them connected to Castle?"

"The poor bastard who died in the basement was a male prostitute named Zach Petrie. He showed up at the emergency room at St. Francis a week before he died, but there's no record of Castle being involved with the case."

"What about the others?"

"Diane Vickers was a prostitute who was treated for a sexually transmitted disease at St. Francis, but as far as we can tell, Castle didn't treat her. David Capp was a runaway, and we can't find any link between him and St. Francis or Justine Castle.

"Now, no one reported Petrie, Vickers or Capp missing, but we'd been treating the disappearance of Kimberly Lyons, the other female victim, as a possible homicide since she went missing a few months ago. Lyons was a student at Portland State. From what we can tell, she was abducted at the Lloyd Center mall. Her car was found there, and she told her friends that she was going to shop for a birthday present for her boyfriend."

"Do you think the others were also random kidnappings?"

McCarthy shrugged.

"How about taking a new look at the old victims to see if we can link them to Castle?"

"I'm already doing that."

Greene smiled. "Sorry, I should have assumed you would be. Anything else new?"

"The DNA test identified the hair in the surgical cap as Castle's. I also talked to the lawyer who was representing Cardoni in his divorce. Castle went through with the divorce after Cardoni disappeared and made out like a bandit."

"How well?"

"She cleared around two million dollars."

Greene whistled. "Two million dollars is a good motive for murdering Cardoni."

"The lawyer also told me Castle was certain that Cardoni had set up secret bank accounts in Switzerland and the Cayman Islands, but she never found them. When I asked when she started looking for them, he said it was well before she filed."

"Why is that important?"

"Four years ago Castle testified at her husband's bail hearing. She said she left him when he raped her, but it looks like she may have been checking into his finances way before that."

"So what do we have, a black widow?"

"It's beginning to look that way, Mike. If she killed Cardoni, it won't be the first time she's offed a husband."

"Oh?"

"It might not even be the second time."

47

The matron closed the door to the visiting room behind Justine Castle, and Amanda motioned to the chair across from her. Justine had lost weight, and there were dark circles under her eyes.

"We've got a problem, Justine," Amanda said.

Justine watched Amanda warily.

"The DNA tests of the hair found in the surgical cap came back positive for you."

Justine seemed to relax a bit, as if she'd expected Amanda to say something else.

"I assumed it would," Justine told Amanda. "Whoever planted the coffee mug and the scalpel obviously took a cap I used during surgery."

"There's more. Mike Greene's developing a theory that you married Vincent Cardoni for his money and killed him to get it."

Justine smiled wearily. "That's utterly ridiculous."

"Greene thinks he can prove it, and he's not simply going to describe you to the jury as a gold digger. He's going to characterize you as one of the most depraved serial killers in history."

Justine leaned back in her chair. Her smile widened.

"Isn't that what they said about Vincent? Aren't they going to have a hard time explaining how I murdered the victims in Milton County when all of the evidence points to him?"

Amanda was surprised that her news had not upset Justine more. She studied her client for a moment. Justine did not blink under the scrutiny.

"You've been thinking about this, haven't you?"

"Why does that surprise you, Amanda? My life is at stake, and I have nothing but time on my hands."

"Well, you're right. The Milton County case hurts Mike, but he can overcome it if he has evidence that you've killed before for money."

Justine's smile faded. "What are you talking about?"

"I reread the autobiography you wrote for me. You left out some things. Like the fact that you shot your first husband to death."

Amanda watched the color drain from Justine's face.

"And I didn't see anything in your bio about the one hundred thousand you cleared on his insurance or the several hundred thousand dollars you inherited when your second husband died a violent death within a year of marrying you. Didn't you think I would be interested in these little tidbits?"

"I shot Gil in self-defense," Justine said, her voice barely above a whisper, "and David's death was an accident. They have nothing to do with this."

"That isn't what Mike Greene thinks. Damn it, Justine, you can't hide something like this. I've got to be prepared. This isn't a shoplifting case. If we make one mistake, the State is going to kill you. And you can be damn sure that the DA will find out every little secret you decide to keep from me."

"I'm sorry."

"Sorry doesn't cut it. Anything you tell me is confidential. Remember me saying that? I don't care how bad it is, you tell me. No one else gets to know, but I've got to know if I'm going to save your life. Okay?"

Justine didn't answer. She just stared past Amanda, who let her collect herself.

"How did they find out?" Justine finally asked.

"The same way Herb Cross did when my father was representing Vincent."

Justine's head snapped up. "Your father had me investigated?"

"Dr. Cardoni told my father that you killed the victims in Milton County. We followed up on the accusation."

"How can you represent me if you think I framed Vincent?" Justine asked angrily.

"I don't think that, and neither does my father. He never believed Cardoni. He was just doing his job."

"Can the DA bring up Gil's and David's deaths?"

"He'll sure as hell try."

"Will it be in the papers?"

"Of course. Even if we keep the evidence from the jury, the legal arguments will be in open court."

Justine squirmed in her chair and her shoulders hunched.

"This is no good," she said, more to herself than Amanda. Then she looked across at her attorney. "You can't let them do this," she pleaded. "No one knows about my past here."

"The DA does. He knows that you insured Gil Manning for a hundred thousand dollars less than a year before you shot him."

"That was for the baby," Justine said desperately. "When we got married, Gil was working construction. He wasn't making enough for us to have our own place. I had to think about how I'd take care of our baby if something happened to him."

"You didn't cancel the policy after your miscarriage," Amanda said softly.

Justine looked stunned.

"After my baby . . . After he . . . I . . . I wasn't thinking very clearly for some time after that happened."

"Alex DeVore interviewed Gil's parents. They believe you murdered Gil."

Anger restored color to Justine's cheeks. She glared at Amanda.

"Do you know why Gil thought it was okay to use me as his private punching bag? He watched his father use his mother that way. Living in that house was like living in hell. Gil and his father were both abusive drunks, and the drinking got worse when high school ended. All of a sudden Gil wasn't a god, and neither one of them could take that. Then I lost my figure when I got pregnant, and Gil wasn't married to the most desirable girl in Carrington anymore. I became an inconvenience, except when Gil needed someone to blame for his problems."

"Why didn't you leave when he started to beat you?"

"Where could I go? My parents wouldn't look at me after Gil knocked me up. I had no money."

"Gil's parents say you drove him to drink and tormented him until he lost his self-control."

"Of course they say that."

"There's an interview with David Barkley's parents in which they accuse you of setting him up."

"That's not true. I loved David."

"They say they warned David that you were after his money. They also say that David didn't drink."

"His parents didn't know the first thing about him. The autopsy showed that David's blood alcohol was point-two-oh. He hated them, and he drank because of the pressure they put on him. I loved David, but he was an alcoholic. I thought I could change him, but I couldn't and he died."

"The neighbors say you and David quarreled the night he died."

Justine looked down at the tabletop.

"He was drinking too much," she said softly. "We had words, and he stormed out and drove away. I couldn't stop him."

"You inherited David's trust fund and the proceeds of another life insurance policy when he was killed."

Justine looked directly into Amanda's eyes when she said, "Yes, I did."

"And there was another policy on Dr. Cardoni."

"Which the insurance company refuses to pay."

"Nevertheless, you see how this looks."

"No, Amanda, I see how the district attorney wants to make it look. I'm counting on you to make a jury see the way it really is."

48

Amanda broke into a smile when the receptionist announced that a Dr. Fiori was calling on line two.

"Hi," Tony said. "I had a great time Friday."

"That makes two of us."

"I got home late from the hospital. That's why I didn't return your message sooner. I was afraid I'd wake you."

"Actually, I was probably up. I've been working on Justine's case into the wee hours. Any luck at the hospital?"

"Hey, I'm a regular Dick Tracy. Not only did I come up with a list, but I've already eliminated a few suspects."

"How?"

"I followed them."

"Don't do that!"

"I thought I'd save you some trouble." Tony sounded hurt.

"I'm serious," Amanda insisted. "It's dangerous. Fax me the list and let my investigator do the rest."

"Don't panic. I'm being very careful."

"Damn it, Tony. Promise me you'll stop."

"Okay, okay, I promise." Tony paused. "Seeing as you're pissed, is this a bad time to ask you out for this Saturday?"

Amanda laughed in spite of herself.

"You're on," she said, "but only if you behave yourself."

"Listen, I've got to run. Think of something nice for Saturday and get back to me."

"Hey, brother, you get back to me."

"Anyone as aggressive as you are can take care of dinner reservations. That'll teach you to bust my balls. And it better be a nice place."

"What ever happened to take-charge guys?"

They both laughed and said goodbye. Amanda was still beaming when Frank rapped on her door-jamb.

"There's a Cheshire cat grin," he said. "Good news, I take it?"

Amanda blushed. "It could be worse."

"Well, I've got good news of my own. Art Prochaska is willing to meet with us."

"When?"

"Now. Grab your coat."

The night that Berkeley won the PAC-10 swimming championships Amanda went carousing with her teammates. One of the bars they hit was a male strip joint. Amanda had cheered and hooted with her friends, but secretly she'd been embarrassed. She felt even more uncomfortable when she entered the Jungle Club with Frank. Onstage, a woman with unnaturally large breasts danced unenthusiastically to a blaring ZZ Top tune. Amanda averted her eyes and followed Frank past the bar to a short hall at the end of which was an office. A man with a bull neck and massive shoulders stood outside the door.

"We're here to see Mr. Prochaska," Frank told him.

"He's expecting you."

Art Prochaska was squeezed behind a desk at one end of the narrow room. He had put on weight since the motion to suppress, but he was no less intimidating. Prochaska's tailored suit gave him an air of quasi-respectability. He and Frank shook hands across the desk.

"It's been a while, Art."

"A coupla years."

"This is my daughter, Amanda." Amanda's hand disappeared in the gangster's massive paw. "You may remember her. She assisted me during the motion in Cedar City."

"Nice to meetcha," Prochaska said. Then he returned his attention to Frank. "Martin said you wanted to talk."

"And I appreciate the quick response."

"I ain't sure I can help, but I'll try. What can I do for you?"

"I'd like to know what happened at the cabin in Milton County four years ago," Amanda said.

Prochaska looked surprised that Amanda had asked a question. When he answered, he turned away from her and spoke to Frank.

"I was never there. I was playing cards that night. I had five witnesses."

Amanda wanted to disabuse Prochaska quickly of the idea that she was Frank's secretary.

"I'm sure they were wonderful witnesses, Mr. Prochaska," she said firmly, "but I was at the cabin, too, and I saw you drive away just as I arrived."

Prochaska turned his attention back to Amanda. She met his stare and held it.

"You're mistaken."

"Probably, if you have five witnesses," Amanda answered with a smile that said that she wasn't buying his bullshit. "But let's say, for the sake of argument, that I wasn't. Why would you have been at the cabin at that time of night?"

"What would it matter?"

"I'm representing Vincent Cardoni's ex-wife, Justine Castle. She's been charged with committing several murders at a farmhouse in Multnomah County. There's a makeshift operating room in the basement of the farmhouse. Other victims were found buried in a graveyard on the farm."

"So?"

"The murder scene is almost identical to the scene of the crime in Milton County."

"Why should I care?"

"It's possible that Vincent Cardoni cut off his own hand four years ago to make everyone think he'd been murdered. If Cardoni was trying to convince everyone that he was dead, it would be convenient for me to see you leaving the cabin just before I discovered his hand."

Prochaska stared at them like a gangster Buddha.

"I'm not interested in getting you in trouble, Mr. Prochaska. In fact, it's my understanding that Martin Breach would be very interested if Cardoni is alive. You should be too if Cardoni tried to set you up."

Prochaska mulled over Amanda's information.

"Anything you tell us will go no further, Art," Frank assured him.

When Prochaska spoke, he directed his remarks at Amanda.

"I was never at that cabin, understand?"

Amanda nodded.

Prochaska leaned forward and spoke so softly that it was almost impossible to hear him over the club's loud music.

"Martin did some business with a doctor at St. Francis. This doctor stiffed Martin for a lot of money, and he wanted it back. Then the doctor turned up as one of the corpses the cops found at that cabin, but the money didn't show up. Martin thought Cardoni had it."

Prochaska waited to see if Amanda was following him. When Amanda nodded, he continued.

"The night you found that hand, outa the blue Cardoni calls and says he wants a truce. He's got the dough at the cabin. Martin should send someone up. Martin sent me. As soon as I saw the hand I knew it was a setup. I got in the car and left. That's all there is to it."

"You didn't find the money?" Amanda asked.

"If Cardoni set me up, there wouldn't be no money, would there?"

Prochaska was on the phone as soon as his visitors closed the door behind them.

"Guess what, Martin? Vincent Cardoni might not be dead."

"That's why Jaffe wanted to see you?"

"He's representing Cardoni's ex-wife." He told Breach about the meeting with the Jaffes.

"Son of a bitch," Breach said when Prochaska was through. "If Cardoni's back in Portland, I want him found before the cops get him."

49

Andrew Volkov moved his cleaning cart against the wall to make way for two internists. They were deep in conversation and didn't even glance at the invisible man in the gray custodian's uniform. When they passed, Volkov moved his cart forward. As he did so, he noticed another doctor watching him from the end of the hall. He ducked his head and the doctor averted his eyes, but it was obvious that Volkov had been the object of his attention.

The physician walked toward Volkov, who turned his cart and pushed it in the opposite direction. A hall led off to the right and he entered it. Halfway down the corridor was the entrance to a stairwell that led to the basement. He left his cart next to it, waited several beats before opening the door, then pushed it wide so that it would take time to close. If the doctor was following him, the door would bait him. If he missed it swinging shut the cart would provide a clue to where he'd gone that only an idiot would miss.

Volkov moved down the stairs slowly, pausing at each landing until he heard the hall door open. He had been right. He was being followed. He waited a moment, then continued to descend the stairs, mak-

ing certain to step heavily enough so that his footsteps created echoes in the stairwell. When he
reached the basement, Volkov opened the door and
let it slam shut. In front of him was a narrow hallway
made narrower by the exposed steam pipes that were
attached to the walls. Low-wattage bulbs, spaced far
apart, kept most of the corridor in shadow. The air
was damp and cool. Volkov moved down the corridor at a steady pace until he was almost at a side hall
that led to the boiler room. He paused until he heard
the basement door open before turning into the side
passage and pressing against the wall. Volkov heard
footsteps drawing closer. They stopped at the entrance to the hallway. Then the doctor stepped
around the corner.

"Why are you following me?" Volkov asked.

The doctor's eyes widened with fright. He pulled
a scalpel out of his pocket and lunged. Volkov
blocked the thrust and lashed out with a front kick.
The doctor leaped back, and the janitor's toe only
grazed him. Volkov's body flowed forward behind
the kick. His fist caught the doctor's shoulder, slam-
ming him against the concrete wall on the other side
of the hallway. Volkov's next kick should have shattered his foe's kneecap, but he was surprised when
his attacker moved into him, nullifying its power.

Volkov felt a sharp pain in his side and realized
that he'd been stabbed. The doctor lashed out again,
and the scalpel ripped through Volkov's shirt, slicing
through skin. Volkov grunted, slashed upward with
an elbow and saw blood gush from a broken nose.
The doctor struck out blindly and stabbed Volkov in
the cheek. The janitor unleashed a kick that connected solidly, driving the doctor backward until he
lost his balance and fell to the floor.

"Andy?"

Arthur West, another janitor, was standing at the far end of the corridor.

"What's going on?" West shouted.

The doctor still held the scalpel and was struggling to his feet. Volkov hesitated. West started walking toward him. Volkov kicked the doctor again and ran toward the exit door at the end of the hallway. He tore it open and fled across the street to the employee parking lot.

50

Amanda walked from the Stockman Building toward the river for several blocks and found Vasquez waiting for her in a booth at the back of O'Brien's Clam Bar.

"What's up?" Vasquez asked

Amanda handed him the list of employees that Tony had faxed to her.

"A friend of mine is a doctor at St. Francis. I told him a little about our case. He thinks that there's a good possibility that the person who planted the scalpel, clothing and coffee mug at the farmhouse works at St. Francis, since all of the evidence came from the hospital. This is a list of men who have been hired at St. Francis during the past two years. I want you to check them out."

"I'll get right on it."

"Great."

A waitress arrived, and Amanda ordered fried clams and an iced tea. Bobby asked for a BLT and coffee.

"Now I have something for you," he said as soon as the waitress left. "I've been trying to find similar killing grounds in the United States and abroad. I

went on the Web initially and found newspaper and
periodical stories about serial murders that were like
our cases. The reporters who wrote the stories gave
me more information about each case and the names
of the detectives who worked them. Most of the cops
talked to me. They'd sent their case information to
the FBI's National Center for the Analysis of Violent
Crimes for investigation by the Investigative Support
Unit and VICAP, the Violent Criminal Apprehension
Program."

The waitress brought their drinks and Bobby continued.

"I know a former FBI agent who owes me a favor.
He talked to some friends at the Bureau and got me
more details on the domestic cases. With the international cases it was harder, but I know someone at the
Interpol office in Salem. She was able to get me information on the foreign cases."

Vasquez handed Amanda a multipage document.
"This is my preliminary list. I've found murders that
are similar to ours in Washington, Colorado, Florida,
New Jersey, Canada, Belgium, Japan, Peru, and Mexico. And it turns out that there was another case right
here in Oregon," he concluded, pointing to the syn-
opsis, which explained that fourteen years ago two
young women had been found buried in the forest
near Ghost Lake, a ski resort in the Cascades.

Something about the entry bothered Amanda, but
her cell phone rang before she could figure out what
it was. She took the phone out of her purse and answered it.

"Is something wrong?" Vasquez asked when she
hung up.

"My friend at St. Francis, the one who got me the
list, has been attacked. I have to go to the hospital."

* * *

Amanda rushed through Emergency until she found Tony slouched in a chair in an examining room. He had black-and-purple bruises under both eyes and a bandaged nose. There was dried blood on his shirt, which was open, revealing ribs wrapped with tape. Amanda stopped in the doorway, shocked by his appearance. Tony stood up when he saw her. The effort made him grimace. Amanda's eyes widened with concern.

"How badly are you hurt?"

"Don't worry. Nothing's broken that can't be fixed."

"What happened?"

"I was on my way to see a patient when I noticed a janitor named Andrew Volkov standing next to a cleaning cart. He's one of the employees on my list. Volkov saw me watching him and got flustered. I followed him into the basement, which was pretty stupid. If I had any brains, I would have realized that he was luring me downstairs. He jumped me and was beating the crap out of me when another janitor came along and scared him off."

"Is Volkov Cardoni?"

"I couldn't honestly say. The body type is right, but I was too busy defending myself to get a good look at him."

Amanda thought for a moment. Then she took out her cell phone.

"I'm going to call Sean McCarthy. He can arrest Volkov for assault and take his prints. We'll know pretty soon if he's Cardoni."

51

It had been three days since the crime lab had matched the prints on Andrew Volkov's custodian's cart to the prints taken four years before from Vincent Cardoni's left hand. Prints found in Volkov's apartment also matched the doctor's. A thorough search of Volkov's locker at the hospital and his apartment provided no clue to Cardoni's whereabouts.

Mike Greene was trying to distract himself while he waited for an update on the case by analyzing a chess game played between Judit Polgar and Viswanathan Anand in a recent tournament in Madrid. He was studying the pivotal position in the game when the phone rang. Greene swiveled his chair and picked up the receiver.

"This is Mike Greene."

"Hi, Mike. This is Roy Bishop."

Bishop was an overbearing criminal defense attorney who was strongly suspected of being a little too friendly with some of the people he represented.

"What's up, Roy?"

"I'm calling on behalf of a client, someone I know you want to talk to. He wants to meet with you."

"Who are we talking about?"

"Vincent Cardoni."

Greene sat up straight.

"If you know where Cardoni is, you better tell me. Harboring a fugitive will get your ticket yanked."

"Ease up, Mike. I've only talked to Cardoni on the phone. I have no idea where he is."

"Does he want to turn himself in?"

"Absolutely not. He made it very clear that he won't meet with you unless he gets a guarantee in writing that he will not be arrested if he shows up and that nothing he says will be used against him."

"That's impossible. The man is a mass murderer."

"He says that he's not. But even if he is, from what he tells me, you don't have grounds to hold him."

Mike Greene looked pale and drawn when Alex De-Vore and Sean McCarthy entered his office at ten the next morning.

"Vincent Cardoni will be here in half an hour," Greene announced. He sounded exhausted.

DeVore looked stunned. McCarthy said, "He's turning himself in?"

Greene shook his head. "He's coming here to talk. I had to guarantee that we would not take him into custody."

"Are you nuts?" DeVore exclaimed.

"You're joking!" McCarthy said simultaneously.

"I was here until ten last night and I was back here at seven this morning hashing this out with Jack, Henry Buchanan and Lillian Po," Greene answered, naming the district attorney for Multnomah County, his chief criminal deputy, and the head of the appellate section. "There's no way we can hold him."

"He killed four people at the farmhouse," McCarthy said.

"He changed his features and lied to get a job at St. Francis so he could steal the coffee mug, the scalpel and the clothes," DeVore argued. "He killed all those people in Milton County."

"It won't wash. Cardoni had access to the items we found at the farmhouse, but there is no way we can prove that he stole them and planted them there. There isn't a single piece of evidence connecting Cardoni to the farmhouse or any of the victims. Believe me, guys, we went round and round on this. I'm as frustrated as you are."

"What about Milton County? He's still under indictment there," McCarthy said.

Mike looked grim.

"There was a massive screwup in the Milton County case, an unbelievable screwup. The judge signed an order granting Cardoni's motion to suppress, which he filed in the clerk's office. Fred Scofield had thirty days to appeal the order if he didn't want it to become final. During the thirty days, Cardoni disappeared and his hand was found in the cabin. Everyone thought that he was dead, and Scofield forgot to file the appeal. That means that Judge Brody's order is final and no evidence seized from the cabin or Cardoni's home in Portland can be used at a trial. Without that evidence, there is no Milton County case."

"I don't believe this," McCarthy said. "You're telling me there's no way to put Cardoni in jail? He's killed at least a dozen people."

"Unless you've got proof that's admissible in court, that's just speculation. I can't arrest a man on a hunch."

"Damn it, there's got to be a way," McCarthy muttered to himself. Suddenly he brightened. "Fiori! Cardoni attacked Dr. Fiori. We can hold him for assault."

"I'm afraid not. Cardoni says Fiori was stalking him. Fiori admits he followed Cardoni into the basement with a scalpel and made the first aggressive move. Cardoni's claiming self-defense.

"Look, guys, we went through these arguments a million times. It always comes out the same way. There isn't a person in this office who doesn't believe that Vincent Cardoni is a homicidal monster, but the sad truth is that there isn't enough evidence to hold him. We've already faxed Bishop our written assurance that we won't arrest Cardoni within twenty-four hours of this meeting."

"If he knows you don't have the evidence to arrest him, why does Cardoni want to meet with you?" DeVore asked.

Before he could answer, the intercom buzzed and the receptionist announced that Dr. Cardoni and Roy Bishop were in the waiting area. Greene told her to show them to the conference room. Then he turned to DeVore.

"You can ask him yourself."

Vincent Cardoni took a seat opposite Mike Greene at the long table in the conference room. A row of stitches crossed Cardoni's cheek. Roy Bishop, a large man with styled brown hair, sat next to his client. Sean McCarthy studied the surgeon carefully. It was hard to believe that this was the man he had arrested four years before.

"Good morning, Dr. Cardoni," McCarthy said.

"I see you're still as polite as you were when you arrested me."

"Except for growing a little grayer, I haven't changed. But you certainly have."

Cardoni smiled.

"Why don't we get down to business, Roy?" Greene said. "I'm dying to know why your client wants to talk to me."

"It's a mystery to me, too, Mike. Dr. Cardoni has not confided his reasons to me."

"I hope you're planning to confess, Doctor," Greene said. "It'll save us a lot of trouble."

"There isn't a thing for me to confess. Contrary to what you believe, I never murdered anyone. Justine killed the people at the farmhouse, and she's responsible for the victims in Milton County."

"Who's responsible for cutting off your hand?" McCarthy asked.

Cardoni held up his right hand and slid down his cuff. Everyone in the room stared at the jagged scar encircling his wrist.

"I did this," Cardoni told McCarthy.

"Plastic surgery, a false identity and self-mutilation? That's pretty extreme behavior for an innocent man."

"I was desperate. I couldn't see any other way to stay alive."

"Want to explain that to us?" Greene prompted.

Cardoni looked at the DA and the two detectives.

"I can tell that you don't believe me, but I swear I'm telling the truth. Justine was Clifford Grant's partner in a black-market organ scheme. She killed him, then set me up so that Martin Breach would think I was the one who ripped him off."

Cardoni took a deep breath. He looked down at the conference table when he spoke.

"You've seen Justine. She's beautiful and brilliant, and she was always two steps ahead of me. Justine knew every one of my weaknesses.

"Look, I know I'm no saint. The pressure in medical school was too intense for me. I used all sorts of pharmaceuticals to cope with it, and they almost destroyed me. Fighting my addiction was exhausting, and it was easy to give in when Justine brought me cocaine. I didn't even realize that she was trying to break me down until it was too late.

"I also didn't know why she saw so much of Clifford Grant until Frank Jaffe told me that Grant was harvesting organs for Martin Breach. He told me about the raid at the airfield. Justine was Grant's silent partner. She framed me to make Breach think I was. Shortly after Frank got me out of jail two of Breach's men attacked me. I was able to get the better of them, and I made one of them tell me why I was attacked. This was the same day I learned that the Milton County DA was trying to reopen the motion to suppress and that there was a good chance I would have to go back to jail. I was strung out on coke, and I figured I was either going to be tortured to death by Martin Breach or end up on death row. My only way out was to convince everyone that I was dead."

"So you chopped off your hand," McCarthy said.

Cardoni fixed on McCarthy. He seemed exasperated.

"Imagine you're accused of a crime you didn't commit. The state of Oregon wants to give you a lethal injection, and a vicious criminal doesn't think that would be a violent enough death. Don't you think you might take desperate measures to save your life?"

"I've got too many real-life problems on my plate to worry about hypothetical ones, Doctor. Maybe you can give me the answer to one of them. Did you steal a coffee mug and a scalpel with Dr. Castle's fingerprints on them and plant them at the farmhouse to implicate her?"

"Haven't you been listening to what I said? She's insane. She's a mass murderer. You've got her now. I'm begging you, don't let her get away with this."

"Dr. Cardoni," Greene said, "I agreed to this meeting in the hopes that you would surrender yourself or at least admit your guilt. Instead you've told us a story that you can't support with one shred of evidence."

Cardoni's head dropped into his hands. Greene continued.

"I'll be frank with you. I don't believe a word you've said. I think you framed Dr. Castle for your own bizarre reasons and set up this meeting in the hopes that you could manipulate me into furthering your plan to send an innocent woman to death row. It's not going to work."

"If you let Justine out, she'll kill again. She is the most dangerous murderer you've ever dealt with. You've got to believe me."

"Well, I don't. Unless you want to surrender or confess, this meeting is over."

52

The guard let Justine Castle into the interview room at the jail. She looked at Amanda expectantly. Amanda waited a beat, then smiled.

"I've got great news. We're holding another release hearing this afternoon. The DA's recommending your release."

"I'll get out of here?" Justine said in disbelief.

"By tonight."

Justine sat down heavily. After a moment she reached across the small table and gripped one of Amanda's hands.

"Thank you, thank you. You have no idea what it's meant to have you as my attorney. I don't think I could have made it through this ordeal without you."

The warmth and intensity of Justine's response caught Amanda by surprise and made her heart swell with pride. She covered Justine's hands and squeezed them.

"You've been incredibly brave, Justine. I think we've turned the corner on this case. With luck, it will be behind you very soon."

Justine was about to say something else when her

features changed from relief and happiness to concern. She released Amanda's hands.

"Why are they letting me go?" Justine asked abruptly. "Have they arrested Vincent?"

Amanda stopped smiling. "No, but they've spoken to him." She related what Mike Greene had told her earlier in the day.

"They just let him walk away?" Justine asked incredulously.

"They can't prosecute him, Justine. They don't have any evidence connecting him to the murders at the farmhouse."

"What about the murders in Milton County?"

"All of the evidence from that case was suppressed."

"This is bad," Justine muttered to herself. "This is very bad."

"You'll be okay, Justine."

Justine fixed Amanda with her eyes. A pulse was throbbing in Justine's temple, and her skin was so tight from tension that Amanda could imagine it ripping.

"You don't understand the way Vincent's mind works. He's insane, he's relentless and he believes that he is infallible. No matter what the odds are against him, he'll come after me."

"He won't try anything with everyone watching."

"That's the worst part, Amanda. Vincent will bide his time before making his move. He waited four years to frame me. Now he'll disappear and wait until everyone has forgotten about him. I'll never be able to sleep, I'll never be able to lead a normal life."

Amanda wanted to comfort her client, but she knew that Justine was right. Cardoni was insane and he was patient, and that was a deadly combination.

"I have an idea," Amanda said. "Do you remember Robert Vasquez, the detective who searched the cabin in Milton County? He's a private detective now. He's been doing some work on this case for me. You might consider hiring him as a bodyguard. I could have him drive you home from the jail."

"He's responsible for Vincent being free, and you want me to hire him?"

"Justine, Bobby Vasquez has been living with his guilt for four years. He's dedicated himself to getting Vincent. This wouldn't just be a job for him. You won't be able to find anyone who would be more committed to protecting you."

Amanda was getting ready to go to the courthouse for the hearing when Vasquez returned her call. Amanda told him about Cardoni. He sounded devastated.

"Cardoni won't be able to control his impulse to kill. There'll be new victims if we don't do something."

"Look, Bobby, I hired you to help on Justine's case. Our job was to clear her, and that's been accomplished."

"Your job was to clear Justine. Mine is to get that motherfucker."

"Don't even think like that. The last time you took the law into your own hands, you blew the State's case out of the water."

Amanda paused to let what she'd said sink in.

"Bobby?"

"Yes?"

"Promise me you won't go after Cardoni on your own."

"Don't worry," Vasquez said a little too quickly. Amanda was not reassured.

"I had another reason for calling you. Justine is going to be released from jail this afternoon. She's worried that Cardoni will come after her. I think she's smart to worry, and I suggested that she hire you for protection."

"As a bodyguard?"

"Right. Will you do it? It'll keep you in the case, and she's really scared."

"With Cardoni out there, she's got a good reason to be."

53

In order to develop expertise, the judges in Multnomah County were assigned to rotations where they heard particular types of cases for set periods of time. There were three judges who handled only homicide cases for one or two years, depending on the judge's preference. Justine Castle's case had been assigned to Mary Campbell, the judge who tried the Dooling case.

At four o'clock the parties met in Judge Campbell's chambers so Mike Greene could explain why the State was willing to release Justine Castle on her own recognizance, even though she was charged with four counts of aggravated murder. Justine, Amanda and Frank were present for the defense. The Multnomah County district attorney accompanied Mike Greene.

"The grand jury had enough evidence to indict Dr. Castle," Judge Campbell said when Greene was through. "That means that you were able to establish probable cause."

"Yes, Your Honor. Our problem is that there is a very real possibility that Dr. Castle was set up by her ex-husband."

"And there was no way to hold him?"

"No, Your Honor. Not at the present time."

"This is very troubling. The idea of releasing the perpetrator of these crimes is repulsive to me, but it is equally repulsive to keep an innocent woman locked in jail." The judge stood up. "Let's go into court and put this on the record. I'm going to grant release on Dr. Castle's recognizance. Keep your statement tight, Mr. Greene, but make certain that the press understands the basis for this motion. Ms. Jaffe, you may speak if you feel the need, but I'll ask you not to use my courtroom as a pulpit. You've already won."

"Don't worry, Your Honor. I don't plan on making any statement in court."

"Very well."

Amanda preceded Justine and her father into the courtroom. Someone had leaked news of the hearing, and every seat was taken. Amanda scanned the faces and saw several that were familiar. Vasquez had found a seat near the front. Amanda nodded to him moments before spotting Art Prochaska in the last row. Seated two rows in front of him was Dr. Carleton Swindell, the hospital administrator, whom Amanda had interviewed as a possible character witness. But the person who captured and held her attention was sitting beside his attorney in the front row, directly behind the defense table. When their eyes met, Vincent Cardoni smiled coldly. Amanda stopped short.

Cardoni shifted his attention to Justine. Amanda had described Cardoni's new look to her client, but Amanda could tell that seeing it in person was a shock. She started to comfort Justine but stopped when she saw that would not be necessary. Justine returned Cardoni's stare with a look of intense hatred. Frank saw what was happening and walked between Justine and Cardoni.

"Good afternoon, Vincent," Frank said in a calm and measured tone.

"I see you're representing a less desirable class of client these days," Cardoni responded.

"I'm going to ask you to act like a gentleman. We're in a court of law, not a barroom."

"Chivalry is usually reserved for the protection of ladies." Frank's features darkened. "But I'll behave myself, out of respect for our friendship."

"Thank you."

Frank took the seat beside Amanda, directly in front of Cardoni. This put Justine as far from her ex-husband as possible. Judge Campbell entered the courtroom. As soon as the judge was seated, Mike Greene moved to have Justine's release conditions changed. He gave the judge a severely abridged version of the reasons he had outlined in chambers for the reversal of the State's position on bail. Amanda found it hard to concentrate on what Mike was saying with Cardoni so close.

Judge Campbell made her ruling swiftly and left the bench. As soon as the judge was gone Justine turned slowly and walked to the rail, her face inches from Cardoni's. Amanda had never seen a face so white with anger. When Justine spoke, her voice was barely audible, but Amanda thought she heard Justine say, "This isn't over, Vincent."

54

Reporters swarmed around Vincent Cardoni as soon as he left the courtroom. Roy Bishop cleared a path, chanting, "No comment." The reporters kept shouting questions as Cardoni descended the marble stairs to the ground-floor lobby. A Town Car was waiting in front of the courthouse. Cardoni and his lawyer ducked inside and the driver took them to the Warwick, a small luxury hotel a few blocks from the Willamette River, where Cardoni had booked a suite. He had no plans to return to the cramped basement apartment he had lived in as Andrew Volkov now that his identity had been discovered.

A mobile van from one of the TV stations followed the Town Car, but the driver phoned ahead and hotel security blocked the reporters from entering the lobby. After a brief consultation, Bishop drove off in the Town Car, and Cardoni took the elevator to his rooms. As soon as he locked the door, he stripped off his clothes and showered under steaming hot water. After the shower, he put on a terry cloth robe and ordered room service. The restaurant at the Warwick was one of Portland's best. The meal was exquisite and the wine superb, but the food and drink could not dull the rage Cardoni felt. Justine would soon be back in his old house, luxuriating in the bath the way she had when they were married. She would be washing away the smell of jail and gloating because she was free and his plan had been thwarted.

By the time room service brought him a bottle of twelve-year-old single-malt scotch and cleared his trays, the sun had fallen below the horizon. Cardoni stood at the window, watching the lights of the city glitter and gleam. The sight soothed him and helped him to put his feelings of failure behind him. Negative thoughts had to be banished. Positive thinking was required if he was going to avenge the loss of his hand and his profession, and his years in exile.

55

Bobby Vasquez was waiting when Justine Castle came out of the jail elevator. He was wearing a sports jacket, a clean blue Oxford shirt and pressed khakis. He had even shaved to make a good impression. Justine paused to study the private detective. He shifted nervously. Justine held out her hand.

"You must be Mr. Vasquez." Her grip was firm, and her hand was cool to the touch.

"Yes, ma'am," Vasquez answered, thinking that she was remarkably composed for someone who had spent several weeks in jail.

"Is your car outside?"

Vasquez nodded.

"Then get me away from here. We can talk while you drive."

Vasquez owned a ten-year-old Ford. It usually looked like a garbage dump, but he had gotten rid of the empty chip bags, old socks and other refuse before driving to the jail. Justine Castle was classier than his usual clientele. She also made him a little nervous. He had seen her confrontation with Cardoni earlier in the day.

"Do you know where I live?" Justine asked when Vasquez drove away from the jail.

"Yes, ma'am. I was at your place when we arrested Dr. Cardoni."

They rode in silence for a while. Vasquez glanced at Justine. She had closed her eyes and was savoring her first moments of freedom.

"So, Mr. Vasquez," she said after a few moments of silence, "tell me what you think of my ex-husband."

"Didn't Miss Jaffe tell you?"

"I want to hear it from you," Justine said, turning so she could observe Vasquez when he answered.

"I don't think he's human. I think he's some kind of mutant, a monster."

"I see we share the same view of Vincent."

"I can't think of many people who wouldn't think that way."

"Will he try to kill me, Mr. Vasquez?"

"I think he has to kill, and he won't stop with you," Bobby answered without hesitation.

"Will the police be able to stop him?"

"Honestly, no. He's going to disappear. Then he's going to surface someplace else. Sooner or later he'll buy another property and start his experiments again. I don't think he can stop himself. I don't think he wants to stop."

"Then what can be done to stop him?" Justine asked. There was a determined set to her jaw.

"What do you mean?" he asked, even though he was certain he knew.

"We both hate Vincent, Mr. Vasquez, and neither one of us thinks the police are capable of dealing with him. I'm certain that he'll try to kill me. If not today or tomorrow, then someday when I least expect it."

Vasquez could feel Justine's eyes boring into him.
"I do not want to live in fear."

"What are you suggesting?"

"How badly do you want to stop Vincent, Mr. Vasquez? How far would you be willing to go?"

56

Vincent Cardoni slept through the night and awoke at nine. He wanted to take a run, but he didn't want to deal with the reporters who were certain to be lurking about, so he moved some furniture and worked up a sweat with calisthenics. After his workout, Cardoni showered, then ordered a light breakfast from room service. He tried reading the newspaper but found that he couldn't concentrate. Cardoni walked to the window. A tanker was passing under the Hawthorne Bridge on the way to Swan Island against the magnificent backdrop of Mt. Hood's snowy slopes. The scene should have brought him peace, but thoughts of Justine kept intruding.

The day passed slowly. By late afternoon Cardoni was thoroughly bored and still had no plan for dealing with his ex-wife. It was soon after the room service waiter cleared his dinner that he spotted the cheap white envelope someone had slipped under his door. The envelope bore no return address. His name was typed on the front. He sat on the sofa in the sitting room and opened it. Inside were two pieces of paper. The first was a map of I-5. A rest area

several miles south of Portland was circled. "11:00 P.M."
was typed on the map.

The second sheet was a photocopy of a journal
entry.

> *Thursday: Subject is still combative after
> four days of applied pain, sleep deprivation and min-
> imal food. 8:10: Subject bound and gagged and
> placed in upstairs closet at end of hall. Turned out
> lights in house, drove off, then parked and doubled
> back. Watched from woods. 8:55: Subject exits
> house, naked and barefoot, armed with kitchen knife.
> Remarkable strength of character. Breaking her will
> be a challenge. 9:00: Subject stunned by my sudden
> appearance, attacks with knife but Taser stops her.
> Subject in shock when told that bonds had been in-
> tentionally loosened to permit escape as test to see
> how fast she would get out compared to other sub-
> jects. Subject sobs as I put on the training hood and
> handcuffs. Will begin pain resistance experiments
> immediately to test whether crushing subject's ex-
> pectation of escape has lowered her resistance.*

Cardoni checked his watch. It was eight-forty-five.
He read the journal entry one more time before going
into his bedroom. DAs and cops said that Roy Bishop
was a criminal lawyer in the truest sense of the
phrase. One advantage of retaining Bishop was the
attorney's willingness to render services that other,
less pricey lawyers were unwilling to provide. Cardoni opened a small valise that Bishop had left for
him and took out a handgun and a hunting knife.

*   *   *

Mike Greene answered his phone after the second ring.

"Hey, Sean. I hope this is good news."

"Would you consider it good news if I could prove that Vincent Cardoni phoned in the nine-one-one on the evening of Justine Castle's arrest and made the call that lured her to the farm? I was rereading the report of the first officer on the scene. There were no phones in the farmhouse, so I asked myself how Cardoni called Dr. Castle and phoned in the nine-one-one. Volkov owned a cell phone. His records show he placed calls to the emergency operator and Dr. Castle's apartment on the evening of Dr. Castle's arrest."

"Great work, Sean!"

"Do we have enough for a warrant for Cardoni's arrest?"

"Meet me at Judge Campbell's house. Let's see what she thinks."

Vasquez knew a maid who worked at the Warwick. Her boyfriend delivered room service. For fifty bucks they were willing to call Vasquez on his cell phone when the doctor left his room. For fifty bucks more one of the garage attendants at the hotel let Vasquez park in a space a few slots down from Cardoni's car. At 9:10 the maid told him that Cardoni was on the move. Vasquez ducked down in his seat and waited. Moments later the surgeon emerged from the elevator and got into his car. He was dressed in jeans, a black turtleneck and a dark windbreaker.

Vasquez had no trouble following Cardoni onto I-5 south. There wasn't much traffic, so he kept a car or two between him and his quarry. When Cardoni turned off at a rest area Vasquez followed him. Cardoni parked near the concrete rest room. The only other vehicle in the rest area was a semi hauling a load of produce. It was parked near the rest room. As he passed by, Vasquez saw that the cab of the truck was empty.

Vasquez parked at the far end of the lot and turned off his engine. Moments later the trucker walked out of the men's room and drove off. Cardoni left his car and entered the rest room. Fifteen minutes later he had not reappeared.

Vasquez got out of his car and moved through the picnic area toward the rest room, using the trees as cover. He circled behind the concrete building and paused to listen. He was about to move again when he heard the sound of someone struggling. Vasquez edged along the side of the building and chanced a quick look around the corner. Something was huddled in the shadows under a bench. It looked like a body. Vasquez was certain that it had not been there when he drove into the lot. He was debating whether to check out the body or wait in the shadows when he heard a noise behind him.

57

Amanda was working on a discovery motion when the intercom buzzed.

"Mary Ann Jager is on line one," the receptionist said.

Amanda recognized the name of the attorney who had purchased the farm.

"This is Amanda Jaffe. How can I help you?"

"I, uh, I'm not sure if I'm calling the right person." Jager sounded nervous. "You represent Justine Castle, right?"

"Yes."

"Is Robert Vasquez working for you?"

"Yes."

"He, uh, he visited my office recently and wanted to know about some property. It's the place where all those people were murdered. I read that Castle was charged with the murders and that you're her lawyer. I can't get in touch with him, so I decided to call you."

"About what?"

"There was someone else who came around asking about the property. Mr. Vasquez showed me a picture but it wasn't him. He, uh, he said there was some money in it if I could tell him who it was. Are you still interested?"

"Yes."

"I never told anyone but Mr. Vasquez about this man, not even the cops, so you'll be the only one who knows."

"Who was it?"

"Vasquez said that he would pay me for that information."

"How much did he say he'd give you?"

"Why don't you come to my office with three hundred dollars? I'm just a few blocks away."

Amanda knocked on Frank's doorjamb.

"Got a second?" she asked when Frank looked up from his work.

"Sure. What's up?"

"I just visited Mary Ann Jager, the attorney who bought the farm where the bodies in the Castle case were found. When Bobby Vasquez interviewed her, she told him that someone else had asked about the property shortly before he did. Bobby showed her an old picture of Cardoni, but she couldn't identify him. Last night she saw the man on the evening news in a story about Justine's case. When she couldn't get in touch with Vasquez, she called me."

"So who is it?"

"Cardoni."

"I thought you said—"

"The picture Vasquez showed her was taken before he had plastic surgery."

Frank's brow furrowed. "That makes no sense. Why would Cardoni expose himself to Jager if he already owned the farm?"

"He wouldn't."

"You're saying . . . ?"

"There are some loose ends in Cardoni's case that always bothered me. For instance, who made the first anonymous call to Vasquez?"

"Martin Breach. Justine." Frank shrugged. "It could have been anyone Cardoni pissed off."

"It couldn't have been Breach," Amanda said. "Why would he want Cardoni in police custody, where he could cut a deal to testify against him? Breach would be more likely to put out a contract on him."

"You're probably right," Frank answered thoughtfully. "And the caller couldn't have been Justine."

"Why?"

"She didn't know about the mountain cabin. Cardoni bought that in secret."

"The police were never able to prove that Cardoni owned the cabin. What if he didn't? What if Justine did?"

"You think Justine is responsible for the murders in Milton County?"

"That's what Cardoni always claimed."

Frank drew into himself for a moment. Then he shook his head.

"It doesn't work. Even if Justine knew about the cabin, how did she know about Martin Breach? The caller said that Cardoni bought his cocaine from Breach.

"In any event, you shouldn't be trying to prove Justine Castle is a murderer. First off, that's a job for the police. Then there's the little fact that Dr. Castle is our client. Even if you had the proof you needed, most of it, like the information you just learned from Jager, is privileged either as an attorney-client confidence or work product. Besides, you're sniffing up a false trail. I don't have any doubts that Cardoni is guilty."

"How can you be so certain?"

"You remember the coffee mug with Cardoni's prints that the police found in the cabin in Milton County?"

Amanda nodded.

"The fact that Cardoni's fingerprints were found on the mug was never made public."

"It wasn't?"

"No. The police always hold something back to weed out false confessions. I became suspicious when a coffee mug was found at the farmhouse with Justine's prints on it. The public didn't know about the coffee mug, but Cardoni did."

"How do you know?"

"I told him his prints had been found on the mug when I was representing him. Only someone who knew about the coffee mug from the Milton County case would go to the trouble of stealing Justine's mug from the hospital and planting it at the farmhouse."

"If it was planted. What if Justine brought the mug with her and drank coffee while she worked?"

Frank's smug look disappeared. "That's a chilling thought."

It dawned on Amanda that another of Frank's conclusions could be wrong as well. He had said that Justine could not have made the anonymous call to Vasquez, because the caller knew about Martin Breach and Justine did not. But Justine would know a great deal about Breach if she was Clifford Grant's partner in the black market organ scheme.

Amanda was about to explain this to her father when the intercom buzzed and the receptionist announced that Sean McCarthy was in the waiting room and needed to talk to Amanda. Frank told her to show McCarthy to his office. The detective looked paler than usual and he moved slowly.

"Good afternoon, Frank, Miss Jaffe," the detective said.

"Good afternoon, Sean," Frank answered. "You look like you can use some coffee. Can I get you some?"

"I'd appreciate it. I haven't been to bed and I'm running on fumes."

Frank buzzed his secretary and asked her to bring a cup of coffee for McCarthy while the detective settled into a chair.

"So, what brings you here?" Frank asked.

"Bobby Vasquez." McCarthy looked at Amanda. "A trucker found him in a rest area on the interstate. He's at the county hospital."

Amanda paled.

"What happened?" Frank asked.

"He was knocked unconscious. The blow to the head was pretty severe. His condition is serious."

Amanda felt dead inside. "Did Cardoni . . . Was he the one who . . . ?"

"We think so," McCarthy answered. "We went to his hotel room to talk to him. He wasn't there, but we found a map in his trash with the rest area circled and a journal excerpt that's similar to the accounts in the journal we found at the farmhouse. We also found your business card in Vasquez's wallet. I thought you might be able to tell me what Bobby was doing in the rest area."

Amanda was about to tell McCarthy that Vasquez was working as Justine's bodyguard, but she stopped herself. Why was Vasquez in the rest area when he was supposed to be guarding Justine? Had Justine sent Vasquez to kill Cardoni? Amanda had no proof that Justine had done anything wrong, and she remembered what Frank had said about her duty to her client.

"Mr. Vasquez was working with me on Dr. Castle's case, but I don't know why he was at the rest area," Amanda told the detective. "Will Bobby be okay?"

"When I left the hospital, the doctors didn't know."

Amanda felt terrible.

"Are you going to arrest Cardoni?" Frank asked.

"We're looking for him. Until we find him, you two should keep your eyes open. We have no reason to believe that Cardoni will go after you, but we're concerned for the safety of anyone connected to him."

Amanda normally dealt with stress by exercising, but she did not have the energy for a workout. Going home was out of the question, because she could not handle being alone. She hesitated a moment, then picked up the phone and called Tony Fiori at the hospital.

"How are you feeling?" she asked.

"Like Sly Stallone at the end of *Rocky*."

"Should you be working?"

"Hey, if Sly could go fifteen rounds with the champ and not quit, I can't let a couple of cracked ribs stop me. What's up?"

"Bobby Vasquez was working with me on the case. Now he's in the hospital. The police think that Cardoni did it."

"Oh, shit. How bad is he?"

"I don't know, but I feel awful."

"Do you need someone to talk to?"

"Yeah, Tony, I do."

"I get off in an hour. Why don't you drive to my place? I'll meet you there."

"That would be great."

"See you in a few hours."

Tony gave Amanda directions to the house he'd purchased when he moved back to Portland. It was in the country, south of the city, several miles east of the interstate on two acres of secluded woodland. Amanda found the curving country lane that led to it. As soon as she got out of her car Tony put his arms around her. They held each other for a moment, then Tony pulled back so he could see Amanda's face.

"You okay?" he asked.

Amanda nodded somberly. "Better now. Thanks."

Rain started to fall, and they hurried inside a modern log cabin with a huge stone fireplace and a high, peaked roof crossed by massive raw beams. No walls separated a large living room from a modern kitchen. On either side of a short hall were an office, a bathroom and the stairs to the basement. A wide stairway led to a sleeping loft that overlooked the first floor.

Logs were stacked in the fireplace, and there was a pile of old newspaper in a wicker basket next to the hearth. Tony used the paper to start a blaze. Amanda listened to the patter of the rain on the roof and the crackle of the flames. The heat from the fire soon took the chill from the room.

"Can I fix you a drink?" he asked when the fire was going. "You look like it might help."

"I don't want a drink." She sounded dragged out.

"Tell me what happened."

"Bobby Vasquez asked me if he could work on Justine's case. My father didn't trust him, but I did, so I argued with Dad until he gave in and let me hire Bobby." Amanda sounded like she had the weight of the world on her shoulders. "When Justine was released from jail I got Vasquez a job as her bodyguard. Now he's badly hurt and I . . . I don't know, it feels like my fault somehow."

Tony sat beside Amanda and took her in his arms.

"It's not, you know. Vasquez is an adult. You just told me that he wanted to work on the case."

Amanda pressed against him, feeling safe and comforted.

"I know you're right. It just doesn't make me feel any better. What if he dies?"

Tony stroked Amanda's hair and kissed her forehead. It was the right thing to do. Amanda wanted to forget Cardoni, Justine Castle and the terrible thing that had happened to Bobby Vasquez. She tilted her face up and their lips met.

"Whatever happens to him, it won't be your fault," he whispered.

That was the right thing to say. Amanda grabbed Tony and kissed him hard. He kissed back just as passionately as they sank onto the white shag rug in front of the fireplace. Tony winced. Amanda drew back, alarmed. She had forgotten Tony's injuries.

"Did I hurt you?"

"A little," he answered with a laugh. "Can you do this gently?"

Amanda placed a hand on Tony's chest. "Lie back."

Tony lowered himself onto the rug as Amanda

stripped off her clothes. Tony reached out and played with her nipples while she tried to undo the buttons on his shirt. The touch of his fingers made it hard to concentrate, and she fumbled a few times. Then she gave up altogether. Tony pulled her to his side. He stroked her thigh with a feathery touch, working his way upward until he slipped his fingers inside her. Amanda closed her eyes and lost herself in Tony's touch. His hands seemed to be everywhere at once, and each stroke made her quiver or flex. Amanda's senses were soon jumbled. Her breath came in gasps, and her body moved involuntarily. When she came the first time she squeezed Tony's fingers tight to keep them in her, straining for more. After a while her legs relaxed and Tony slipped his hand out. She opened her eyes. It took a few seconds to focus. He was watching her, still fully clothed. Her breathing was ragged. Tony smiled.

"You've got strong legs." He shook his fingers slowly. "These might be broken. I'm not sure I can finish unbuttoning my shirt."

Amanda flushed.

"Think maybe you can do the job this time?" he asked.

Amanda nodded, still too wasted to speak. Tony lay down beside her and she started undressing him. As she worked he played with her body. By the time they were both naked, she had no idea where she was.

Amanda lay in Tony's arms. She could feel the heat from the fire on her back. The rain beat a tattoo on the roof.

"Maybe it would be a good idea if you stayed here

for a while," Tony said. "I don't like the idea of you being alone with Cardoni on the loose."

"I don't think he'll go after me. Why would he?"

"Why did he go after any of the people he killed? Cardoni doesn't think logically."

Amanda remembered the way Cardoni had stared at her at the release hearing. She also remembered McCarthy's warning.

"Hey, it's not like going to prison," Tony said. "I make much better meals than they serve in the joint."

Amanda smiled. "Okay, I'm sold."

"Speaking of food, I'm starving. There's a shower upstairs and a warm-up suit in the closet that you can slip on. While you're showering I'll whip up some dinner."

It occurred to Amanda that she had not eaten for hours. Tony grabbed his jeans and shirt and limped toward the downstairs bathroom to wash up. Amanda picked up her crumpled clothes from the floor and climbed the stairs to the loft. A king-size bed sat beneath high windows. Amanda straightened her clothes as best she could and folded them over a chair. A blue warm-up suit was hanging in Tony's closet.

Amanda turned on the light in the bathroom. Tony had a large shower stall with multiple shower heads, and a Jacuzzi. Amanda set down the suit on the tiled counter next to the sink and turned on the shower. She watched the rain spatter on the skylight for a moment before stepping into the shower stall. It was chilly in the bathroom, and the cascade of hot water felt wonderful. Amanda closed her eyes, tilted her head back and let it run over her, trying to lose herself in the pulsating spray. But she couldn't. The Castle case kept intruding on her thoughts.

For all intents and purposes, her involvement in Justine's case was over. Justine was out of jail and the charges against her would soon be dismissed. She should feel triumphant, but she didn't. And the case wasn't really over. Cardoni was somewhere in the night, and Bobby Vasquez, his latest victim, was suffering in a hospital while Justine Castle lived in fear. The ending was unsatisfactory, not at all like a work of fiction where all the loose ends were tied up with a well-constructed knot.

58

In the morning Tony left for St. Francis and Amanda returned to her apartment to dress for work and pack some clothes to take to Tony's at the end of the day. Amanda called the county hospital, only to find that the doctors weren't letting Vasquez have visitors. Then she tried Justine to find out why Vasquez was following Cardoni instead of guarding her. She got the machine and left a message asking Justine to call.

Tony phoned Amanda shortly before noon and told her to come by at nine. By the time she pulled into Tony's driveway, she was ravenous. The aroma of simmering tomatoes, herbs and spices assaulted Amanda as soon as she walked through the front door. Tony was dressed in jeans and a T-shirt spotted with tomato sauce.

"Let me at the food, I'm starving," Amanda said, slipping an arm around his waist.

"You're going to have to show maturity and self-control. I just beat you home."

"Do you have any tree bark I can chew on?"

"No," Tony replied with a laugh, "but there's a loaf of olive bread sitting on the counter next to a great bottle of Chianti. If you want white, there's a bottle of Orvieto chilling in the fridge. Now, give me your bag."

Tony took Amanda's valise from her and carried it up to the loft. Amanda shucked her coat and wandered across the living room to the kitchen. A cast-iron pot filled with tomato sauce was bubbling on the stove next to a larger pot of boiling water. A fire crackled in the hearth. Amanda poured a glass of Chianti, cut a slice of bread and wandered over to the couch. She remembered curling up with Tony after dinner on their first date, four years ago. That had been a great evening, an evening she had replayed in her mind many times.

"What are you daydreaming about?" Tony asked as he came down the stairs from the loft.

"How nice it is to be with you."

Tony smiled warmly. "Me too."

A timer bell went off in the kitchen. He groaned. "Duty calls."

Ten minutes later the pasta was ready. When they were through with dinner, Amanda carried the dishes into the kitchen. Then they settled down in front of the fire.

"Tell me about Justine Castle," Amanda asked abruptly.

Tony looked surprised. "What do you want to know?"

"What's she like?"

"I don't know, really. I see her at the hospital, but we aren't intimate anymore, if that's what you're worried about."

"I'm not jealous. I just want to get a handle on her."

"And you haven't while you've been representing her?"

"She's very controlled most of the time. And she

lies, or at least she withholds information. What was she like when you were close to her?"

"You want to know what she was like when we were lovers?" Tony sounded uncomfortable. Amanda nodded, flushing slightly because she was embarrassed to pry and worried that Tony would think that she was jealous.

"I was only with Justine a few times. The sex was okay, but sometimes I wasn't sure if she knew I was there. And she was tough to talk to if we weren't talking shop. She's a brilliant surgeon, but she didn't seem to have any interests outside medicine. I don't know what else to say."

"Do you think that Justine is capable of murder?"

Tony paused and gave the question some thought.

"I guess anyone is under the right circumstances," he answered finally.

"I'm talking about something else. I'm talking about . . . Cardoni always claimed that Justine was framing him, that she killed the people at the cabin."

Tony shook his head. "I just can't see her as a serial killer."

Amanda wanted to tell Tony about the way Justine's first two husbands had died, but her duty to her client sealed her lips.

"What makes you think that Cardoni isn't responsible for the killings?" Tony asked.

"I can't tell you very much. A lot of what I know is confidential."

"Have you thought of a way to prove your suspicions?"

"Vasquez compiled a list of other serial murders with possible similar MOs. I can see if Justine lived in any of these places when the murders were committed."

"I'm not a lawyer, but don't you have a duty to Justine? She's your client. Should you be investigating her?"

"No, I shouldn't." Amanda sighed. "It's just that I feel responsible for what happened to Vasquez and that I should do something."

Tony yawned. "Well, I know what to do," he said. "We should get to bed. I'm beat and I've got to get up at the crack of dawn."

"Let me help you clean up."

"Not necessary. Why don't you use the bathroom while I load the dishwasher? It'll only take me a minute."

Amanda walked over to Tony. He took her in his arms, and she leaned her head against his shoulder.

"It's nice being here."

He kissed her forehead. "It's nice having you."

Tony patted her on the butt. "Now let me clean up before I fall asleep."

Amanda gave him a quick kiss and went upstairs to the loft. She heard the disposal run as she started to enter the bathroom. It stopped. She opened her valise and took out her makeup case. She was headed for the bathroom when her cell phone rang. It was in her purse, and it took a moment to find it.

"Hello?"

"Amanda?"

"Justine?"

Amanda heard heavy breathing on the other end.

"You have to come to my house, now. We have to talk. It's about Vincent. It's . . . it's urgent."

Justine was speaking in gasps. She sounded very upset.

"What do you—"

"Please come right away."

"Justine, I can't—"

The phone went dead. Downstairs the dishwasher started. Amanda leaned over the loft wall and yelled down to Tony.

"What is it?"

"Justine just called me on my cell phone."

Tony walked to the bottom of the stairs, a damp dishrag dangling from his hand. Amanda repeated the phone call as she descended.

"Should we call the police?" she asked when she reached the bottom.

"What would you tell them? Wouldn't she have called the cops if she was in danger?"

"She sounded so upset."

Tony thought for a moment. "Let's drive over."

He walked to a drawer in the kitchen and took out a pistol. Amanda's eyes widened.

"Do you know how to use that?"

"Oh, yeah," Tony said. "The care and use of handguns is one of the things my father taught me. He was a gun nut. I never liked shooting, but now I'm glad I know how."

Justine's Dutch Colonial looked eerie and deserted. The limbs of the barren shade trees swayed in the chill night air like skeletal hands. There were no lights on in the downstairs rooms, but two of the upstairs dormer windows glowed pale yellow like cat's eyes.

"Justine should be expecting us. Why is it dark downstairs?"

"I don't like this," Tony said as they climbed out of the car.

He rang the doorbell as Amanda glanced nervously over her shoulder and to either side. When

Justine did not answer after the second ring, Tony tried the door.

"It's locked."

The curtains on the front windows were drawn, but Amanda pointed out a small gap between the sill and the bottom of the curtain. Tony slipped through a row of boxwood hedges and squatted so that he could see into the front room. Amanda started to say something, but Tony put his finger to his lips and hurried back to her.

"Go to the car and lock yourself in," he whispered urgently. "Call nine-one-one. Justine is in there. She's tied to a chair."

"Is she—"

"Go now," he said, pushing her away from him. "Ask for an ambulance. Go!"

Tony disappeared around the side of the house. Amanda ducked behind the car and called 911 on her cell phone. The dispatcher took the information and told her that help was on the way. As soon as she hung up Amanda reached for the door handle, but she stopped when she realized that Tony had the ignition key. If she locked herself in, she would be trapped with no way to escape if Cardoni came for her.

Amanda hesitated for a moment, then followed the path that Tony had taken to the rear of Justine's house, crouching low and listening for any sound. Just as she reached the backyard Amanda heard a shot. She froze, terrified. A second, louder shot followed. Amanda edged along the side of the house until she was able to see through the windowpanes into a large, modern kitchen. Vincent Cardoni was sprawled against the wall next to the refrigerator. Tony stood over him, gun in hand. Amanda opened

the door. There was a smell of gunpowder in the air.
Tony swung the gun toward her, his eyes wide with
panic.

"It's me," Amanda yelled, thrusting her arms toward him, hands out.

"Jesus!" Tony lowered the gun. "I told you to stay
in the car."

"I called nine-one-one, but I didn't want to stay
alone."

"I could have shot you."

Amanda remembered the first shot. "Are you
okay?"

Tony nodded.

"What happened?"

"He tried to kill me," Tony said, pointing to a
head-high hole in the wall next to the back door. "He
was in the kitchen. He fired when I stepped through
the door." Tony shook his head. He looked dazed. "I
shot him."

Amanda flipped on the kitchen light and knelt beside Cardoni. There was a gun lying near his hand,
and blood was spreading across his shirt. Cardoni's
eyes were closed, and his head lolled to one side. He
was alive, but just barely. Tony took a handkerchief
out of his pocket and picked up the gun. Amanda
looked at him quizzically.

"Cardoni's prints will be on the gun. I don't want
the police thinking that I shot him in cold blood."

Amanda suddenly remembered the reason they'd
driven to the house in the middle of the night. She
took Tony's hand.

"It's okay. It was self-defense. Now we've got to
check on Justine."

Amanda pushed through the door that led to the
living room. As she groped for a light switch she

could see a figure silhouetted against the shaded window, and she could smell the rustlike scent of blood.

Amanda stopped searching for the light and crossed the room. When she drew closer, she saw that Justine's arms and legs were secured to a straight-back chair with thick strips of masking tape in a way that made the front of her naked body vulnerable to assault.

"Justine," Amanda whispered in a trembling voice.

Justine's head was down and her chin rested on her chest. A lamp sat on an end table near the chair. As Amanda switched it on she noticed a blood-smeared hunting knife resting next to the base.

Weak yellow light illuminated the room. Amanda's back was to Justine, and it took all her courage to turn around. A sob caught in Amanda's throat, and her stomach clenched. She wanted to turn away, but she'd lost control of her body and could only stare with horror at what had once been a beautiful woman.

Tony knelt beside Justine and checked for a pulse. Then he turned to Amanda with sad eyes and shook his head.

59

They waited in the kitchen for the ambulance and the patrol cars that were coming in response to Amanda's 911 call. While Tony watched Cardoni, Amanda phoned homicide. Sean McCarthy arrived soon after the ambulance and the first patrol car. While the medics were loading Cardoni onto a stretcher, McCarthy took the couple into the den where Amanda had watched the videotape of Mary Sandowski's torture four years before. The TV and VCR were still there. Amanda could not bring herself to look at them.

McCarthy could see that Amanda and Tony were emotionally drained and made arrangements to talk to them at the Justice Center. Amanda's father arrived soon after the police. Frank insisted that Amanda spend the night in her old room. He also offered to put up Tony for the night.

Amanda was in bed by three. For the first time since she was a little girl, she kept a light on. The horror of what she had seen and her guilt at suspecting Justine tormented her every time she shut her eyes. When she did drift into sleep she found herself in a pitch-black room. She tried to sit up, but her body was secured by leather restraints. As she struggled to get loose a door opened, admitting a bright, blinding light. When her eyes adjusted, Amanda saw that she was strapped to an operating table.

"Who's there?" she called, her heart beating faster.

A bare lightbulb dangled from the ceiling over Amanda's head. A face covered by a surgical mask suddenly moved between Amanda and the light. A cap covered the doctor's head. In one of his hands was a shiny scalpel, in the other a coffee mug.

"I see our patient is awake," the surgeon said. Then the mug slipped from the doctor's fingers and fell in slow motion, spilling its contents. Blood, not coffee, flew through space. The mug smashed against the concrete floor and exploded into ceramic shards. Amanda lurched up in bed, her heart pounding. It took her half an hour to fall asleep again.

Amanda was up by seven-thirty, feeling ragged and bleary-eyed but unable to get back to sleep. Through the front windows she saw a crowd of reporters massing near the curb. Frank had taken the phone off the hook and asked McCarthy to send an officer to keep the mob off his lawn.

Tony was very subdued when he came downstairs. No one had much of an appetite. Frank had put up a pot of coffee, and the couple carried their mugs onto the back porch where the reporters could not see them. The shade trees in the backyard were denuded of leaves, and the gray weather had bleached the color out of the grass and hedges. It was cold and blustery, but it was not raining.

"Couldn't sleep?" Tony asked. Amanda shook her head.

"Me either."

They were quiet for a moment.

"Whenever I closed my eyes I saw myself shooting Cardoni." Tony shook his head as if to clear it of the image. "I don't know why I feel bad. I mean, the guy was a monster and I stopped him. I should feel great, but I don't."

Amanda laid a hand on his arm.

"That's only natural, Tony. Cops who shoot criminals in the line of duty feel guilty even when they know they've done the right thing."

Tony stared straight ahead, nodding bravely.

"He would have killed again." Amanda put her hand over his. "Think of the lives you've saved."

Tony looked away.

Amanda grabbed him by the chin and forced him to look at her.

"You're a hero, do you know that? Not everyone would have gone into Justine's house knowing that Cardoni might be inside."

"Amanda, I—"

Amanda put her finger on his lips. She kissed him, then laid her head on Tony's chest.

"Amanda, you don't still think that Justine killed all those people, do you?"

"No. I feel terrible for suspecting her."

Amanda remembered what Cardoni had done to Justine. She fought back tears. After a moment, she took a deep breath and pulled away from Tony.

"We should get ready," she said, wiping her eyes. "We have to go downtown and talk to Sean McCarthy."

* * *

McCarthy had instructed Frank to park under the Justice Center in the police garage so they could avoid the media. As soon as they arrived at the homicide bureau, Alex DeVore escorted Tony into one interrogation room and McCarthy escorted Amanda into another. McCarthy was kind and his questions were gentle. Three-quarters of an hour after he started, the detective told Amanda that he was done. As he opened the door for her, Mike Greene stepped into the room.

"Can we have a minute?" Greene asked.

"Sure, I'm done. Thanks, Amanda," he said closing the door behind him.

"Am I going to need an attorney?" Amanda asked with a weary smile.

"Yeah, I'd get the Dream Team on this, right away." He smiled. "How you doin'?"

"I'm okay."

"You have no idea how horrible I felt when Sean told me what Cardoni did to Justine Castle."

"Why should you feel responsible?"

"I'm the one who decided that we didn't have enough evidence to hold that lunatic."

Amanda's weary eyes softened. "You didn't have a choice. You'd have been breaking the law if you'd done anything different."

"The worst part is that we had enough evidence to arrest Cardoni. We just couldn't find the son of a bitch."

Mike told her about the cell phone bill that proved that Cardoni had phoned in the 911 and called Justine's house on the evening of Justine's arrest.

"We were also following up on an idea Sean had four years ago but stopped pursuing after Cardoni disappeared. You know that Cardoni practiced at a hospital in Denver before he came to Portland?"

Amanda nodded.

"I just heard from the Colorado state police this morning. Two years ago they uncovered a killing ground similar to ours in a rural area about an hour outside of Denver. The bodies had been buried for some time. A Colorado lawyer, who has since been disbarred, purchased the property where the graves were found. He was contacted by an anonymous buyer through the mail and paid in cashier's checks."

"Cardoni's MO."

Mike nodded.

"I might have some extra ammo to use against Cardoni," Amanda said. "You know that Bobby Vasquez is working for me, right?"

"Sean mentioned it."

"He gave me a preliminary list of serial murders that might have the same MO as Cardoni's killings. I'll get it to you in case he found something that your investigators missed."

"Great," he answered distractedly. "Listen, about Bobby . . ."

"Have you gotten an update on his condition?"

"It's not good. The doctors don't know if he's going to make it."

Amanda's shoulders slumped. "What about Cardoni?"

Mike looked grim. "The bastard's doing fine. That's the bad news. The good news is that he'll be fit for trial soon, so I'll be able to send him to death row. I trust you won't be representing him this time."

Amanda forced a smile and shook her head.

"Am I done here? I'd love to get home and take a long, hot bath."

"You're done," Mike said, holding her chair for her as she stood. Then he took her hand and gave it an affectionate squeeze.

"If there's anything I can do, let me know," Greene said quietly with a warmth that surprised her. She looked at the DA quizzically, and he blushed.

"I enjoy butting heads with you," he said, "so take care of yourself."

60

Even with Cardoni locked in the secure wing at St. Francis, Amanda was afraid to stay by herself. But she turned Tony down when he invited her to stay at his house. Amanda never ran from something that scared her, and she wasn't going to start now.

That night, alone in her apartment, Amanda watched an old movie until her eyes grew heavy, then went to bed around one. She dreamed again about the operating room, the masked surgeon and the coffee mug filled with blood. When the mug slipped from the surgeon's fingers, a wave of blood arced through the air. Amanda jerked up in bed when the mug shattered. It was the second time she'd had that dream, and both times she had woken feeling at loose ends.

No reporters were lurking outside the offices of Jaffe, Katz, Lehane and Brindisi when Amanda arrived at eight the next morning. She had been putting off work on her other cases while she concentrated on Justine Castle. Before she could get to them she had to put Justine's files in order. It was while she was performing this chore that Amanda spotted Bobby Vasquez's list of possible killing grounds. She remembered her promise to send it to Mike Greene. As she scanned the list her eye lit on the Ghost Lake, Oregon, entry. Something about Ghost Lake tickled her memory again, but she was interrupted before she could give it much thought.

"There's a call for you on line three," the receptionist told her.

"Who is it?"

"He says he's Vincent Cardoni," the receptionist answered nervously. "He asked for Mr. Jaffe. When I told him he was out of town, he insisted on speaking to you."

Amanda hesitated. It would be easy to have the receptionist tell Cardoni that she would not take the call, but her curiosity got the better of her.

"Why are you calling this firm, Dr. Cardoni?" Amanda demanded as soon as she picked up the receiver. "Roy Bishop is your attorney."

"Bishop has no credibility with the district attorney or the police."

"That may be, but we are no longer your lawyers."

"I paid your father a lot of money to represent me. He's still under retainer."

"You can discuss that with him when he comes back to Portland at the end of the week. As far as I'm concerned, our professional relationship ended when you murdered my client."

"But I didn't. Please come to St. Francis. I have to talk to you."

"You must be insane to think that I would come anywhere near you after what you did to Justine."

"You have to come." Cardoni's voice was raw and needy.

"The last time I agreed to meet with you, it didn't turn out so well. I think I'll pass."

"This is more important than you know," Cardoni pleaded. "You're in danger, and you're the only person who knows enough to understand."

Amanda hesitated. She had no interest in meeting Cardoni. The idea of being in the same room with him scared the hell out of her. But he sounded so disturbed and unsure of himself.

"Listen carefully, Dr. Cardoni. You think we still have an attorney-client relationship, but we don't. If you say anything incriminating, I'll walk straight from your hospital room to police headquarters and tell them every word you told me."

"I'll take that chance."

Amanda was surprised by the response. "Let me make myself clear, Doctor. I would like nothing better than to be the one who gives you your lethal injection."

"I said I'll take that chance."

Amanda thought for a moment. She could hear Cardoni's ragged breathing on the other end of the line.

"I will talk to you on one condition. I am going to bring a release with me. Once you sign it, the attorney-client privilege will no longer apply and I'll be free to tell the police anything you tell me. I'll also be free to testify against you in court. Will you sign the release?"

"Yes, I will."

A massive steel door separated the secured ward at St. Francis from a small entry area opposite the elevator. An orderly manned a desk in front of the door. He inspected Amanda's ID and briefcase, then pressed a button. Another orderly studied Amanda through a window made of bulletproof glass that was centered in the top half of the door. When he was satisfied, he let Amanda into the ward, relocked the door and escorted her to Cardoni's room. A policeman was sitting outside. He stood up when he heard footsteps tapping down the narrow hallway. Amanda handed her bar card and driver's license to the policeman.

"I'm Dr. Cardoni's attorney."

"Can you please open your briefcase?"

Amanda complied, and he thumbed through her paperwork and inspected all of the compartments.

"You'll have to leave the briefcase out here. You can bring in your papers and a pen, but don't give the pen to Dr. Cardoni."

"I have a paper he has to sign."

"Okay. I'll come in with you. He can sign in my presence."

Cardoni was dressed in a hospital gown and propped up on a hospital bed with his head slightly elevated. His arms were lying on top of his blanket, and Amanda saw the jagged scar that circled the surgeon's arm just above his right wrist. Cardoni's eyes followed Amanda as she crossed the room. She moved a chair near the bed but was careful to stay far enough away so he could not reach her. The policeman positioned himself at the end of the bed. Cardoni glanced at him.

"You don't need a bodyguard," he said quietly. "I'm not going to hurt you."

Cardoni looked tired and subdued. The bravado she had so often noticed was not present.

"The policeman will leave as soon as you sign the release."

Cardoni held out his hand, and Amanda gave him

the document and a pen. He read it quickly, signed and returned the pen.

"I'll be watching through the window," the officer assured Amanda before leaving the room. Amanda sat stiffly, feeling very uncomfortable in the doctor's presence.

"Thank you for coming," Cardoni said as soon as the lock clicked into place.

"What did you want to tell me?"

Cardoni closed his eyes and rested for a moment. He seemed weak and exhausted. "I was wrong about Justine."

"Clever move, Doctor. Who are you going to blame for your crimes now?"

"I know I'm fighting an uphill battle trying to convince you that I'm innocent, but please hear me out. Four years ago, after Justine buried me at my bail hearing, I was certain that she had framed me. And after I did this," Cardoni said, pointing at his scarred wrist, "all I could think about was revenge for my hand, the time I'd spent in jail and the destruction of the life I'd built. I wanted her to suffer the way I was suffering."

Cardoni held his wrist out. "Do you have any idea what it's like to saw off your own hand, to lose a part of yourself? Can you imagine what it would be like for a surgeon whose life is his hands? And the new hand." Cardoni laughed bitterly. "Picking up a glass was like climbing Everest. Holding a pen, writing; my God, the hours I spent trying to master that simple task."

He paused and rubbed his eyes. "And, of course, there were the victims. I believed that Justine would continue to kill and that no one would try to stop her because everyone thought that I was guilty.

"I returned to Portland and took a job at St. Francis so I could keep an eye on Justine. I was certain that she had a new killing ground. It took me almost a year to find it. I spent hours looking at records, visiting properties that fit the profile, talking to attorneys until I discovered Mary Ann Jager on the Thursday before Justine was arrested. That night I went to the farm and found that poor bastard in the basement. He was already dead."

Cardoni closed his eyes again and took a deep, rasping breath before continuing. He looked as though he were trying to banish a bad dream.

"I went back to the hospital and took the coffee mug. I already had a surgical cap with some of Justine's hair and a scalpel with her prints. I'd been saving them.

"After planting everything at the farmhouse, I parked down the street from Justine's house and phoned her from my cell phone. She left and I followed. When I saw her make the turn from the highway onto the road that led to the farm, I called in the nine-one-one. I hoped that the police would find her at the farm. If she got away before they arrived, her prints would be on the items I left and everything she touched when she was there. An anonymous tip would lead the police to her."

Cardoni paused again. He looked depressed.

"When I found the victim in the basement, I studied him so I could write a journal entry detailing what I was certain she had done to him. I learned the writing style when I read the journal in the farmhouse bedroom. As soon as I was sure that Justine was going to the farm, I wrote the journal entry on the computer in her house and left a copy."

Cardoni rubbed his eyes and sighed.

"I was so certain that I was doing the right thing. I was so certain that Justine had framed me and killed all of those people. Seeing that man in the basement . . . I was so certain . . ."

Cardoni's voice trailed off.

"Everything was going exactly the way I planned it until Tony Fiori blew my cover. I knew the police would release Justine as soon as they realized that I was alive. I was desperate, so I had Roy Bishop set up that meeting with Mike Greene to try to convince him that Justine was guilty."

"It didn't work."

"No, it didn't, but something did happen. I received instructions to come to a rest area off the interstate. A diary excerpt was enclosed. It was an account of the torture of one of the victims. Only the killer would have that journal. So I went to the rest area early to lay a trap, but I outsmarted myself. The killer was there ahead of me, and I was hit with a tranquilizer dart."

Amanda held up her hand as though she were stopping traffic.

"Please. If you're going to tell me that Bobby Vasquez is the killer, I'll walk out right now."

"No, no. I didn't even know that he had followed me to the rest area until McCarthy questioned me after Justine's murder."

"So who is it now? The butler?"

Cardoni answered her sarcasm with a murderous glare. Then his anger faded and he looked defeated. Amanda folded her arms across her chest but stayed seated.

"The first time I woke up after being tranquilized I was in total darkness and disoriented. I'm not even certain that this really happened. I thought I saw light and I think that someone gave me a shot, then I was out again.

"The next time I came to I was in Justine's kitchen. I remember Fiori shooting me. The next thing I remember, I was in the hospital."

Amanda stood up. "This has been a very interesting story, Dr. Cardoni. I suggest you try selling it to Hollywood. Perhaps you can start a writing career while you're on death row."

"I have proof. Have them test my blood. The hospital draws blood before an operation. Have the hospital run a screen for tranquilizers. I was still heavily sedated when Fiori shot me."

"You can have your attorney do that. My firm doesn't represent you anymore."

Amanda pressed a button next to the door.

"I know who killed Justine," Cardoni shouted at her. "It's your boyfriend, Tony Fiori."

Amanda burst out laughing. "If I were you, I'd go with the butler. It's a hell of a lot more believable."

"He tried to kill me at the hospital," Cardoni cried out desperately. "Then he shot me at Justine's house. I was on the floor when he came through the door. I was barely conscious. Why would he shoot someone who was no threat to him? I think he needed me dead to stop the investigation. I think he was afraid that the police would figure out that I'm innocent if they kept looking into these murders."

Amanda turned to face Cardoni. The fear she'd felt was long gone, replaced by a cold hatred.

"He shot you because you tried to kill him, Dr. Cardoni. I saw your gun."

"I never fired a shot. I swear."

Amanda banged on the door and the guard opened it immediately. She turned back to face Cardoni.

"I was with Tony when Justine called from her house and asked me to come over. She was alive then, but she was dead when Tony and I arrived. You were the only other person at the house. You tried to kill Tony and you murdered Justine."

"Miss Jaffe, please," Cardoni pleaded. But Amanda was already out the door.

61

Amanda was furious with herself for visiting Cardoni and furious with the surgeon for thinking so little of her that he would try to fool her with his ridiculous story. During the return trip to the Stockman Building, she thought about things Cardoni had said that would help nail him. He'd confessed to planting the mug, scalpel and surgical cap at the farmhouse. This tied him to the scene of four murders, but it didn't prove that he'd killed anybody. Amanda wanted something more. Justine's death demanded it.

It was while she was parking that Amanda remembered the Ghost Lake murders that Bobby Vasquez had included on his list. Back at her desk, she ran an Internet search. She found several stories about Betty Francis, a senior at Sunset High School, who had disappeared seventeen years before during a winter break ski trip, and Nancy Hamada, a sophomore at Oregon State, who had disappeared the next year, also while skiing at the Ghost Lake resort during winter break. Their bodies had been discovered fourteen years ago when a cross-country skier stumbled across them.

Amanda phoned the sheriff's department in Ghost

Lake. No one in the department had been with the sheriff's office fourteen years earlier, but the secretary, who had grown up in Ghost Lake, remembered that Sally and Tom Findlay's boy, Jeff, had been a deputy when the bodies were discovered. Amanda called the Findlays and learned that their son was working in Portland.

Zimmer Scrap and Iron was an ugly stretch of chain-link fence, piles of twisted and rusting chunks of iron and herds of monster cranes that spread along the shores of the Willamette River. Just after four-thirty Amanda parked her car in front of the corporate headquarters, a three-story brick building surrounded by chaos and ruin. Amanda asked the receptionist if Jeff Findlay was in. Moments later a tall, square-jawed man with sandy hair walked into the waiting area. His pale blue eyes fixed on Amanda, and he flashed her a confused smile.

"What did you want to see me about, Miss Jaffe?"

"Two murders you helped investigate at Ghost Lake fourteen years ago. You were a deputy with the county sheriff's office at the time."

Findlay stopped smiling. "What's your interest in those cases?"

"They may be connected to a larger series of murders that were committed over the past four years."

"Let's go inside."

Amanda followed Findlay to a small, unoccupied office.

"I can see you remember the case," Amanda said.

"That was the worst thing I've ever seen. Two months after the girls were dug up I quit law enforcement for good. I enrolled in an accounting program at a community college, then finished up at Portland State. I think I was trying to find a profession that would keep me as far away from dead bodies as I could get."

"If Betty Francis and Nancy Hamada looked anything like the victims I've seen, I don't blame you."

Amanda told Findlay about the Cardoni and Castle cases.

"We've always thought that the killings in Milton and Multnomah Counties weren't Cardoni's first," Amanda concluded. "We were hoping to find an earlier murder that we could connect to him."

"And you think this is it?"

"It might be."

"Cardoni's name never came up in our investigation," Findlay said.

"Where were the bodies found?" Amanda asked.

"In separate graves in the forest that borders the ski resort."

"Who owned that land?"

"Ghost Lake Resort."

"Cardoni's practice has been to buy property in a remote area and bury the bodies near the house where he tortures his victims. Was there private property near the burial site?"

Findlay shook his head. "No, there . . . Oh, wait. There was a cabin a couple of miles away. Funny thing is, there was a double murder at the cabin a year before we found the bodies. We looked hard for a connection, but the only one we could find was that all four murders were during winter break."

"Did the double murder at the cabin involve torture?"

"Not that we could tell. The cabin was torched and the bodies were badly burned. If I remember, the medical examiner concluded that the man had been bludgeoned."

Amanda frowned. There was something very familiar about this case.

"Who were the victims?" she asked.

"One was a young woman. She'd gone up to the ski resort with her boyfriend and disappeared. Or at least that's what the boyfriend said. They were having problems. We interviewed several witnesses who heard loud arguments on the evening the woman disappeared.

"The popular theory was that she'd been upset with her boyfriend, met the guy who owned the cabin and gone off with him. The boyfriend finds out, goes to the cabin, kills them and burns the place down. Trouble was, we never had any evidence to support the theory, so no one was ever arrested."

A thought flickered through Amanda's mind, but she could not hold on to it.

"Do you remember the names of the victims?"

"No, but I seem to remember that the man was a lot older than the woman. I think he was an attorney with a Portland firm."

The blood drained from Amanda's face.

"Are you okay?" Findlay asked, concerned by Amanda's ash gray coloring.

Amanda did not answer. It dawned on her suddenly that she knew the name of the attorney who died at Ghost Lake, and, just as quickly, she understood the significance of her dream about the blood-filled coffee mug.

The meeting with Jeff Findlay had taken half an hour, and it took another hour before Amanda was sufficiently composed to return to the office. Frank was still working at six o'clock when she knocked on his doorjamb.

"Hey, princess."

"What're you working on?" Amanda asked, to see if she was in control of her voice.

Frank leaned back and folded his hands across his stomach.

"You know that drug bust in Union County?"

Amanda nodded.

"We've picked up one of the defendants."

Amanda forced a smile and sat down across from her father. Outside, the lights of downtown Portland shone bright, but storm clouds covered the moon.

"Thank God for the rising crime rate, huh?"

"It does help pay the rent," Frank said. "How come you're here after quitting time?"

"I wanted to ask you something."

"Shoot."

"Remember the night I picked you up at the airport? The day after I found Cardoni's hand?"

Frank laughed. "How could I forget? It's not every day a father gets a call from his daughter informing him that she's discovered the amputated limb of a psychopath."

"I guess it was a memorable occasion. Anyway, on the ride back I told you about finding Tony with Justine Castle and you said that Tony might not be the best person to get serious with. What made you say that?"

"Why do you want to know?"

"Tony and I, we've gotten pretty close since he returned from New York."

Frank's eyebrows went up.

"When you said that about Tony, four years ago,

he was leaving Oregon and I didn't see any reason to press you. But now . . . I mean, is there some reason you don't like him?"

"No, I guess I just didn't like him hurting my little girl." Frank smiled ruefully. "You know, it doesn't matter whether that little girl is five or twenty-five when you're her father." Frank paused. "So, how serious is this?"

Amanda forced a smile and shrugged. "I don't know, Dad. But there was nothing specific, right?"

Frank hesitated. Then he sat up straight.

"You know that Dominic, Tony's father, was one of my original law partners?"

Amanda nodded.

"Dom was in my study group in law school. So was Ernie Katz. We called ourselves the Three Musketeers because we were all young guys with families who were working our way through night school.

"Dom was the life of the party, the hardest drinker, the one who always wanted to go for a beer. I never understood how he could always be on the go without collapsing, but you do that sort of thing when you're young and never think about it. Nowadays they have names for Dom's problem: bipolar disorder, manic-depression. We just thought of Dom as an iron man, and we rarely saw him when he was down.

"Once we formed our partnership it became obvious that Dom had problems. His wife left him and Tony when Tony was in high school. There were rumors that he was abusive to both of them. Tony was pretty wild by then. I helped him out of two scrapes in high school, and I was able to keep his record clean. When he went to Colgate I hoped that being away from Dom would help him get his life together.

"Dom was very smart and he was a good lawyer when his motor was going, but he was arrogant and lazy. He was also a heavy drinker and a womanizer. He cost us two good secretaries before we caught on. You were a sophomore in high school when Ernie and I asked Dom to leave the firm. It was a bad scene.

"Two days later a detective came to the office. It was winter break and we were supposed to go skiing, but I had to call off the trip, remember?"

Amanda nodded.

"Dom had a cabin in the mountains—"

"Near Ghost Lake, wasn't it?"

Frank nodded, and Amanda felt sick.

"The detective told us that it had burned to the ground. Dom and a young woman were inside when the fire started. The police determined that it was arson."

"Where was Tony?" Amanda asked, using every ounce of will to keep her tone casual.

"He was in Mexico for winter break. I'm the one who had to phone him and tell him that his father was dead." Frank shook his head sadly as he remembered the call.

"So you talked to him, you spoke to him?"

"Not right away. If I remember, I left a message at his hotel asking him to call. I think he got in touch a day or so later. Then he flew home."

"What does his father's murder or his problems have to do with you not liking Tony? You can't blame him for his father's sins."

Frank thought for a moment before replying.

"What Tony's done, becoming a doctor, is admirable, but growing up the way he did can affect a young man; it leaves scars. Sometimes they're permanent and they prevent a man from ever figuring out how to relate to a woman. Tony's father was a drunk and a womanizer, and he was physically abusive. That's the lesson he taught Tony. When you told me he was dating you and seeing another woman at the same time, it made me think of the way Dom treated women."

Amanda stood up. It was all she could do to keep her legs from shaking.

"Thanks, Dad. I've got to go now."

"Sure. I hope I didn't upset you."

"No, I'm fine."

Amanda flashed a smile and hoped it masked her fear. Then she turned and left the office, fighting hard to keep from running.

62

The orderly on duty outside the secured ward looked up when two men wearing white coats over casual clothes got out of the elevator. Dimitri Novikov and Igor Timoshenko were arguing about this year's prospects for the Seattle Mariners. They both carried cups of coffee. Timoshenko had a stethoscope around his neck. The guard relaxed. That's when Novikov pressed his silenced pistol against the guard's temple.

"Please ring for your friend who is inside," Dimitri asked politely in barely accented English. "I will be lowering my pistol as soon as you do, but my companion is also armed and he will kill you if there is any trouble."

As soon as the guard pressed the button, the weapon disappeared. A moment later a face pressed against the bulletproof glass in the door to the ward.

"We're here to examine Dr. Cardoni," Novikov said into the intercom next to the door. Then he turned to Timoshenko and continued to press his position that the Mariners had no chance of winning their division.

"Their relievers are pathetic," he said emphatically.

He was midway through listing the earned-run averages of the team's relief pitchers when the door opened. He stopped arguing long enough to press his gun against the orderly's stomach.

"One word and I will kill you. Lead us to Dr. Cardoni's room."

The orderly's eyes widened. He turned without speaking and started down the corridor. He was so frightened that the *pfft* made by Timoshenko's silenced pistol did not register. Timoshenko closed the door to the ward, locked it and followed Novikov and the orderly. On the other side of the door, blood from a fatal head wound spread over the surface of the guard's desk.

Timoshenko and Novikov were Russians who lived in Seattle. Martin Breach had used their talents before for special jobs. The previous evening they had met Art Prochaska in a video arcade in Vancouver, Washington. Prochaska had paid them $25,000 and promised another $25,000 if they delivered Vincent Cardoni to Breach alive and relatively unharmed. He had given the Russians a floor plan of the hospital and a detailed diagram of the secured ward. An elevator inside the ward was used to move prisoners. An ambulance driven by another Russian was parked outside a ground-floor door of the hospital. All Novikov and Timoshenko had to do was gain access to Cardoni's room, sedate him and take him down the elevator. Breach did not care how they accomplished their task as long as they delivered their package.

The policeman who was sitting outside Cardoni's room was surprised to see two doctors following the orderly down the corridor. He knew the schedule by heart, and no one was supposed to be examining the prisoner at two o'clock in the morning. The officer stood and took one step forward before Timoshenko shot him in the forehead. Blood from the exit wound splattered across the window in the door to Cardoni's room. The orderly made a half turn, but he was dead before he could complete it. It was always best to leave no witnesses.

Novikov took the orderly's keys and opened the door. He put his pistol in the pocket of his white coat and withdrew a syringe. The room was dark, but Novikov could make out a large shape under a blanket and sheet. He moved quietly, not wanting to wake Cardoni. Prochaska had made it clear that there would be no more money if Cardoni was killed or badly injured, and Novikov did not want to have to explain failure to Martin Breach.

Cardoni's blanket covered him from head to toe. Novikov was standing over the bed before he could make out the top of the surgeon's head in the darkened room. The Russian pulled the covers back slowly. He was leaning down to inject Cardoni when the surgeon plunged a bedspring through Novikov's ear and into his brain. It was the same bedspring he had broken off from the underside of his bed and spent hours straightening and sharpening in the dark while planning his escape. The hypodermic fell to the floor and shattered. Cardoni propped up the Russian, who twitched for a moment before becoming limp.

Timoshenko glanced down the hall, then looked through the window to see how his partner was doing. Novikov's body was bent forward, shielding Cardoni from Timoshenko, whose view was partially obscured by the blood that had spattered across the window in the steel door. Cardoni slid out from under his attacker and lowered Novikov's body onto the bed. He found the Russian's weapon while Timoshenko was figuring out that something unplanned had occurred in the darkened room. Cardoni shot the Russian while he was charging through the door.

When Cardoni was certain that his assailants were dead, the surgeon stripped Novikov, who was closest to his size and whose clothes were unstained by blood. In a few minutes Cardoni was dressed in street clothes covered by a doctor's white coat. A stethoscope was draped around his neck. He took the elevator to the ground floor and walked out of St. Francis Medical Center.

Sean McCarthy's call awakened Mike Greene from a deep sleep at five-thirty. He had been bleary-eyed when he picked up the receiver, but the news of Cardoni's escape acted like a double shot of espresso. Greene was so distracted that he recalled little of the drive through the darkened streets of Portland. The first thing that did make an impression was the large bloodstain that covered the desk outside the secured ward. He shivered involuntarily as he walked through the law enforcement personnel who jammed the corridor outside Cardoni's room.

Sean McCarthy was talking to a fingerprint expert. A policeman and a man in an orderly's clothes lay on the green linoleum floor in pools of blood a few feet from the detective. Greene smelled the dead men before he saw them. He looked up so that the bodies were only in his peripheral vision.

As soon as he spotted the deputy district attorney, McCarthy walked to meet him.

"Let's get out of here," McCarthy said. "I need some coffee."

"How did he get away?" Greene asked as soon as they were in the elevator.

"We're not sure yet. We found five bodies. We've identified three of them: the orderly who mans the desk in front of the elevator and the policeman and orderly who were found outside Cardoni's room. Here's where it gets weird. There are two dead men in Cardoni's room. One man was shot as he came through the door. He was dressed like a doctor, but he was holding a pistol with a silencer. The techs think it's the weapon that was used to kill the cop and the two orderlies.

"The second man was killed with a sharpened bedspring. Cardoni worked it off the bottom of his bed. The second man is only wearing underwear, and we found Cardoni's hospital gown on the floor. We assume Cardoni's wearing the dead man's clothing."

"Was the guy a doctor?"

"We don't know, but no doctors were scheduled to visit Cardoni and no one from St. Francis has been able to identify either man."

The elevator doors opened. McCarthy bought two coffees from a vending machine while Greene took a table in the deserted cafeteria.

"One interesting thing," McCarthy told the DA after taking a sip from his cup. "Cardoni had a visitor yesterday afternoon, Amanda Jaffe."

"What was she doing with Cardoni?"

"Her firm represented him when he was charged in Milton County. Maybe he wants her to continue the representation."

"There's no way the Jaffes could do that," Mike said. "She's a witness, and he murdered one of the

firm's clients. There's a clear conflict. Have you
talked to her?"

"I phoned her apartment, but her answering machine was on."

"Have someone go there. It's a long shot, but Cardoni may have said something to Amanda that will
give us a clue to where he's gone."

Before McCarthy could answer, McCarthy's partner, Alex DeVore, walked into the cafeteria.

"We've got an ID on the two men in Cardoni's
room," he said. "Dimitri Novikov and Igor Timoshenko, Russian Mafia from Seattle."

"What were they doing down here?" McCarthy
asked.

"Remember the Colombians who tried to move in
on Martin Breach two years ago?"

"I still have trouble eating when I think about the
crime scene," Greene answered.

"The word is that Novikov was in on that."

"So you think Breach brought in out-of-town talent to do Cardoni?"

"Breach never forgives and he never forgets," Mc-
Carthy answered.

Mike Greene's pager started to beep. He took a
look at the number on the screen, then pulled out a
cell phone and dialed immediately.

"Amanda? It's Mike."

"We've got to talk."

She sounded upset, almost near tears.

"I can't right now. I'm at St. Francis. Cardoni's escaped."

"What! How?"

"We're not really certain."

"We still have to talk. Please. What I have to say
may be more important than the escape."

"I find that hard to believe."

"There's a possibility that Vincent Cardoni is innocent."

"Come on, Amanda. Cardoni murdered Justine
Castle almost under your nose. We've got five dead
men here. The man is a homicidal maniac."

"Listen to me closely, Mike. Before a patient has
surgery the hospital draws a blood sample. You have
to find out if there was any trace of sedatives, anesthetic or tranquilizers in Cardoni's sample. If his
blood wasn't tested for those substances, I want you
to run one and tell me the results. If the test results are
what I think they'll be, you'll change your opinion."

63

Sean McCarthy and Alex DeVore followed Mike Greene into the conference room at the district attorney's office. Greene stared at Amanda Jaffe. Her shoulders slumped and her complexion was ashen.

"What the hell happened to you?" Greene asked as he took a seat next to her. When Amanda answered, he had to strain to hear her.

"We've all been fools." Her voice caught, and she paused to collect herself. Mike thought that she might begin to cry. "Cardoni is innocent. So was Justine."

"It's going to take a lot to convince me of that."

Amanda took a deep breath, as if the mere act of speaking had wasted her. She sipped from a glass of water.

"Fifteen years ago a member of my father's law firm drove to a cabin he owned near the Ghost Lake ski resort. A few days later my father learned that he had died in an arson fire. The body of a young woman was also found in the cabin."

"What does this have to do with Cardoni?"

"Nothing. The lawyer's name was Dominic Fiori. He was Tony's father. The following year, the bodies of two young women were found in shallow graves a mile or so from the Fiori cabin. One had been reported missing the year before the arson during winter break. The other was reported missing two years before, also during winter break."

Amanda paused. She ran her hand hard back and forth across her forehead and fought to regain control of her emotions.

"Are you okay?" Mike asked, concerned by Amanda's obvious distress.

"No, Mike. I feel sick. I can't . . ."

Greene cast a quick glance at McCarthy, who looked equally concerned.

Amanda gathered herself. When she spoke, Greene was certain he'd misunderstood her.

"What did you say?"

"I said the women at Ghost Lake were Tony Fiori's first victims." Amanda's voice broke as tears flooded her eyes. "He killed them, Mike. He killed them all."

"How is that possible, Amanda? Tony was with you when Justine called you for help. The medical examiner said that Justine died within an hour of your arrival at her house. You told Sean that you were with Fiori for two hours before Justine called."

Amanda wiped her eyes. When she spoke, her voice was devoid of emotion.

"When I visited him at the hospital, Cardoni told me that he was knocked out with a tranquilizer dart at the rest area. I think Tony kept him a prisoner somewhere, then brought Cardoni to Justine's house before I came over to Tony's house on the night Justine died."

"But what about the phone call?" Mike asked. "How could Tony kill Justine? He was never out of your sight."

"That's not true. I didn't see Tony while I was

making the nine-one-one call at Justine's house. I've given this a lot of thought. What if Tony tortured Justine earlier in the afternoon and forced her to make a tape? He could have left Cardoni sedated in Justine's kitchen and Justine sedated and tied to the chair in the living room. I took Justine's call in the loft on my cell phone. Tony could have played the tape over his phone in his kitchen. I couldn't see Tony when I spoke to Justine. None of her statements was responsive to anything I said. The call was short. She said my name, then she told me to come over and she hung up."

"I don't know, " Greene said. "That's quite a stretch."

Amanda sat up straight in her chair and her features hardened.

"Cardoni had traces of heavy-duty tranquilizers in his blood. That's what you told me. Why would he tranquilize himself?"

Greene didn't answer.

"After Tony told me that Justine was tied up in the living room, he told me to stay in the car and lock myself in when I called nine-one-one. He was counting on my following his orders. I think he ran into the house and cut Justine's throat. He'd calculated when the anesthetic he'd given Cardoni would wear off. Maybe he even gave Cardoni something to bring him around. After that, all he had to do was place the second gun in Cardoni's hand while Cardoni was still groggy and fire the first shot. Then he shot Cardoni with his own gun. I'm betting that Tony would have finished him off if I'd stayed in the car. Tony needed Cardoni dead so you'd stop investigating his crimes. He was afraid you'd stumble onto something that would prove he was the killer."

"This sounds crazy, Amanda," Greene said.

"Tony Fiori has been killing since he was a junior in high school and no one has ever suspected him. He was supposed to be in Mexico during winter break when his father died, but that was his alibi. I think his father walked in on him while he was working on his third victim and Tony killed him. My father is the one who called Mexico to tell Tony that Dominic was dead. I asked him about that last night. He said it took the people at his hotel a day to find him."

"You have to do better than this."

Amanda reminded Mike Greene of the killing ground in Colorado and told him about the killing ground in Peru. She also told him her dream about the blood-filled coffee cup and what it meant.

"It's possible," McCarthy said when she was through, "but there's nowhere near enough for an indictment."

"There's no concrete evidence at all," Mike added.

"I know," Amanda answered, her voice unsteady but filled with determination. "That's why you have to let me get you your evidence."

64

"God, it's good to see you, Tony," Amanda said, reaching up to give him a hug. "Thanks for letting me stay here."

In a van parked on a side road a short distance from Tony's house, Alex DeVore, Sean McCarthy and Mike Greene heard every word broadcast through the listening devices that had been planted while Fiori was at the hospital.

"To tell the truth, I haven't felt like staying alone, either, since I heard Cardoni escaped."

"We probably don't have anything to worry about. Sean McCarthy's convinced that Cardoni is long gone."

"You wouldn't be staying here if you believed that."

Amanda smiled coyly. "I might have ulterior motives."

"You are such a slut."

Tony put his hands around Amanda's waist, pulled her close and kissed her. She pulled back slightly, and he looked confused.

"Everything all right?"

"Sure," she said, fighting to keep from sounding

nervous. "Cardoni's escape just has me rattled. Say, I'm starving. What's for dinner?"

"Veal piccata, but I just got home fifteen minutes ago, so I don't have dinner up yet."

"Busy day at the hospital?" Amanda asked, to keep Tony talking.

"It was a madhouse. All anyone was talking about was Cardoni's killing spree. Then we had a five-car pileup on the interstate."

Amanda followed Tony into the kitchen. He filled a pot of water, then took two strips of veal scaloppini out of a shopping bag and laid them between sheets of wax paper.

"I may have proof of Cardoni's guilt soon," Amanda said as Tony pounded the veal lightly to flatten it.

"Oh?"

"Bobby Vasquez discovered two murders that occurred in Oregon that are very similar to the killings in Milton County and the murders at the farm."

"No kidding. When was this?"

"One woman was killed seventeen years ago and the other sixteen years ago."

"Where were the murders?"

"The Ghost Lake ski resort. The women were found in the forest, half a mile from one of the runs. This could have been Cardoni's first killing ground, so he may not have been as careful as he is now."

Tony blended flour with salt and pepper, then dipped the meat in the mixture until there was a light coating of flour on the veal.

"Did you tell McCarthy that Cardoni accused me?" he asked casually.

"No. Why should I waste his time with that ridiculous story? Cardoni was just desperate. He even claimed that he was drugged when he was at Justine's house. He wanted me to have the blood that was drawn prior to his operation screened for tranquilizers."

"Who was supposed to have drugged him? Me?" Tony asked as he put olive oil and butter in a skillet, placed the skillet on a burner on the stove and turned on the heat under the pot of water.

"Yeah," Amanda answered, shaking her head in disbelief. "He said that he was coming to when you shot him."

"Coming at me is more like it. What did McCarthy think about that little gem?"

"I didn't mention it to him. Like I said, why waste his time with Cardoni's crap?" Amanda shook her head. "I do have to give Cardoni credit, though. He had me going for a minute."

"You've got to be kidding."

"He's a skilled liar, Tony. You have no idea how convincing he can be."

Tony looked alarmed. "You actually thought I . . . that I could do that?"

"No, but he made a pretty good case against you."

"How, if I didn't do it?"

"Whether you did it or not is irrelevant. Lawyers convince juries all the time that things that didn't happen are true." Amanda smiled. "I bet I could convince you that you're guilty, using my exceptional forensic skills."

"Bullshit."

"That's not a challenge, is it?"

"Loser does the dishes."

"You're on."

"Okay, Ally McJaffe. Prove I did it."

"Let's see." Amanda stroked her chin dramatically. "First, there's the killing ground in Colorado."

"What killing ground?"

"It was on the list that Bobby Vasquez compiled for me of murder cases with MOs similar to the Oregon cases. The bodies of several torture victims were found on farmland near Boulder. The farm was purchased using the MO used to purchase the farmhouse in Multnomah County and the home in Milton County."

"How does that prove I'm a killer?" Tony asked with a skeptical smile.

"You were a ski instructor in Colorado, and you went to school at the University of Colorado at Boulder."

"That's true, but Cardoni worked in Denver. And, come to think of it, so did Justine. You won't get much mileage out of that point. Next?"

The water started to boil. Tony turned the heat up under the skillet.

"There's the coffee mug."

Tony looked puzzled. "What coffee mug?"

"The one the police found at the cabin in Milton County."

"What about it?"

"The police never told the press or the public that Cardoni's prints were on it."

"So?"

"You knew."

"I did?"

"Four years ago, at your house, we were talking about Cardoni's case after dinner. I told you about serial killer profiles, and I mentioned that organized nonsocials have active fantasy lives that enable them to visualize their crimes in advance. I said that this trait helped them anticipate errors that could lead to their capture. You commented that Cardoni did not anticipate the errors that led to his capture. You said that it was really dumb to leave a scalpel and a coffee mug with his fingerprints at the scene of the crime."

"I don't remember saying that."

"Well, you did."

"Come on." Tony laughed. "How can you possibly remember what we talked about four years ago?"

Amanda stopped smiling. "It was our first date, Tony. I remember everything about it. I was really taken with you and replayed the evening in my head a lot of times. It meant something to me."

"Well, you got the conversation wrong. I never mentioned anything about a coffee mug. I don't think I even knew the cops found a mug at the cabin, unless you told me about it. That might be where I heard about it, if I did. You said yourself that we talked about the case."

The butter and olive oil were heating up, and Tony put the veal in the sizzling pan.

"There was another killing ground in Peru."

Tony froze.

"Cardoni was living in the States when the victims disappeared and Justine was never in Peru, but you were in medical school in Lima then."

"There were similar murders when I was studying in Peru?"

Amanda nodded.

"Wow. That's amazing." Tony shrugged and smiled. "Well, I didn't do it. Besides, you're forgetting that Cardoni admitted framing Justine by planting evidence at the farmhouse. That proves he was at the scene of the crime."

"Ah, but it doesn't prove he committed the crime. Cardoni claimed that he framed Justine because he believed that she framed him four years ago."

"Why would Justine do that?"

"Clifford Grant made a deal with Martin Breach to deliver a heart that was supposed to be transplanted into a wealthy Canadian. The police raided the airport when Grant arrived with it, but Grant escaped with the money and the organ. Grant had a partner. Breach didn't know the partner's name. The partner killed Grant to keep him from talking and buried him at the cabin. Cardoni's story is that the partner created a fall guy to throw Breach off the scent. With his addiction to cocaine and erratic behavior, Cardoni was the perfect patsy. Cardoni thought Justine was Grant's partner, so he framed her to get even. Now he claims that you were Grant's partner."

"Of course he does. With Justine dead, he couldn't very well carry on with his ridiculous story that she framed him."

"Oh, it's pretty clear that Cardoni was framed."

"Yeah?" Tony said as he dropped several handfuls of pasta into the boiling water.

"Cardoni didn't know about the farm until shortly before he framed Justine. I talked to Mary Ann Jager, the lawyer who bought the property. She said that Cardoni showed up at her office a few days before Justine was arrested and tried to find out who owned it and how it had been purchased. Why would he do that if he already owned it?"

Tony clapped his hands and laughed. "Very impressive, Amanda. You're a terrific lawyer. You almost have me convinced that I killed everyone."

"That's why I get paid the big bucks," Amanda said, making a small bow.

"Still, when you add everything up, your case against me is purely circumstantial and pretty skinny."

"I've won with less," she answered with a confident smile.

Tony sighed. "Are you taking me in before dinner or do I get a last meal?"

Amanda pointed to the skillet. "That smells too good to waste. I think I'll wait until after we eat to bring you in."

"Here's a reward for your kindness."

Tony secured a slender piece of veal on the tines of a fork and held it just out of reach of Amanda's lips.

"Take a taste," he said, feeding the slice to Amanda. As soon as it was in her mouth, Tony swung his fist as hard as he could and caught Amanda flush on the jaw. She staggered. Tony pulled her to the ground and applied a choke hold. Amanda was unconscious in moments.

"**H**ow about opening the wine?" Tony said as he pressed tape over Amanda's mouth. He kept up a dialogue about his day at work, interspersed with cooking instructions, while he searched Amanda for a wire. If she was here on her own, he had no problems. If she was wired or the police had gotten into the house and planted listening devices, he would have to disappear. He didn't think the police were watching him on a concealed camera because they would have moved as soon as he hit Amanda.

Amanda began to stir. Tony rolled her over and secured her hands behind her back with a set of plastic restraints. He hastily scribbled a short note and took a sharp knife out of a drawer while regaling

Amanda with a funny story about a screwup by a new intern. As soon as Amanda's eyes opened Tony pressed the knife to her throat and held up a note: ONE SOUND AND I WILL BLIND YOU.

Amanda's eyes showed her fear, but she did not make a sound. Tony motioned her to her feet. Amanda scrambled up and stood unsteadily, still groggy from being rendered unconscious. Tony had removed all of her clothes during the search, but she was too terrified to be embarrassed. He pointed toward the basement door with his knife. Amanda hesitated, and he stabbed her in the arm. Amanda gasped. Tony put the knife to her eye and she stumbled down the hall.

"Is that a great Chianti or what?" Tony asked cheerfully.

65

"Something's wrong," Mike Greene said. He, Alex DeVore, Sean McCarthy and a technician were squeezed in the back of a van jammed with electronic equipment.

"They're talking," Alex DeVore said.

"No, *he's* talking. She hasn't spoken in more than five minutes. I put a watch on them. She's got to be nervous. Hell, she's got to be terrified. Someone in that state should be talking a blue streak. It's her only contact with us."

"Mike might be right," McCarthy said.

"If we send the men in now, we blow it," DeVore cautioned.

"If we don't and something happens to Amanda, I—"

"Hold it," the tech interrupted. "They're in the basement. I can hear them going down the stairs."

"Send the men in, now," McCarthy yelled, ripping off his headset.

DeVore yanked the mike from the tech's hand.

"Go, go, go," he yelled. "They're in the basement."

* * *

SWAT team members rose from their positions in the woods surrounding Tony's house and moved in. The first group went in the back door and the second through the front. When they experienced no resistance, the first group opened the cellar door. It was pitch black. The first man through the door crouched low and scanned the basement with night vision goggles. He edged down the stairs, weapon at the ready. Two other SWAT team members followed. They fanned out when they were in the basement. There was little to see: a floor-to-ceiling wine rack, the furnace, a water heater, a racing bike.

"Lights," the team leader ordered. The men removed their goggles and the man at the top of the stairs flipped the switch.

"Where are they?" one of the men asked.

"There has to be another way out," the team leader said. "Find it."

"Over here," one of the men yelled. He was kneeling next to a trap door that was flush with the floor. It had been covered with a rug. Three of the men surrounded the door and aimed their assault rifles at it. The fourth man opened the door in one smooth movement while the team leader looked on. There was a narrow depression in the earth no wider or deeper than a coffin. There were blood spots on the dirt. A rank smell issued forth.

"The basement is deserted," the team leader reported to the men in the van.

"So is the rest of the house," the tech in the van answered. The second team had already briefed him.

"We found a hidden trap door covering a coffin-size hole with what appears to be dried blood and excrement in it. He may have been holding people down there."

"Keep looking for another way out," McCarthy said. "If there's one hidden door, there might be another."

Tony Fiori had met his first victim on the slopes of the Ghost Lake resort. He had taken her to the family cabin, tortured her to death and buried her in the woods. Everything went so smoothly that Tony gave no thought to being caught. Teenagers don't do much planning, anyway. Tony's luck held with his second victim. Then Dominic Fiori walked in on his son in the act of torturing victim number three, and it suddenly occurred to Tony that it would be wise to take precautions.

Tony had enough money from his father's estate and life insurance to secure a private place to conduct his experiments in pain, and he soon developed a foolproof technique for purchasing his "research facilities." Then he studied forensic techniques to avoid detection by police specialists. Finally he created an escape plan if the worst-case scenario occurred.

As soon as they were in the basement, Tony placed a hood over Amanda's head, slid the moveable wine rack aside and pushed her into the escape tunnel. A flashlight hung on a hook just inside the door. Beneath it was a backpack with a pistol, cash, a change of clothing, materials for a disguise, a fake passport and other false identification.

Tony barred the entrance to the tunnel from the inside, grabbed the flashlight and located the backpack. The tunnel extended a quarter of a mile under the woods behind his house. Amanda ran stooped over because of the low ceiling. Stones and roots cut her bare feet; her buttocks and the backs of her thighs bled from gashes made by Tony's knife as he jabbed her when she slowed. A half mile from the tunnel exit a car purchased with false ID was waiting. Several hundred miles away in a small Montana town was his new laboratory. Amanda Jaffe would be its inaugural subject. It was stocked with enough food to last several months. When the search for him and Amanda died down, he would leave the country and plan his future. Amanda, or what was left of her, would stay behind in Montana.

Tony felt energized by the chase. He'd heard the back door crash open seconds before he closed and bolted the door to the tunnel, and it gave him a sense of satisfaction to know that he had outwitted the police.

As they hustled along, Tony admired the way Amanda's buttocks moved ahead of him. They were lithe and well muscled, like her legs. Tony thought about the time he would spend with Amanda. Tony liked best those first lovely moments when his subjects fully appreciated the horror of their situation. He watched with night vision goggles as they awoke in the dark, confused, frightened and unaware that they were under observation. There was always a widening of the eyes, a racing of the pulse, the mad attempt to break free from their bonds. He would lose this moment with Amanda. In her case, though, there would be other compensations.

"You present me with a rare opportunity," Tony told Amanda as he prodded her forward. "Most of my subjects have been runaways, addicts or prostitutes. They haven't been in the best of physical condition, and I've often wondered what effect that had on their ability to tolerate pain. I'm interested to see how much pain a well-conditioned athlete can endure.

We'll both learn a lot about pain in the weeks to come."

Tony suddenly grabbed Amanda's arm and yanked her to an abrupt stop while he listened for movement in the tunnel. When he was certain they were not being followed, he slapped her with the blade of his knife. She lurched forward and collided with the tunnel wall before Tony set her straight.

"You were so easy to fool," Tony taunted, breathing easily as they ran. "I dated you to milk you for information, just as I used Justine to find out what I needed to know to frame Vincent. Did you think our reunion at St. Francis was a coincidence? Justine told me about the interview."

Tony chuckled. "You weren't much of a challenge, though I must say that your reactions to sexual stimulus were often interesting. I may see if I can bring you to climax while you're in pain. I've tried it before on male and female subjects with interesting results."

Amanda was becoming exhausted and disoriented. It was hard to breathe in the hood with the tape across her mouth, and her fear was quickly sapping her strength.

"You can take some comfort in the fact that you're aiding science. You know, it was my father who inspired my interest in pain, but he wasn't very scientific or imaginative. Belts and fists were the limits of his creativity. I've far surpassed him, as you'll soon learn.

"I would have loved using Vincent as a subject, but I couldn't because the medical examiner would have seen the marks. If you hadn't stopped me from killing Cardoni, the investigation would have ended and I wouldn't have had to worry about someone like you discovering my work in Peru and Ghost Lake. I bet you wish you'd stayed in the car."

They were almost at the end of the tunnel when they heard the explosion.

"Looks like the police have found my escape hatch. But don't get your hopes up. They're a quarter mile behind."

Tony shoved open a trap door concealed under a layer of earth. He pushed Amanda up a short ladder, closed the door and rolled a boulder over it. Then he urged Amanda through the woods. There was no trail, but Tony knew every inch of the route to the car by heart. He did practice runs each month.

Amanda gasped for air as she stumbled forward over the stones that cut her feet. Only fear of what Tony would do if she slowed down kept her moving. Her legs trembled and she stayed upright by sheer force of will. Finally, just when she was certain that she could not go another step, she ran into the side of a car.

"Stop," Tony ordered.

Amanda doubled over. Her lungs heaved. She heard the trunk pop open. Once she was in the trunk, it would be all over. Tony would drive away and her fate would be sealed.

Amanda broke away from the car and was in the woods before Tony could react. She hit a tree with her shoulder, spun and drove forward blindly. She expected to feel Tony's grip any moment, but she was still running free when a log sent her sprawling. Pain shot through her shins as she flew through space. Her head cracked against a tree trunk. She lay on the ground, stunned, yet somehow gathered herself, rolled to her side and regained her feet. A car motor started. She heard tires spinning and distant shouts. Amanda raced toward the voices, stumbled and fell to her knees.

"She's over here," someone shouted.

"It's okay," someone else said.

Amanda collapsed as kind hands took hold of her. Someone cut through the plastic restraints that bound her hands behind her, and someone else draped a coat over her shoulders. Another person removed the hood and the tape that sealed her mouth. With eyes blurred by tears and exhaustion, Amanda saw the SWAT team members who were scouring the woods.

"Do you have him?" someone shouted.

"He's gone. He's disappeared," someone else answered.

"**A**manda, it's me."

Amanda opened her eyes and saw Mike Greene leaning over her in the back of the ambulance.

"Is she okay?" Greene asked the medic.

"She'll be fine," he answered. "She's disoriented and frightened, but her cuts are all superficial."

"Did they get him?" Amanda asked.

Greene shook his head.

"But don't worry. He won't get far," Mike said bravely, though without conviction. He sat next to Amanda, trying to think of something else to say. The medic gave Amanda a cup of steaming tea. She thanked him automatically and took a sip while her eyes stared ahead vacantly. Finally, at a loss for words, Mike Greene laid a reassuring hand on her shoulder and gave it a squeeze.

66

Tony Fiori came to slowly. His vision was blurred, his cheek pressed against cold, damp concrete. Fiori's hands were bound tightly behind his back. Tape covered his mouth; he tried to stand, but his ankles were also bound.

"Good, you're awake."

Fiori recognized the voice. He rolled over and saw Vincent Cardoni watching him.

"We're in a warehouse in Portland, if you're interested," Cardoni said as he reached down to check the ankle and wrist restraints. Fiori tried to wrench away from him, but it was useless.

"I'd conserve your strength if I were you. You're going to need it."

Cardoni saw fear in Fiori's eyes and smiled. "Oh, no, you don't have to worry about me. But you do need to be afraid."

Cardoni took out his cell phone.

"I followed Amanda Jaffe to your house and spotted the SWAT team, so I stayed in the woods to see what would happen."

Cardoni listened to someone on the other end of the phone. "Mr. Breach, please.

"It was luck that I saw you emerge from your tunnel," he continued as he waited for Breach to take his call. "Bad luck for you." Cardoni smiled. "You've made my life hell since the day you framed me. But you're going to put things right. You're going to square me with Martin Breach."

Cardoni's attention returned to the phone. "Mr. Breach," he said, "have you checked with your police friends?" Cardoni paused. "Good. Then you know that Tony Fiori was Dr. Grant's partner and that I had nothing to do with the heart?"

Cardoni paused again and nodded at something Breach said. When he spoke, he looked at Fiori so that he could enjoy his reaction.

"No, no, Mr. Breach, I don't want any money. Dr. Fiori cost me my hand and my career, and he made me live underground like an animal for four years. What we both want, I believe, is revenge: something more fitting than a quick and painless death by lethal injection."

Cardoni watched with great satisfaction as understanding, then terror, registered in Fiori's eyes. He tried to speak, but the tape muffled his words. As he thrashed on the ground Cardoni gave Breach the address of the warehouse, then disconnected.

"They'll be here soon, so I have to leave," Cardoni said. "Mr. Breach did want me to tell you something, though. It seems that a contact in the police department gave him a copy of your pain journals. He says he found them quite interesting and is looking forward to trying the techniques you found most effective."

Fiori's eyes stretched open as far as possible. He strained uselessly against his bonds. Cardoni watched him for a moment more, then threw his head back and began to laugh. His laughter continued to echo in the cold, hollow space as he disappeared into the night.

67

Two weeks after her escape, Amanda was reviewing case notes in the corridor outside a courtroom when she looked up to find Mike Greene smiling down at her.

"Mr. Greene, are you spying on me?" she asked, matching his smile with one of her own.

Mike sat beside her on the bench. "Nope, I'm just checking to see if you're okay."

"Thanks, Mike, I'm fine."

"This must be really hard for you. You were very close to Fiori, weren't you?"

Amanda smiled sadly. "He used me to find out about the investigation, Mike. I never meant anything to him, and he doesn't mean a thing to me now. I'll tell you one thing, though—I'm through dating serial killers."

Mike barked out a laugh. Then he sobered and looked at Amanda uneasily. She sensed that he wanted to say something, but Greene looked uncharacteristically nervous.

"Have you heard anything more about Bobby Vasquez?" Amanda asked when the silence went on too long.

"He'll be out of the hospital by next week," Greene said. He seemed grateful for the easy question. "He's made a great recovery."

"Thank God for that." She paused. "Have you . . . ?"

Mike shook his head. "There's nothing new on Fiori. He's dropped off the face of the earth."

Amanda sighed. She nodded toward the police officer sitting a few benches away.

"It sure would be nice to know that I didn't need protection anymore."

"Well, you're going to get it until we know you're safe. I don't want anything happening to you—at least outside court."

Amanda smiled. "I think I can take pretty good care of myself there."

"That you can," Mike agreed. Then he hesitated. "You know, I could take over as your bodyguard this Saturday if you're interested."

Amanda looked confused. Mike smiled nervously.

"Do you like jazz?"

"What?"

"There's a really good trio playing at a club in Old Town next week."

Amanda couldn't hide her surprise.

"Are you asking me out, like on a date?"

"I've wanted to ask you out for a long time." Mike blushed. "No guts. But I figured if you could be brave enough to go up against Fiori, I could muster the courage to ask you out."

"I love jazz."

Mike's face lit up. "Okay."

"Give me a call and let me know when we're going."

"I will. This is great."

Amanda laughed. "Does this mean you'll go easier on me the next time we have a case together?"

"Not a chance," Mike answered, grinning unabashedly. "Not a chance."

Epilogue

The three men who were playing cards looked up when Martin Breach walked through the door to the warehouse.

"Hey, Marty," Art Prochaska said.

Breach waved, then glanced down at the man who lay on the bloodstained mattress. It was almost impossible to tell that he was human. After a moment Fiori looked up listlessly with his one good eye. Breach lost interest and walked to the card players.

"You think we got everything out of him?" Breach asked Prochaska.

"Our guy in the islands cleaned out the account. I don't think he's got another one. If he ain't talked by now, nothing else we do is gonna make him. It's been a month."

Breach nodded. "Get rid of him," he told Prochaska.

Prochaska breathed a sigh of relief. His enjoyment in torturing Fiori had waned considerably after the first few days, although Marty's enthusiasm had lasted much, much longer.

"Oh, and Arty," Breach said, pulling a can of beer from a cooler, "let's leave a little something so the cops know he's dead. I don't want them to keep wasting their time on a big manhunt. Those are my tax dollars they're spending."

"How about we send them a hand?" Prochaska asked with a smile. Breach considered the suggestion for a moment, then shook his head.

"That would be poetic, but I want the cops to know he's really dead. And Frank's daughter, I want her to know, too. She's a good kid, and Frank's always done right by me. I don't want them worrying."

Breach popped the tab on his beer and took a long, satisfying drink.

"So what's it gonna be, Marty?"

Breach thought for a moment. Then he looked down at Fiori and smiled.

"The head, Arty. Send them the head."

PHILLIP MARGOLIN is the author of *Lost Lake,
Sleeping Beauty, Ties That Bind,* and eight other *New York
Times* bestsellers. He is a longtime criminal defense
attorney and lives in Portland, Oregon. You can visit his
website at *www.phillipmargolin.com.*